The Last Halloween
1: CHILDREN

ABBY HOWARD

IRON
CIRCUS
COMICS

strange and amazing

inquiry@ironcircus.com   www.ironcircus.com

WRITER & ARTIST
Abby Howard

PUBLISHER
C. Spike Trotman

EDITOR
Kel McDonald

ART DIRECTOR & COVER DESIGN
Matt Sheridan

BOOK DESIGN & PRINT TECHNICIAN
Beth Scorzato

PROOFREADER
Abby Lehrke

PUBLISHED BY
Iron Circus Comics
329 West 18th Street, Suite 604
Chicago, IL 60616
ironcircus.com

FIRST EDITION: September 2020

ISBN: 978-1-945820-66-3

10 9 8 7 6 5 4 3 2 1

Printed in China

THE LAST HALLOWEEN VOLUME 1: CHILDREN

Publisher's Cataloging-In-Publication Data
(Prepared by The Donohue Group, Inc.)

Names: Howard, Abby (Comic artist), author, illustrator.
Title: The last Halloween. Volume 1, Children / by Abby Howard.
Other Titles: Children
Description: First Edition. | Chicago, IL : Iron Circus Comics, 2020. | Series: Last Halloween ; [1] | Summary: "In a gothic adventure at the end of the world, a ten-year-old girl and a motley crew of ghouls must stop an invading horde of monsters on a fateful Halloween night"– Provided by publisher.
Identifiers: ISBN 9781945820663
Subjects: LCSH: Halloween–Comic books, strips, etc. | Monsters–Comic books, strips, etc. | Ghouls and ogres–Comic books, strips, etc. | CYAC: Halloween–Fiction. | Monsters–Fiction. | Ghouls and ogres–Fiction. | LCGFT: Graphic novels. | Horror comic books, strips, etc. | Horror comics. | Gothic fiction. | Action and adventure comics.
Classification: LCC PZ7.7.H73 La 2020 | DDC 741.5973 [Fic]–dc23

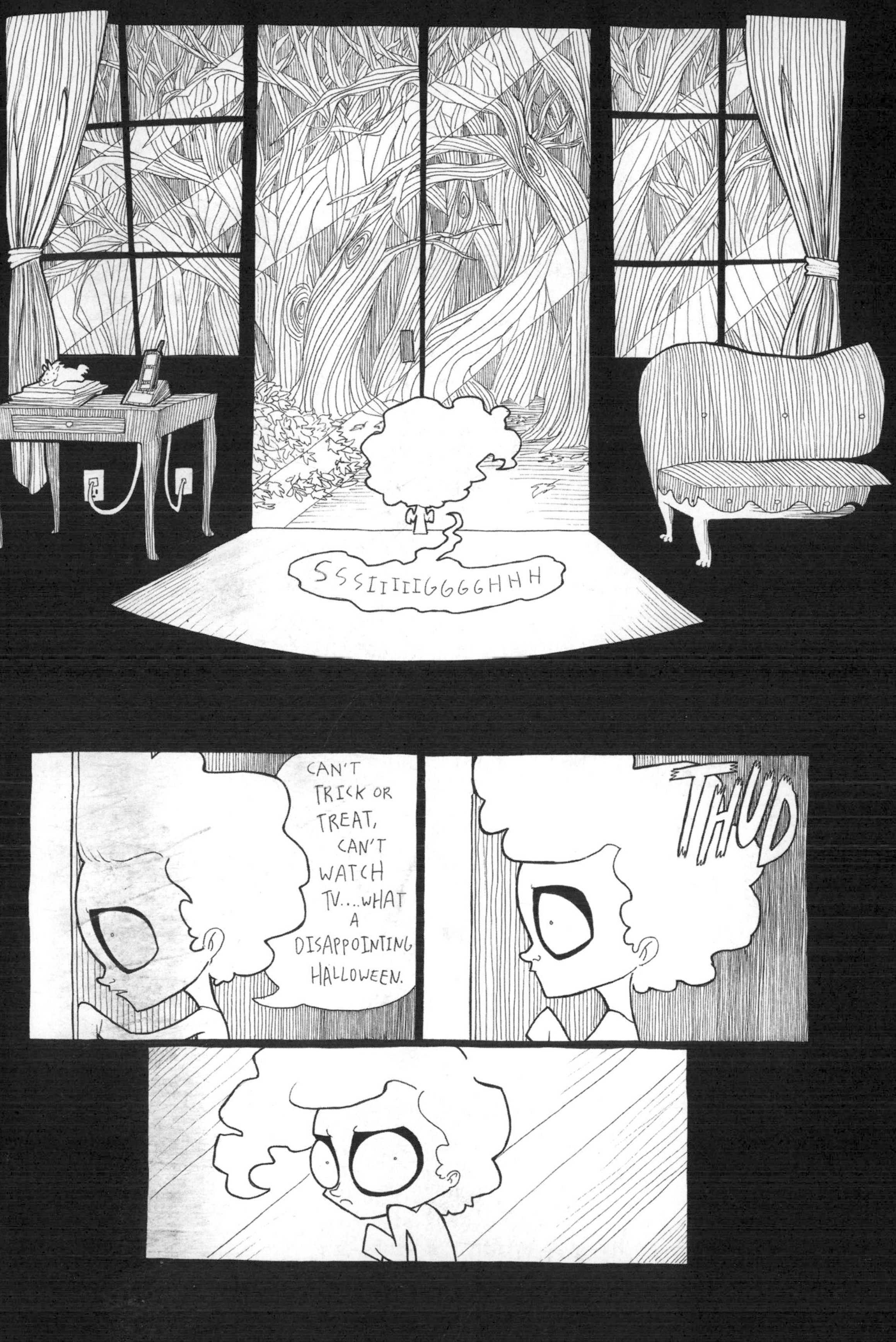
SSSIIIIIGGGGHHH
CAN'T TRICK OR TREAT, CAN'T WATCH TV....WHAT A DISAPPOINTING HALLOWEEN.
THUD

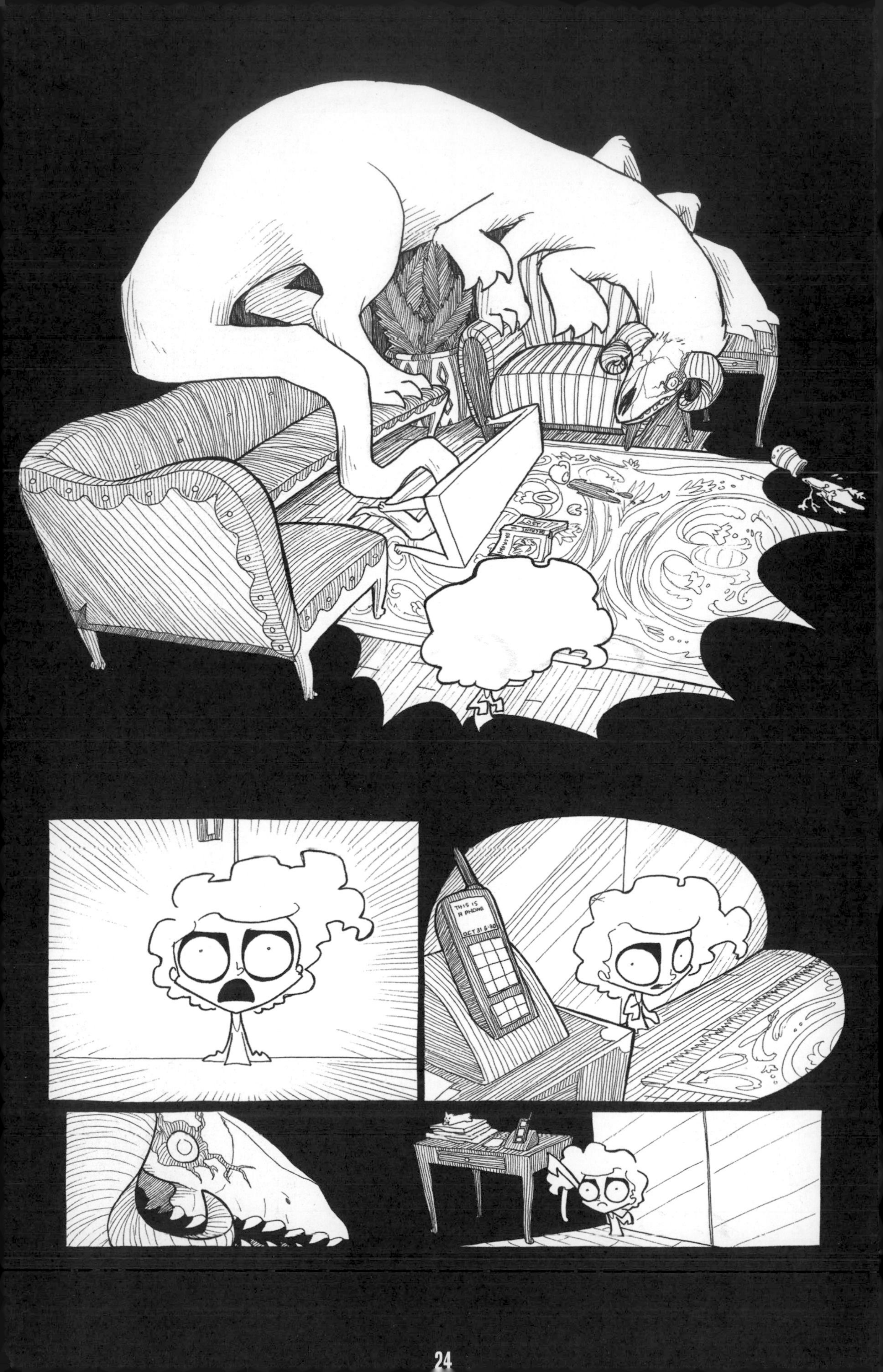
THIS IS
A PHONE
OCT 31 6:30

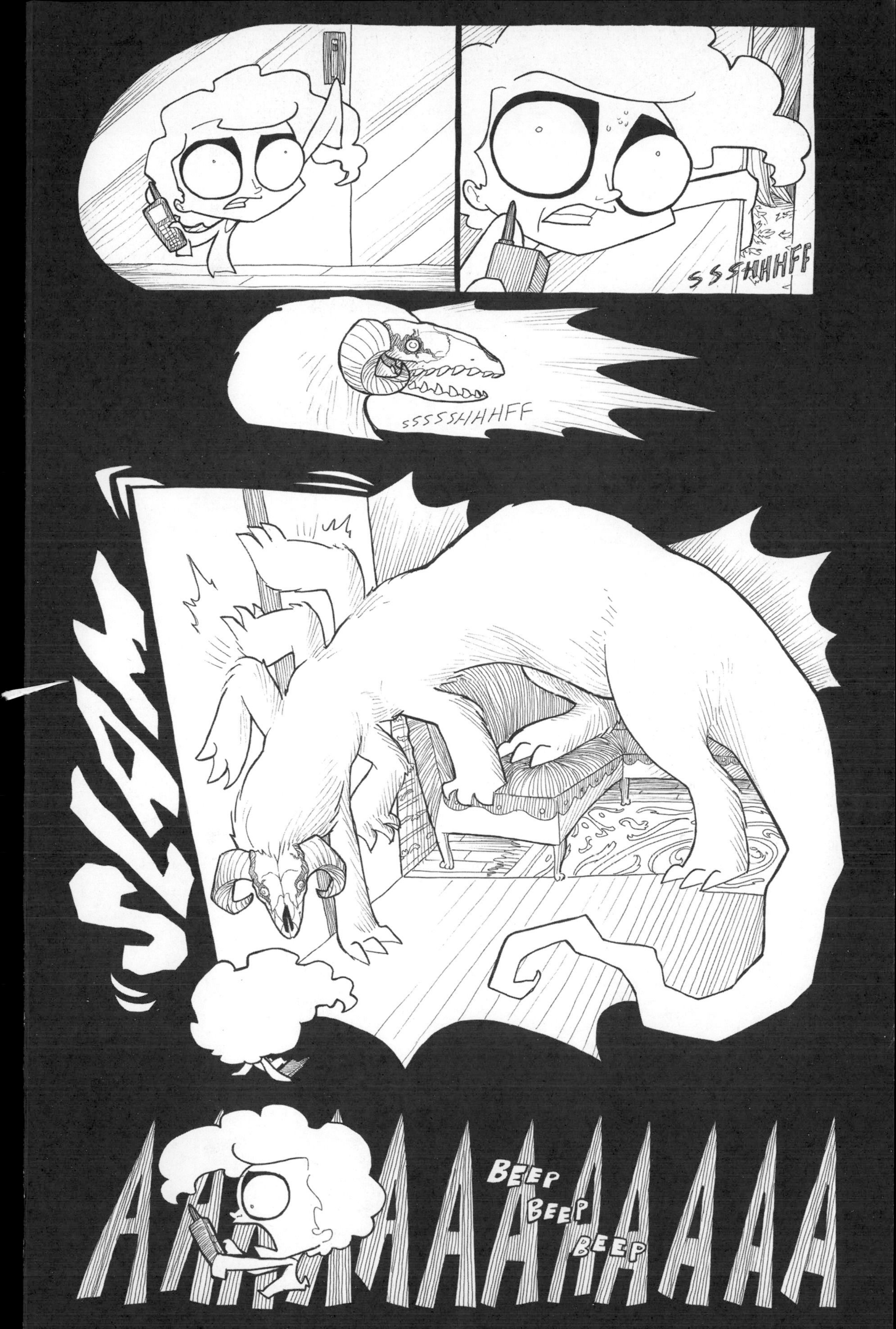
SSSHHHFF
sssssHHHFF
SLAM
AAAAAAAAAAAA
BEEP
BEEP
BEEP

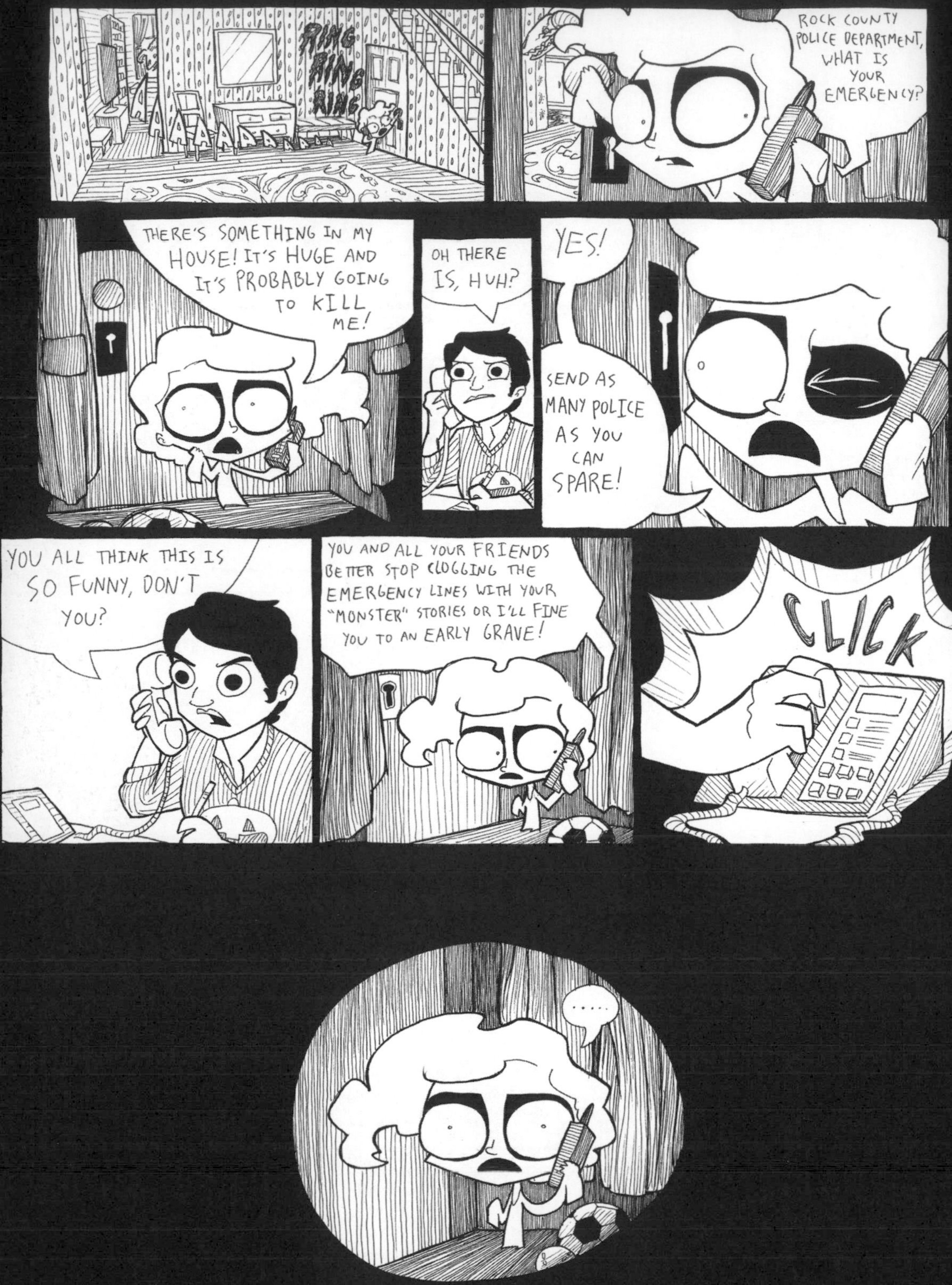
RING RING RING
AAAAAAAAAAAA
ROCK COUNTY POLICE DEPARTMENT, WHAT IS YOUR EMERGENCY?
THERE'S SOMETHING IN MY HOUSE! IT'S HUGE AND IT'S PROBABLY GOING TO KILL ME!
OH THERE IS, HUH?
YES!
SEND AS MANY POLICE AS YOU CAN SPARE!
YOU ALL THINK THIS IS SO FUNNY, DON'T YOU?
YOU AND ALL YOUR FRIENDS BETTER STOP CLOGGING THE EMERGENCY LINES WITH YOUR "MONSTER" STORIES OR I'LL FINE YOU TO AN EARLY GRAVE!
CLICK
.....

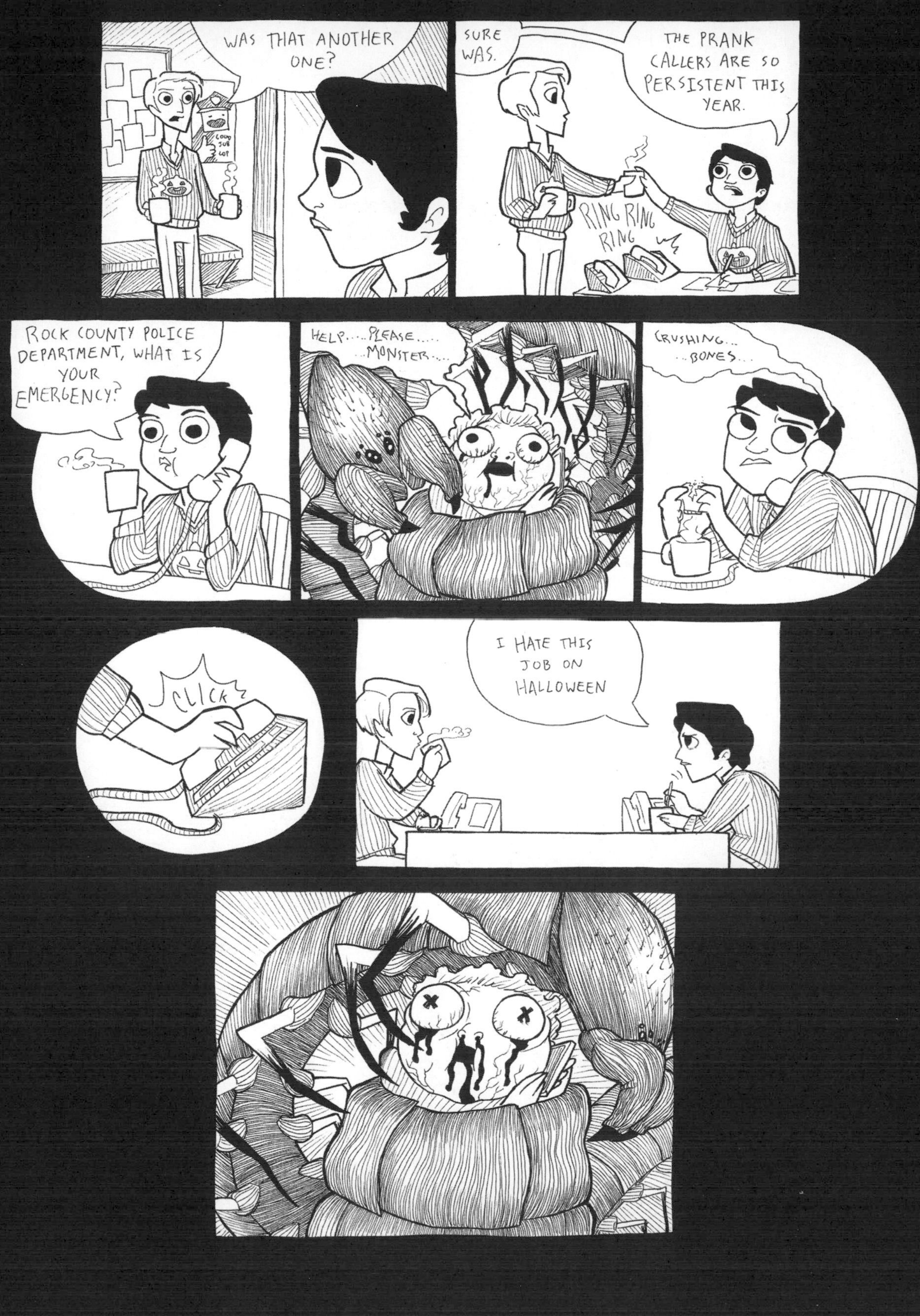
WAS THAT ANOTHER ONE?
SURE WAS.
THE PRANK CALLERS ARE SO PERSISTENT THIS YEAR.
RING RING RING
ROCK COUNTY POLICE DEPARTMENT, WHAT IS YOUR EMERGENCY?
HELP.....PLEASE..... ...MONSTER.....
CRUSHING... ...BONES...
CLICK
I HATE THIS JOB ON HALLOWEEN

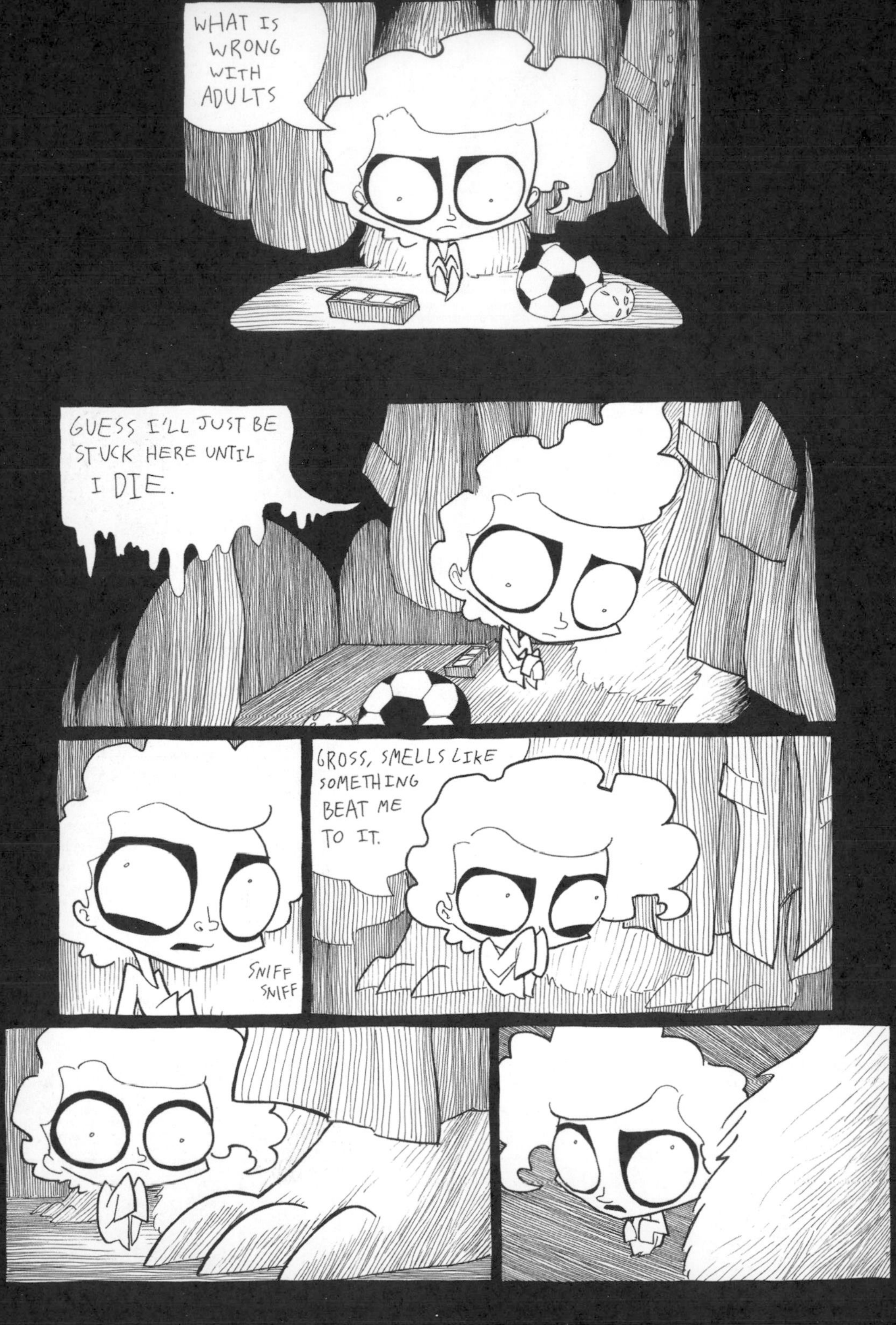
WHAT IS WRONG WITH ADULTS
GUESS I'LL JUST BE STUCK HERE UNTIL I DIE.
SNIFF SNIFF
GROSS, SMELLS LIKE SOMETHING BEAT ME TO IT.

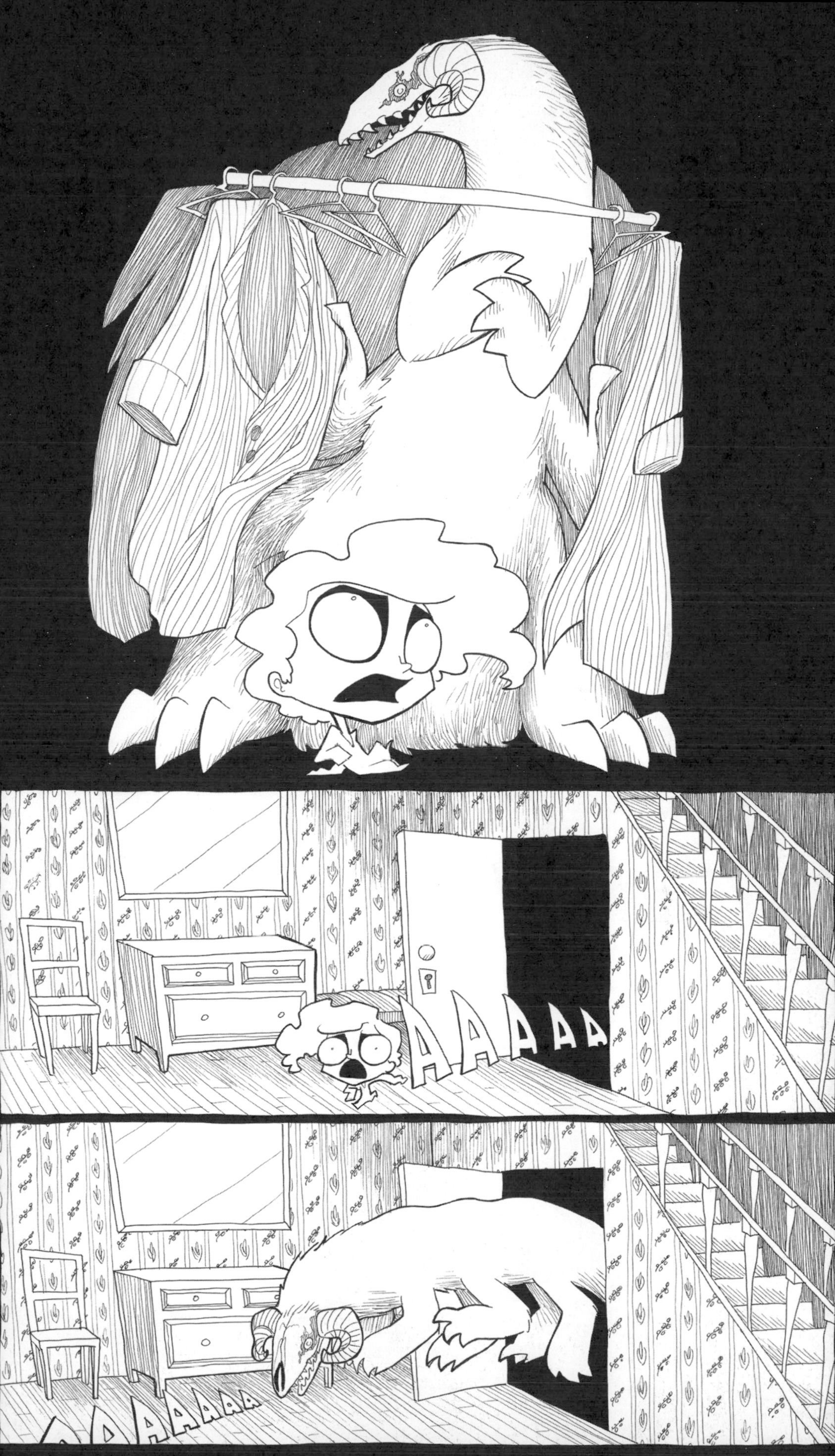
AAAAA
AAAAAA

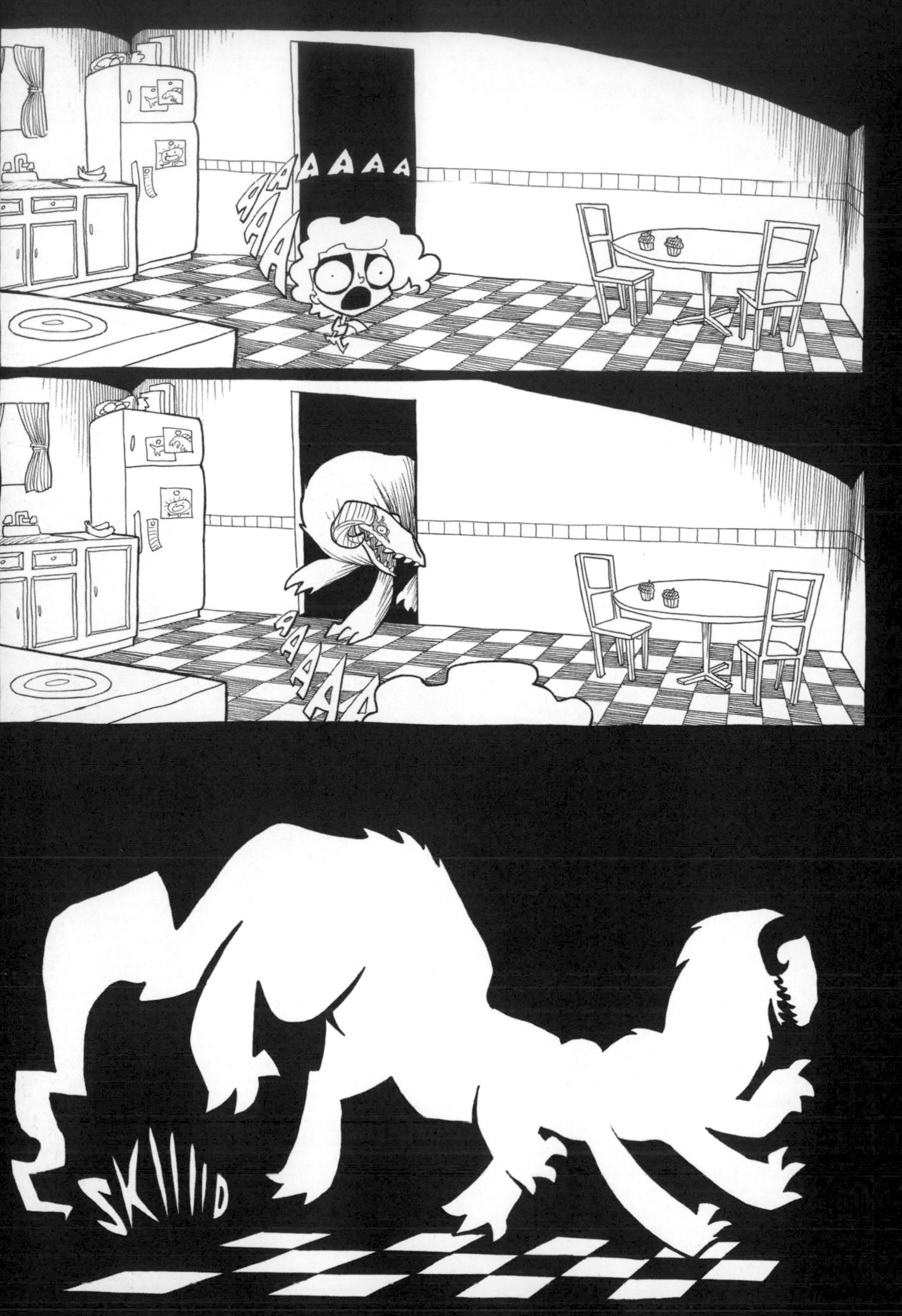
AAAAAAAA
AAAAAA
SKIIIID

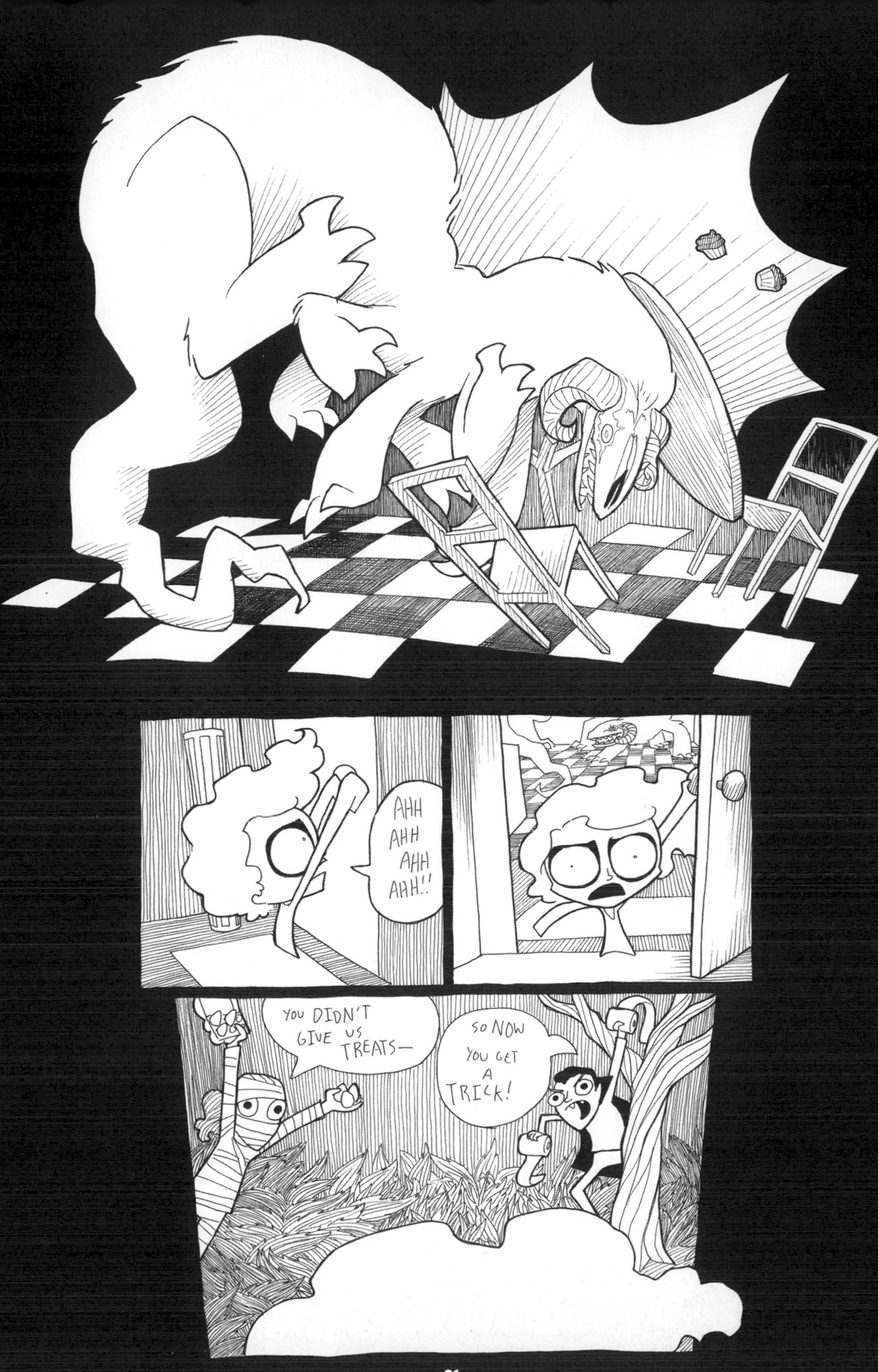
AHH
AHH
AHH
AHH!!
YOU DIDN'T GIVE US TREATS—
SO NOW YOU GET A TRICK!

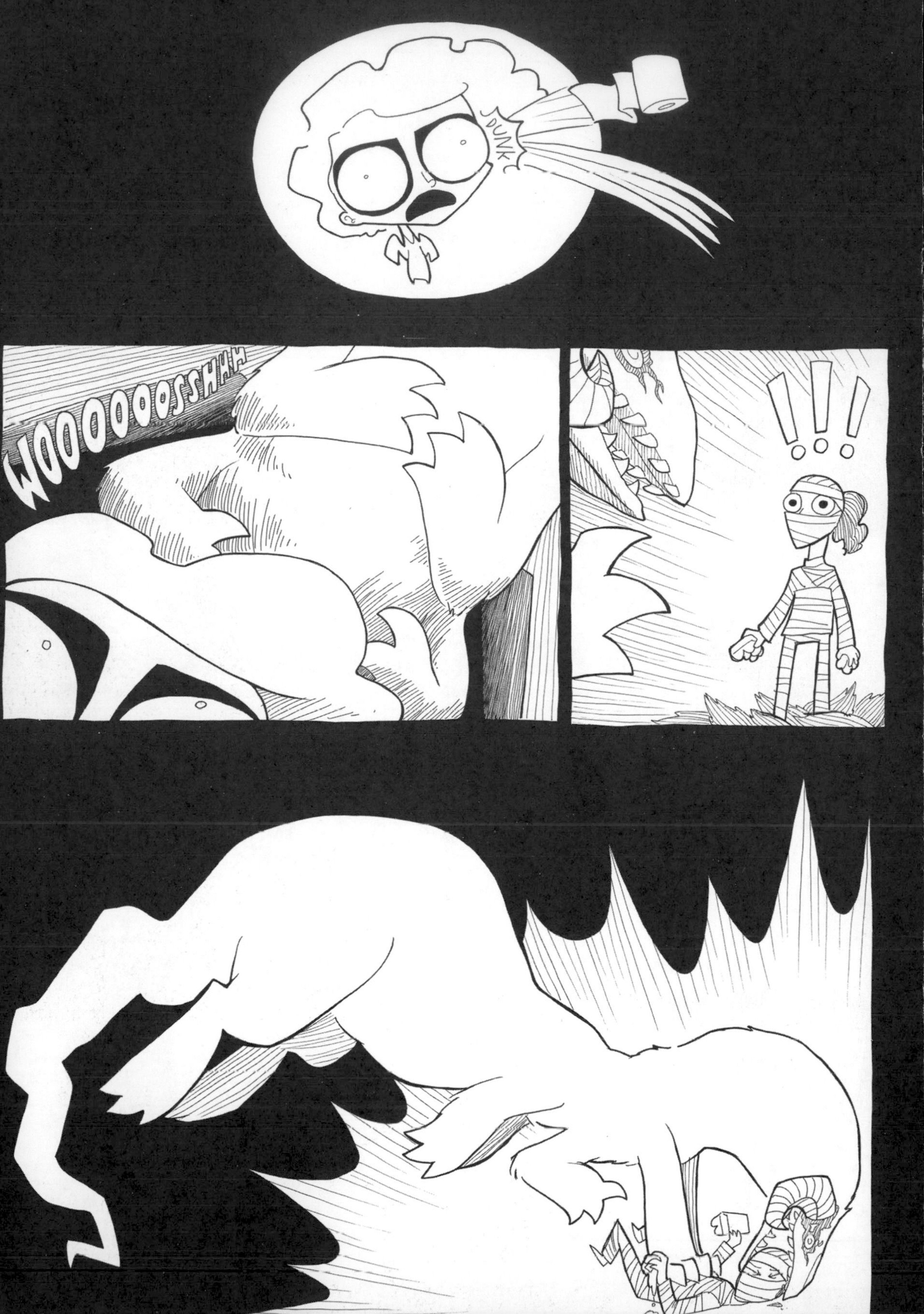
DUNK
WOOOOOOSSHHH
!!!

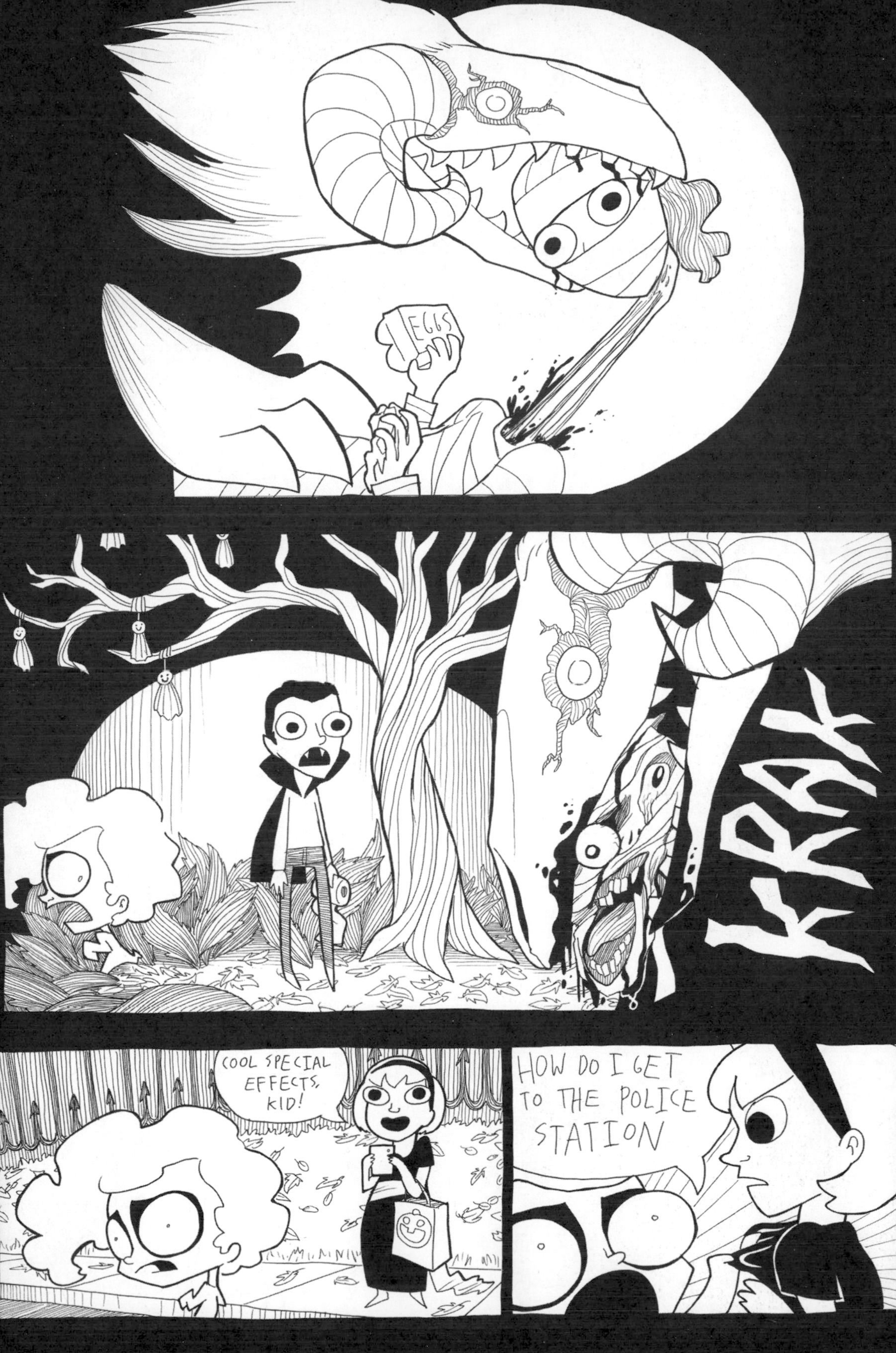
EGGS
KRAK
COOL SPECIAL EFFECTS, KID!
HOW DO I GET TO THE POLICE STATION

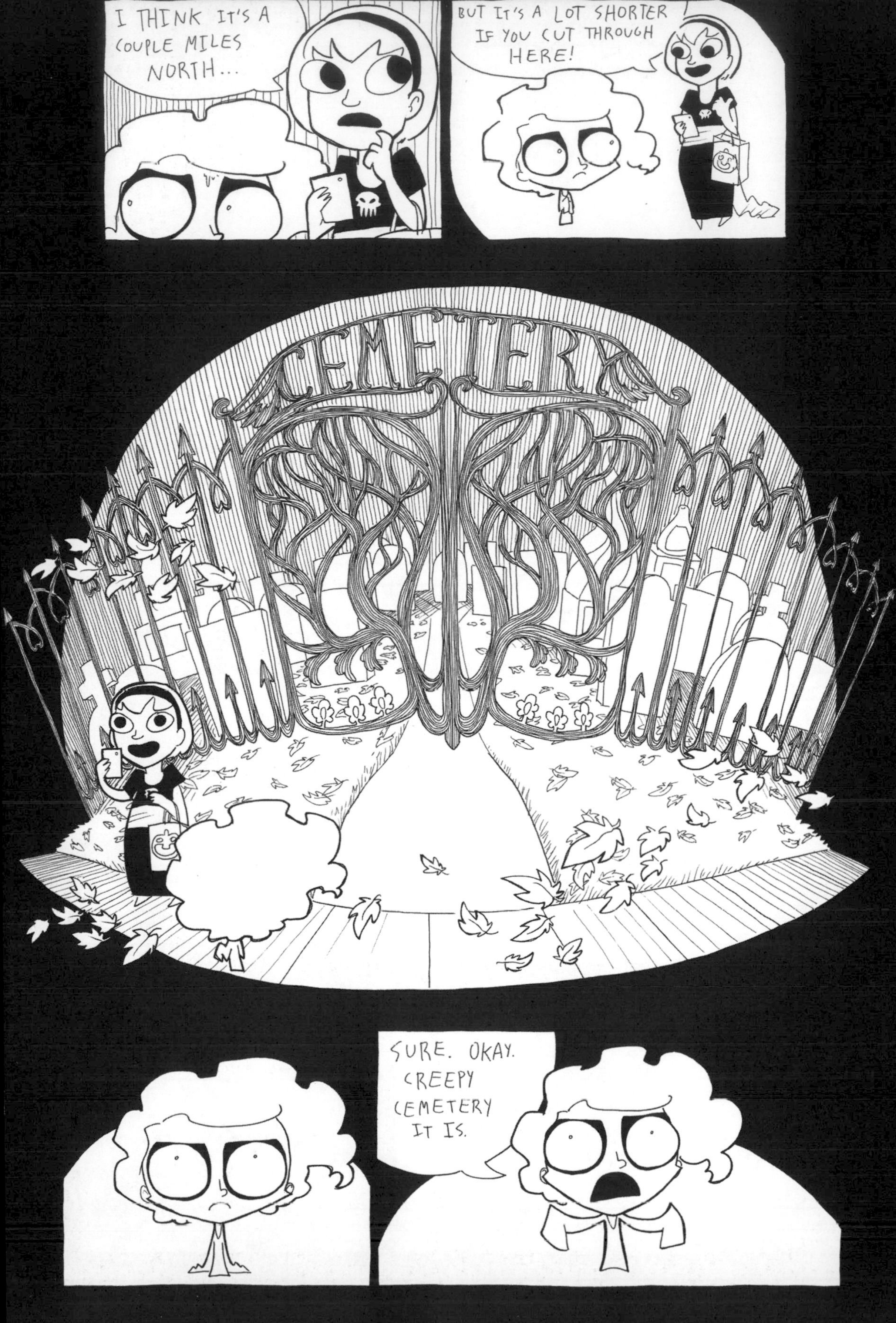

I THINK IT'S A COUPLE MILES NORTH...
BUT IT'S A LOT SHORTER IF YOU CUT THROUGH HERE!
CEMETERY
SURE. OKAY. CREEPY CEMETERY IT IS.

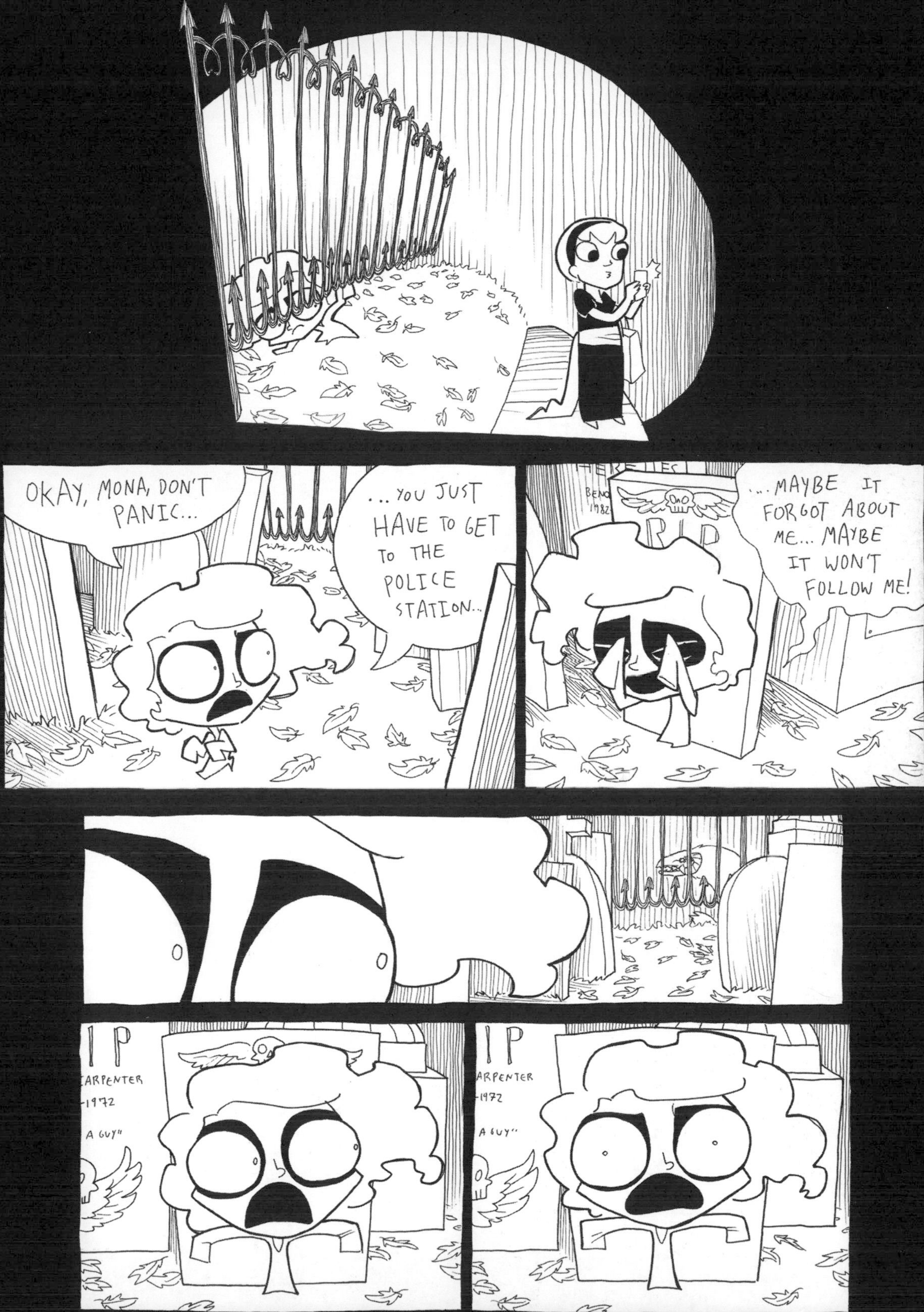

OKAY, MONA, DON'T PANIC...
...YOU JUST HAVE TO GET TO THE POLICE STATION...
...MAYBE IT FORGOT ABOUT ME... MAYBE IT WON'T FOLLOW ME!

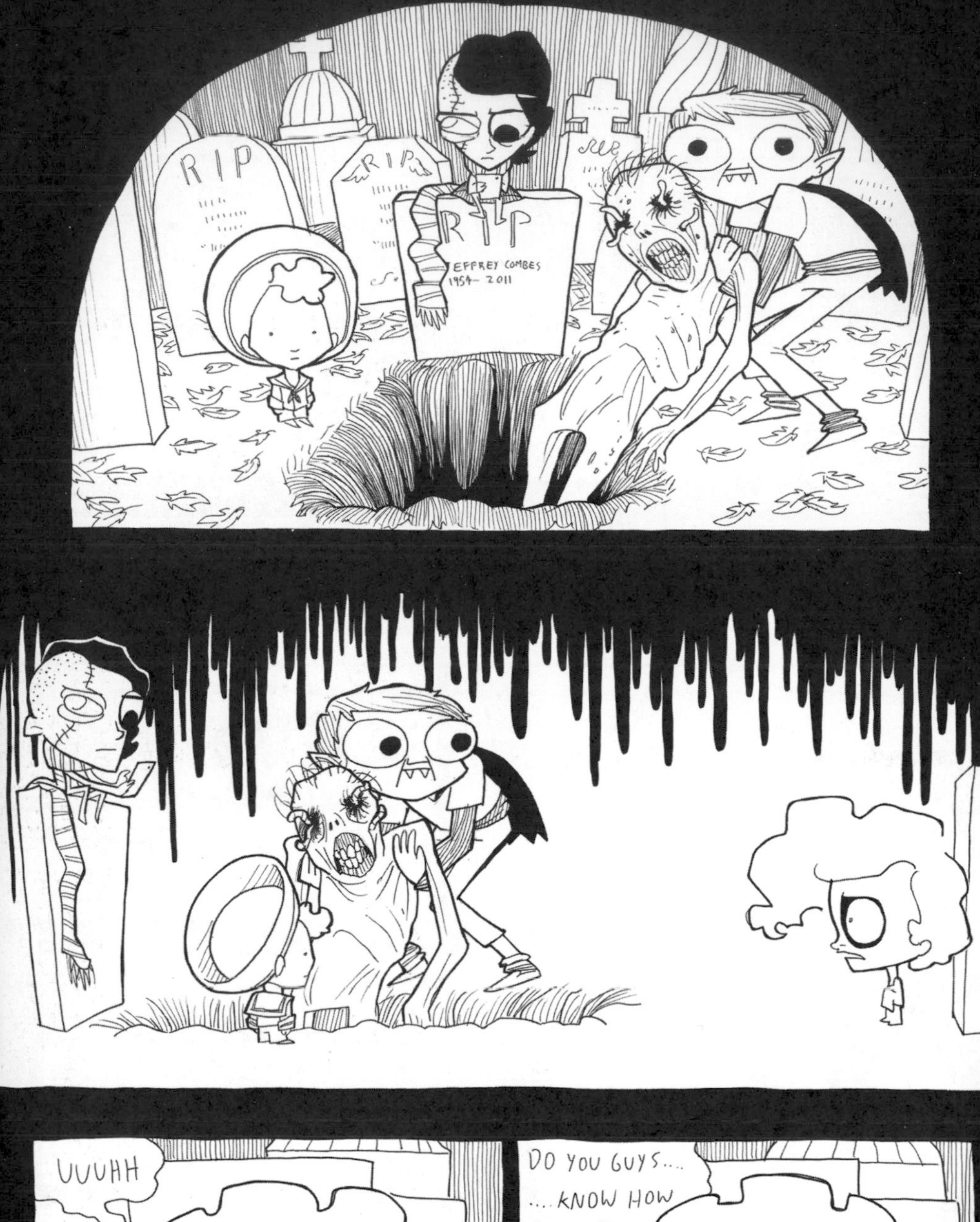
RIP
RIP
RIP
EFFREY COMBES
1954– 2011
UUUHH
DO YOU GUYS....
....KNOW HOW TO GET TO THE POLICE STATION

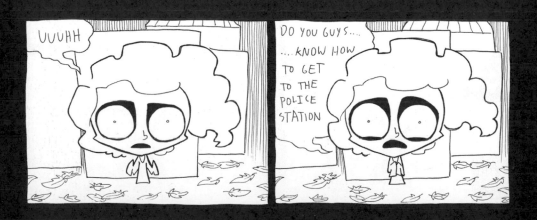

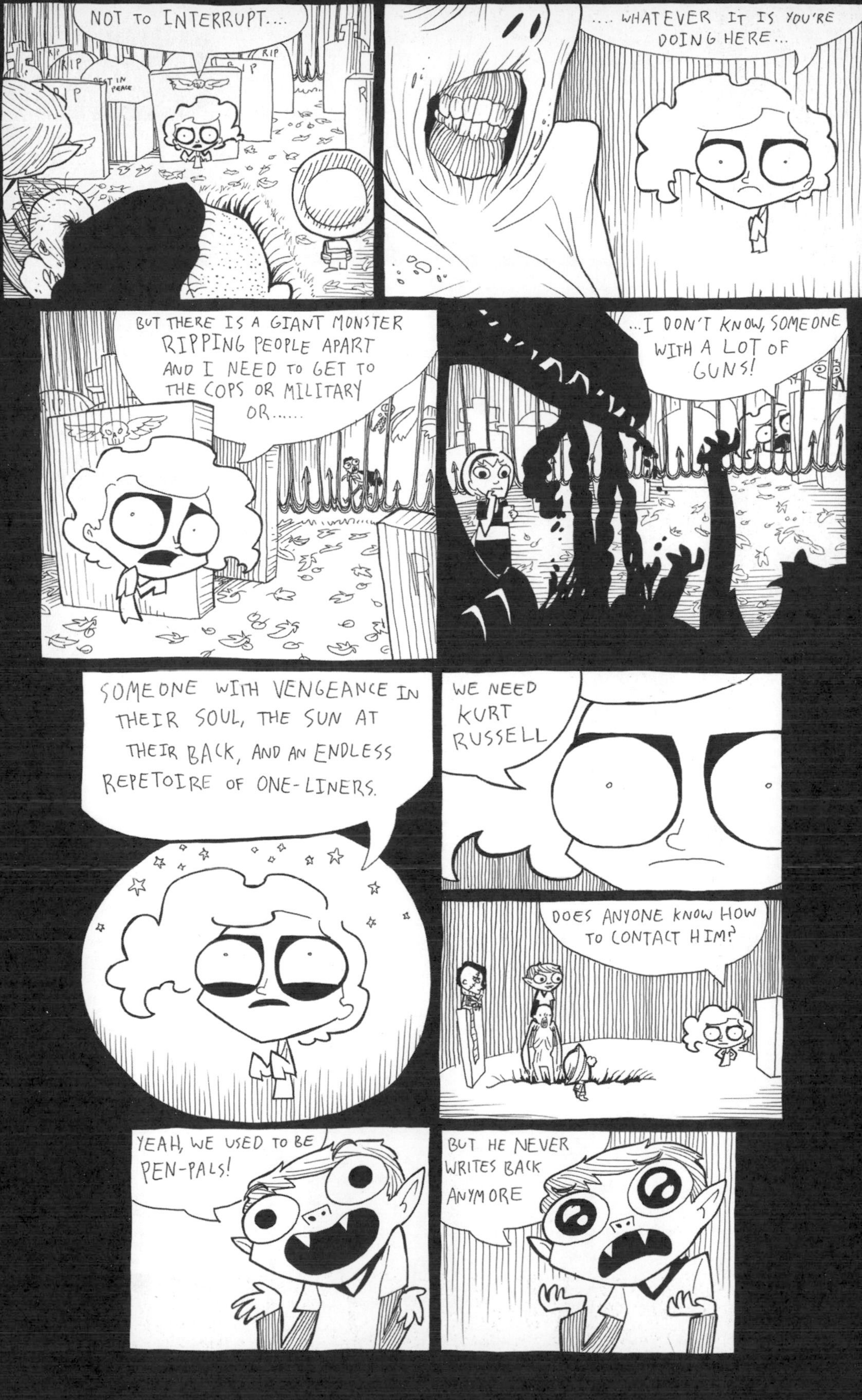
NOT TO INTERRUPT....
RIP
RIP
REST IN PEACE
RIP
RIP
.... WHATEVER IT IS YOU'RE DOING HERE...
BUT THERE IS A GIANT MONSTER RIPPING PEOPLE APART AND I NEED TO GET TO THE COPS OR MILITARY OR......
...I DON'T KNOW, SOMEONE WITH A LOT OF GUNS!
SOMEONE WITH VENGEANCE IN THEIR SOUL, THE SUN AT THEIR BACK, AND AN ENDLESS REPETOIRE OF ONE-LINERS.
WE NEED KURT RUSSELL
DOES ANYONE KNOW HOW TO CONTACT HIM?
YEAH, WE USED TO BE PEN-PALS!
BUT HE NEVER WRITES BACK ANYMORE

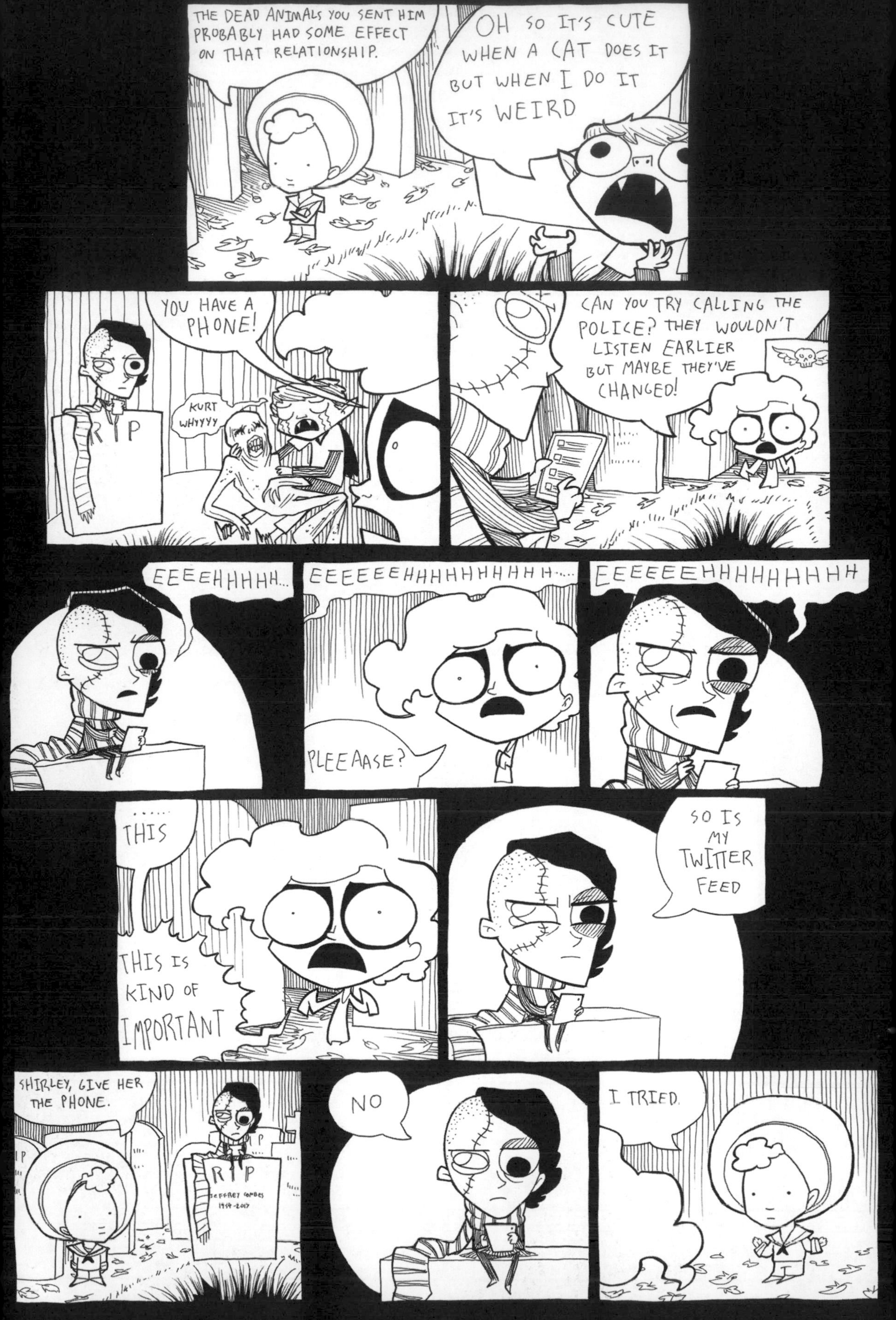
THE DEAD ANIMALS YOU SENT HIM PROBABLY HAD SOME EFFECT ON THAT RELATIONSHIP.
OH SO IT'S CUTE WHEN A CAT DOES IT BUT WHEN I DO IT IT'S WEIRD
YOU HAVE A PHONE!
KURT WHYYYY
R I P
CAN YOU TRY CALLING THE POLICE? THEY WOULDN'T LISTEN EARLIER BUT MAYBE THEY'VE CHANGED!
EEEEHHHHH...
EEEEEEHHHHHHHHHH.....
EEEEEEHHHHHHHHHH
PLEEAASE?
......
THIS
THIS IS KIND OF IMPORTANT
SO IS MY TWITTER FEED
SHIRLEY, GIVE HER THE PHONE.
R I P
NO
I TRIED.

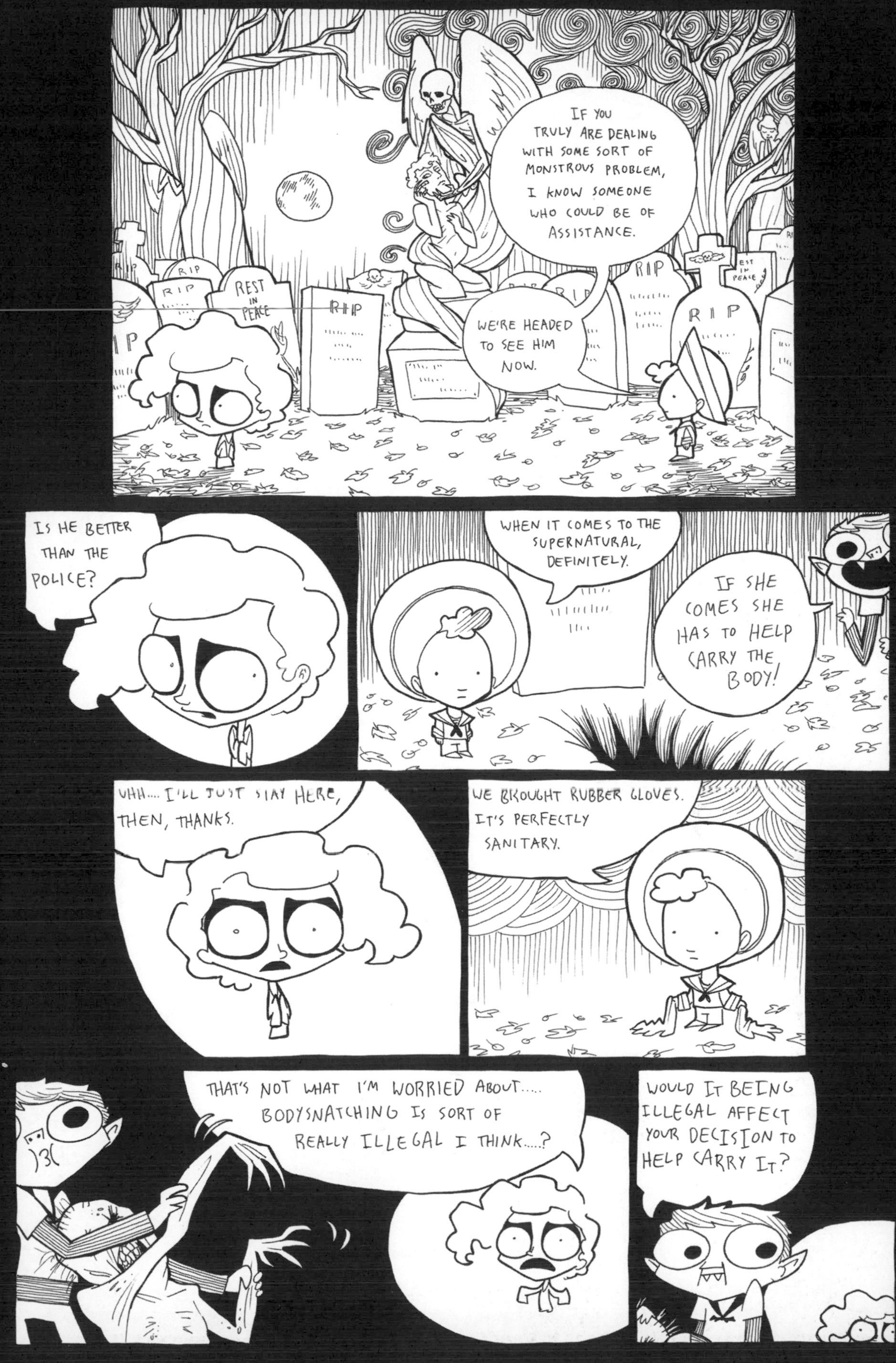

IF YOU TRULY ARE DEALING WITH SOME SORT OF MONSTROUS PROBLEM, I KNOW SOMEONE WHO COULD BE OF ASSISTANCE.
WE'RE HEADED TO SEE HIM NOW.
REST IN PEACE
RIP
IS HE BETTER THAN THE POLICE?
WHEN IT COMES TO THE SUPERNATURAL, DEFINITELY.
IF SHE COMES SHE HAS TO HELP CARRY THE BODY!
UHH.... I'LL JUST STAY HERE, THEN, THANKS.
WE BROUGHT RUBBER GLOVES. IT'S PERFECTLY SANITARY.
THAT'S NOT WHAT I'M WORRIED ABOUT..... BODYSNATCHING IS SORT OF REALLY ILLEGAL I THINK.....?
WOULD IT BEING ILLEGAL AFFECT YOUR DECISION TO HELP CARRY IT?

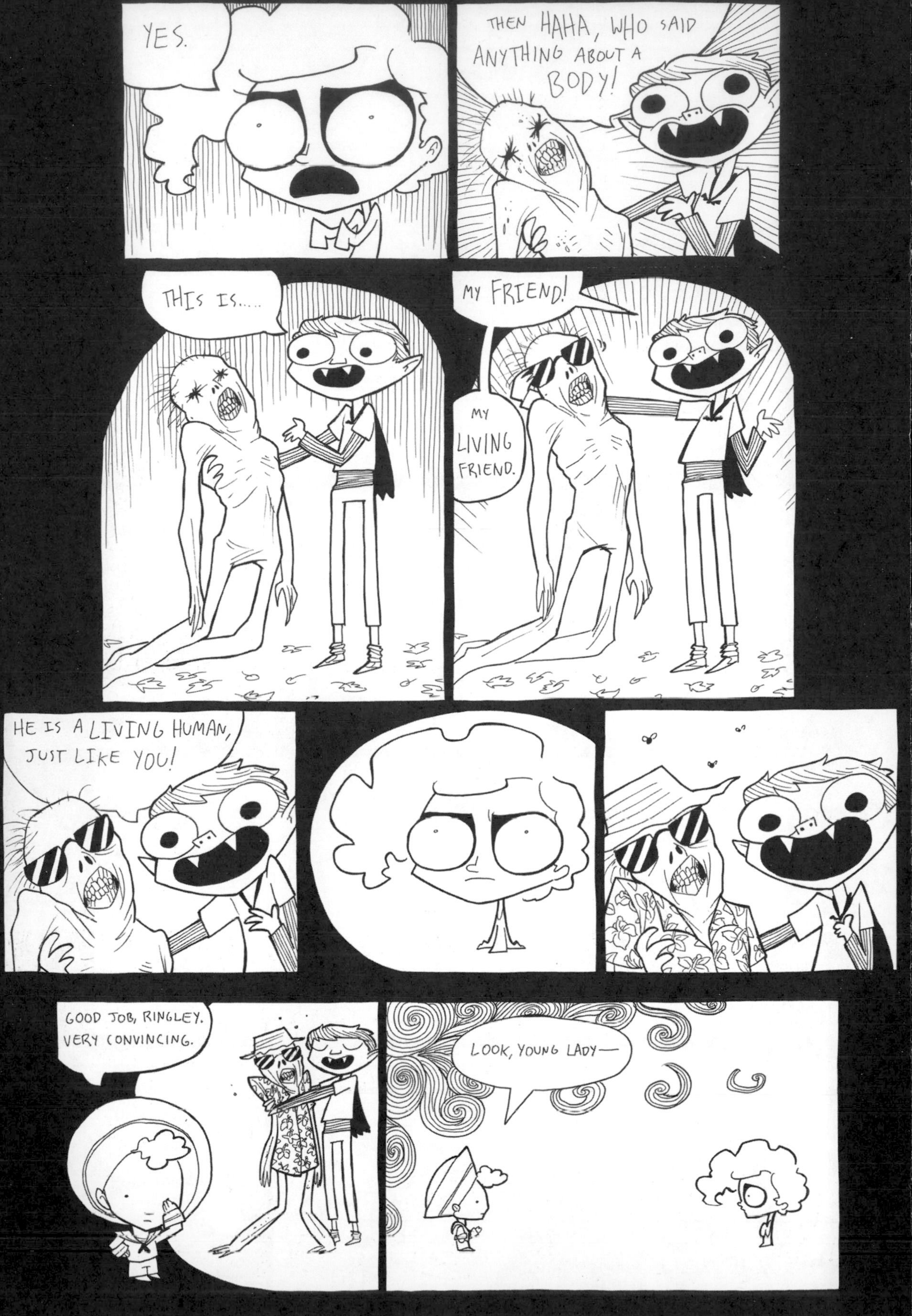
YES.
THEN HAHA, WHO SAID ANYTHING ABOUT A BODY!
THIS IS.....
MY FRIEND!
MY LIVING FRIEND.
HE IS A LIVING HUMAN, JUST LIKE YOU!
GOOD JOB, RINGLEY. VERY CONVINCING.
LOOK, YOUNG LADY—

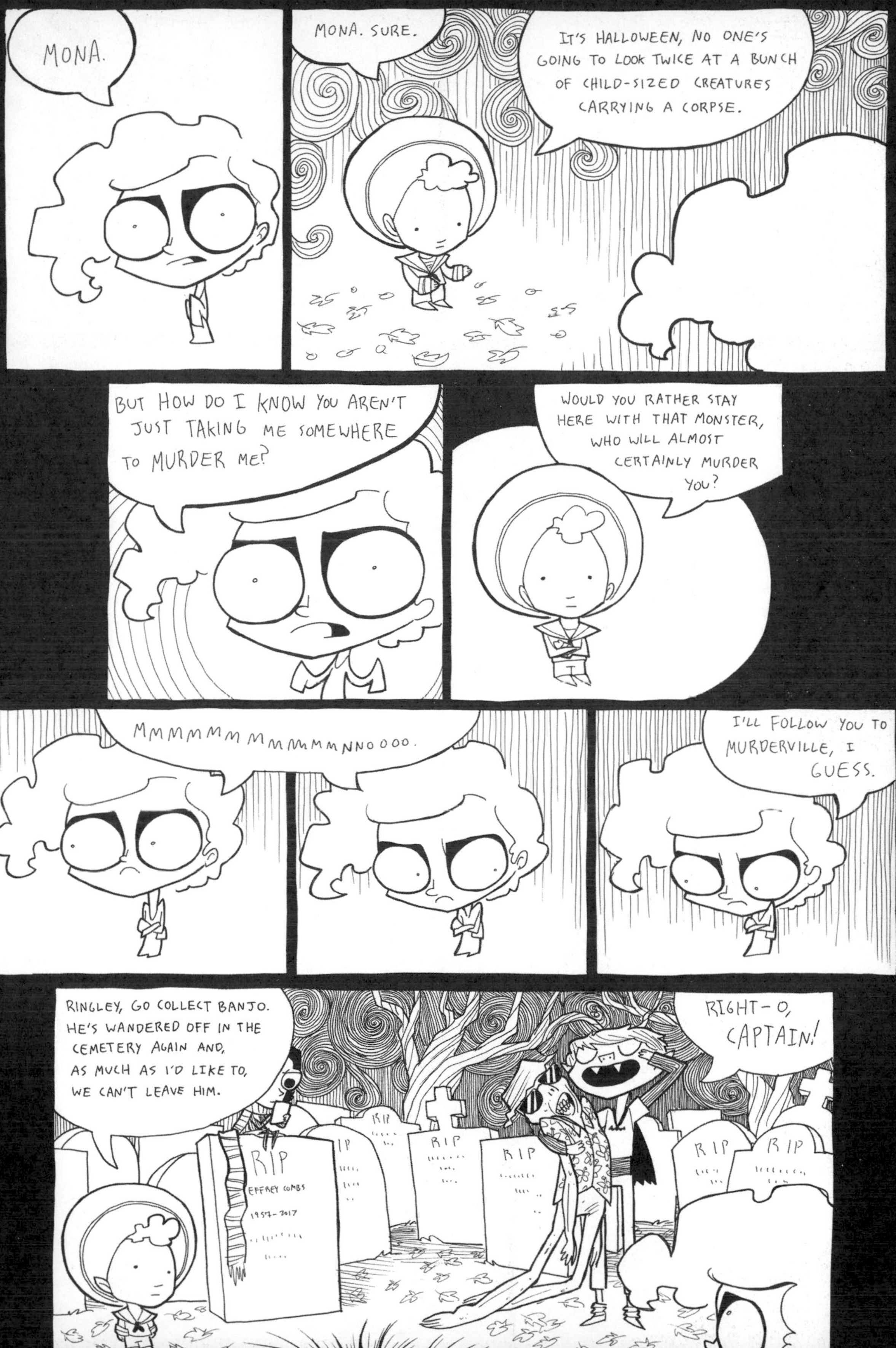
MONA.
MONA. SURE.
IT'S HALLOWEEN, NO ONE'S GOING TO LOOK TWICE AT A BUNCH OF CHILD-SIZED CREATURES CARRYING A CORPSE.
BUT HOW DO I KNOW YOU AREN'T JUST TAKING ME SOMEWHERE TO MURDER ME?
WOULD YOU RATHER STAY HERE WITH THAT MONSTER, WHO WILL ALMOST CERTAINLY MURDER YOU?
MMMMMMMMMMMMMNNOOOO.
I'LL FOLLOW YOU TO MURDERVILLE, I GUESS.
RINGLEY, GO COLLECT BANJO. HE'S WANDERED OFF IN THE CEMETERY AGAIN AND, AS MUCH AS I'D LIKE TO, WE CAN'T LEAVE HIM.
RIGHT-O, CAPTAIN!
RIP
EFFREY COMBS
1957-2017

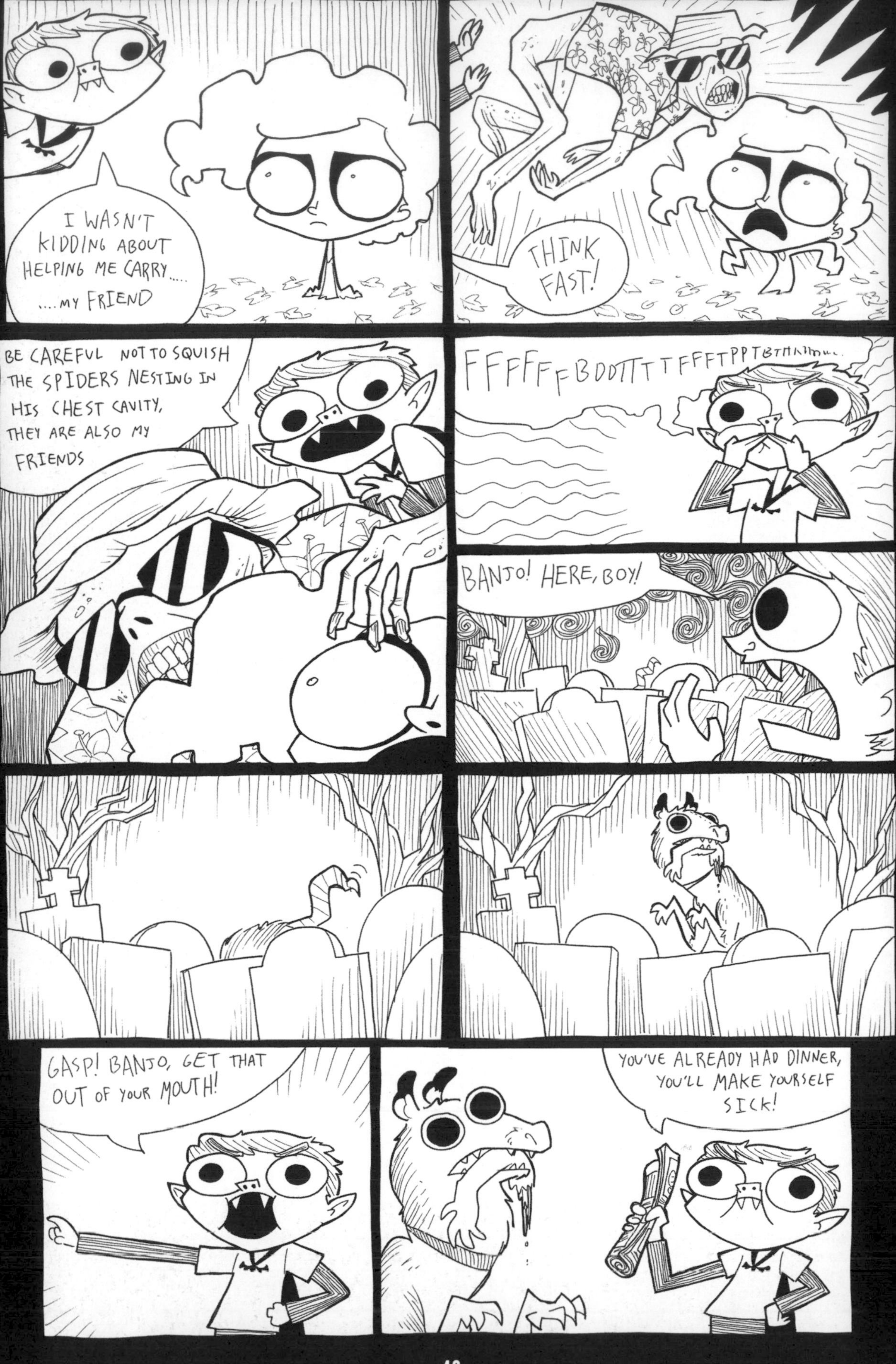
I WASN'T KIDDING ABOUT HELPING ME CARRY.....
....MY FRIEND
THINK FAST!
BE CAREFUL NOT TO SQUISH THE SPIDERS NESTING IN HIS CHEST CAVITY, THEY ARE ALSO MY FRIENDS
FFFFFFBOOTTTTTFFFTPPT
BANJO! HERE, BOY!
GASP! BANJO, GET THAT OUT OF YOUR MOUTH!
YOU'VE ALREADY HAD DINNER, YOU'LL MAKE YOURSELF SICK!

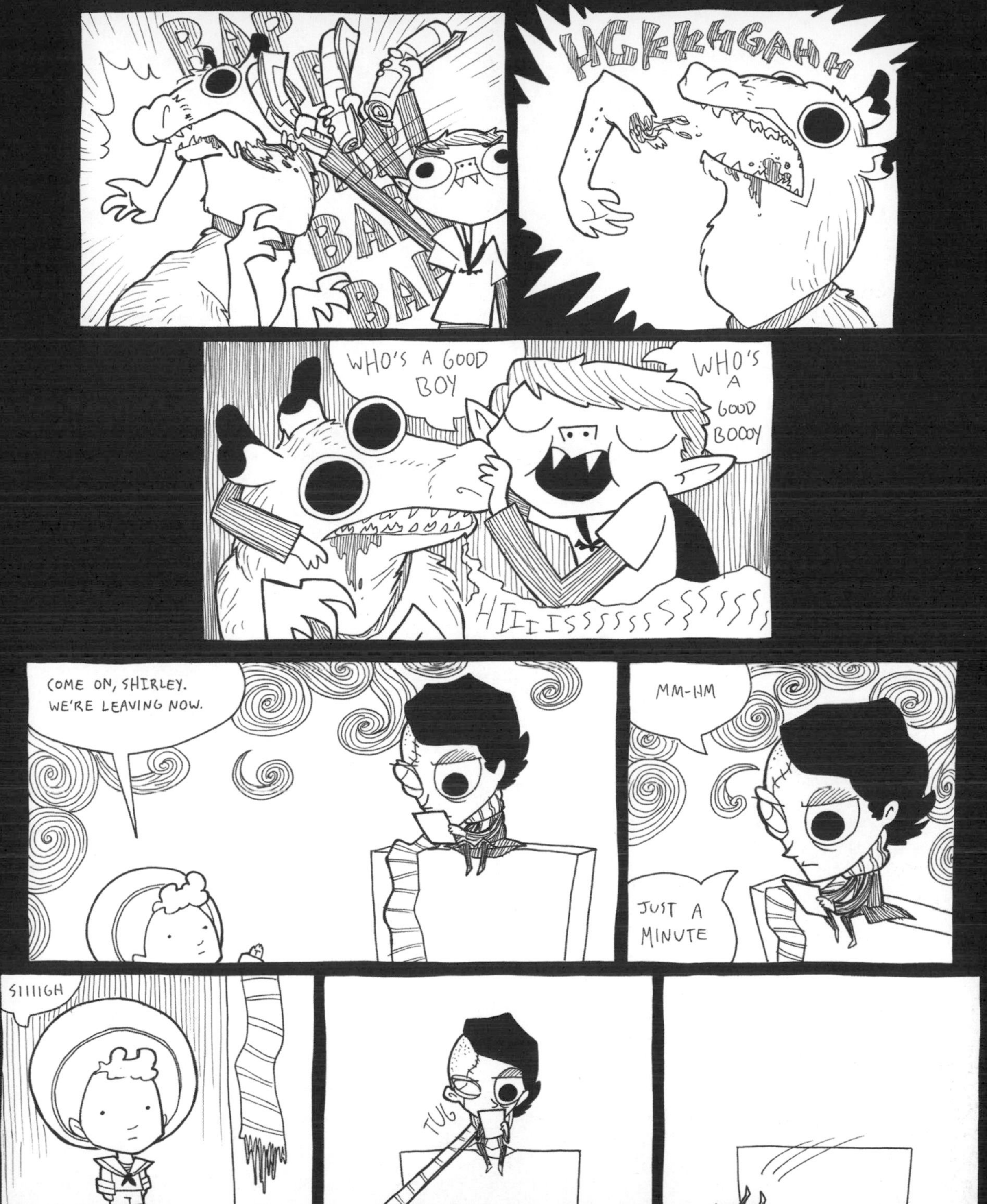

BAP
BAP
BAP
HGEKHGAHH
WHO'S A GOOD BOY
WHO'S A GOOD BOOOY
HIIISSSSSSSSSSSS
COME ON, SHIRLEY. WE'RE LEAVING NOW.
MM-HM
JUST A MINUTE
SIIIIGH
TUG

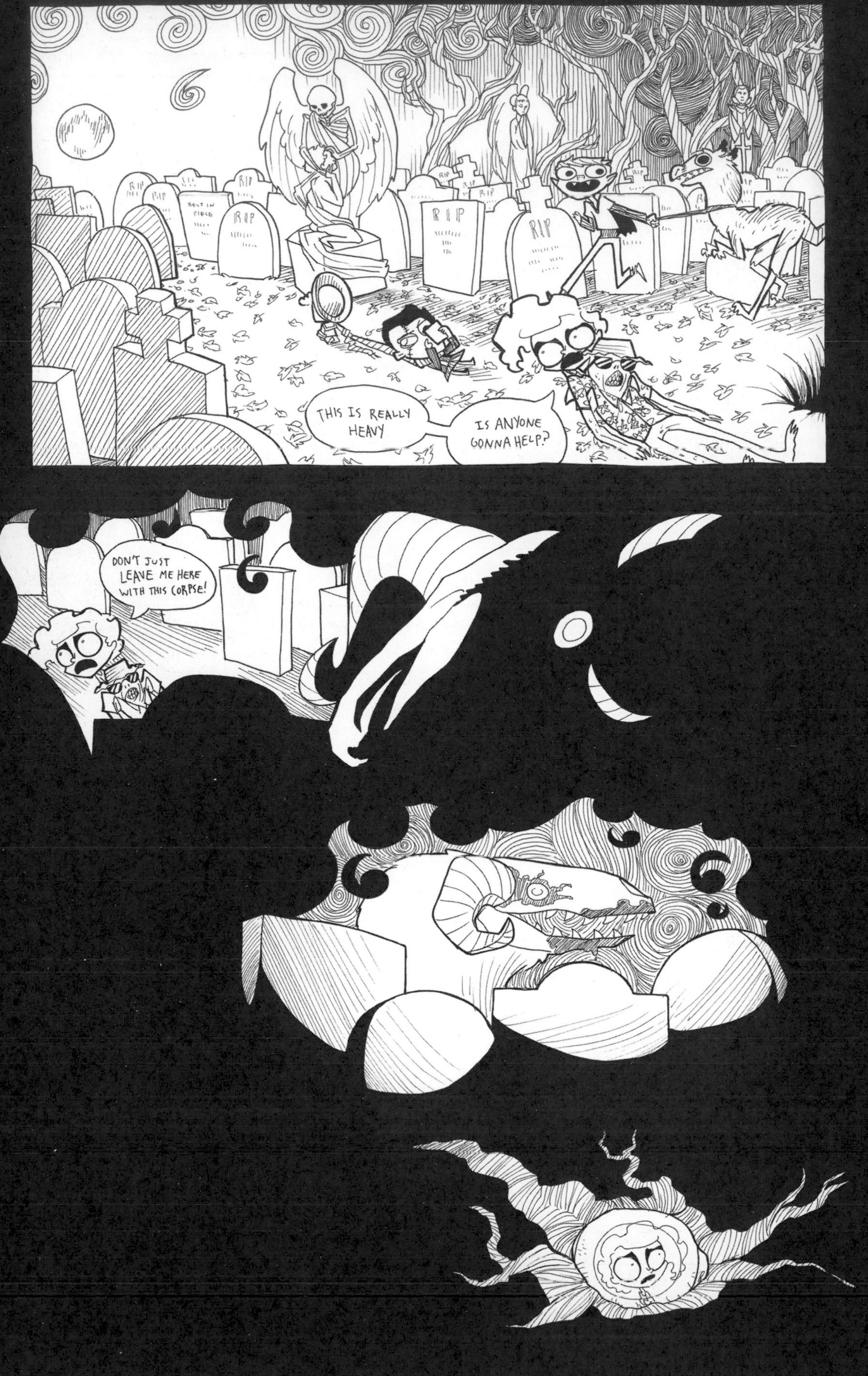
THIS IS REALLY HEAVY
IS ANYONE GONNA HELP?
DON'T JUST LEAVE ME HERE WITH THIS CORPSE!

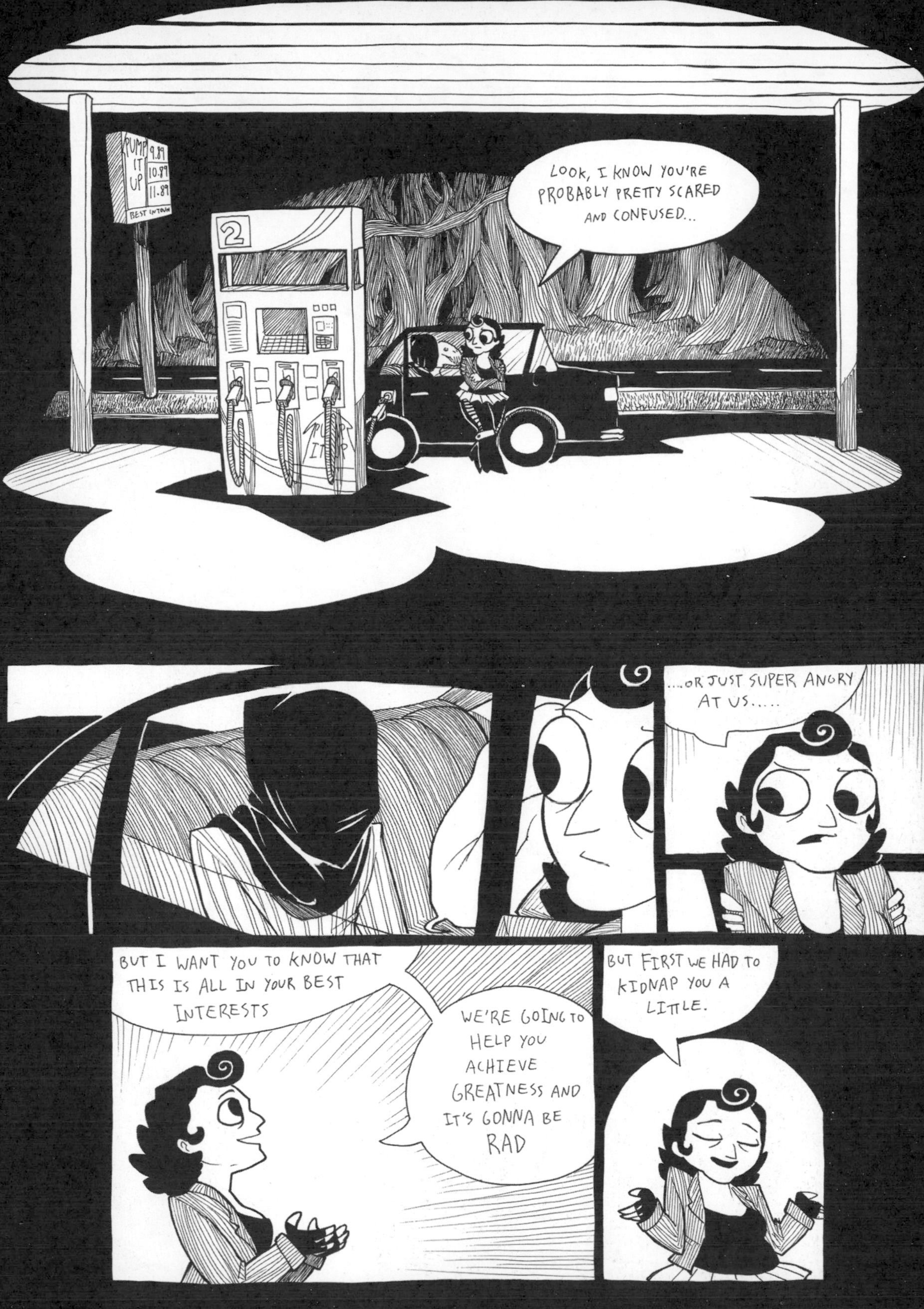
PUMP IT UP 9.89 10.89 11.89
BEST IN TOWN
2
LOOK, I KNOW YOU'RE PROBABLY PRETTY SCARED AND CONFUSED...
...OR JUST SUPER ANGRY AT US.....
BUT I WANT YOU TO KNOW THAT THIS IS ALL IN YOUR BEST INTERESTS
WE'RE GOING TO HELP YOU ACHIEVE GREATNESS AND IT'S GONNA BE RAD
BUT FIRST WE HAD TO KIDNAP YOU A LITTLE.

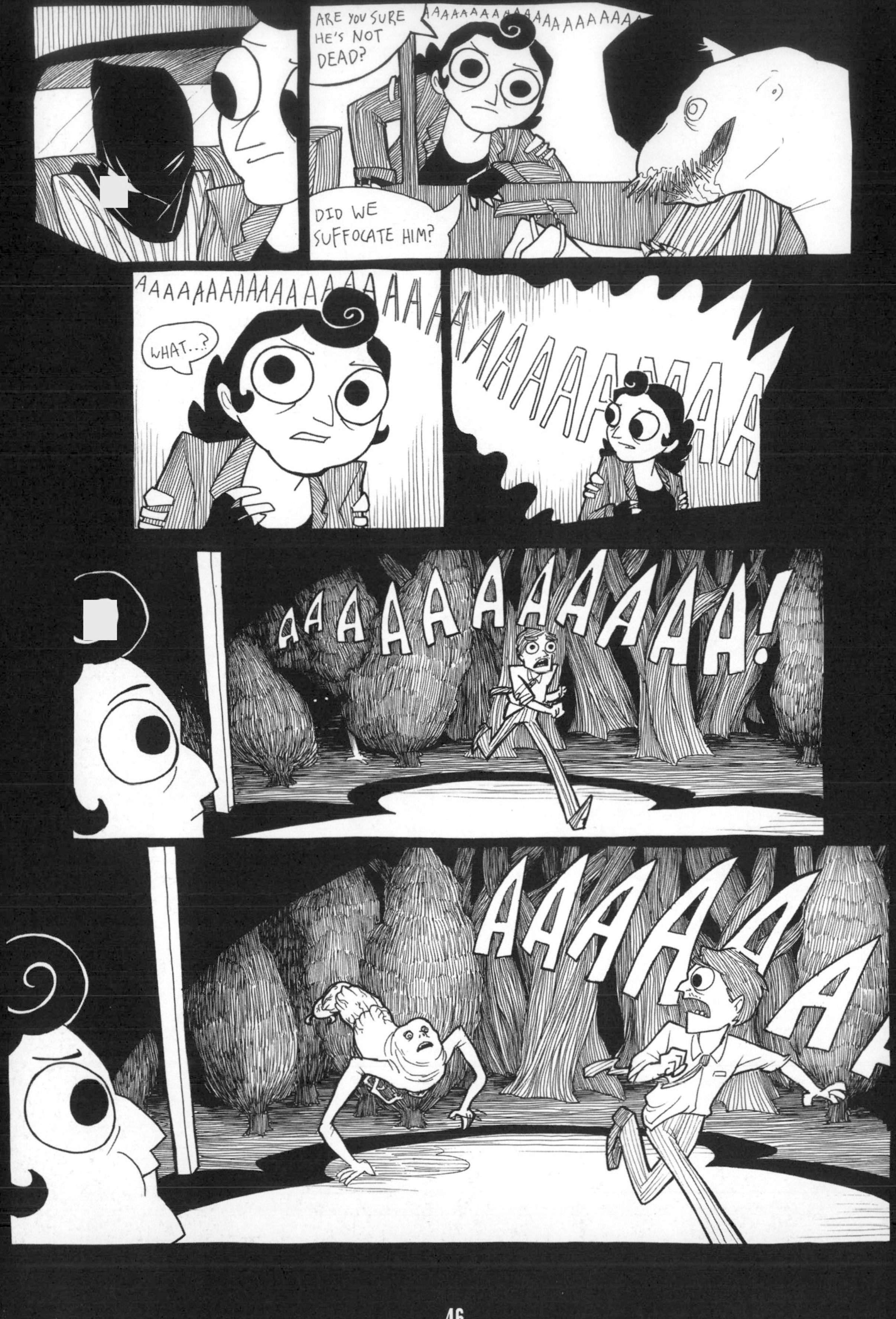
ARE YOU SURE HE'S NOT DEAD?
AAAAAAAAAAAAAAAAAA
DID WE SUFFOCATE HIM?
AAAAAAAAAAAAAAAAA
WHAT...?
AAAAAAAAAAAAA
AAAAAAAAAAAAA!
AAAAAAA

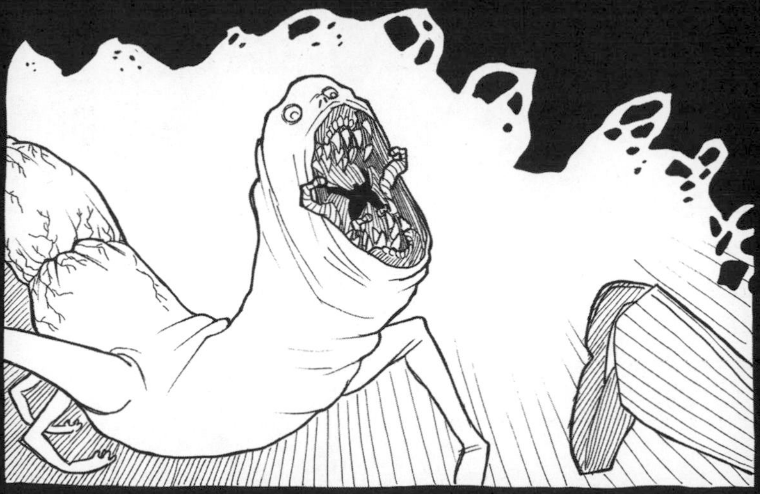

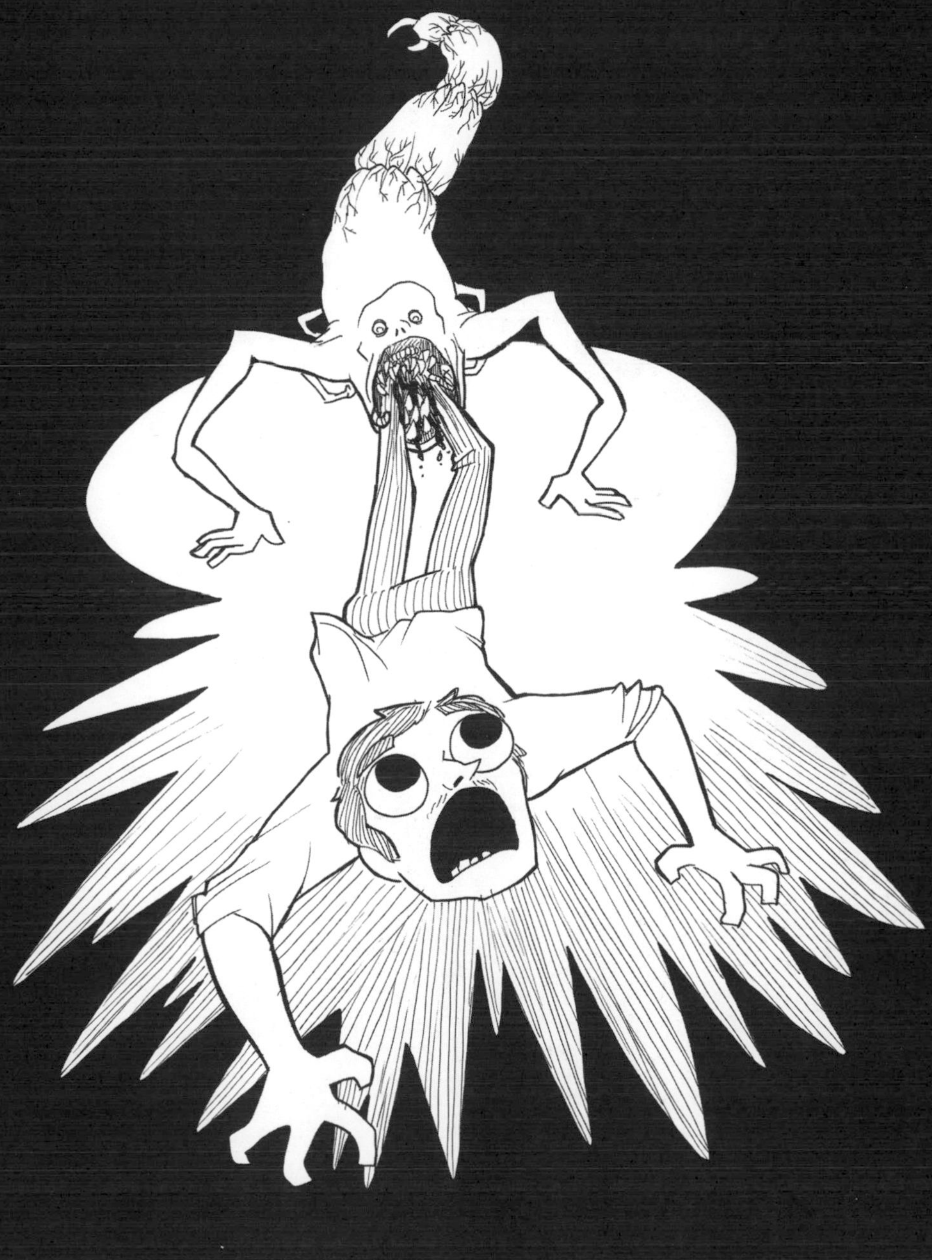

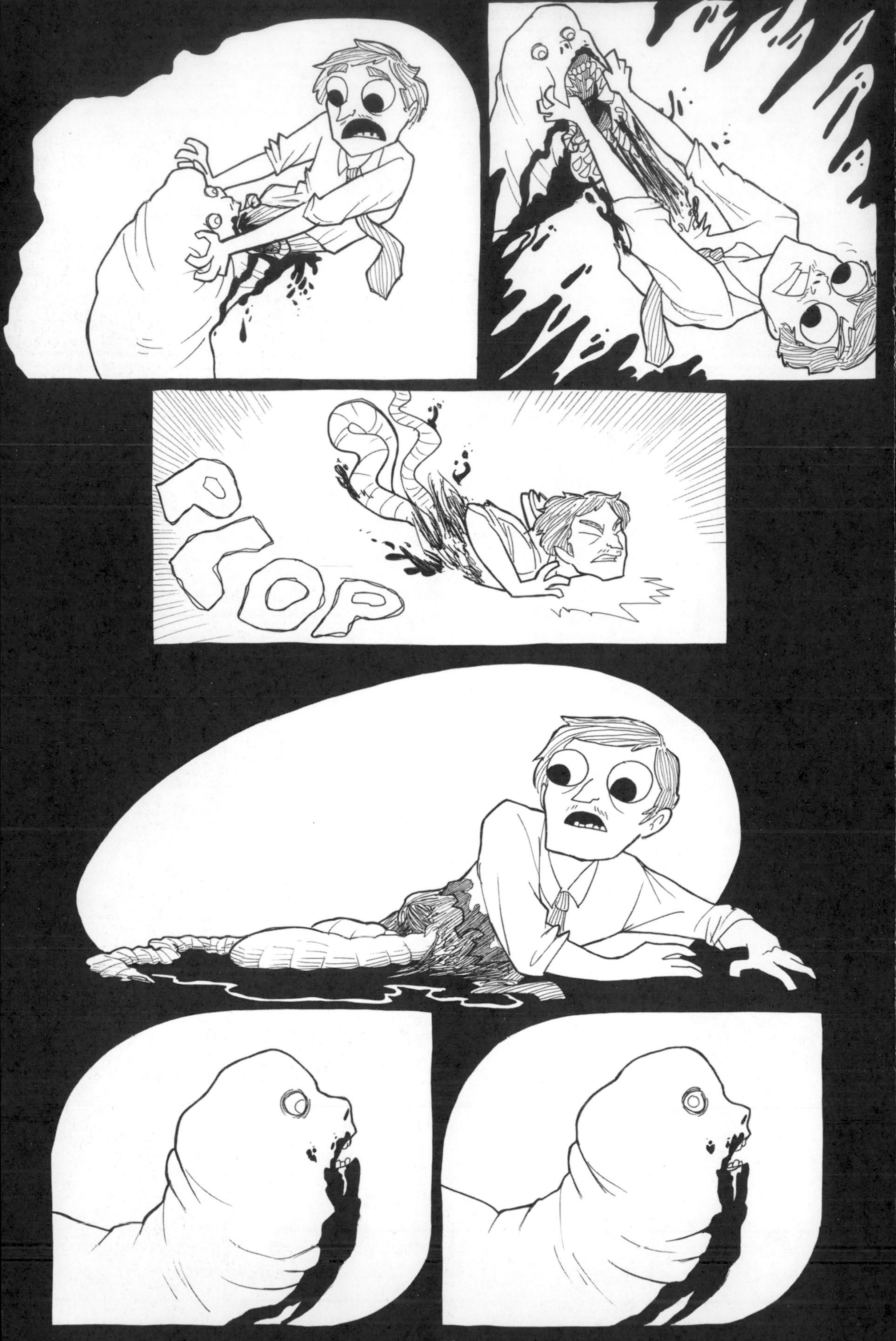
PLOP

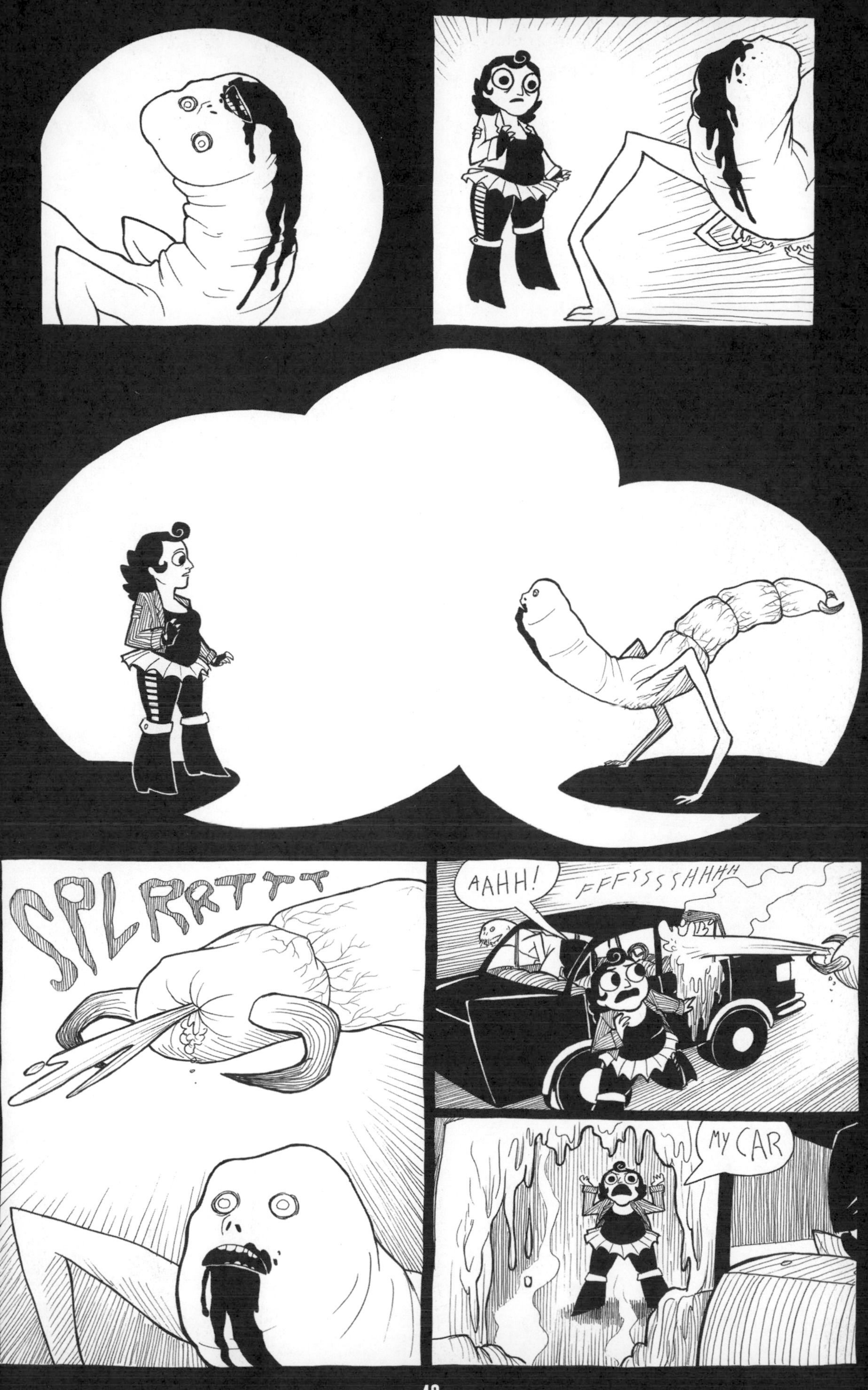
SPLRRTTT
AAHH!
FFFSSSSHHHH
MY CAR

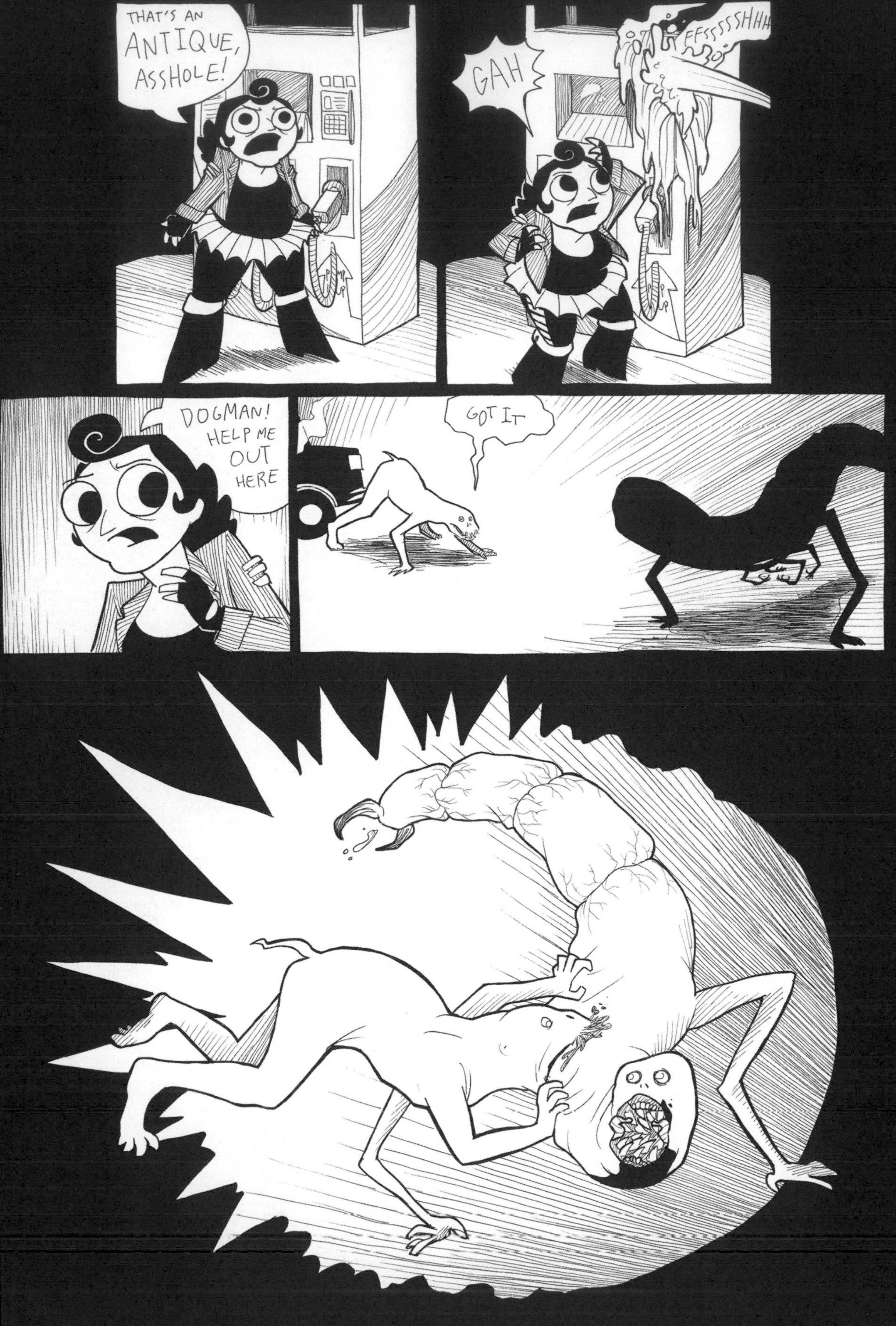
THAT'S AN ANTIQUE, ASSHOLE!
GAH
FFSSSSSSHHH
DOGMAN! HELP ME OUT HERE
GOT IT

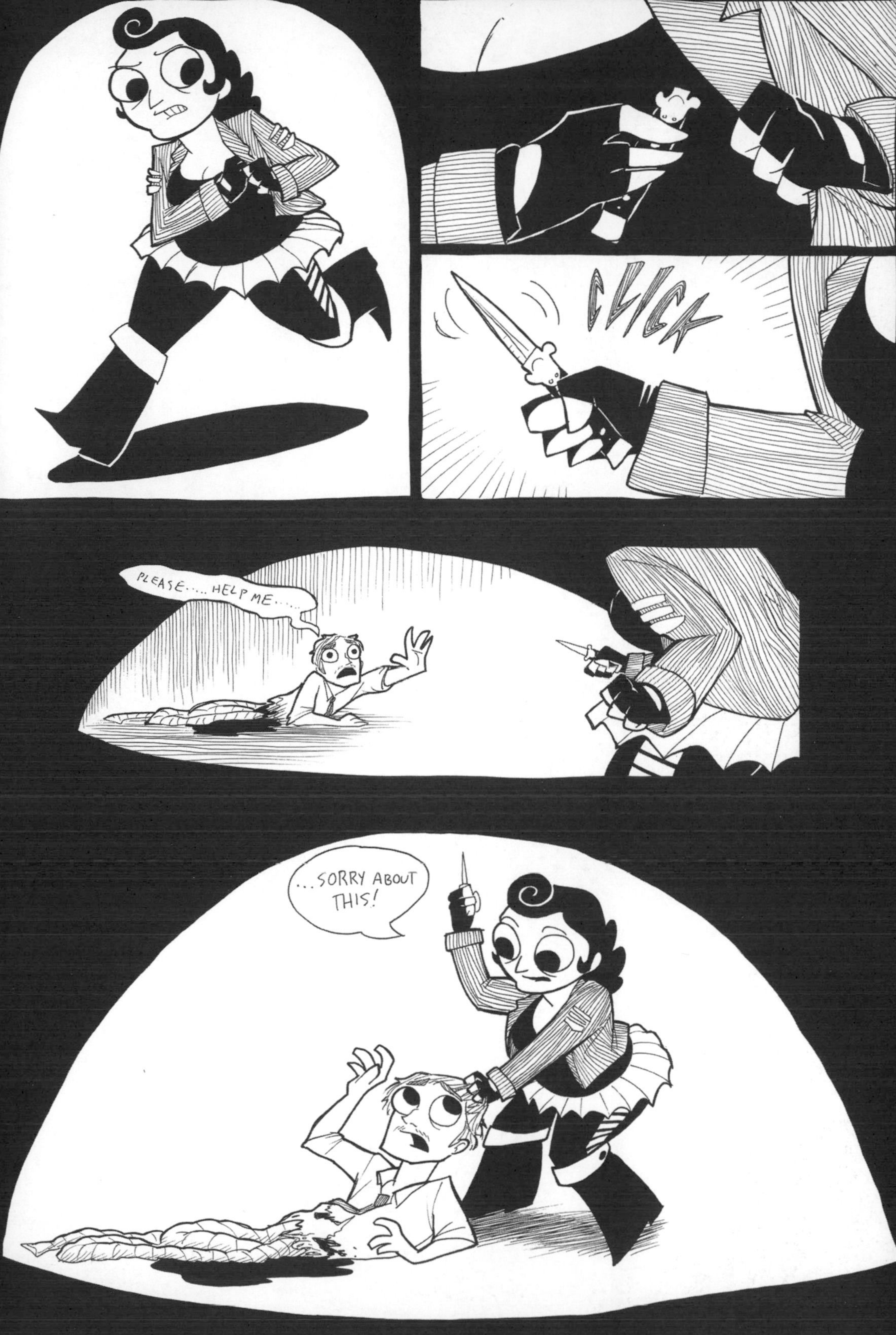
CLICK
PLEASE..... HELP ME.....
...SORRY ABOUT THIS!

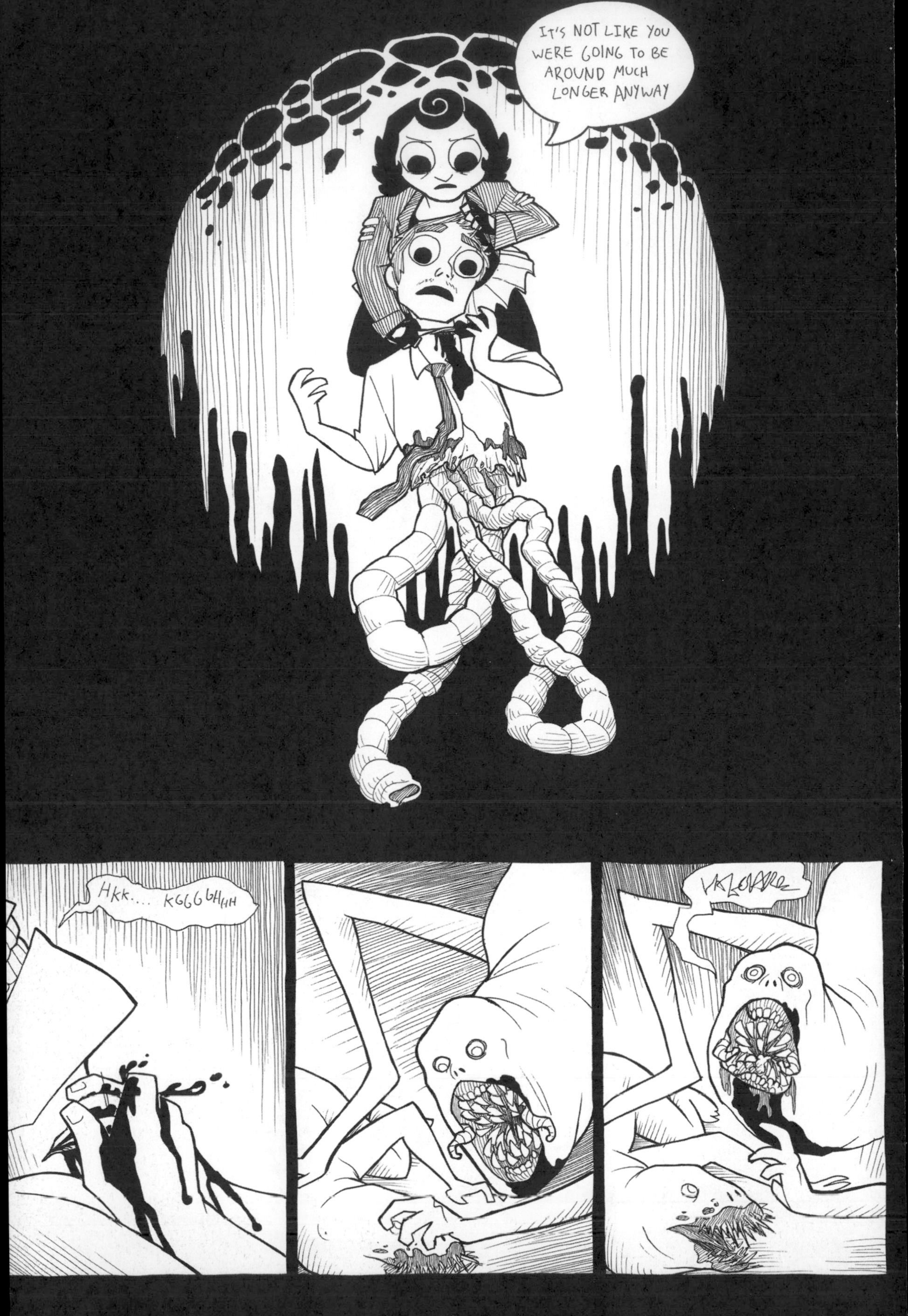
IT'S NOT LIKE YOU WERE GOING TO BE AROUND MUCH LONGER ANYWAY
HKK.... KGGGGHHH

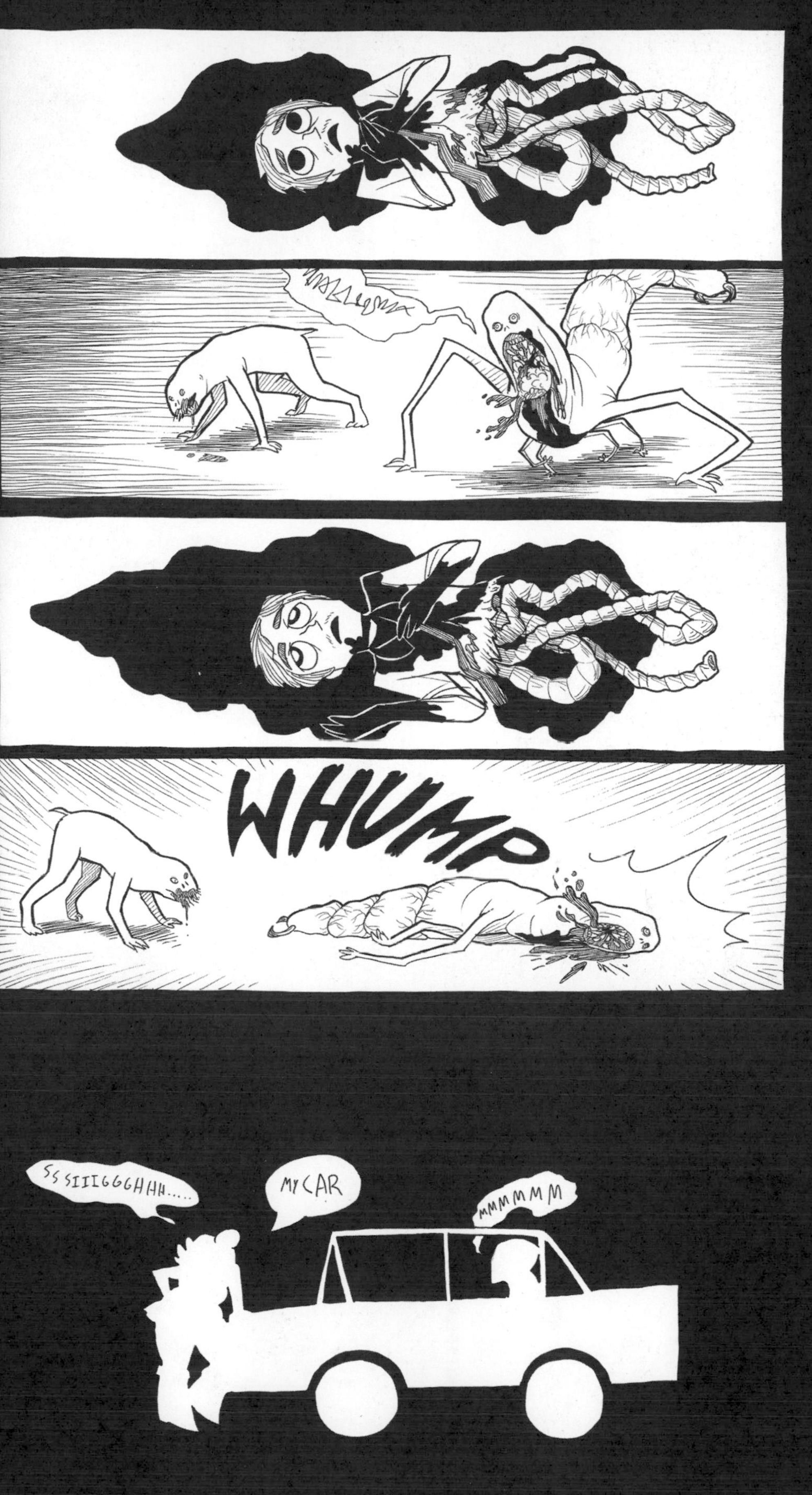
WHUMP
SSSIIIGGGHHH.....
MY CAR
MMMMMM

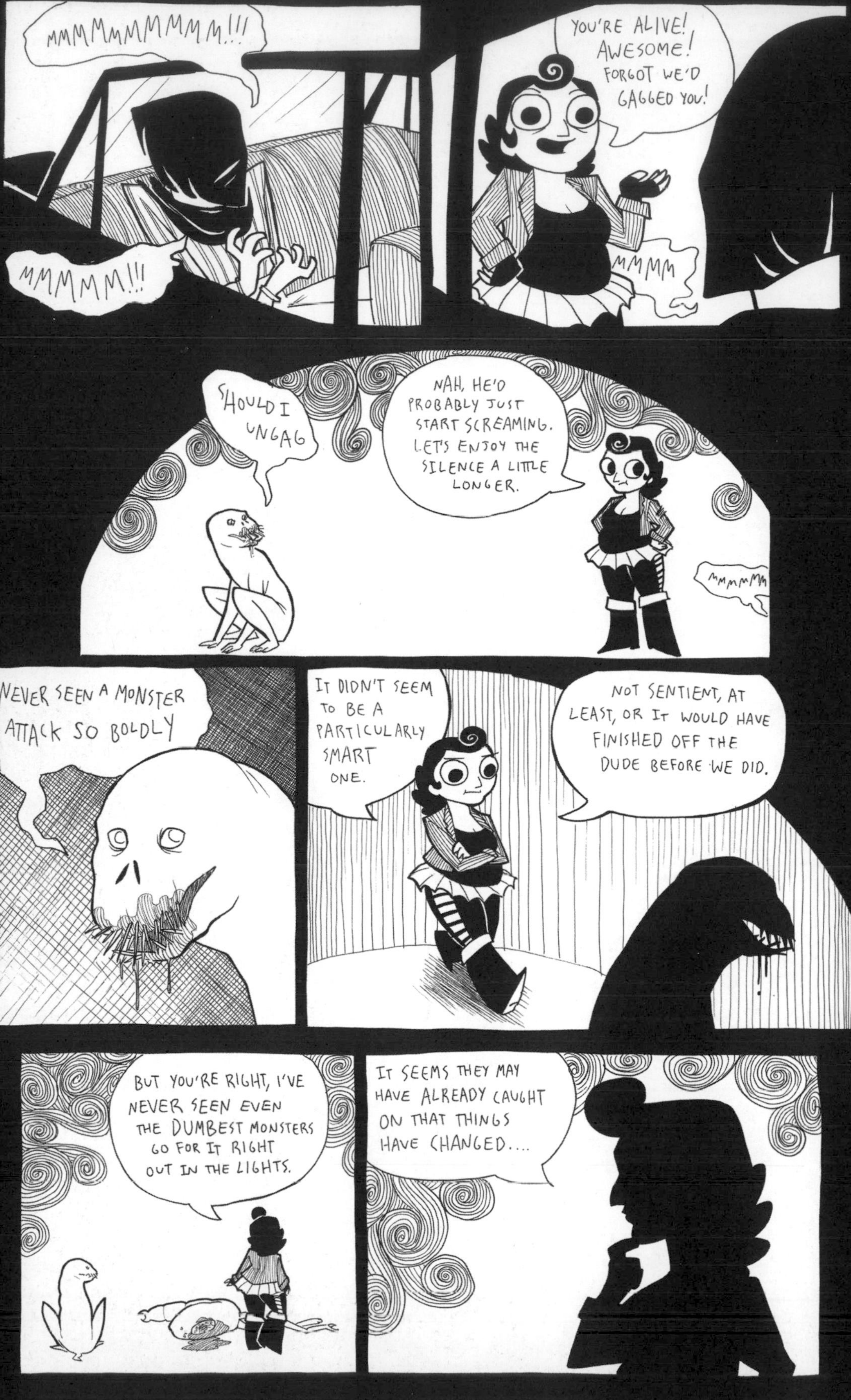
MMMMMMMMMM!!!
MMMMM!!!
YOU'RE ALIVE! AWESOME! FORGOT WE'D GAGGED YOU!
MMMM
SHOULD I UNGAG
NAH, HE'D PROBABLY JUST START SCREAMING. LET'S ENJOY THE SILENCE A LITTLE LONGER.
MMMMMM
NEVER SEEN A MONSTER ATTACK SO BOLDLY
IT DIDN'T SEEM TO BE A PARTICULARLY SMART ONE.
NOT SENTIENT, AT LEAST, OR IT WOULD HAVE FINISHED OFF THE DUDE BEFORE WE DID.
BUT YOU'RE RIGHT, I'VE NEVER SEEN EVEN THE DUMBEST MONSTERS GO FOR IT RIGHT OUT IN THE LIGHTS.
IT SEEMS THEY MAY HAVE ALREADY CAUGHT ON THAT THINGS HAVE CHANGED....

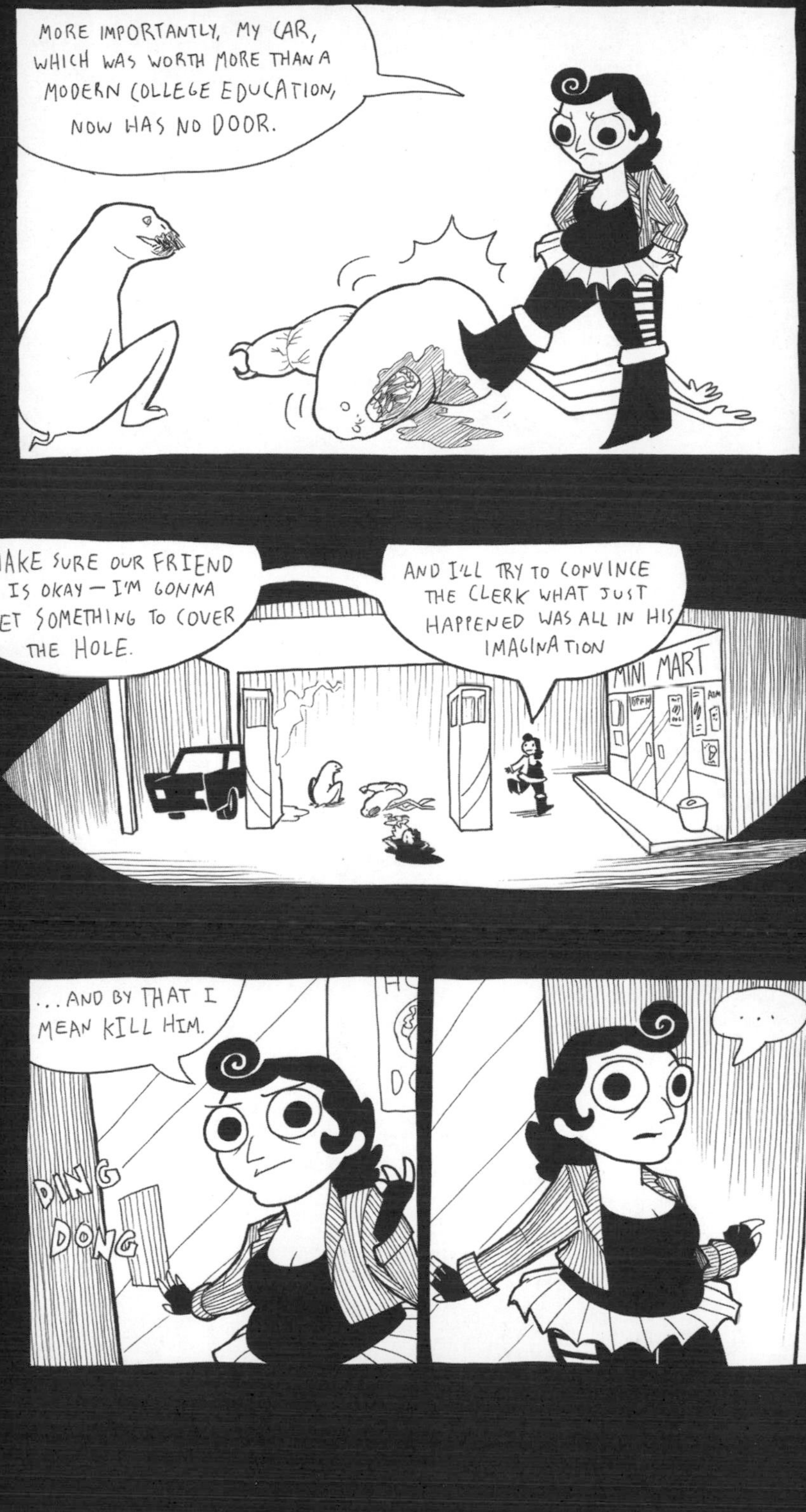
MORE IMPORTANTLY, MY CAR, WHICH WAS WORTH MORE THAN A MODERN COLLEGE EDUCATION, NOW HAS NO DOOR.
MAKE SURE OUR FRIEND IS OKAY — I'M GONNA GET SOMETHING TO COVER THE HOLE.
AND I'LL TRY TO CONVINCE THE CLERK WHAT JUST HAPPENED WAS ALL IN HIS IMAGINATION
MINI MART
...AND BY THAT I MEAN KILL HIM.
DING DONG
...

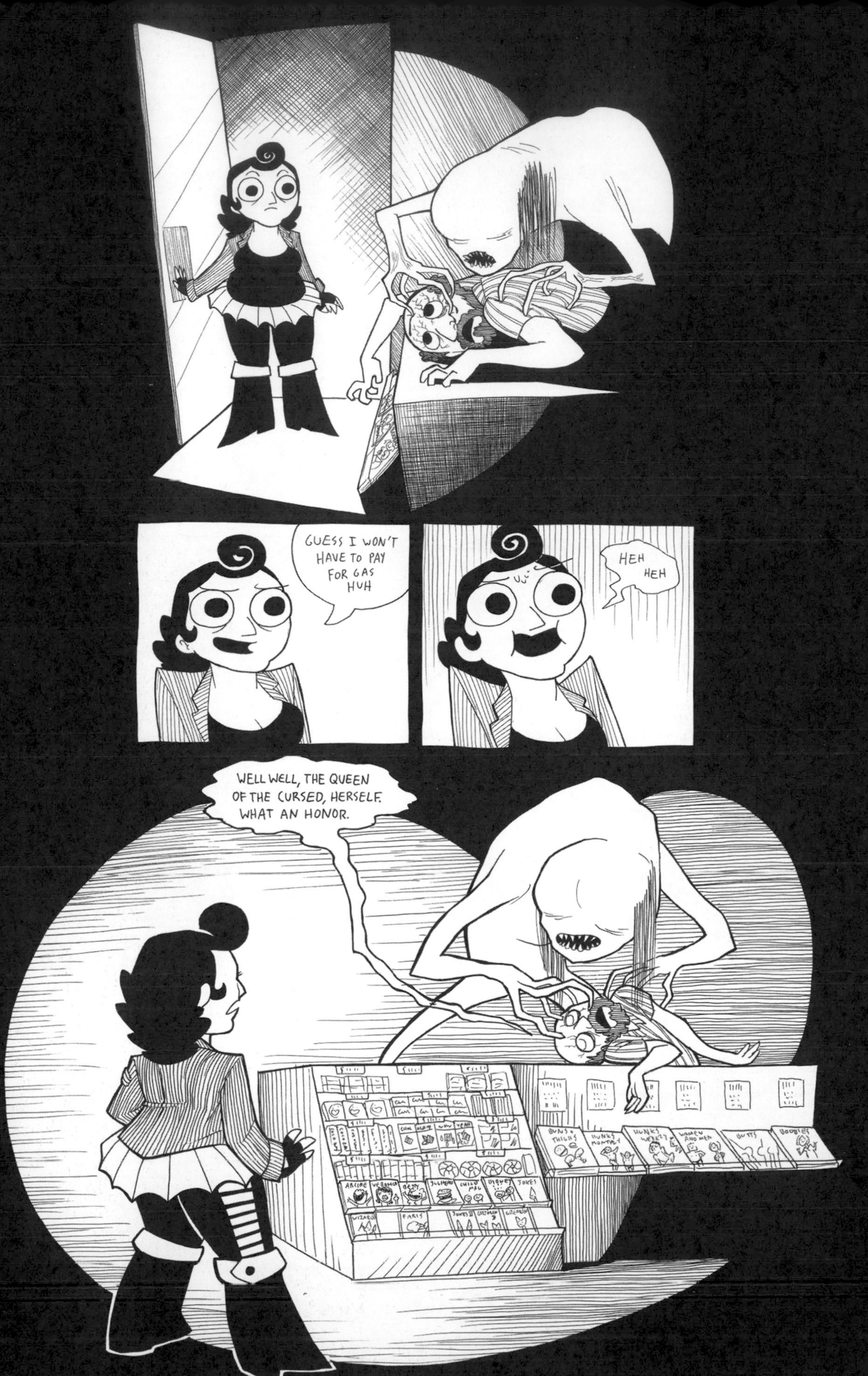
GUESS I WON'T HAVE TO PAY FOR GAS HUH
HEH HEH
WELL WELL, THE QUEEN OF THE CURSED, HERSELF. WHAT AN HONOR.

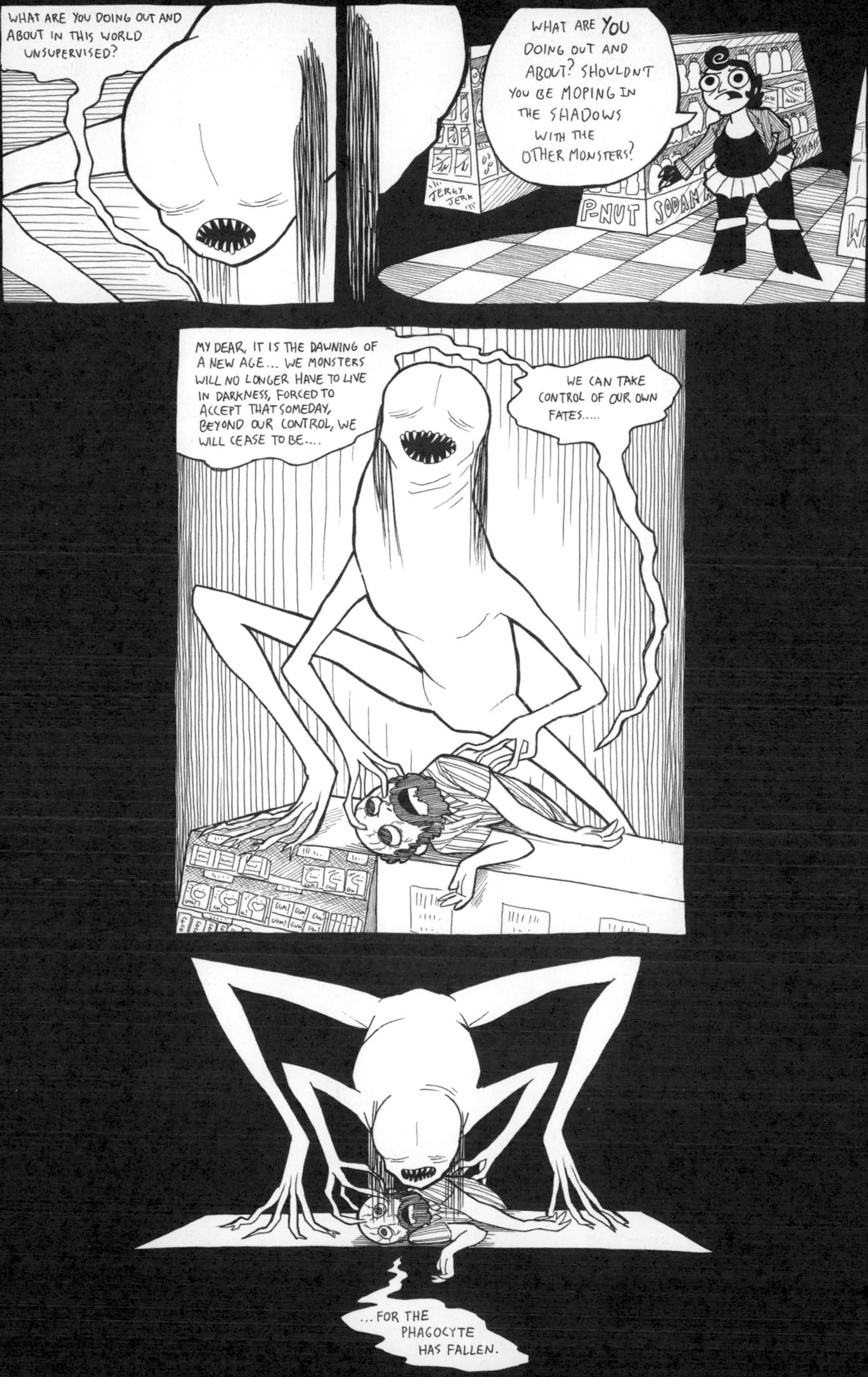
WHAT ARE YOU DOING OUT AND ABOUT IN THIS WORLD UNSUPERVISED?
WHAT ARE YOU DOING OUT AND ABOUT? SHOULDN'T YOU BE MOPING IN THE SHADOWS WITH THE OTHER MONSTERS?
JERKY JERK
P-NUT
SODA
MY DEAR, IT IS THE DAWNING OF A NEW AGE... WE MONSTERS WILL NO LONGER HAVE TO LIVE IN DARKNESS, FORCED TO ACCEPT THAT SOMEDAY, BEYOND OUR CONTROL, WE WILL CEASE TO BE....
WE CAN TAKE CONTROL OF OUR OWN FATES.....
GUM!
...FOR THE PHAGOCYTE HAS FALLEN.

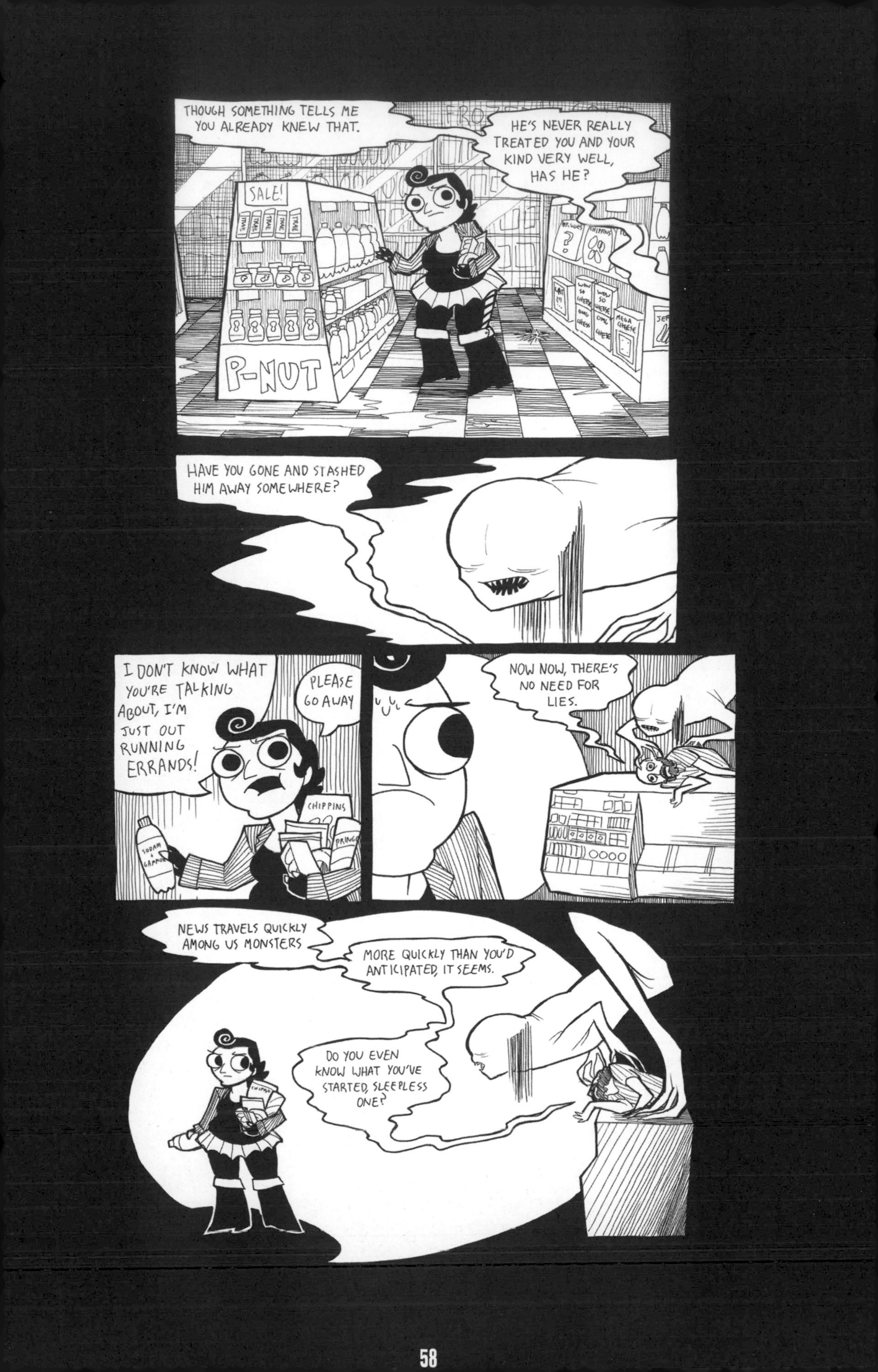
THOUGH SOMETHING TELLS ME YOU ALREADY KNEW THAT.
HE'S NEVER REALLY TREATED YOU AND YOUR KIND VERY WELL, HAS HE?
SALE!
P-NUT
HAVE YOU GONE AND STASHED HIM AWAY SOMEWHERE?
I DON'T KNOW WHAT YOU'RE TALKING ABOUT, I'M JUST OUT RUNNING ERRANDS!
PLEASE GO AWAY
CHIPPINS
NOW NOW, THERE'S NO NEED FOR LIES.
NEWS TRAVELS QUICKLY AMONG US MONSTERS
MORE QUICKLY THAN YOU'D ANTICIPATED, IT SEEMS.
DO YOU EVEN KNOW WHAT YOU'VE STARTED, SLEEPLESS ONE?

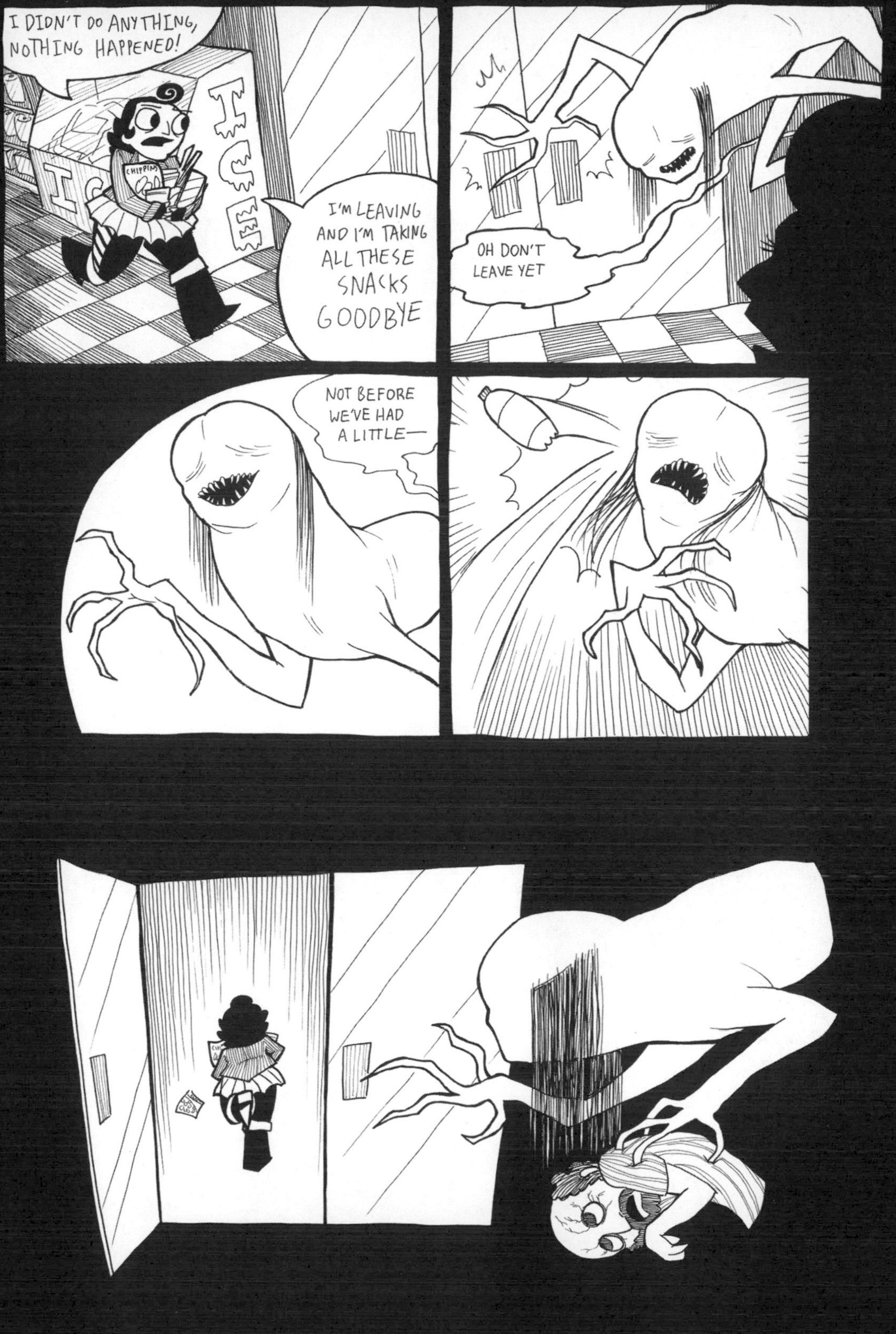
I DIDN'T DO ANYTHING, NOTHING HAPPENED!
I'M LEAVING AND I'M TAKING ALL THESE SNACKS GOODBYE
OH DON'T LEAVE YET
NOT BEFORE WE'VE HAD A LITTLE—

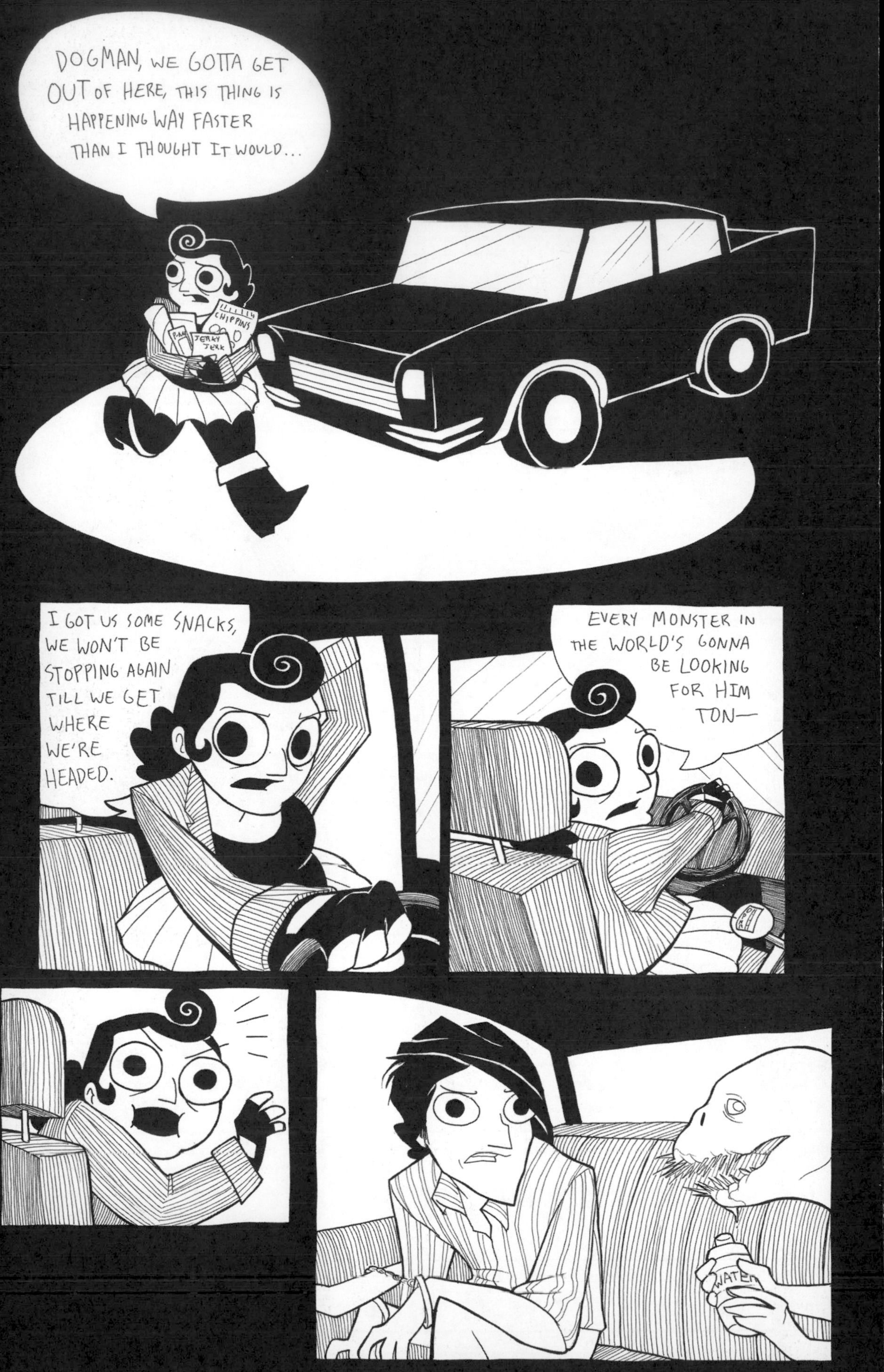
DOGMAN, WE GOTTA GET OUT OF HERE, THIS THING IS HAPPENING WAY FASTER THAN I THOUGHT IT WOULD...
CHIPPINS
JERKY JERK
I GOT US SOME SNACKS, WE WON'T BE STOPPING AGAIN TILL WE GET WHERE WE'RE HEADED.
EVERY MONSTER IN THE WORLD'S GONNA BE LOOKING FOR HIM TON—
WATER

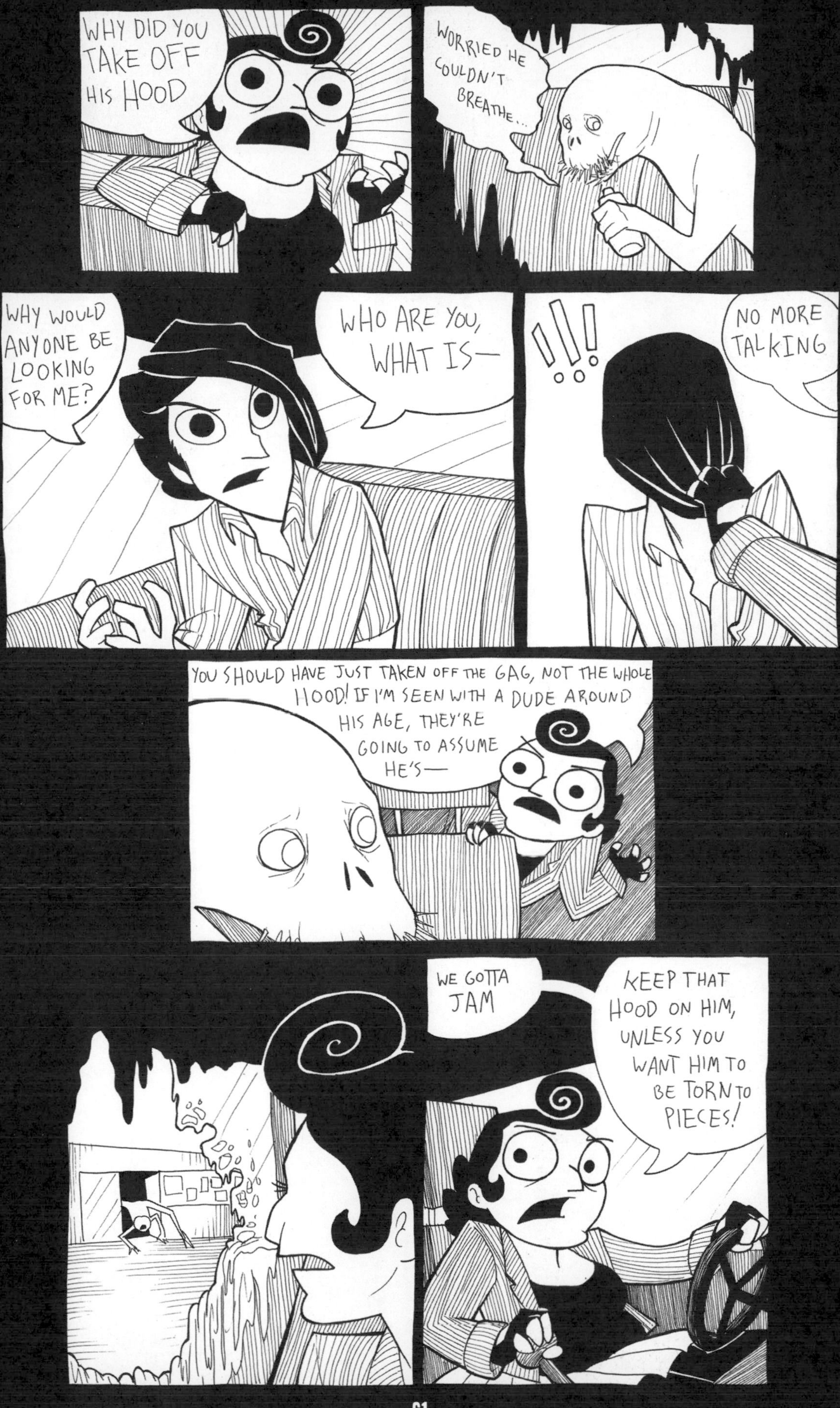
WHY DID YOU TAKE OFF HIS HOOD
WORRIED HE COULDN'T BREATHE...
WHY WOULD ANYONE BE LOOKING FOR ME?
WHO ARE YOU, WHAT IS—
!!!
NO MORE TALKING
YOU SHOULD HAVE JUST TAKEN OFF THE GAG, NOT THE WHOLE HOOD! IF I'M SEEN WITH A DUDE AROUND HIS AGE, THEY'RE GOING TO ASSUME HE'S—
WE GOTTA JAM
KEEP THAT HOOD ON HIM, UNLESS YOU WANT HIM TO BE TORN TO PIECES!

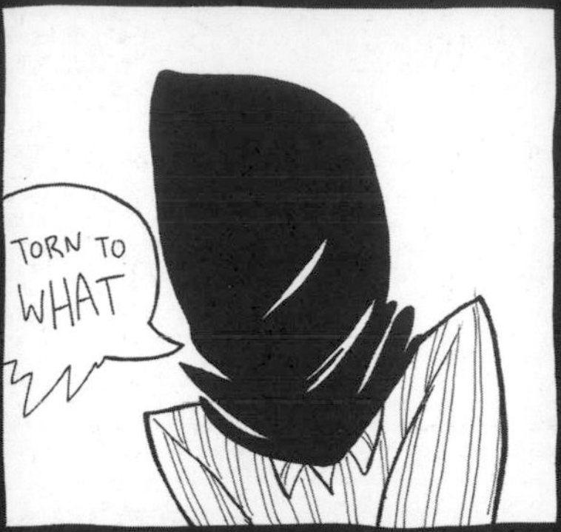
TORN TO WHAT

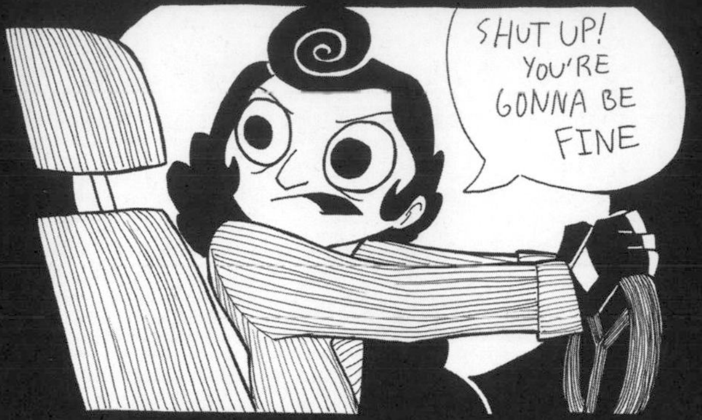
SHUT UP! YOU'RE GONNA BE FINE

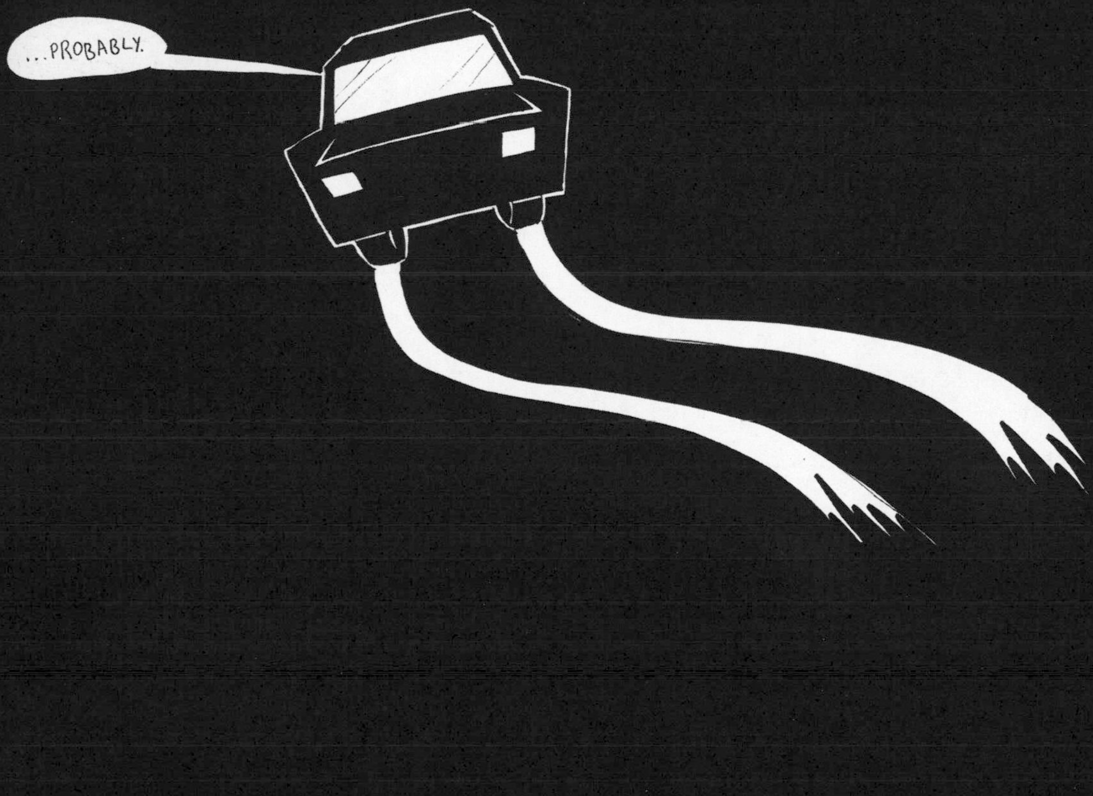
...PROBABLY.

CHAPTER 2

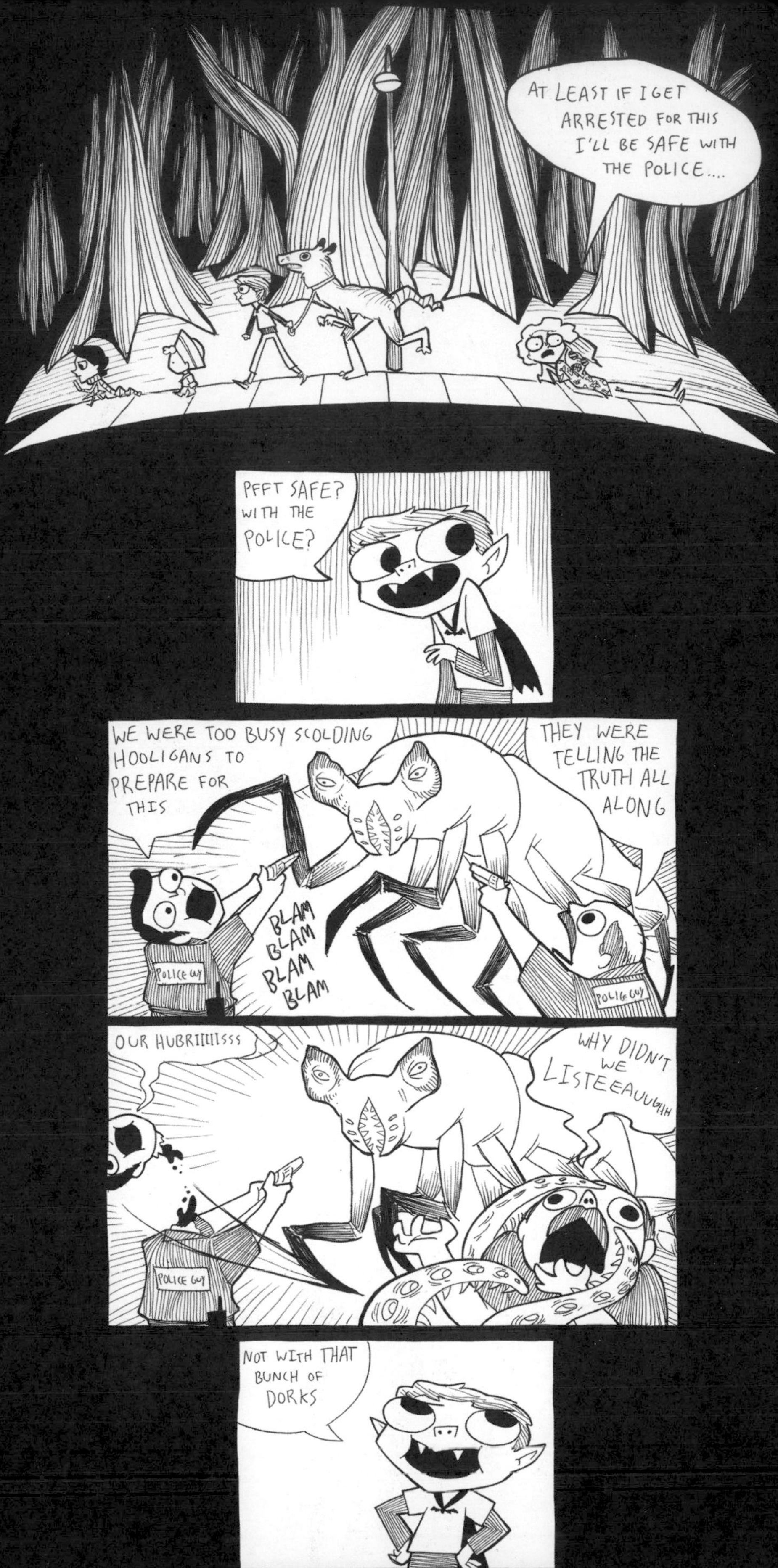
AT LEAST IF I GET ARRESTED FOR THIS I'LL BE SAFE WITH THE POLICE....
PFFT SAFE? WITH THE POLICE?
WE WERE TOO BUSY SCOLDING HOOLIGANS TO PREPARE FOR THIS
THEY WERE TELLING THE TRUTH ALL ALONG
BLAM BLAM BLAM BLAM
POLICE GUY
POLICE GUY
OUR HUBRIIIIIISSS
WHY DIDN'T WE LISTEEAUUGHH
POLICE GUY
NOT WITH THAT BUNCH OF DORKS

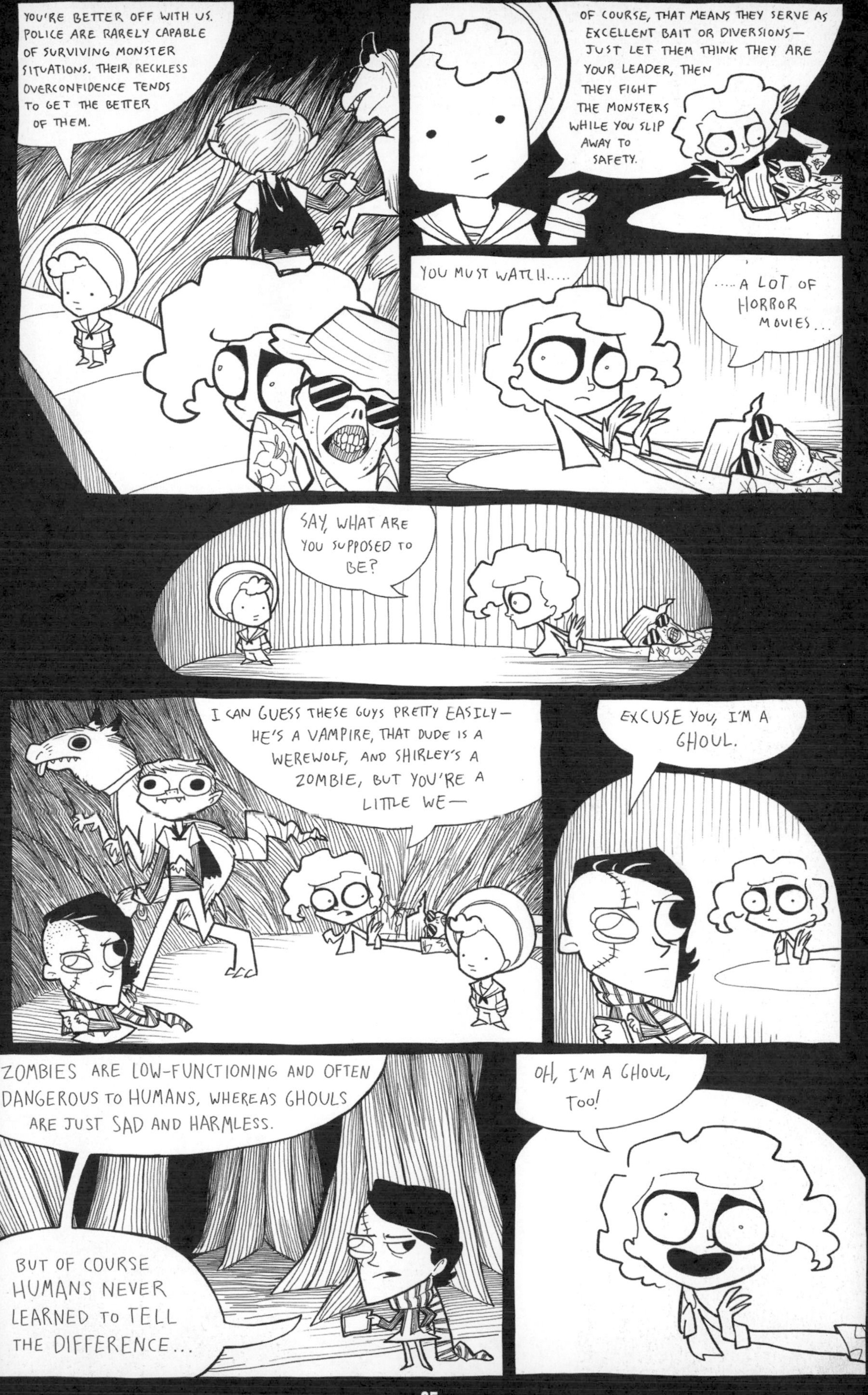
YOU'RE BETTER OFF WITH US. POLICE ARE RARELY CAPABLE OF SURVIVING MONSTER SITUATIONS. THEIR RECKLESS OVERCONFIDENCE TENDS TO GET THE BETTER OF THEM.
OF COURSE, THAT MEANS THEY SERVE AS EXCELLENT BAIT OR DIVERSIONS— JUST LET THEM THINK THEY ARE YOUR LEADER, THEN THEY FIGHT THE MONSTERS WHILE YOU SLIP AWAY TO SAFETY.
YOU MUST WATCH.....
.....A LOT OF HORROR MOVIES...
SAY, WHAT ARE YOU SUPPOSED TO BE?
I CAN GUESS THESE GUYS PRETTY EASILY— HE'S A VAMPIRE, THAT DUDE IS A WEREWOLF, AND SHIRLEY'S A ZOMBIE, BUT YOU'RE A LITTLE WE—
EXCUSE YOU, I'M A GHOUL.
ZOMBIES ARE LOW-FUNCTIONING AND OFTEN DANGEROUS TO HUMANS, WHEREAS GHOULS ARE JUST SAD AND HARMLESS.
BUT OF COURSE HUMANS NEVER LEARNED TO TELL THE DIFFERENCE...
OH, I'M A GHOUL, TOO!

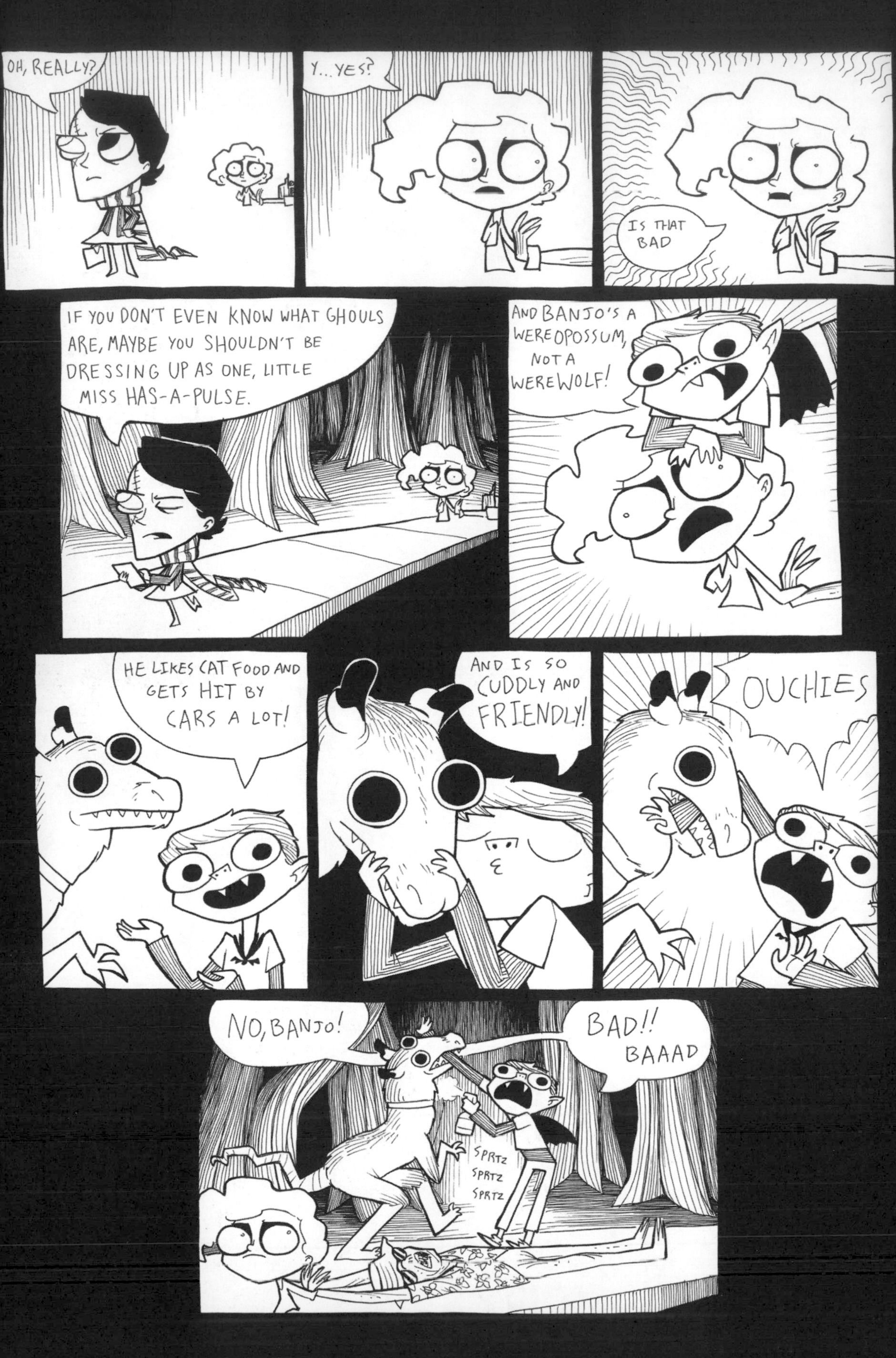
OH, REALLY?
Y... YES?
IS THAT BAD
IF YOU DON'T EVEN KNOW WHAT GHOULS ARE, MAYBE YOU SHOULDN'T BE DRESSING UP AS ONE, LITTLE MISS HAS-A-PULSE.
AND BANJO'S A WEREOPOSSUM, NOT A WEREWOLF!
HE LIKES CAT FOOD AND GETS HIT BY CARS A LOT!
AND IS SO CUDDLY AND FRIENDLY!
OUCHIES
NO, BANJO!
BAD!! BAAAD
SPRTZ
SPRTZ
SPRTZ

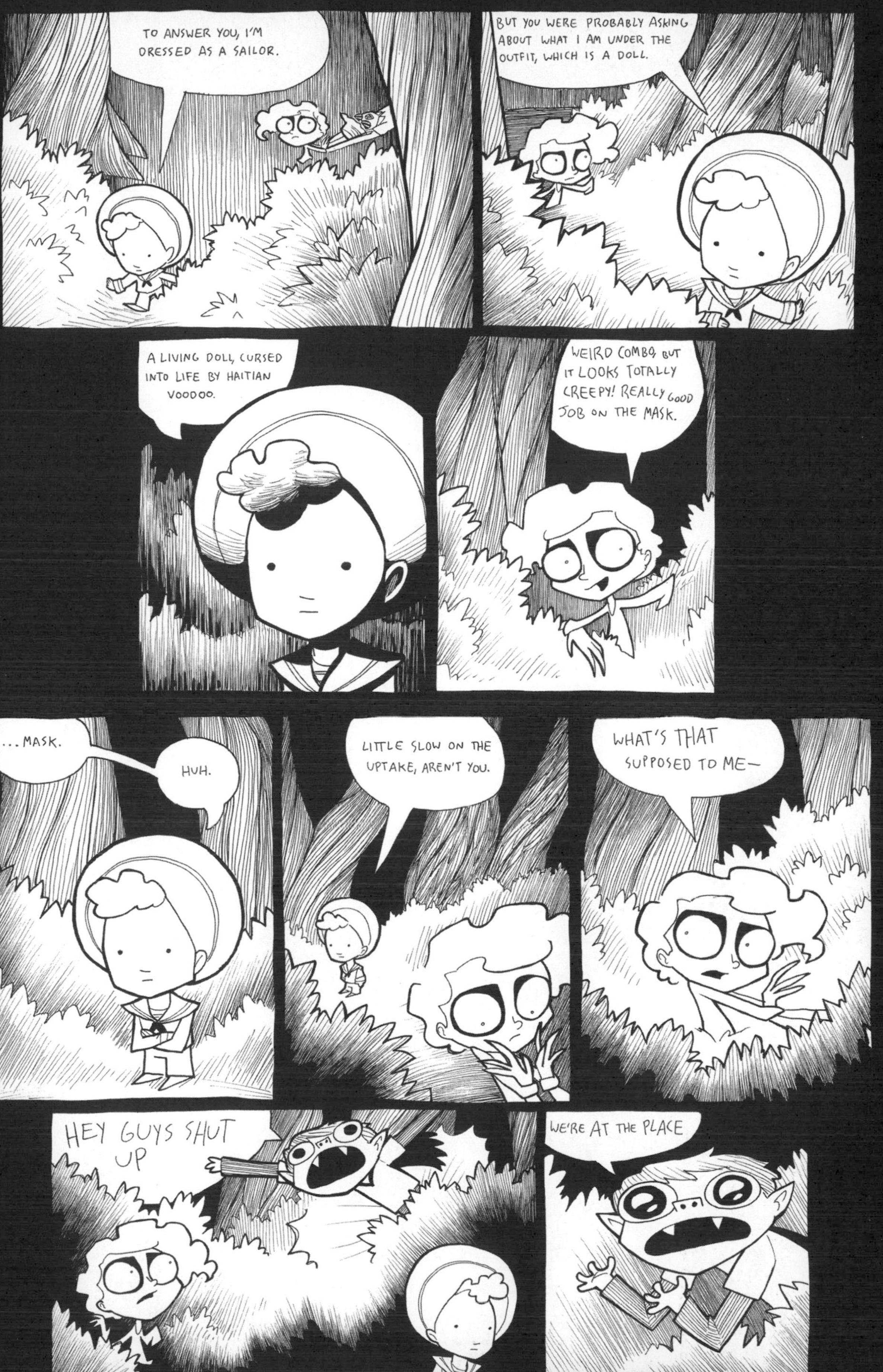
TO ANSWER YOU, I'M DRESSED AS A SAILOR.
BUT YOU WERE PROBABLY ASKING ABOUT WHAT I AM UNDER THE OUTFIT, WHICH IS A DOLL.
A LIVING DOLL, CURSED INTO LIFE BY HAITIAN VOODOO.
WEIRD COMBO, BUT IT LOOKS TOTALLY CREEPY! REALLY GOOD JOB ON THE MASK.
...MASK.
HUH.
LITTLE SLOW ON THE UPTAKE, AREN'T YOU.
WHAT'S THAT SUPPOSED TO ME—
HEY GUYS SHUT UP
WE'RE AT THE PLACE

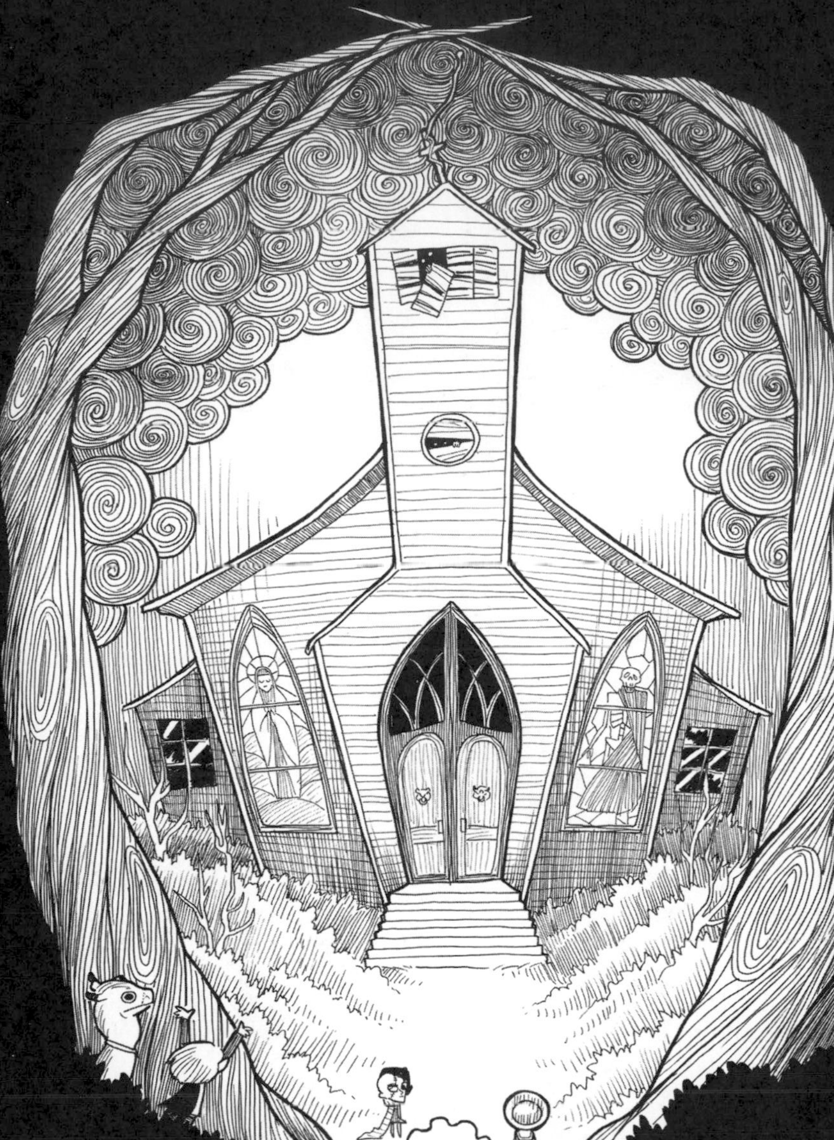

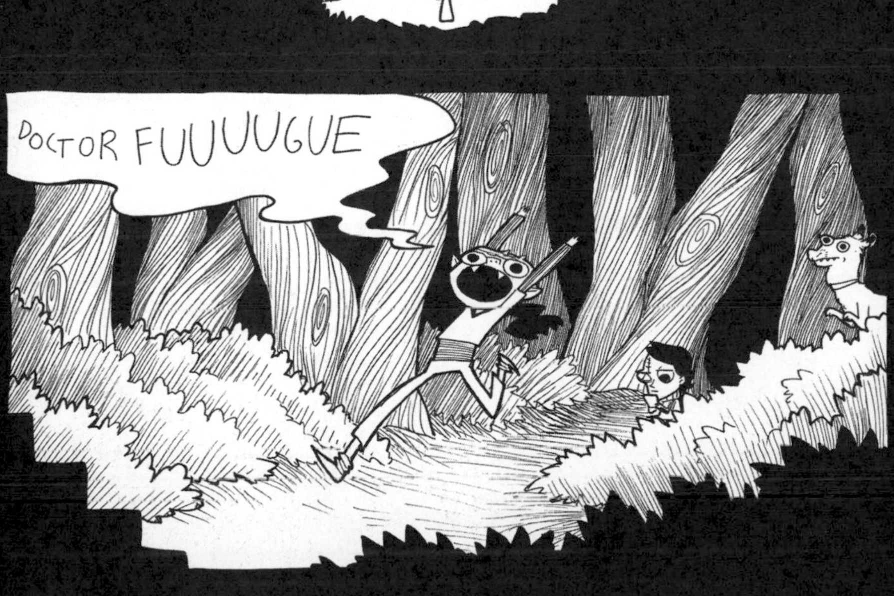
DOCTOR FUUUUGUE

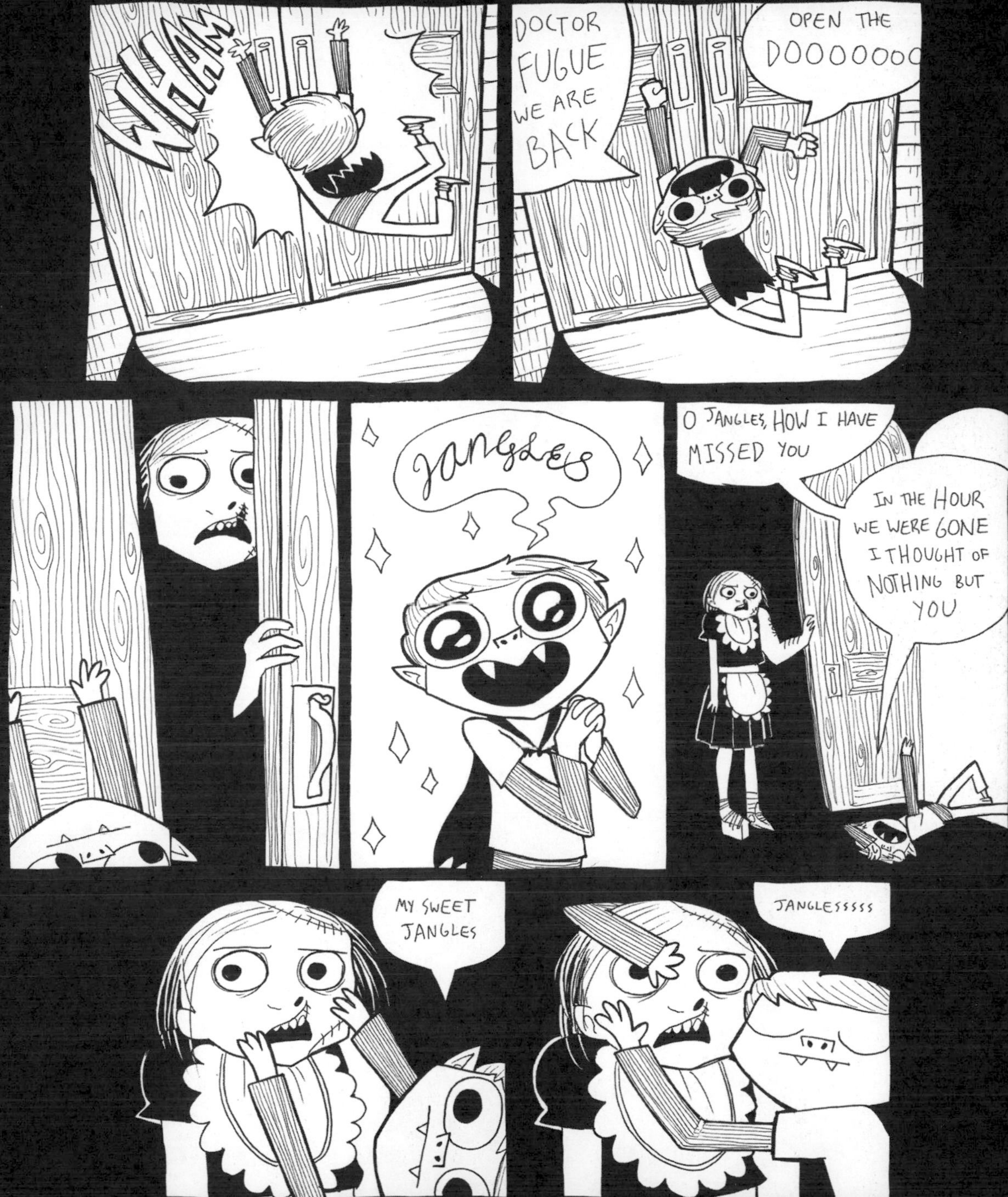
WHAM
DOCTOR FUGUE WE ARE BACK
OPEN THE DOOOOOOOO
JANGLES
O JANGLES, HOW I HAVE MISSED YOU
IN THE HOUR WE WERE GONE I THOUGHT OF NOTHING BUT YOU
MY SWEET JANGLES
JANGLESSSSS

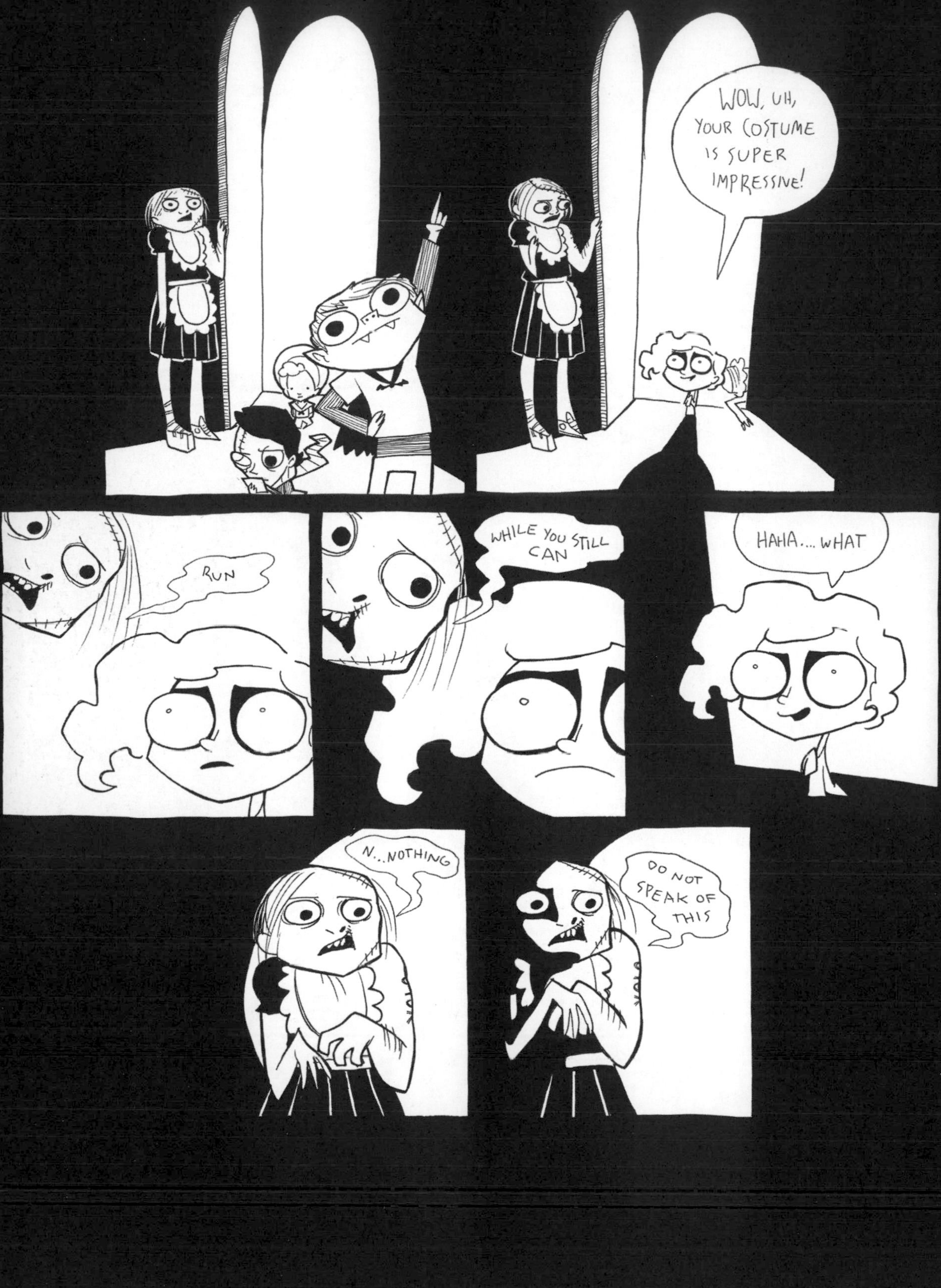
WOW, UH, YOUR COSTUME IS SUPER IMPRESSIVE!
RUN
WHILE YOU STILL CAN
HAHA.... WHAT
N...NOTHING
DO NOT SPEAK OF THIS

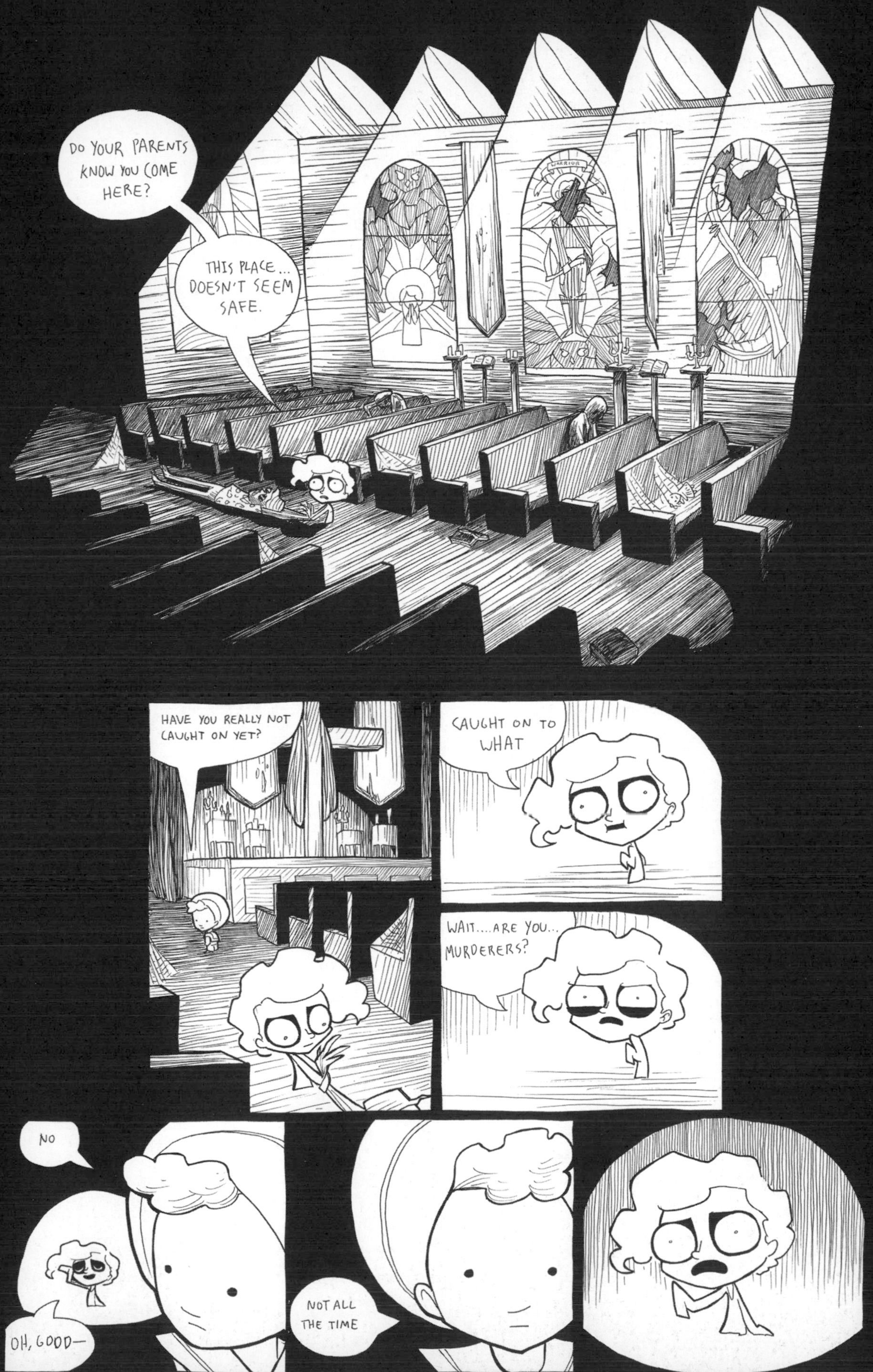
DO YOUR PARENTS KNOW YOU COME HERE?
THIS PLACE... DOESN'T SEEM SAFE.
HAVE YOU REALLY NOT CAUGHT ON YET?
CAUGHT ON TO WHAT
WAIT....ARE YOU... MURDERERS?
NO
OH, GOOD—
NOT ALL THE TIME

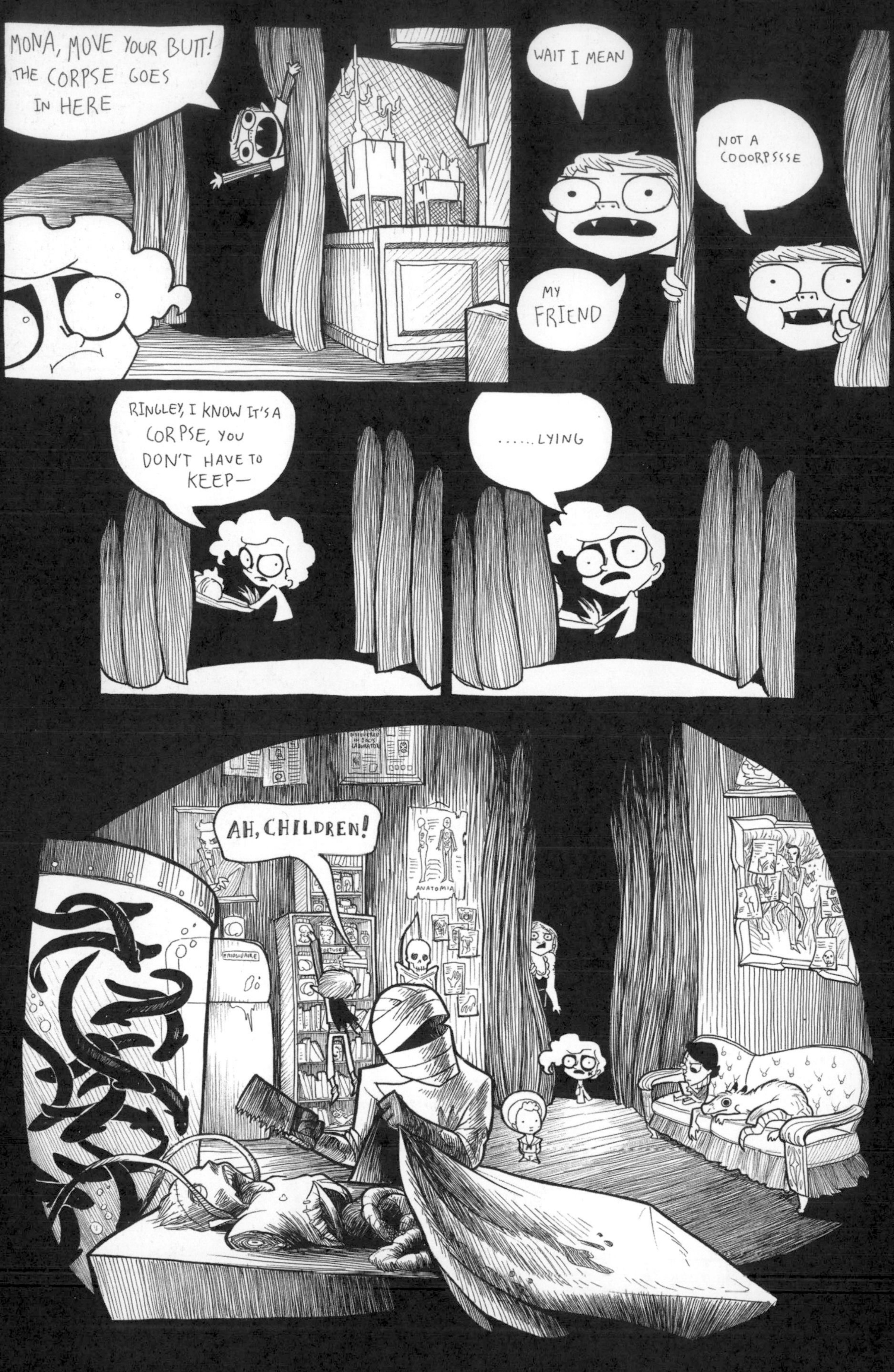
MONA, MOVE YOUR BUTT! THE CORPSE GOES IN HERE
WAIT I MEAN
NOT A COOORPSSSE
MY FRIEND
RINGLEY, I KNOW IT'S A CORPSE, YOU DON'T HAVE TO KEEP—
......LYING
AH, CHILDREN!
ANATOMIA

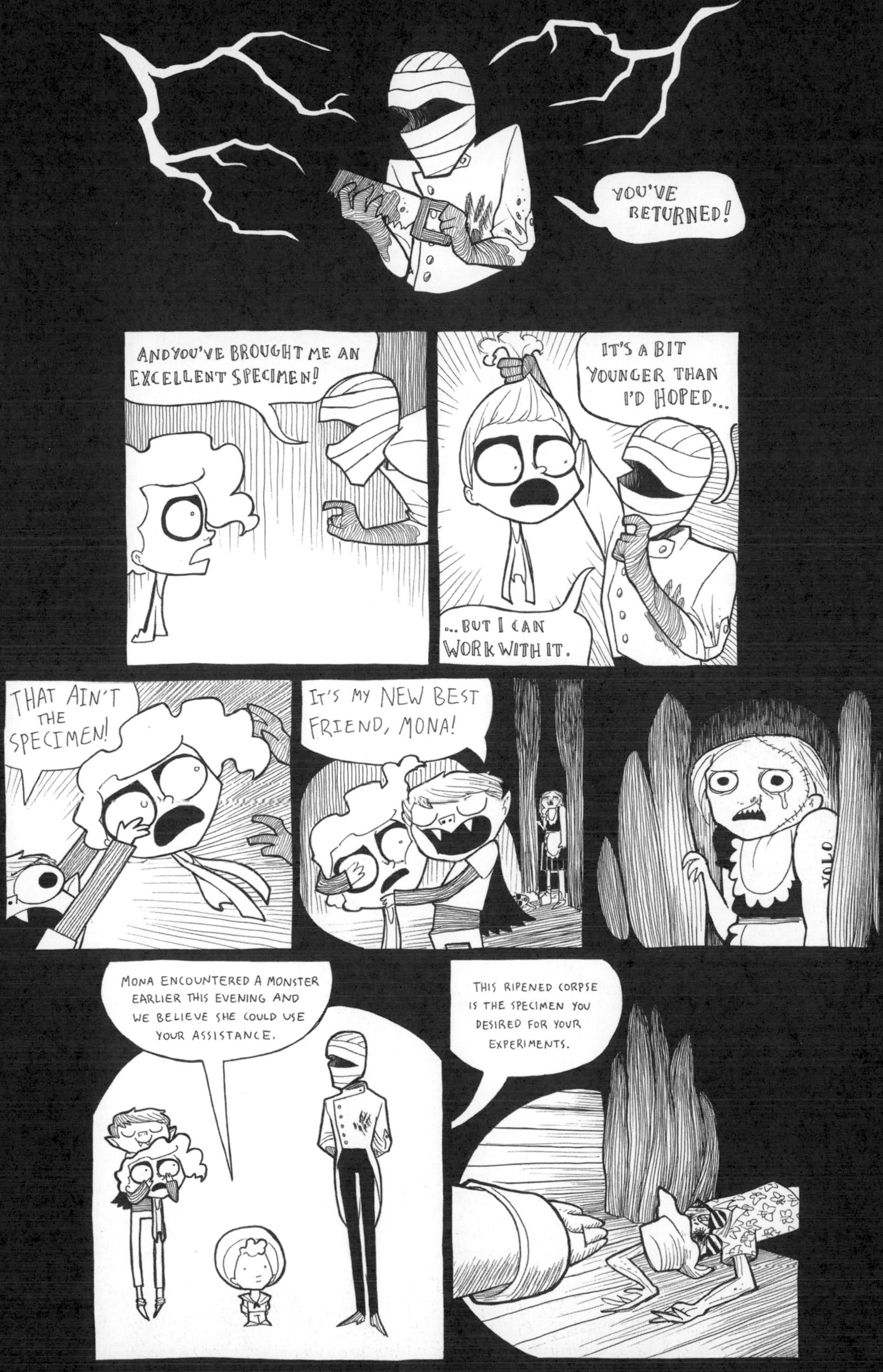
YOU'VE RETURNED!
AND YOU'VE BROUGHT ME AN EXCELLENT SPECIMEN!
IT'S A BIT YOUNGER THAN I'D HOPED...
...BUT I CAN WORK WITH IT.
THAT AIN'T THE SPECIMEN!
IT'S MY NEW BEST FRIEND, MONA!
YOLO
MONA ENCOUNTERED A MONSTER EARLIER THIS EVENING AND WE BELIEVE SHE COULD USE YOUR ASSISTANCE.
THIS RIPENED CORPSE IS THE SPECIMEN YOU DESIRED FOR YOUR EXPERIMENTS.

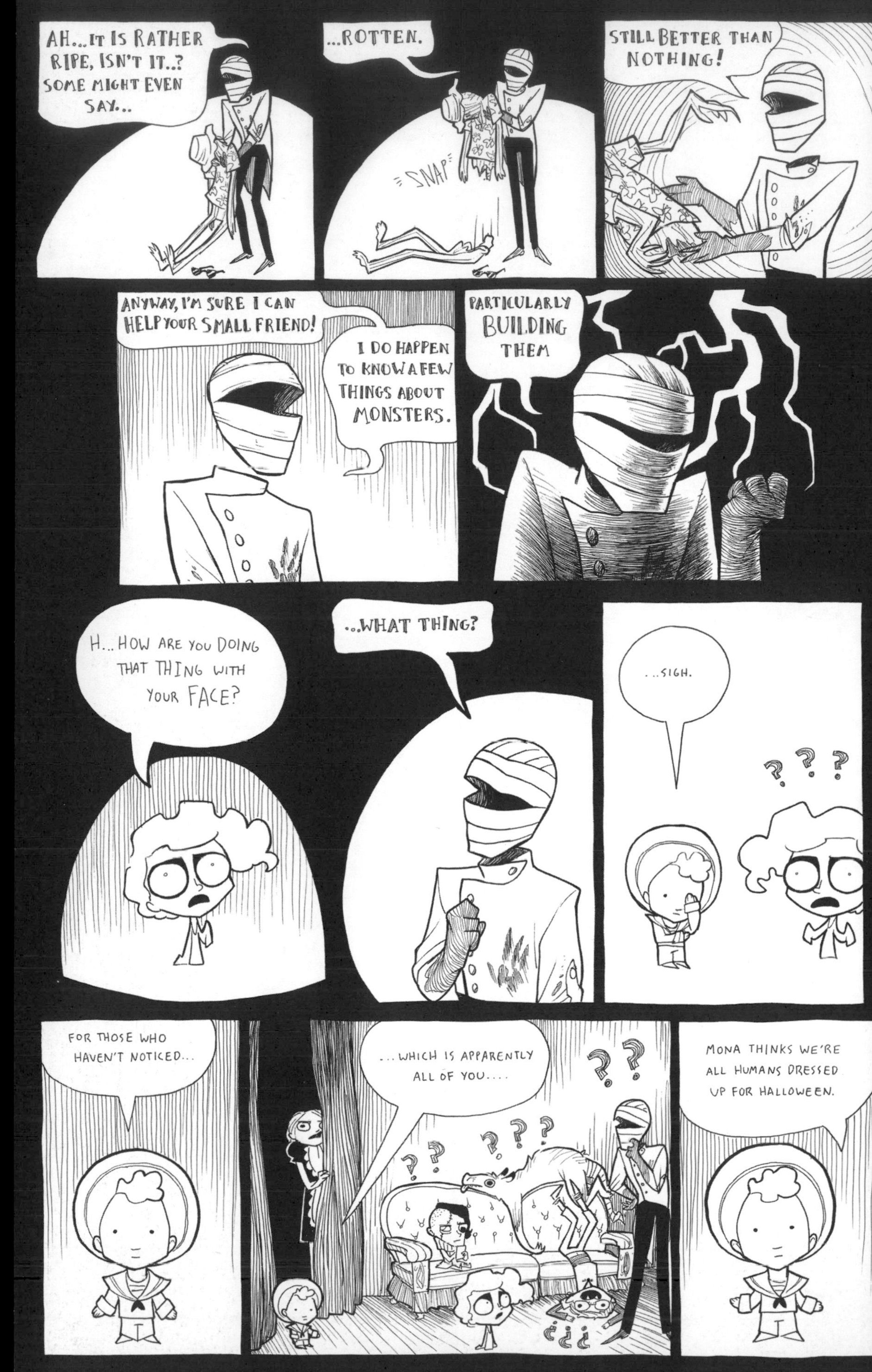
AH... IT IS RATHER RIPE, ISN'T IT..? SOME MIGHT EVEN SAY...
...ROTTEN.
SNAP
STILL BETTER THAN NOTHING!
ANYWAY, I'M SURE I CAN HELP YOUR SMALL FRIEND!
I DO HAPPEN TO KNOW A FEW THINGS ABOUT MONSTERS.
PARTICULARLY BUILDING THEM
H... HOW ARE YOU DOING THAT THING WITH YOUR FACE?
...WHAT THING?
...SIGH.
???
FOR THOSE WHO HAVEN'T NOTICED...
...WHICH IS APPARENTLY ALL OF YOU....
MONA THINKS WE'RE ALL HUMANS DRESSED UP FOR HALLOWEEN.

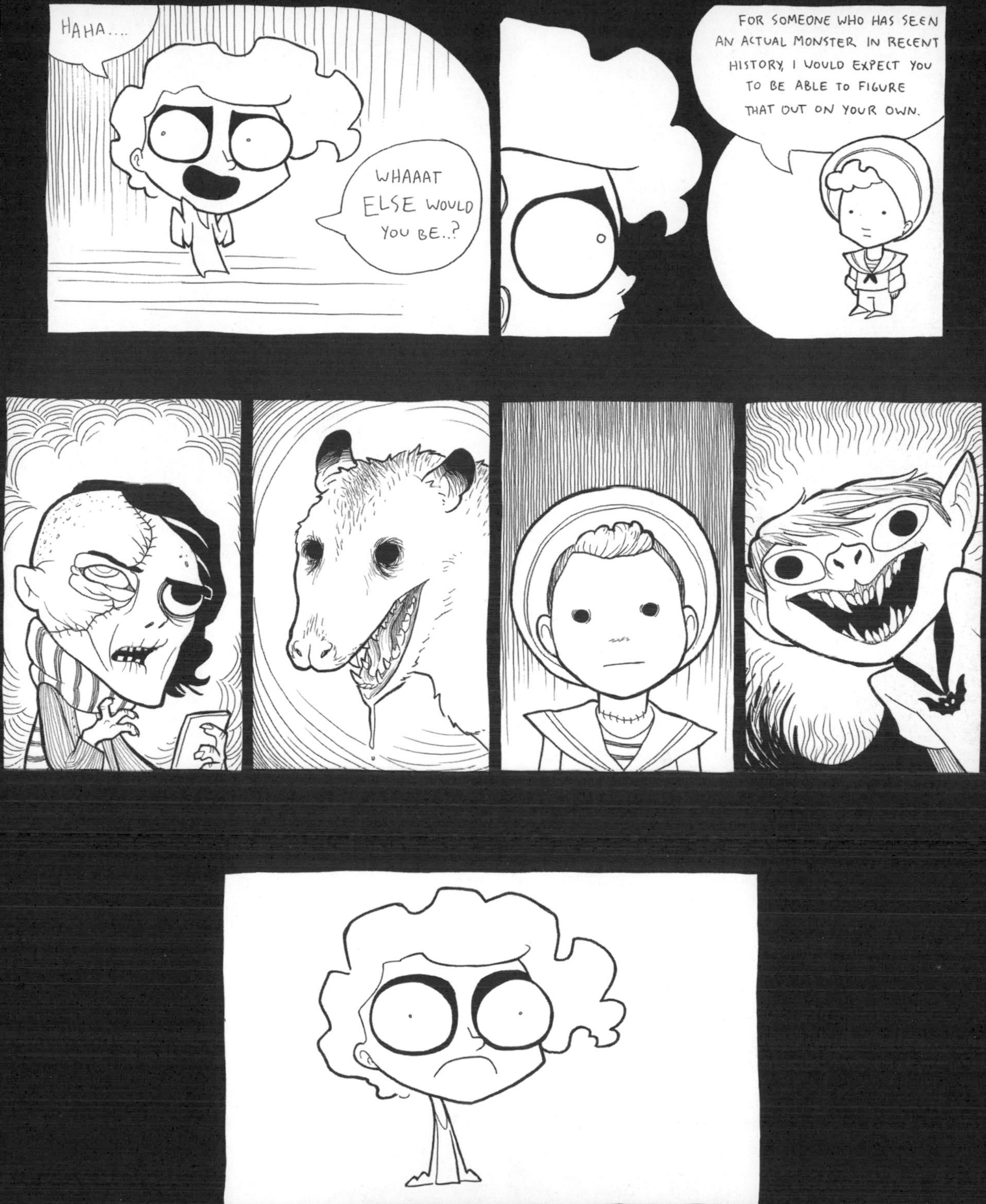
HAHA....
WHAAAT ELSE WOULD YOU BE..?
FOR SOMEONE WHO HAS SEEN AN ACTUAL MONSTER IN RECENT HISTORY, I WOULD EXPECT YOU TO BE ABLE TO FIGURE THAT OUT ON YOUR OWN.

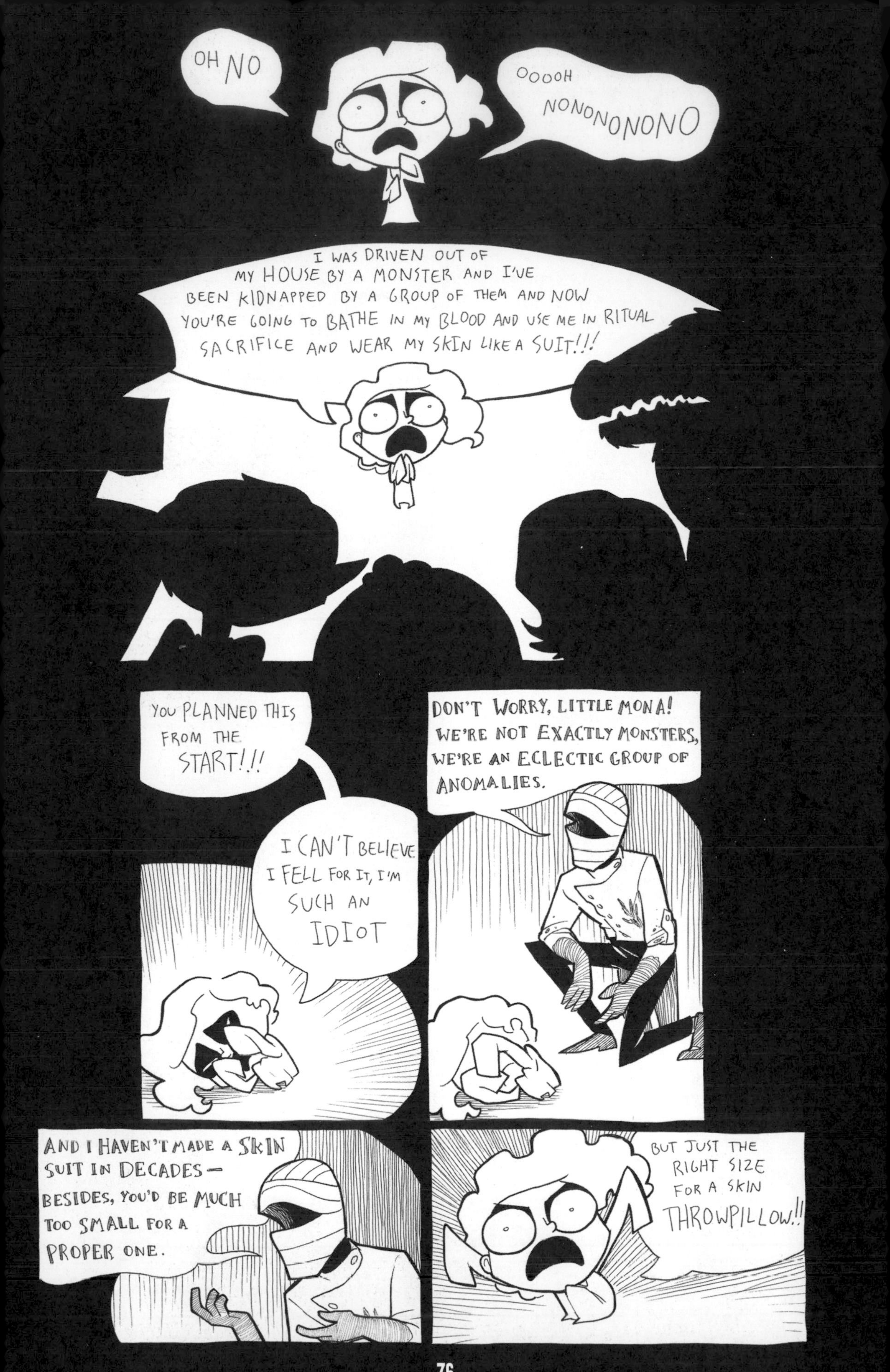
OH NO
OOOOH NONONONONO
I WAS DRIVEN OUT OF MY HOUSE BY A MONSTER AND I'VE BEEN KIDNAPPED BY A GROUP OF THEM AND NOW YOU'RE GOING TO BATHE IN MY BLOOD AND USE ME IN RITUAL SACRIFICE AND WEAR MY SKIN LIKE A SUIT!!!
YOU PLANNED THIS FROM THE START!!!
I CAN'T BELIEVE I FELL FOR IT, I'M SUCH AN IDIOT
DON'T WORRY, LITTLE MONA! WE'RE NOT EXACTLY MONSTERS, WE'RE AN ECLECTIC GROUP OF ANOMALIES.
AND I HAVEN'T MADE A SKIN SUIT IN DECADES— BESIDES, YOU'D BE MUCH TOO SMALL FOR A PROPER ONE.
BUT JUST THE RIGHT SIZE FOR A SKIN THROWPILLOW!!

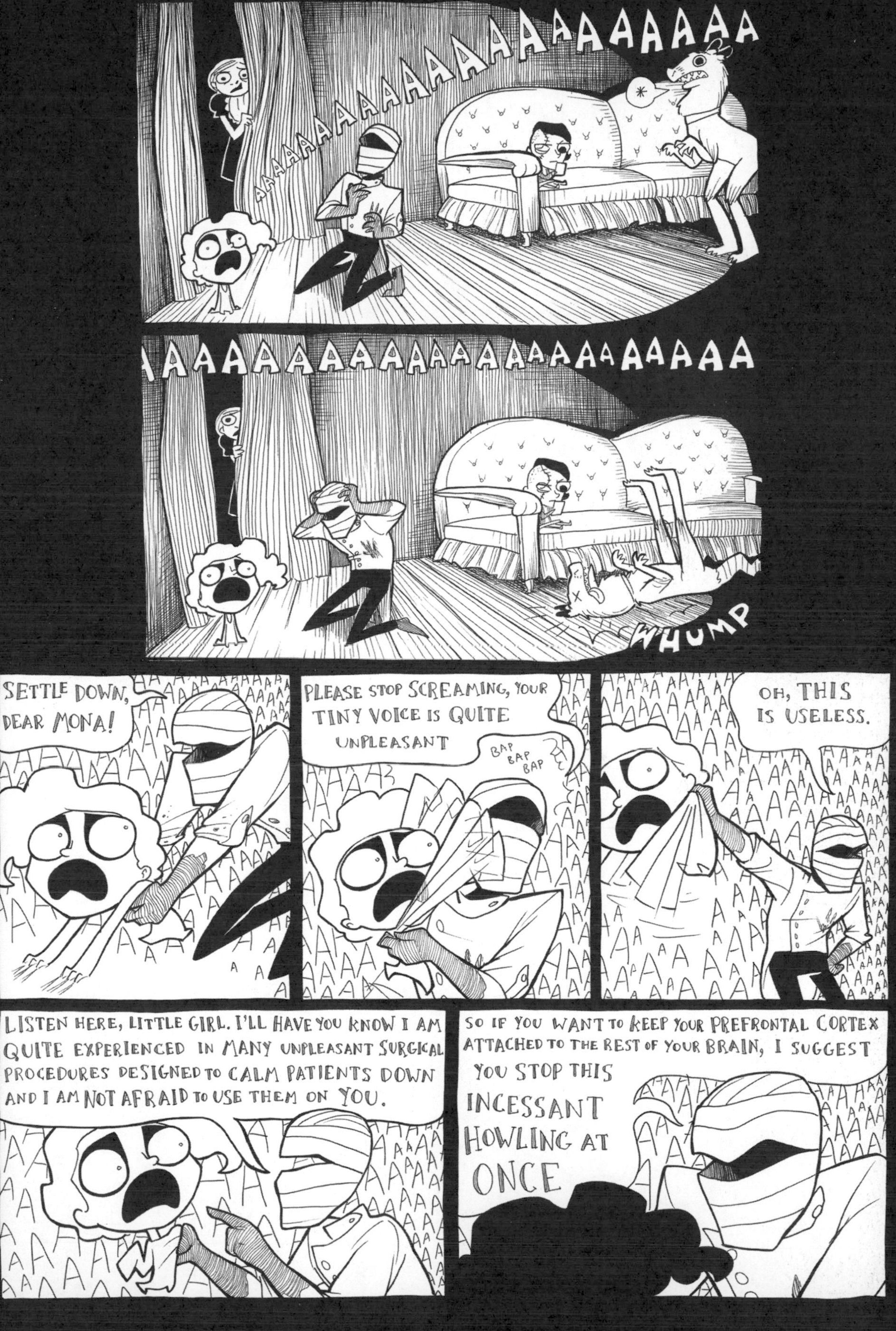
AAAAAAAAAAAAAAAAAAAAAAAAAA
AAAAAAAAAAAAAAAAAAAAAAA
WHUMP
SETTLE DOWN, DEAR MONA!
PLEASE STOP SCREAMING, YOUR TINY VOICE IS QUITE UNPLEASANT
BAP BAP BAP
OH, THIS IS USELESS.
LISTEN HERE, LITTLE GIRL. I'LL HAVE YOU KNOW I AM QUITE EXPERIENCED IN MANY UNPLEASANT SURGICAL PROCEDURES DESIGNED TO CALM PATIENTS DOWN AND I AM NOT AFRAID TO USE THEM ON YOU.
SO IF YOU WANT TO KEEP YOUR PREFRONTAL CORTEX ATTACHED TO THE REST OF YOUR BRAIN, I SUGGEST YOU STOP THIS INCESSANT HOWLING AT ONCE

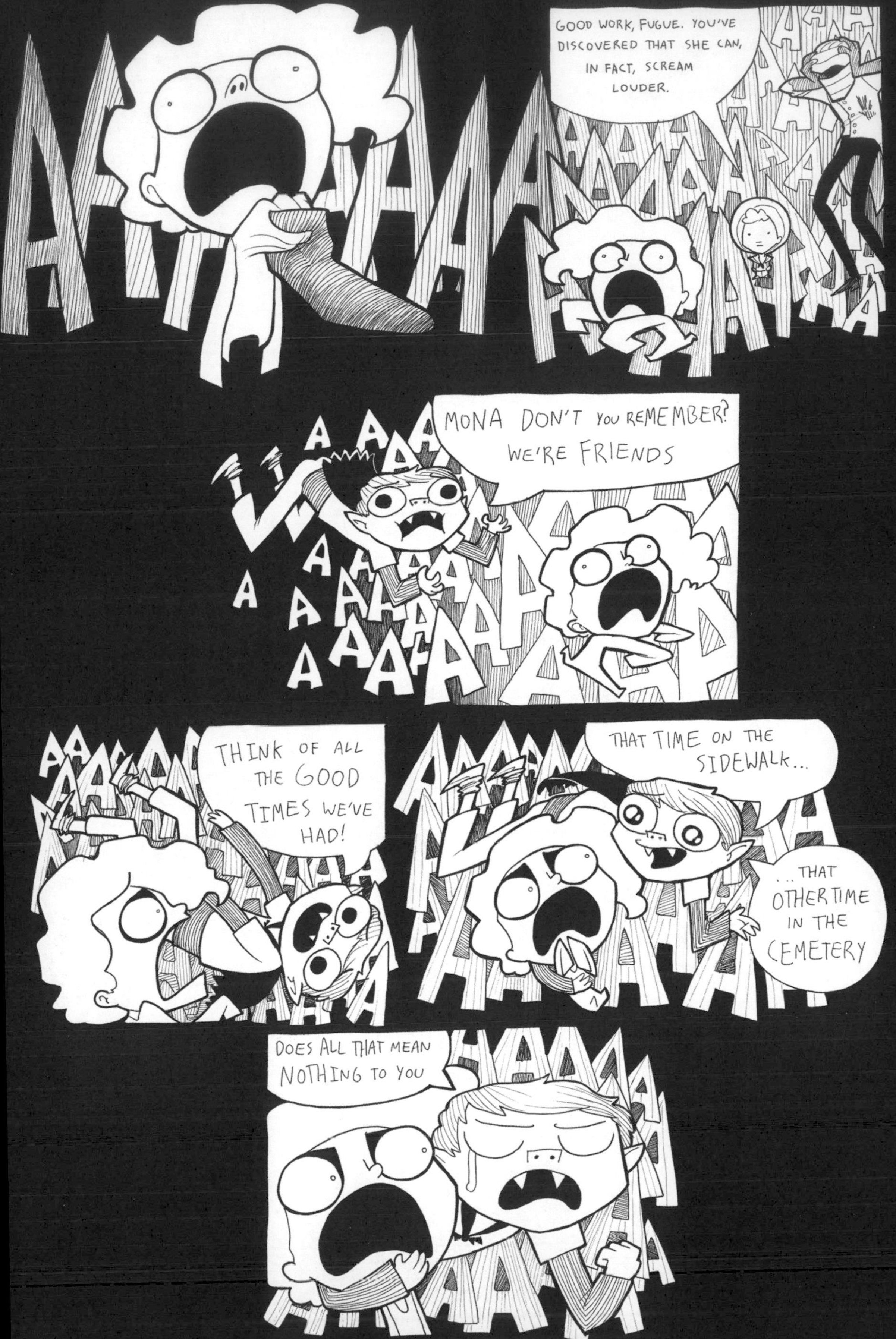
GOOD WORK, FUGUE. YOU'VE DISCOVERED THAT SHE CAN, IN FACT, SCREAM LOUDER.
MONA DON'T YOU REMEMBER? WE'RE FRIENDS
THINK OF ALL THE GOOD TIMES WE'VE HAD!
THAT TIME ON THE SIDEWALK...
...THAT OTHER TIME IN THE CEMETERY
DOES ALL THAT MEAN NOTHING TO YOU

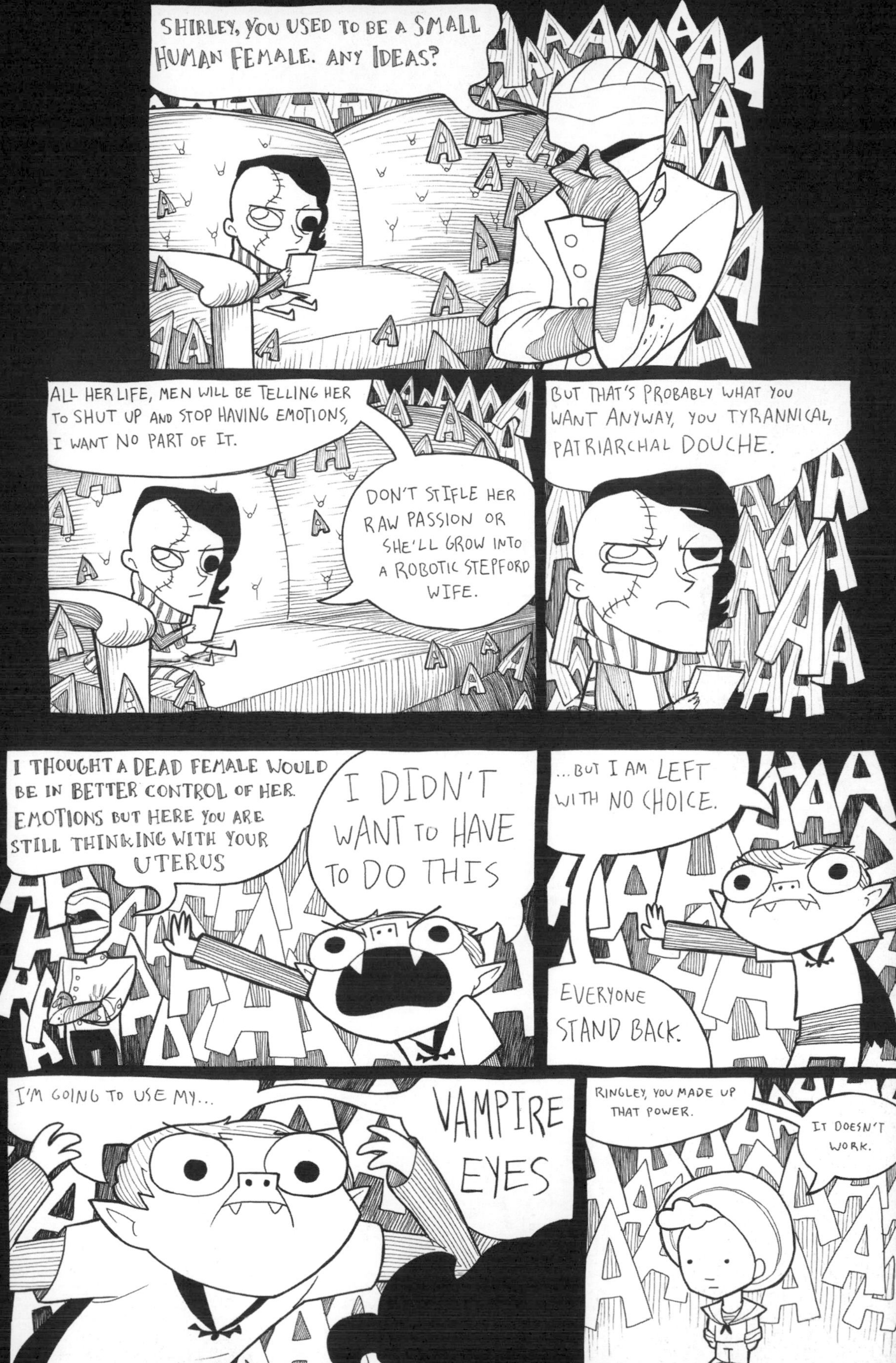
SHIRLEY, YOU USED TO BE A SMALL HUMAN FEMALE. ANY IDEAS?
ALL HER LIFE, MEN WILL BE TELLING HER TO SHUT UP AND STOP HAVING EMOTIONS, I WANT NO PART OF IT.
DON'T STIFLE HER RAW PASSION OR SHE'LL GROW INTO A ROBOTIC STEPFORD WIFE.
BUT THAT'S PROBABLY WHAT YOU WANT ANYWAY, YOU TYRANNICAL, PATRIARCHAL DOUCHE.
I THOUGHT A DEAD FEMALE WOULD BE IN BETTER CONTROL OF HER EMOTIONS BUT HERE YOU ARE STILL THINKING WITH YOUR UTERUS
I DIDN'T WANT TO HAVE TO DO THIS
...BUT I AM LEFT WITH NO CHOICE.
EVERYONE STAND BACK.
I'M GOING TO USE MY...
VAMPIRE EYES
RINGLEY, YOU MADE UP THAT POWER.
IT DOESN'T WORK.

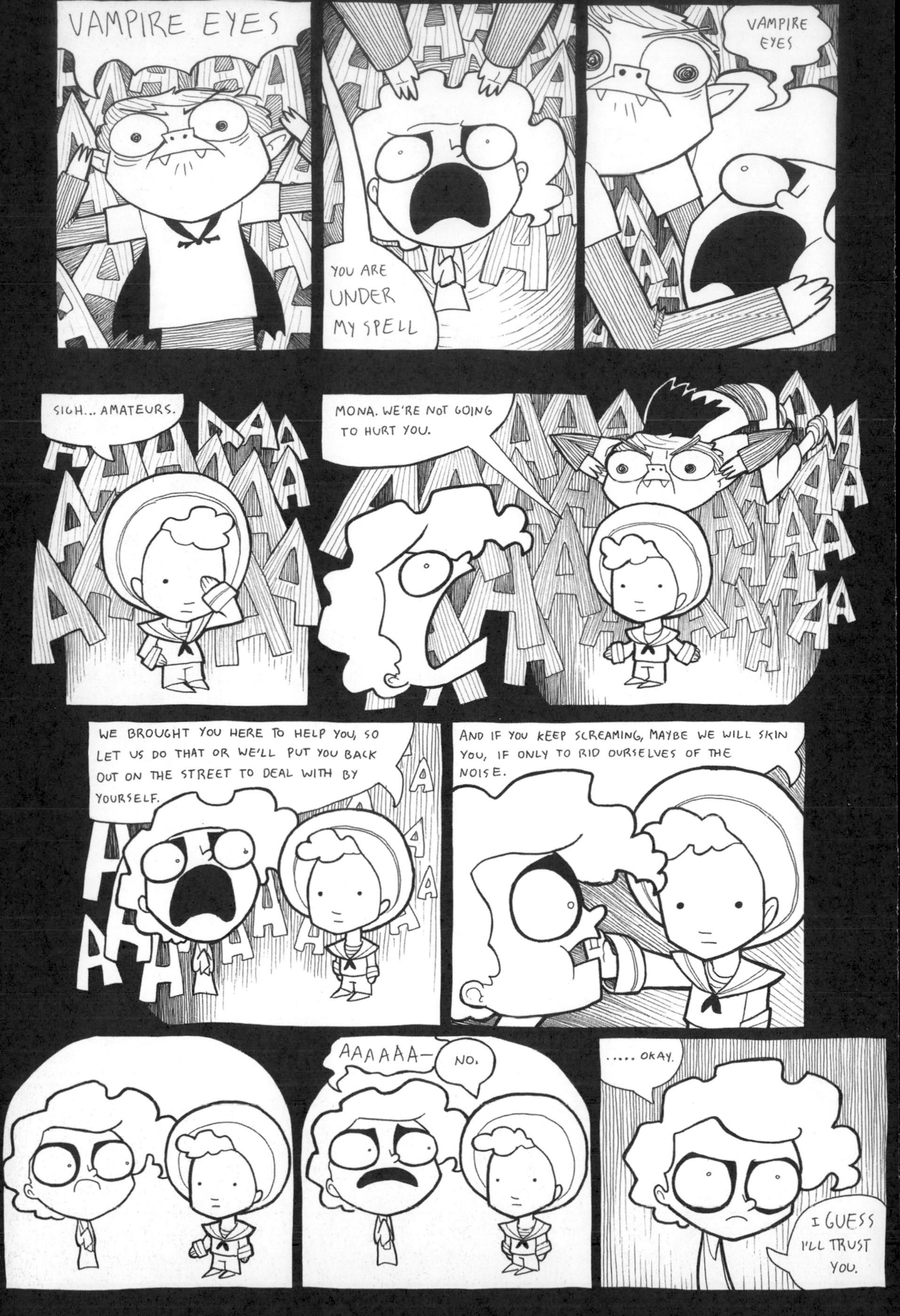
VAMPIRE EYES
YOU ARE UNDER MY SPELL
VAMPIRE EYES
SIGH... AMATEURS.
MONA. WE'RE NOT GOING TO HURT YOU.
WE BROUGHT YOU HERE TO HELP YOU, SO LET US DO THAT OR WE'LL PUT YOU BACK OUT ON THE STREET TO DEAL WITH BY YOURSELF.
AND IF YOU KEEP SCREAMING, MAYBE WE WILL SKIN YOU, IF ONLY TO RID OURSELVES OF THE NOISE.
AAAAAA—
NO.
..... OKAY.
I GUESS I'LL TRUST YOU.

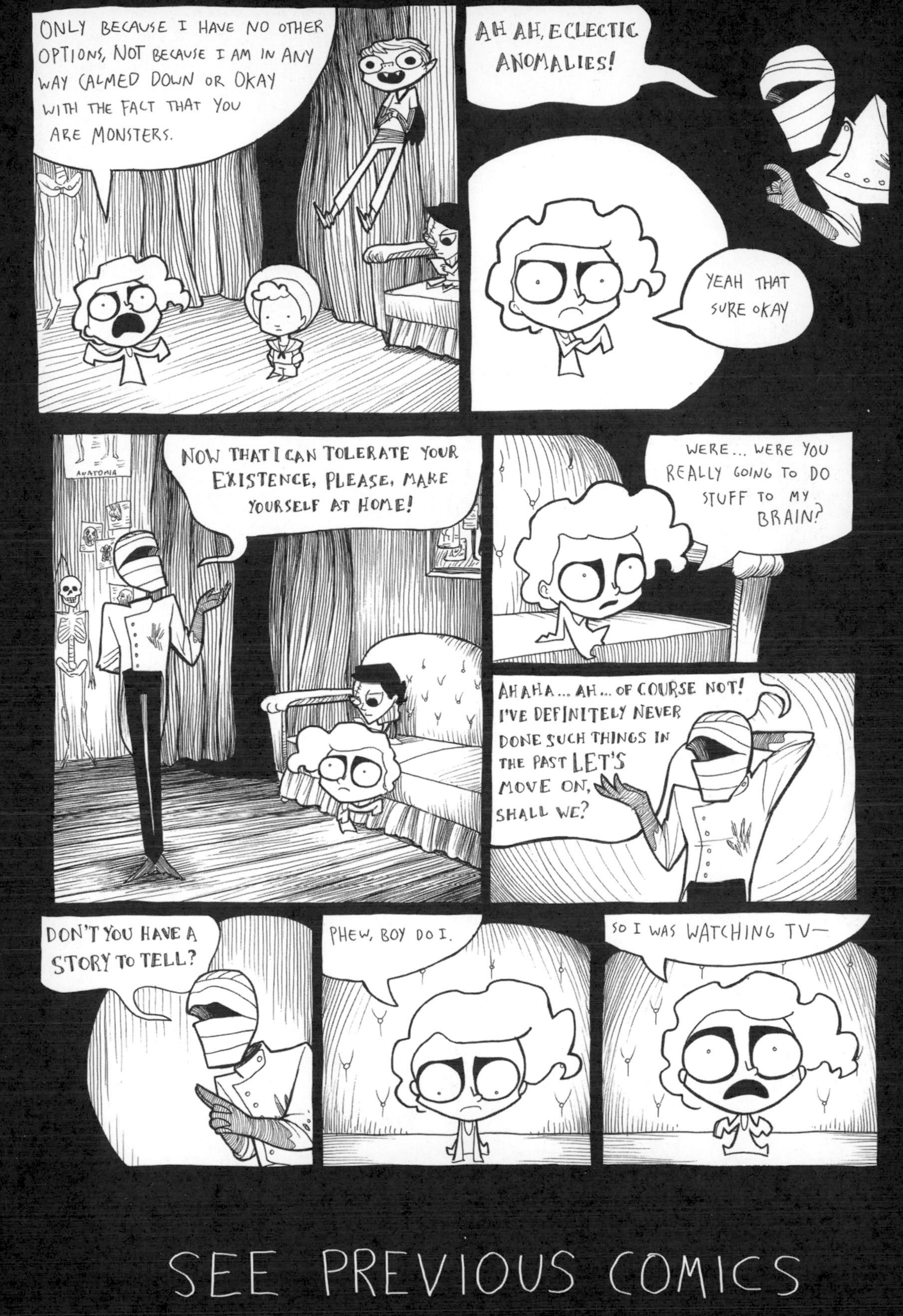
ONLY BECAUSE I HAVE NO OTHER OPTIONS, NOT BECAUSE I AM IN ANY WAY CALMED DOWN OR OKAY WITH THE FACT THAT YOU ARE MONSTERS.
AH AH, ECLECTIC ANOMALIES!
YEAH THAT SURE OKAY
NOW THAT I CAN TOLERATE YOUR EXISTENCE, PLEASE, MAKE YOURSELF AT HOME!
ANATOMIA
WERE... WERE YOU REALLY GOING TO DO STUFF TO MY BRAIN?
AHAHA... AH... OF COURSE NOT! I'VE DEFINITELY NEVER DONE SUCH THINGS IN THE PAST LET'S MOVE ON, SHALL WE?
DON'T YOU HAVE A STORY TO TELL?
PHEW, BOY DO I.
SO I WAS WATCHING TV—

SEE PREVIOUS COMICS

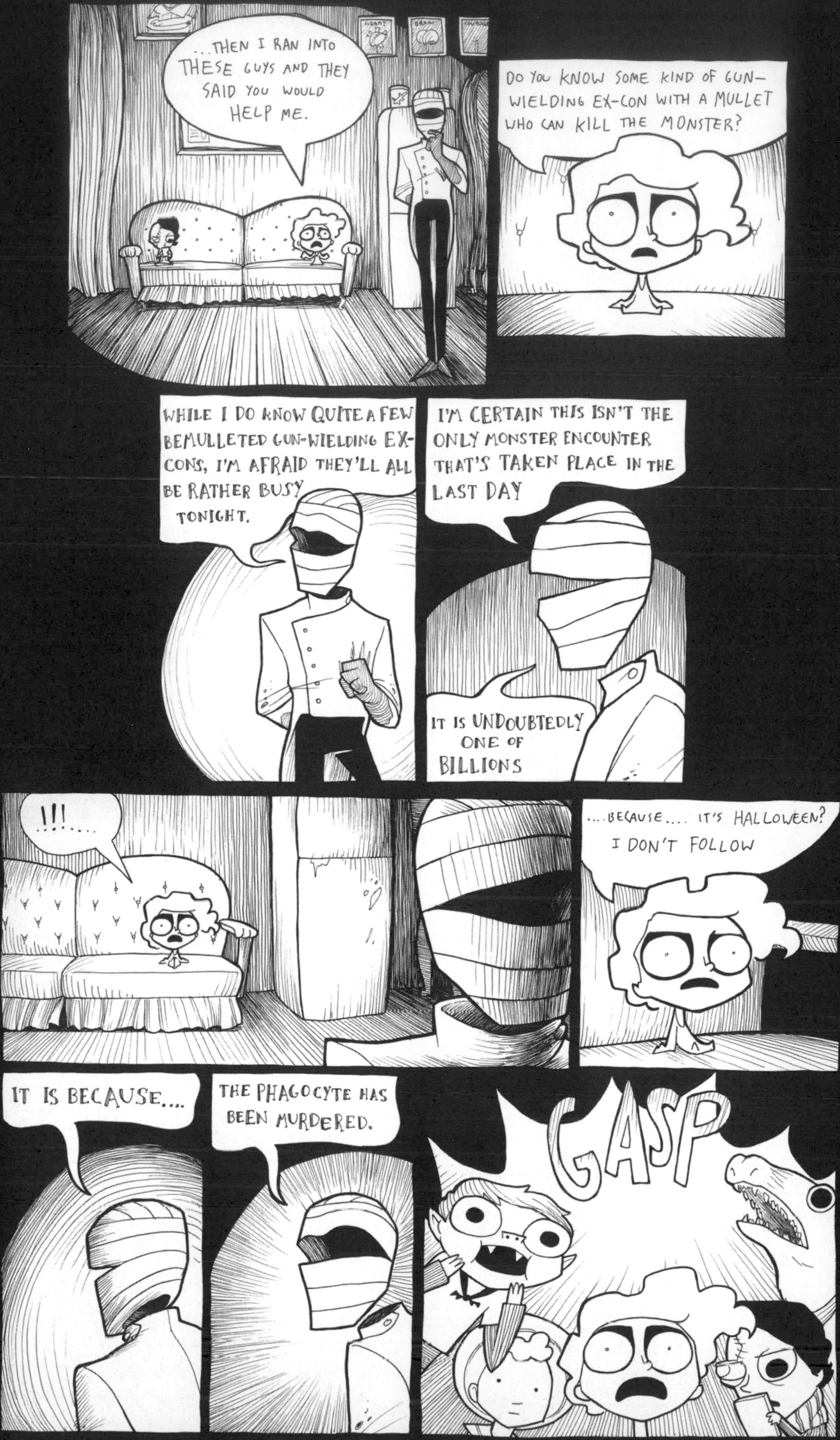
...THEN I RAN INTO THESE GUYS AND THEY SAID YOU WOULD HELP ME.
DO YOU KNOW SOME KIND OF GUN-WIELDING EX-CON WITH A MULLET WHO CAN KILL THE MONSTER?
WHILE I DO KNOW QUITE A FEW BEMULLETED GUN-WIELDING EX-CONS, I'M AFRAID THEY'LL ALL BE RATHER BUSY TONIGHT.
I'M CERTAIN THIS ISN'T THE ONLY MONSTER ENCOUNTER THAT'S TAKEN PLACE IN THE LAST DAY
IT IS UNDOUBTEDLY ONE OF BILLIONS
!!!.....
....BECAUSE.... IT'S HALLOWEEN? I DON'T FOLLOW
IT IS BECAUSE....
THE PHAGOCYTE HAS BEEN MURDERED.
GASP

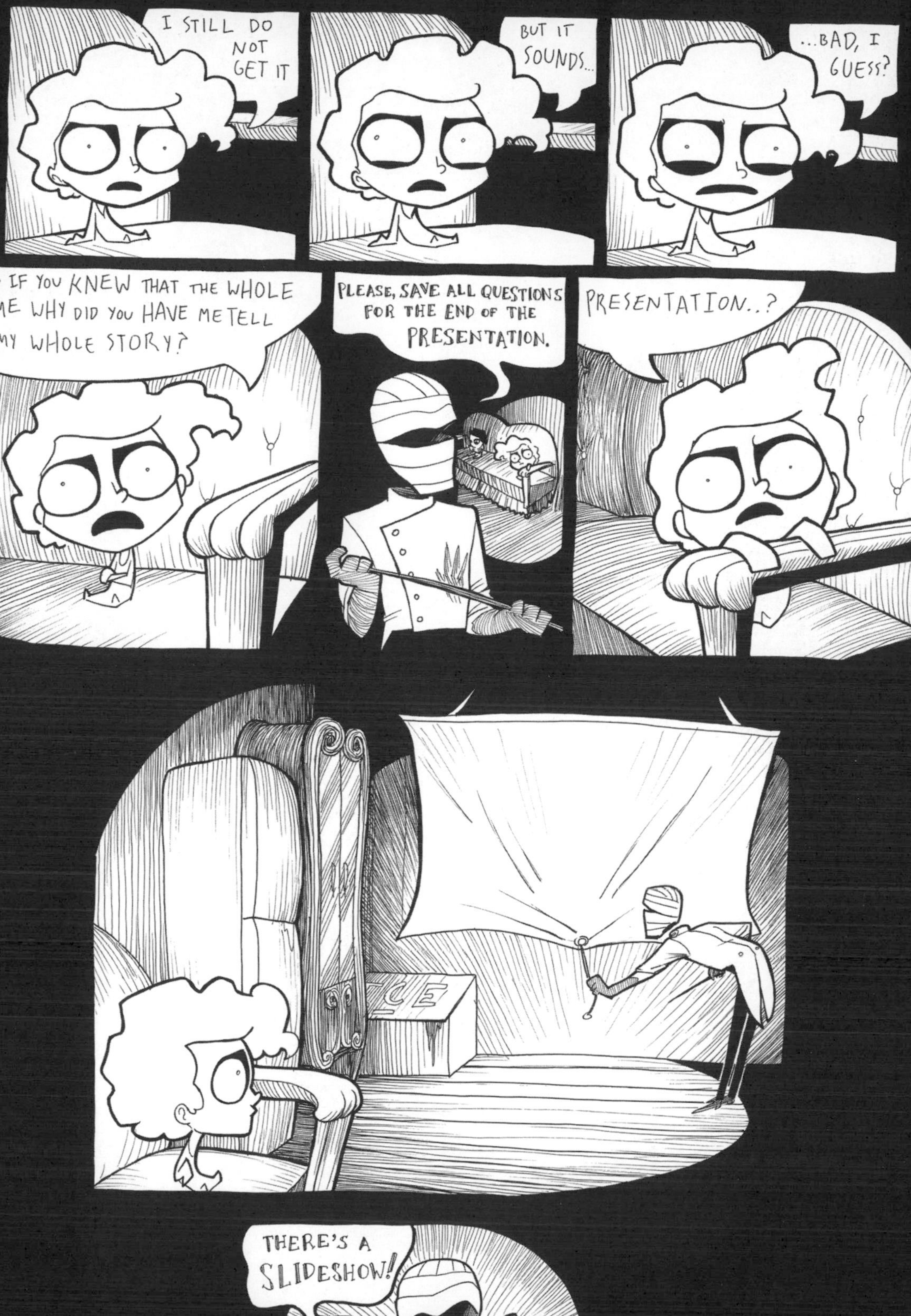

I STILL DO NOT GET IT
BUT IT SOUNDS...
...BAD, I GUESS?
AND IF YOU KNEW THAT THE WHOLE TIME WHY DID YOU HAVE ME TELL MY WHOLE STORY?
PLEASE, SAVE ALL QUESTIONS FOR THE END OF THE PRESENTATION.
PRESENTATION..?
ICE
THERE'S A SLIDESHOW!

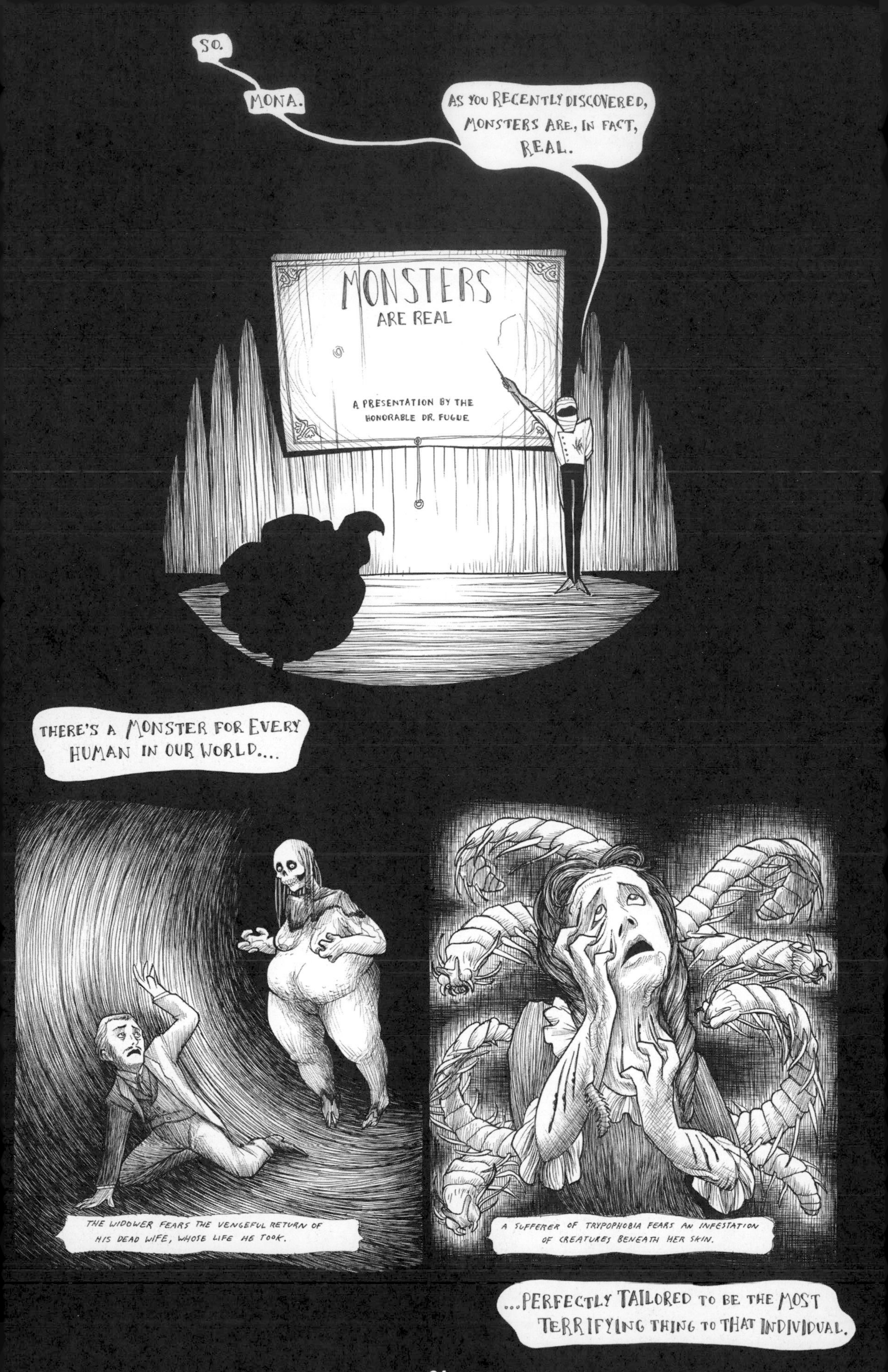
SO.
MONA.
AS YOU RECENTLY DISCOVERED, MONSTERS ARE, IN FACT, REAL.
MONSTERS
ARE REAL
A PRESENTATION BY THE HONORABLE DR. FUGUE
THERE'S A MONSTER FOR EVERY HUMAN IN OUR WORLD....
THE WIDOWER FEARS THE VENGEFUL RETURN OF HIS DEAD WIFE, WHOSE LIFE HE TOOK.
A SUFFERER OF TRYPOPHOBIA FEARS AN INFESTATION OF CREATURES BENEATH HER SKIN.
...PERFECTLY TAILORED TO BE THE MOST TERRIFYING THING TO THAT INDIVIDUAL.

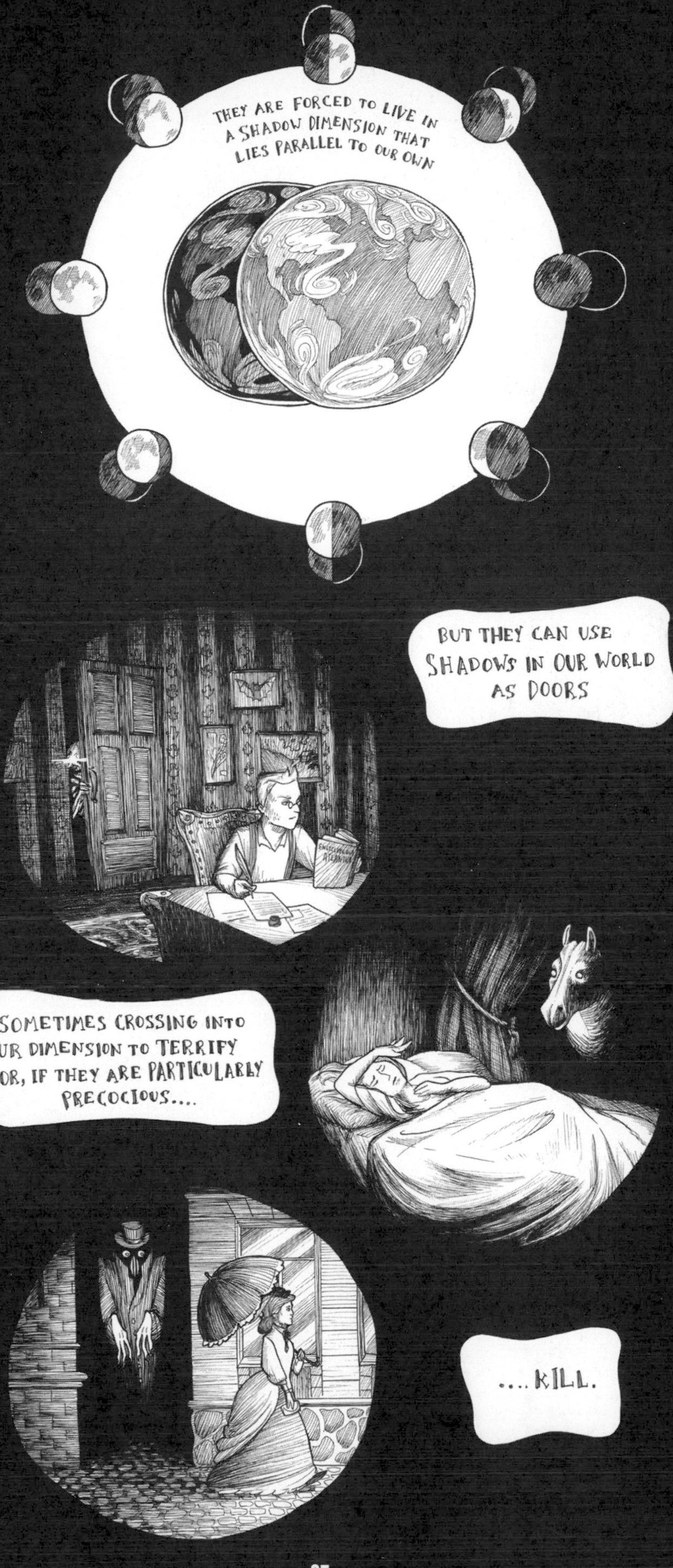
THEY ARE FORCED TO LIVE IN A SHADOW DIMENSION THAT LIES PARALLEL TO OUR OWN
BUT THEY CAN USE SHADOWS IN OUR WORLD AS DOORS
SOMETIMES CROSSING INTO OUR DIMENSION TO TERRIFY OR, IF THEY ARE PARTICULARLY PRECOCIOUS....
....KILL.

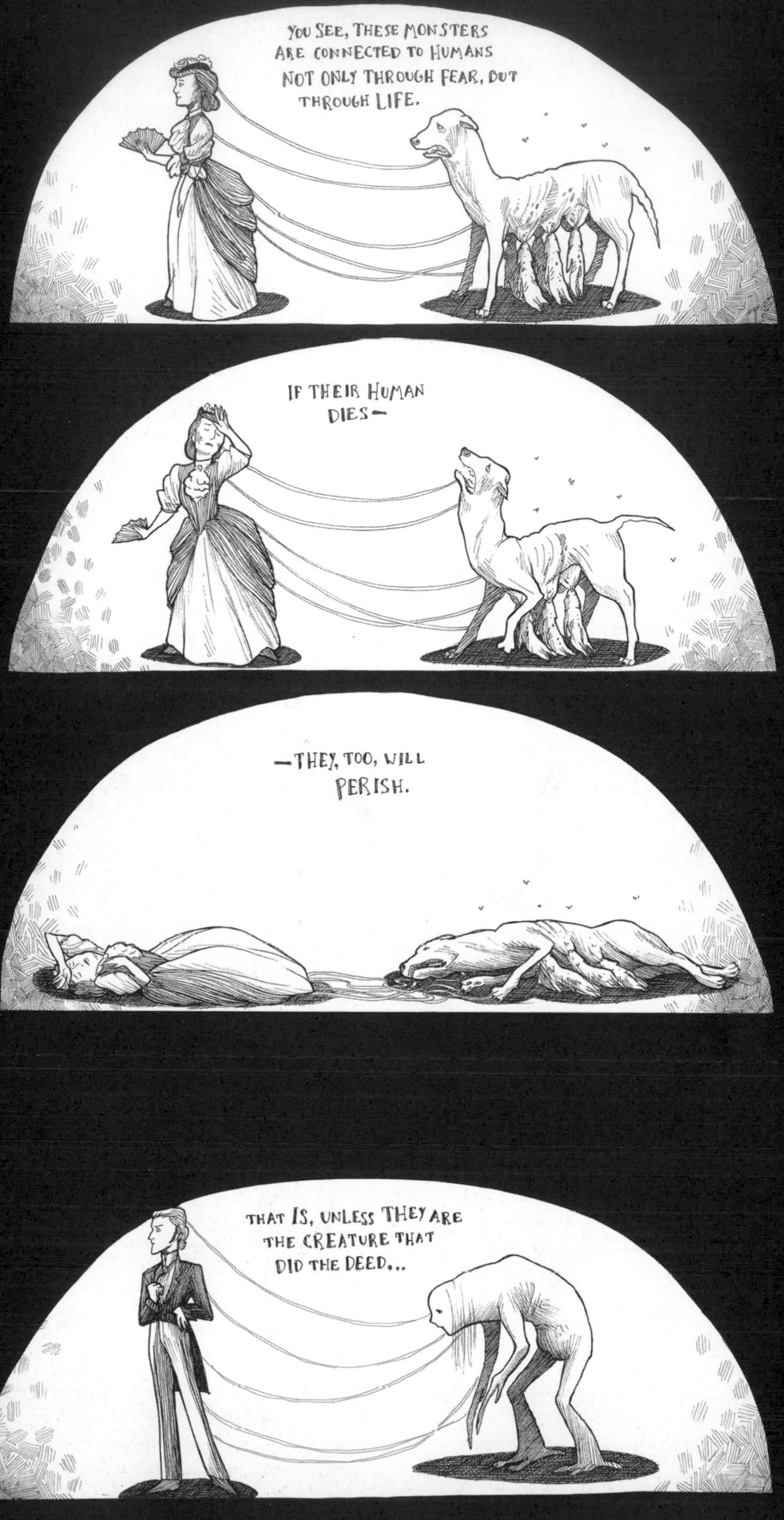
YOU SEE, THESE MONSTERS ARE CONNECTED TO HUMANS NOT ONLY THROUGH FEAR, BUT THROUGH LIFE.
IF THEIR HUMAN DIES—
—THEY, TOO, WILL PERISH.
THAT IS, UNLESS THEY ARE THE CREATURE THAT DID THE DEED...

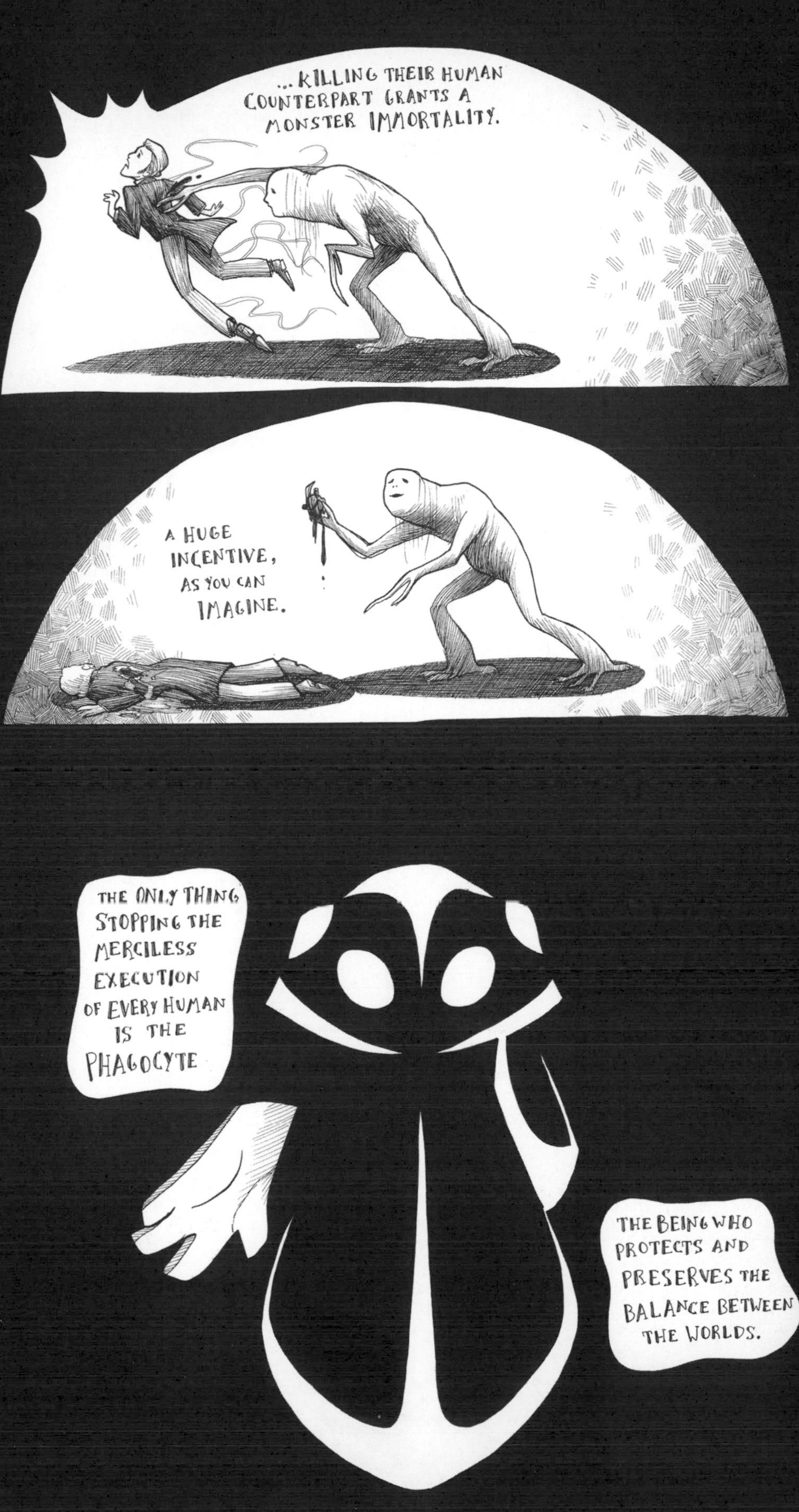
...KILLING THEIR HUMAN COUNTERPART GRANTS A MONSTER IMMORTALITY.
A HUGE INCENTIVE, AS YOU CAN IMAGINE.
THE ONLY THING STOPPING THE MERCILESS EXECUTION OF EVERY HUMAN IS THE PHAGOCYTE
THE BEING WHO PROTECTS AND PRESERVES THE BALANCE BETWEEN THE WORLDS.

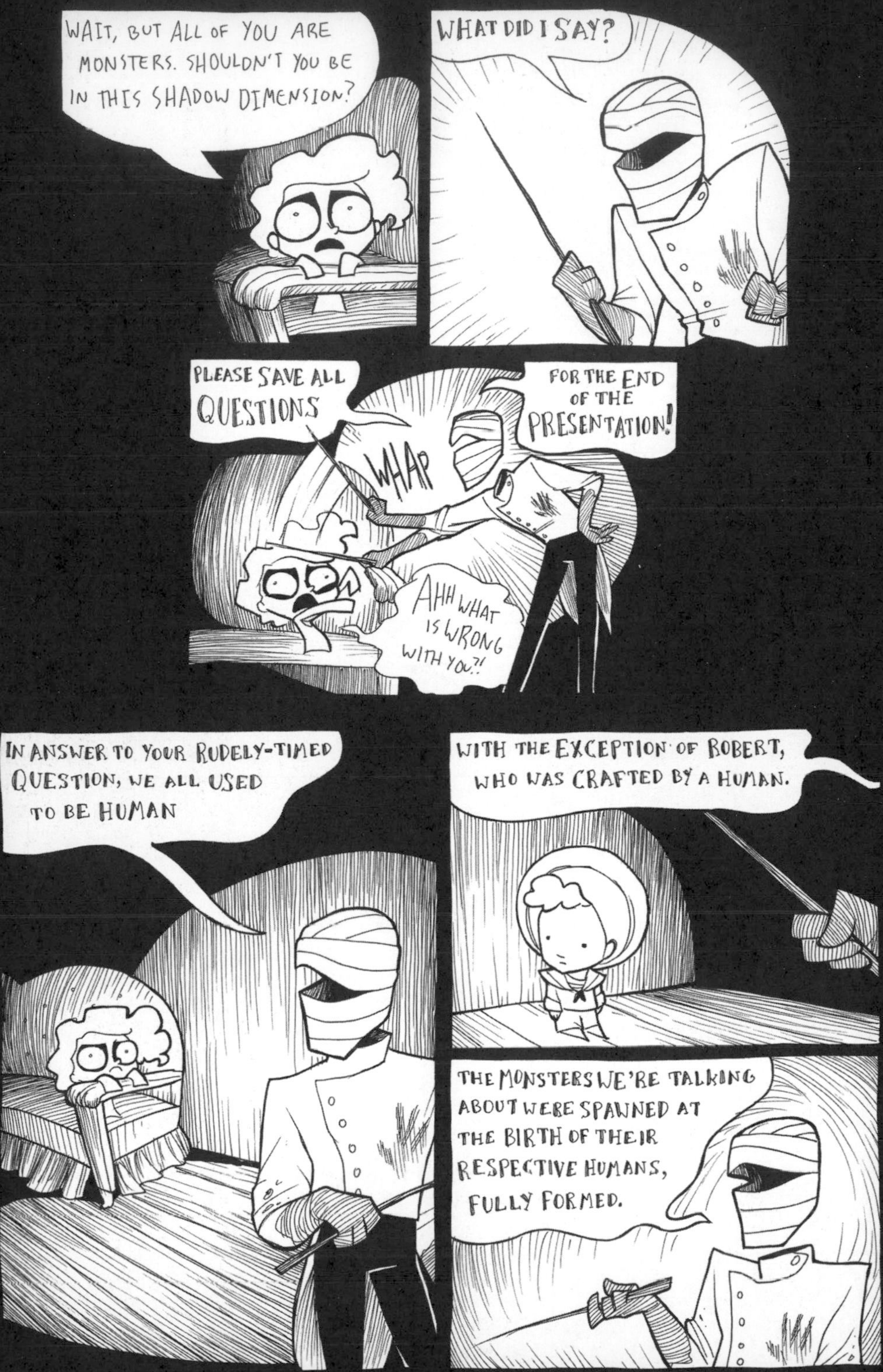
WAIT, BUT ALL OF YOU ARE MONSTERS. SHOULDN'T YOU BE IN THIS SHADOW DIMENSION?
WHAT DID I SAY?
PLEASE SAVE ALL QUESTIONS
FOR THE END OF THE PRESENTATION!
WHAP
AHH WHAT IS WRONG WITH YOU?!
IN ANSWER TO YOUR RUDELY-TIMED QUESTION, WE ALL USED TO BE HUMAN
WITH THE EXCEPTION OF ROBERT, WHO WAS CRAFTED BY A HUMAN.
THE MONSTERS WE'RE TALKING ABOUT WERE SPAWNED AT THE BIRTH OF THEIR RESPECTIVE HUMANS, FULLY FORMED.

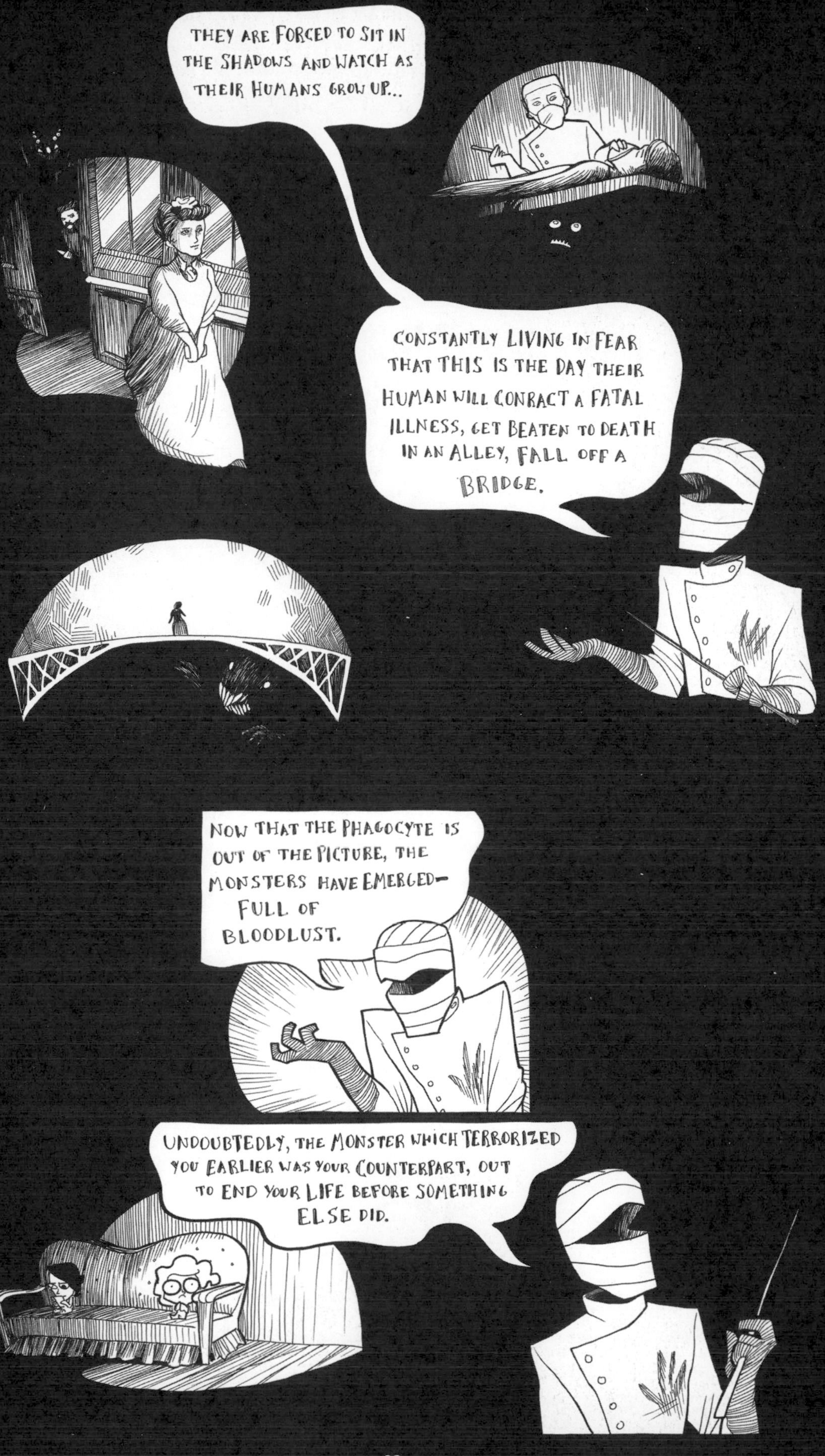
THEY ARE FORCED TO SIT IN THE SHADOWS AND WATCH AS THEIR HUMANS GROW UP...
CONSTANTLY LIVING IN FEAR THAT THIS IS THE DAY THEIR HUMAN WILL CONRACT A FATAL ILLNESS, GET BEATEN TO DEATH IN AN ALLEY, FALL OFF A BRIDGE.
NOW THAT THE PHAGOCYTE IS OUT OF THE PICTURE, THE MONSTERS HAVE EMERGED— FULL OF BLOODLUST.
UNDOUBTEDLY, THE MONSTER WHICH TERRORIZED YOU EARLIER WAS YOUR COUNTERPART, OUT TO END YOUR LIFE BEFORE SOMETHING ELSE DID.

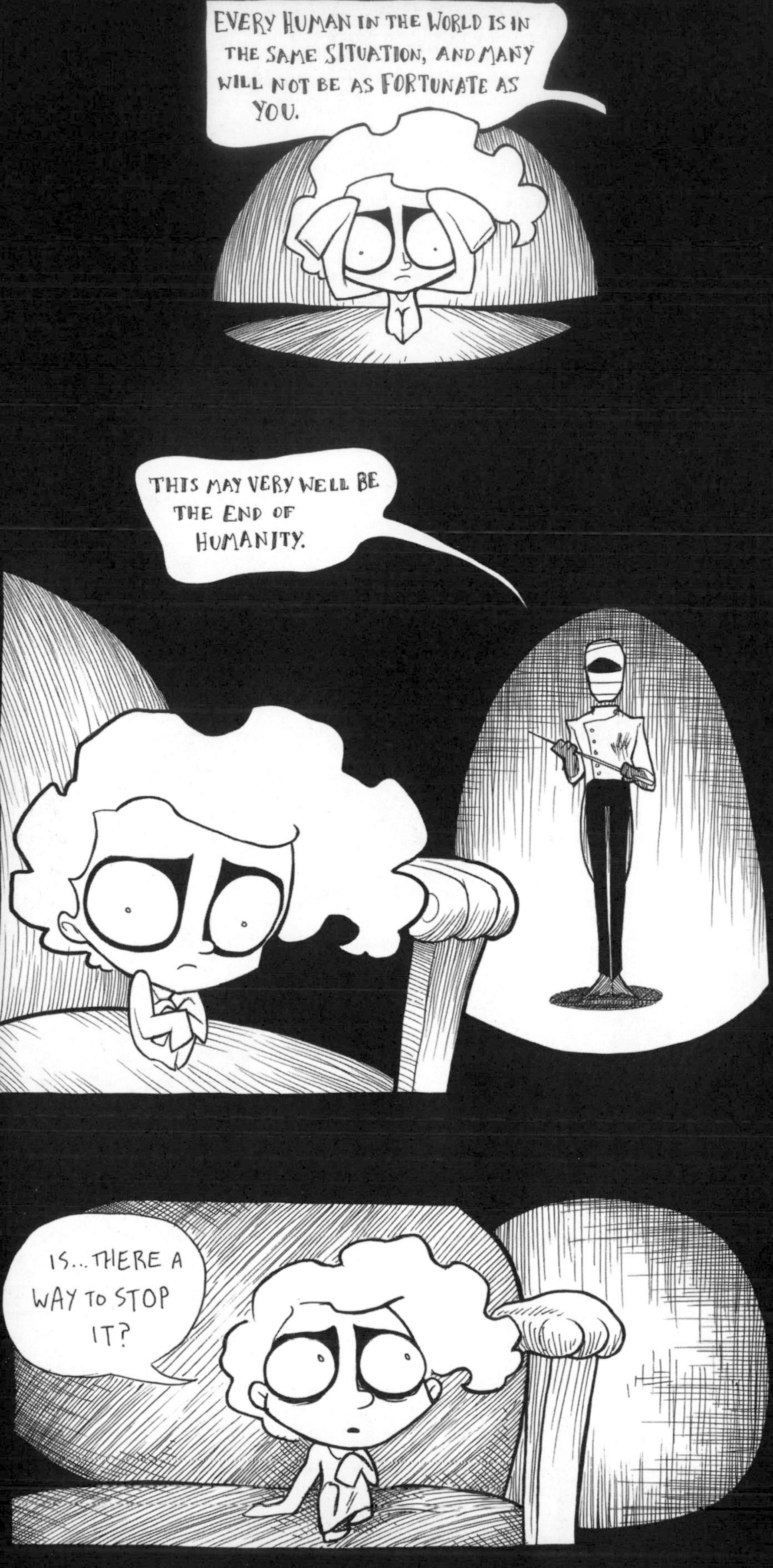
EVERY HUMAN IN THE WORLD IS IN THE SAME SITUATION, AND MANY WILL NOT BE AS FORTUNATE AS YOU.
THIS MAY VERY WELL BE THE END OF HUMANITY.
IS... THERE A WAY TO STOP IT?

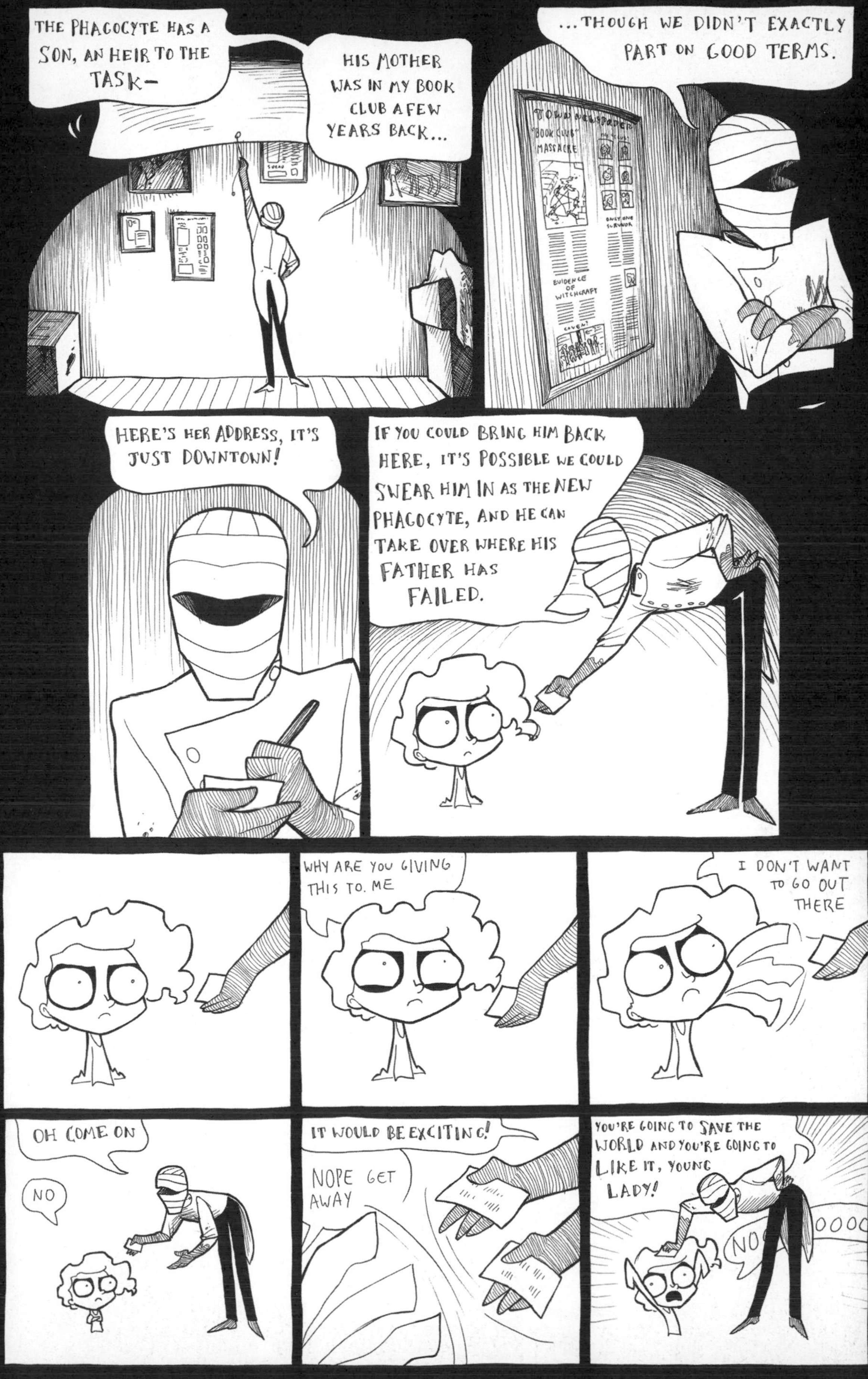
THE PHAGOCYTE HAS A SON, AN HEIR TO THE TASK—
HIS MOTHER WAS IN MY BOOK CLUB A FEW YEARS BACK...
...THOUGH WE DIDN'T EXACTLY PART ON GOOD TERMS.
TOWN NEWSPAPER
"BOOK CLUB" MASSACRE
ONLY ONE SURVIVOR
EVIDENCE OF WITCHCRAFT
COVEN?
HERE'S HER ADDRESS, IT'S JUST DOWNTOWN!
IF YOU COULD BRING HIM BACK HERE, IT'S POSSIBLE WE COULD SWEAR HIM IN AS THE NEW PHAGOCYTE, AND HE CAN TAKE OVER WHERE HIS FATHER HAS FAILED.
WHY ARE YOU GIVING THIS TO. ME
I DON'T WANT TO GO OUT THERE
OH COME ON
NO
IT WOULD BE EXCITING!
NOPE GET AWAY
YOU'RE GOING TO SAVE THE WORLD AND YOU'RE GOING TO LIKE IT, YOUNG LADY!
NOOOOO

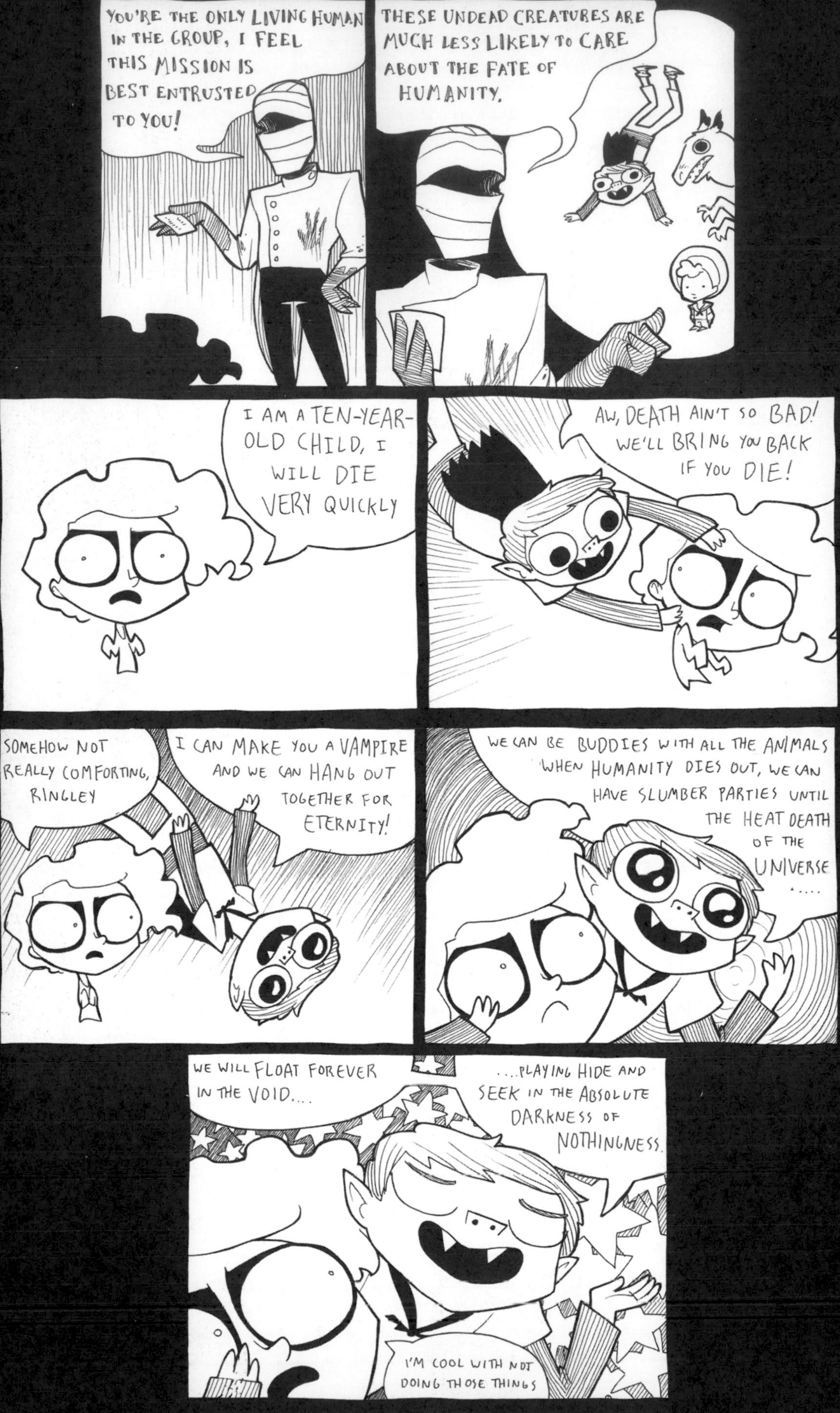
YOU'RE THE ONLY LIVING HUMAN IN THE GROUP, I FEEL THIS MISSION IS BEST ENTRUSTED TO YOU!
THESE UNDEAD CREATURES ARE MUCH LESS LIKELY TO CARE ABOUT THE FATE OF HUMANITY.
I AM A TEN-YEAR-OLD CHILD, I WILL DIE VERY QUICKLY
AW, DEATH AIN'T SO BAD! WE'LL BRING YOU BACK IF YOU DIE!
SOMEHOW NOT REALLY COMFORTING, RINGLEY
I CAN MAKE YOU A VAMPIRE AND WE CAN HANG OUT TOGETHER FOR ETERNITY!
WE CAN BE BUDDIES WITH ALL THE ANIMALS WHEN HUMANITY DIES OUT, WE CAN HAVE SLUMBER PARTIES UNTIL THE HEAT DEATH OF THE UNIVERSE.....
WE WILL FLOAT FOREVER IN THE VOID....
....PLAYING HIDE AND SEEK IN THE ABSOLUTE DARKNESS OF NOTHINGNESS.
I'M COOL WITH NOT DOING THOSE THINGS

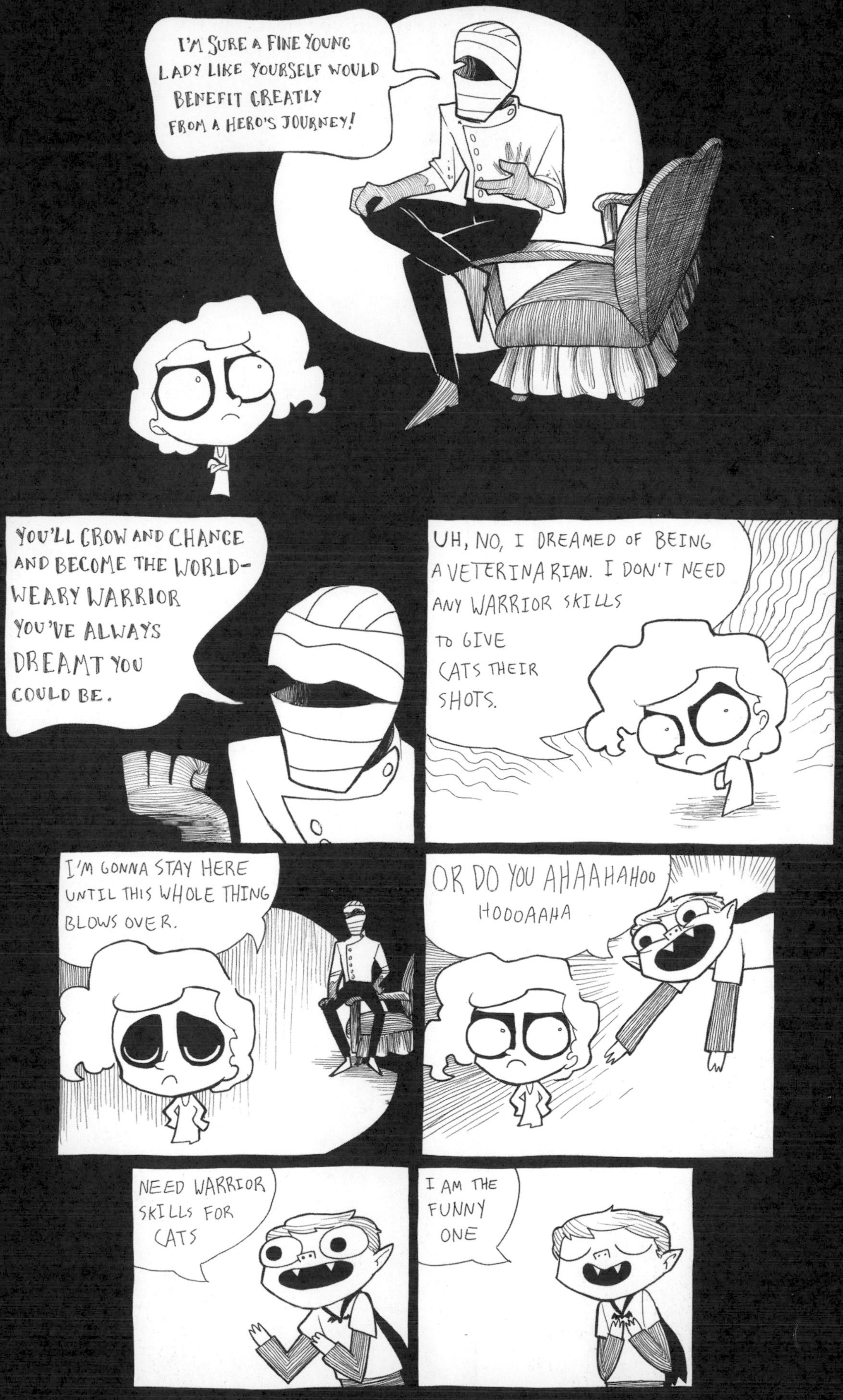
I'M SURE A FINE YOUNG LADY LIKE YOURSELF WOULD BENEFIT GREATLY FROM A HERO'S JOURNEY!
YOU'LL GROW AND CHANGE AND BECOME THE WORLD-WEARY WARRIOR YOU'VE ALWAYS DREAMT YOU COULD BE.
UH, NO, I DREAMED OF BEING A VETERINARIAN. I DON'T NEED ANY WARRIOR SKILLS TO GIVE CATS THEIR SHOTS.
I'M GONNA STAY HERE UNTIL THIS WHOLE THING BLOWS OVER.
OR DO YOU AHAAHAHOO HOOOAAHA
NEED WARRIOR SKILLS FOR CATS
I AM THE FUNNY ONE

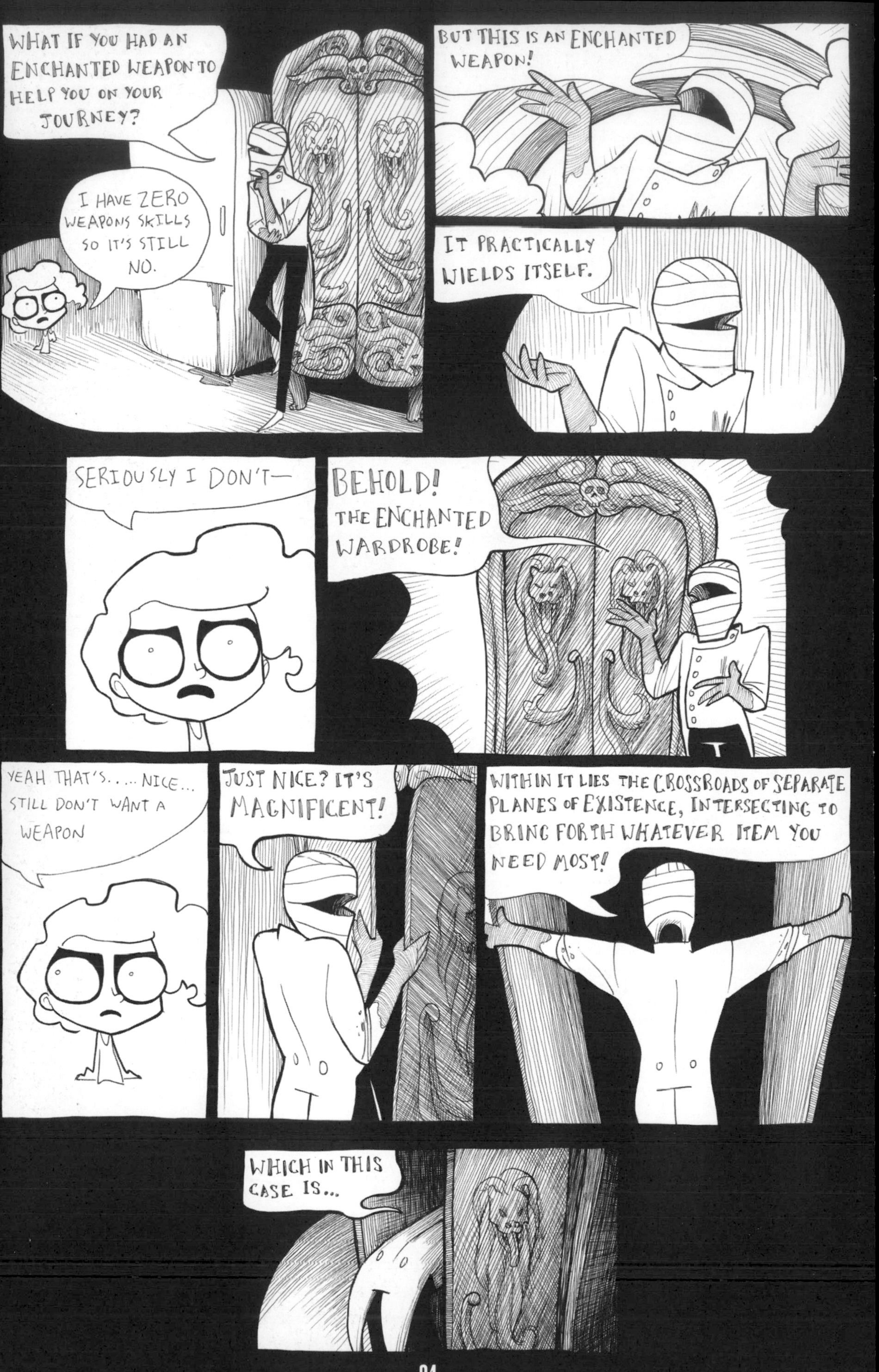
WHAT IF YOU HAD AN ENCHANTED WEAPON TO HELP YOU ON YOUR JOURNEY?
I HAVE ZERO WEAPONS SKILLS SO IT'S STILL NO.
BUT THIS IS AN ENCHANTED WEAPON!
IT PRACTICALLY WIELDS ITSELF.
SERIOUSLY I DON'T—
BEHOLD! THE ENCHANTED WARDROBE!
YEAH THAT'S.....NICE... STILL DON'T WANT A WEAPON
JUST NICE? IT'S MAGNIFICENT!
WITHIN IT LIES THE CROSSROADS OF SEPARATE PLANES OF EXISTENCE, INTERSECTING TO BRING FORTH WHATEVER ITEM YOU NEED MOST!
WHICH IN THIS CASE IS...

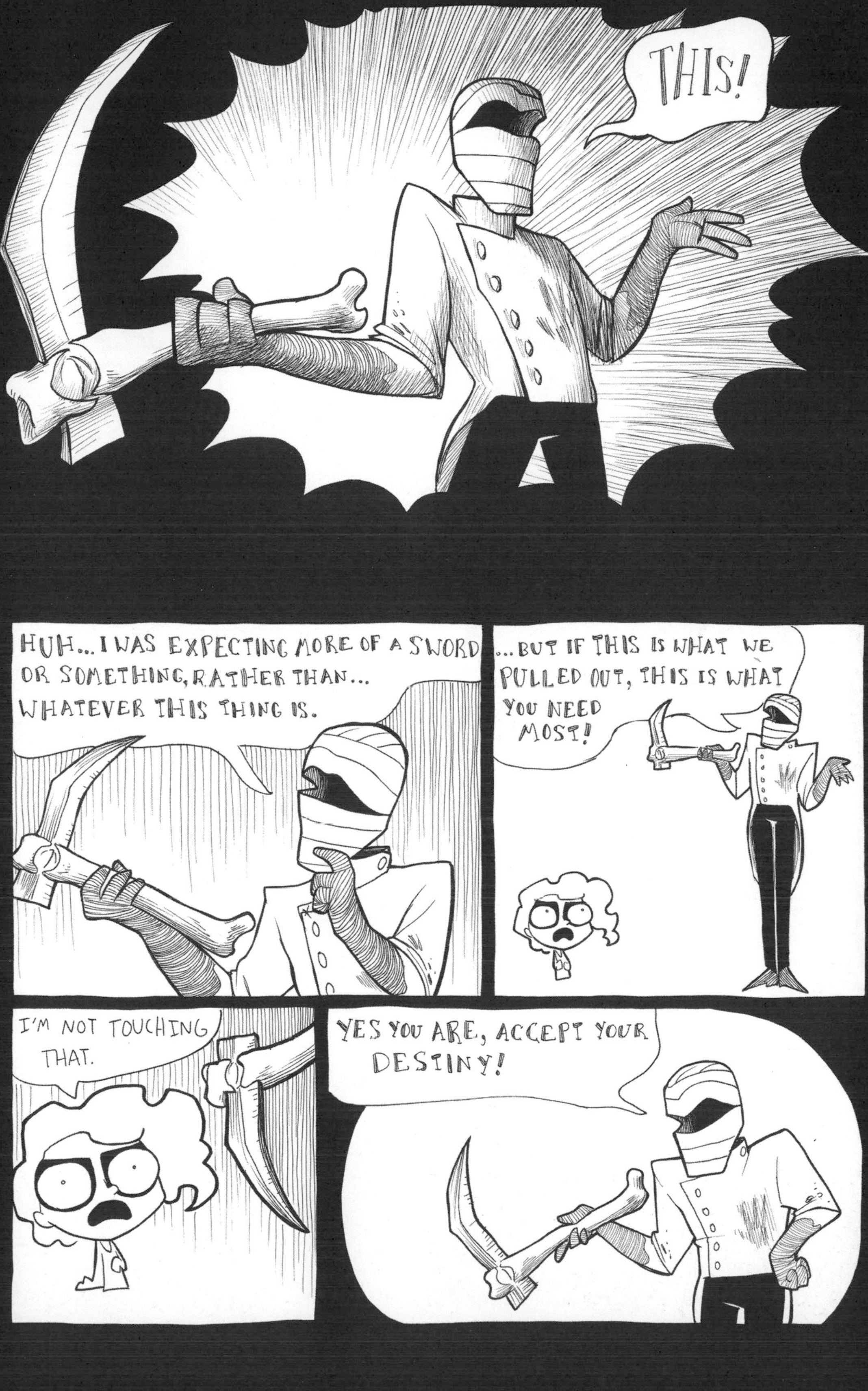
THIS!
HUH... I WAS EXPECTING MORE OF A SWORD OR SOMETHING, RATHER THAN... WHATEVER THIS THING IS.
...BUT IF THIS IS WHAT WE PULLED OUT, THIS IS WHAT YOU NEED MOST!
I'M NOT TOUCHING THAT.
YES YOU ARE, ACCEPT YOUR DESTINY!

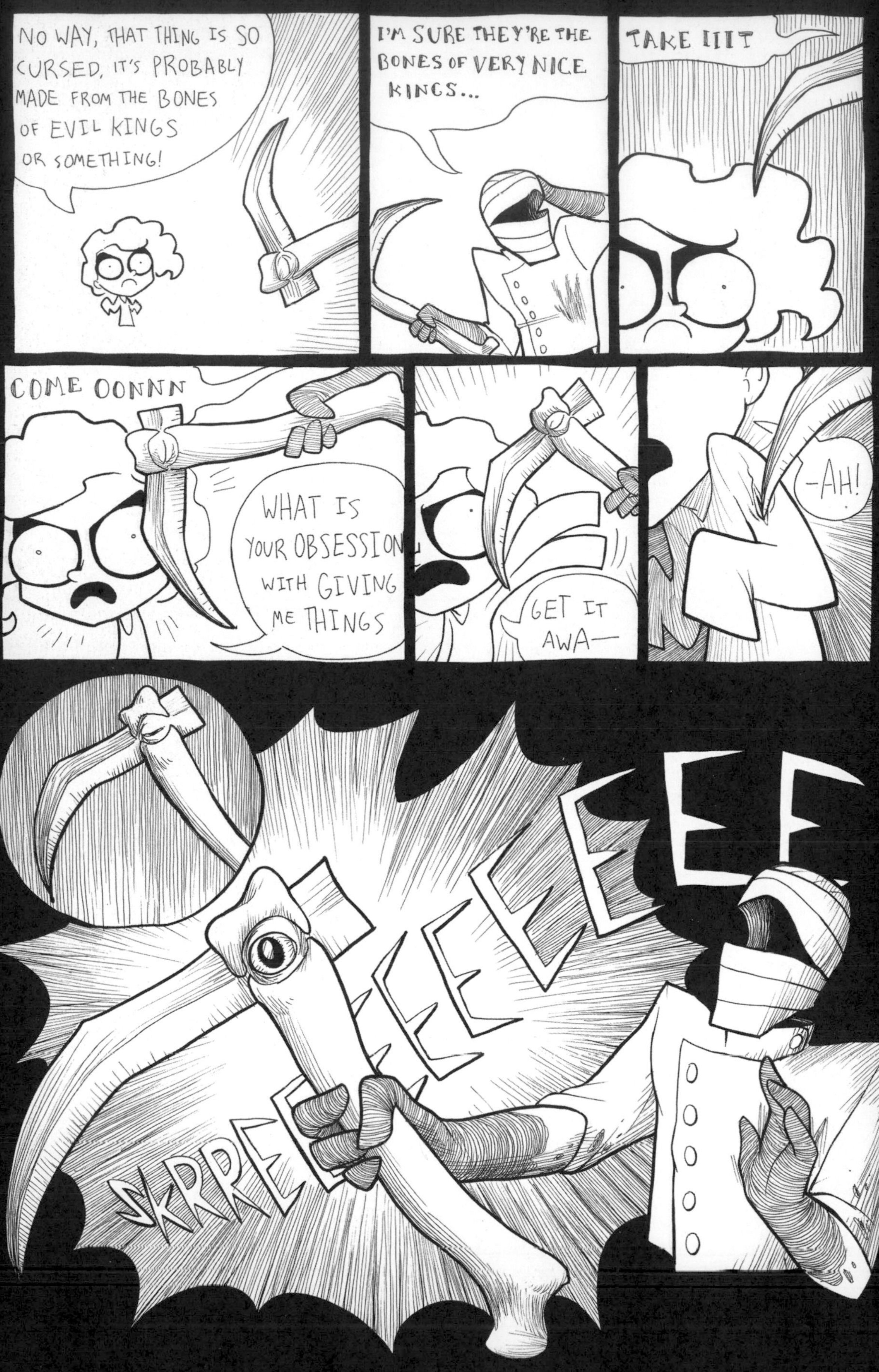
NO WAY, THAT THING IS SO CURSED, IT'S PROBABLY MADE FROM THE BONES OF EVIL KINGS OR SOMETHING!
I'M SURE THEY'RE THE BONES OF VERY NICE KINGS...
TAKE IIIT
COME OONNN
WHAT IS YOUR OBSESSION WITH GIVING ME THINGS
GET IT AWA—
-AH!
SKRREEEEEEEEE

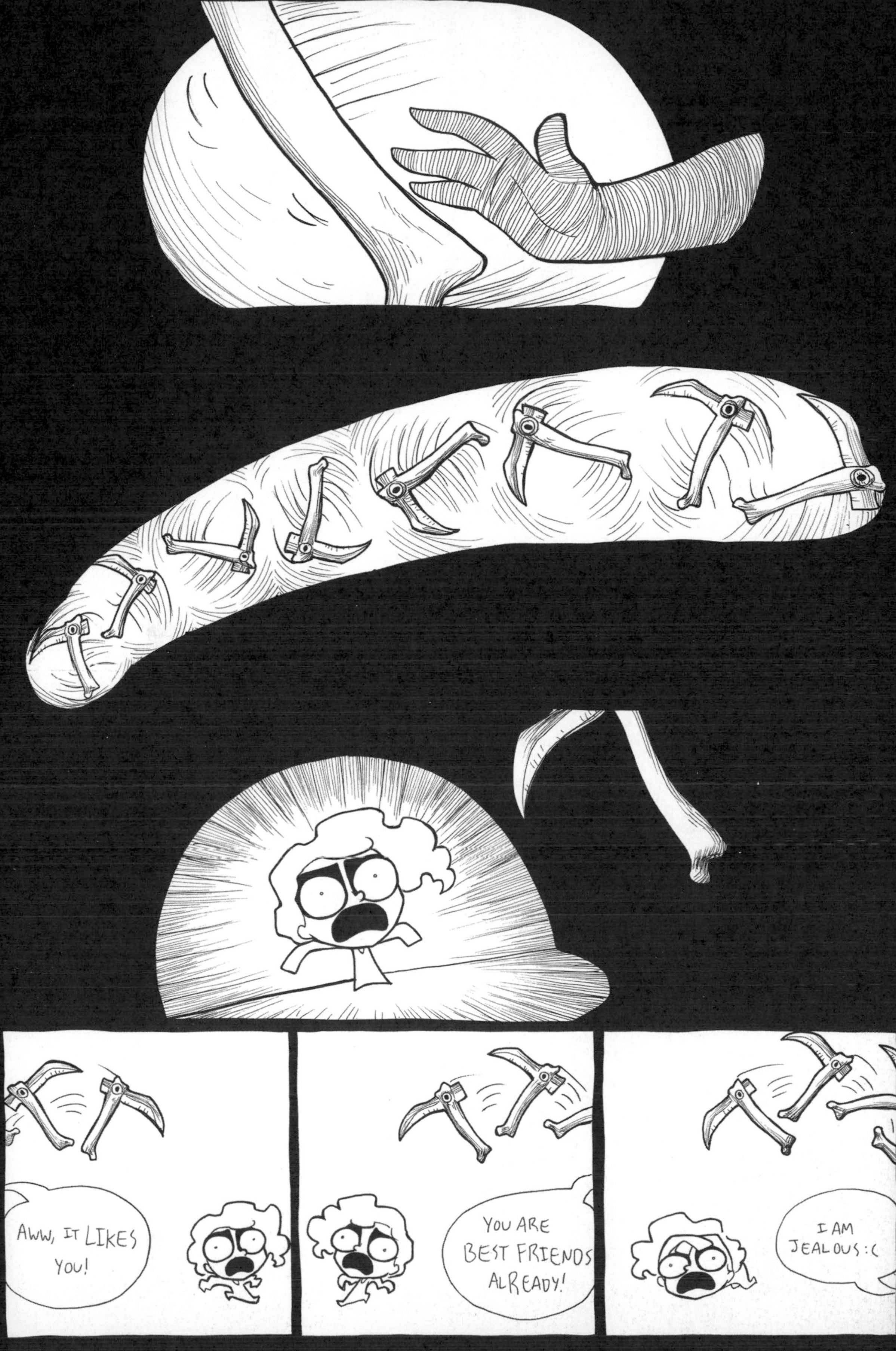
AWW, IT LIKES YOU!
YOU ARE BEST FRIENDS ALREADY!
I AM JEALOUS :(

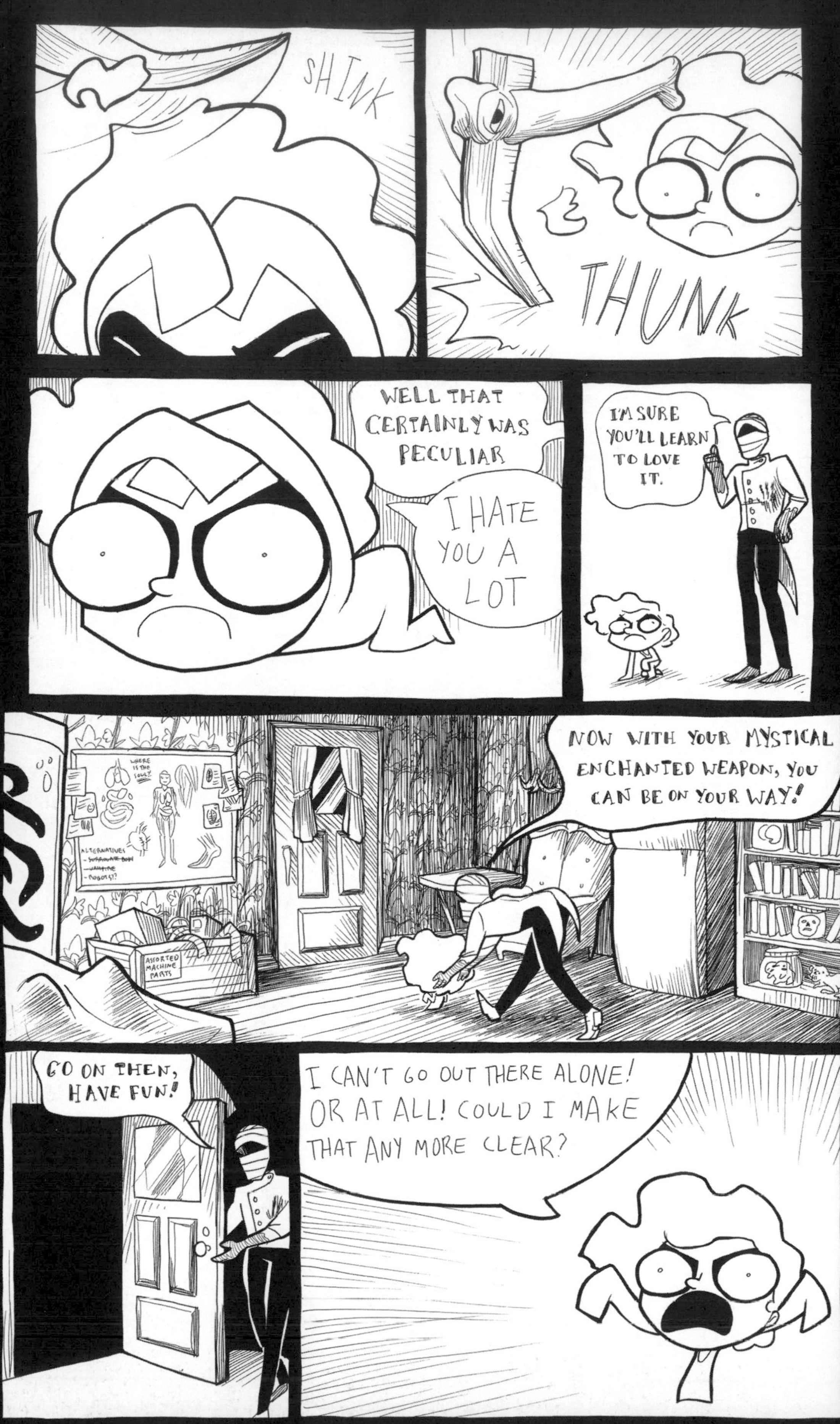
SHINK
THUNK
WELL THAT CERTAINLY WAS PECULIAR
I HATE YOU A LOT
I'M SURE YOU'LL LEARN TO LOVE IT.
WHERE IS THE SOUL?
ALTERNATIVES
- ROBOTS?!
ASSORTED MACHINE PARTS
NOW WITH YOUR MYSTICAL ENCHANTED WEAPON, YOU CAN BE ON YOUR WAY!
GO ON THEN, HAVE FUN!
I CAN'T GO OUT THERE ALONE! OR AT ALL! COULD I MAKE THAT ANY MORE CLEAR?

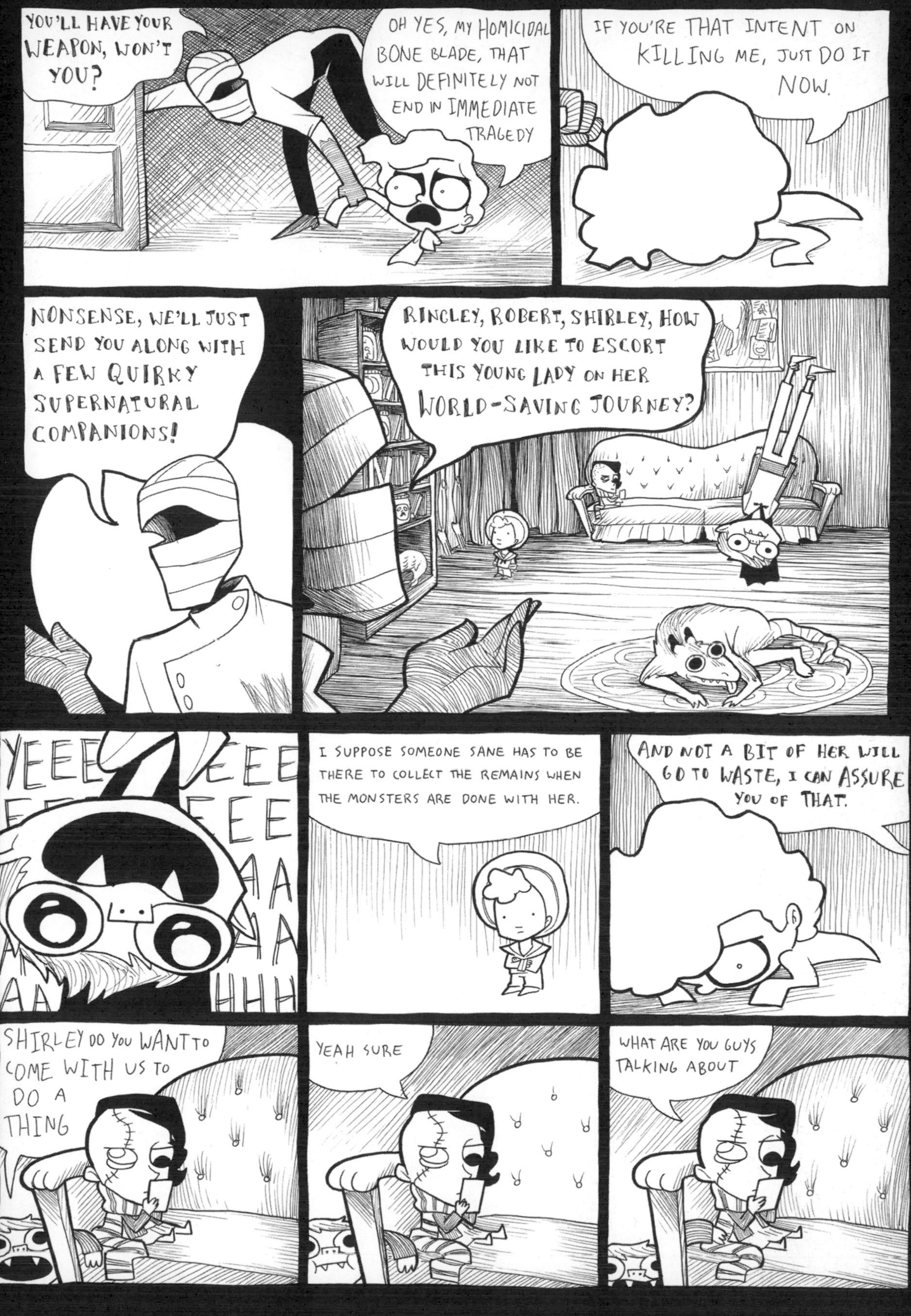
YOU'LL HAVE YOUR WEAPON, WON'T YOU?
OH YES, MY HOMICIDAL BONE BLADE, THAT WILL DEFINITELY NOT END IN IMMEDIATE TRAGEDY
IF YOU'RE THAT INTENT ON KILLING ME, JUST DO IT NOW.
NONSENSE, WE'LL JUST SEND YOU ALONG WITH A FEW QUIRKY SUPERNATURAL COMPANIONS!
RINGLEY, ROBERT, SHIRLEY, HOW WOULD YOU LIKE TO ESCORT THIS YOUNG LADY ON HER WORLD-SAVING JOURNEY?
YEEEEEEEEEAAAAAAHHH
I SUPPOSE SOMEONE SANE HAS TO BE THERE TO COLLECT THE REMAINS WHEN THE MONSTERS ARE DONE WITH HER.
AND NOT A BIT OF HER WILL GO TO WASTE, I CAN ASSURE YOU OF THAT.
SHIRLEY DO YOU WANT TO COME WITH US TO DO A THING
YEAH SURE
WHAT ARE YOU GUYS TALKING ABOUT

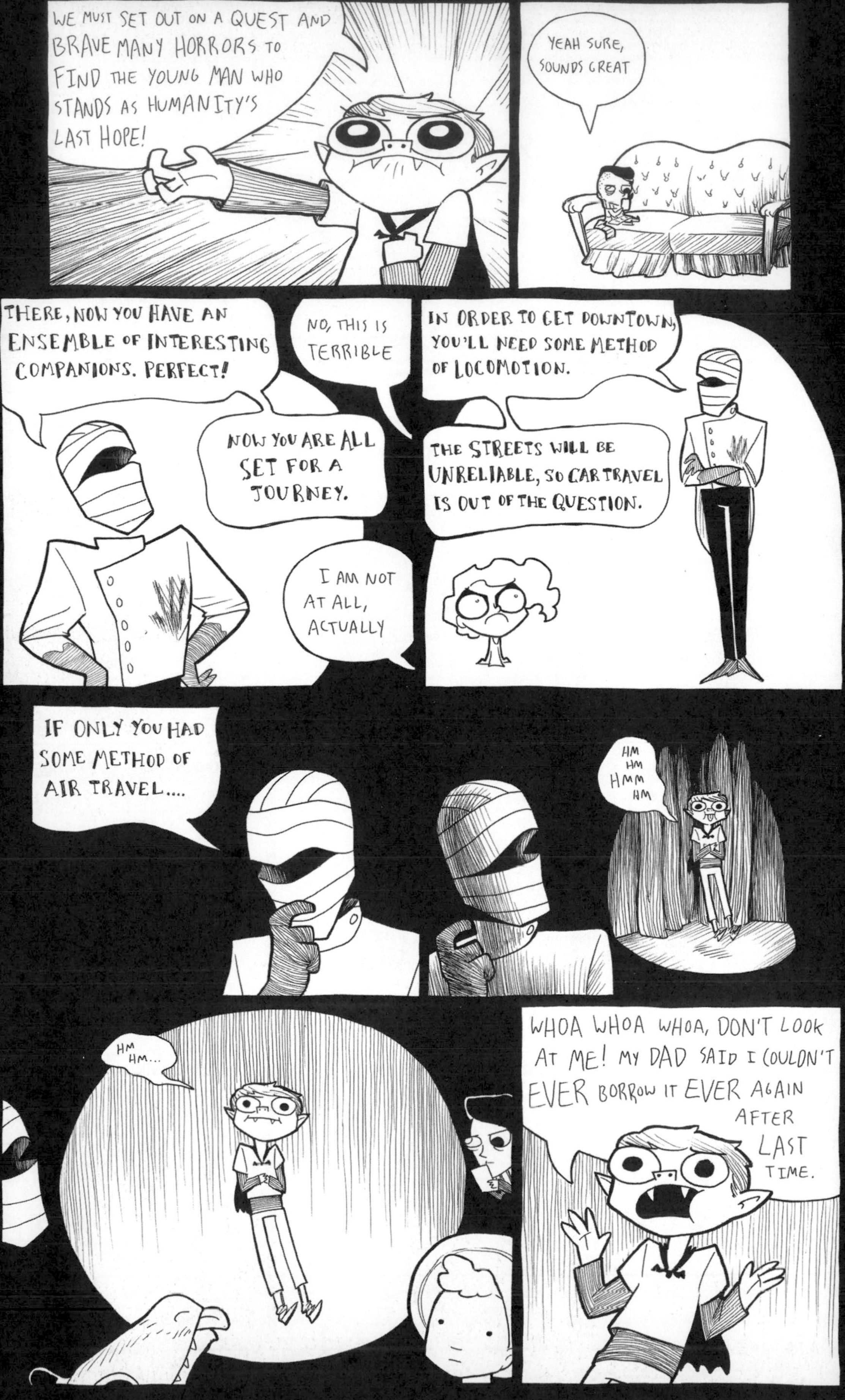
WE MUST SET OUT ON A QUEST AND BRAVE MANY HORRORS TO FIND THE YOUNG MAN WHO STANDS AS HUMANITY'S LAST HOPE!
YEAH SURE, SOUNDS GREAT
THERE, NOW YOU HAVE AN ENSEMBLE OF INTERESTING COMPANIONS. PERFECT!
NO, THIS IS TERRIBLE
NOW YOU ARE ALL SET FOR A JOURNEY.
I AM NOT AT ALL, ACTUALLY
IN ORDER TO GET DOWNTOWN, YOU'LL NEED SOME METHOD OF LOCOMOTION.
THE STREETS WILL BE UNRELIABLE, SO CAR TRAVEL IS OUT OF THE QUESTION.
IF ONLY YOU HAD SOME METHOD OF AIR TRAVEL....
HM HM HMM HM
HM HM...
WHOA WHOA WHOA, DON'T LOOK AT ME! MY DAD SAID I COULDN'T EVER BORROW IT EVER AGAIN AFTER LAST TIME.

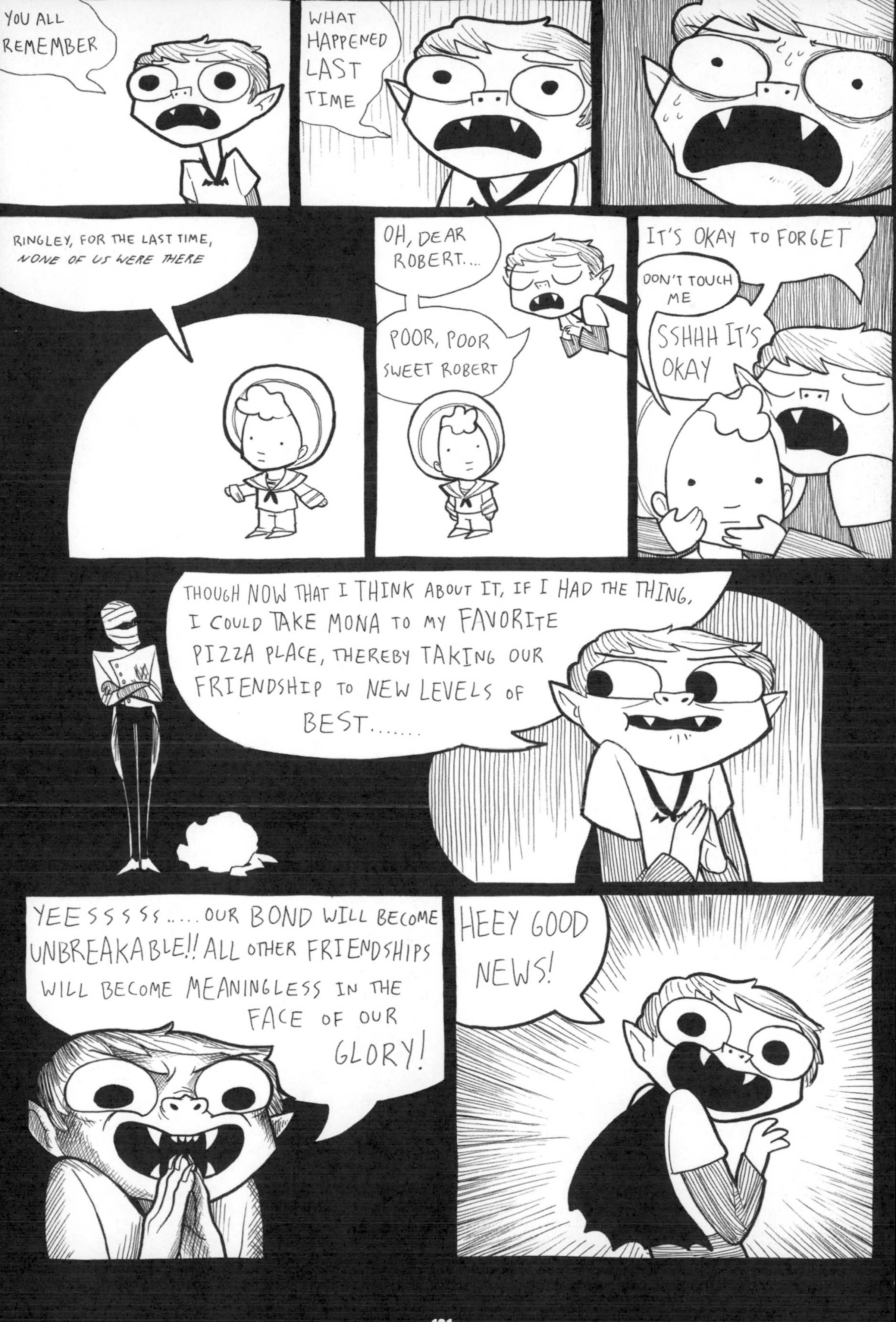
YOU ALL REMEMBER
WHAT HAPPENED LAST TIME
RINGLEY, FOR THE LAST TIME, NONE OF US WERE THERE
OH, DEAR ROBERT....
POOR, POOR SWEET ROBERT
IT'S OKAY TO FORGET
DON'T TOUCH ME
SSHHH IT'S OKAY
THOUGH NOW THAT I THINK ABOUT IT, IF I HAD THE THING, I COULD TAKE MONA TO MY FAVORITE PIZZA PLACE, THEREBY TAKING OUR FRIENDSHIP TO NEW LEVELS OF BEST.......
YEESSSSS.....OUR BOND WILL BECOME UNBREAKABLE!! ALL OTHER FRIENDSHIPS WILL BECOME MEANINGLESS IN THE FACE OF OUR GLORY!
HEEY GOOD NEWS!

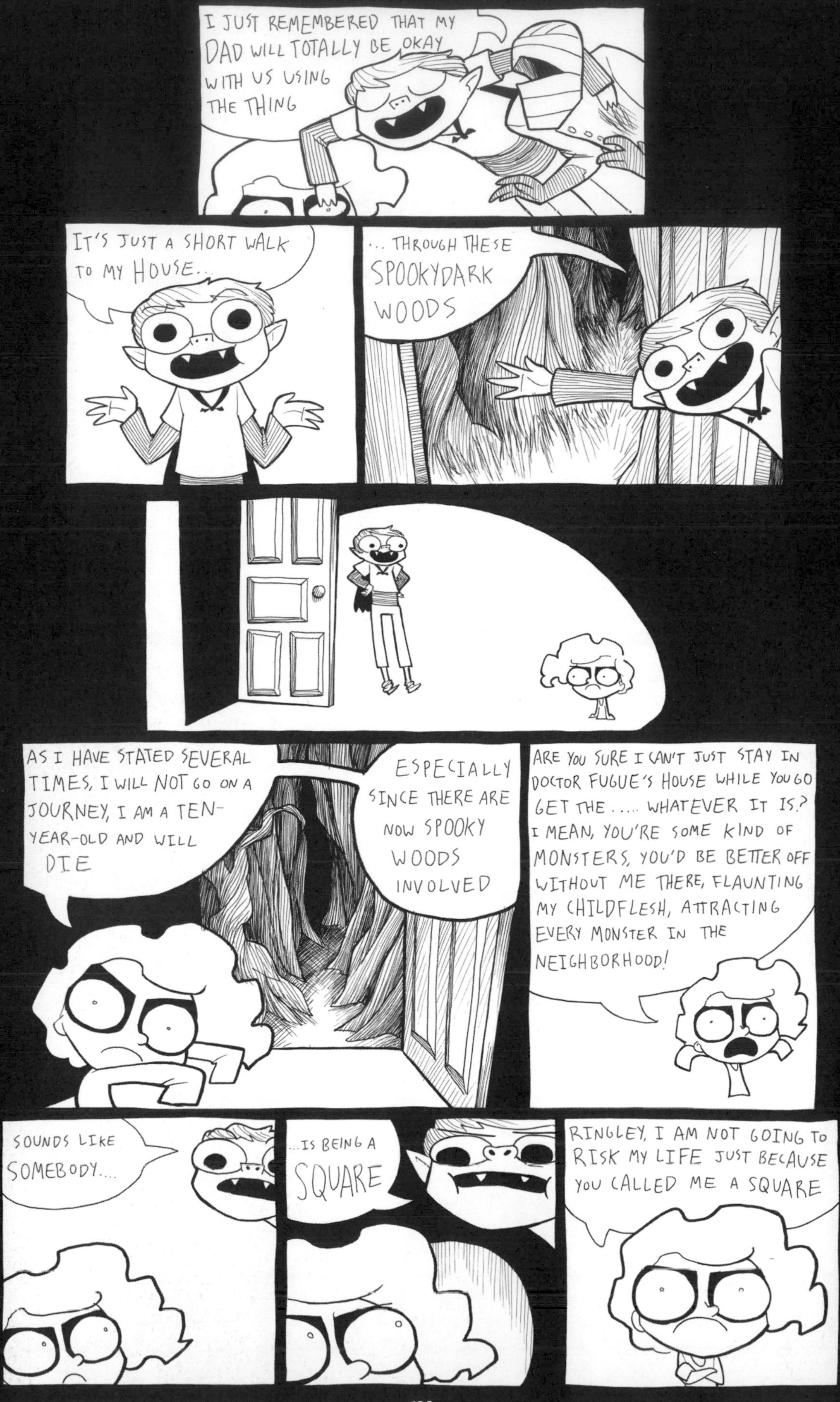
I JUST REMEMBERED THAT MY DAD WILL TOTALLY BE OKAY WITH US USING THE THING
IT'S JUST A SHORT WALK TO MY HOUSE...
...THROUGH THESE SPOOKYDARK WOODS
AS I HAVE STATED SEVERAL TIMES, I WILL NOT GO ON A JOURNEY, I AM A TEN-YEAR-OLD AND WILL DIE
ESPECIALLY SINCE THERE ARE NOW SPOOKY WOODS INVOLVED
ARE YOU SURE I CAN'T JUST STAY IN DOCTOR FUGUE'S HOUSE WHILE YOU GO GET THE..... WHATEVER IT IS? I MEAN, YOU'RE SOME KIND OF MONSTERS, YOU'D BE BETTER OFF WITHOUT ME THERE, FLAUNTING MY CHILDFLESH, ATTRACTING EVERY MONSTER IN THE NEIGHBORHOOD!
SOUNDS LIKE SOMEBODY....
...IS BEING A SQUARE
RINGLEY, I AM NOT GOING TO RISK MY LIFE JUST BECAUSE YOU CALLED ME A SQUARE

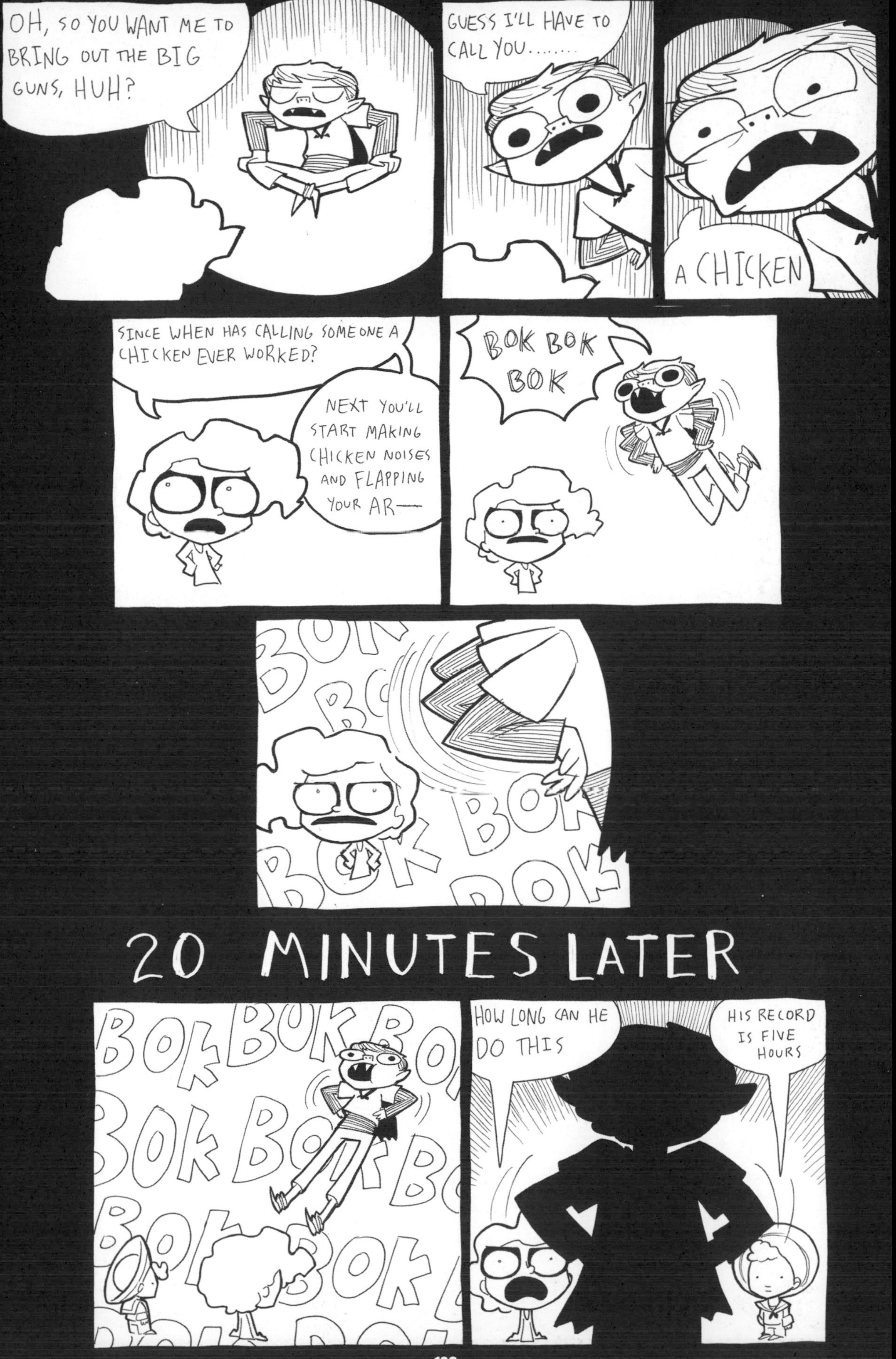
OH, SO YOU WANT ME TO BRING OUT THE BIG GUNS, HUH?
GUESS I'LL HAVE TO CALL YOU.......
A CHICKEN
SINCE WHEN HAS CALLING SOMEONE A CHICKEN EVER WORKED?
NEXT YOU'LL START MAKING CHICKEN NOISES AND FLAPPING YOUR AR—
BOK BOK BOK
20 MINUTES LATER
HOW LONG CAN HE DO THIS
HIS RECORD IS FIVE HOURS

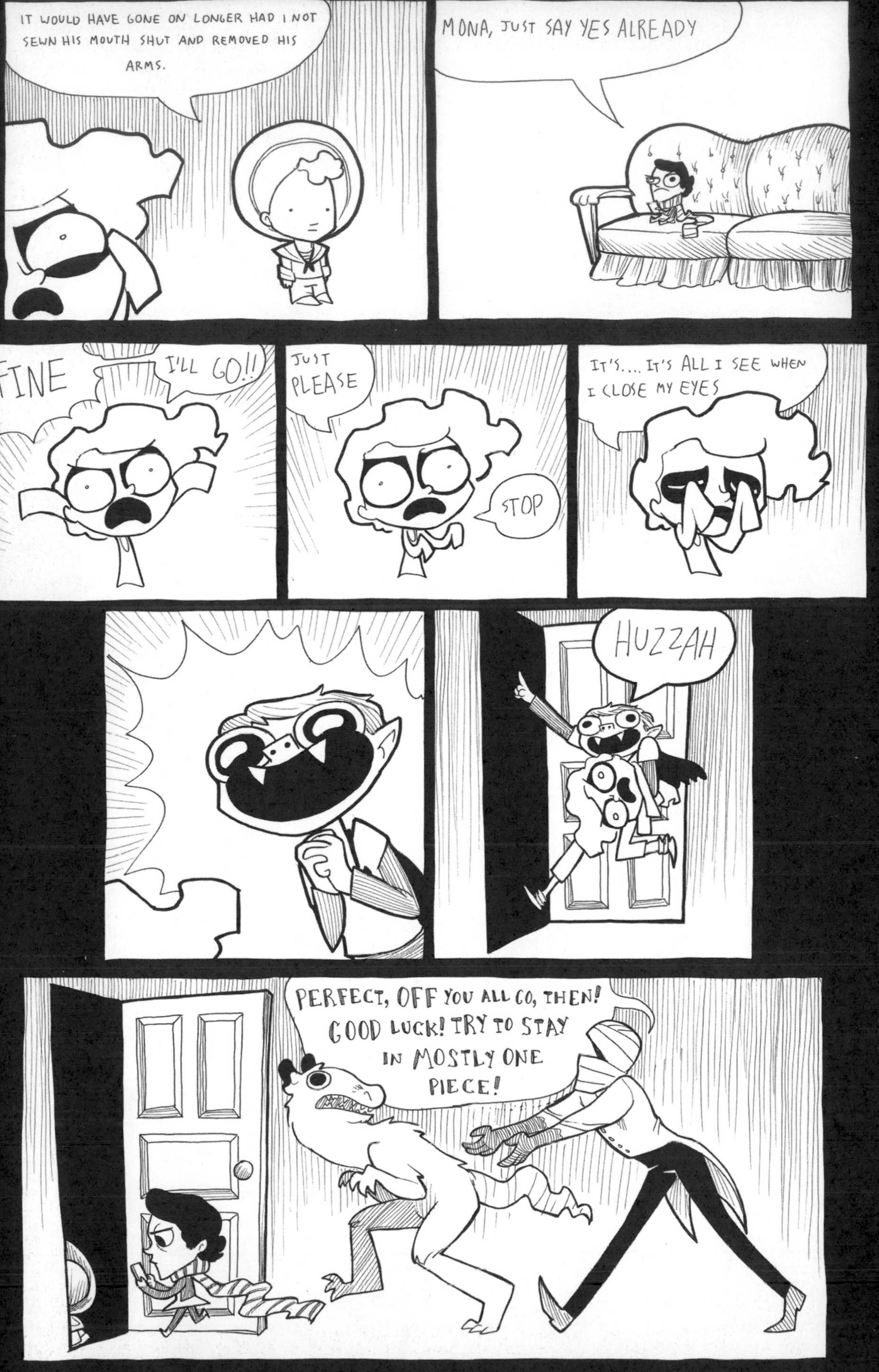
IT WOULD HAVE GONE ON LONGER HAD I NOT SEWN HIS MOUTH SHUT AND REMOVED HIS ARMS.
MONA, JUST SAY YES ALREADY
FINE
I'LL GO!!
JUST PLEASE
STOP
IT'S.... IT'S ALL I SEE WHEN I CLOSE MY EYES
HUZZAH
PERFECT, OFF YOU ALL GO, THEN! GOOD LUCK! TRY TO STAY IN MOSTLY ONE PIECE!

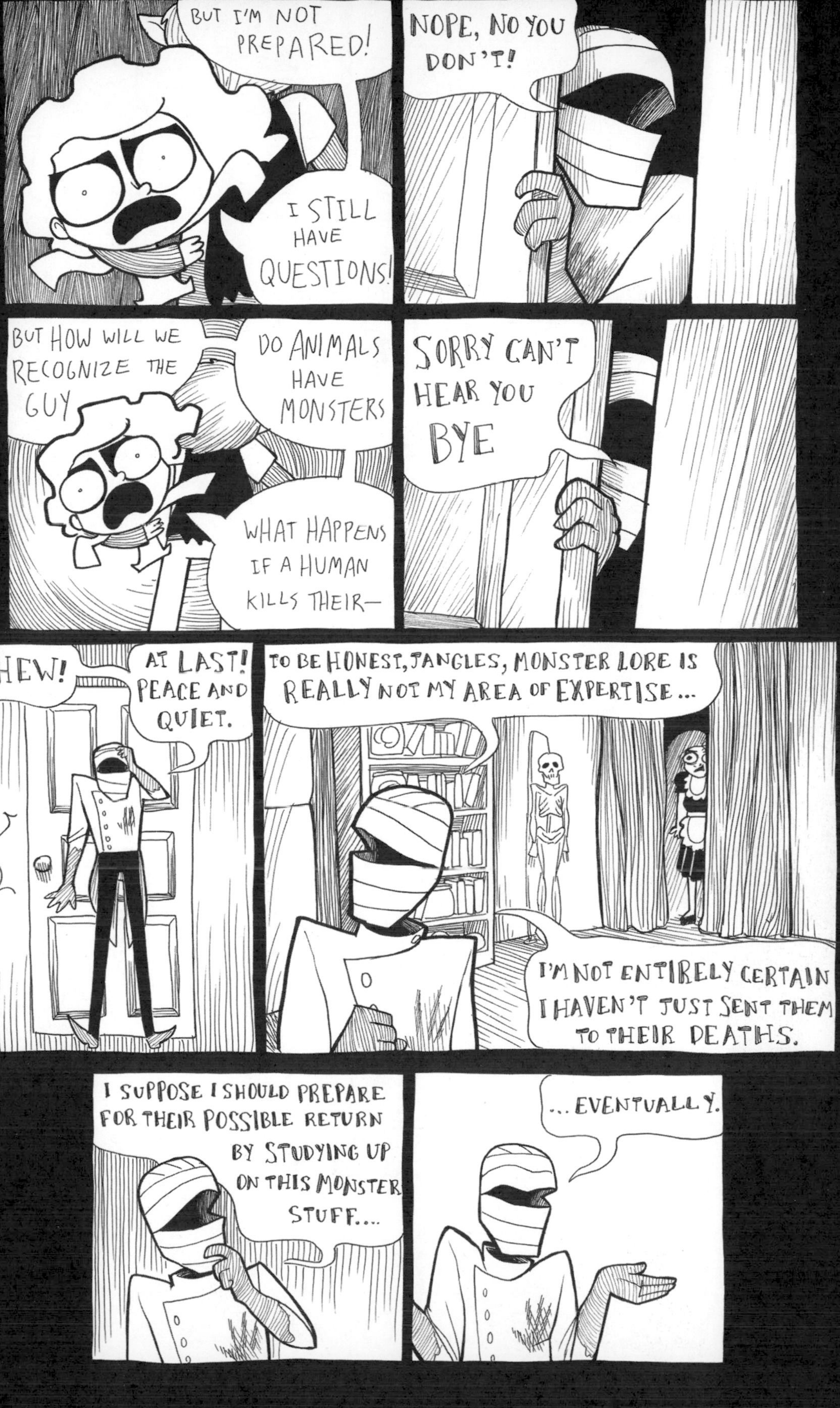
BUT I'M NOT PREPARED!
I STILL HAVE QUESTIONS!
NOPE, NO YOU DON'T!
BUT HOW WILL WE RECOGNIZE THE GUY
DO ANIMALS HAVE MONSTERS
WHAT HAPPENS IF A HUMAN KILLS THEIR—
SORRY CAN'T HEAR YOU BYE
PHEW!
AT LAST! PEACE AND QUIET.
TO BE HONEST, JANGLES, MONSTER LORE IS REALLY NOT MY AREA OF EXPERTISE...
I'M NOT ENTIRELY CERTAIN I HAVEN'T JUST SENT THEM TO THEIR DEATHS.
I SUPPOSE I SHOULD PREPARE FOR THEIR POSSIBLE RETURN BY STUDYING UP ON THIS MONSTER STUFF....
...EVENTUALLY.

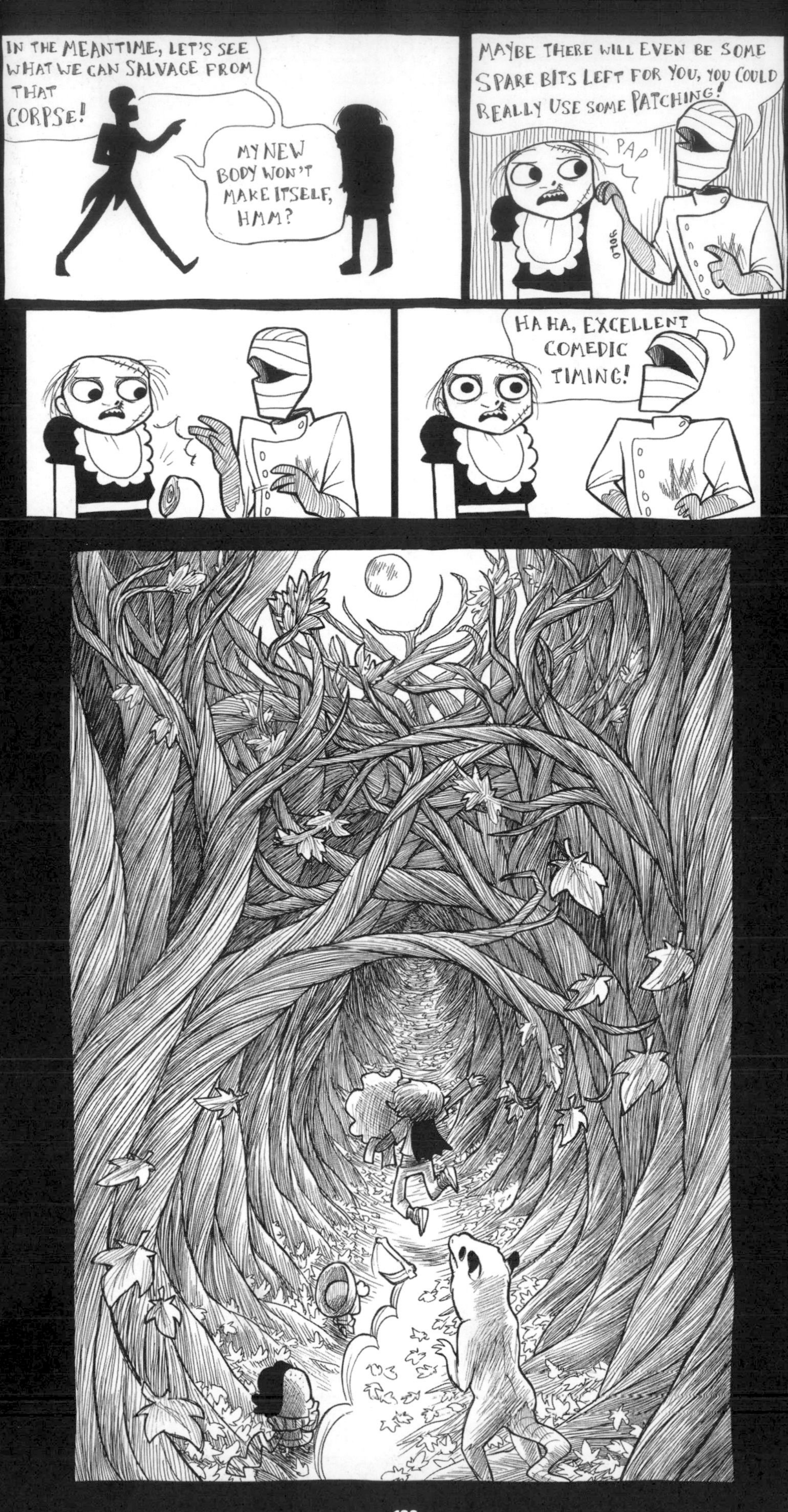
IN THE MEANTIME, LET'S SEE WHAT WE CAN SALVAGE FROM THAT CORPSE!
MY NEW BODY WON'T MAKE ITSELF, HMM?
MAYBE THERE WILL EVEN BE SOME SPARE BITS LEFT FOR YOU, YOU COULD REALLY USE SOME PATCHING!
PAP
HA HA, EXCELLENT COMEDIC TIMING!

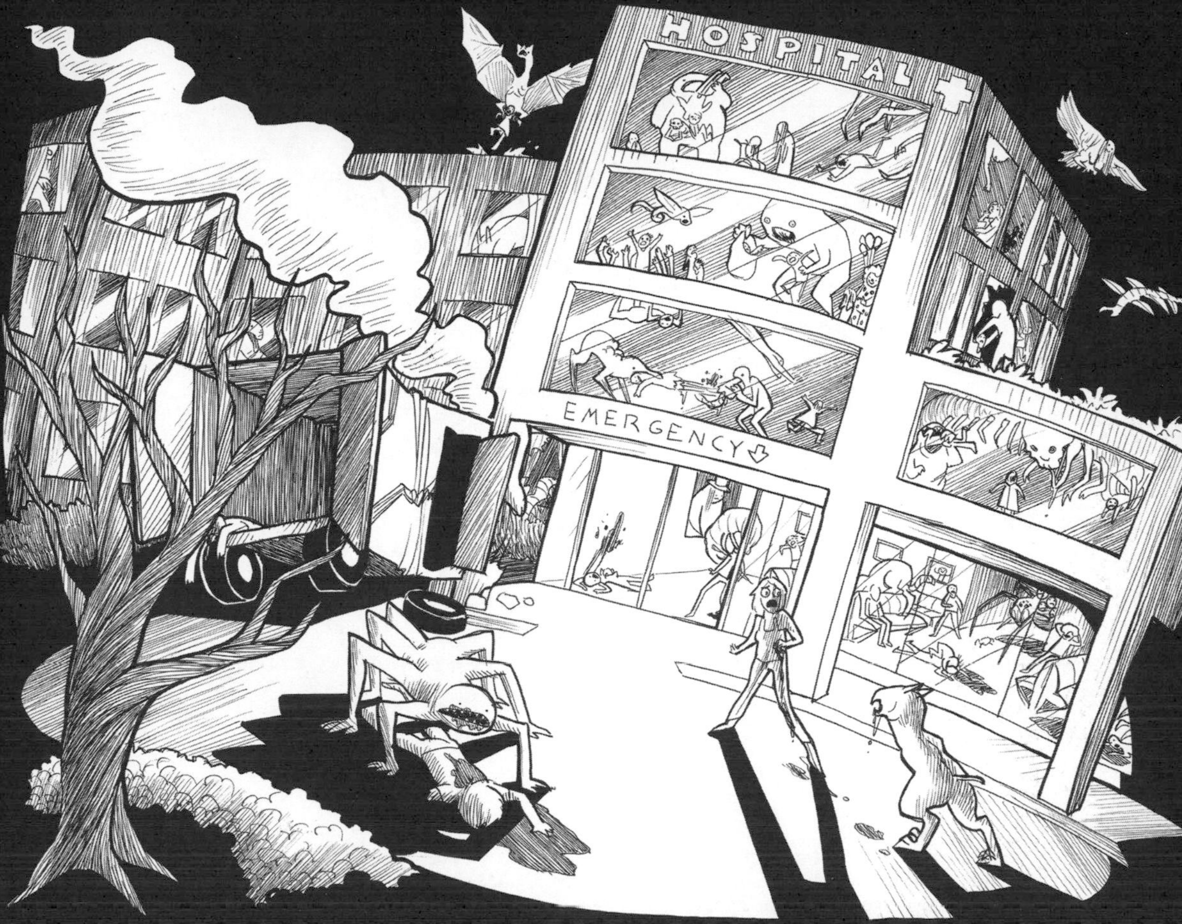
HOSPITAL
EMERGENCY

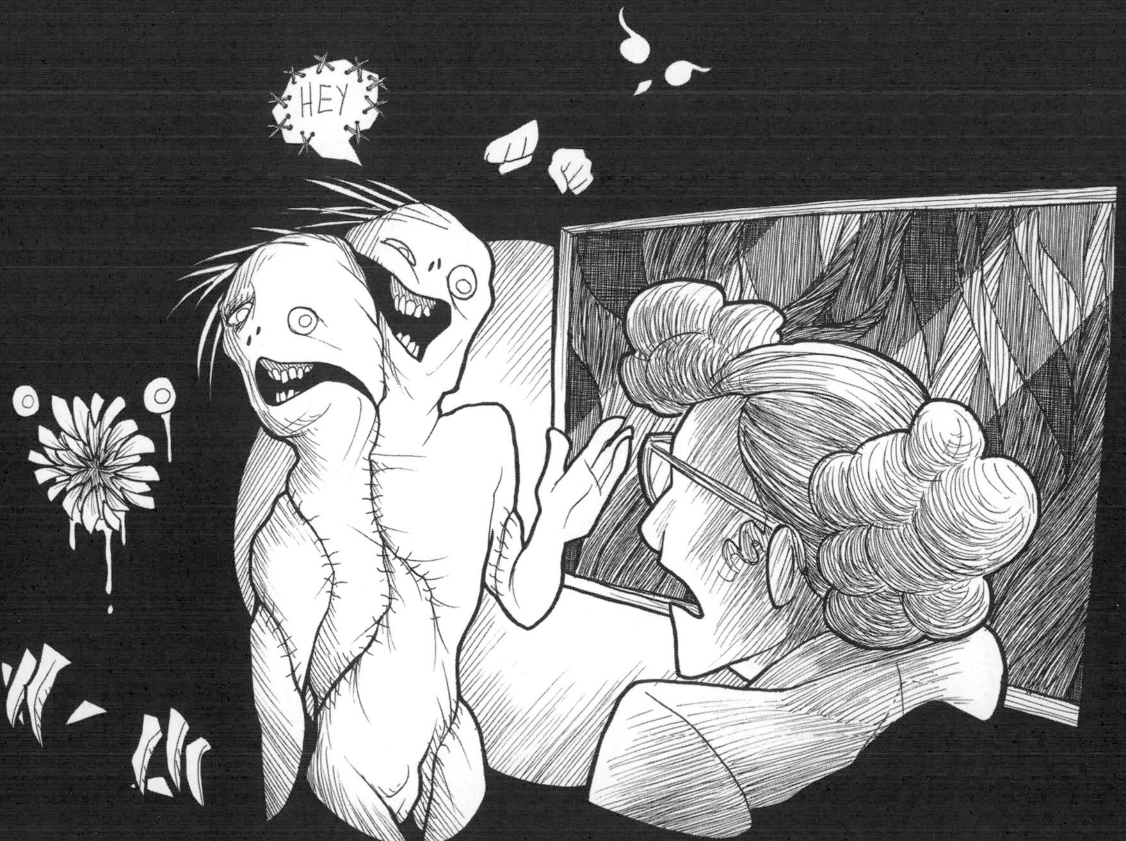
HEY

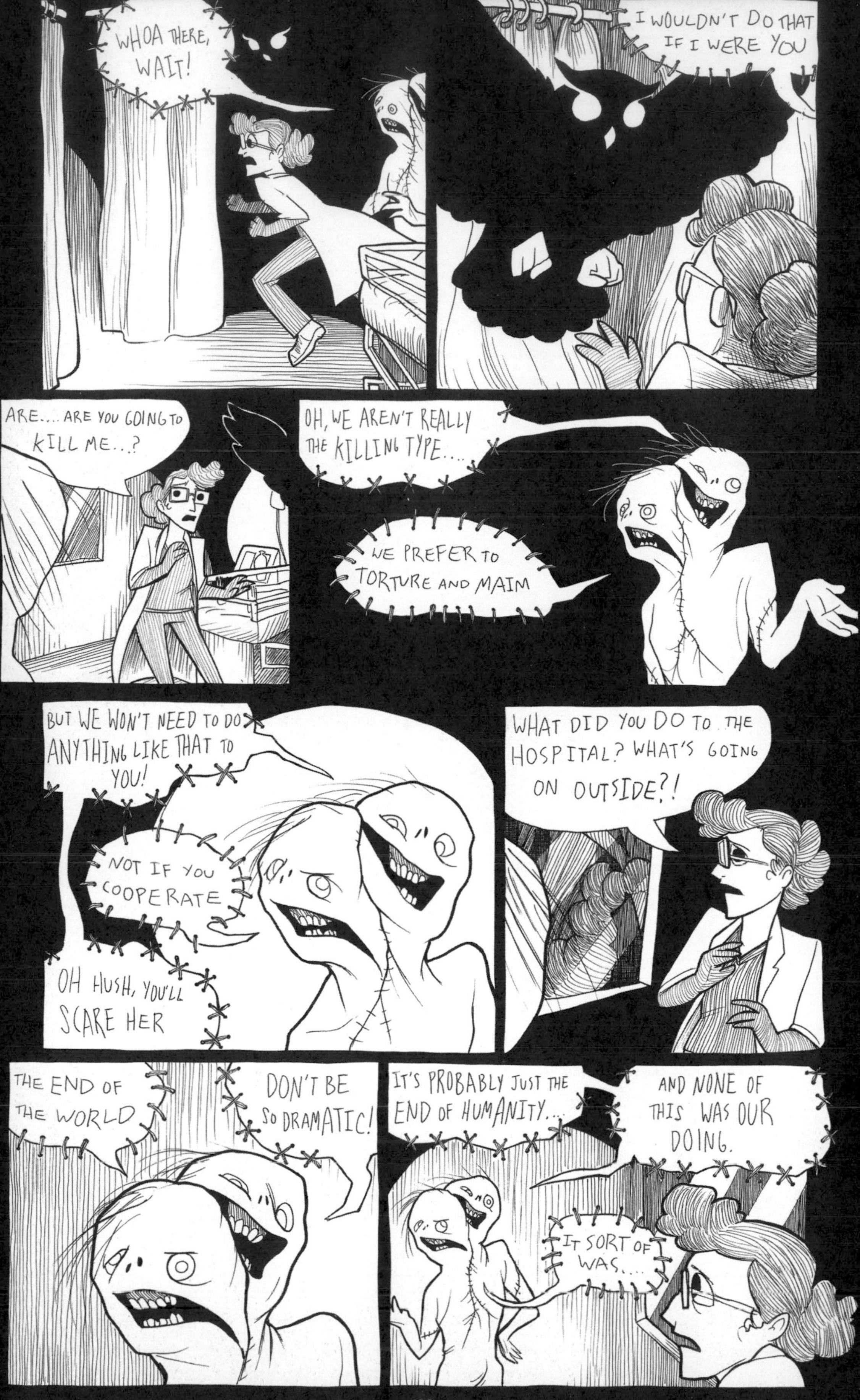
WHOA THERE, WAIT!
I WOULDN'T DO THAT IF I WERE YOU
ARE.... ARE YOU GOING TO KILL ME...?
OH, WE AREN'T REALLY THE KILLING TYPE....
WE PREFER TO TORTURE AND MAIM
BUT WE WON'T NEED TO DO ANYTHING LIKE THAT TO YOU!
NOT IF YOU COOPERATE
OH HUSH, YOU'LL SCARE HER
WHAT DID YOU DO TO THE HOSPITAL? WHAT'S GOING ON OUTSIDE?!
THE END OF THE WORLD
DON'T BE SO DRAMATIC!
IT'S PROBABLY JUST THE END OF HUMANITY....
AND NONE OF THIS WAS OUR DOING.
IT SORT OF WAS....

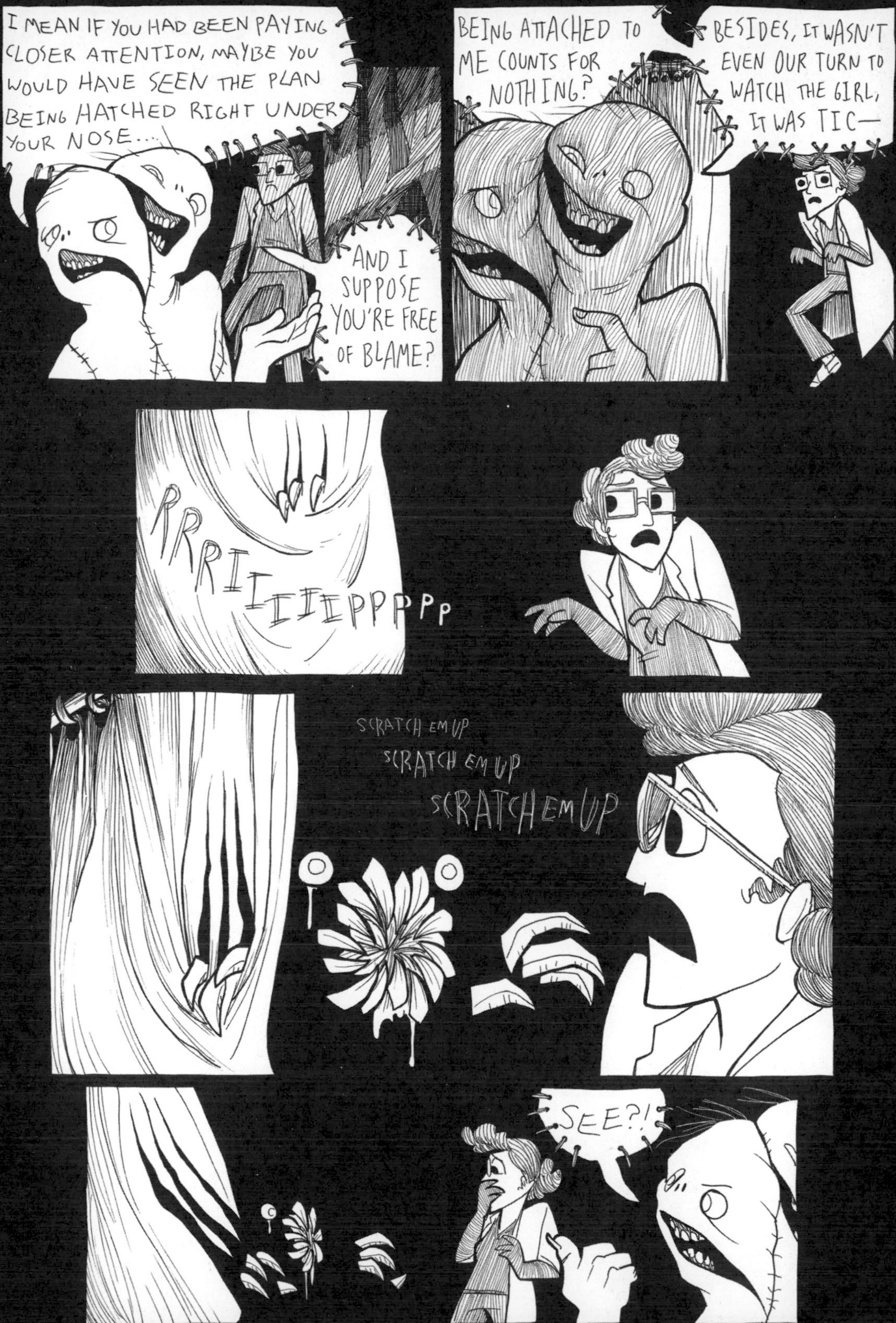
I MEAN IF YOU HAD BEEN PAYING CLOSER ATTENTION, MAYBE YOU WOULD HAVE SEEN THE PLAN BEING HATCHED RIGHT UNDER YOUR NOSE....
AND I SUPPOSE YOU'RE FREE OF BLAME?
BEING ATTACHED TO ME COUNTS FOR NOTHING?
BESIDES, IT WASN'T EVEN OUR TURN TO WATCH THE GIRL, IT WAS TIC—
RRRIIIIEPPPPP
SCRATCH EM UP
SCRATCH EM UP
SCRATCH EM UP
SEE?!

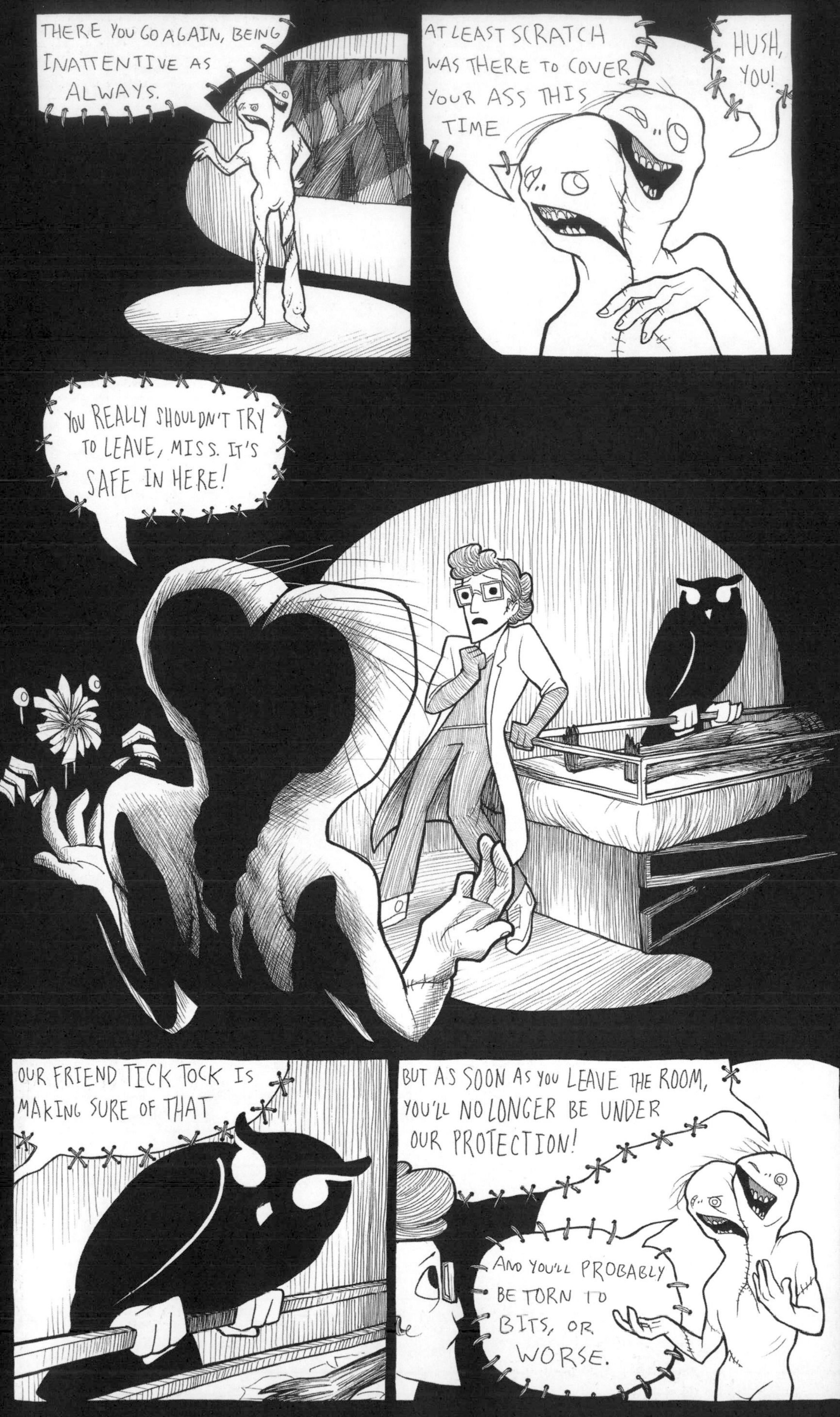
THERE YOU GO AGAIN, BEING INATTENTIVE AS ALWAYS.
AT LEAST SCRATCH WAS THERE TO COVER YOUR ASS THIS TIME
HUSH, YOU!
YOU REALLY SHOULDN'T TRY TO LEAVE, MISS. IT'S SAFE IN HERE!
OUR FRIEND TICK TOCK IS MAKING SURE OF THAT
BUT AS SOON AS YOU LEAVE THE ROOM, YOU'LL NO LONGER BE UNDER OUR PROTECTION!
AND YOU'LL PROBABLY BE TORN TO BITS, OR WORSE.

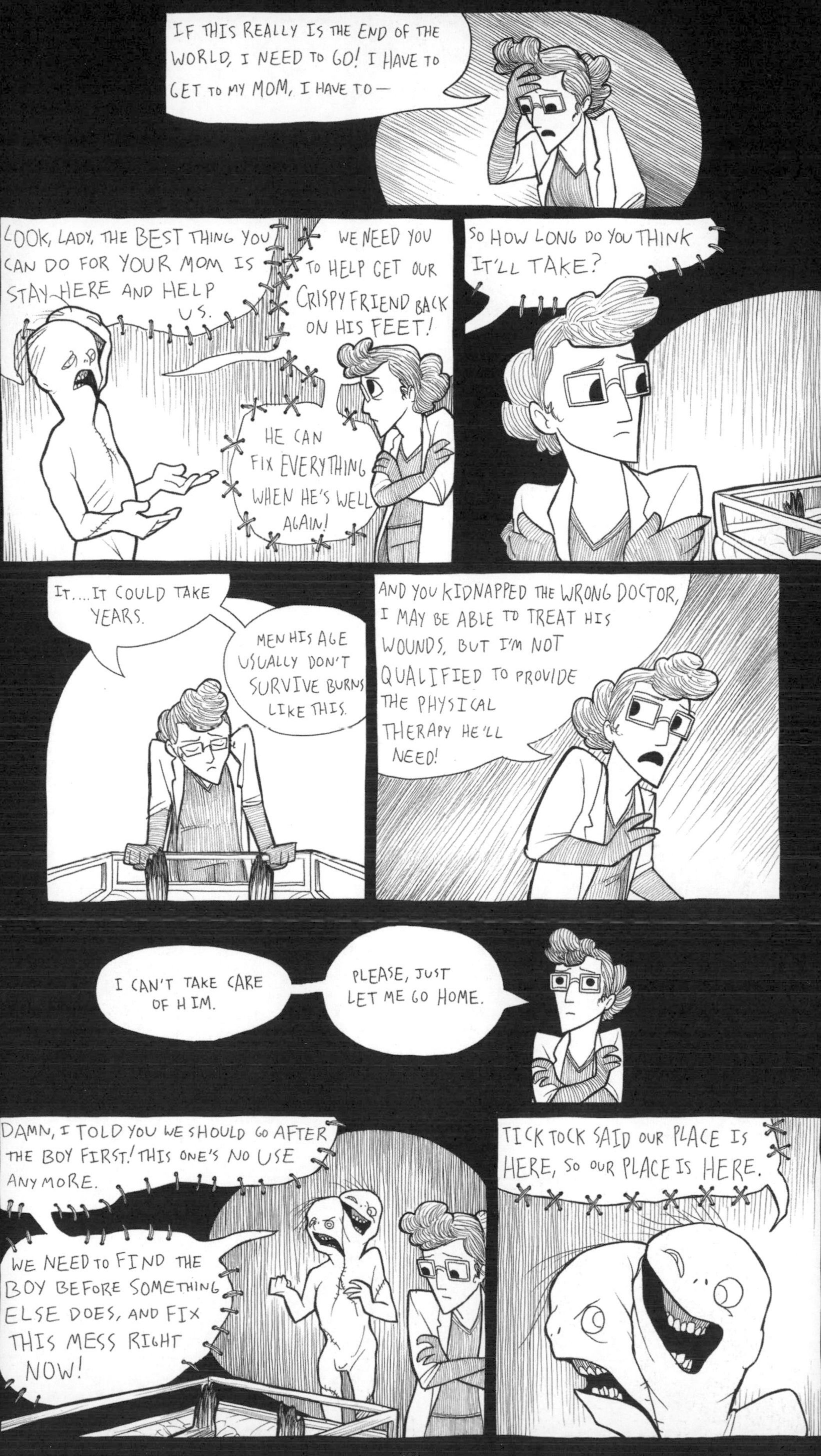
IF THIS REALLY IS THE END OF THE WORLD, I NEED TO GO! I HAVE TO GET TO MY MOM, I HAVE TO—
LOOK, LADY, THE BEST THING YOU CAN DO FOR YOUR MOM IS STAY HERE AND HELP US.
WE NEED YOU TO HELP GET OUR CRISPY FRIEND BACK ON HIS FEET!
HE CAN FIX EVERYTHING WHEN HE'S WELL AGAIN!
SO HOW LONG DO YOU THINK IT'LL TAKE?
IT.... IT COULD TAKE YEARS.
MEN HIS AGE USUALLY DON'T SURVIVE BURNS LIKE THIS.
AND YOU KIDNAPPED THE WRONG DOCTOR, I MAY BE ABLE TO TREAT HIS WOUNDS, BUT I'M NOT QUALIFIED TO PROVIDE THE PHYSICAL THERAPY HE'LL NEED!
I CAN'T TAKE CARE OF HIM.
PLEASE, JUST LET ME GO HOME.
DAMN, I TOLD YOU WE SHOULD GO AFTER THE BOY FIRST! THIS ONE'S NO USE ANYMORE.
WE NEED TO FIND THE BOY BEFORE SOMETHING ELSE DOES, AND FIX THIS MESS RIGHT NOW!
TICK TOCK SAID OUR PLACE IS HERE, SO OUR PLACE IS HERE.

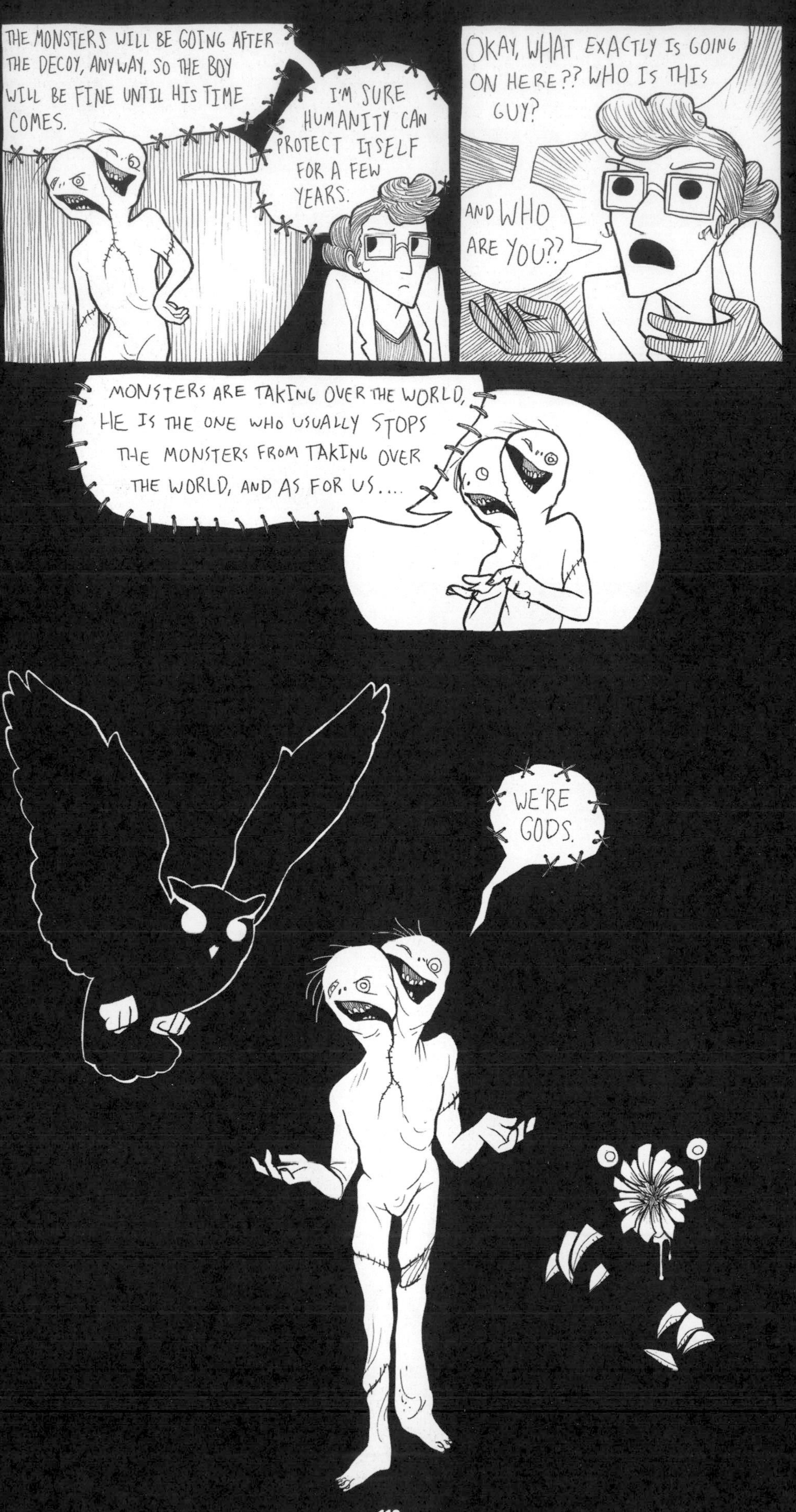
THE MONSTERS WILL BE GOING AFTER THE DECOY, ANYWAY, SO THE BOY WILL BE FINE UNTIL HIS TIME COMES.
I'M SURE HUMANITY CAN PROTECT ITSELF FOR A FEW YEARS.
OKAY, WHAT EXACTLY IS GOING ON HERE?? WHO IS THIS GUY?
AND WHO ARE YOU??
MONSTERS ARE TAKING OVER THE WORLD, HE IS THE ONE WHO USUALLY STOPS THE MONSTERS FROM TAKING OVER THE WORLD, AND AS FOR US....
WE'RE GODS.

CHAPTER 3

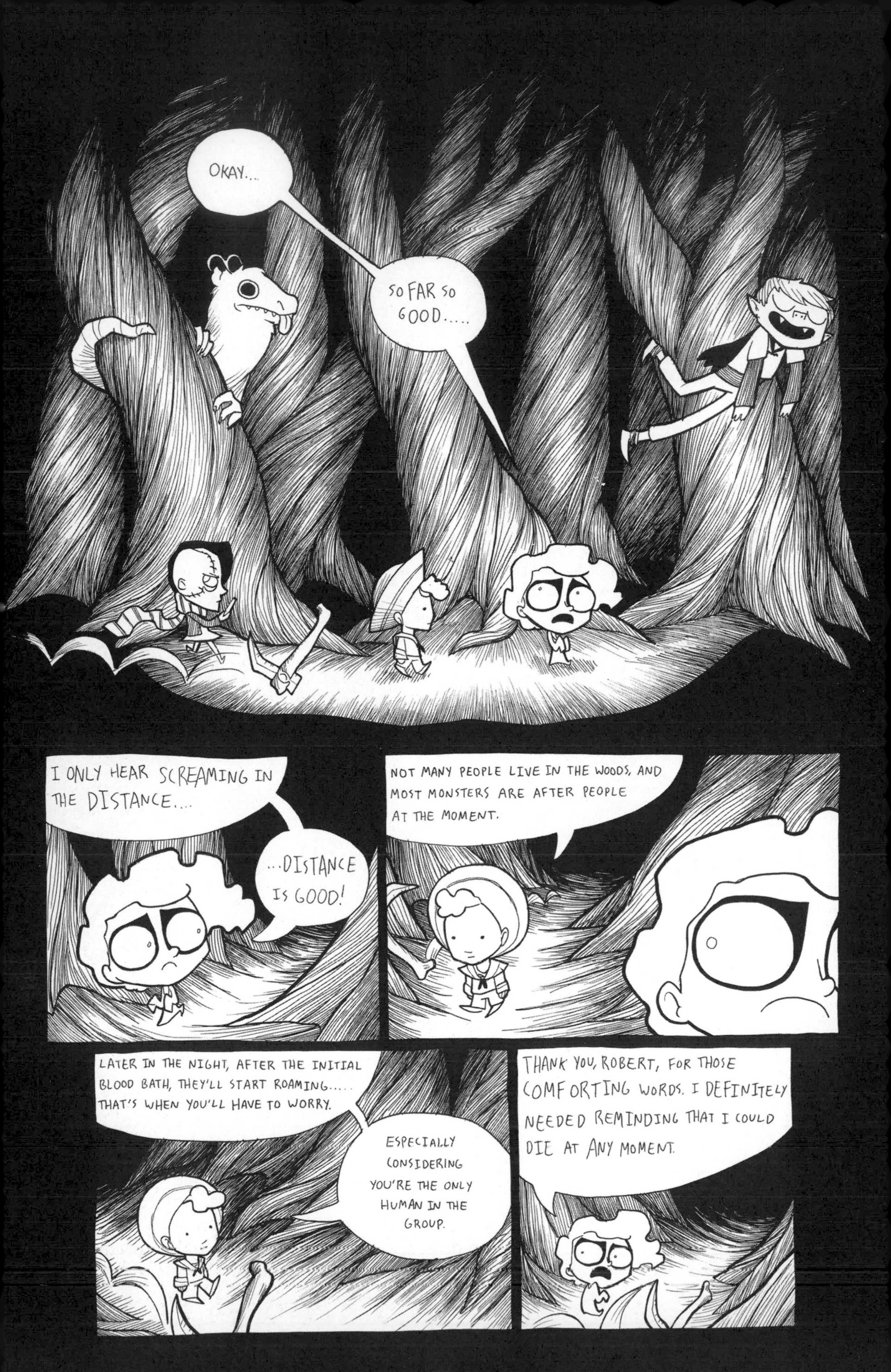

OKAY...
SO FAR SO GOOD.....
I ONLY HEAR SCREAMING IN THE DISTANCE....
...DISTANCE IS GOOD!
NOT MANY PEOPLE LIVE IN THE WOODS, AND MOST MONSTERS ARE AFTER PEOPLE AT THE MOMENT.
LATER IN THE NIGHT, AFTER THE INITIAL BLOOD BATH, THEY'LL START ROAMING..... THAT'S WHEN YOU'LL HAVE TO WORRY.
ESPECIALLY CONSIDERING YOU'RE THE ONLY HUMAN IN THE GROUP.
THANK YOU, ROBERT, FOR THOSE COMFORTING WORDS. I DEFINITELY NEEDED REMINDING THAT I COULD DIE AT ANY MOMENT.

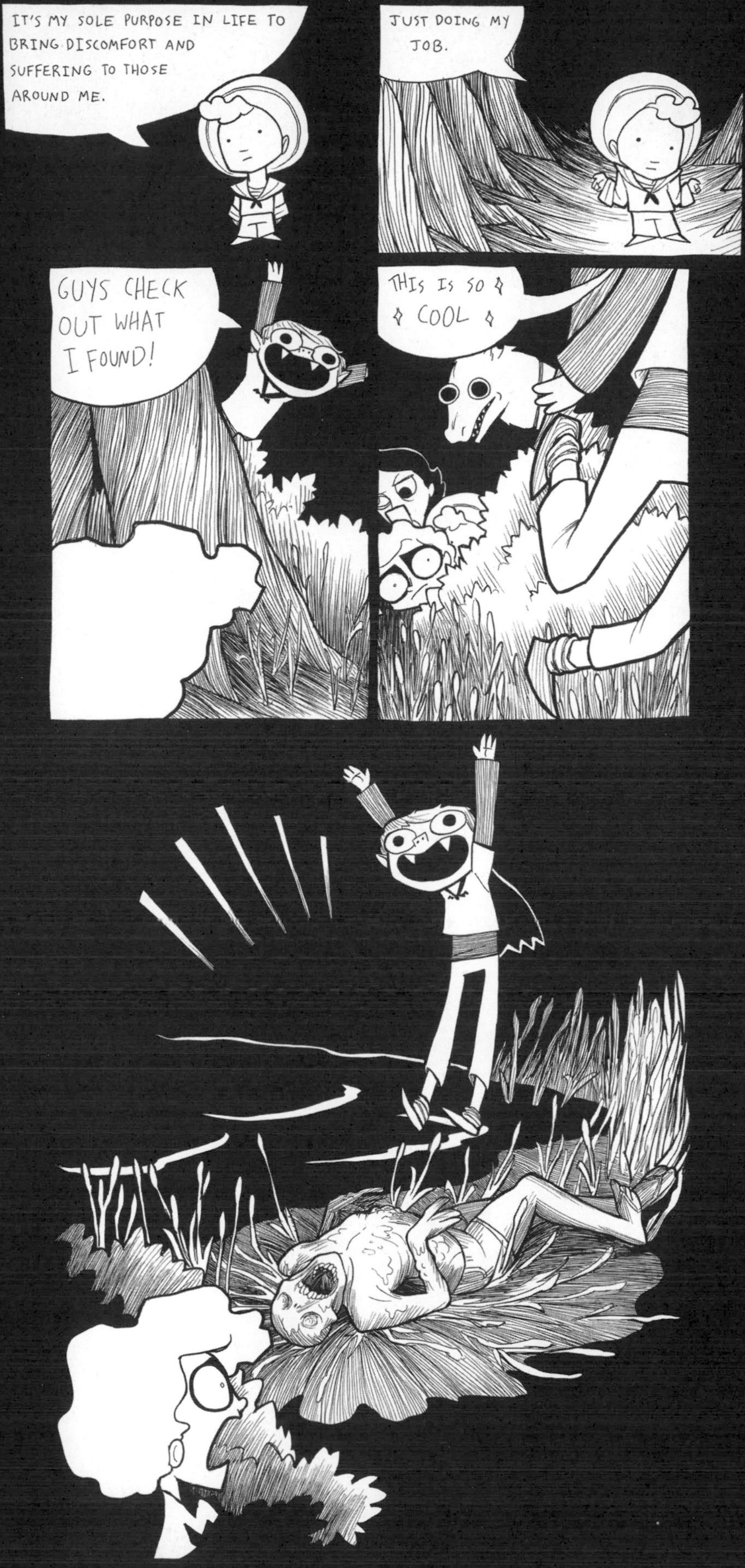
IT'S MY SOLE PURPOSE IN LIFE TO BRING DISCOMFORT AND SUFFERING TO THOSE AROUND ME.
JUST DOING MY JOB.
GUYS CHECK OUT WHAT I FOUND!
THIS IS SO COOL

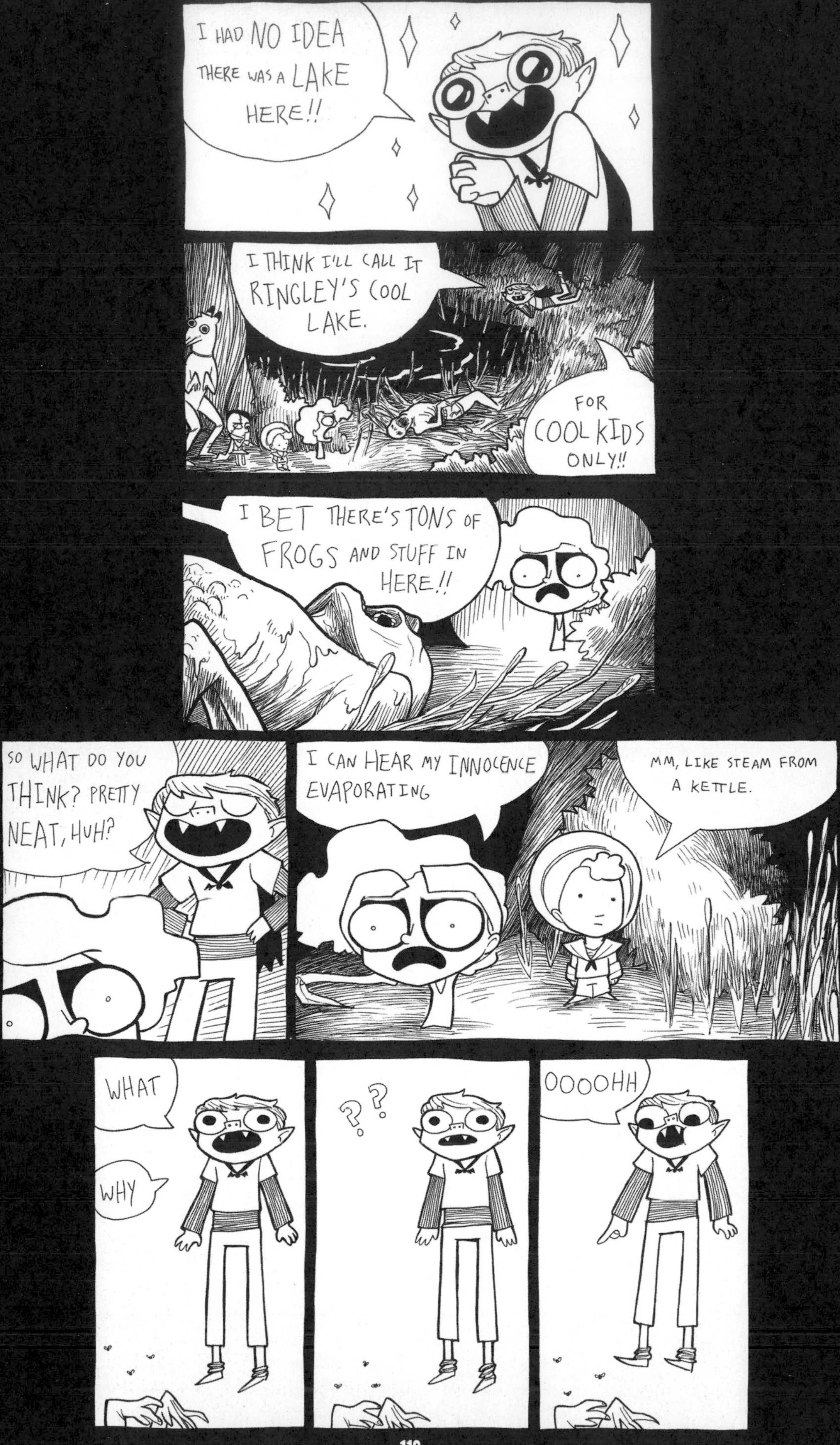
I HAD NO IDEA THERE WAS A LAKE HERE!!
I THINK I'LL CALL IT RINGLEY'S COOL LAKE.
FOR COOL KIDS ONLY!!
I BET THERE'S TONS OF FROGS AND STUFF IN HERE!!
SO WHAT DO YOU THINK? PRETTY NEAT, HUH?
I CAN HEAR MY INNOCENCE EVAPORATING
MM, LIKE STEAM FROM A KETTLE.
WHAT
WHY
??
OOOOHH

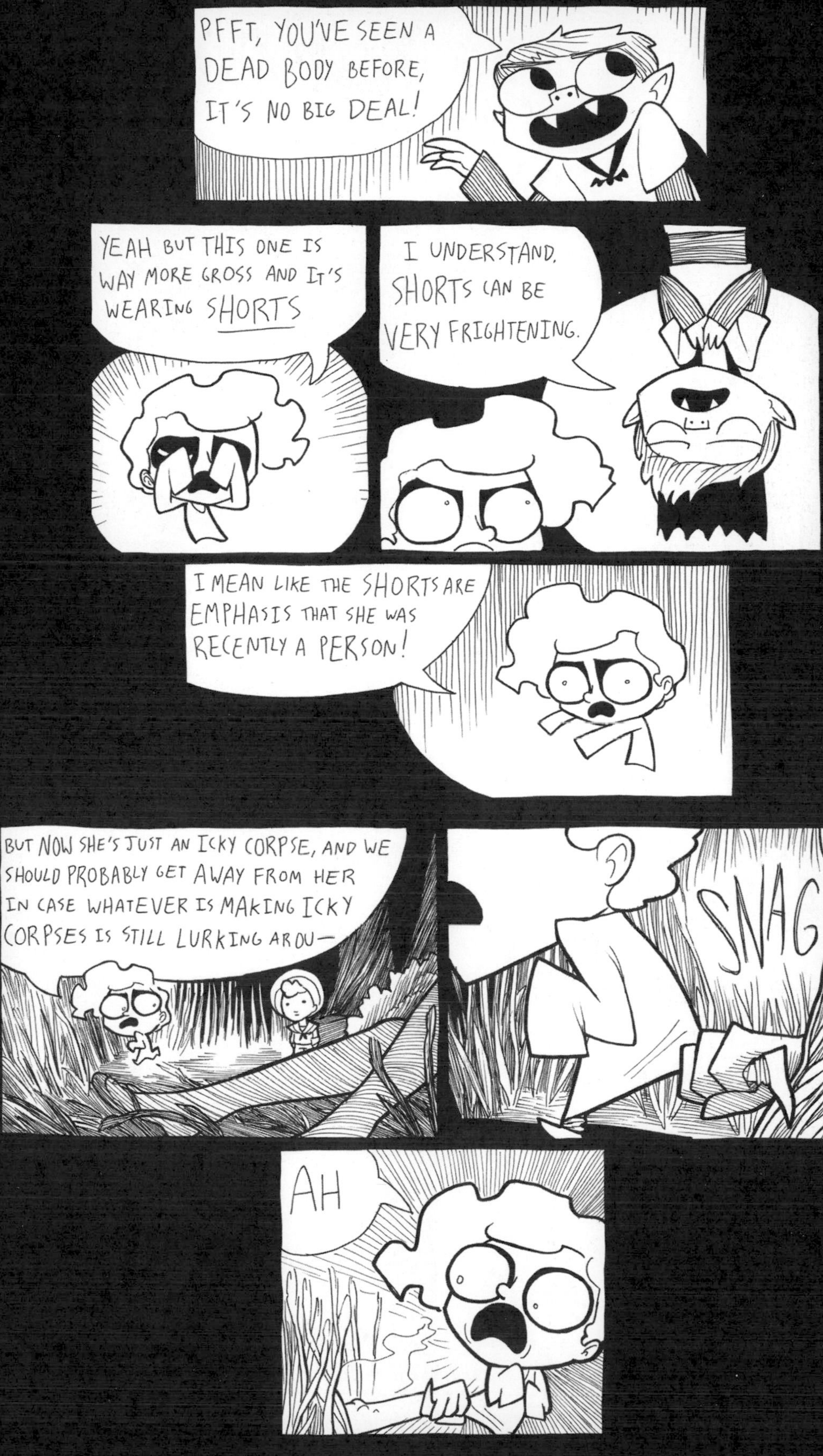
PFFT, YOU'VE SEEN A DEAD BODY BEFORE, IT'S NO BIG DEAL!
YEAH BUT THIS ONE IS WAY MORE GROSS AND IT'S WEARING SHORTS
I UNDERSTAND. SHORTS CAN BE VERY FRIGHTENING.
I MEAN LIKE THE SHORTS ARE EMPHASIS THAT SHE WAS RECENTLY A PERSON!
BUT NOW SHE'S JUST AN ICKY CORPSE, AND WE SHOULD PROBABLY GET AWAY FROM HER IN CASE WHATEVER IS MAKING ICKY CORPSES IS STILL LURKING AROU—
SNAG
AH

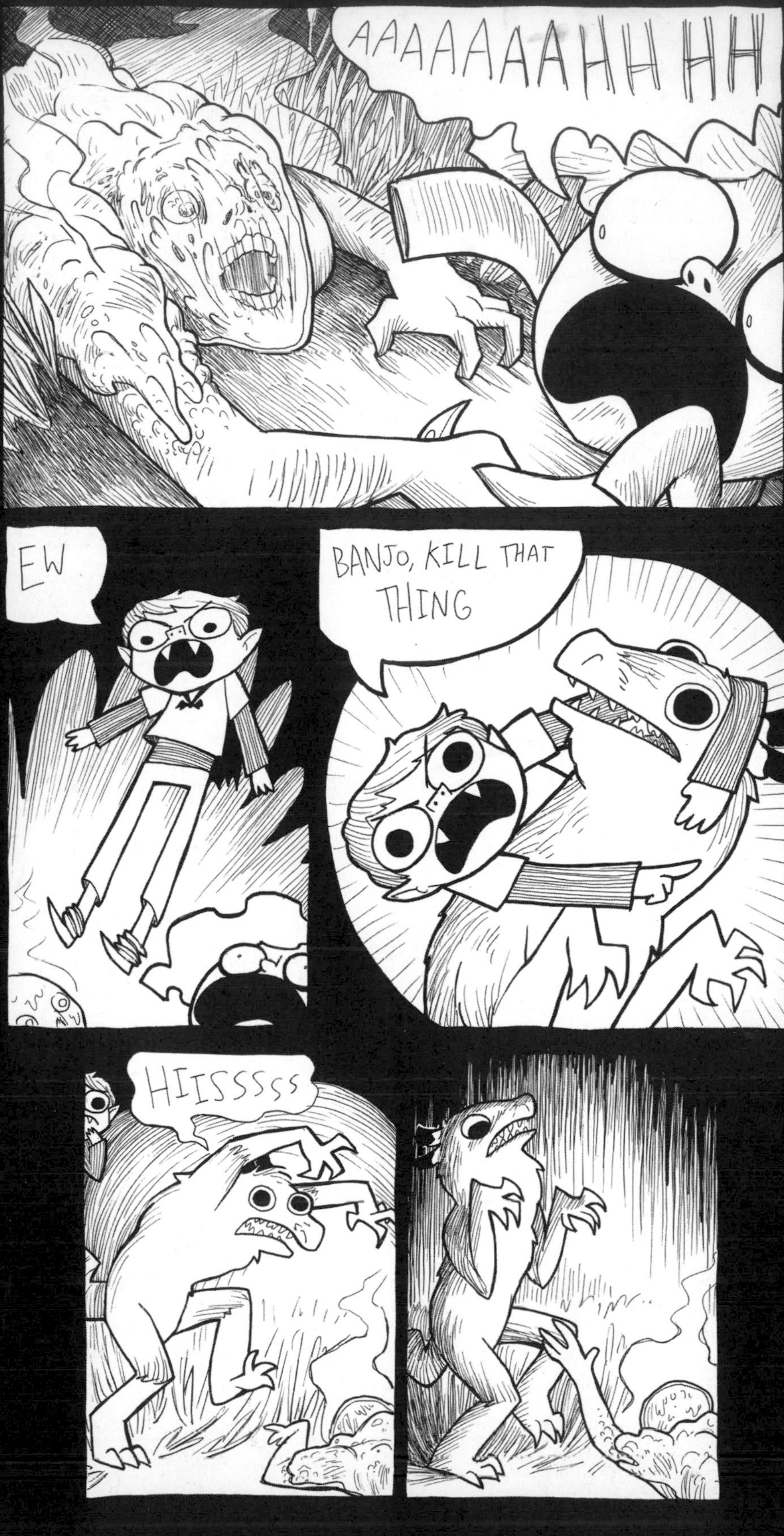
AAAAAAAHHHHH
EW
BANJO, KILL THAT THING
HIISSSSS

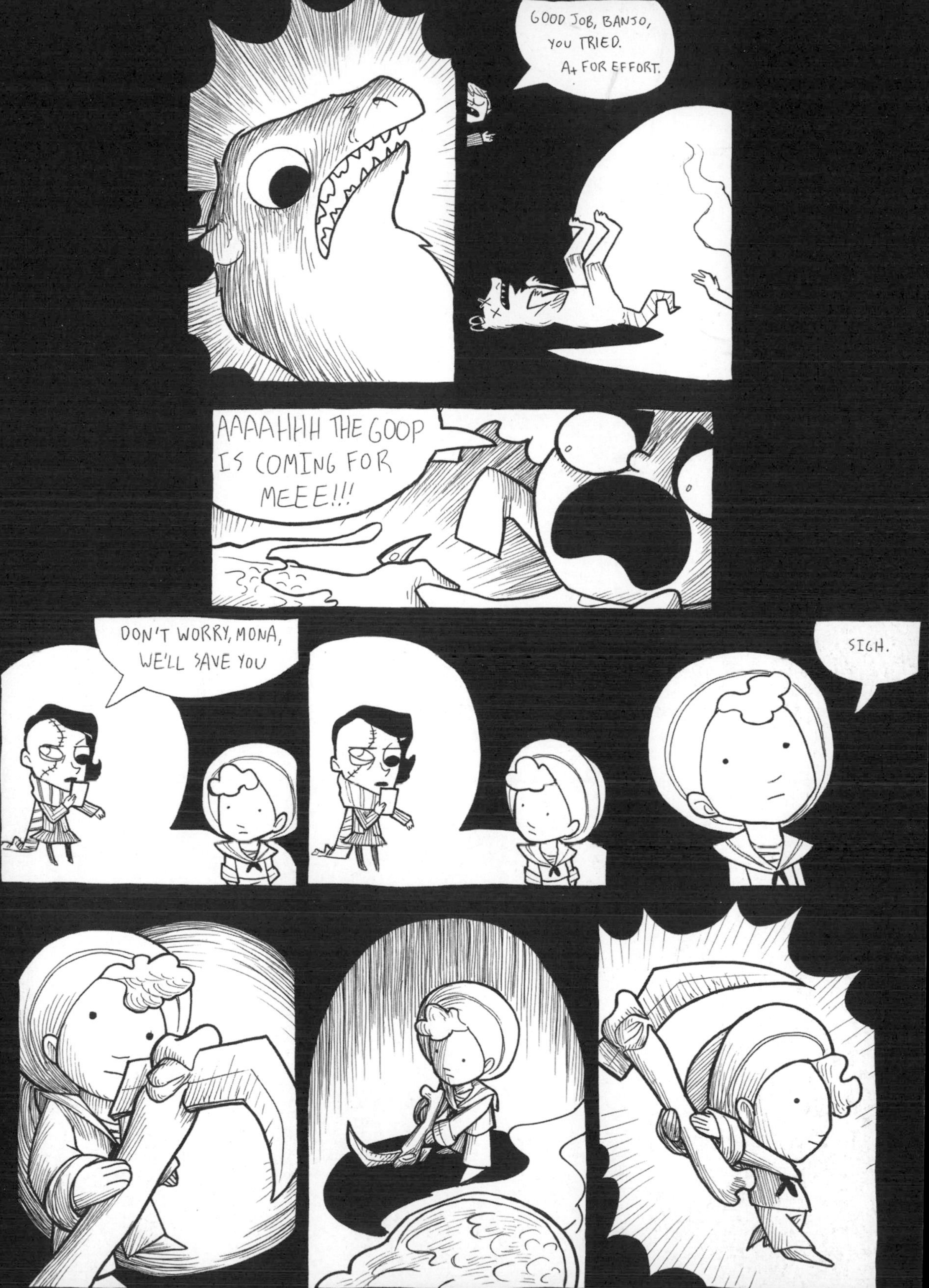
GOOD JOB, BANJO, YOU TRIED. A+ FOR EFFORT.
AAAAHHH THE GOOP IS COMING FOR MEEE!!!
DON'T WORRY, MONA, WE'LL SAVE YOU
SIGH.

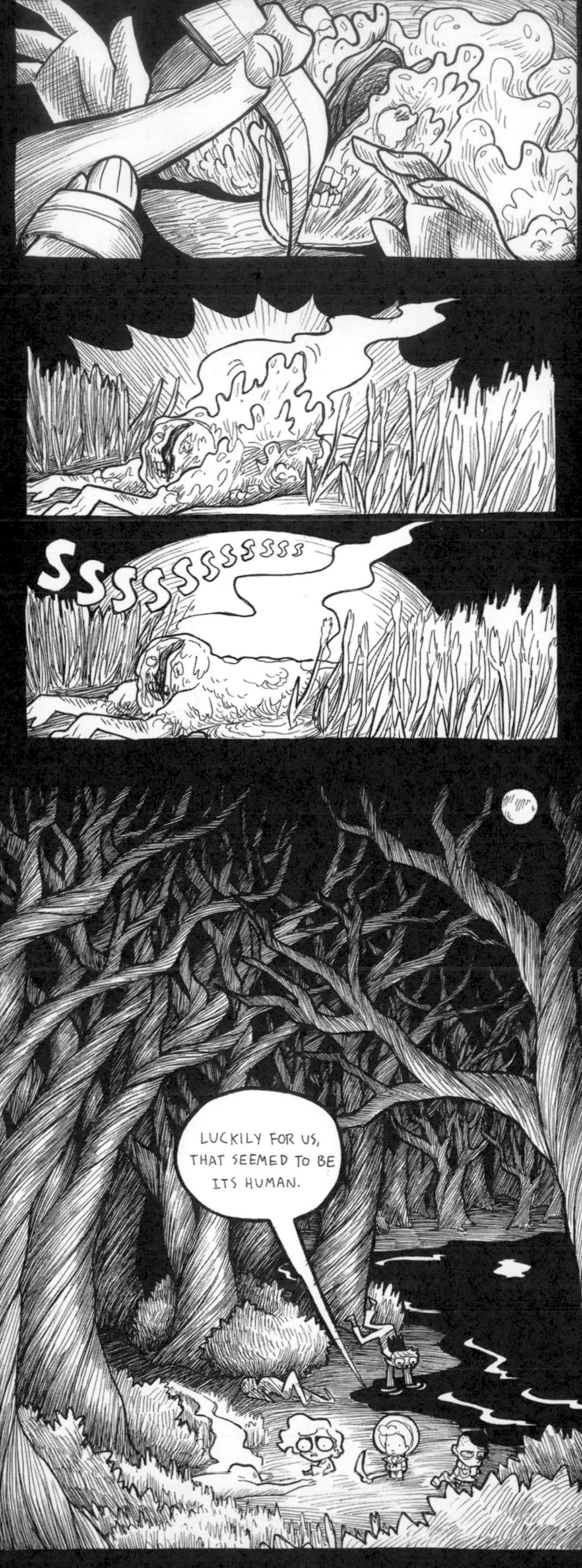
SSSSSSSSSSSSS
LUCKILY FOR US, THAT SEEMED TO BE ITS HUMAN.

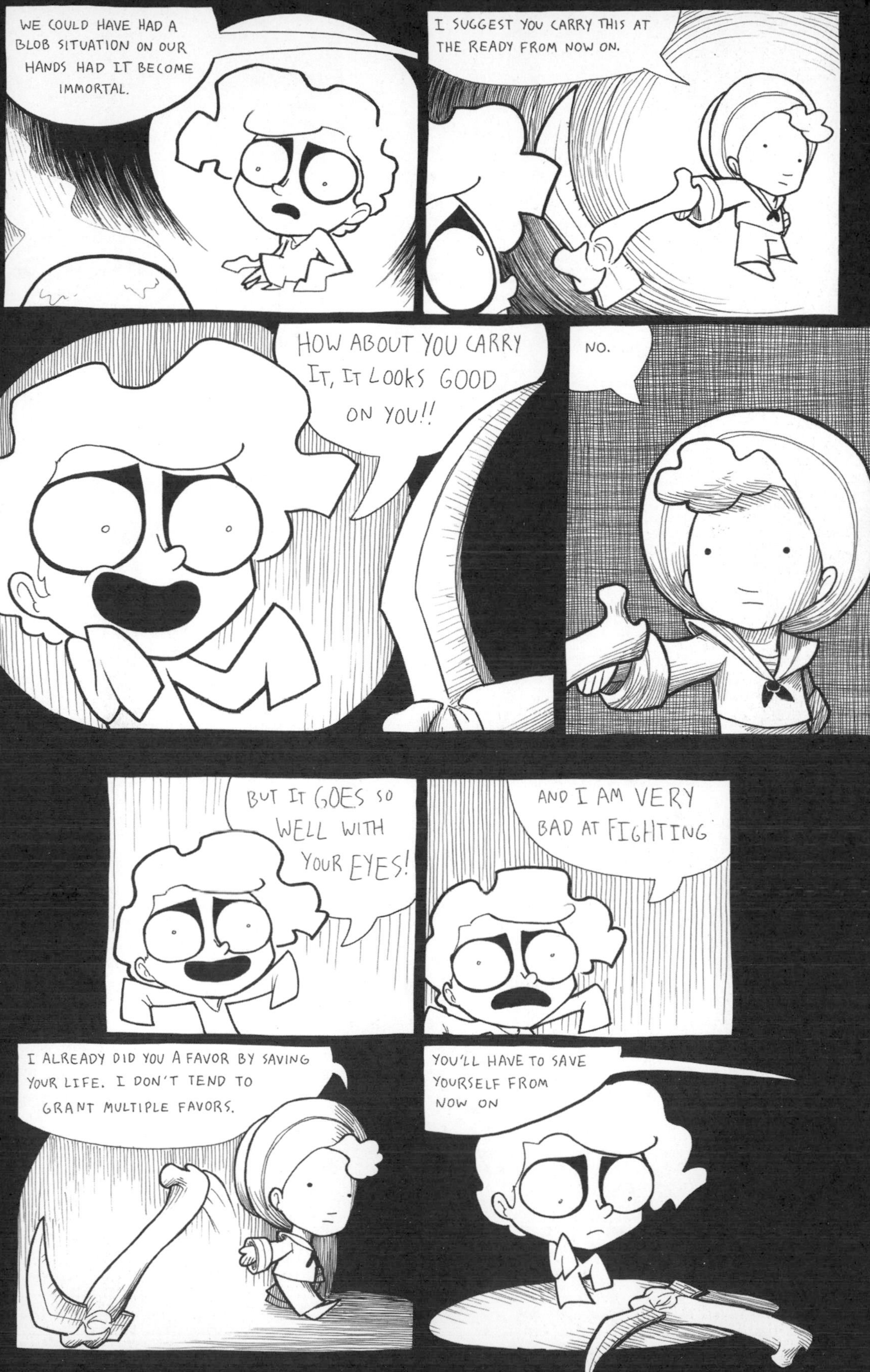
WE COULD HAVE HAD A BLOB SITUATION ON OUR HANDS HAD IT BECOME IMMORTAL.
I SUGGEST YOU CARRY THIS AT THE READY FROM NOW ON.
HOW ABOUT YOU CARRY IT, IT LOOKS GOOD ON YOU!!
NO.
BUT IT GOES SO WELL WITH YOUR EYES!
AND I AM VERY BAD AT FIGHTING
I ALREADY DID YOU A FAVOR BY SAVING YOUR LIFE. I DON'T TEND TO GRANT MULTIPLE FAVORS.
YOU'LL HAVE TO SAVE YOURSELF FROM NOW ON

OR YOU WON'T BE SAVED AT ALL.

SIIGH, WELL, YOU SCARED OFF ALL THE FROGS

LET'S JUST GO, ALL THE MAGIC'S BEEN TAKEN FROM THIS PLACE.

THIS IS THE GREATEST TRAGEDY OF MY LIFE....

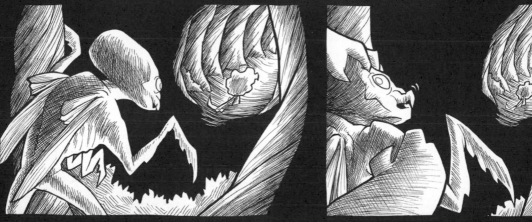

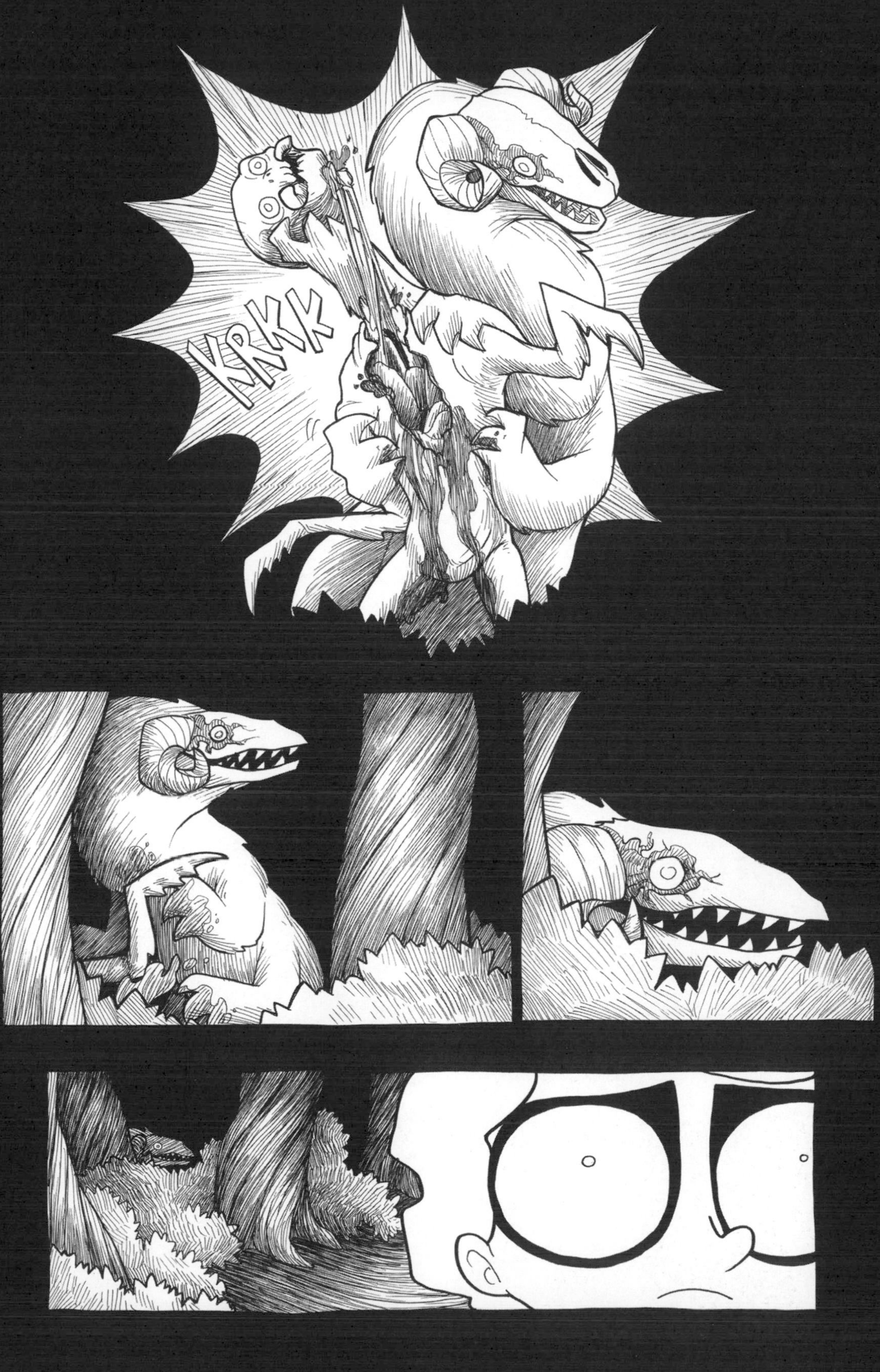
KRKK

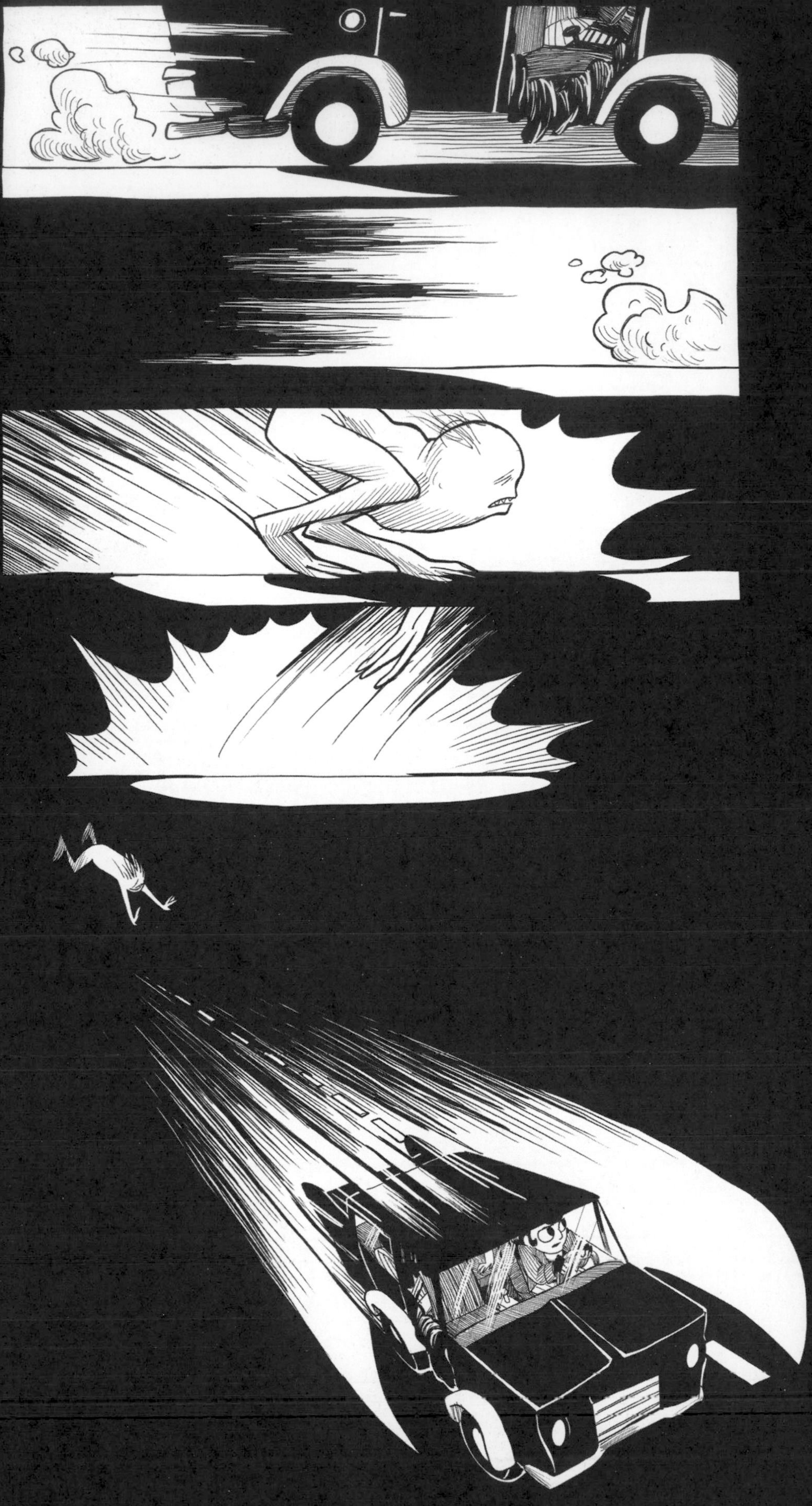

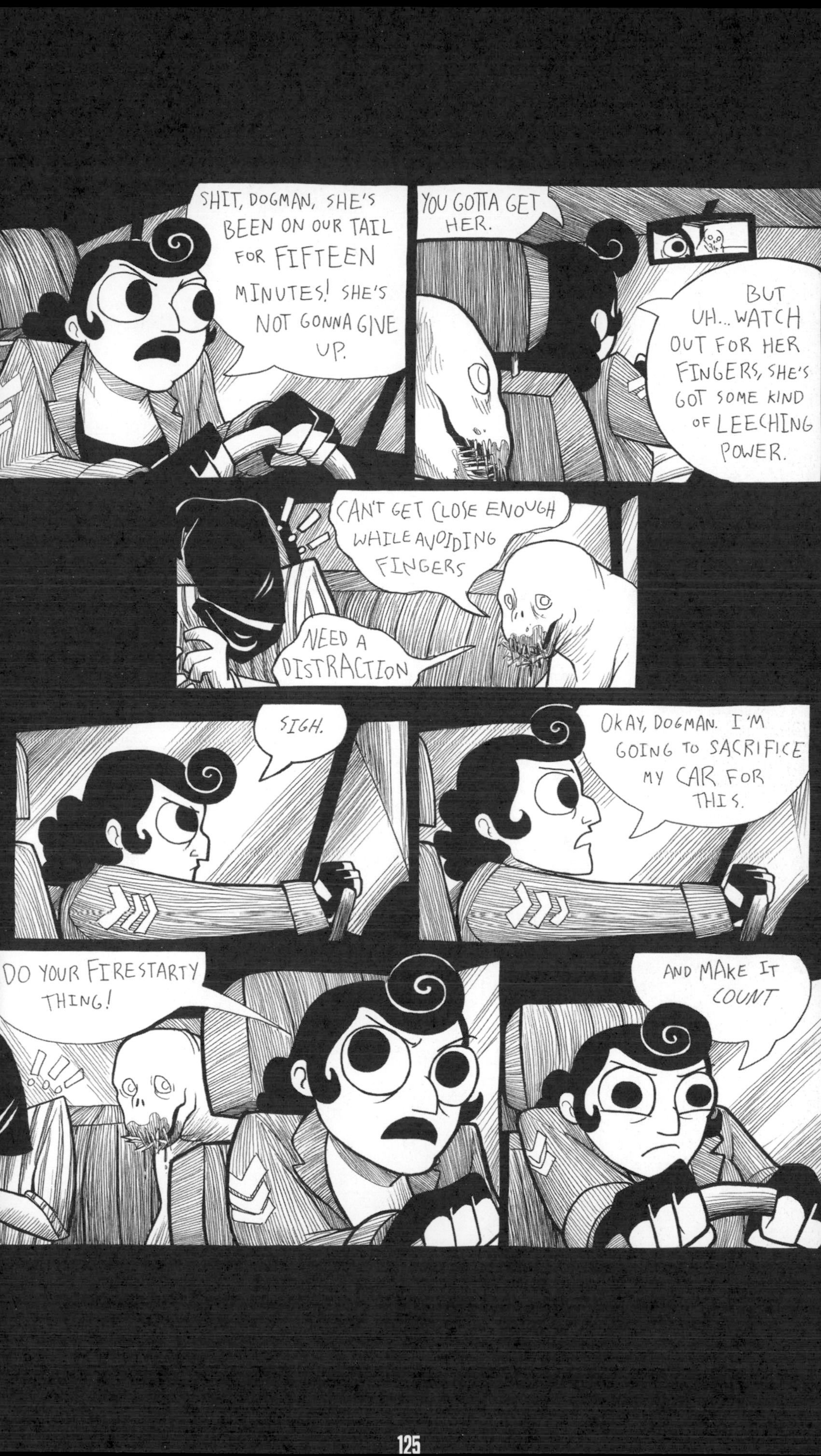
SHIT, DOGMAN, SHE'S BEEN ON OUR TAIL FOR FIFTEEN MINUTES! SHE'S NOT GONNA GIVE UP.
YOU GOTTA GET HER.
BUT UH... WATCH OUT FOR HER FINGERS, SHE'S GOT SOME KIND OF LEECHING POWER.
CAN'T GET CLOSE ENOUGH WHILE AVOIDING FINGERS
NEED A DISTRACTION
SIGH.
OKAY, DOGMAN. I'M GOING TO SACRIFICE MY CAR FOR THIS.
DO YOUR FIRESTARTY THING!
AND MAKE IT COUNT

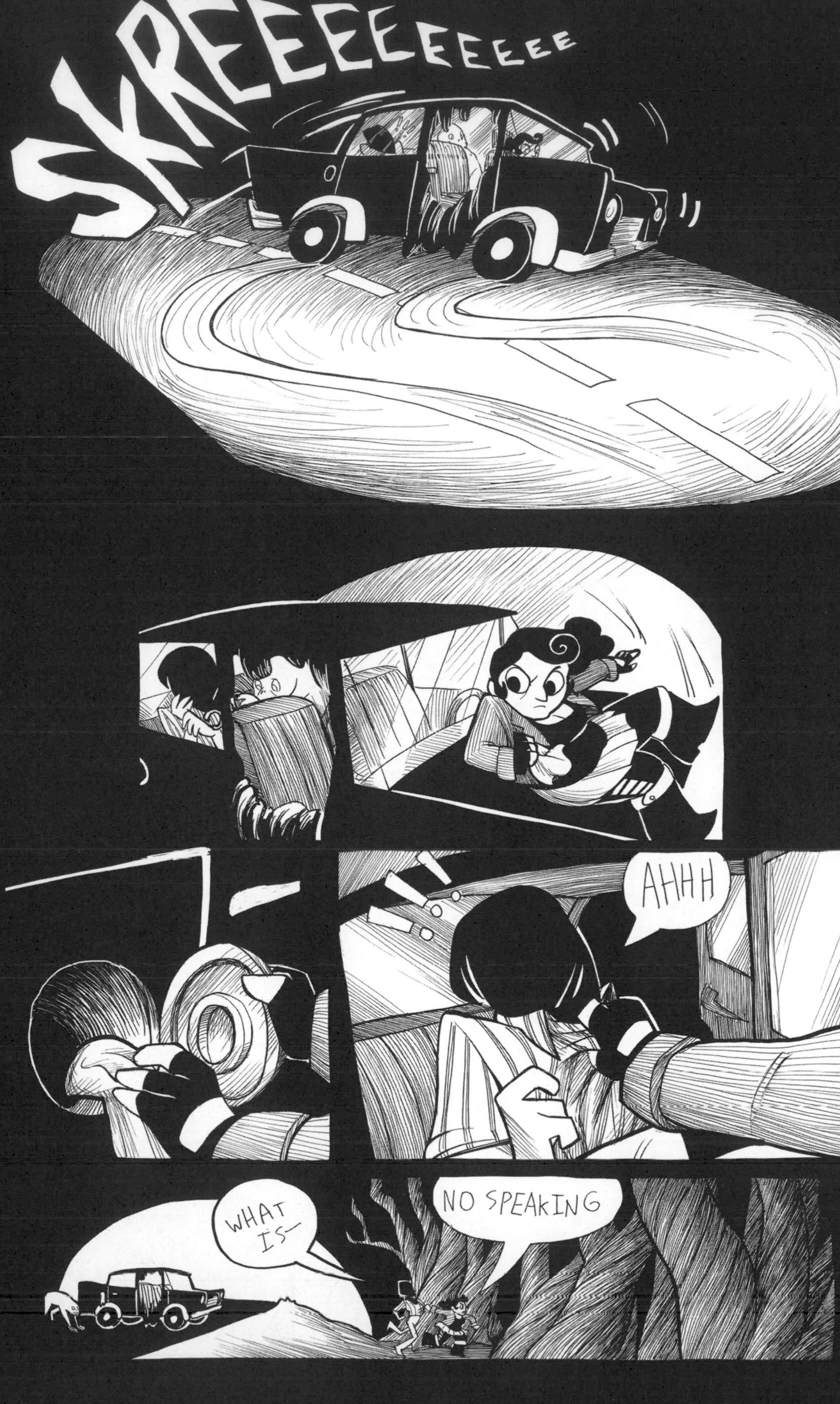
SKREEEEEEEEEE
AHHH
WHAT IS—
NO SPEAKING

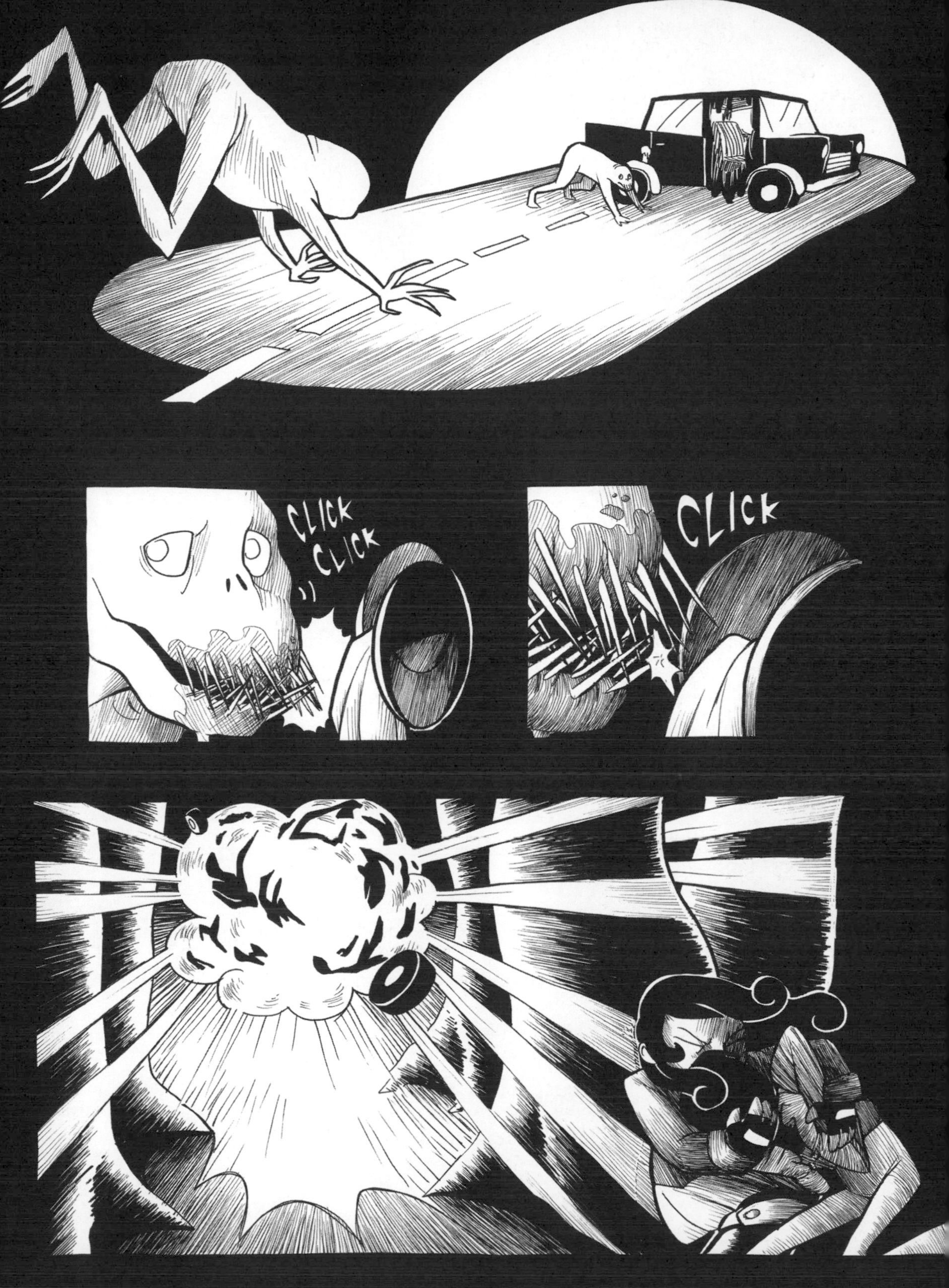
CLICK
CLICK
CLICK

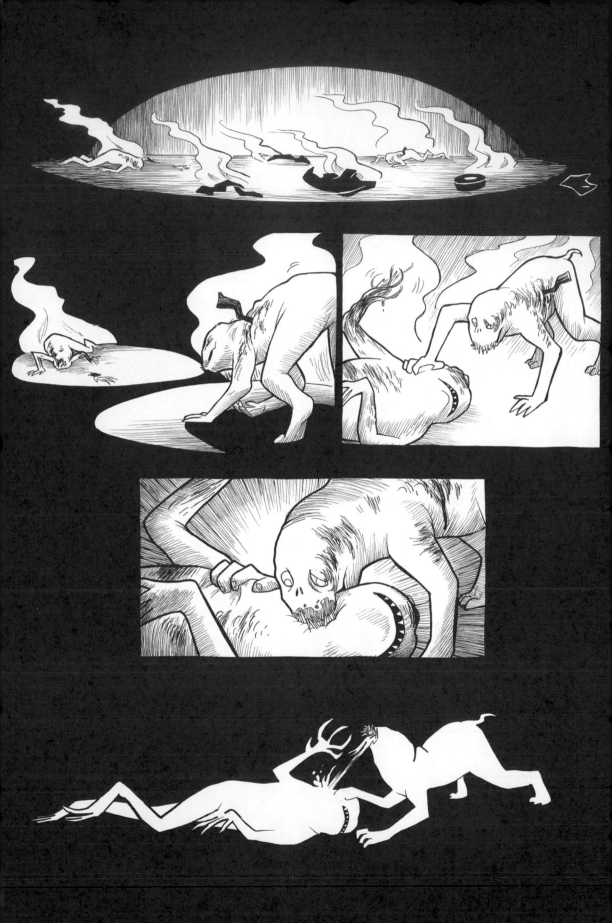

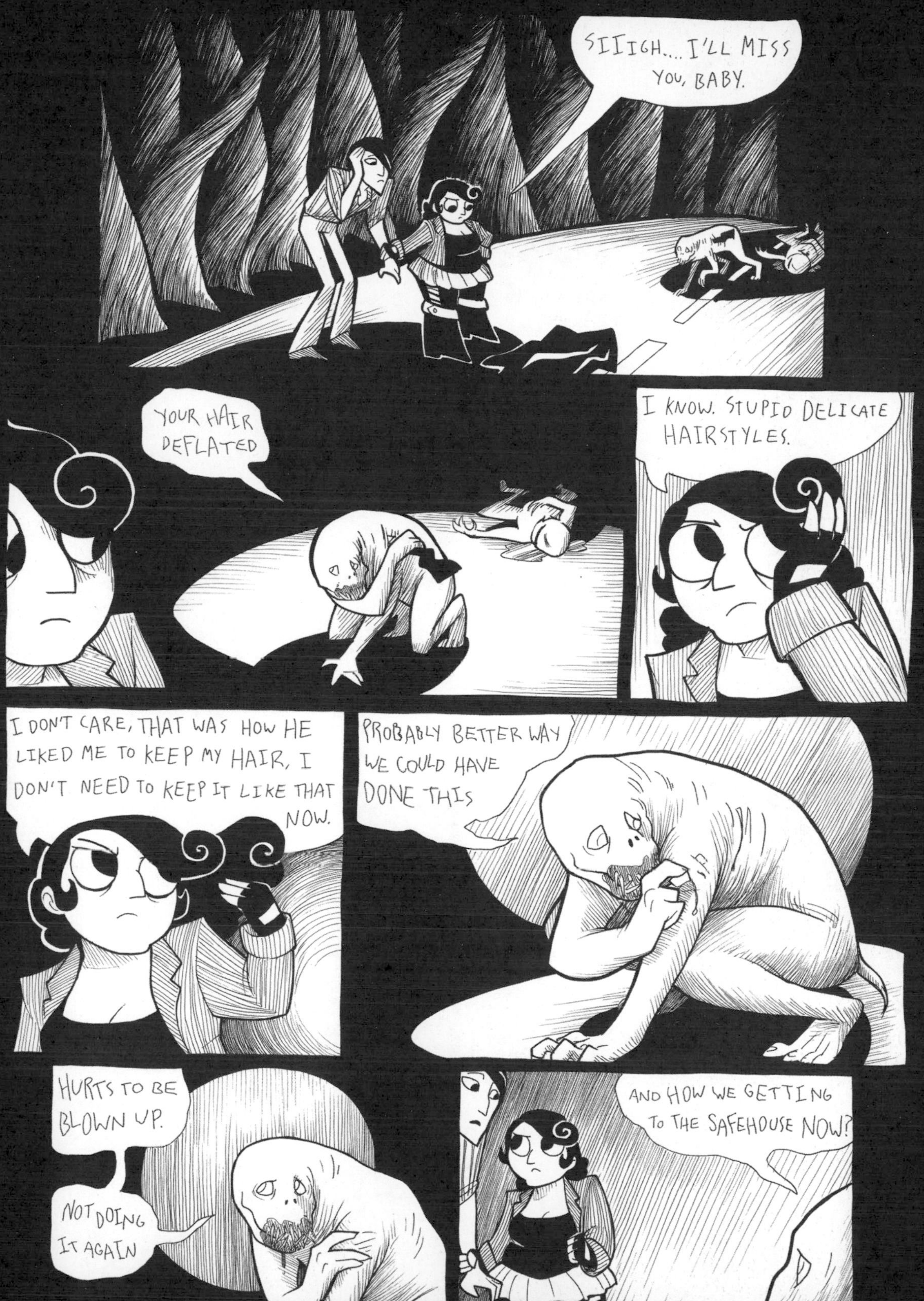
SIIIGH.... I'LL MISS YOU, BABY.
YOUR HAIR DEFLATED
I KNOW. STUPID DELICATE HAIRSTYLES.
I DON'T CARE, THAT WAS HOW HE LIKED ME TO KEEP MY HAIR, I DON'T NEED TO KEEP IT LIKE THAT NOW.
PROBABLY BETTER WAY WE COULD HAVE DONE THIS
HURTS TO BE BLOWN UP.
NOT DOING IT AGAIN
AND HOW WE GETTING TO THE SAFEHOUSE NOW?

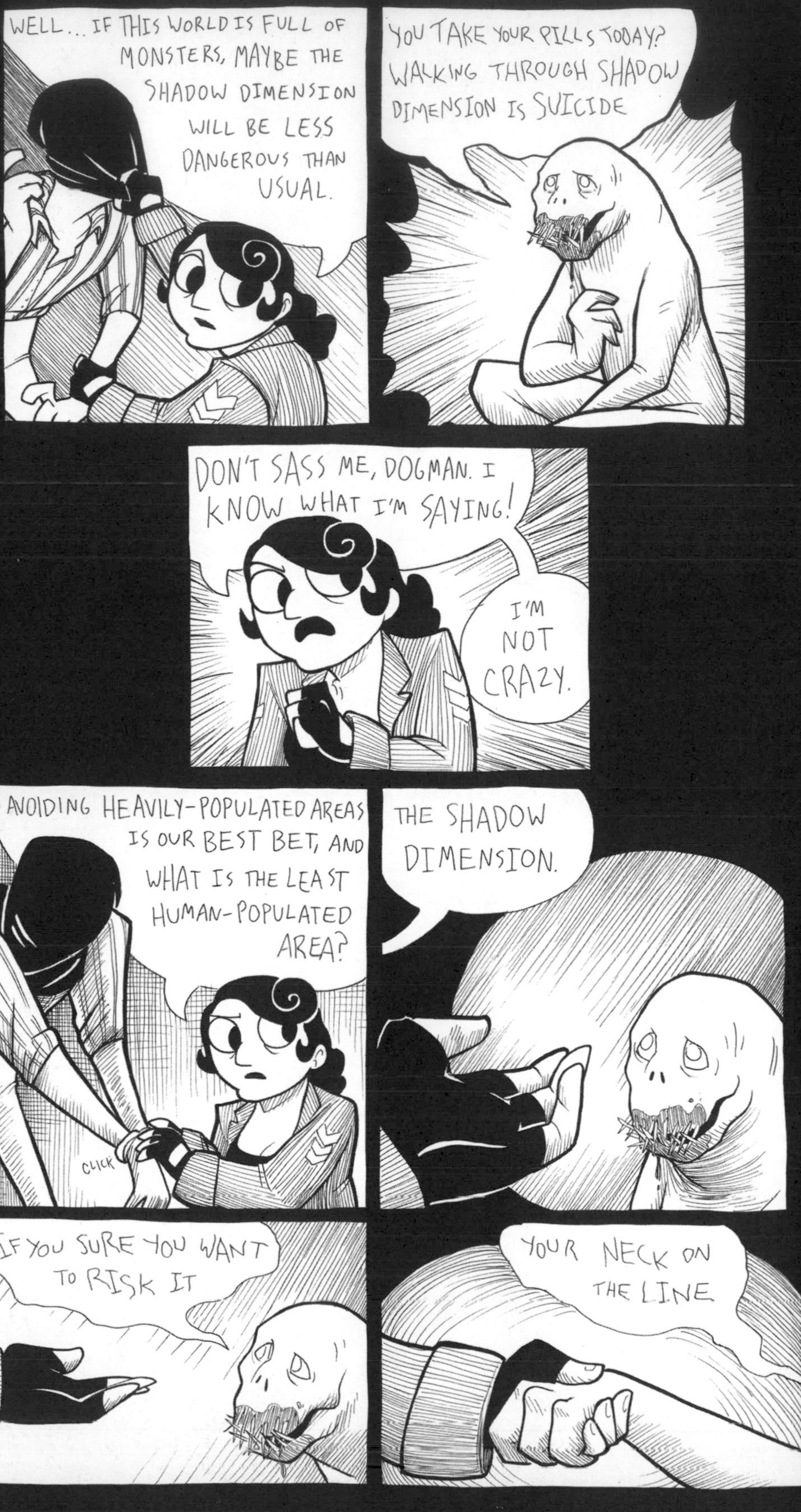
WELL... IF THIS WORLD IS FULL OF MONSTERS, MAYBE THE SHADOW DIMENSION WILL BE LESS DANGEROUS THAN USUAL.
YOU TAKE YOUR PILLS TODAY? WALKING THROUGH SHADOW DIMENSION IS SUICIDE
DON'T SASS ME, DOGMAN. I KNOW WHAT I'M SAYING!
I'M NOT CRAZY.
AVOIDING HEAVILY-POPULATED AREAS IS OUR BEST BET, AND WHAT IS THE LEAST HUMAN-POPULATED AREA?
CLICK
THE SHADOW DIMENSION.
IF YOU SURE YOU WANT TO RISK IT
YOUR NECK ON THE LINE

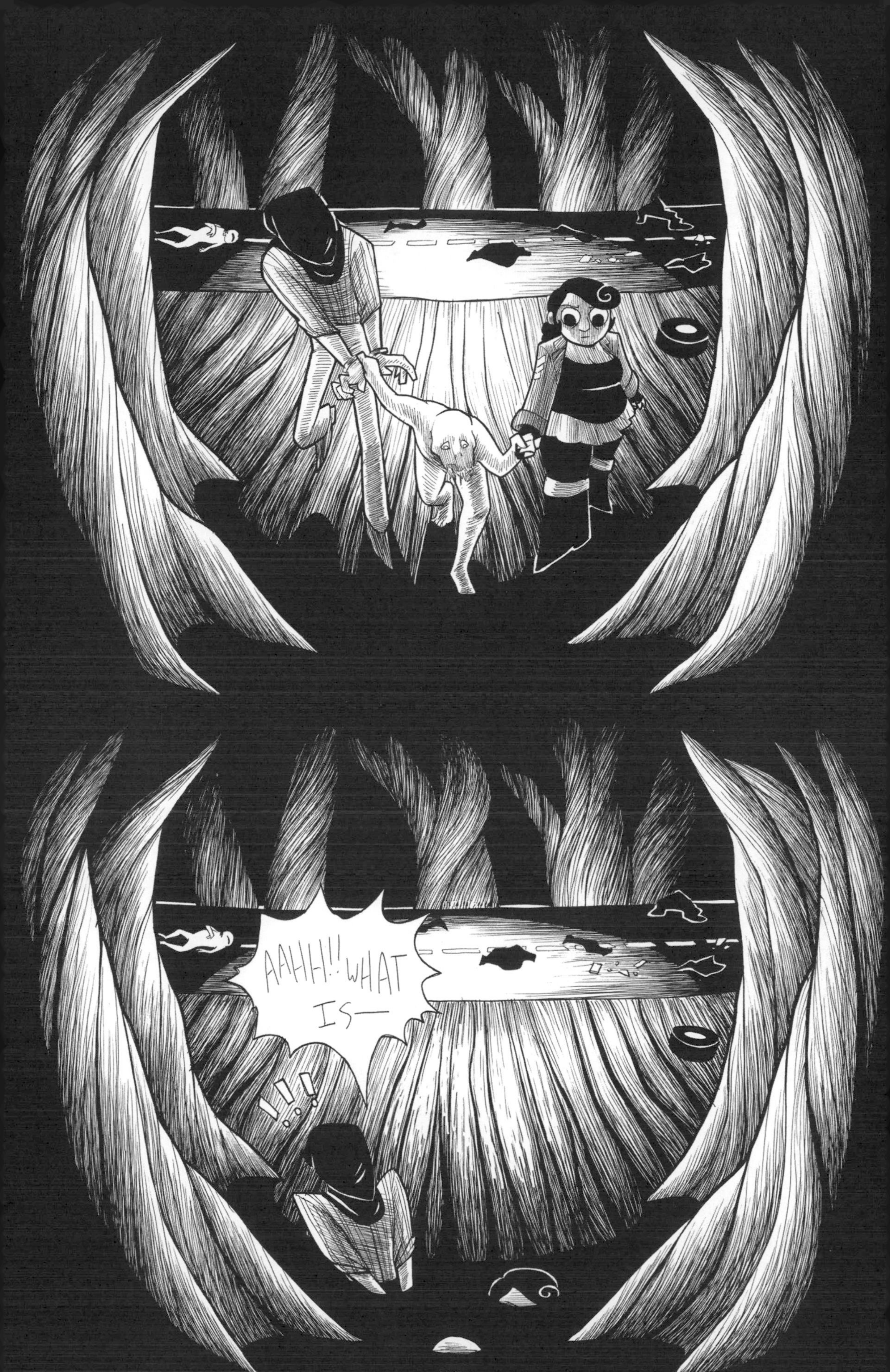
AAHH!! WHAT IS—
!!!

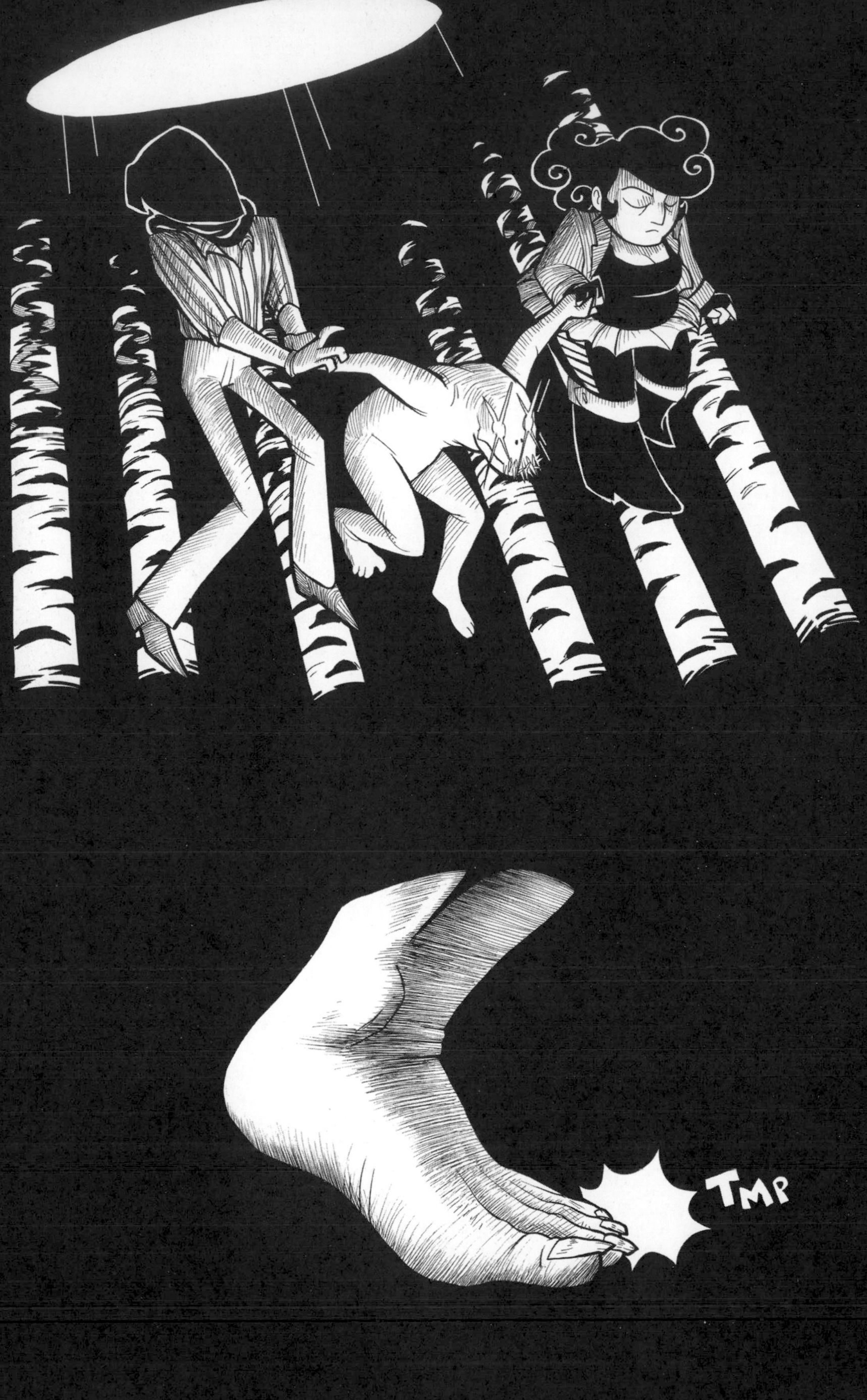
TMP

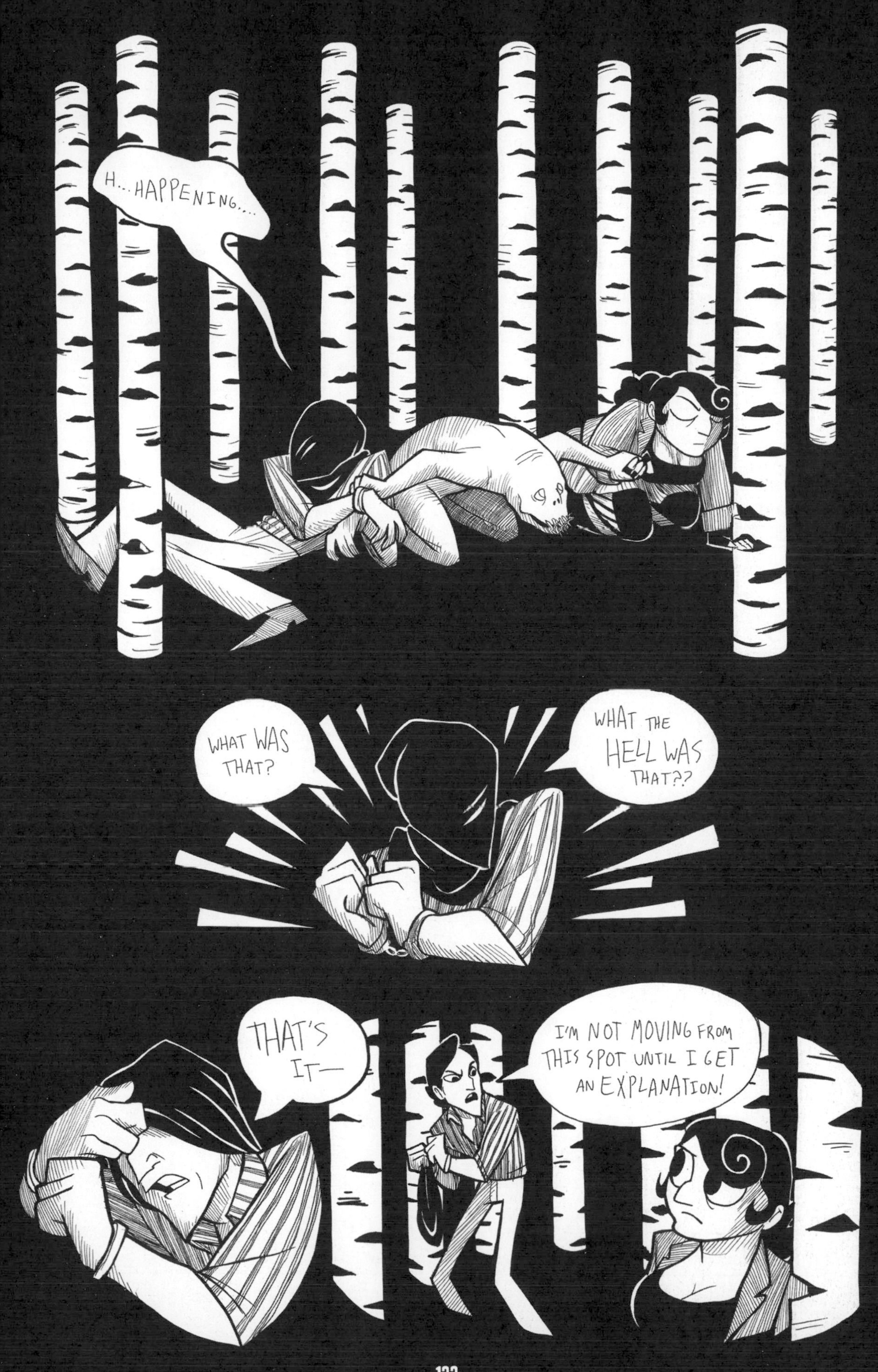
H...HAPPENING....
WHAT WAS THAT?
WHAT THE HELL WAS THAT??
THAT'S IT—
I'M NOT MOVING FROM THIS SPOT UNTIL I GET AN EXPLANATION!

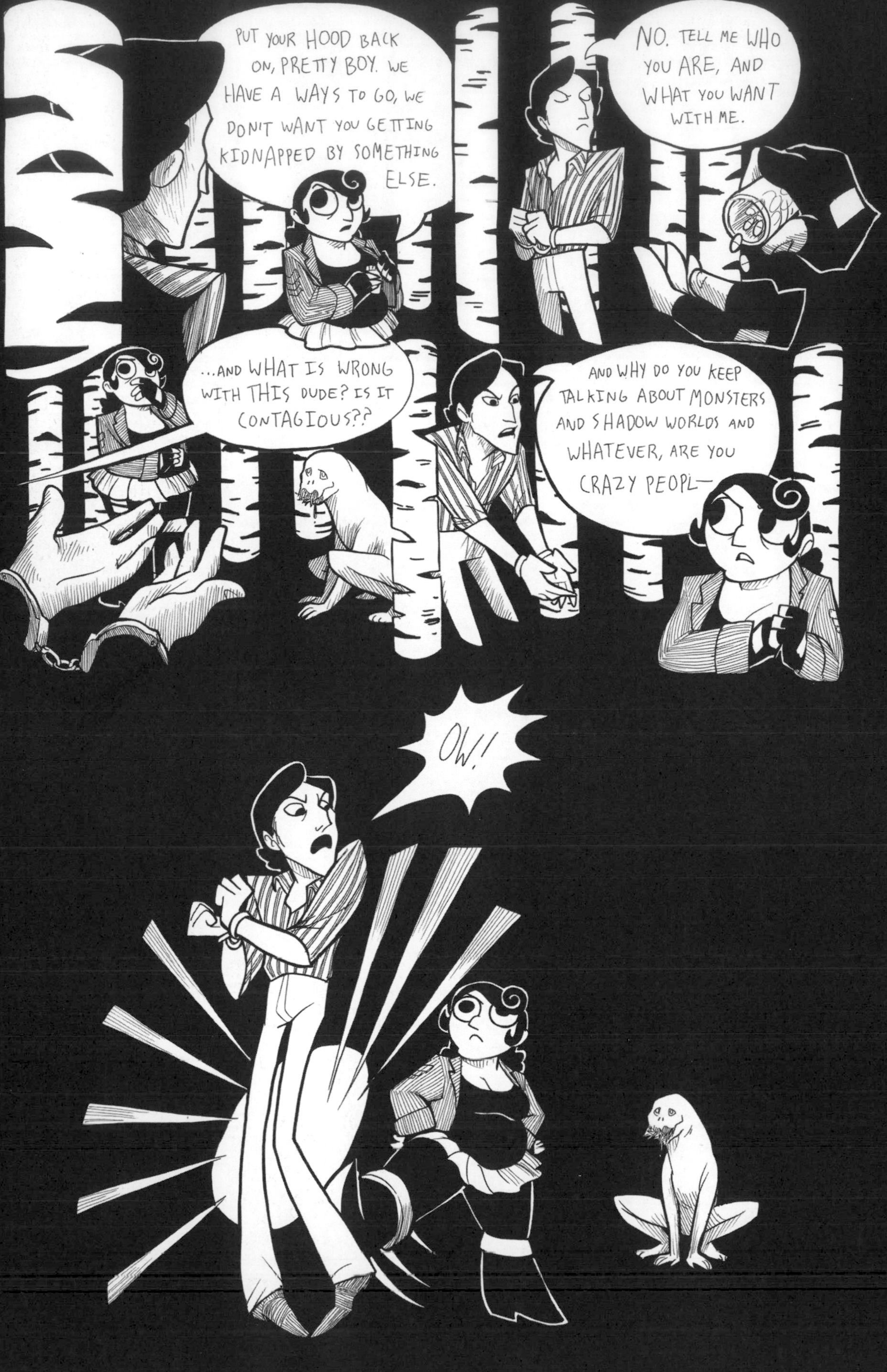
PUT YOUR HOOD BACK ON, PRETTY BOY. WE HAVE A WAYS TO GO, WE DON'T WANT YOU GETTING KIDNAPPED BY SOMETHING ELSE.
NO. TELL ME WHO YOU ARE, AND WHAT YOU WANT WITH ME.
...AND WHAT IS WRONG WITH THIS DUDE? IS IT CONTAGIOUS??
AND WHY DO YOU KEEP TALKING ABOUT MONSTERS AND SHADOW WORLDS AND WHATEVER, ARE YOU CRAZY PEOPL—
OW!

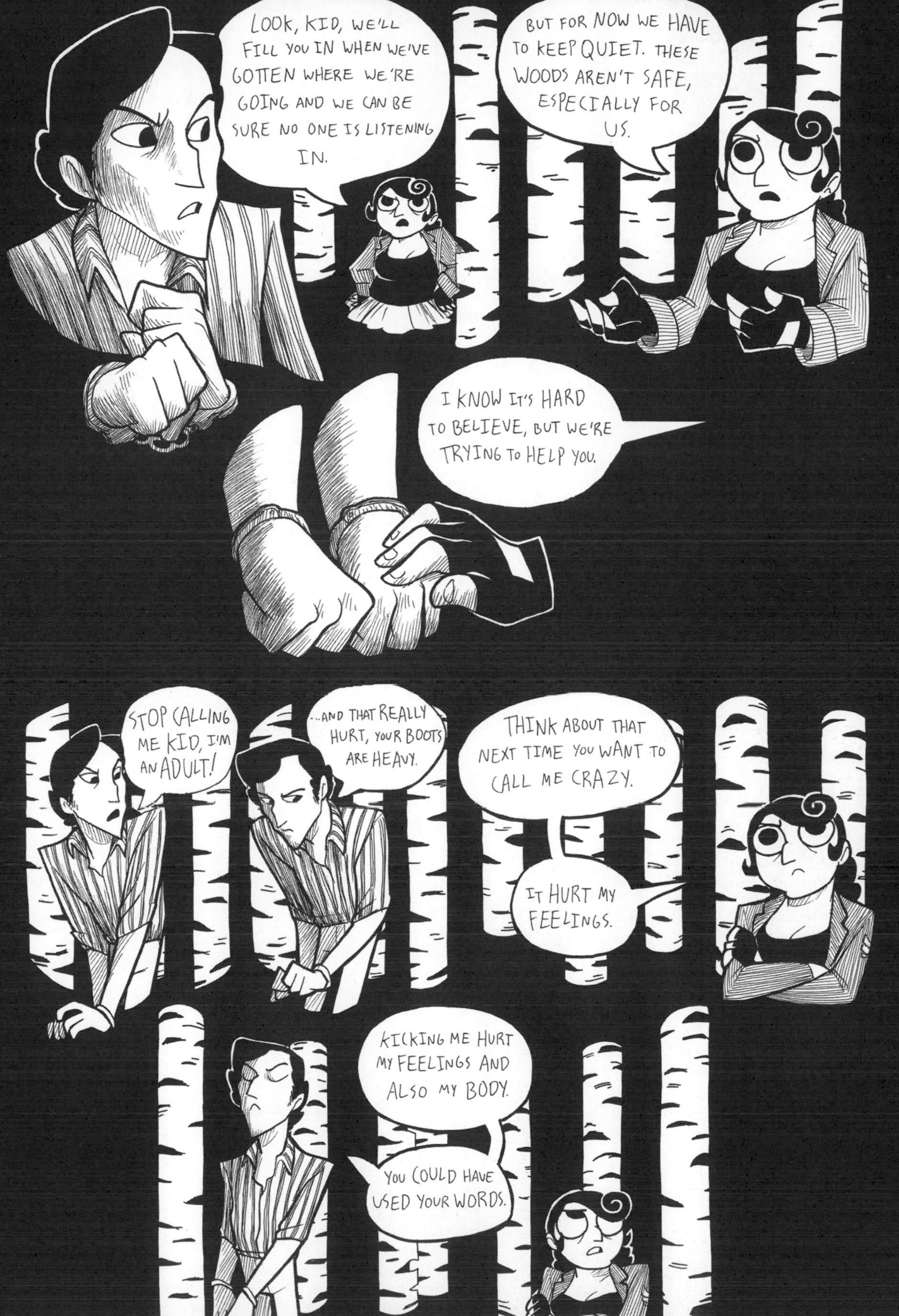
LOOK, KID, WE'LL FILL YOU IN WHEN WE'VE GOTTEN WHERE WE'RE GOING AND WE CAN BE SURE NO ONE IS LISTENING IN.
BUT FOR NOW WE HAVE TO KEEP QUIET. THESE WOODS AREN'T SAFE, ESPECIALLY FOR US.
I KNOW IT'S HARD TO BELIEVE, BUT WE'RE TRYING TO HELP YOU.
STOP CALLING ME KID, I'M AN ADULT!
...AND THAT REALLY HURT, YOUR BOOTS ARE HEAVY.
THINK ABOUT THAT NEXT TIME YOU WANT TO CALL ME CRAZY.
IT HURT MY FEELINGS.
KICKING ME HURT MY FEELINGS AND ALSO MY BODY.
YOU COULD HAVE USED YOUR WORDS.

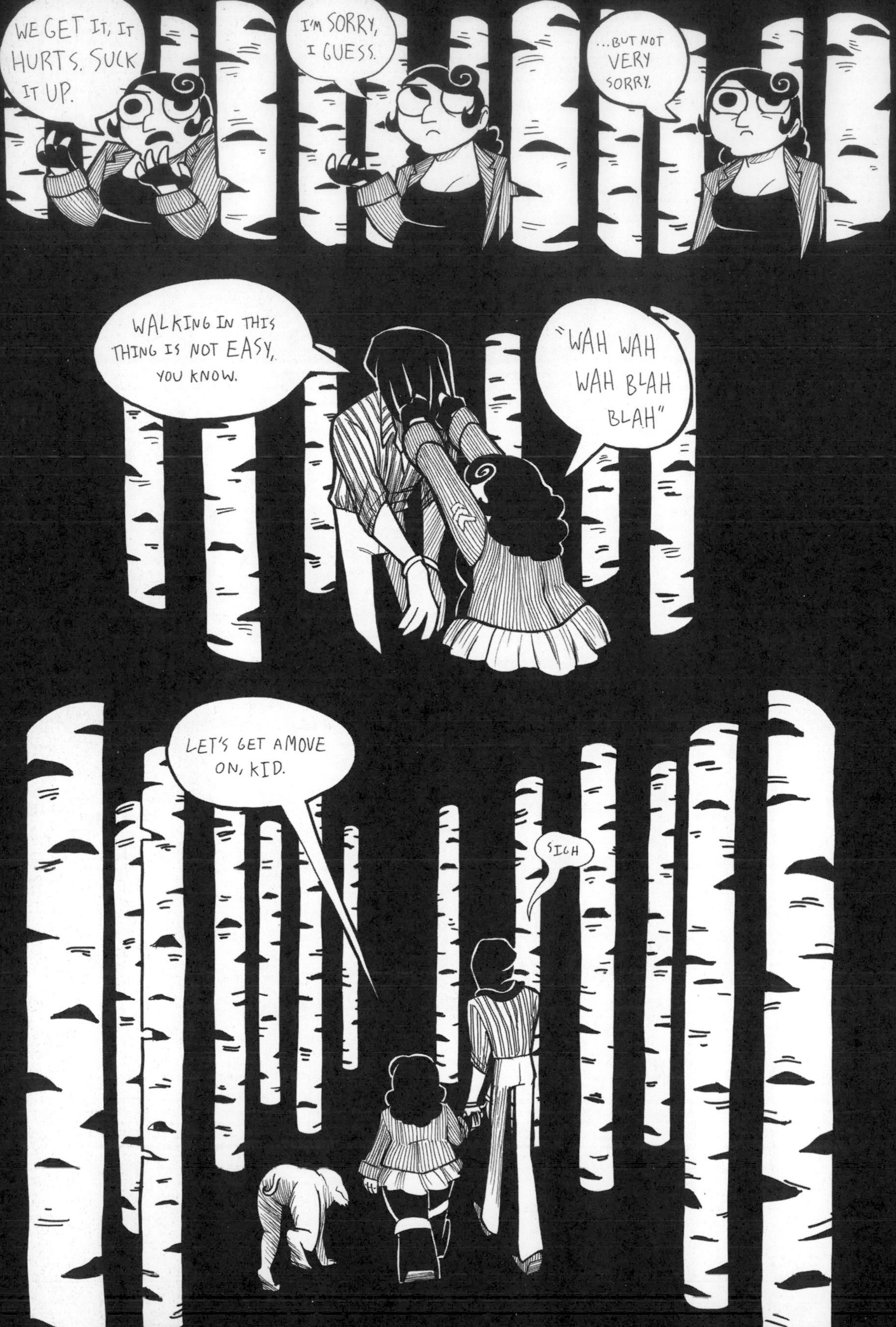
WE GET IT, IT HURTS. SUCK IT UP.
I'M SORRY, I GUESS.
...BUT NOT VERY SORRY.
WALKING IN THIS THING IS NOT EASY, YOU KNOW.
"WAH WAH WAH BLAH BLAH"
LET'S GET A MOVE ON, KID.
SIGH

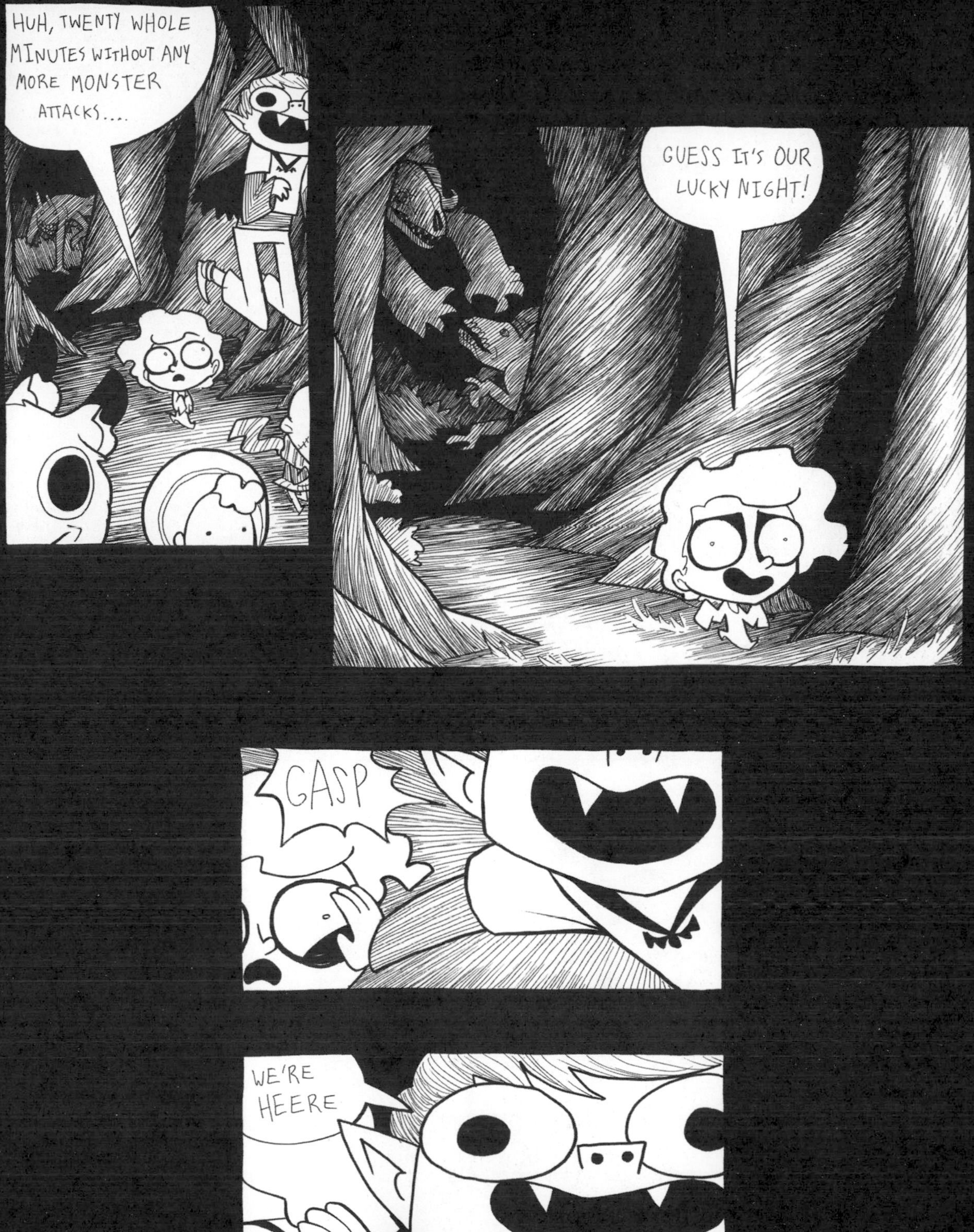
HUH, TWENTY WHOLE MINUTES WITHOUT ANY MORE MONSTER ATTACKS....
GUESS IT'S OUR LUCKY NIGHT!
GASP
WE'RE HEERE

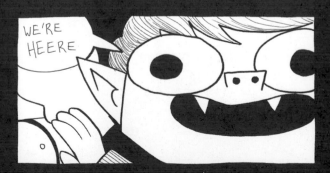

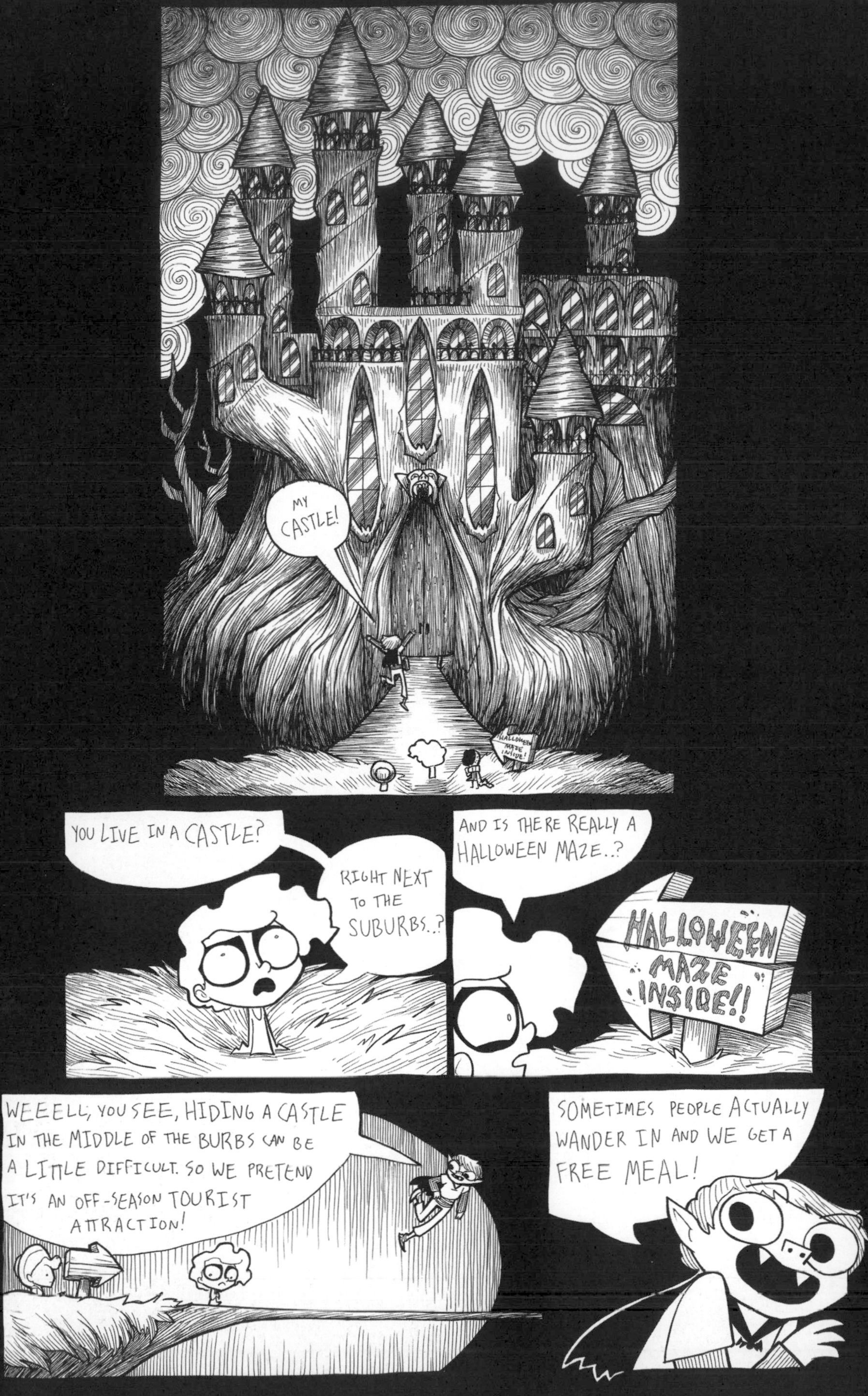
MY CASTLE!
HALLOWEEN MAZE INSIDE!
YOU LIVE IN A CASTLE?
RIGHT NEXT TO THE SUBURBS..?
AND IS THERE REALLY A HALLOWEEN MAZE..?
HALLOWEEN MAZE INSIDE!!
WEEELL, YOU SEE, HIDING A CASTLE IN THE MIDDLE OF THE BURBS CAN BE A LITTLE DIFFICULT. SO WE PRETEND IT'S AN OFF-SEASON TOURIST ATTRACTION!
SOMETIMES PEOPLE ACTUALLY WANDER IN AND WE GET A FREE MEAL!

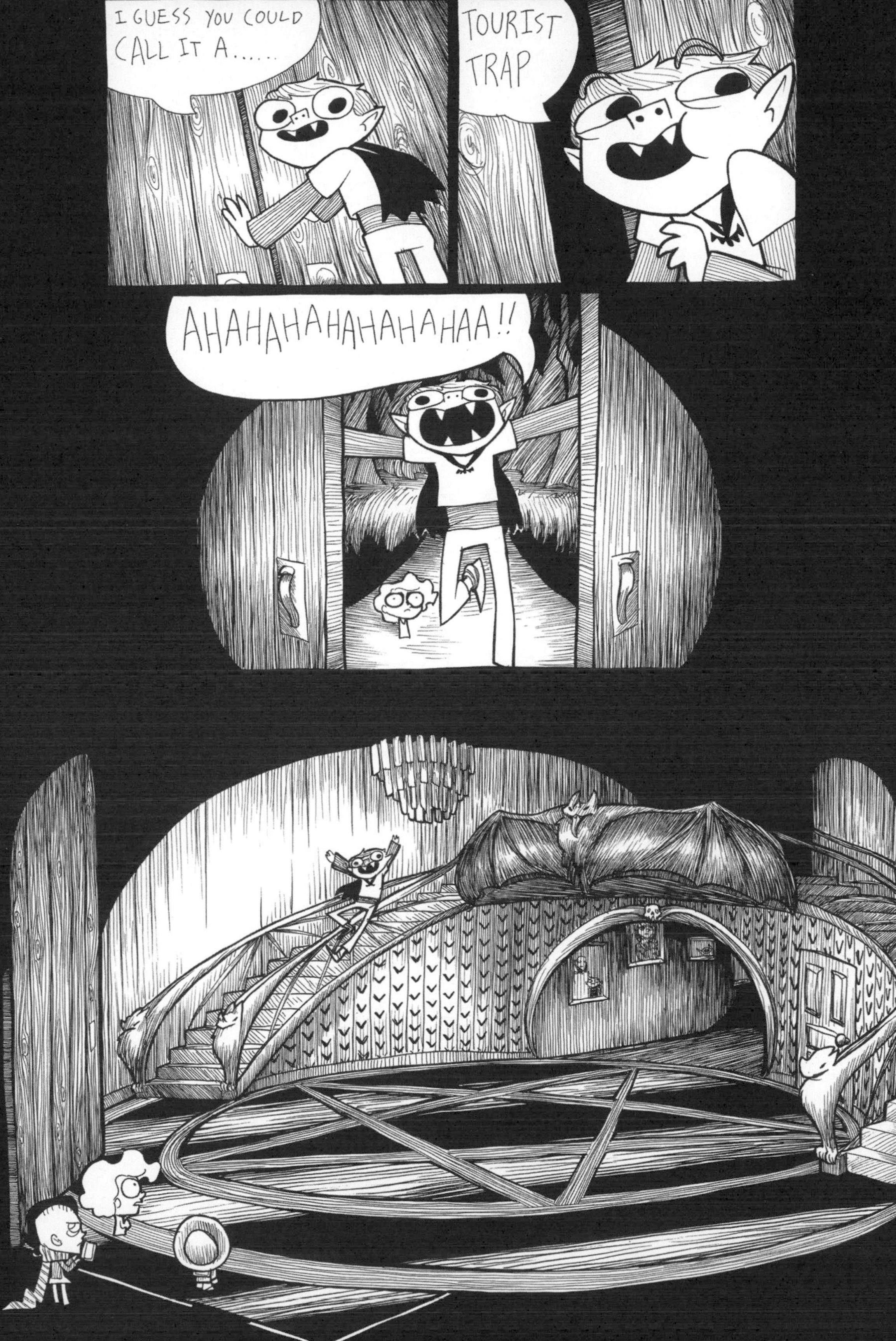

I GUESS YOU COULD CALL IT A......
TOURIST TRAP
AHAHAHAHAHAHAHAHAA!!

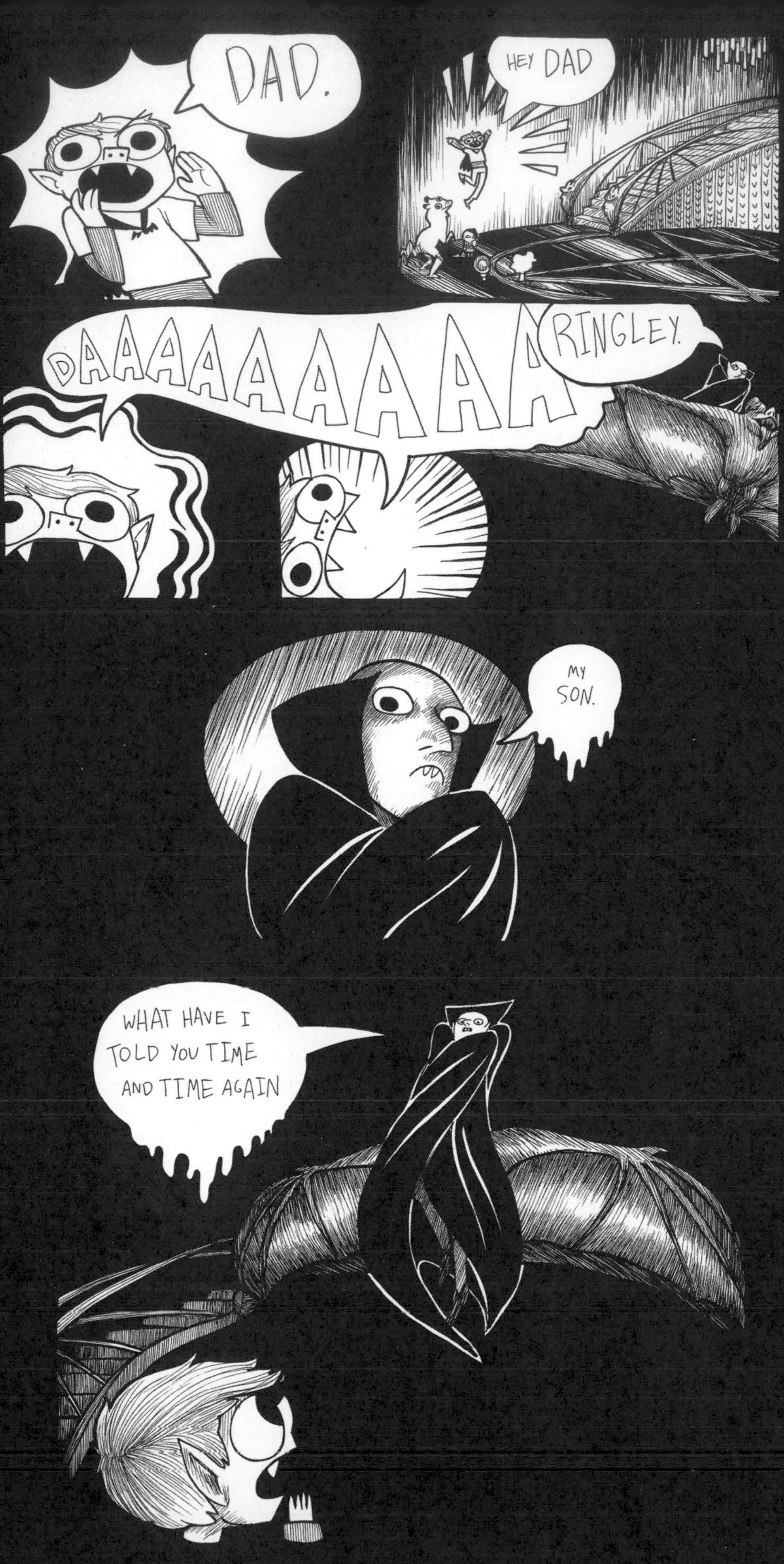
DAD.
HEY DAD
DAAAAAAAAAA
RINGLEY.
MY SON.
WHAT HAVE I TOLD YOU TIME AND TIME AGAIN

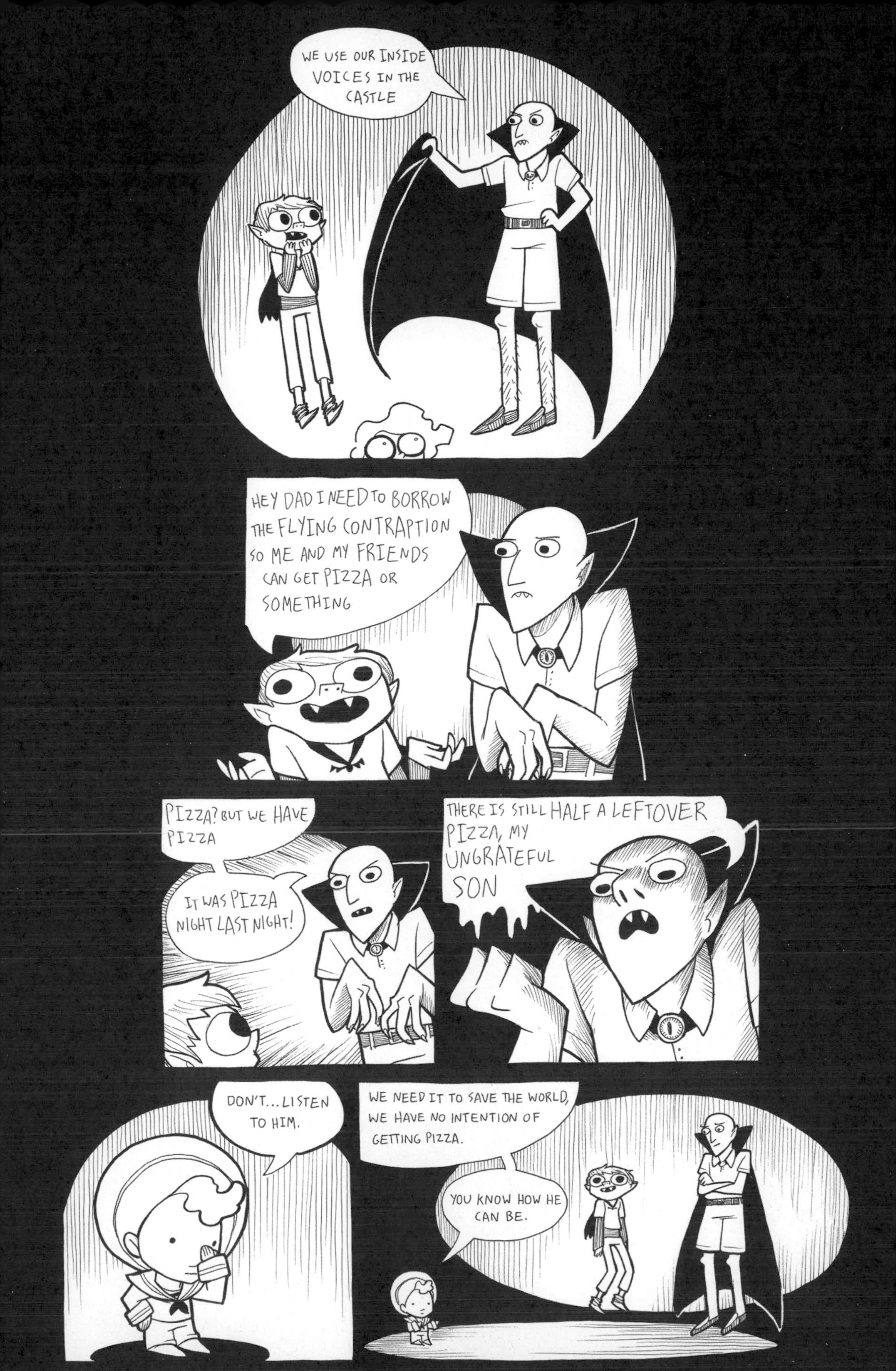
WE USE OUR INSIDE VOICES IN THE CASTLE
HEY DAD I NEED TO BORROW THE FLYING CONTRAPTION SO ME AND MY FRIENDS CAN GET PIZZA OR SOMETHING
PIZZA? BUT WE HAVE PIZZA
IT WAS PIZZA NIGHT LAST NIGHT!
THERE IS STILL HALF A LEFTOVER PIZZA, MY UNGRATEFUL SON
DON'T... LISTEN TO HIM.
WE NEED IT TO SAVE THE WORLD, WE HAVE NO INTENTION OF GETTING PIZZA.
YOU KNOW HOW HE CAN BE.

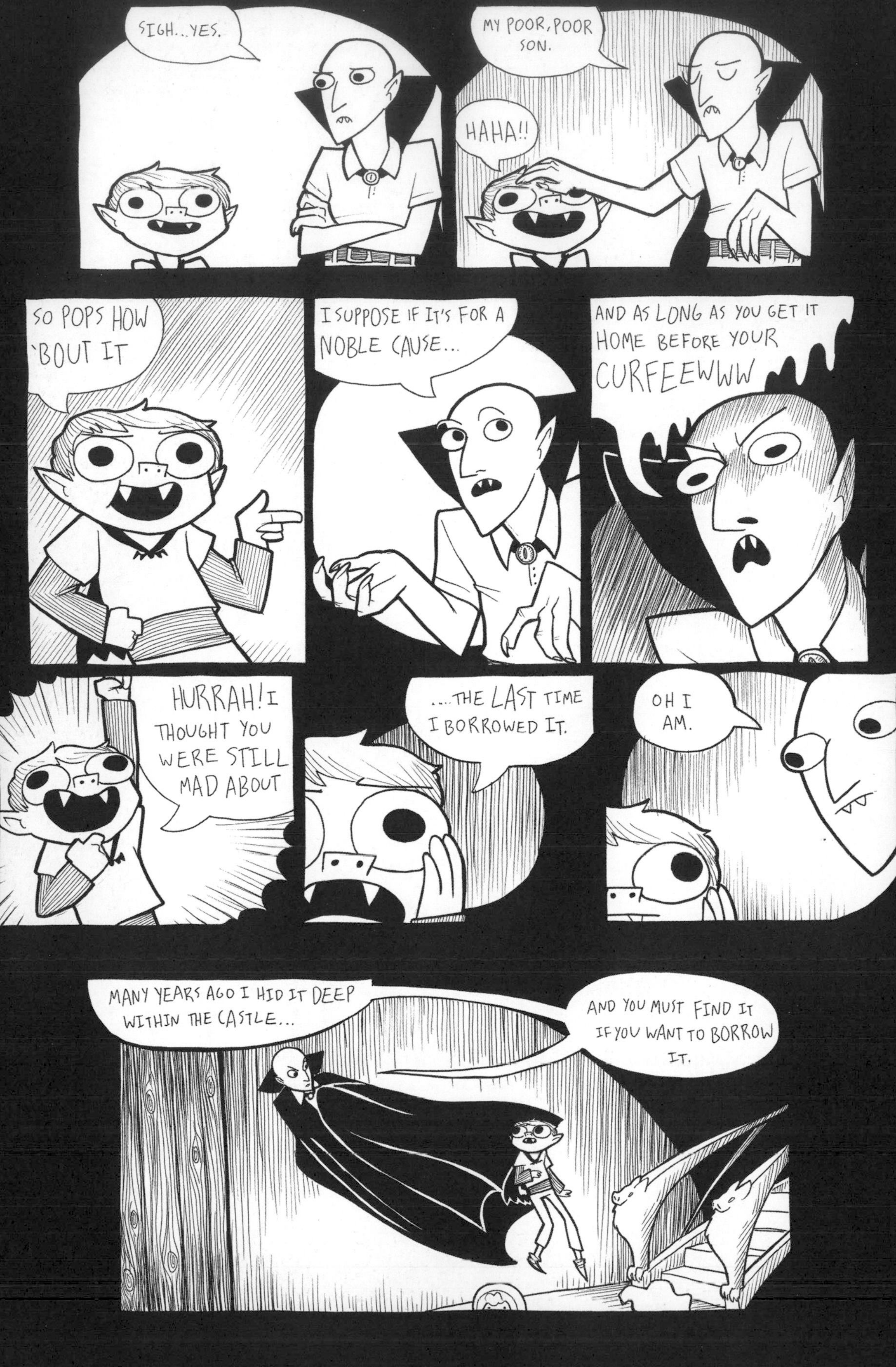
SIGH...YES.
MY POOR, POOR SON.
HAHA!!
SO POPS HOW 'BOUT IT
I SUPPOSE IF IT'S FOR A NOBLE CAUSE...
AND AS LONG AS YOU GET IT HOME BEFORE YOUR CURFEEWWW
HURRAH! I THOUGHT YOU WERE STILL MAD ABOUT
....THE LAST TIME I BORROWED IT.
OH I AM.
MANY YEARS AGO I HID IT DEEP WITHIN THE CASTLE...
AND YOU MUST FIND IT IF YOU WANT TO BORROW IT.

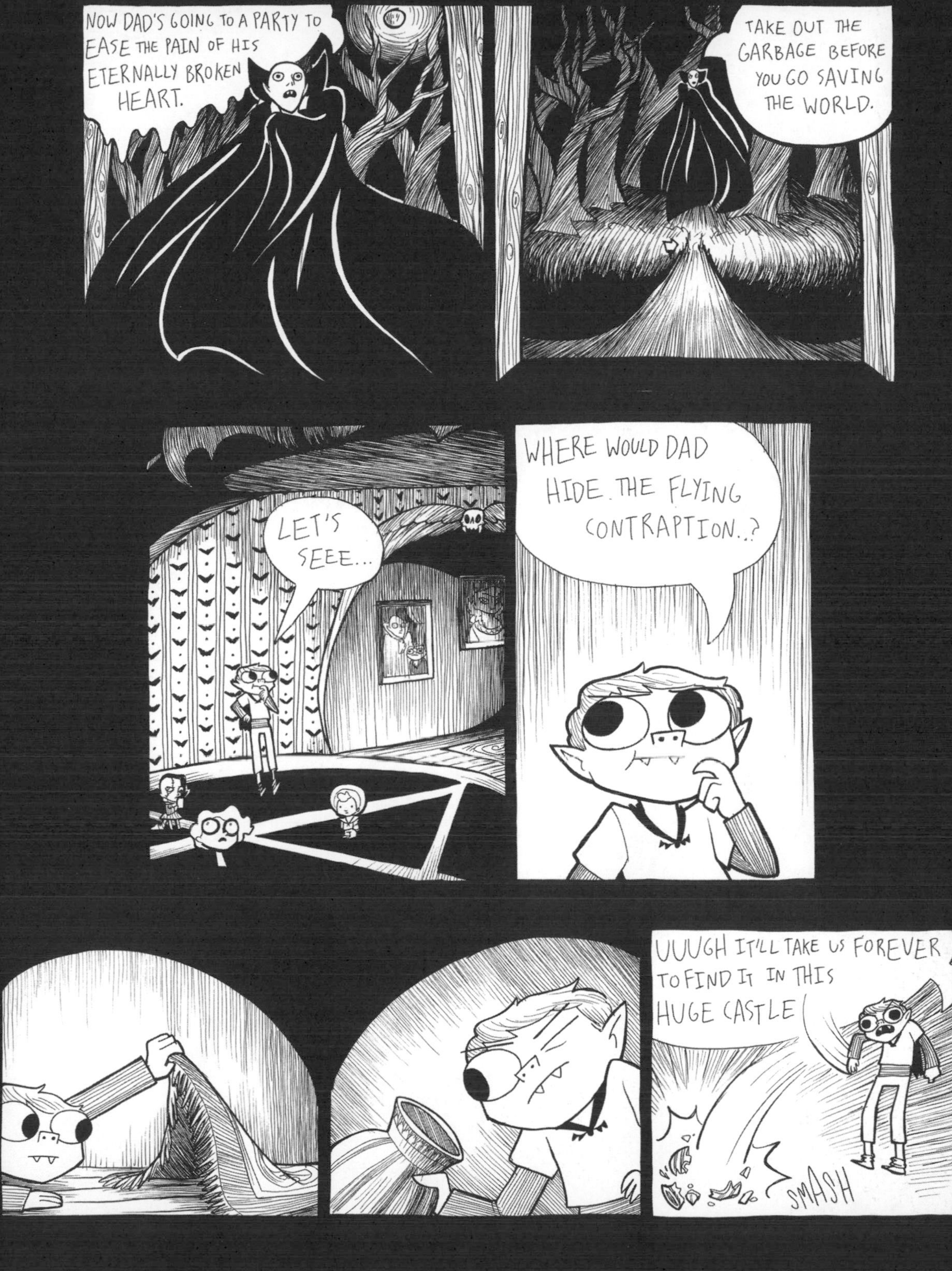
NOW DAD'S GOING TO A PARTY TO EASE THE PAIN OF HIS ETERNALLY BROKEN HEART.
TAKE OUT THE GARBAGE BEFORE YOU GO SAVING THE WORLD.
LET'S SEEE...
WHERE WOULD DAD HIDE THE FLYING CONTRAPTION..?
UUUGH IT'LL TAKE US FOREVER TO FIND IT IN THIS HUGE CASTLE
SMASH

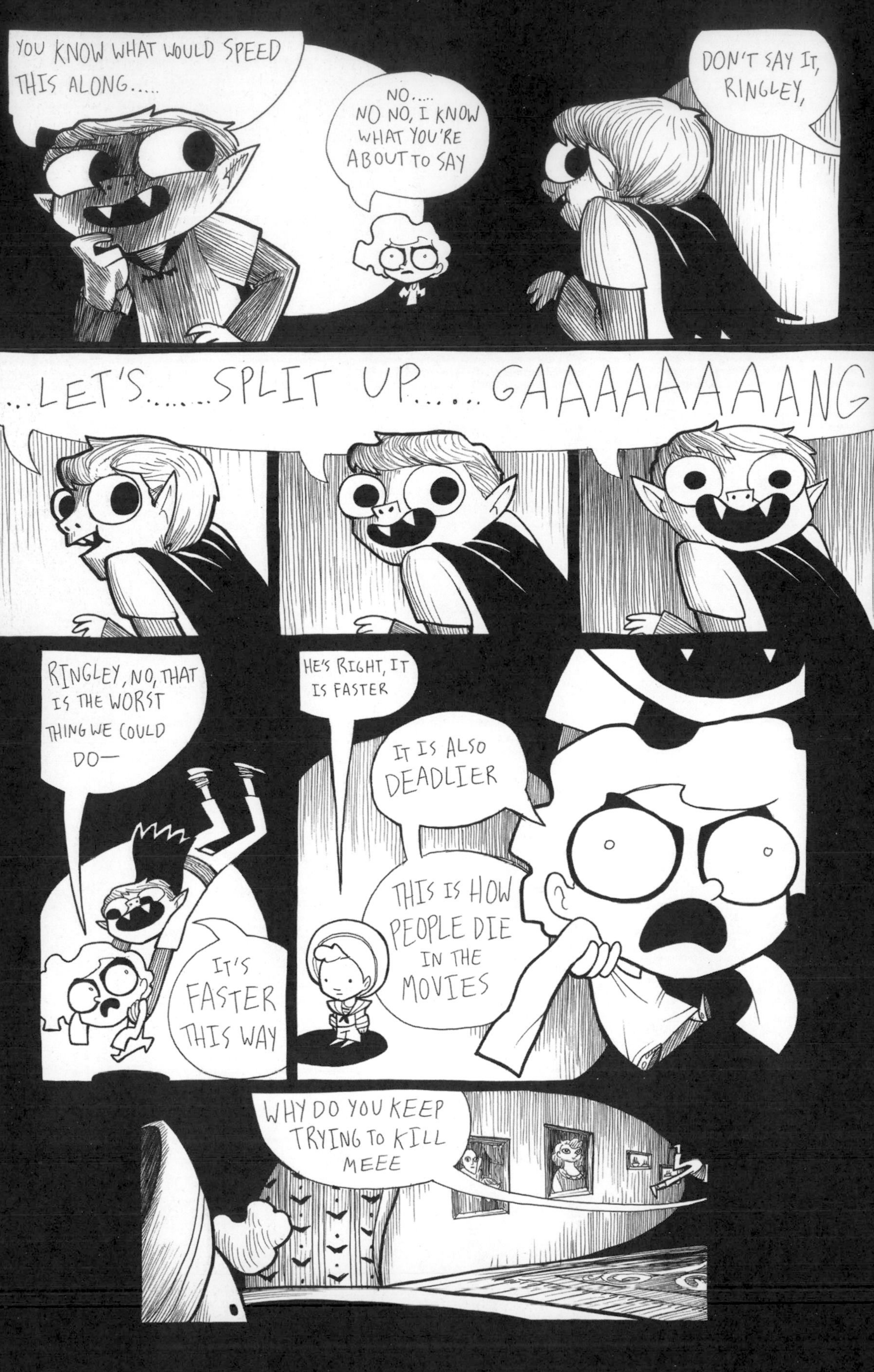

YOU KNOW WHAT WOULD SPEED THIS ALONG.....
NO..... NO NO, I KNOW WHAT YOU'RE ABOUT TO SAY
DON'T SAY IT, RINGLEY,
.....LET'S.......SPLIT UP......GAAAAAAAAANG
RINGLEY, NO, THAT IS THE WORST THING WE COULD DO—
IT'S FASTER THIS WAY
HE'S RIGHT, IT IS FASTER
IT IS ALSO DEADLIER
THIS IS HOW PEOPLE DIE IN THE MOVIES
WHY DO YOU KEEP TRYING TO KILL MEEE

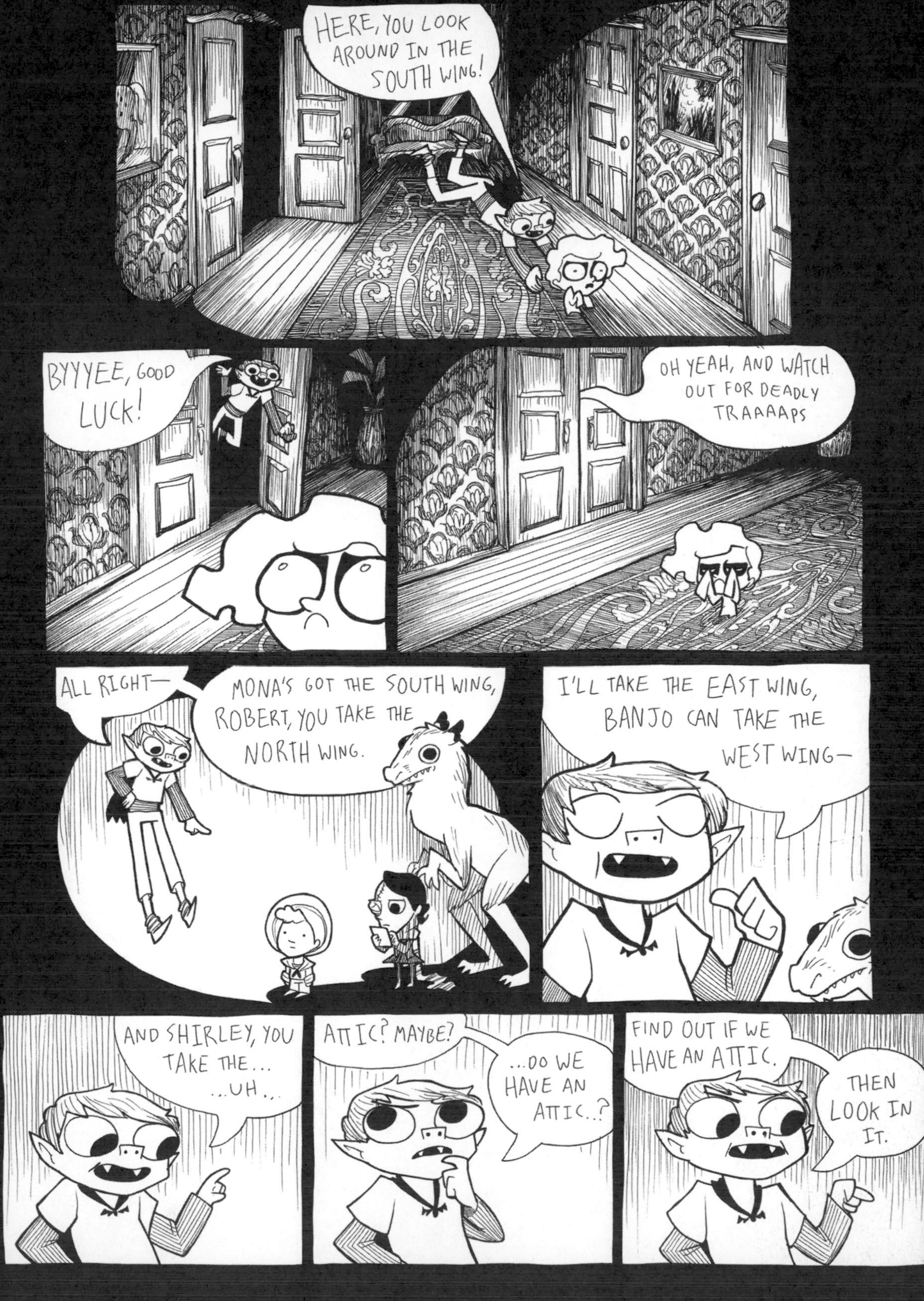
HERE, YOU LOOK AROUND IN THE SOUTH WING!
BYYYEE, GOOD LUCK!
OH YEAH, AND WATCH OUT FOR DEADLY TRAAAAPS
ALL RIGHT—
MONA'S GOT THE SOUTH WING, ROBERT, YOU TAKE THE NORTH WING.
I'LL TAKE THE EAST WING, BANJO CAN TAKE THE WEST WING—
AND SHIRLEY, YOU TAKE THE... ...UH...
ATTIC? MAYBE?
...DO WE HAVE AN ATTIC...?
FIND OUT IF WE HAVE AN ATTIC.
THEN LOOK IN IT.

AND SO....

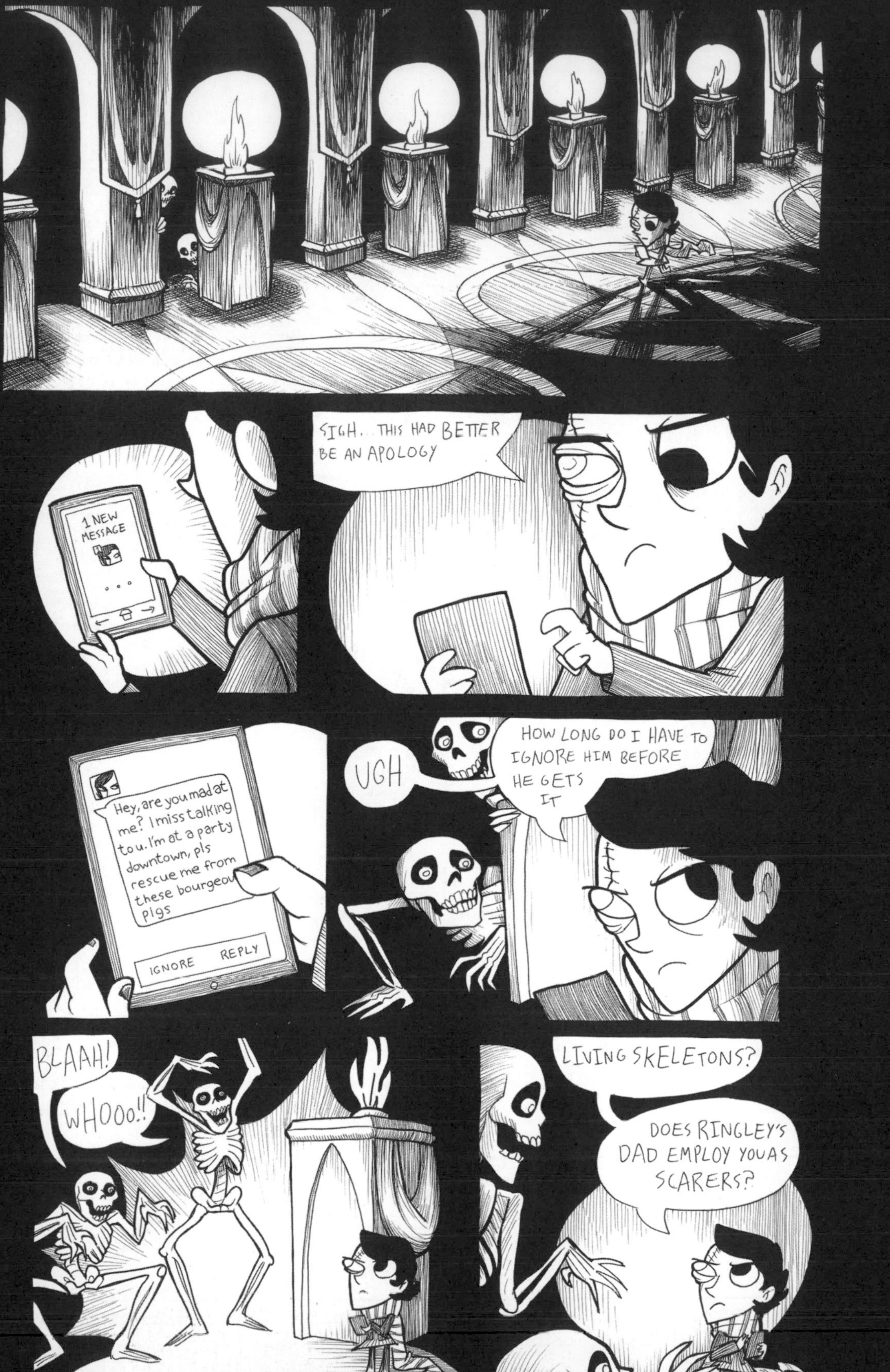
1 NEW MESSAGE
SIGH... THIS HAD BETTER BE AN APOLOGY
Hey, are you mad at me? I miss talking to u. I'm at a party downtown, pls rescue me from these bourgeou pigs
IGNORE
REPLY
UGH
HOW LONG DO I HAVE TO IGNORE HIM BEFORE HE GETS IT
BLAAH!
WHOOo!!
LIVING SKELETONS?
DOES RINGLEY'S DAD EMPLOY YOU AS SCARERS?

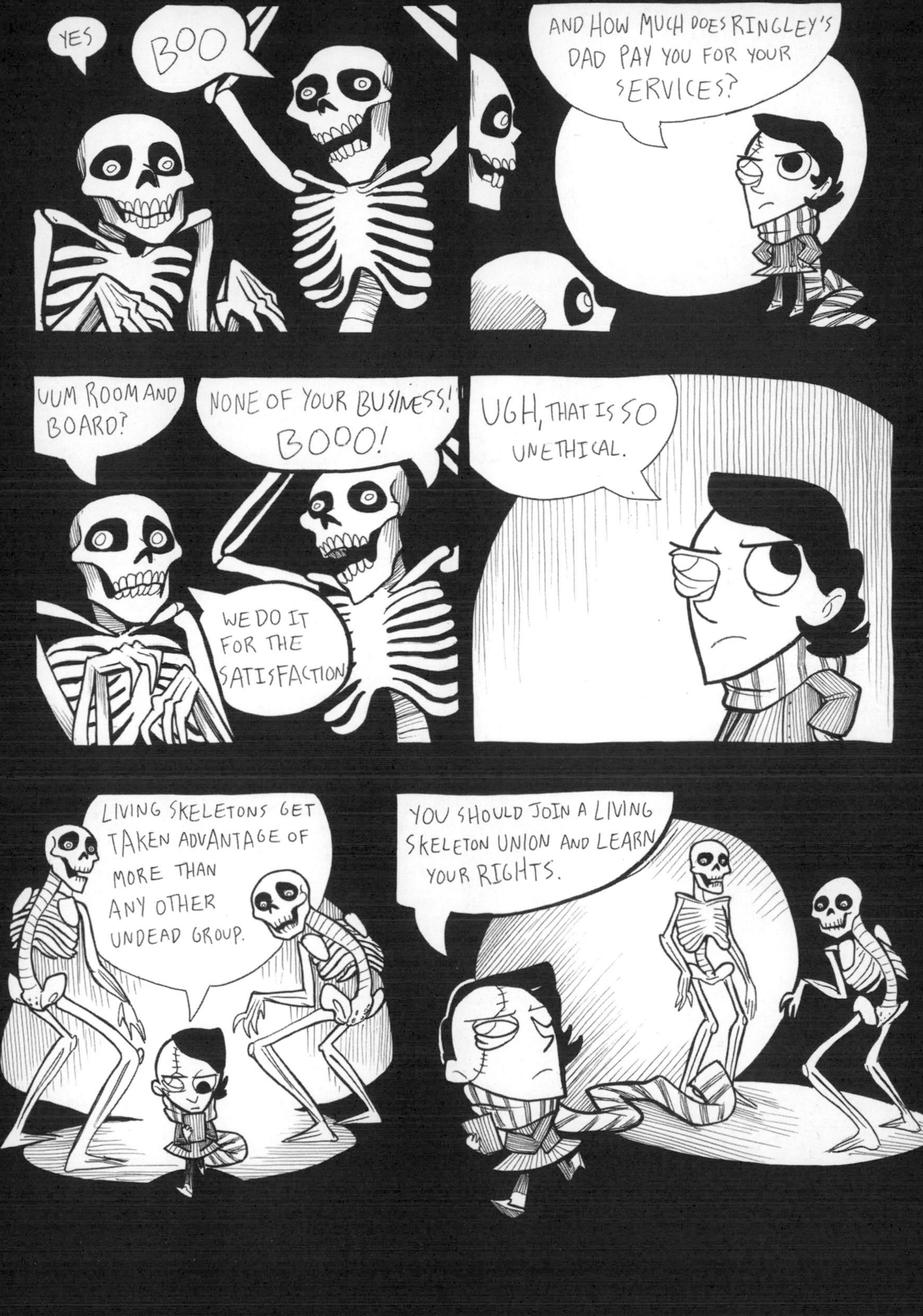
YES
BOO
AND HOW MUCH DOES RINGLEY'S DAD PAY YOU FOR YOUR SERVICES?
UUM ROOM AND BOARD?
NONE OF YOUR BUSINESS!
BOOO!
WE DO IT FOR THE SATISFACTION
UGH, THAT IS SO UNETHICAL.
LIVING SKELETONS GET TAKEN ADVANTAGE OF MORE THAN ANY OTHER UNDEAD GROUP.
YOU SHOULD JOIN A LIVING SKELETON UNION AND LEARN YOUR RIGHTS.

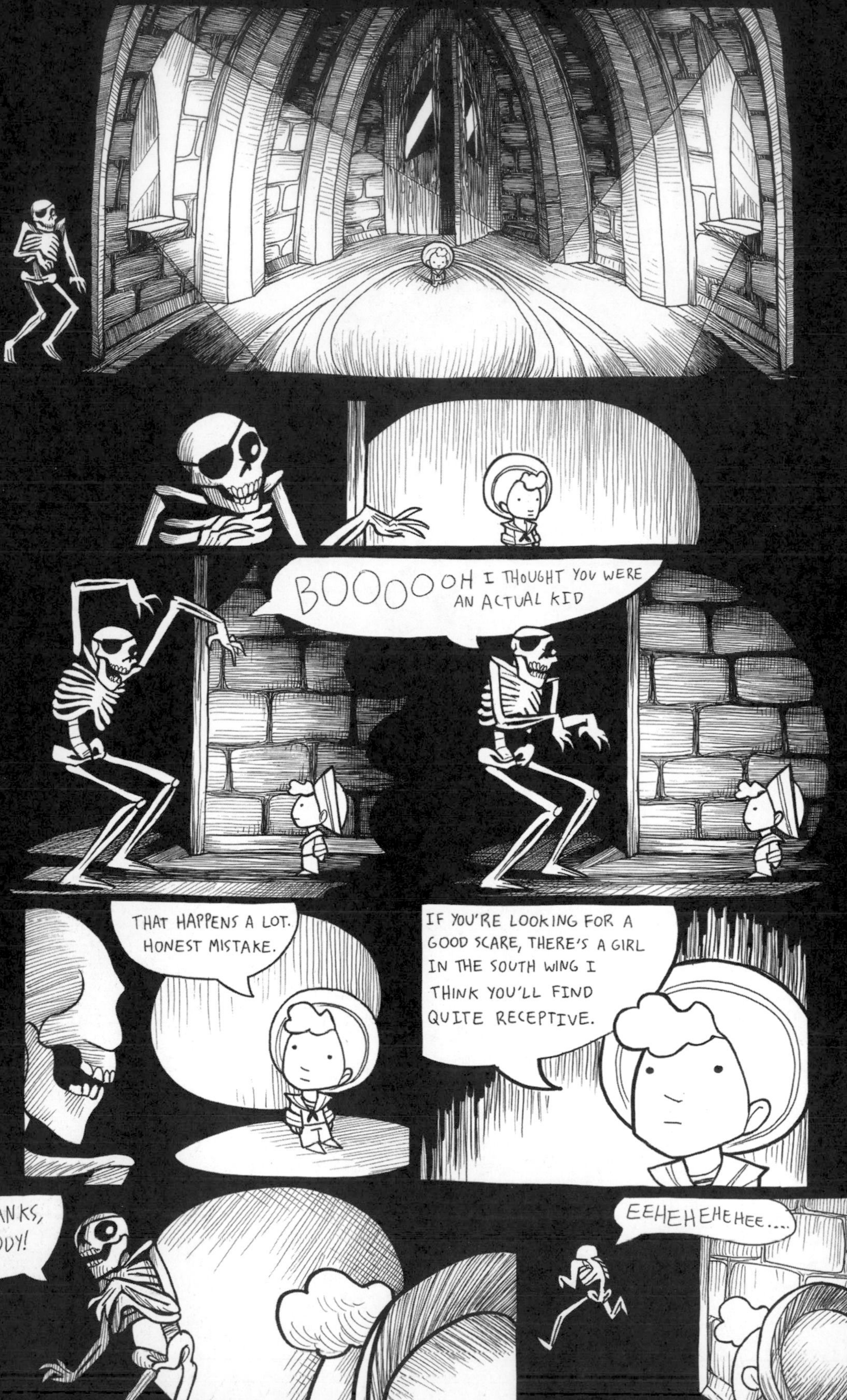
BOOOOOOH I THOUGHT YOU WERE AN ACTUAL KID
THAT HAPPENS A LOT. HONEST MISTAKE.
IF YOU'RE LOOKING FOR A GOOD SCARE, THERE'S A GIRL IN THE SOUTH WING I THINK YOU'LL FIND QUITE RECEPTIVE.
THANKS, BUDDY!
EEHEHEHEHEE....

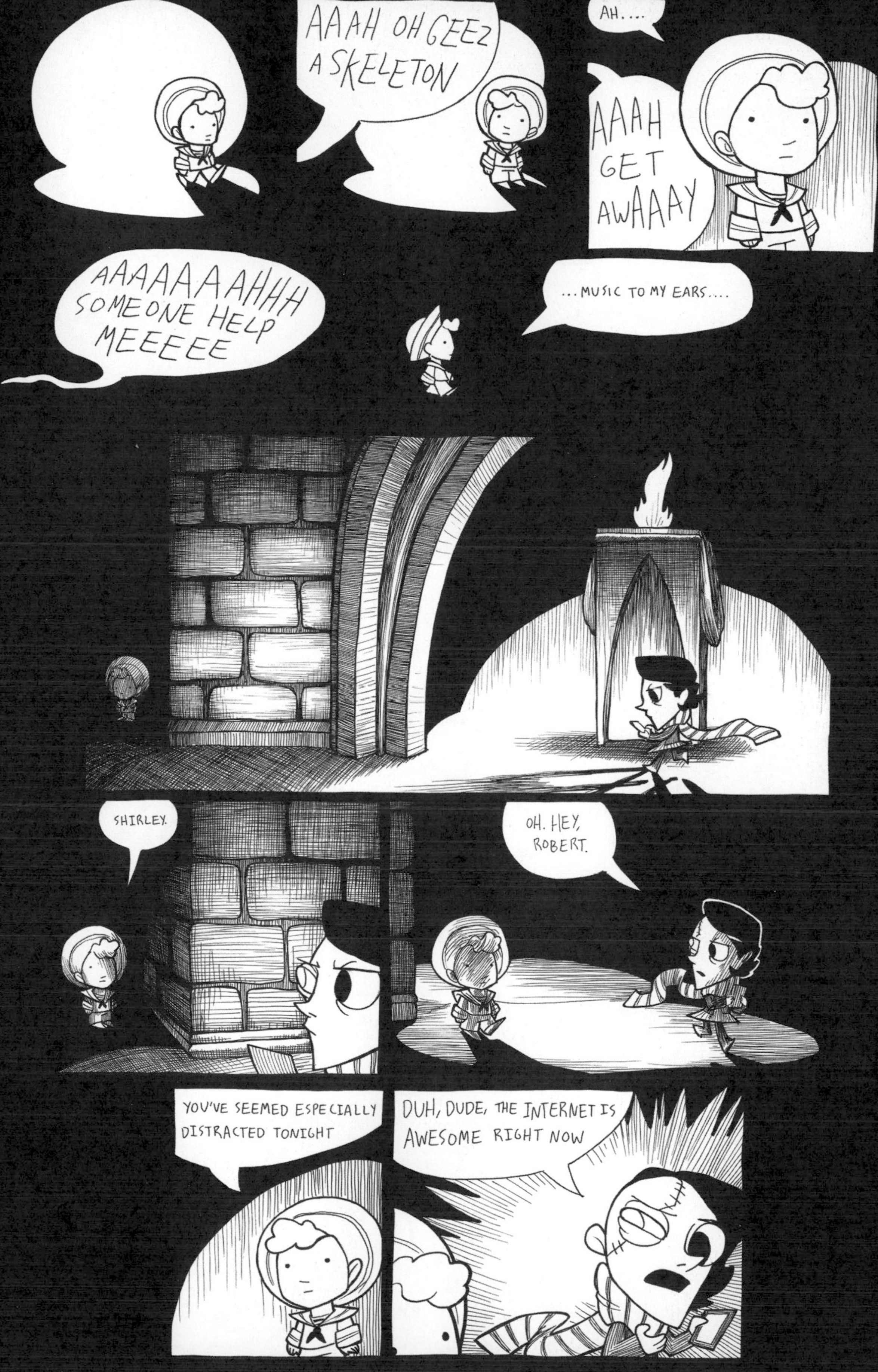

AAAH OH GEEZ A SKELETON
AH....
AAAH GET AWAAAY
AAAAAAAHHH SOMEONE HELP MEEEEE
...MUSIC TO MY EARS....
SHIRLEY.
OH. HEY, ROBERT.
YOU'VE SEEMED ESPECIALLY DISTRACTED TONIGHT
DUH, DUDE, THE INTERNET IS AWESOME RIGHT NOW

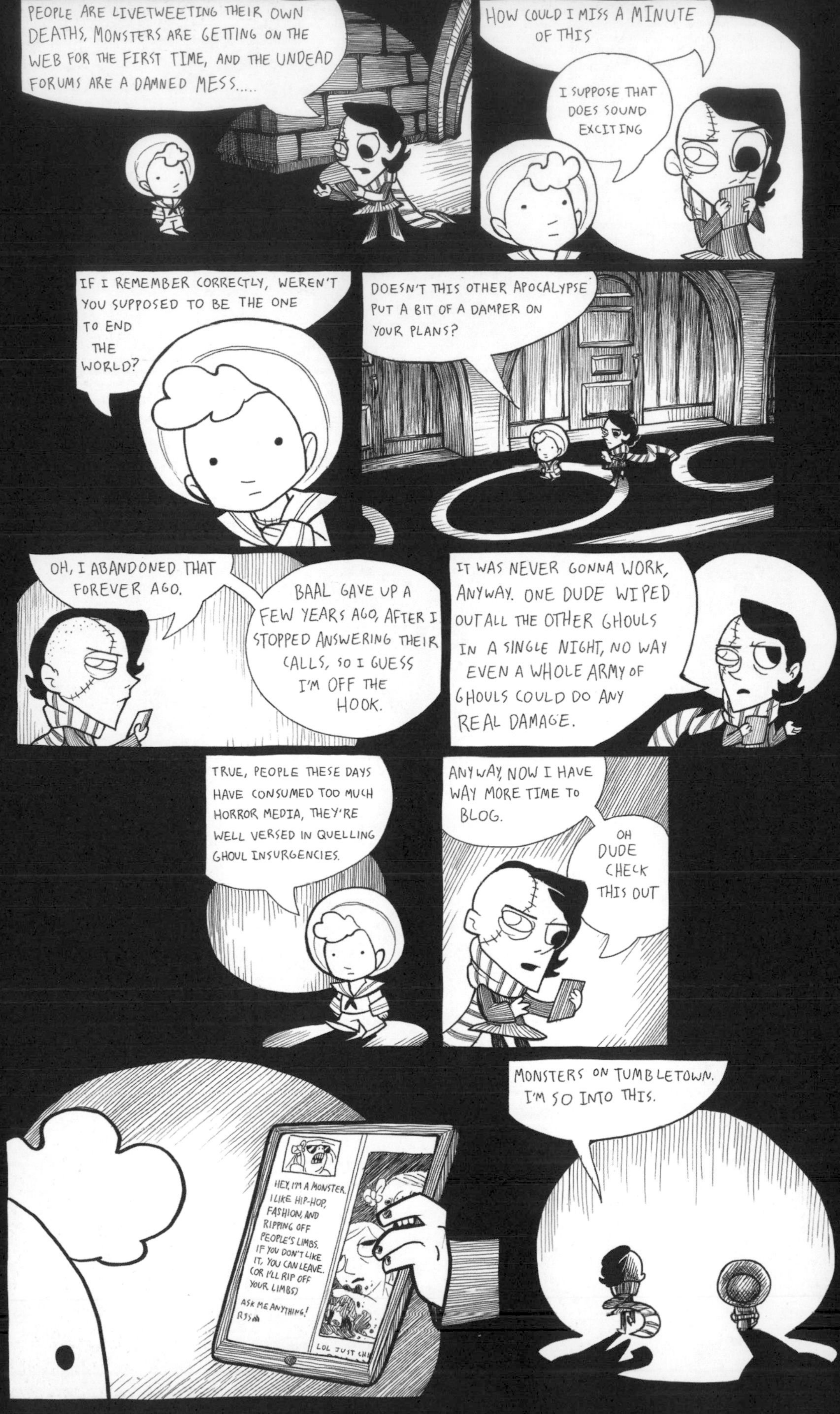
PEOPLE ARE LIVETWEETING THEIR OWN DEATHS, MONSTERS ARE GETTING ON THE WEB FOR THE FIRST TIME, AND THE UNDEAD FORUMS ARE A DAMNED MESS.....
HOW COULD I MISS A MINUTE OF THIS
I SUPPOSE THAT DOES SOUND EXCITING
IF I REMEMBER CORRECTLY, WEREN'T YOU SUPPOSED TO BE THE ONE TO END THE WORLD?
DOESN'T THIS OTHER APOCALYPSE PUT A BIT OF A DAMPER ON YOUR PLANS?
OH, I ABANDONED THAT FOREVER AGO.
BAAL GAVE UP A FEW YEARS AGO, AFTER I STOPPED ANSWERING THEIR CALLS, SO I GUESS I'M OFF THE HOOK.
IT WAS NEVER GONNA WORK, ANYWAY. ONE DUDE WIPED OUT ALL THE OTHER GHOULS IN A SINGLE NIGHT, NO WAY EVEN A WHOLE ARMY OF GHOULS COULD DO ANY REAL DAMAGE.
TRUE, PEOPLE THESE DAYS HAVE CONSUMED TOO MUCH HORROR MEDIA, THEY'RE WELL VERSED IN QUELLING GHOUL INSURGENCIES.
ANYWAY, NOW I HAVE WAY MORE TIME TO BLOG.
OH DUDE CHECK THIS OUT
HEY, I'M A MONSTER. I LIKE HIP-HOP, FASHION, AND RIPPING OFF PEOPLE'S LIMBS. IF YOU DON'T LIKE IT, YOU CAN LEAVE. (OR I'LL RIP OFF YOUR LIMBS)
ASK ME ANYTHING!
MONSTERS ON TUMBLETOWN. I'M SO INTO THIS.

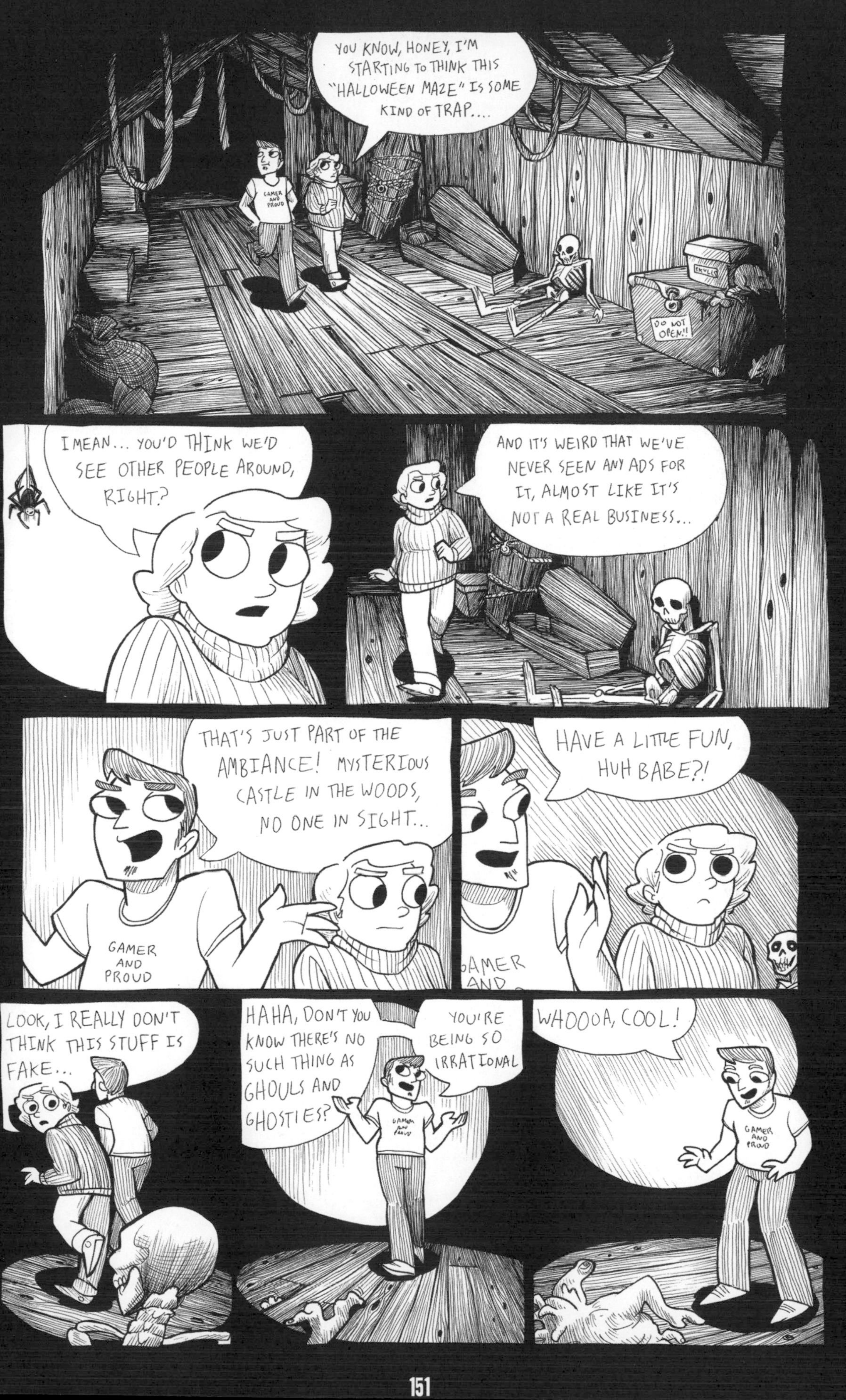

YOU KNOW, HONEY, I'M STARTING TO THINK THIS "HALLOWEEN MAZE" IS SOME KIND OF TRAP....
GAMER AND PROUD
SKULLS
DO NOT OPEN!!
I MEAN... YOU'D THINK WE'D SEE OTHER PEOPLE AROUND, RIGHT?
AND IT'S WEIRD THAT WE'VE NEVER SEEN ANY ADS FOR IT, ALMOST LIKE IT'S NOT A REAL BUSINESS...
THAT'S JUST PART OF THE AMBIANCE! MYSTERIOUS CASTLE IN THE WOODS, NO ONE IN SIGHT...
GAMER AND PROUD
HAVE A LITTLE FUN, HUH BABE?!
LOOK, I REALLY DON'T THINK THIS STUFF IS FAKE...
HAHA, DON'T YOU KNOW THERE'S NO SUCH THING AS GHOULS AND GHOSTIES?
YOU'RE BEING SO IRRATIONAL
WHOOOA, COOL!
GAMER AND PROUD

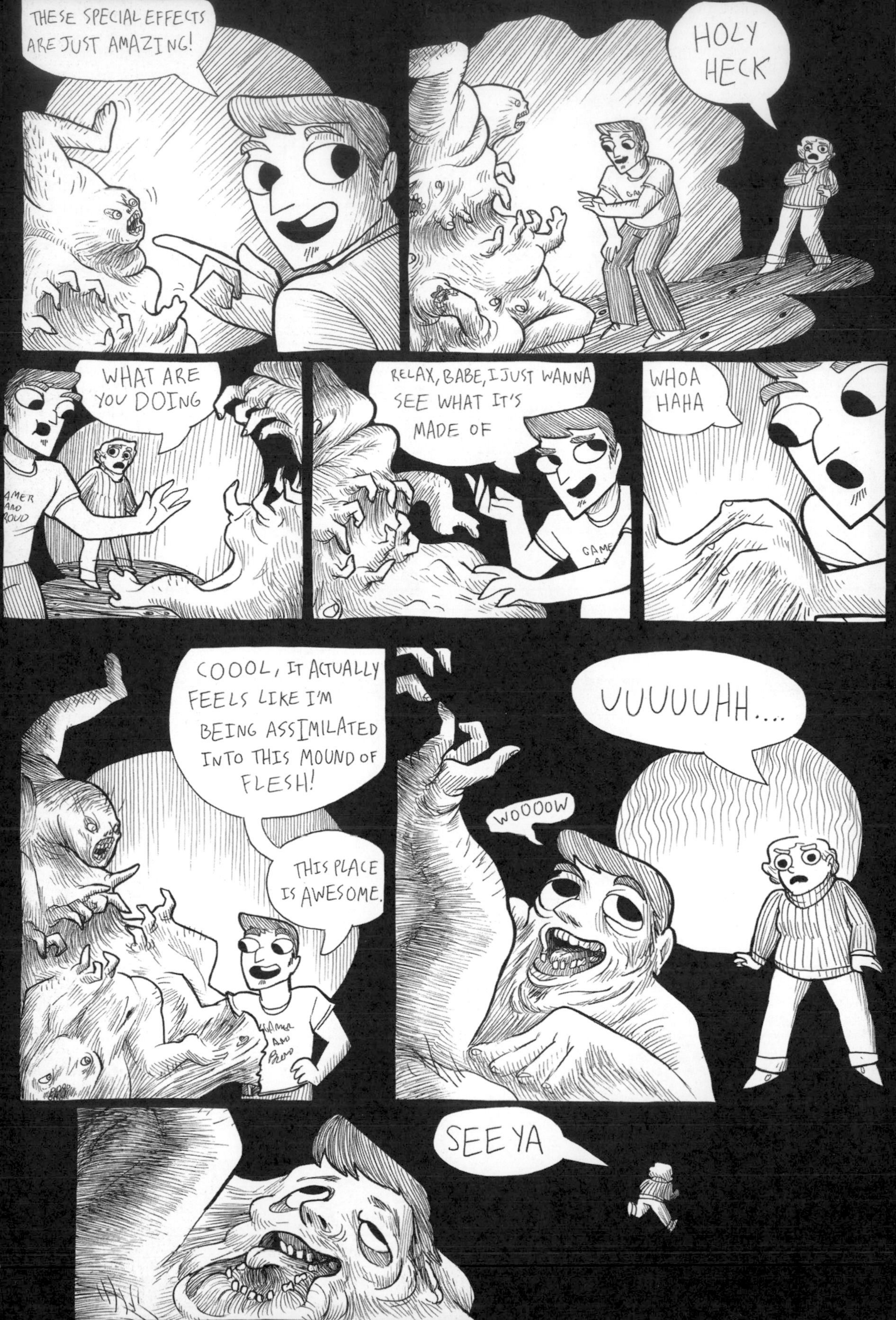

THESE SPECIAL EFFECTS ARE JUST AMAZING!
HOLY HECK
WHAT ARE YOU DOING
RELAX, BABE, I JUST WANNA SEE WHAT IT'S MADE OF
WHOA HAHA
COOOL, IT ACTUALLY FEELS LIKE I'M BEING ASSIMILATED INTO THIS MOUND OF FLESH!
THIS PLACE IS AWESOME.
UUUUUHH....
WOOOOW
SEE YA

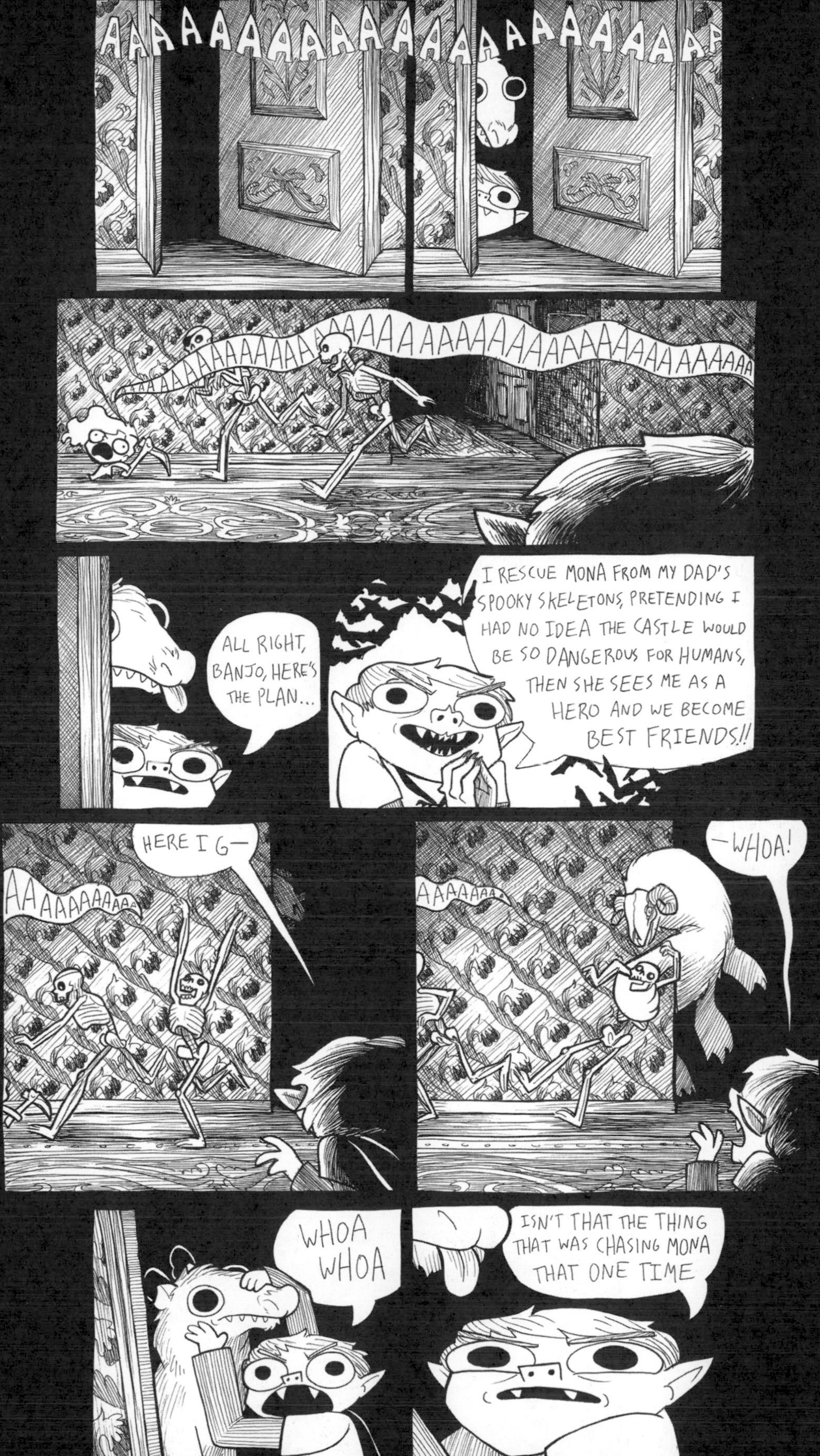
AAAAAAAAAAAAAAAAAAAAP
AAAAAAAAAAAAAAAAAAAAAAAAAAAAAAAAAA
ALL RIGHT, BANJO, HERE'S THE PLAN...
I RESCUE MONA FROM MY DAD'S SPOOKY SKELETONS, PRETENDING I HAD NO IDEA THE CASTLE WOULD BE SO DANGEROUS FOR HUMANS, THEN SHE SEES ME AS A HERO AND WE BECOME BEST FRIENDS!!
AAAAAAAAAA
HERE I G—
AAAAAAA
—WHOA!
WHOA WHOA
ISN'T THAT THE THING THAT WAS CHASING MONA THAT ONE TIME

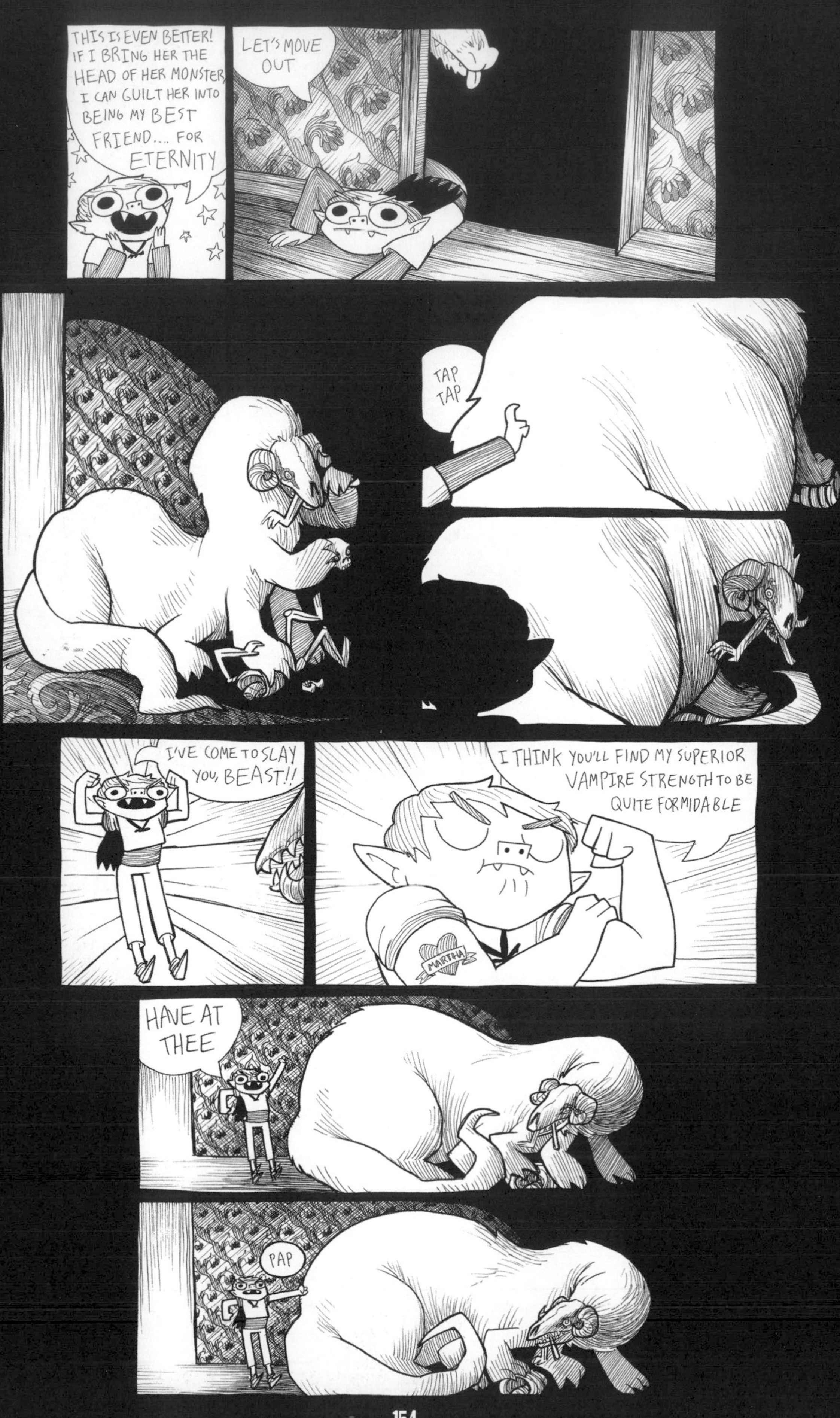
THIS IS EVEN BETTER! IF I BRING HER THE HEAD OF HER MONSTER, I CAN GUILT HER INTO BEING MY BEST FRIEND.... FOR ETERNITY
LET'S MOVE OUT
TAP TAP
I'VE COME TO SLAY YOU, BEAST!!
I THINK YOU'LL FIND MY SUPERIOR VAMPIRE STRENGTH TO BE QUITE FORMIDABLE
MARTHA
HAVE AT THEE
PAP

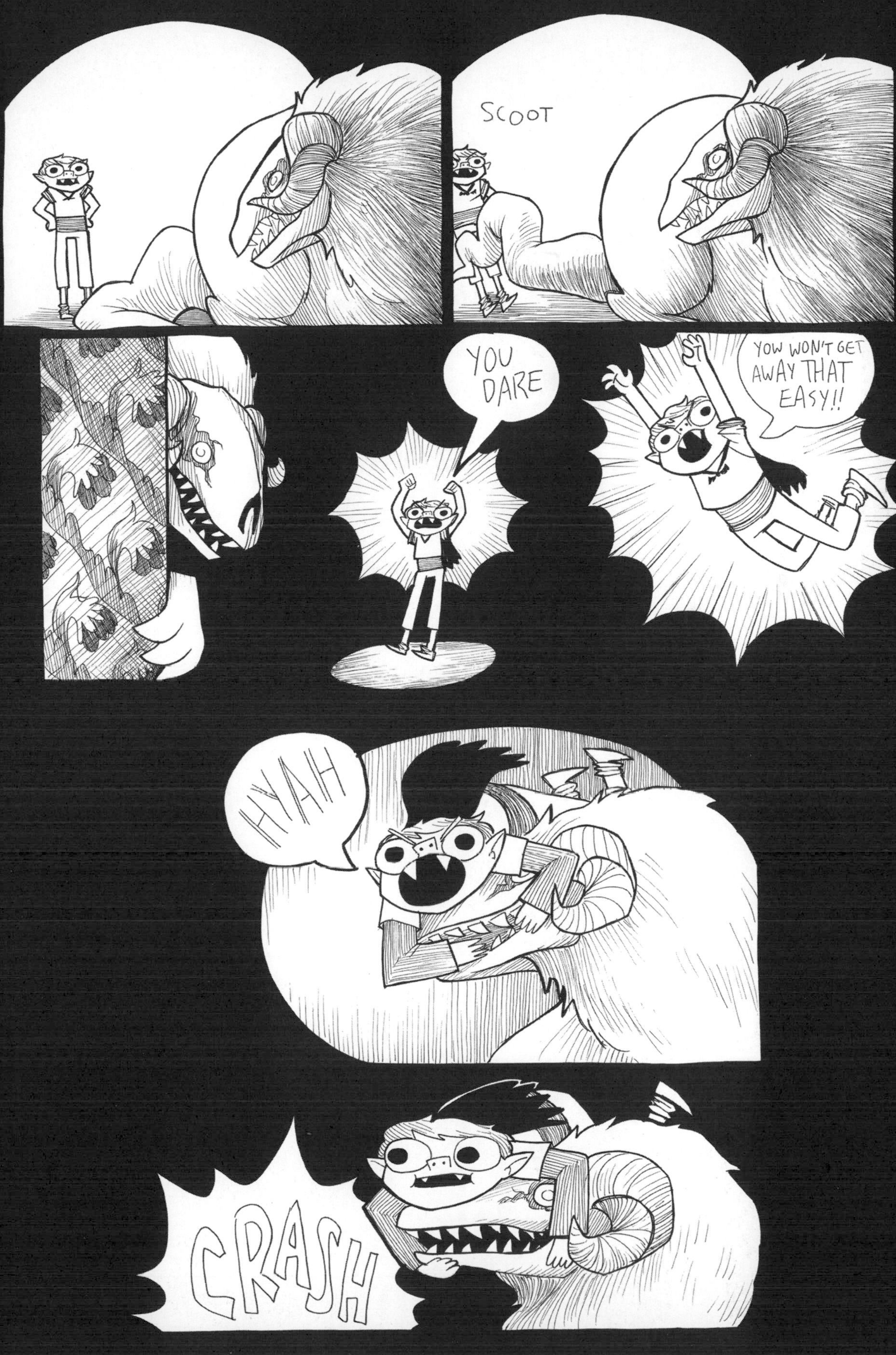
SCOOT
YOU DARE
ST
YOW WON'T GET AWAY THAT EASY!!
HYAH
CRASH

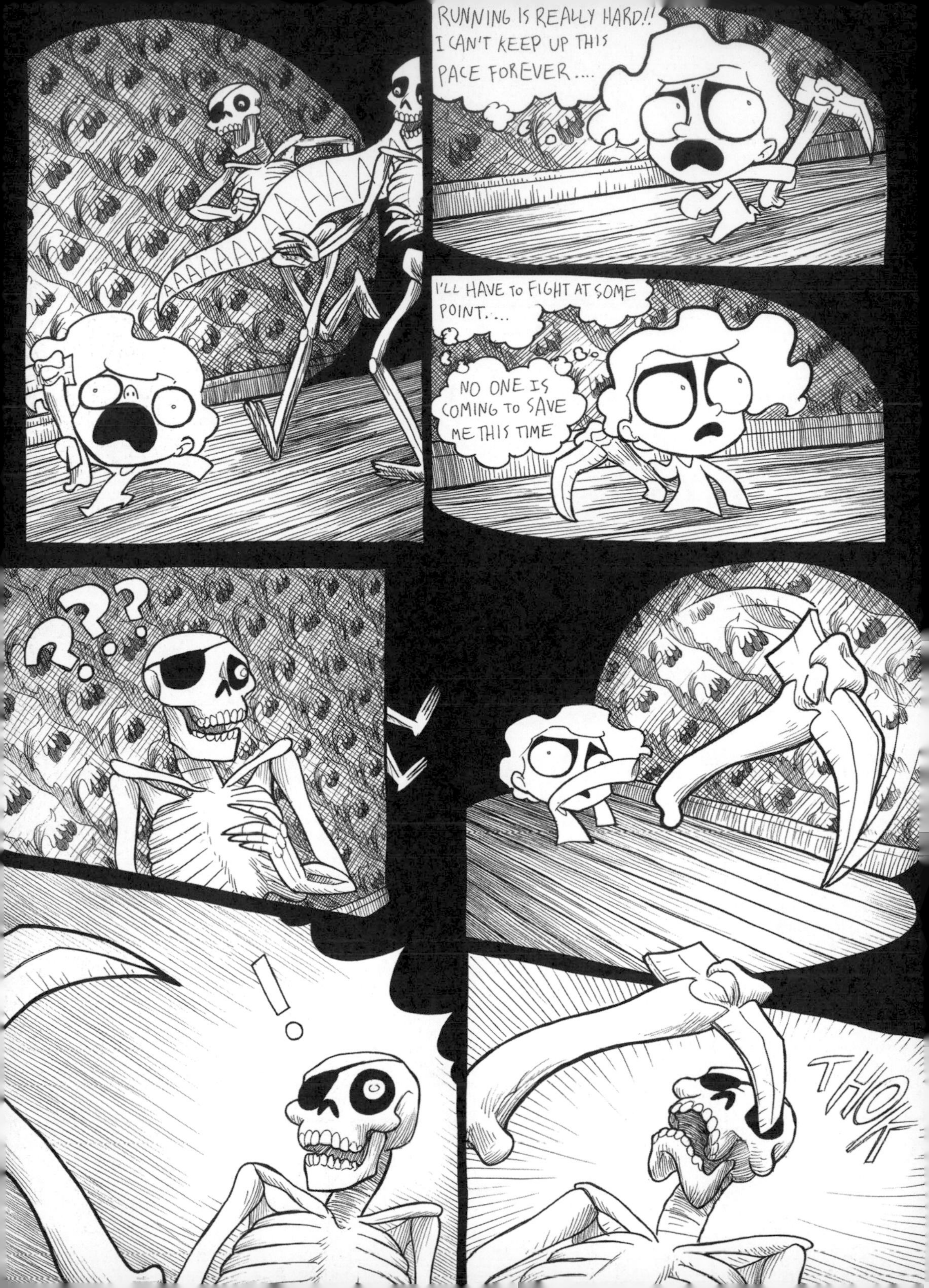
AAAAAAAAAAAAAAAAA
RUNNING IS REALLY HARD!! I CAN'T KEEP UP THIS PACE FOREVER....
I'LL HAVE TO FIGHT AT SOME POINT....
NO ONE IS COMING TO SAVE ME THIS TIME
???
!
THOK

AAAHH MY GOOD EYE

UUUH THAT'S WHAT YOU GET.!!

IF YOU MESS WITH ME!!

NOW THAT I'M BLIND I WON'T BE ABLE TO DO MY JOB....

NOW MY WIFE WILL HAVE TO GET A THIRD JOB TO SUPPORT OUR KIDS....

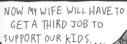

WELL WHAT WERE YOU EXPECTING WHEN YOU ACTED LIKE YOU WERE GOING TO KILL ME?

THAT YOU WOULD RUN AND HIDE, NOT TURN AROUND AND ROB ME OF MY SIGHT

UM MAYBE YOU CAN.... GET A NEW EYE? FROM ANOTHER SKELETON?

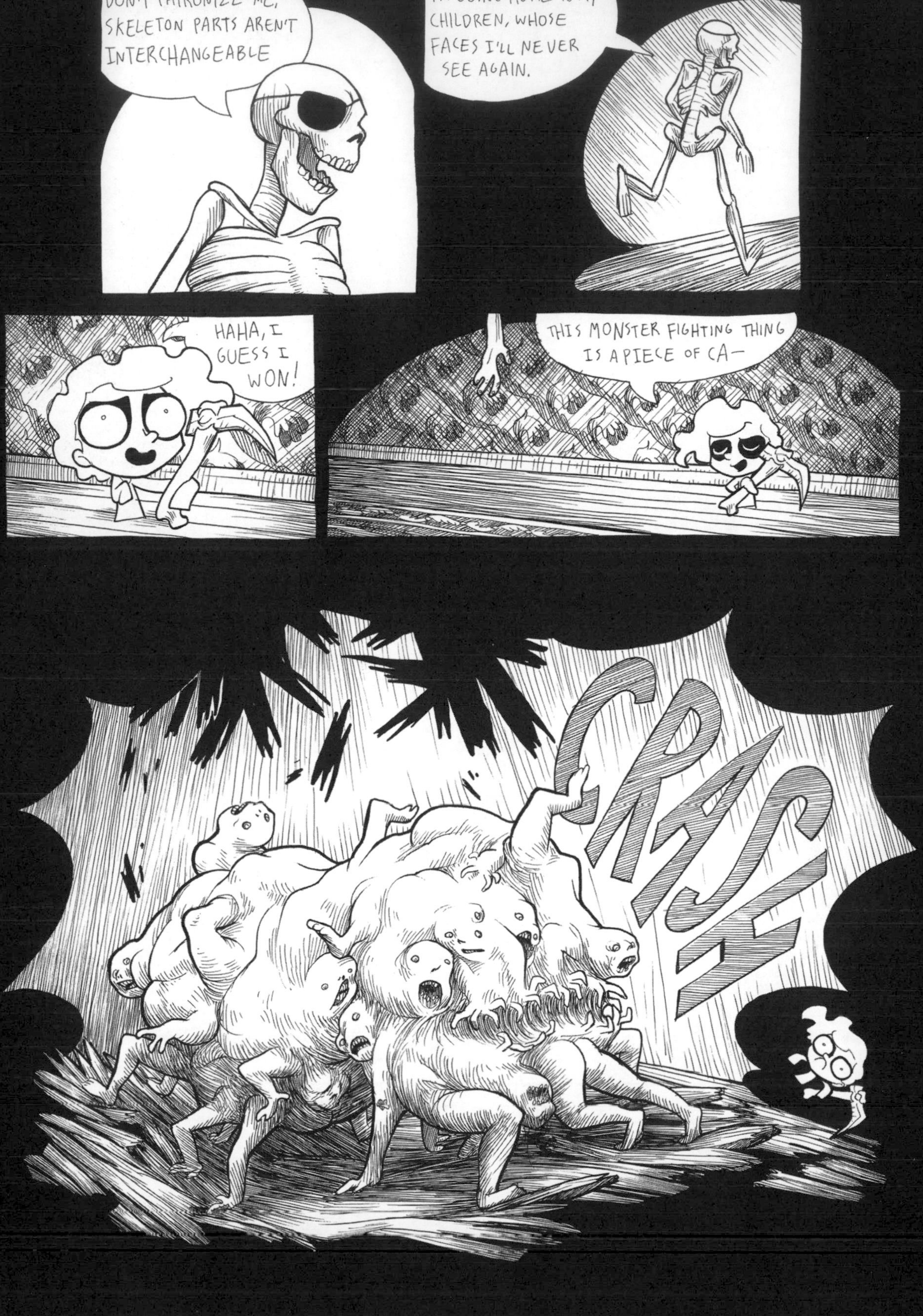
DON'T PATRONIZE ME, SKELETON PARTS AREN'T INTERCHANGEABLE
I'M GOING HOME TO MY CHILDREN, WHOSE FACES I'LL NEVER SEE AGAIN.
HAHA, I GUESS I WON!
THIS MONSTER FIGHTING THING IS A PIECE OF CA—
CRASH

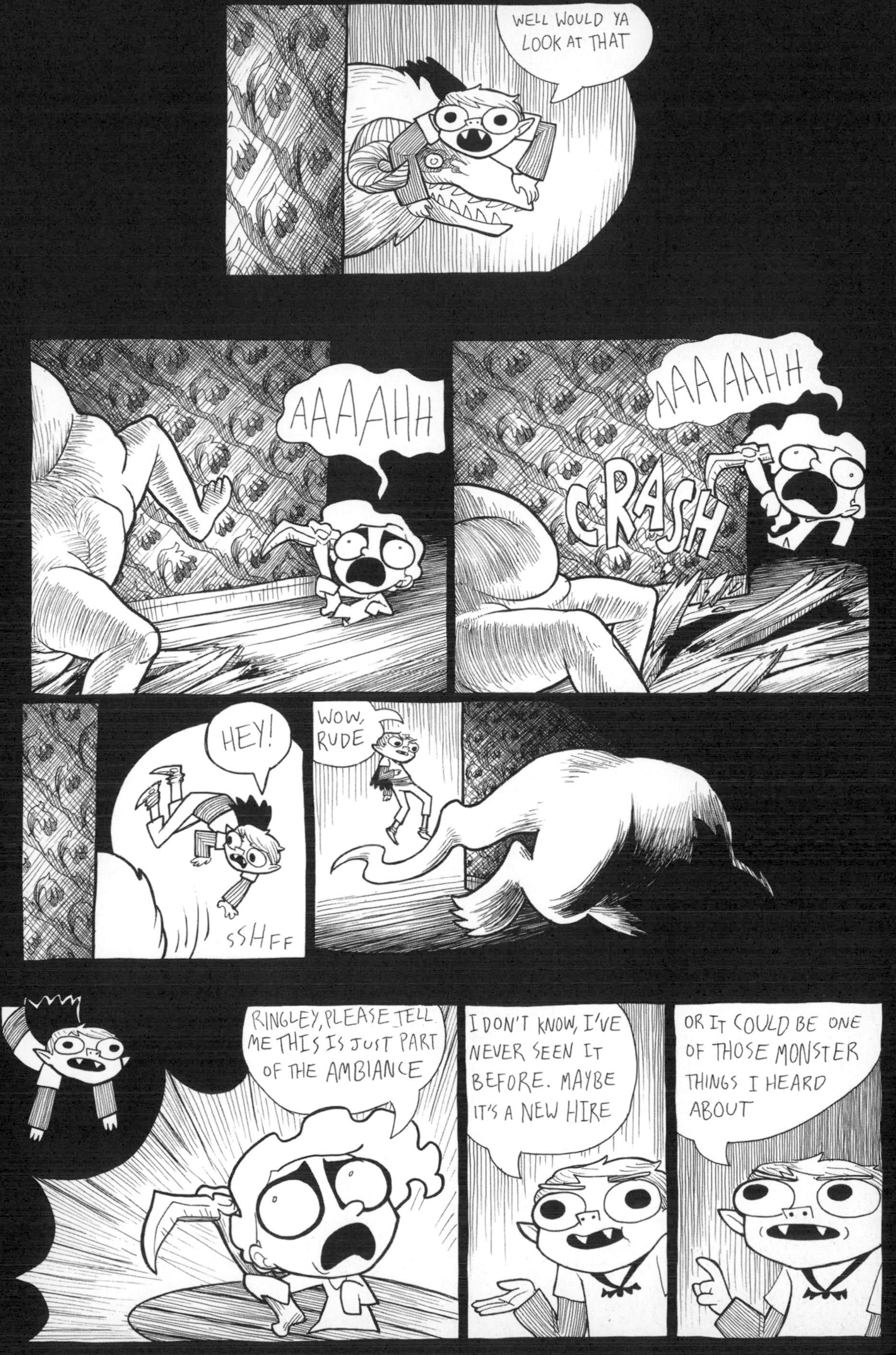
WELL WOULD YA LOOK AT THAT
AAAAHH
AAAAAHH
CRASH
HEY!
SSHFF
WOW, RUDE
RINGLEY, PLEASE TELL ME THIS IS JUST PART OF THE AMBIANCE
I DON'T KNOW, I'VE NEVER SEEN IT BEFORE. MAYBE IT'S A NEW HIRE
OR IT COULD BE ONE OF THOSE MONSTER THINGS I HEARD ABOUT

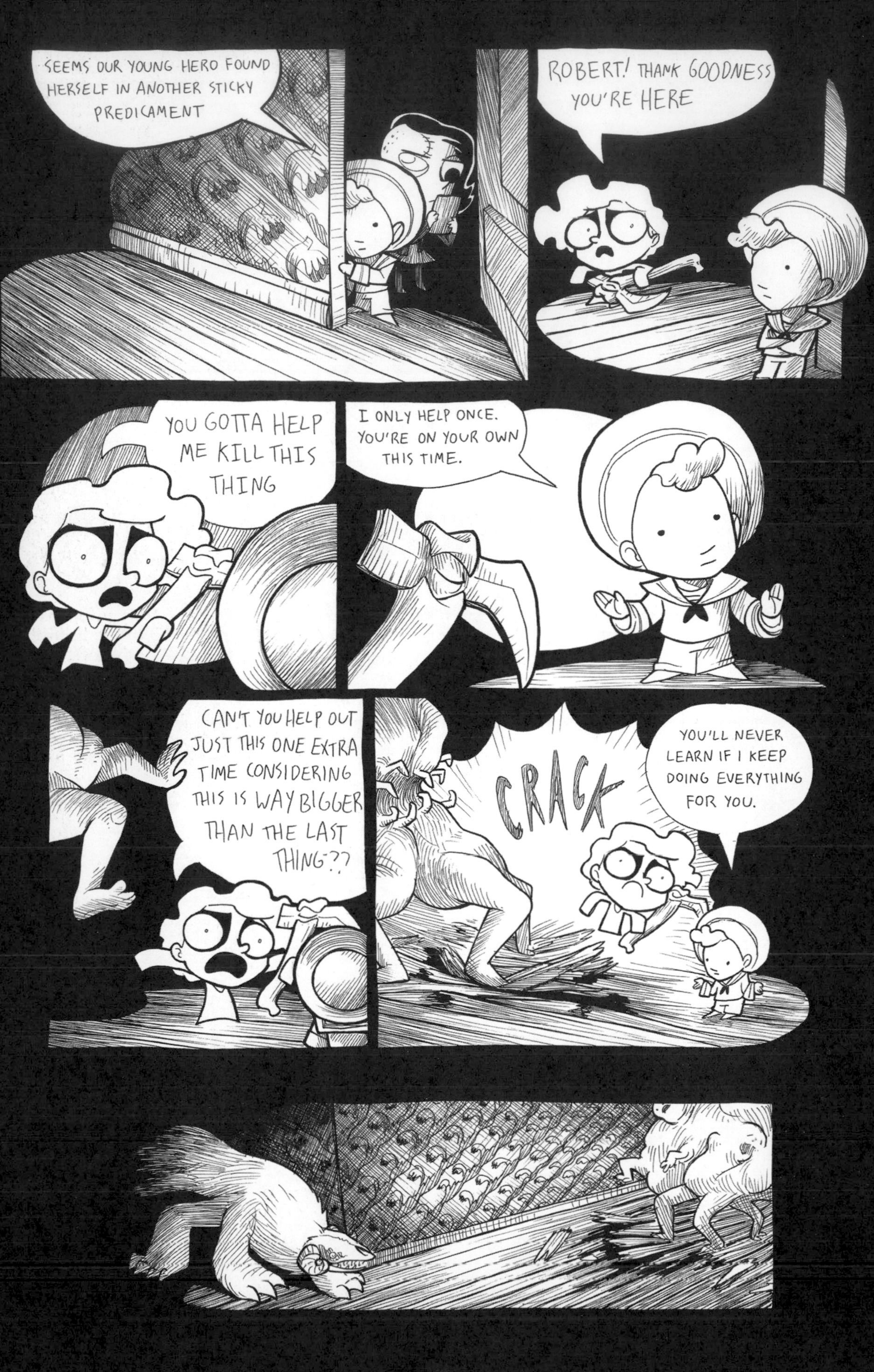
SEEMS OUR YOUNG HERO FOUND HERSELF IN ANOTHER STICKY PREDICAMENT
ROBERT! THANK GOODNESS YOU'RE HERE
YOU GOTTA HELP ME KILL THIS THING
I ONLY HELP ONCE. YOU'RE ON YOUR OWN THIS TIME.
CAN'T YOU HELP OUT JUST THIS ONE EXTRA TIME CONSIDERING THIS IS WAY BIGGER THAN THE LAST THING??
CRACK
YOU'LL NEVER LEARN IF I KEEP DOING EVERYTHING FOR YOU.

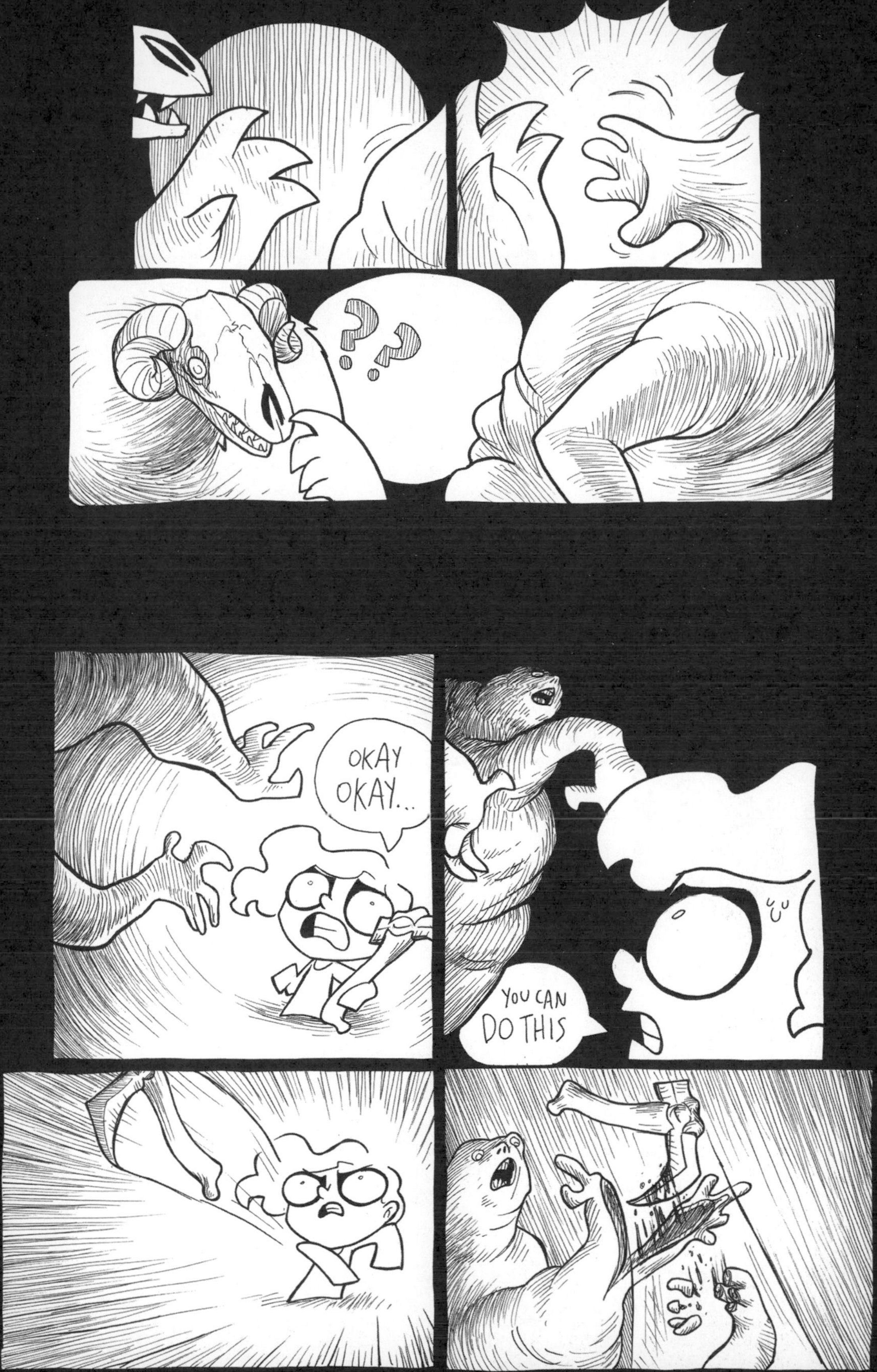
??
OKAY OKAY...
YOU CAN DO THIS

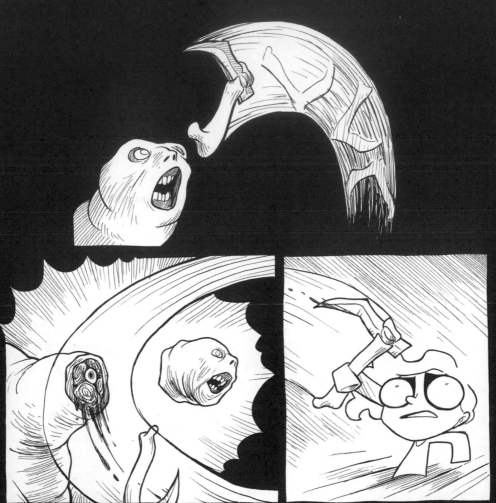

HAH! I DID IT!!

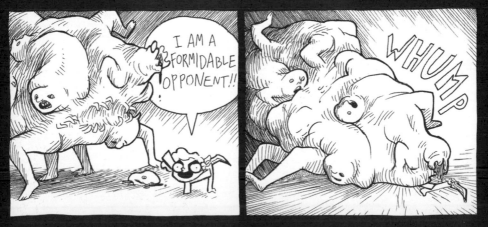

I AM A ₃FORMIDABLE OPPONENT!!

WHUMP

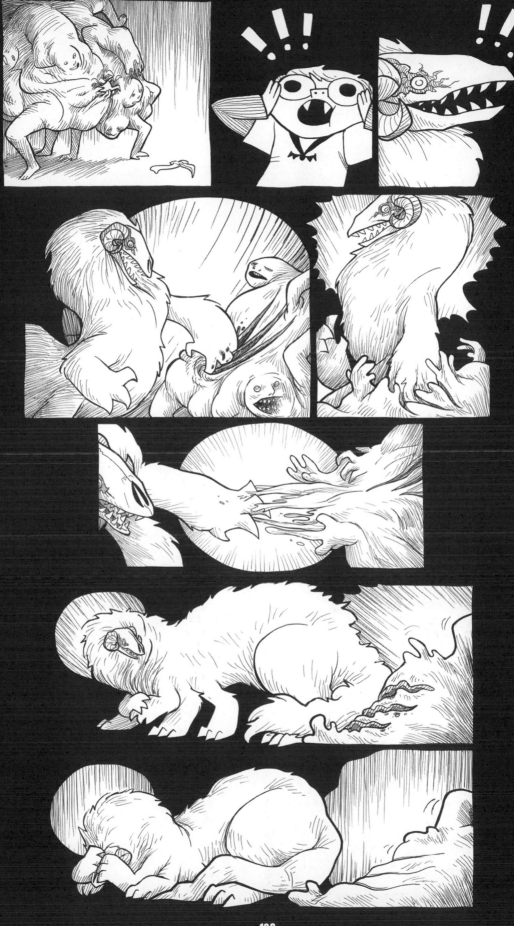

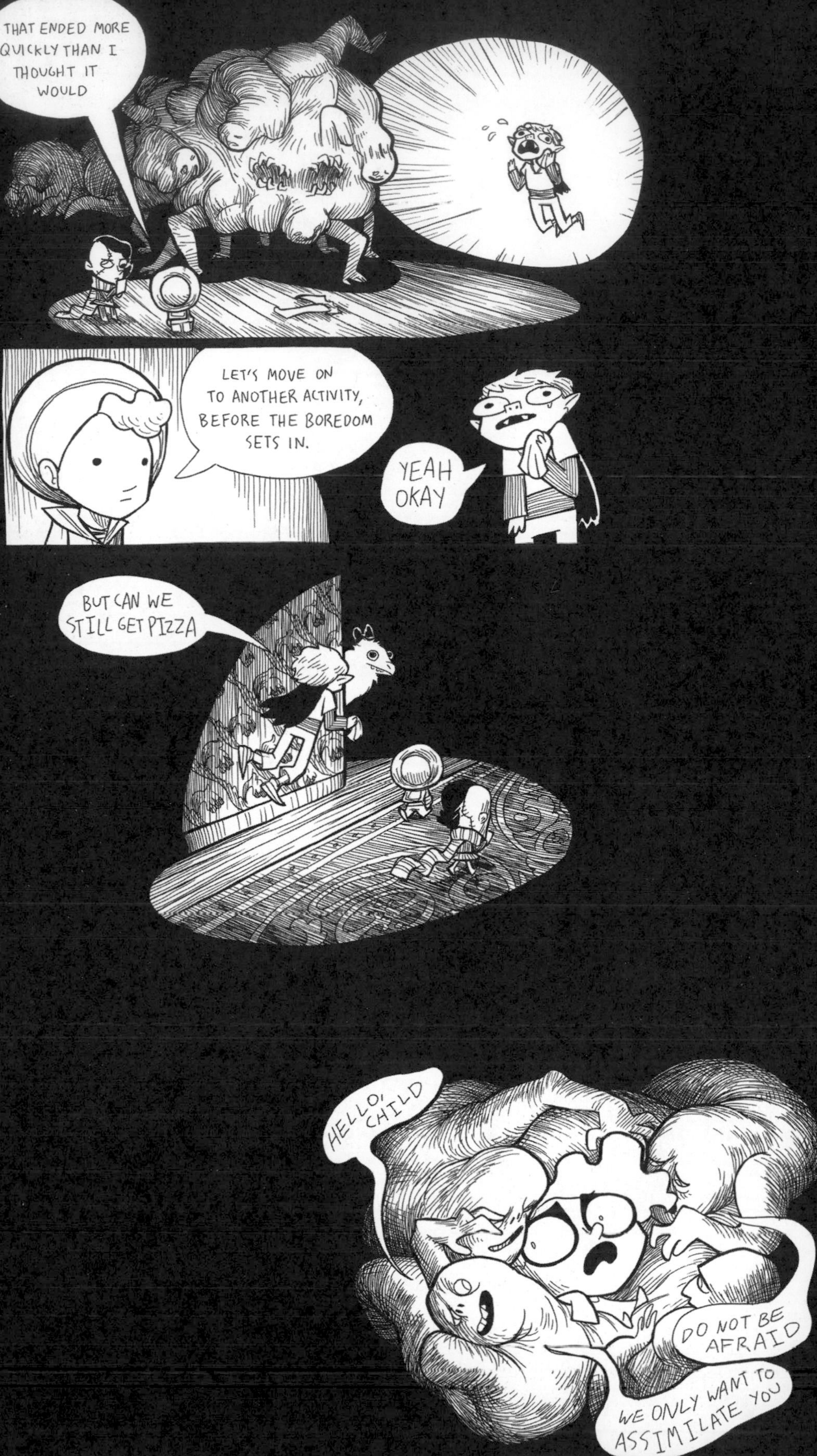
THAT ENDED MORE QUICKLY THAN I THOUGHT IT WOULD
LET'S MOVE ON TO ANOTHER ACTIVITY, BEFORE THE BOREDOM SETS IN.
YEAH OKAY
BUT CAN WE STILL GET PIZZA
HELLO, CHILD
DO NOT BE AFRAID
WE ONLY WANT TO ASSIMILATE YOU

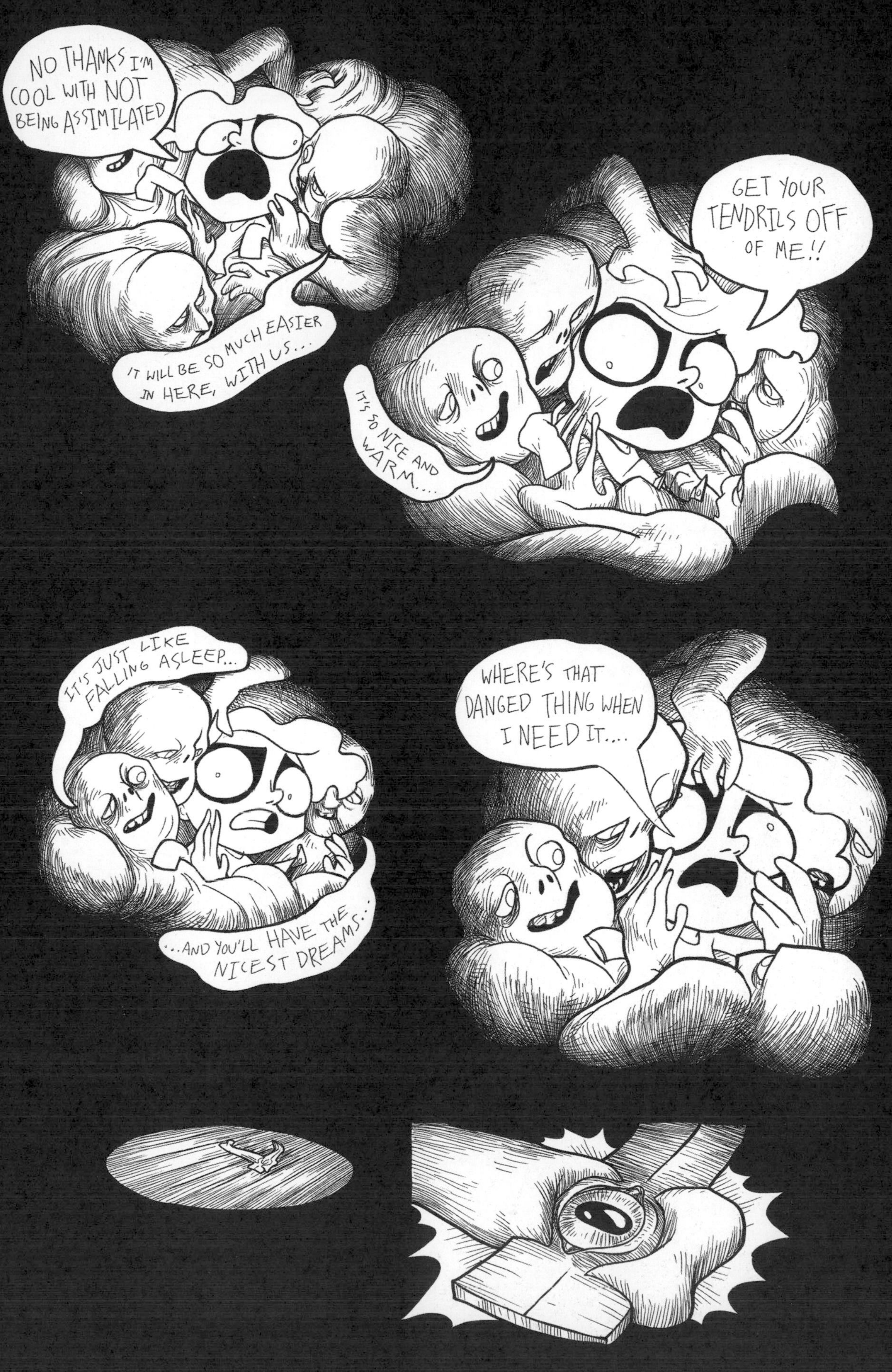
NO THANKS I'M COOL WITH NOT BEING ASSIMILATED
IT WILL BE SO MUCH EASIER IN HERE, WITH US...
GET YOUR TENDRILS OFF OF ME!!
IT'S SO NICE AND WARM....
IT'S JUST LIKE FALLING ASLEEP...
...AND YOU'LL HAVE THE NICEST DREAMS...
WHERE'S THAT DANGED THING WHEN I NEED IT....

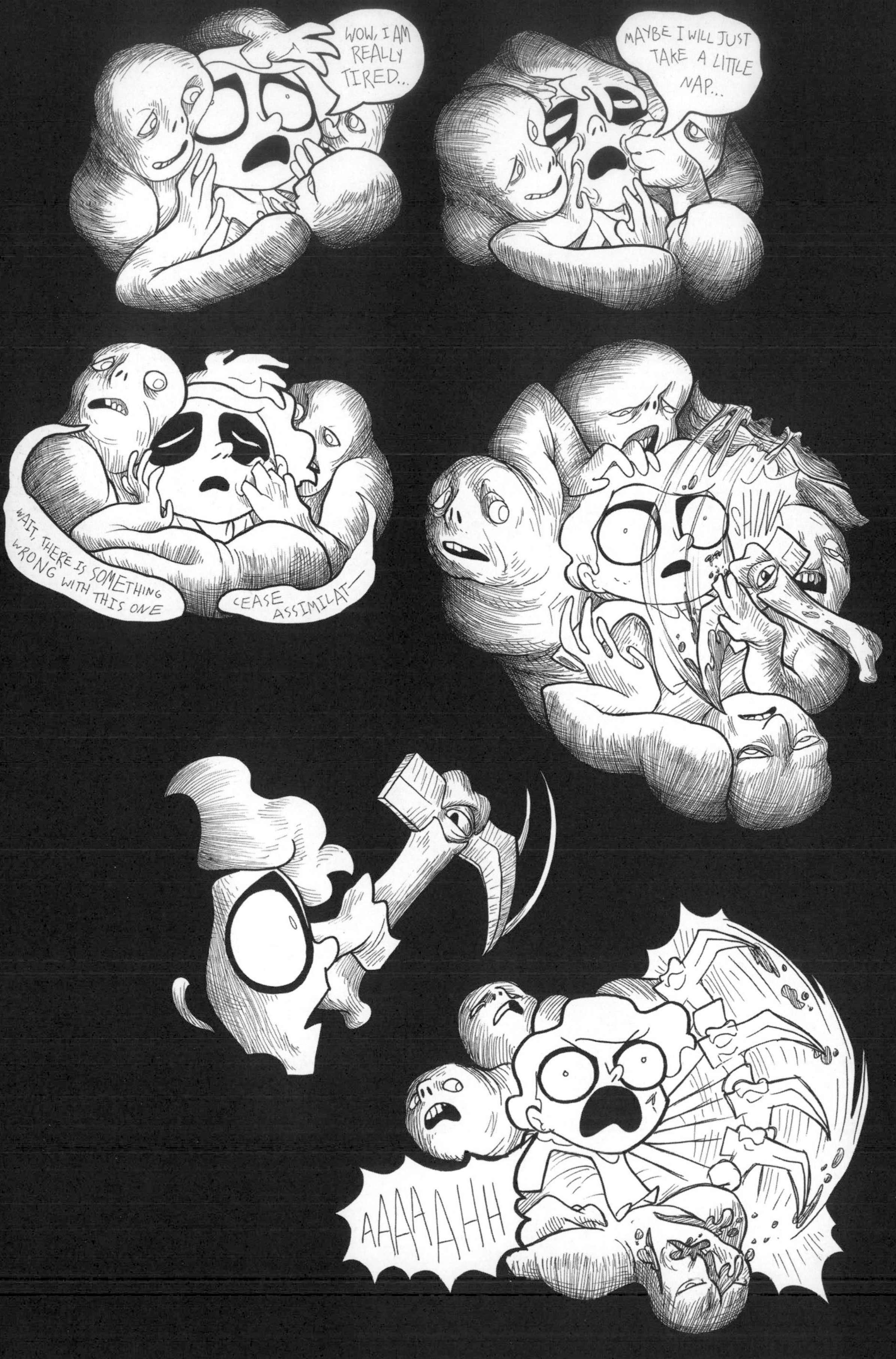
WOW, I AM REALLY TIRED...
MAYBE I WILL JUST TAKE A LITTLE NAP...
WAIT, THERE IS SOMETHING WRONG WITH THIS ONE
CEASE ASSIMILAT—
SHING
AAAAAHH

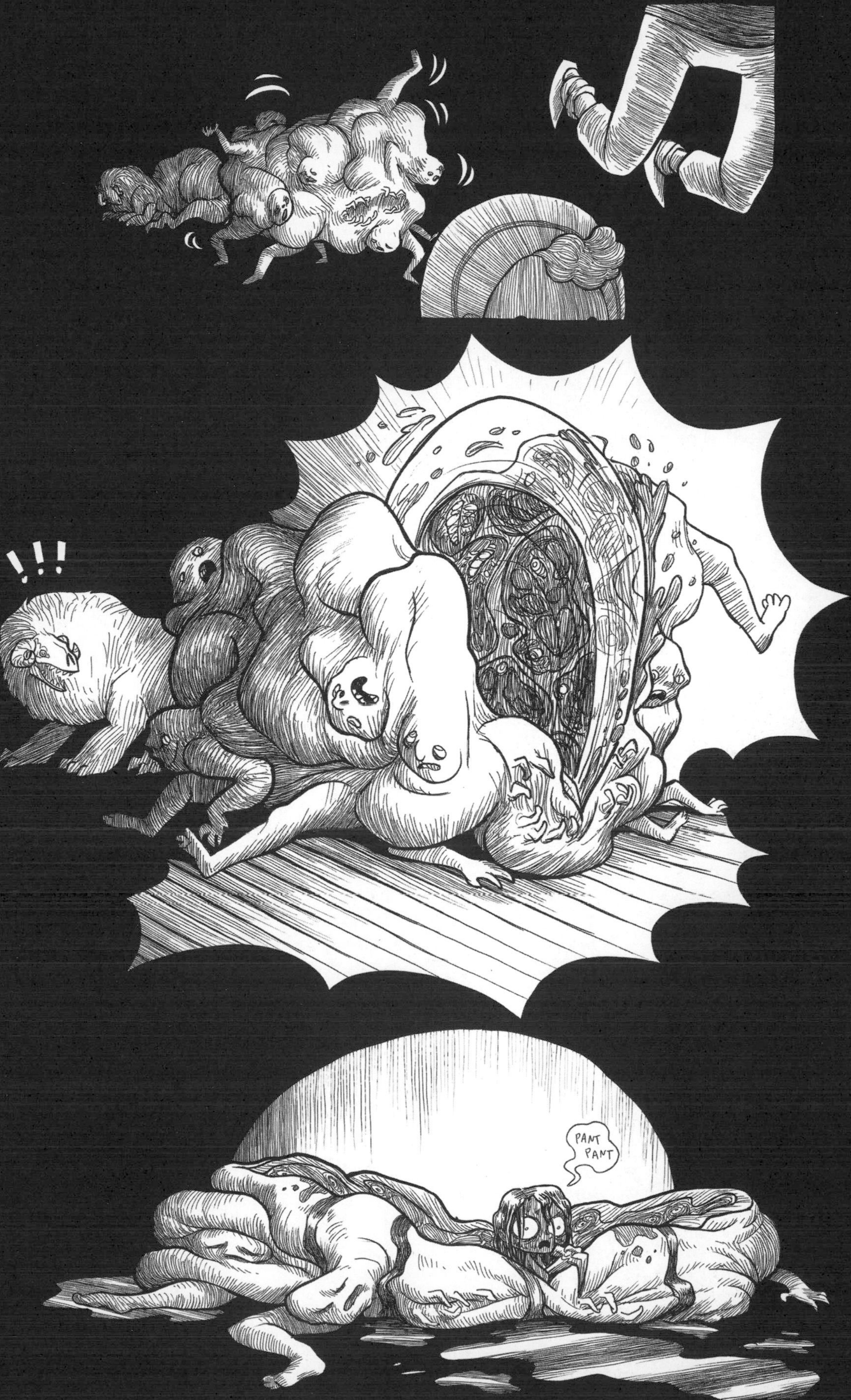
!!!
PANT PANT

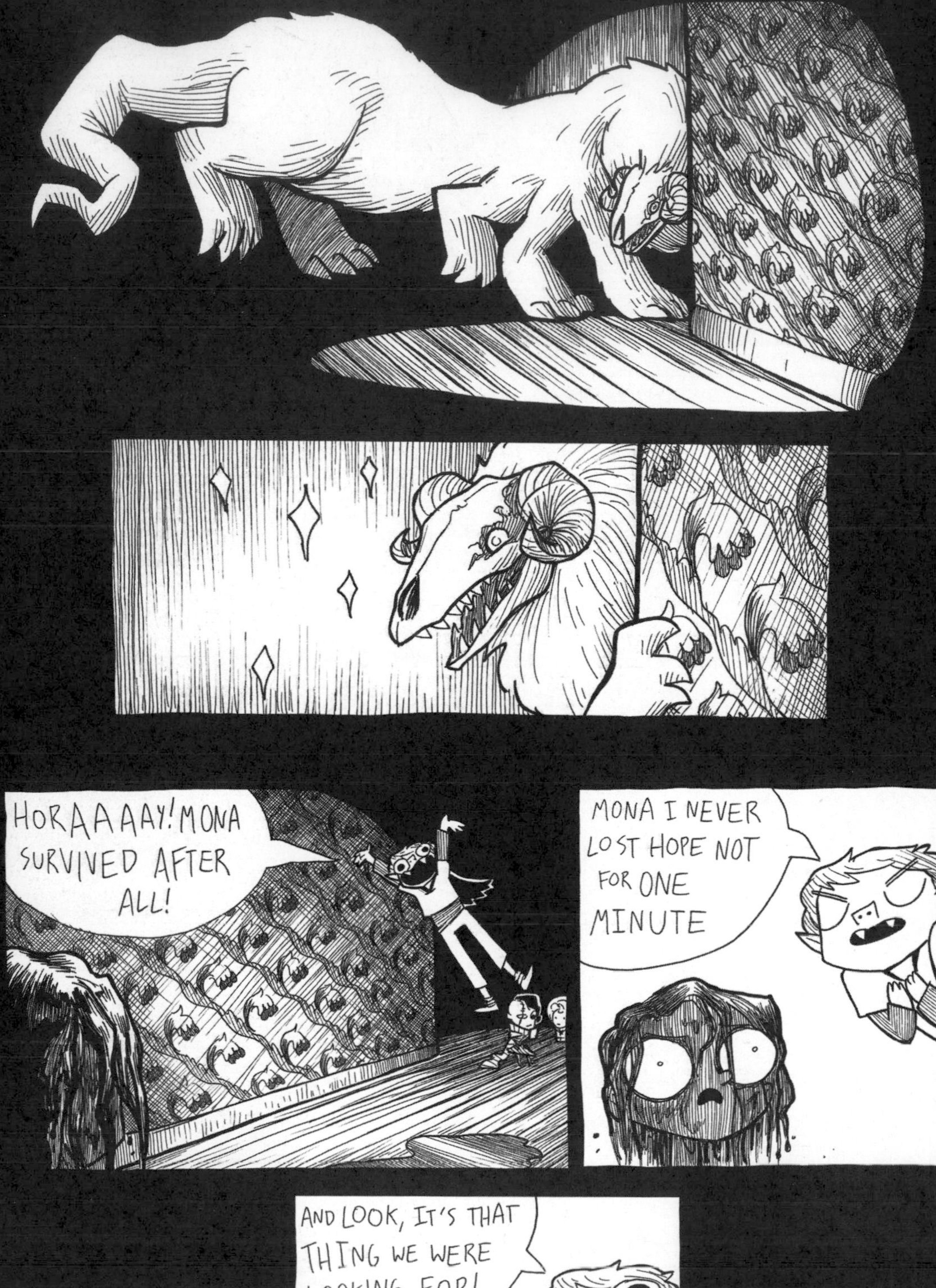
HORAAAAY! MONA SURVIVED AFTER ALL!
MONA I NEVER LOST HOPE NOT FOR ONE MINUTE
AND LOOK, IT'S THAT THING WE WERE LOOKING FOR!

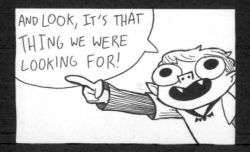

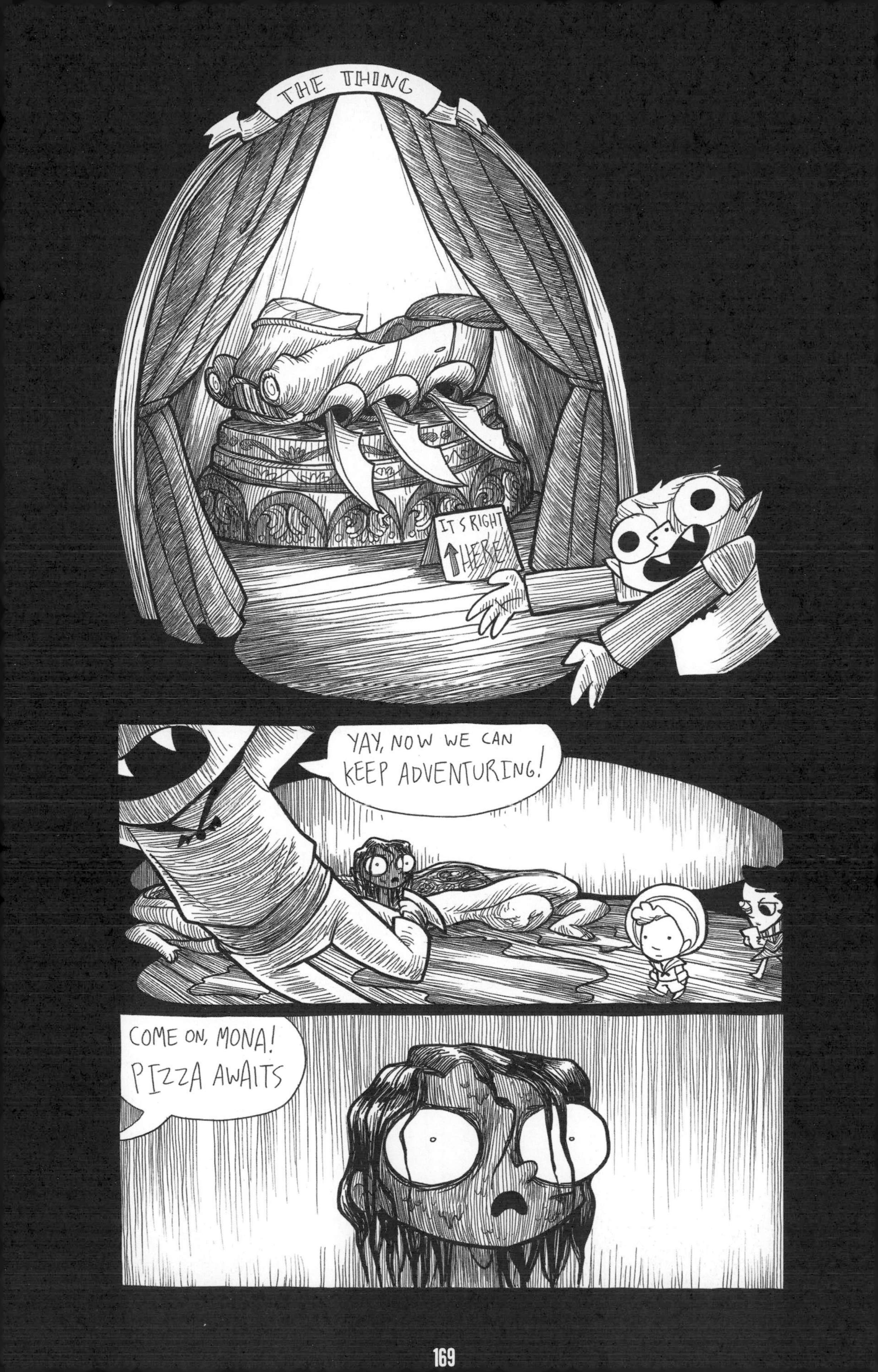
THE THING
IT'S RIGHT HERE!
YAY, NOW WE CAN KEEP ADVENTURING!
COME ON, MONA! PIZZA AWAITS

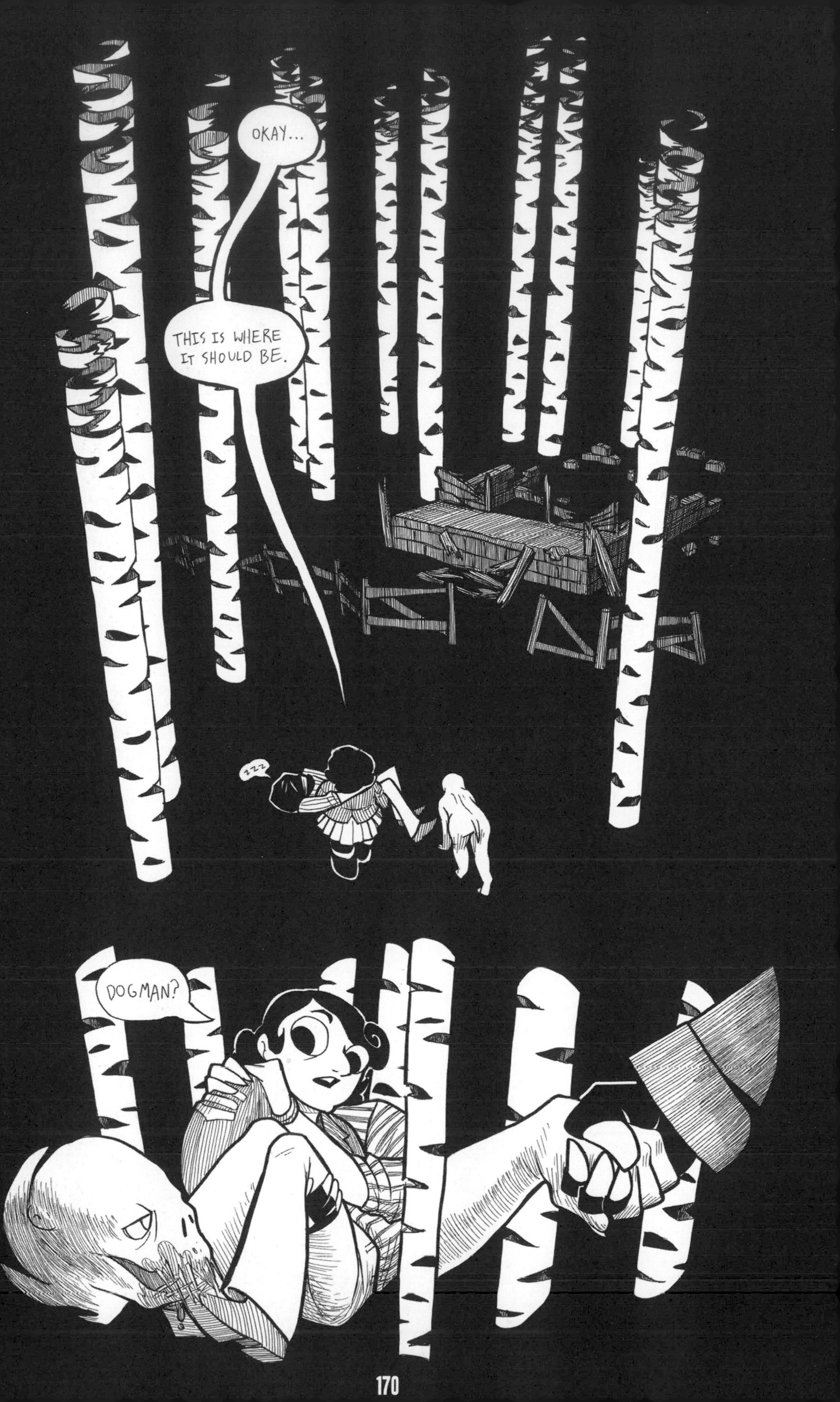
OKAY...
THIS IS WHERE IT SHOULD BE.
ZZZ
DOGMAN?

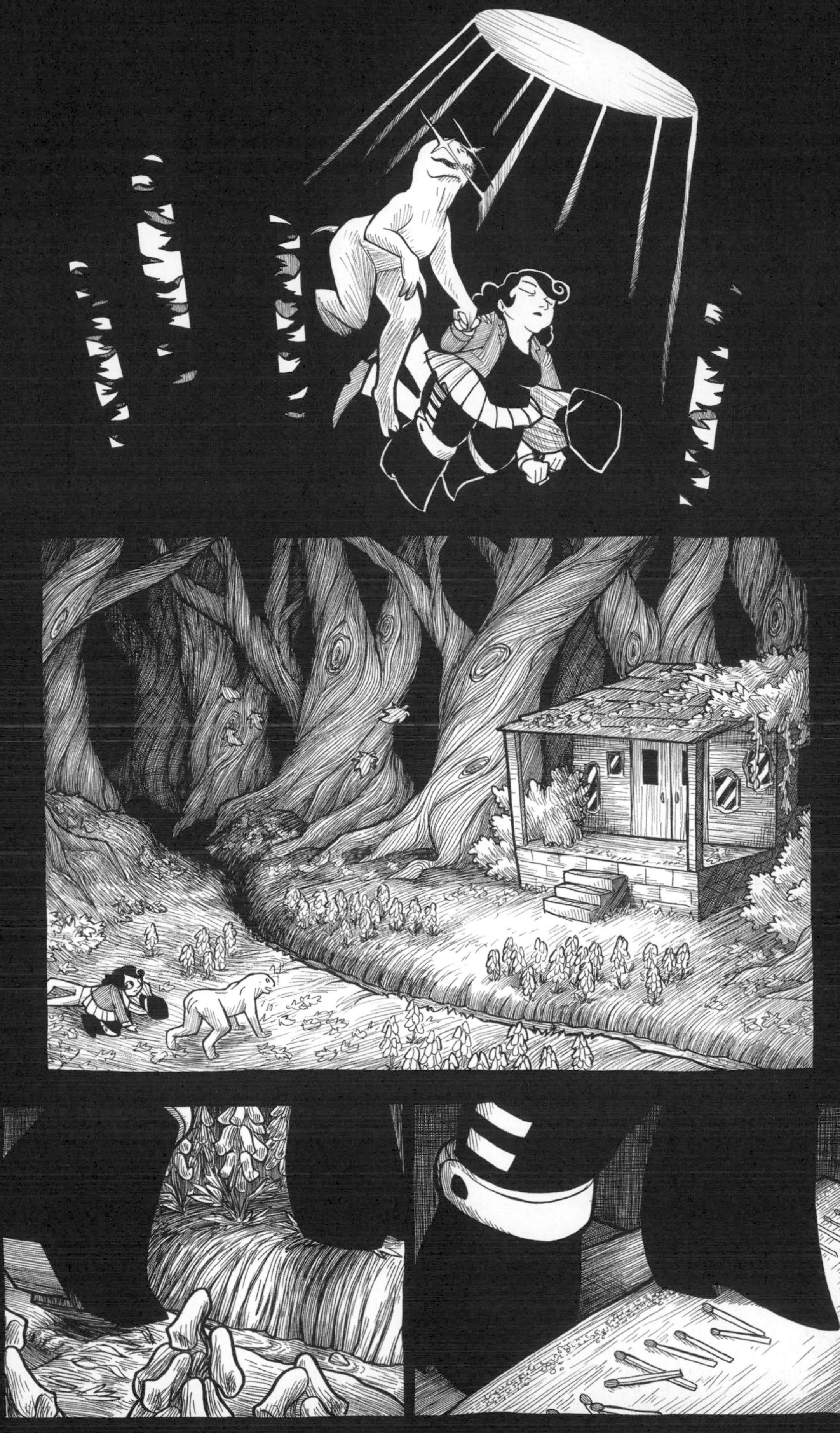

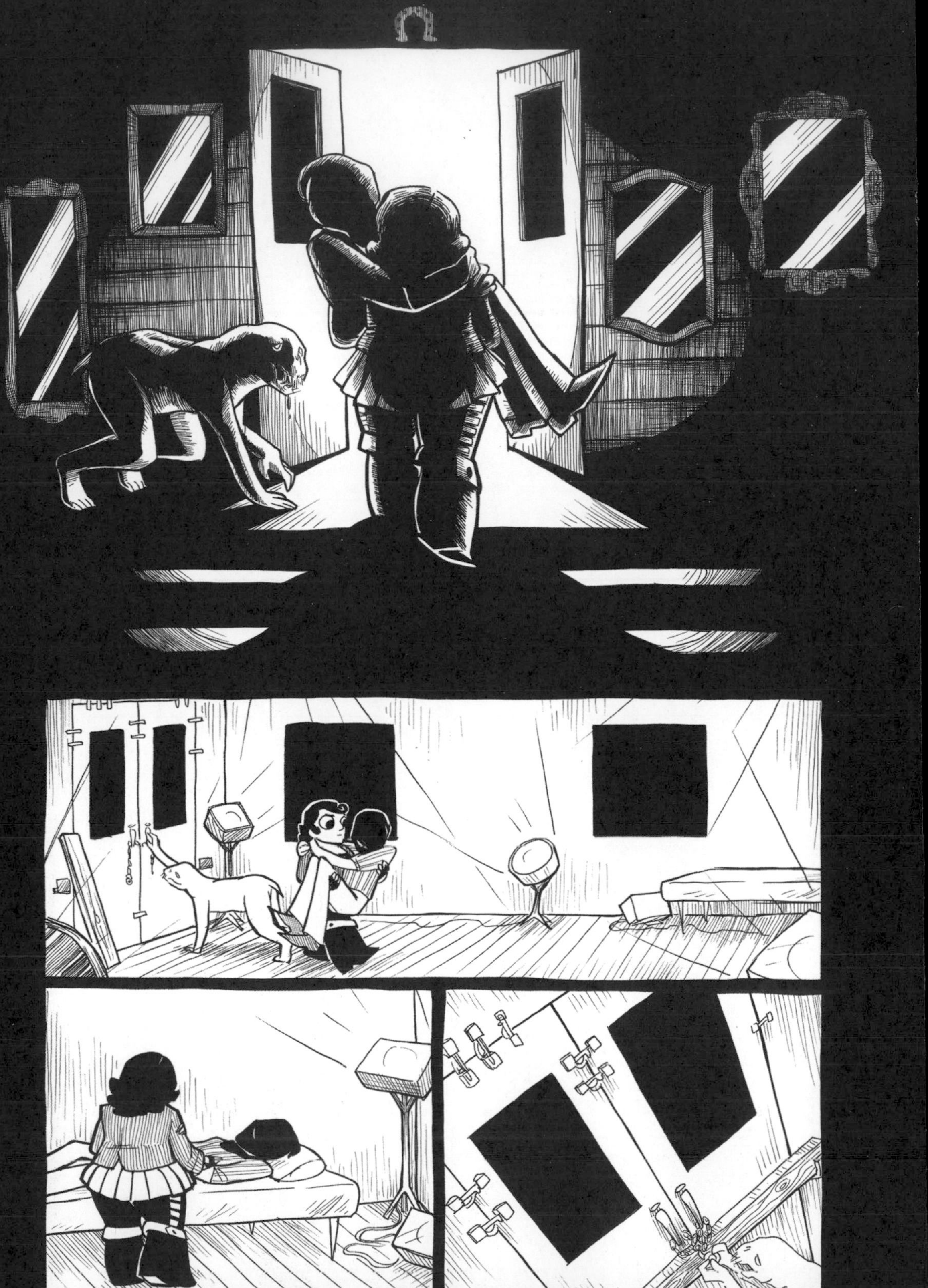

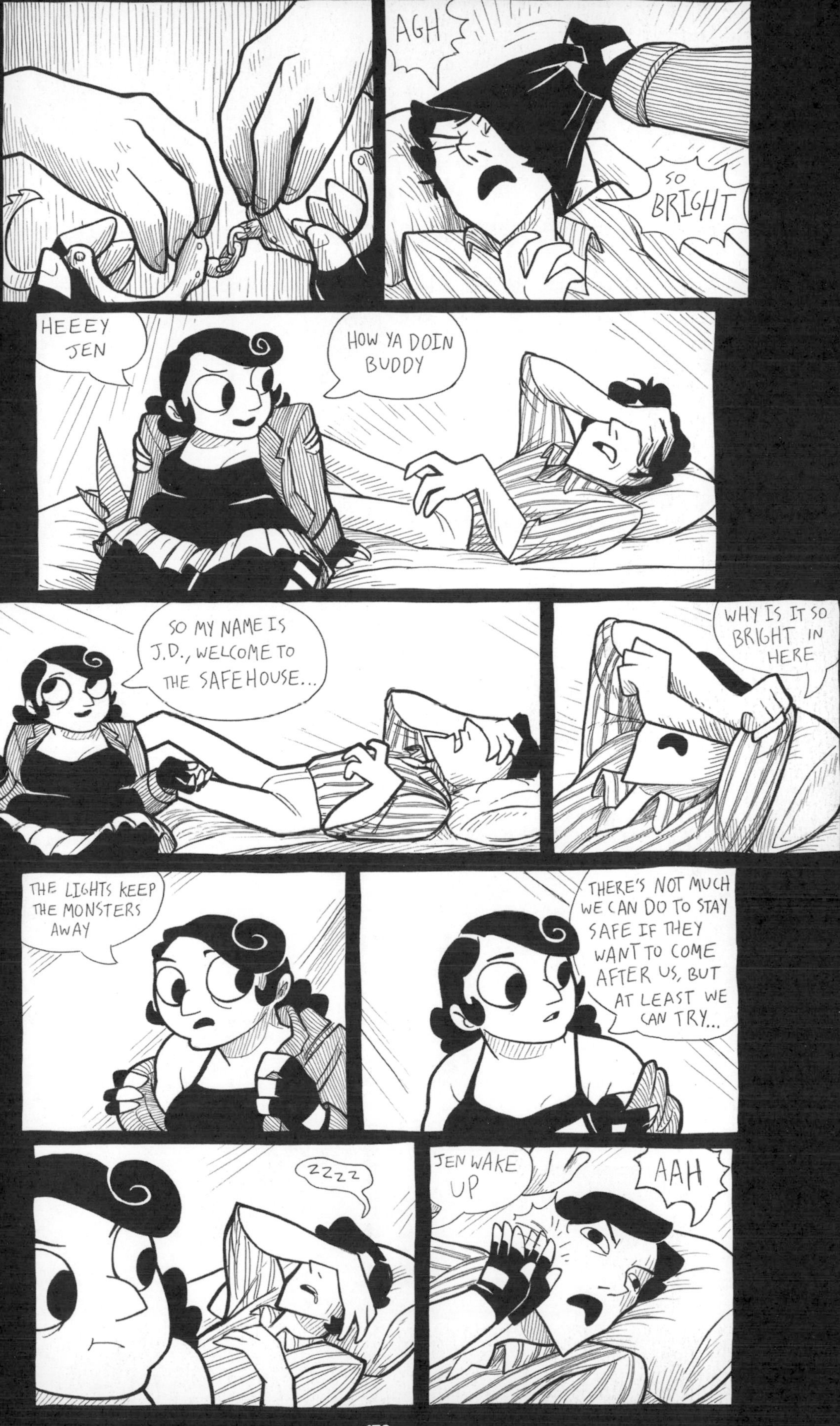
AGH
SO BRIGHT
HEEEY JEN
HOW YA DOIN BUDDY
SO MY NAME IS J.D., WELCOME TO THE SAFEHOUSE...
WHY IS IT SO BRIGHT IN HERE
THE LIGHTS KEEP THE MONSTERS AWAY
THERE'S NOT MUCH WE CAN DO TO STAY SAFE IF THEY WANT TO COME AFTER US, BUT AT LEAST WE CAN TRY...
ZZZZ
JEN WAKE UP
AAH

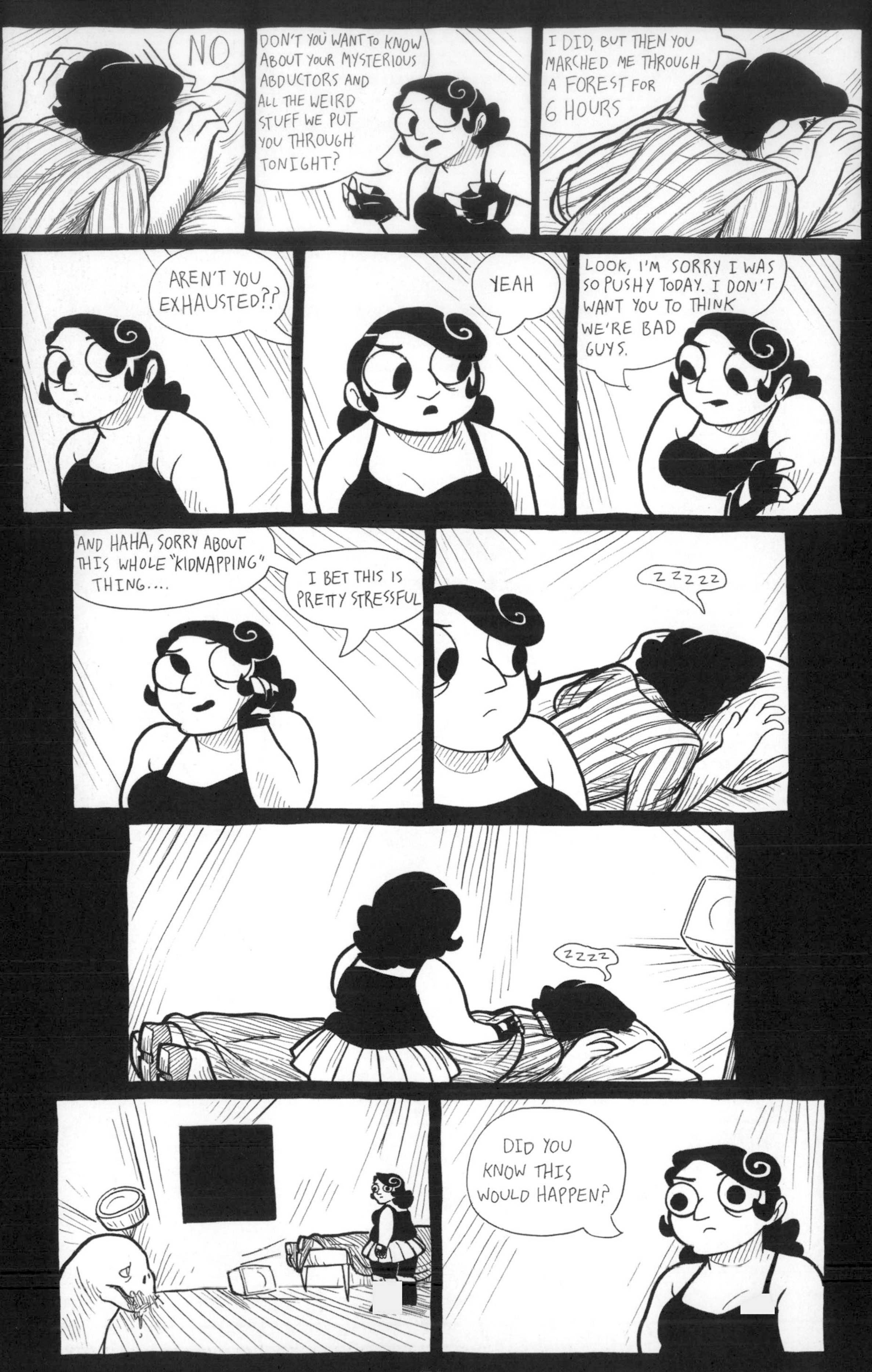
NO
DON'T YOU WANT TO KNOW ABOUT YOUR MYSTERIOUS ABDUCTORS AND ALL THE WEIRD STUFF WE PUT YOU THROUGH TONIGHT?
I DID, BUT THEN YOU MARCHED ME THROUGH A FOREST FOR 6 HOURS
AREN'T YOU EXHAUSTED??
YEAH
LOOK, I'M SORRY I WAS SO PUSHY TODAY. I DON'T WANT YOU TO THINK WE'RE BAD GUYS.
AND HAHA, SORRY ABOUT THIS WHOLE "KIDNAPPING" THING....
I BET THIS IS PRETTY STRESSFUL
ZZZZZ
ZZZZ
DID YOU KNOW THIS WOULD HAPPEN?

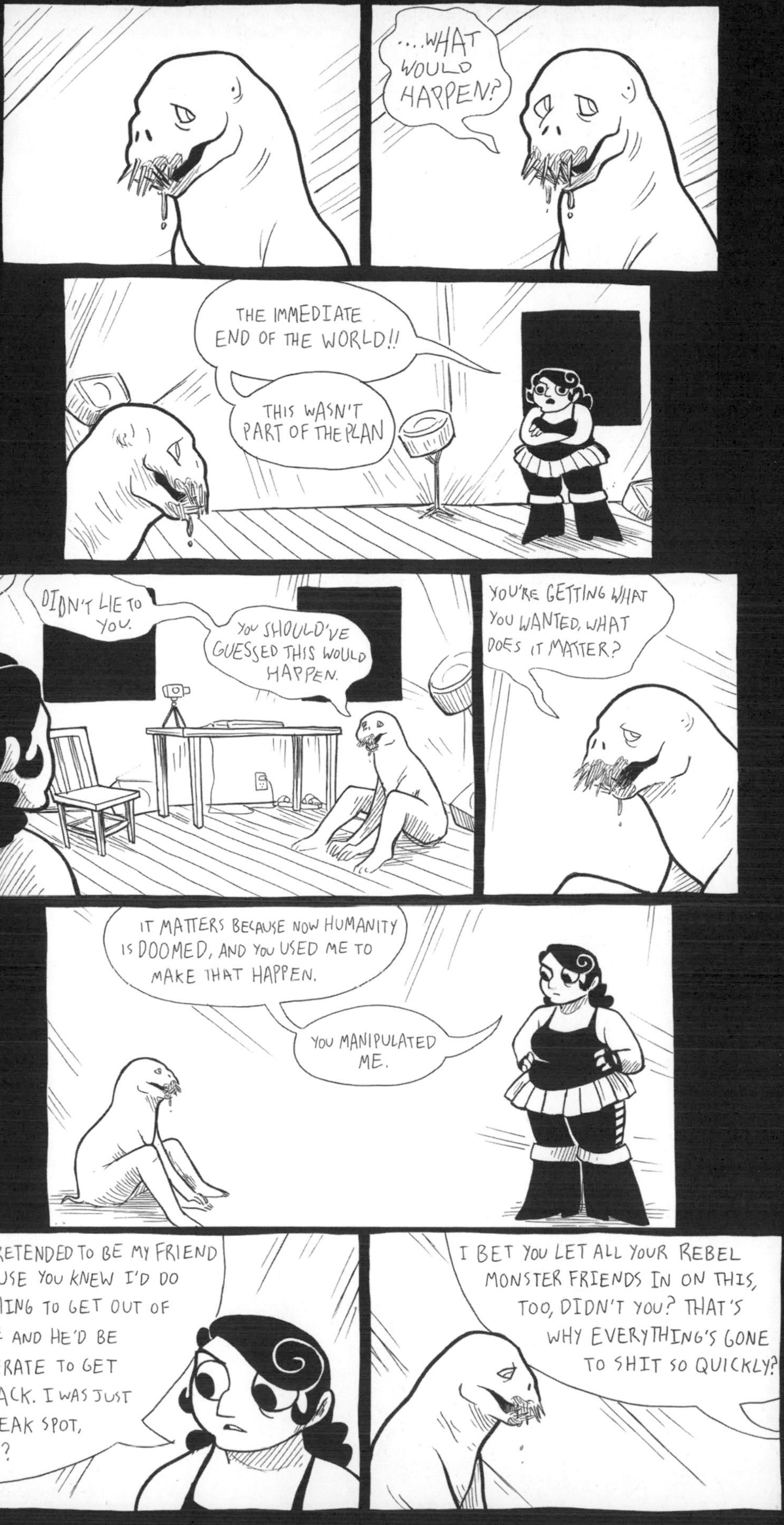

....WHAT WOULD HAPPEN?
THE IMMEDIATE END OF THE WORLD!!
THIS WASN'T PART OF THE PLAN
DIDN'T LIE TO YOU.
YOU SHOULD'VE GUESSED THIS WOULD HAPPEN.
YOU'RE GETTING WHAT YOU WANTED, WHAT DOES IT MATTER?
IT MATTERS BECAUSE NOW HUMANITY IS DOOMED, AND YOU USED ME TO MAKE THAT HAPPEN.
YOU MANIPULATED ME.
YOU PRETENDED TO BE MY FRIEND BECAUSE YOU KNEW I'D DO ANYTHING TO GET OUT OF THERE AND HE'D BE DESPERATE TO GET ME BACK. I WAS JUST HIS WEAK SPOT, HUH?
I BET YOU LET ALL YOUR REBEL MONSTER FRIENDS IN ON THIS, TOO, DIDN'T YOU? THAT'S WHY EVERYTHING'S GONE TO SHIT SO QUICKLY?

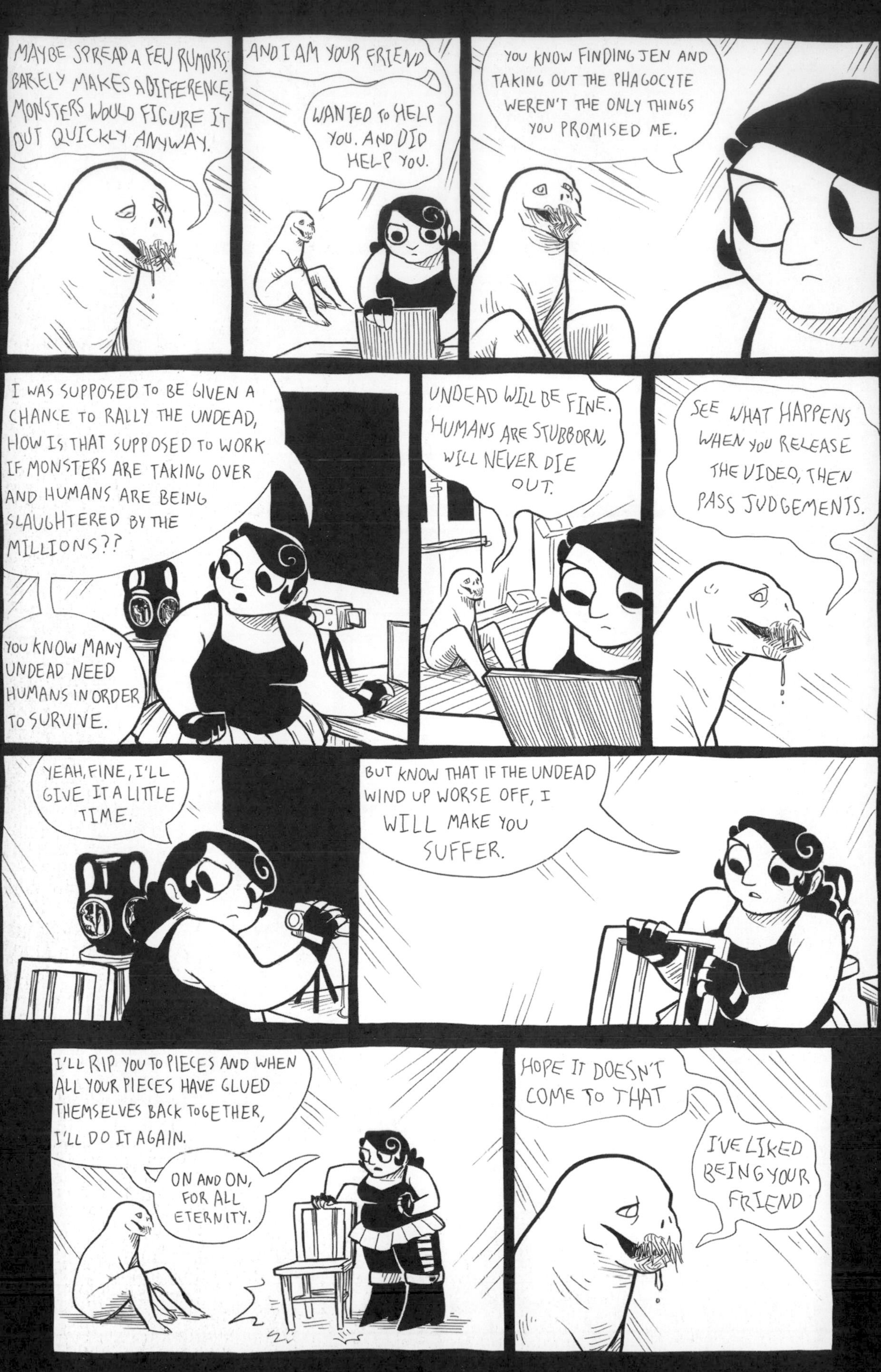
MAYBE SPREAD A FEW RUMORS: BARELY MAKES A DIFFERENCE; MONSTERS WOULD FIGURE IT OUT QUICKLY ANYWAY.
AND I AM YOUR FRIEND
WANTED TO HELP YOU. AND DID HELP YOU.
YOU KNOW FINDING JEN AND TAKING OUT THE PHAGOCYTE WEREN'T THE ONLY THINGS YOU PROMISED ME.
I WAS SUPPOSED TO BE GIVEN A CHANCE TO RALLY THE UNDEAD, HOW IS THAT SUPPOSED TO WORK IF MONSTERS ARE TAKING OVER AND HUMANS ARE BEING SLAUGHTERED BY THE MILLIONS??
YOU KNOW MANY UNDEAD NEED HUMANS IN ORDER TO SURVIVE.
UNDEAD WILL BE FINE. HUMANS ARE STUBBORN, WILL NEVER DIE OUT.
SEE WHAT HAPPENS WHEN YOU RELEASE THE VIDEO, THEN PASS JUDGEMENTS.
YEAH, FINE, I'LL GIVE IT A LITTLE TIME.
BUT KNOW THAT IF THE UNDEAD WIND UP WORSE OFF, I WILL MAKE YOU SUFFER.
I'LL RIP YOU TO PIECES AND WHEN ALL YOUR PIECES HAVE GLUED THEMSELVES BACK TOGETHER, I'LL DO IT AGAIN.
ON AND ON, FOR ALL ETERNITY.
HOPE IT DOESN'T COME TO THAT
I'VE LIKED BEING YOUR FRIEND

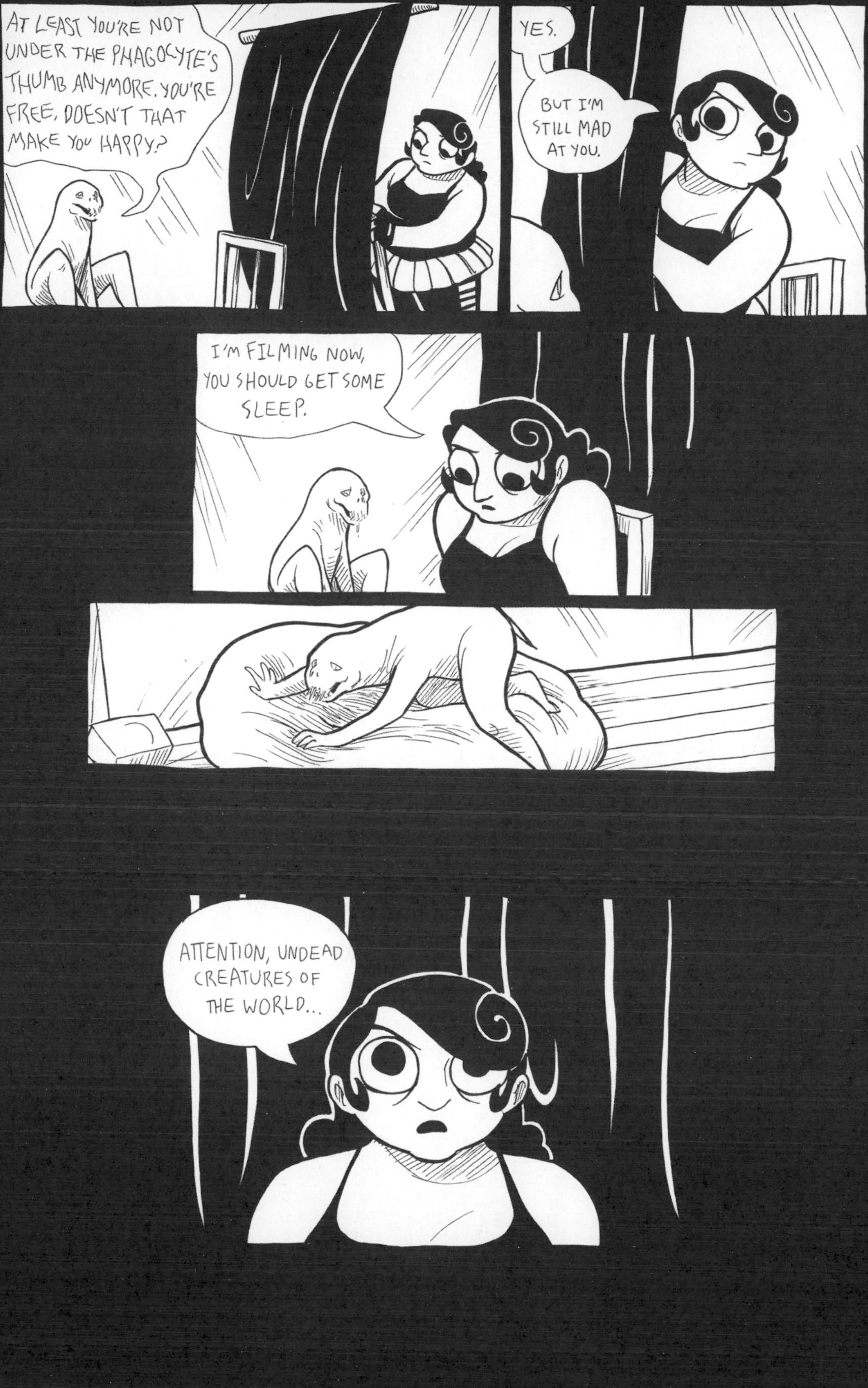
AT LEAST YOU'RE NOT UNDER THE PHAGOCYTE'S THUMB ANYMORE. YOU'RE FREE, DOESN'T THAT MAKE YOU HAPPY?
YES.
BUT I'M STILL MAD AT YOU.
I'M FILMING NOW, YOU SHOULD GET SOME SLEEP.
ATTENTION, UNDEAD CREATURES OF THE WORLD...

CHAPTER 4

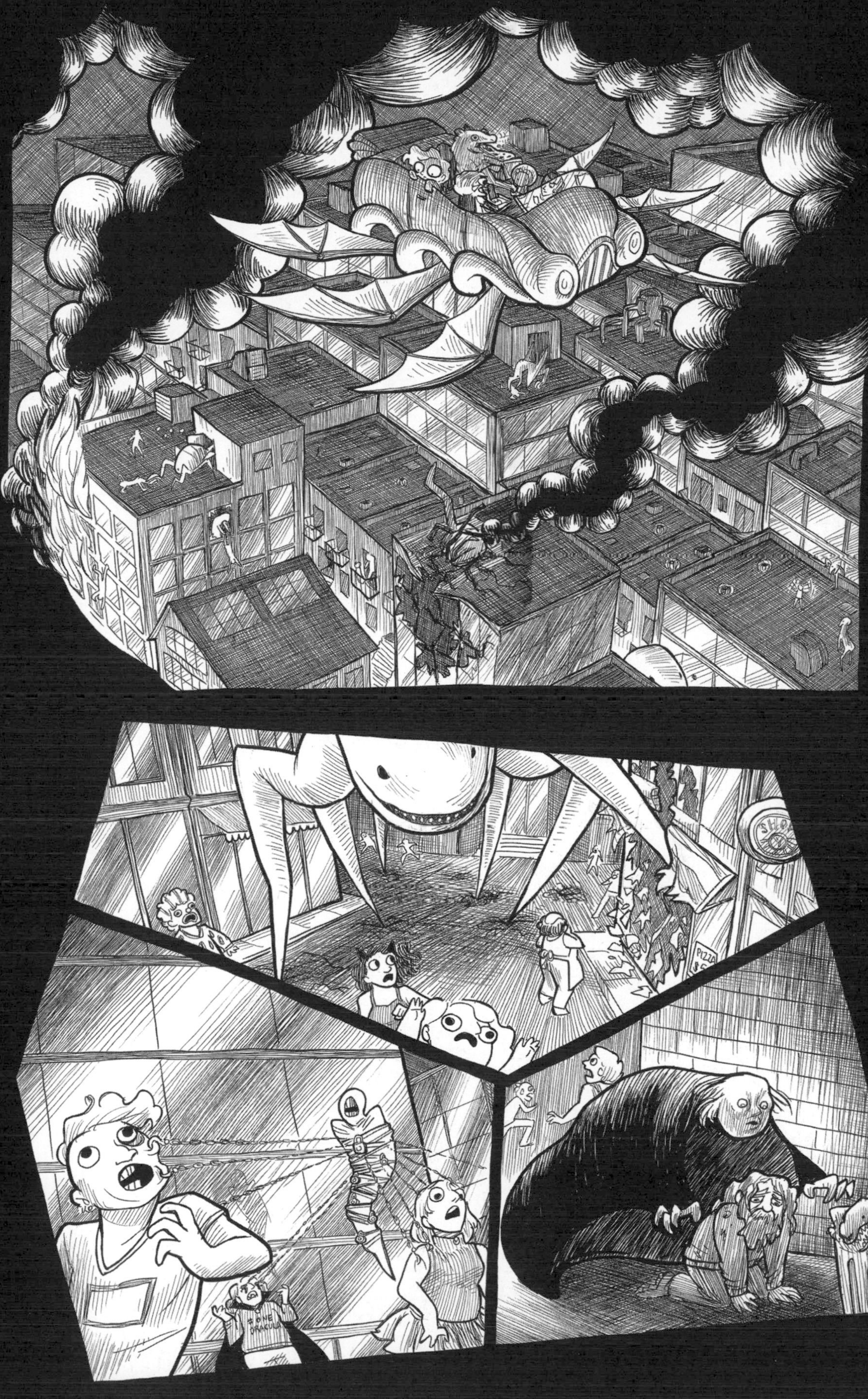
PIZZA
#ONE DRACULA

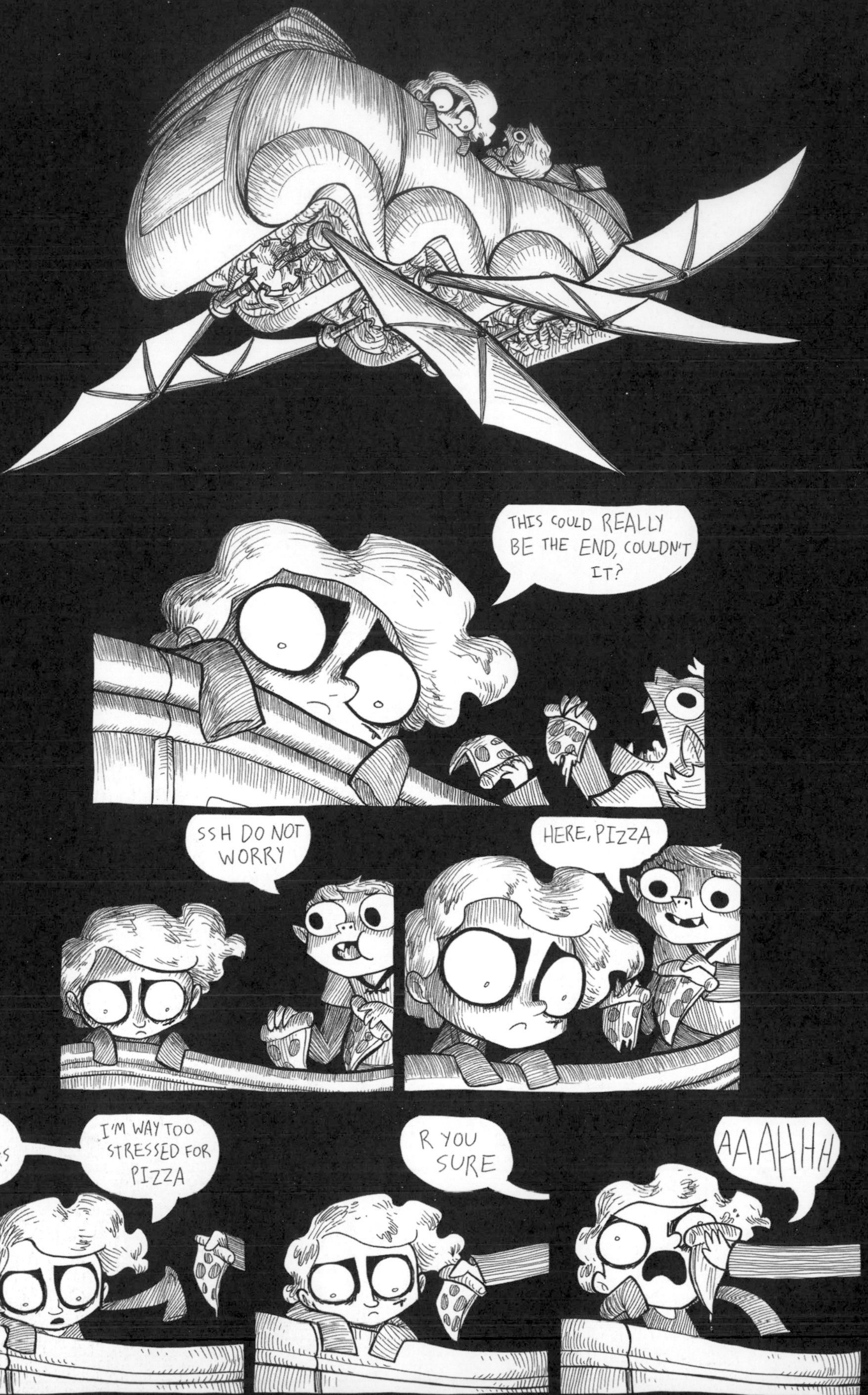
THIS COULD REALLY BE THE END, COULDN'T IT?
SSH DO NOT WORRY
HERE, PIZZA
NO THANKS
I'M WAY TOO STRESSED FOR PIZZA
R YOU SURE
AAAHHH

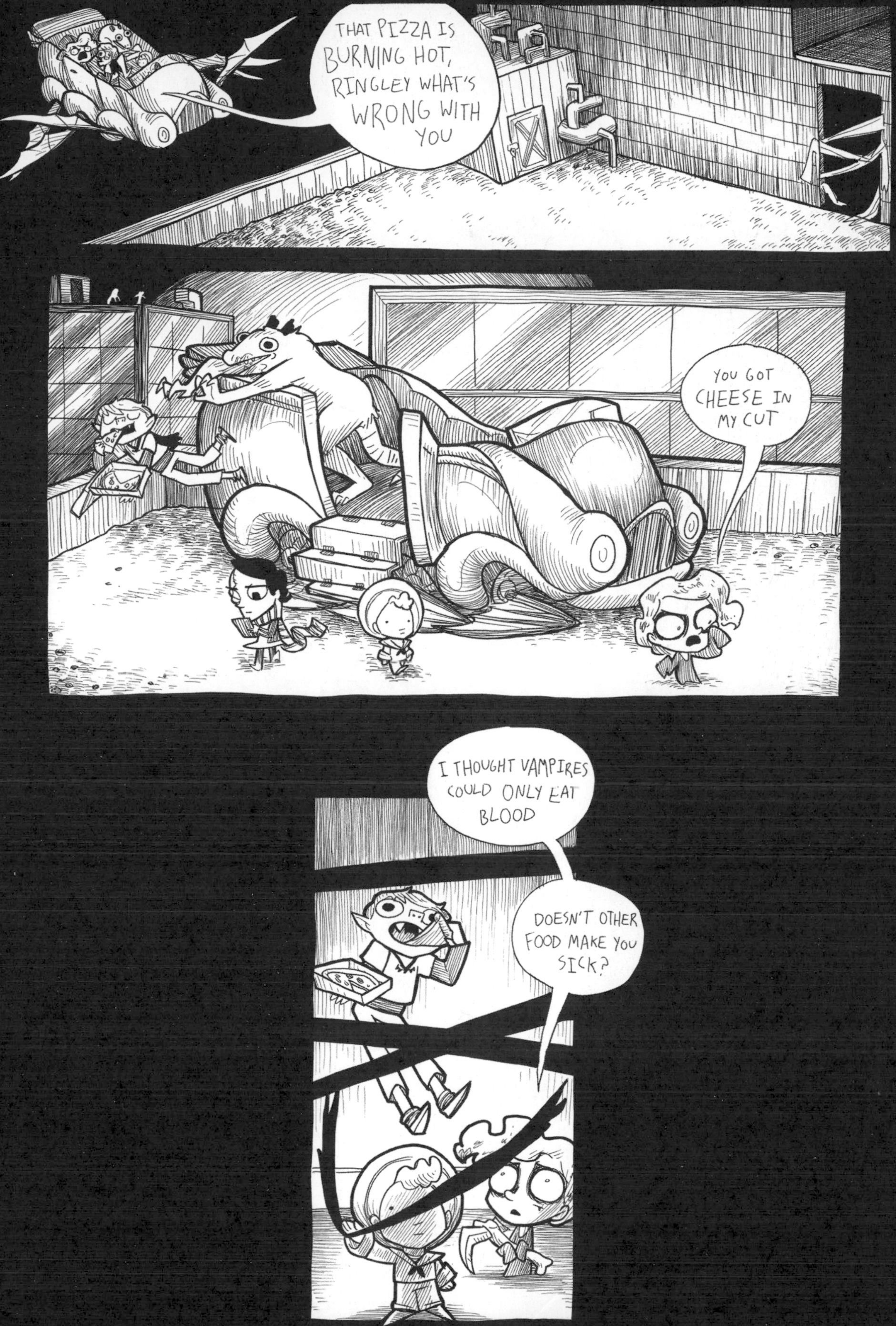
THAT PIZZA IS BURNING HOT, RINGLEY WHAT'S WRONG WITH YOU
YOU GOT CHEESE IN MY CUT
I THOUGHT VAMPIRES COULD ONLY EAT BLOOD
DOESN'T OTHER FOOD MAKE YOU SICK?

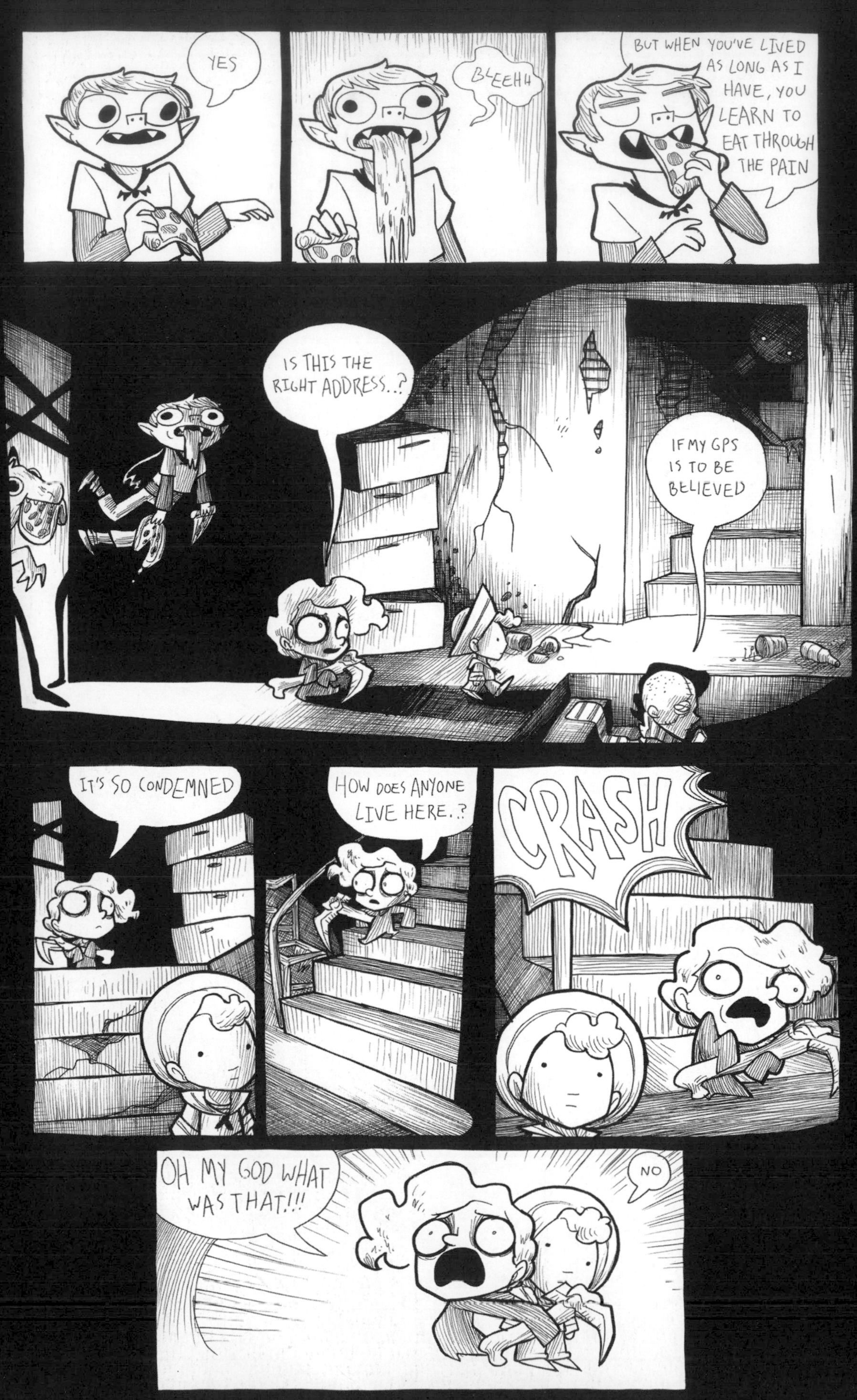
YES
BLEEHH
BUT WHEN YOU'VE LIVED AS LONG AS I HAVE, YOU LEARN TO EAT THROUGH THE PAIN
IS THIS THE RIGHT ADDRESS..?
IF MY GPS IS TO BE BELIEVED
IT'S SO CONDEMNED
HOW DOES ANYONE LIVE HERE..?
CRASH
OH MY GOD WHAT WAS THAT!!!
NO

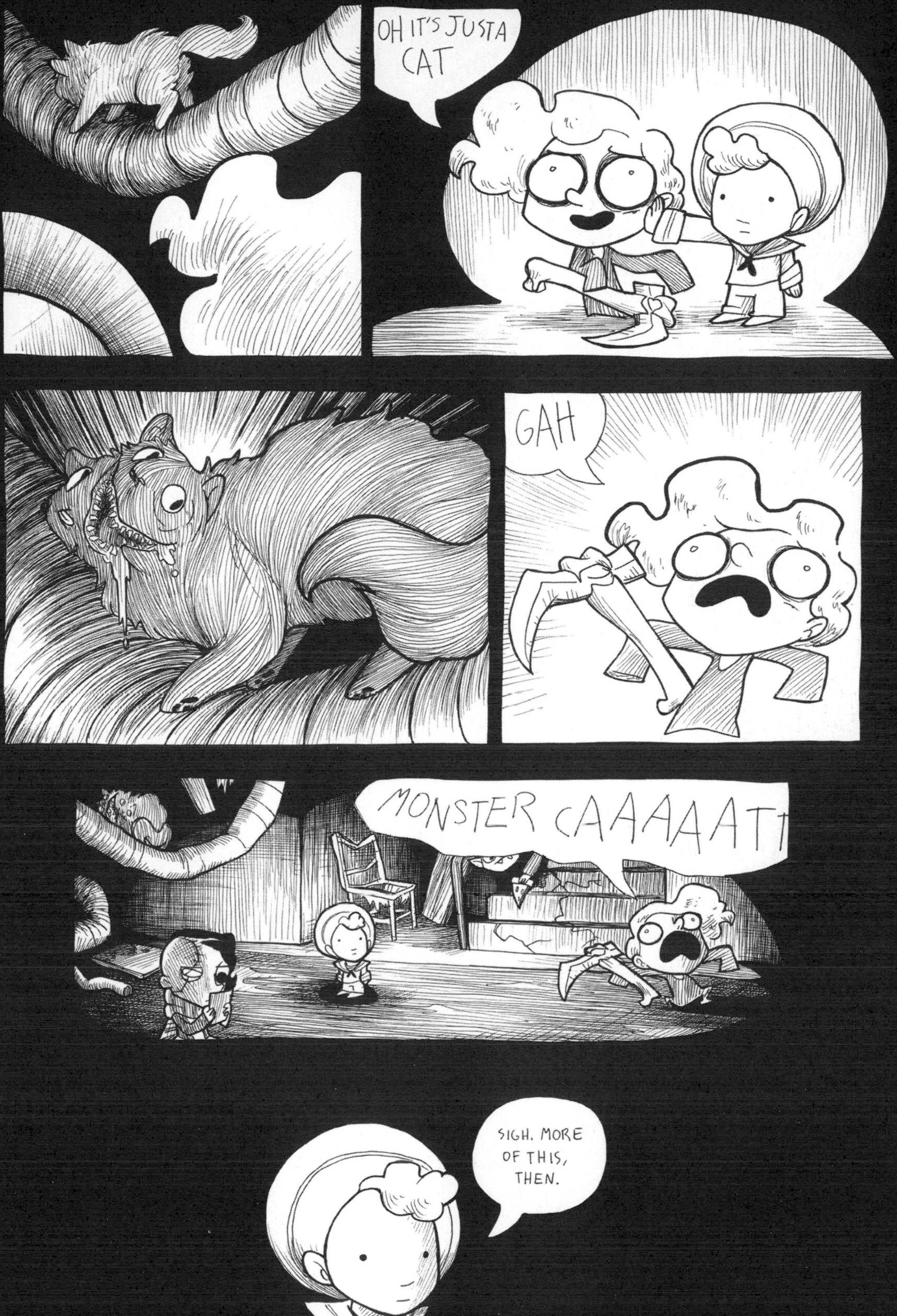
OH IT'S JUSTA CAT
GAH
MONSTER CAAAAATT
SIGH. MORE OF THIS, THEN.

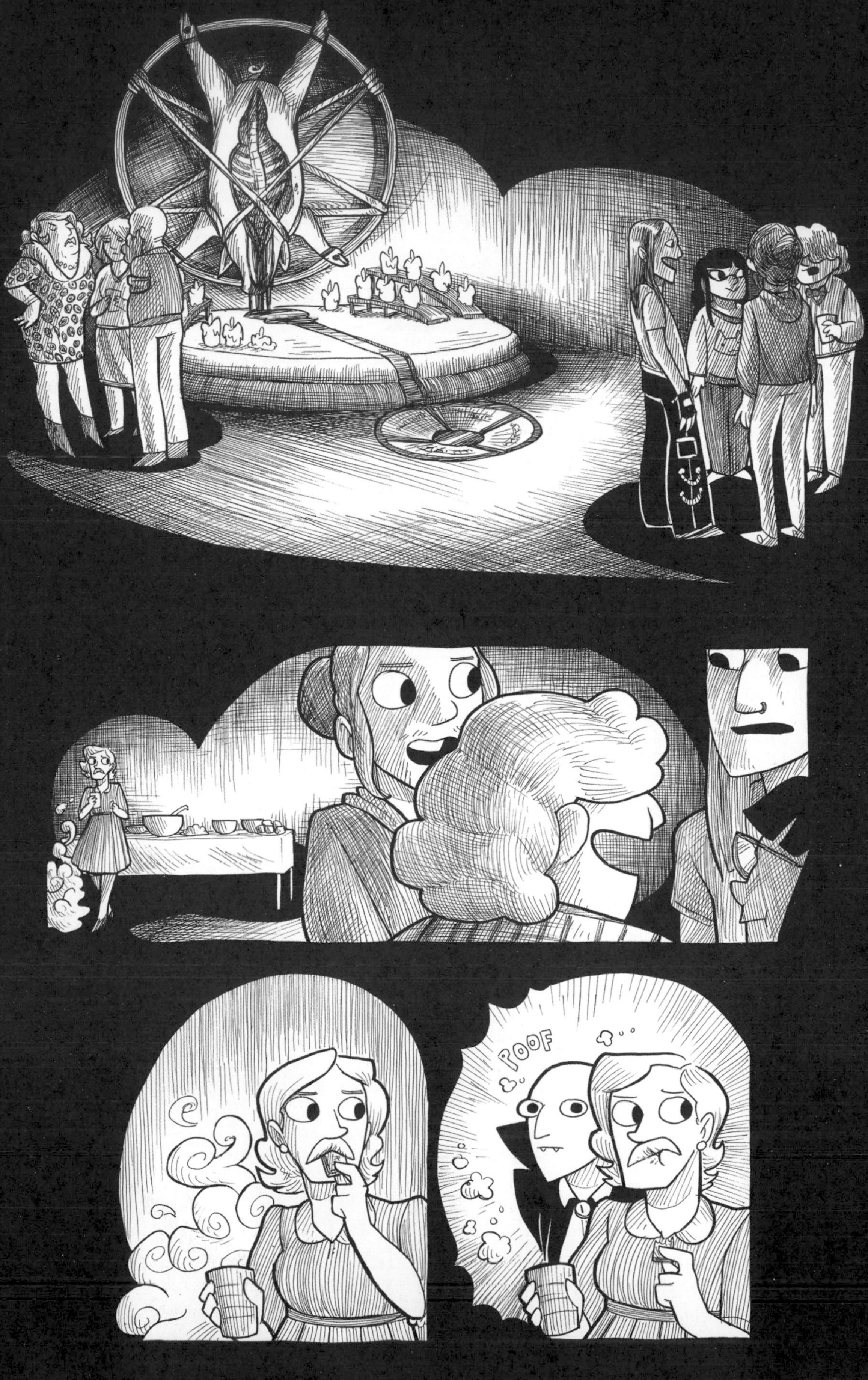
POOF

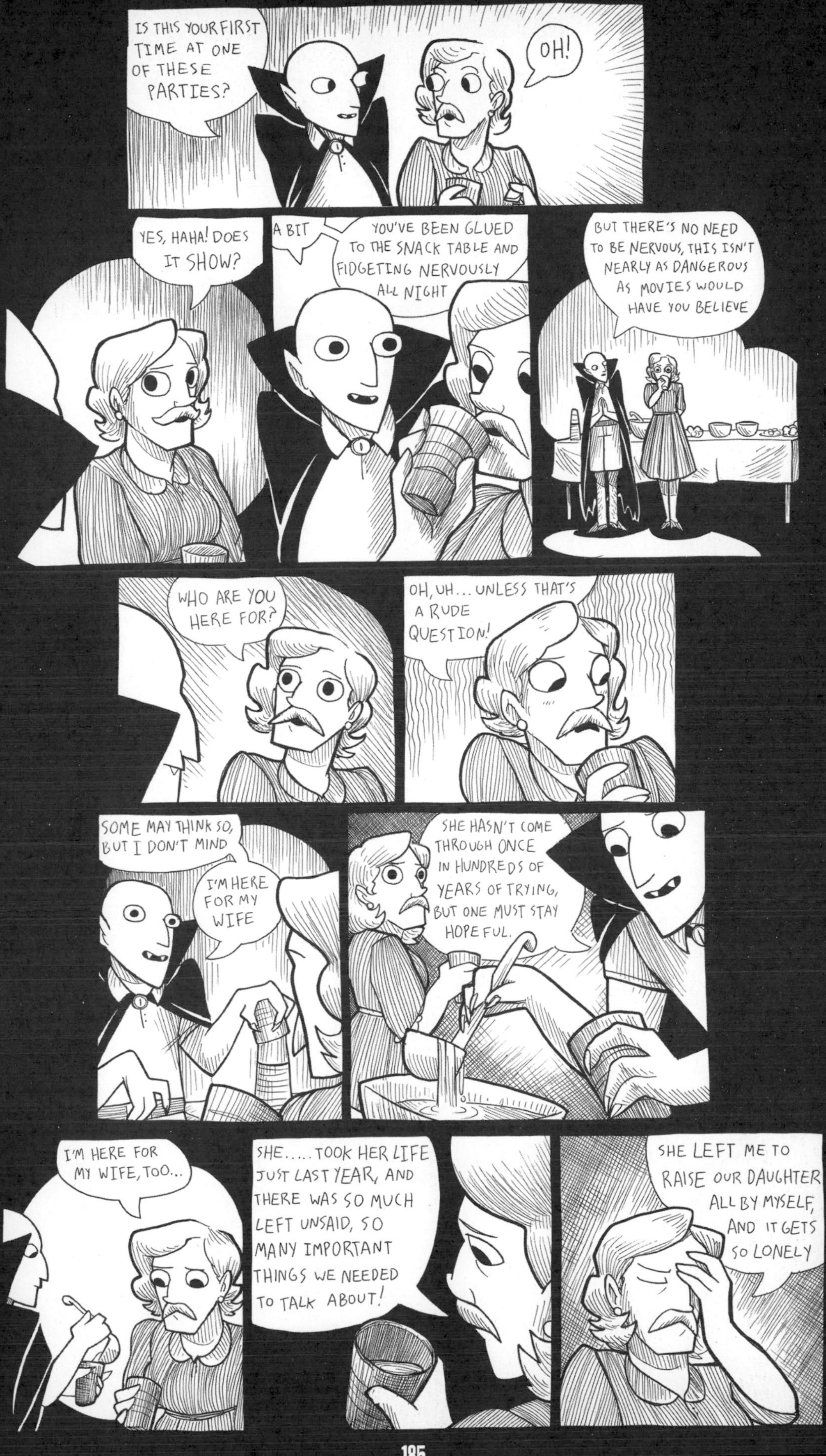
IS THIS YOUR FIRST TIME AT ONE OF THESE PARTIES?
OH!
YES, HAHA! DOES IT SHOW?
A BIT
YOU'VE BEEN GLUED TO THE SNACK TABLE AND FIDGETING NERVOUSLY ALL NIGHT
BUT THERE'S NO NEED TO BE NERVOUS, THIS ISN'T NEARLY AS DANGEROUS AS MOVIES WOULD HAVE YOU BELIEVE
WHO ARE YOU HERE FOR?
OH, UH... UNLESS THAT'S A RUDE QUESTION!
SOME MAY THINK SO, BUT I DON'T MIND
I'M HERE FOR MY WIFE
SHE HASN'T COME THROUGH ONCE IN HUNDREDS OF YEARS OF TRYING, BUT ONE MUST STAY HOPEFUL.
I'M HERE FOR MY WIFE, TOO...
SHE..... TOOK HER LIFE JUST LAST YEAR, AND THERE WAS SO MUCH LEFT UNSAID, SO MANY IMPORTANT THINGS WE NEEDED TO TALK ABOUT!
SHE LEFT ME TO RAISE OUR DAUGHTER ALL BY MYSELF, AND IT GETS SO LONELY

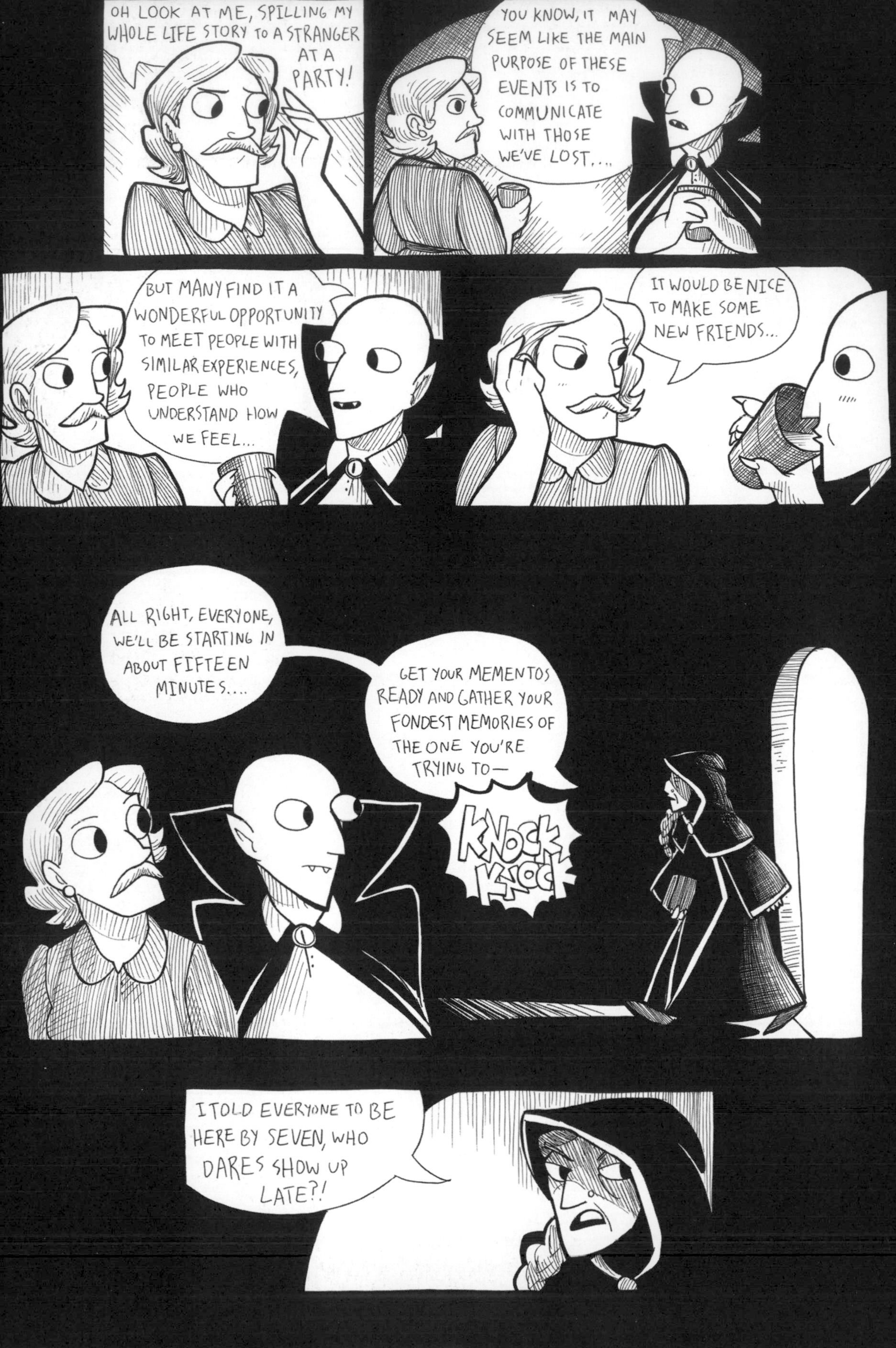
OH LOOK AT ME, SPILLING MY WHOLE LIFE STORY TO A STRANGER AT A PARTY!
YOU KNOW, IT MAY SEEM LIKE THE MAIN PURPOSE OF THESE EVENTS IS TO COMMUNICATE WITH THOSE WE'VE LOST....
BUT MANY FIND IT A WONDERFUL OPPORTUNITY TO MEET PEOPLE WITH SIMILAR EXPERIENCES, PEOPLE WHO UNDERSTAND HOW WE FEEL...
IT WOULD BE NICE TO MAKE SOME NEW FRIENDS...
ALL RIGHT, EVERYONE, WE'LL BE STARTING IN ABOUT FIFTEEN MINUTES....
GET YOUR MEMENTOS READY AND GATHER YOUR FONDEST MEMORIES OF THE ONE YOU'RE TRYING TO—
KNOCK KNOCK
I TOLD EVERYONE TO BE HERE BY SEVEN, WHO DARES SHOW UP LATE?!

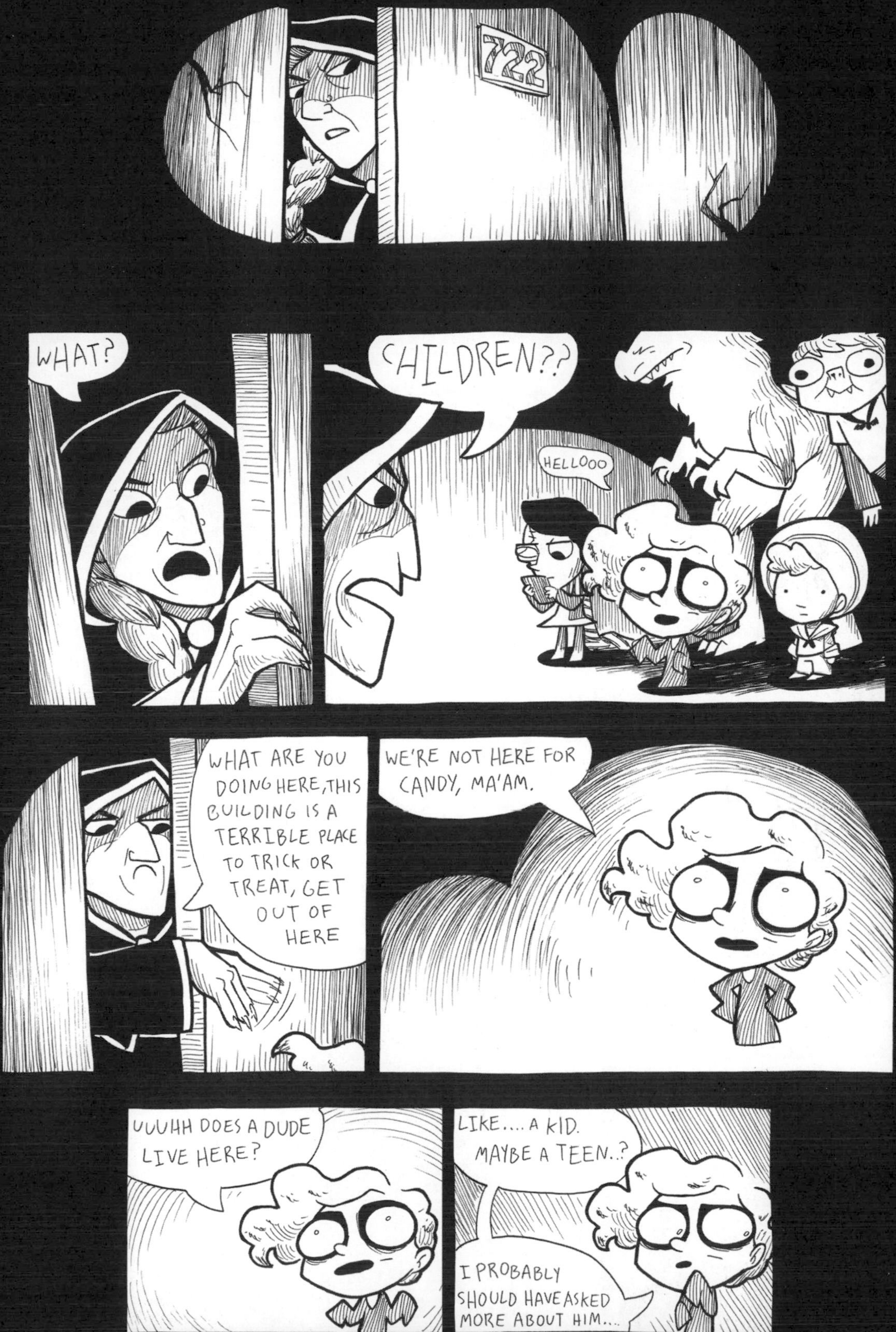
722
WHAT?
CHILDREN??
HELLOOO
WHAT ARE YOU DOING HERE, THIS BUILDING IS A TERRIBLE PLACE TO TRICK OR TREAT, GET OUT OF HERE
WE'RE NOT HERE FOR CANDY, MA'AM.
UUUHH DOES A DUDE LIVE HERE?
LIKE.... A KID. MAYBE A TEEN..?
I PROBABLY SHOULD HAVE ASKED MORE ABOUT HIM...

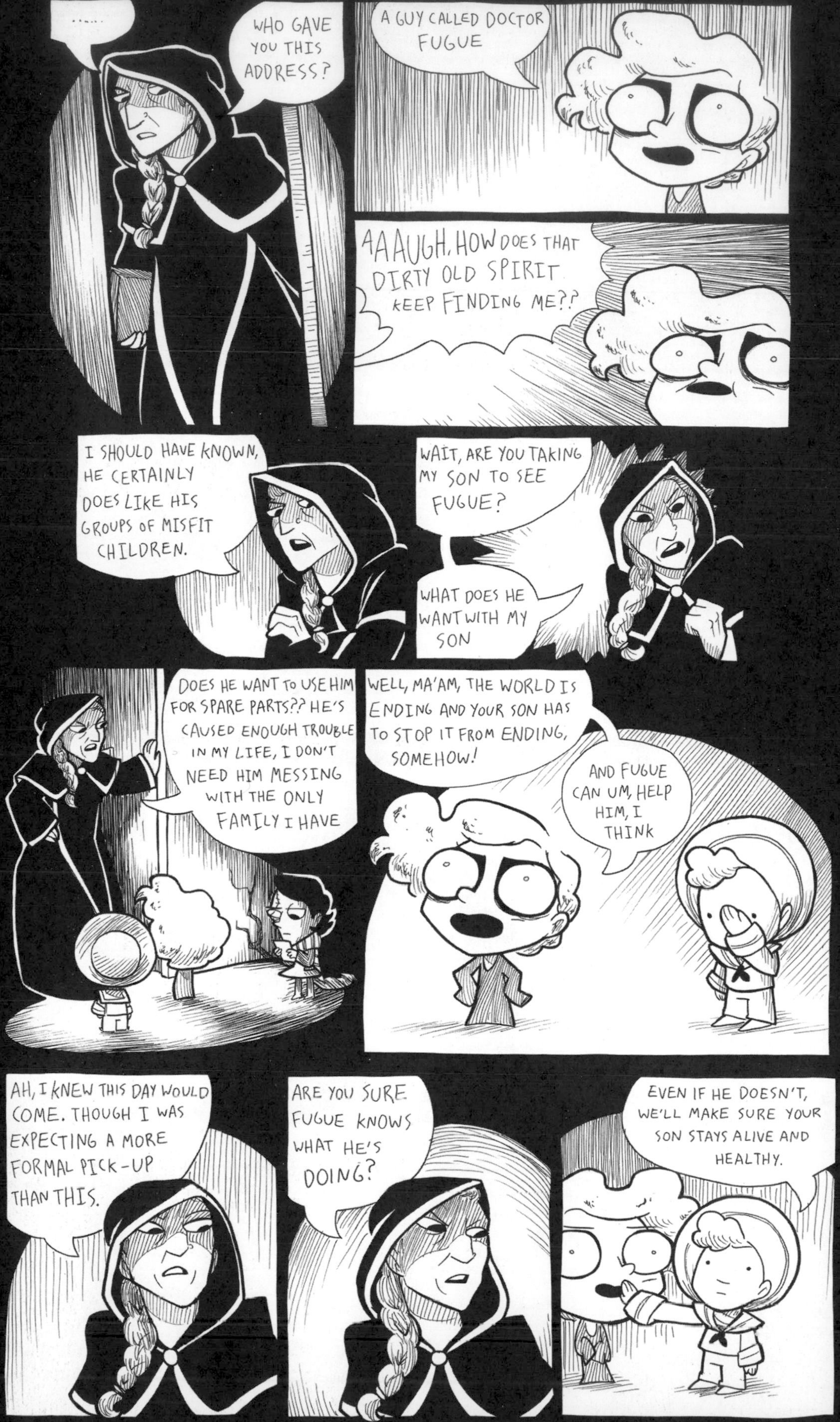
......
WHO GAVE YOU THIS ADDRESS?
A GUY CALLED DOCTOR FUGUE
AAAUGH, HOW DOES THAT DIRTY OLD SPIRIT KEEP FINDING ME??
I SHOULD HAVE KNOWN, HE CERTAINLY DOES LIKE HIS GROUPS OF MISFIT CHILDREN.
WAIT, ARE YOU TAKING MY SON TO SEE FUGUE?
WHAT DOES HE WANT WITH MY SON
DOES HE WANT TO USE HIM FOR SPARE PARTS?? HE'S CAUSED ENOUGH TROUBLE IN MY LIFE, I DON'T NEED HIM MESSING WITH THE ONLY FAMILY I HAVE
WELL, MA'AM, THE WORLD IS ENDING AND YOUR SON HAS TO STOP IT FROM ENDING, SOMEHOW!
AND FUGUE CAN UM, HELP HIM, I THINK
AH, I KNEW THIS DAY WOULD COME. THOUGH I WAS EXPECTING A MORE FORMAL PICK-UP THAN THIS.
ARE YOU SURE FUGUE KNOWS WHAT HE'S DOING?
EVEN IF HE DOESN'T, WE'LL MAKE SURE YOUR SON STAYS ALIVE AND HEALTHY.

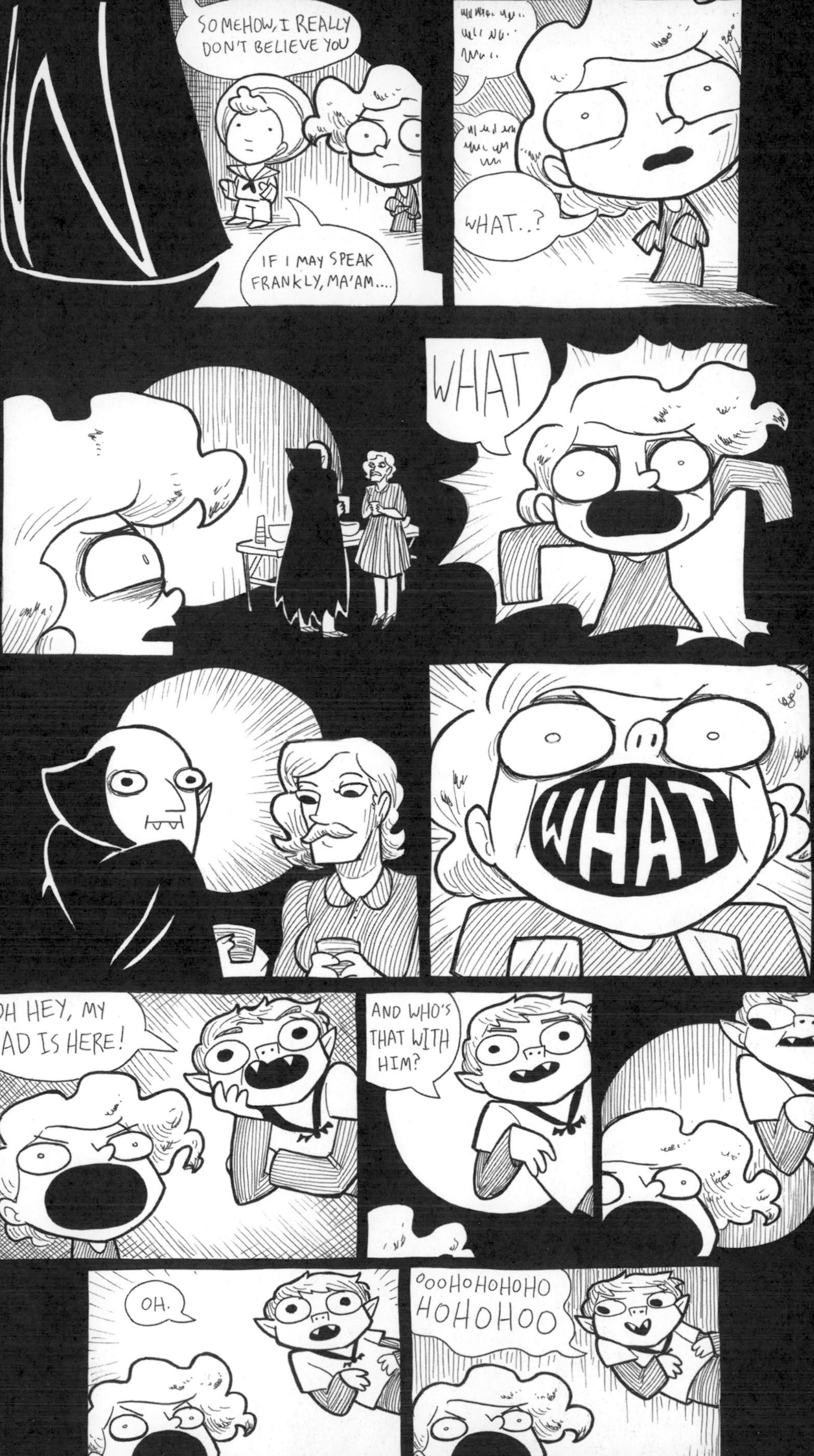
SOMEHOW, I REALLY DON'T BELIEVE YOU
IF I MAY SPEAK FRANKLY, MA'AM....
WHAT..?
WHAT
WHAT
OH HEY, MY DAD IS HERE!
AND WHO'S THAT WITH HIM?
OH.
OOOHOHOHOHO HOHOHOO

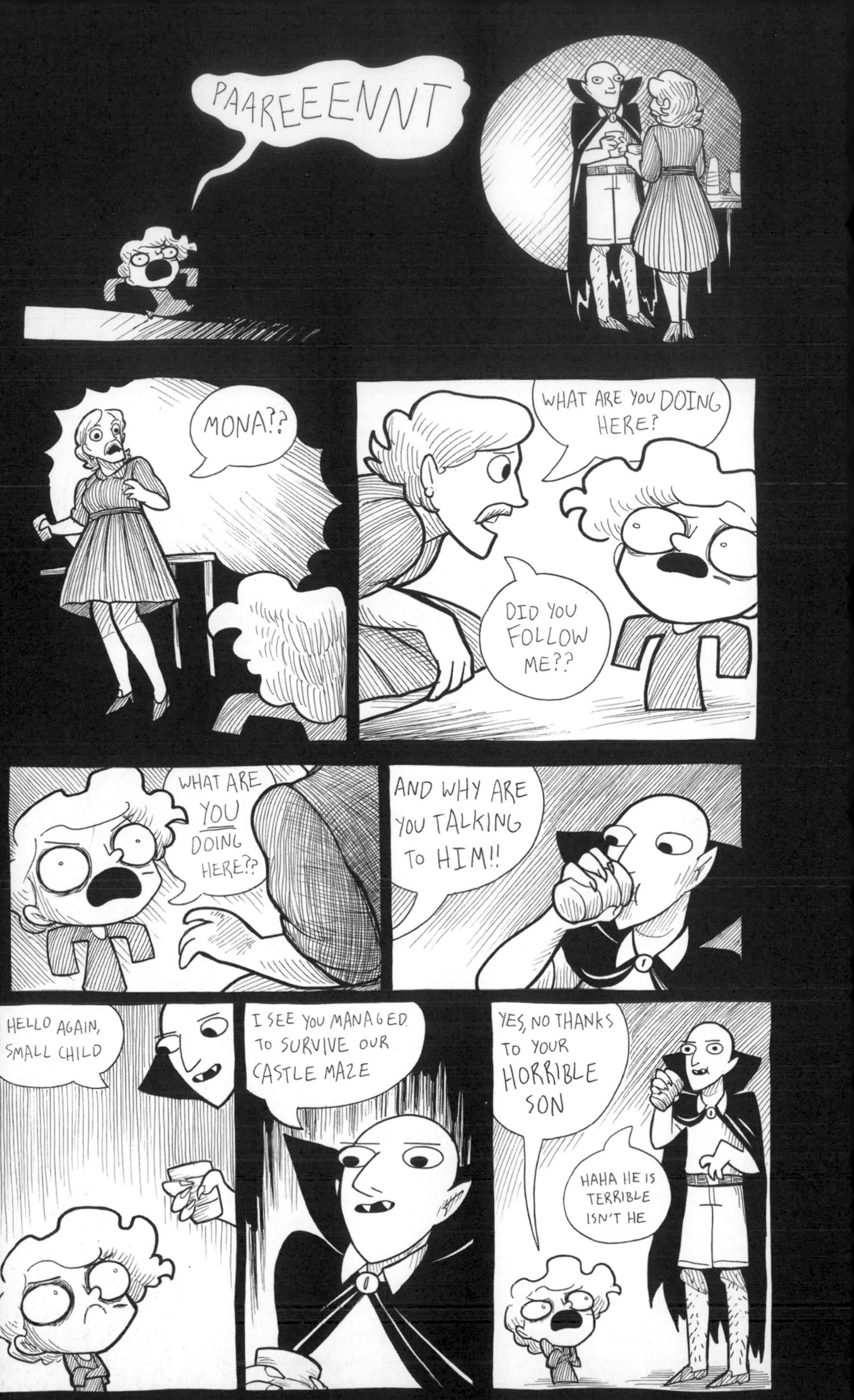
PAAREEEENNT
MONA??
WHAT ARE YOU DOING HERE?
DID YOU FOLLOW ME??
WHAT ARE YOU DOING HERE??
AND WHY ARE YOU TALKING TO HIM!!
HELLO AGAIN, SMALL CHILD
I SEE YOU MANAGED TO SURVIVE OUR CASTLE MAZE
YES, NO THANKS TO YOUR HORRIBLE SON
HAHA HE IS TERRIBLE ISN'T HE

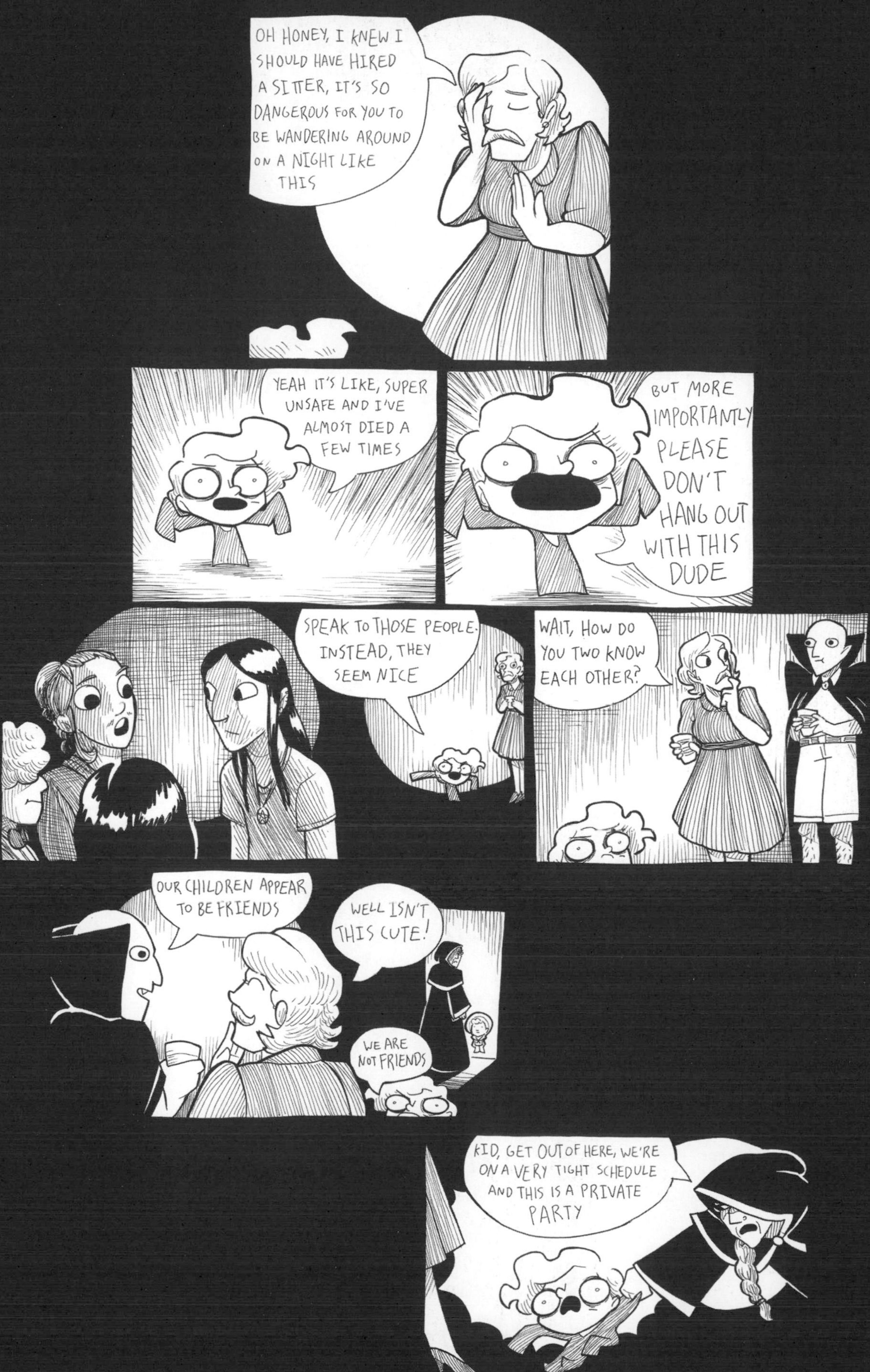
OH HONEY, I KNEW I SHOULD HAVE HIRED A SITTER, IT'S SO DANGEROUS FOR YOU TO BE WANDERING AROUND ON A NIGHT LIKE THIS
YEAH IT'S LIKE, SUPER UNSAFE AND I'VE ALMOST DIED A FEW TIMES
BUT MORE IMPORTANTLY PLEASE DON'T HANG OUT WITH THIS DUDE
SPEAK TO THOSE PEOPLE. INSTEAD, THEY SEEM NICE
WAIT, HOW DO YOU TWO KNOW EACH OTHER?
OUR CHILDREN APPEAR TO BE FRIENDS
WELL ISN'T THIS CUTE!
WE ARE NOT FRIENDS
KID, GET OUT OF HERE, WE'RE ON A VERY TIGHT SCHEDULE AND THIS IS A PRIVATE PARTY

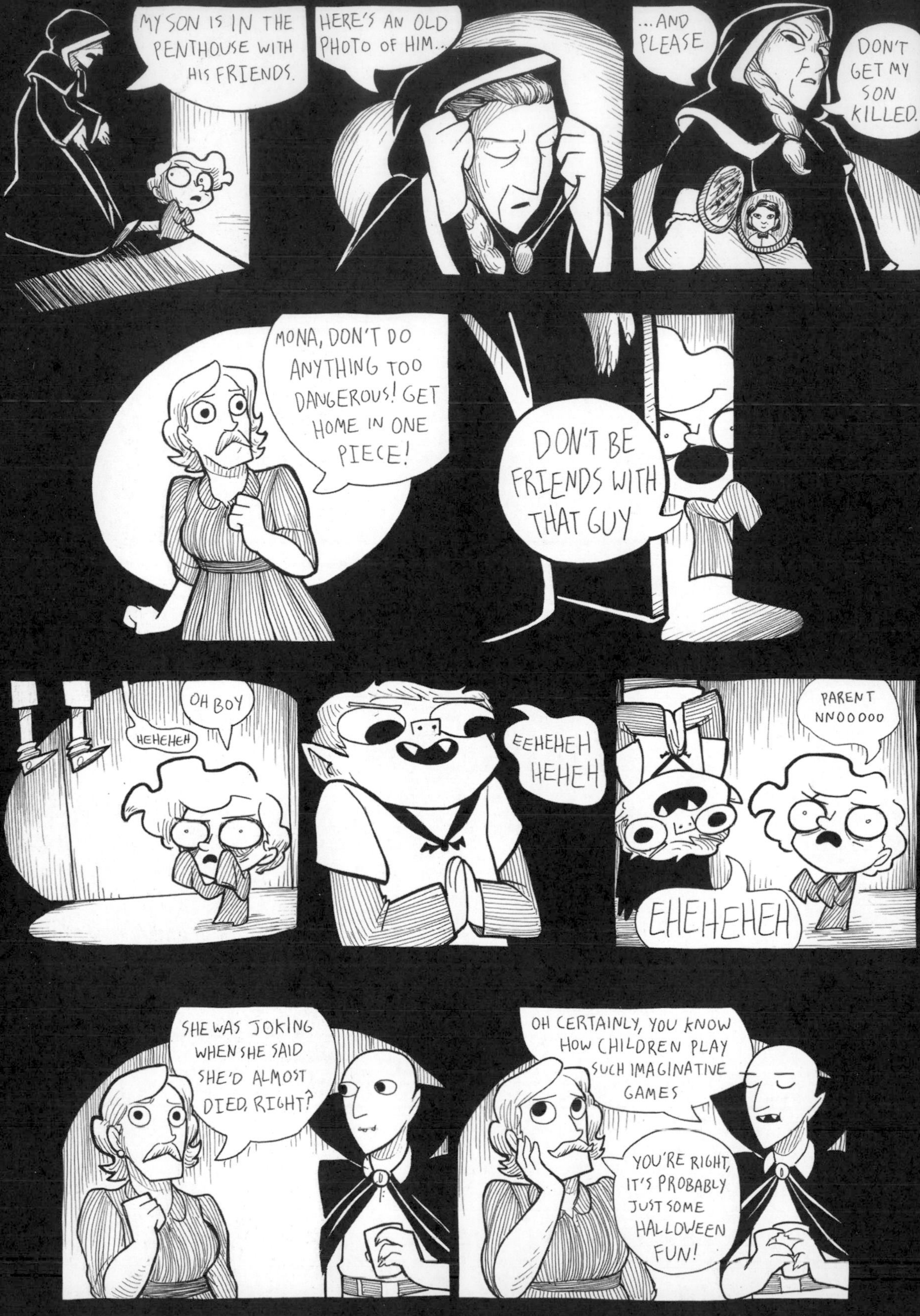
MY SON IS IN THE PENTHOUSE WITH HIS FRIENDS.
HERE'S AN OLD PHOTO OF HIM...
...AND PLEASE
DON'T GET MY SON KILLED.
MONA, DON'T DO ANYTHING TOO DANGEROUS! GET HOME IN ONE PIECE!
DON'T BE FRIENDS WITH THAT GUY
OH BOY
HEHEHEH
EEHEHEH HEHEH
PARENT NNOOOOO
EHEHEHEH
SHE WAS JOKING WHEN SHE SAID SHE'D ALMOST DIED, RIGHT?
OH CERTAINLY, YOU KNOW HOW CHILDREN PLAY SUCH IMAGINATIVE GAMES
YOU'RE RIGHT, IT'S PROBABLY JUST SOME HALLOWEEN FUN!

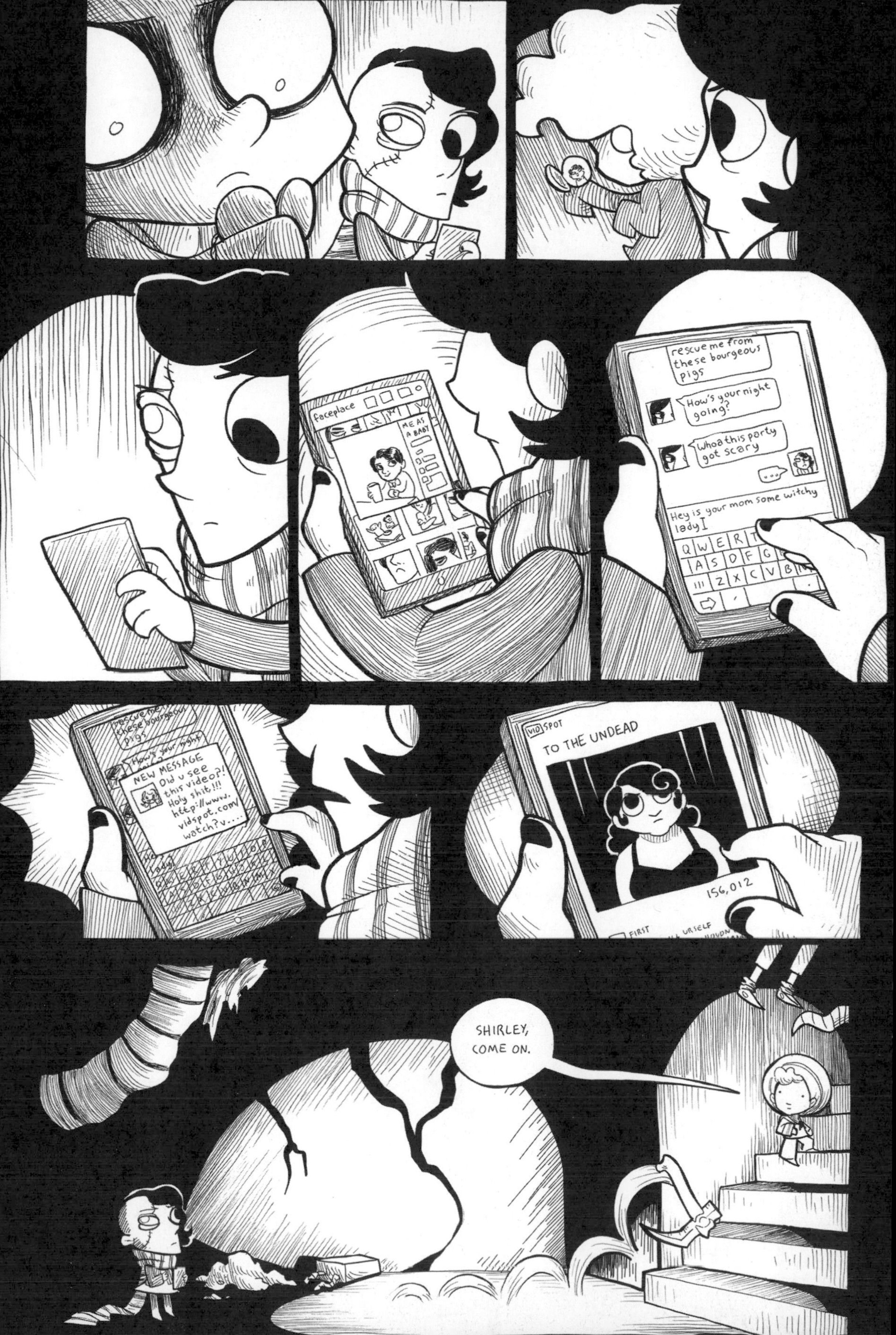
faceplace
ME AS A BABY
rescue me from these bourgeous pigs
How's your night going?
Whoa this party got scary
Hey is your mom some witchy lady
NEW MESSAGE
Did u see this video?! Holy shit!!! http://www.vidspot.com/watch?v....
VIDSPOT
TO THE UNDEAD
156,012
SHIRLEY, COME ON.

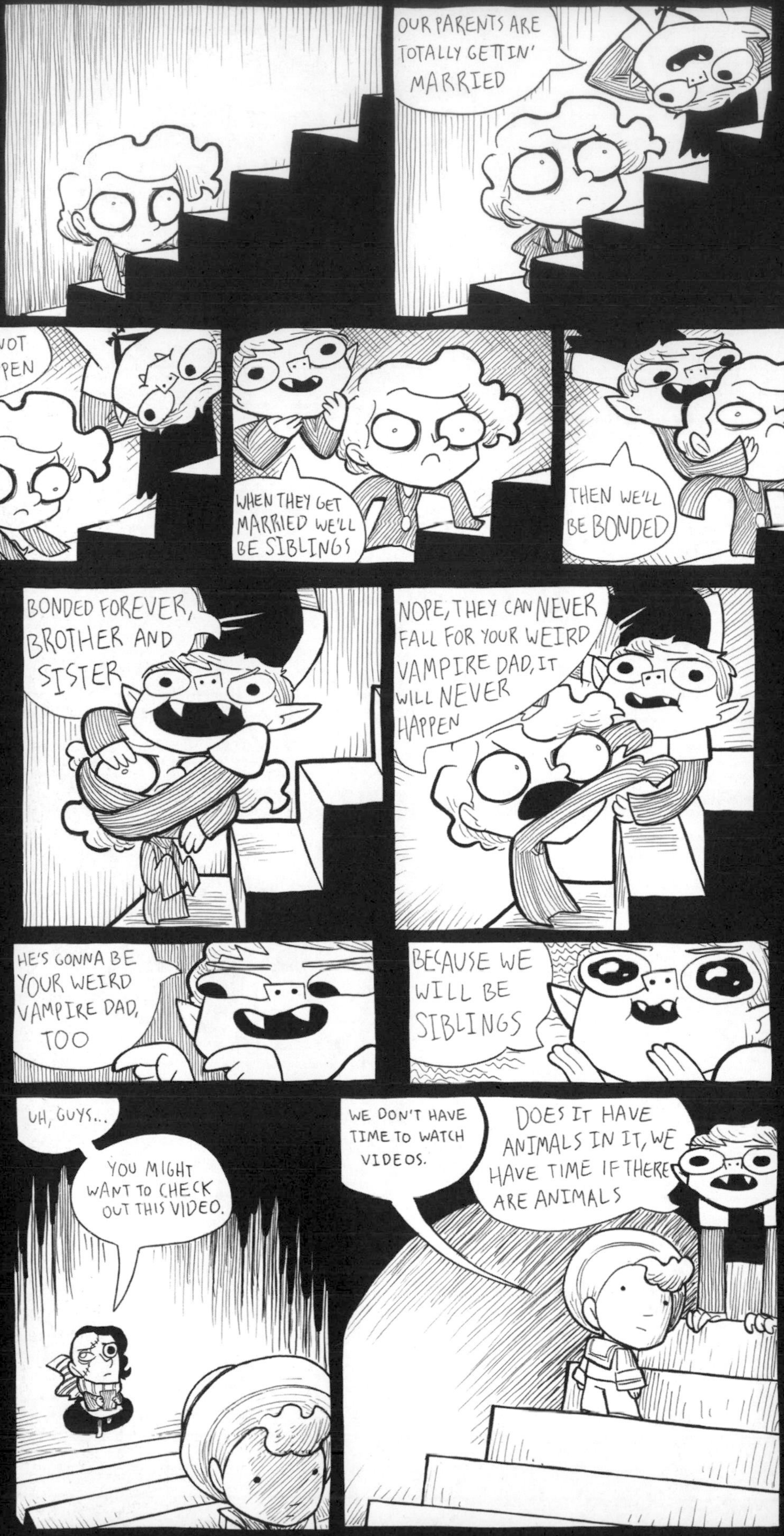
OUR PARENTS ARE TOTALLY GETTIN' MARRIED
NO, THAT'S NOT GONNA HAPPEN
WHEN THEY GET MARRIED WE'LL BE SIBLINGS
THEN WE'LL BE BONDED
BONDED FOREVER, BROTHER AND SISTER
NOPE, THEY CAN NEVER FALL FOR YOUR WEIRD VAMPIRE DAD, IT WILL NEVER HAPPEN
HE'S GONNA BE YOUR WEIRD VAMPIRE DAD, TOO
BECAUSE WE WILL BE SIBLINGS
UH, GUYS...
YOU MIGHT WANT TO CHECK OUT THIS VIDEO.
WE DON'T HAVE TIME TO WATCH VIDEOS.
DOES IT HAVE ANIMALS IN IT, WE HAVE TIME IF THERE ARE ANIMALS

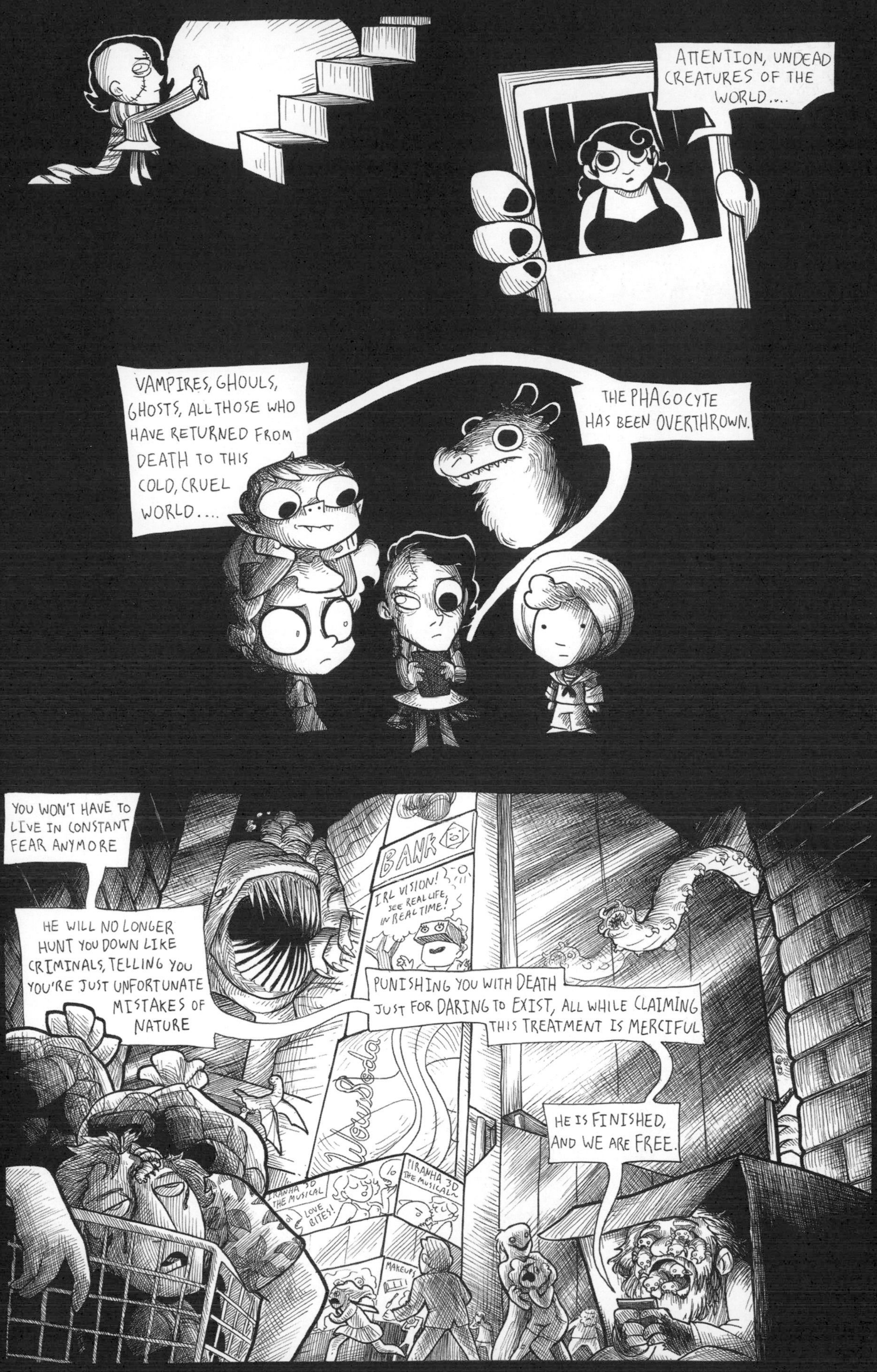
ATTENTION, UNDEAD CREATURES OF THE WORLD....
VAMPIRES, GHOULS, GHOSTS, ALL THOSE WHO HAVE RETURNED FROM DEATH TO THIS COLD, CRUEL WORLD....
THE PHAGOCYTE HAS BEEN OVERTHROWN.
YOU WON'T HAVE TO LIVE IN CONSTANT FEAR ANYMORE
HE WILL NO LONGER HUNT YOU DOWN LIKE CRIMINALS, TELLING YOU YOU'RE JUST UNFORTUNATE MISTAKES OF NATURE
PUNISHING YOU WITH DEATH JUST FOR DARING TO EXIST, ALL WHILE CLAIMING THIS TREATMENT IS MERCIFUL
HE IS FINISHED, AND WE ARE FREE.
BANK
IRL VISION! SEE REAL LIFE, IN REAL TIME!
PIRANHA 3D THE MUSICAL
LOVE BITES!
MAKEUP

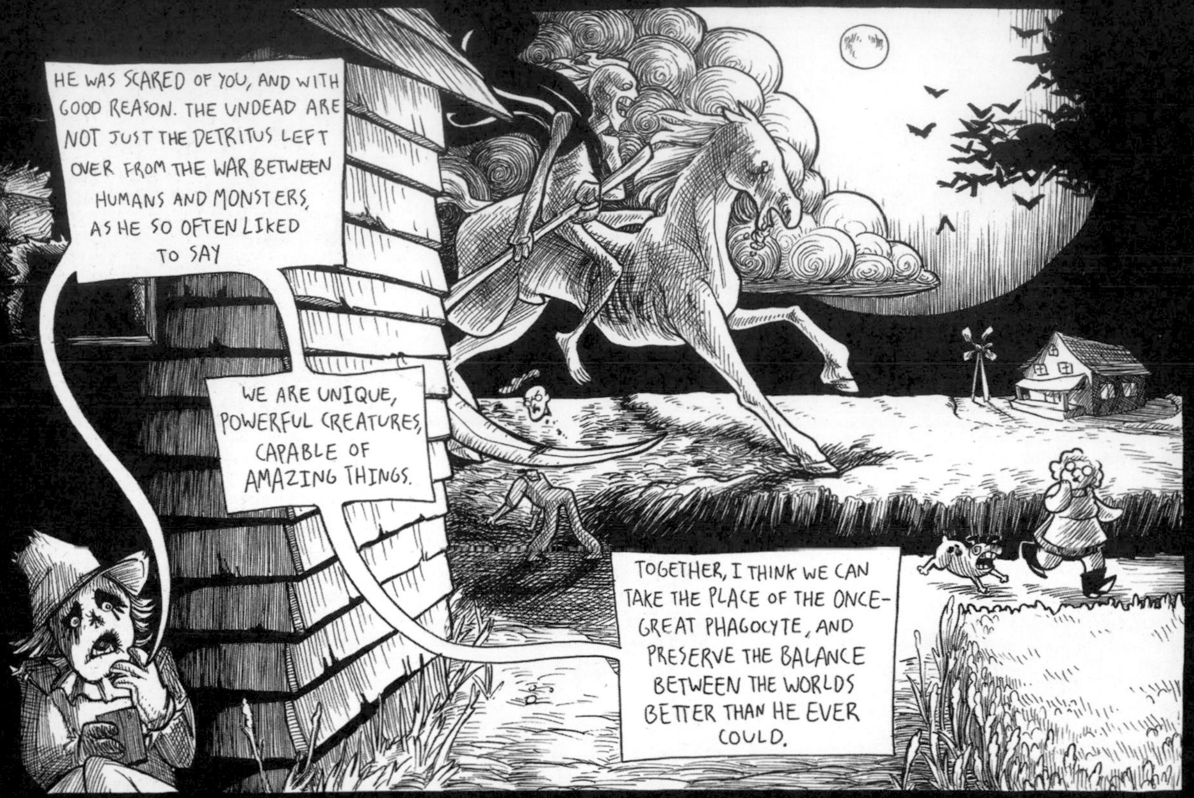
HE WAS SCARED OF YOU, AND WITH GOOD REASON. THE UNDEAD ARE NOT JUST THE DETRITUS LEFT OVER FROM THE WAR BETWEEN HUMANS AND MONSTERS, AS HE SO OFTEN LIKED TO SAY
WE ARE UNIQUE, POWERFUL CREATURES, CAPABLE OF AMAZING THINGS.
TOGETHER, I THINK WE CAN TAKE THE PLACE OF THE ONCE-GREAT PHAGOCYTE, AND PRESERVE THE BALANCE BETWEEN THE WORLDS BETTER THAN HE EVER COULD.

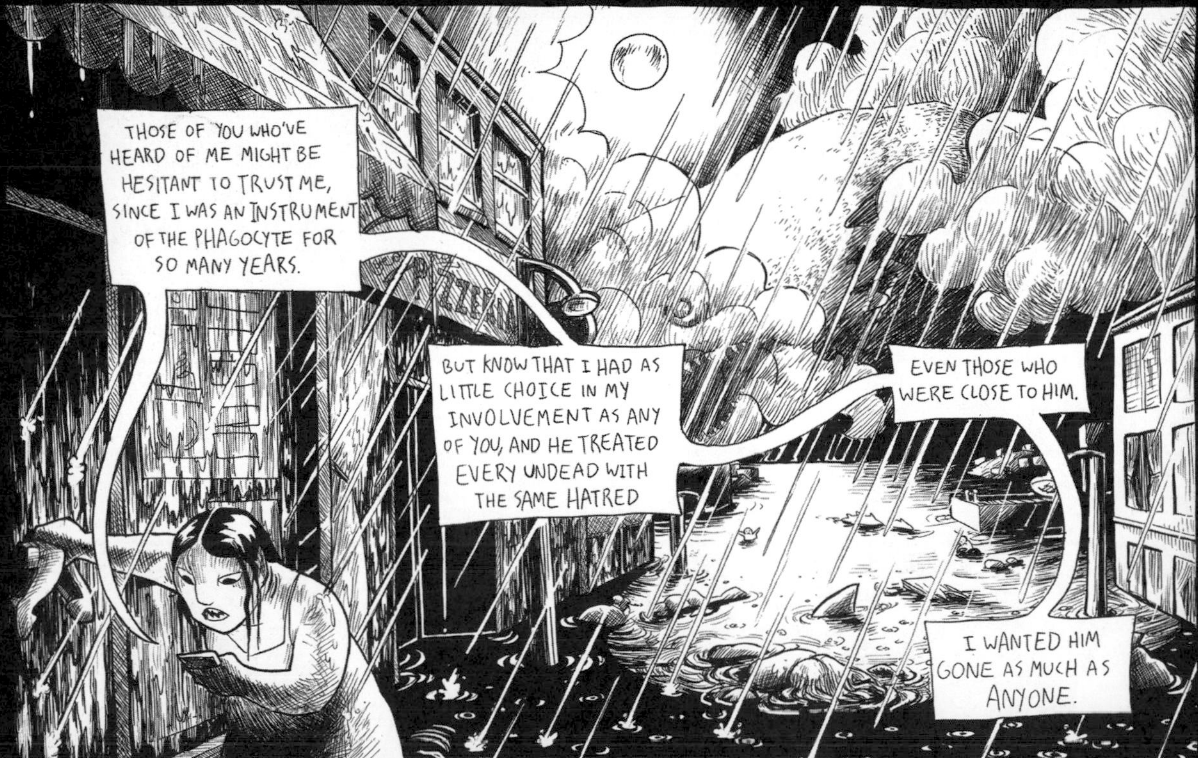
THOSE OF YOU WHO'VE HEARD OF ME MIGHT BE HESITANT TO TRUST ME, SINCE I WAS AN INSTRUMENT OF THE PHAGOCYTE FOR SO MANY YEARS.
BUT KNOW THAT I HAD AS LITTLE CHOICE IN MY INVOLVEMENT AS ANY OF YOU, AND HE TREATED EVERY UNDEAD WITH THE SAME HATRED
EVEN THOSE WHO WERE CLOSE TO HIM.
I WANTED HIM GONE AS MUCH AS ANYONE.

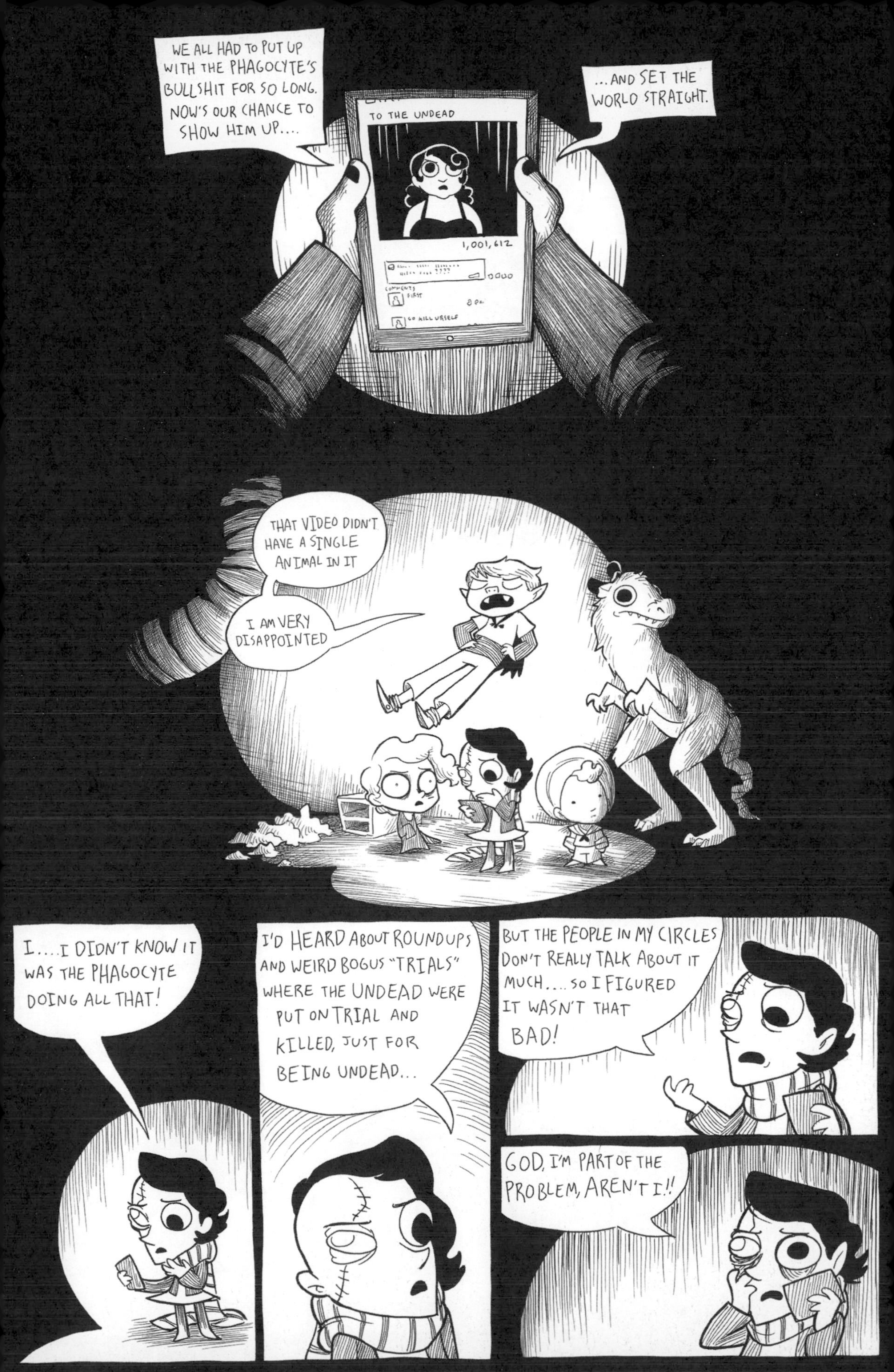
WE ALL HAD TO PUT UP WITH THE PHAGOCYTE'S BULLSHIT FOR SO LONG. NOW'S OUR CHANCE TO SHOW HIM UP....
TO THE UNDEAD
1,001,612
COMMENTS
FIRST
GO KILL URSELF
...AND SET THE WORLD STRAIGHT.
THAT VIDEO DIDN'T HAVE A SINGLE ANIMAL IN IT
I AM VERY DISAPPOINTED
I....I DIDN'T KNOW IT WAS THE PHAGOCYTE DOING ALL THAT!
I'D HEARD ABOUT ROUNDUPS AND WEIRD BOGUS "TRIALS" WHERE THE UNDEAD WERE PUT ON TRIAL AND KILLED, JUST FOR BEING UNDEAD...
BUT THE PEOPLE IN MY CIRCLES DON'T REALLY TALK ABOUT IT MUCH.... SO I FIGURED IT WASN'T THAT BAD!
GOD, I'M PART OF THE PROBLEM, AREN'T I!!

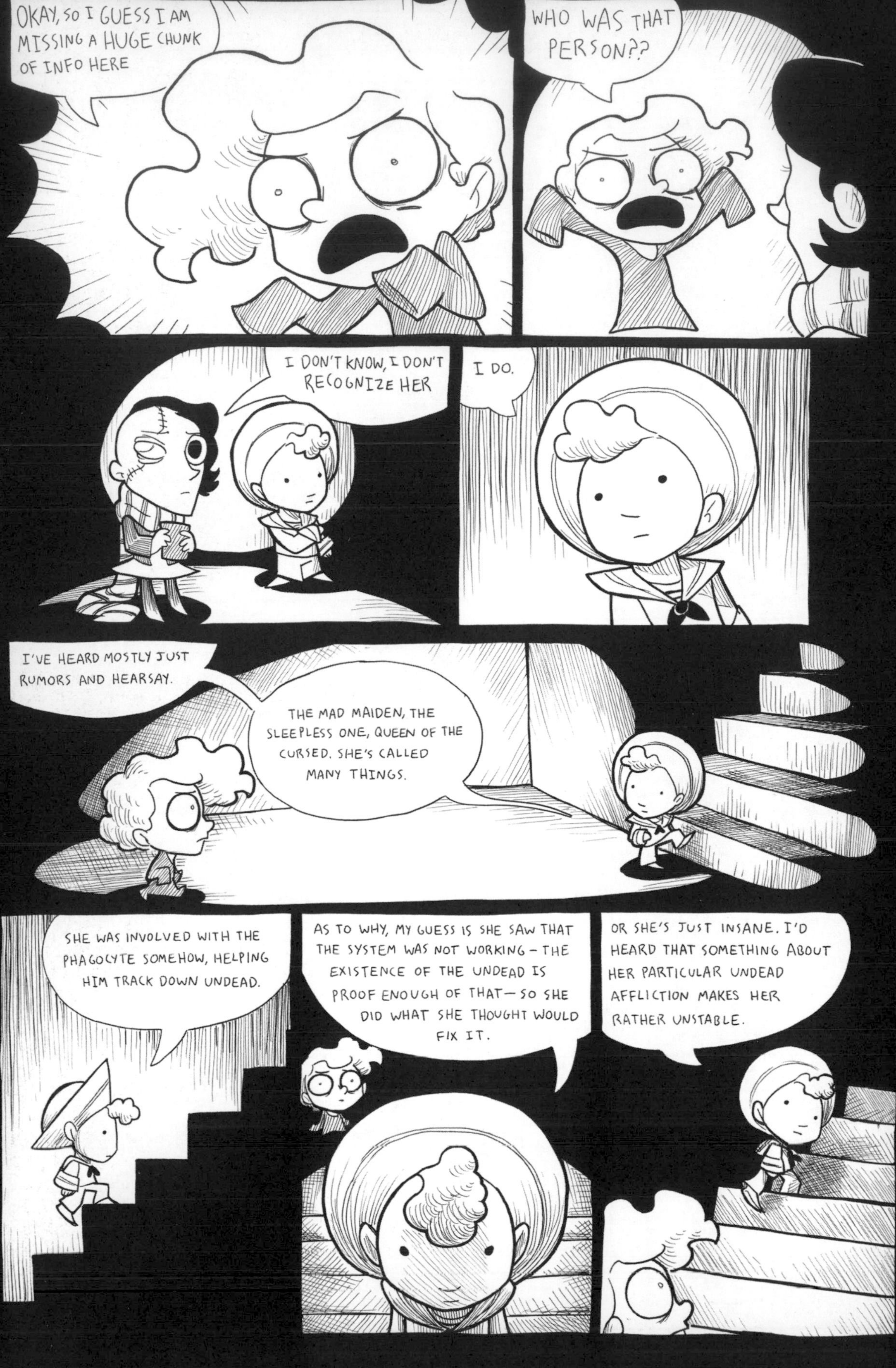
OKAY, SO I GUESS I AM MISSING A HUGE CHUNK OF INFO HERE
WHO WAS THAT PERSON??
I DON'T KNOW, I DON'T RECOGNIZE HER
I DO.
I'VE HEARD MOSTLY JUST RUMORS AND HEARSAY.
THE MAD MAIDEN, THE SLEEPLESS ONE, QUEEN OF THE CURSED. SHE'S CALLED MANY THINGS.
SHE WAS INVOLVED WITH THE PHAGOCYTE SOMEHOW, HELPING HIM TRACK DOWN UNDEAD.
AS TO WHY, MY GUESS IS SHE SAW THAT THE SYSTEM WAS NOT WORKING – THE EXISTENCE OF THE UNDEAD IS PROOF ENOUGH OF THAT – SO SHE DID WHAT SHE THOUGHT WOULD FIX IT.
OR SHE'S JUST INSANE. I'D HEARD THAT SOMETHING ABOUT HER PARTICULAR UNDEAD AFFLICTION MAKES HER RATHER UNSTABLE.

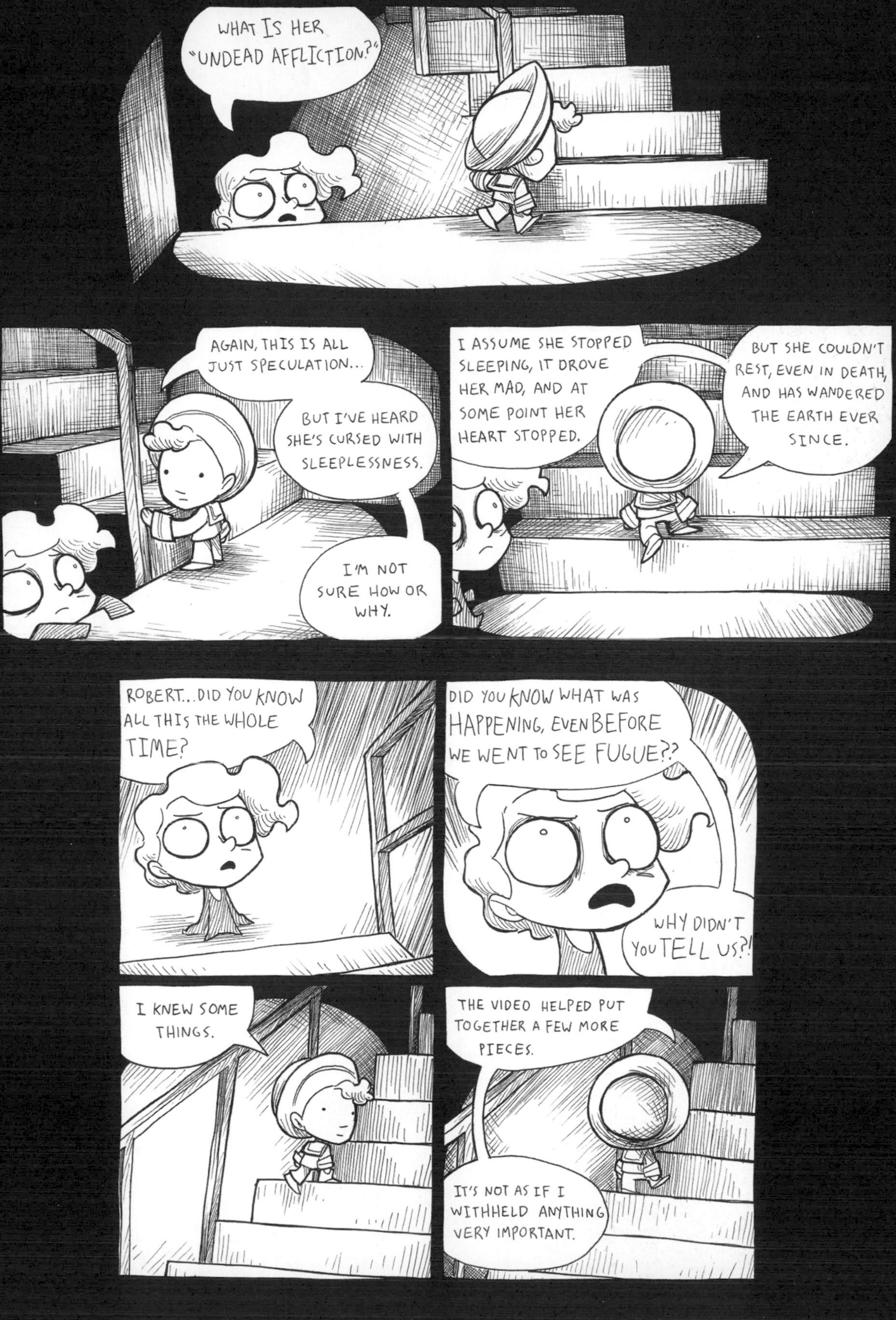

WHAT IS HER "UNDEAD AFFLICTION?"
AGAIN, THIS IS ALL JUST SPECULATION...
BUT I'VE HEARD SHE'S CURSED WITH SLEEPLESSNESS.
I'M NOT SURE HOW OR WHY.
I ASSUME SHE STOPPED SLEEPING, IT DROVE HER MAD, AND AT SOME POINT HER HEART STOPPED.
BUT SHE COULDN'T REST, EVEN IN DEATH, AND HAS WANDERED THE EARTH EVER SINCE.
ROBERT... DID YOU KNOW ALL THIS THE WHOLE TIME?
DID YOU KNOW WHAT WAS HAPPENING, EVEN BEFORE WE WENT TO SEE FUGUE??
WHY DIDN'T YOU TELL US?!
I KNEW SOME THINGS.
THE VIDEO HELPED PUT TOGETHER A FEW MORE PIECES.
IT'S NOT AS IF I WITHHELD ANYTHING VERY IMPORTANT.

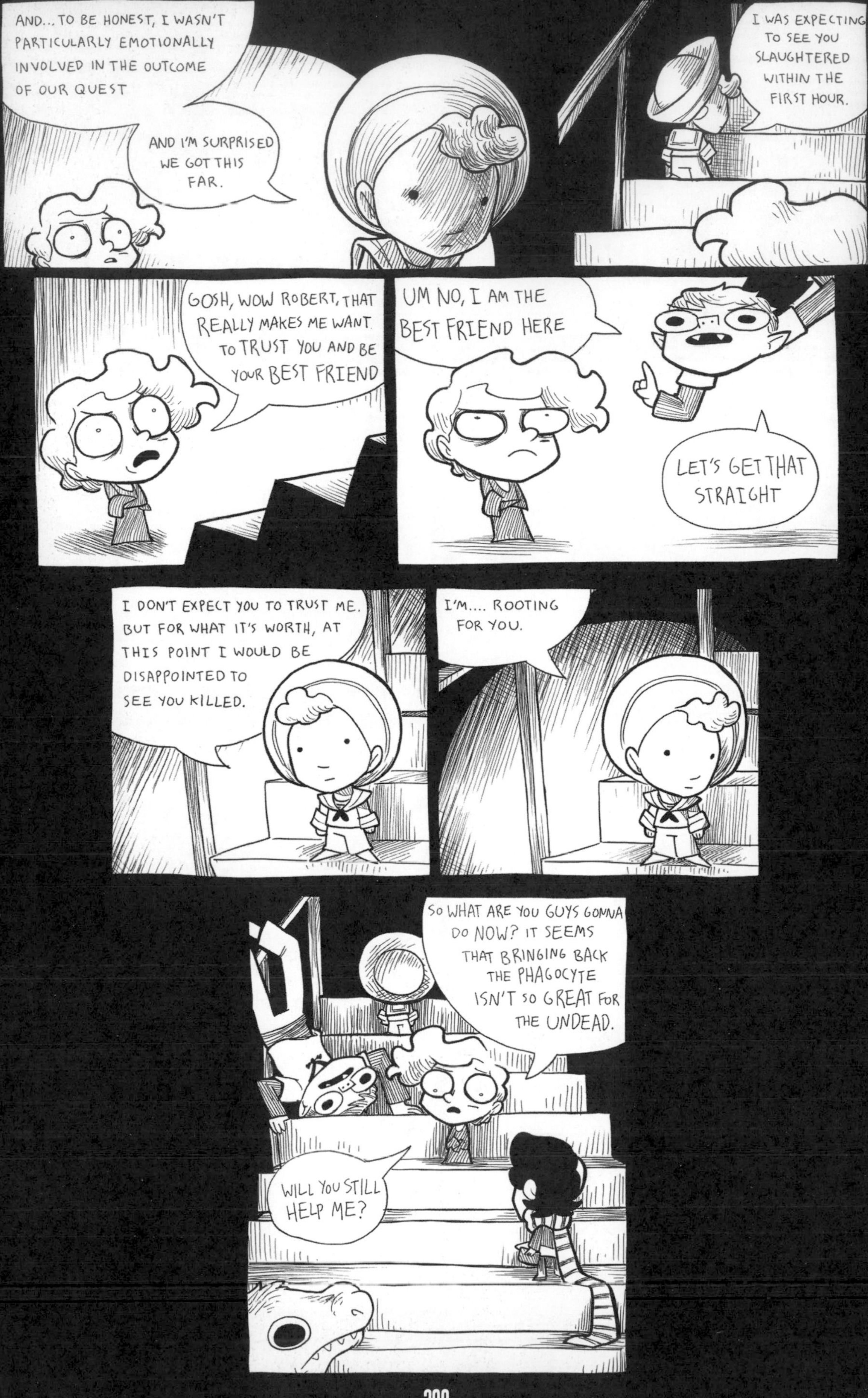
AND... TO BE HONEST, I WASN'T PARTICULARLY EMOTIONALLY INVOLVED IN THE OUTCOME OF OUR QUEST
AND I'M SURPRISED WE GOT THIS FAR.
I WAS EXPECTING TO SEE YOU SLAUGHTERED WITHIN THE FIRST HOUR.
GOSH, WOW ROBERT, THAT REALLY MAKES ME WANT TO TRUST YOU AND BE YOUR BEST FRIEND
UM NO, I AM THE BEST FRIEND HERE
LET'S GET THAT STRAIGHT
I DON'T EXPECT YOU TO TRUST ME. BUT FOR WHAT IT'S WORTH, AT THIS POINT I WOULD BE DISAPPOINTED TO SEE YOU KILLED.
I'M.... ROOTING FOR YOU.
SO WHAT ARE YOU GUYS GONNA DO NOW? IT SEEMS THAT BRINGING BACK THE PHAGOCYTE ISN'T SO GREAT FOR THE UNDEAD.
WILL YOU STILL HELP ME?

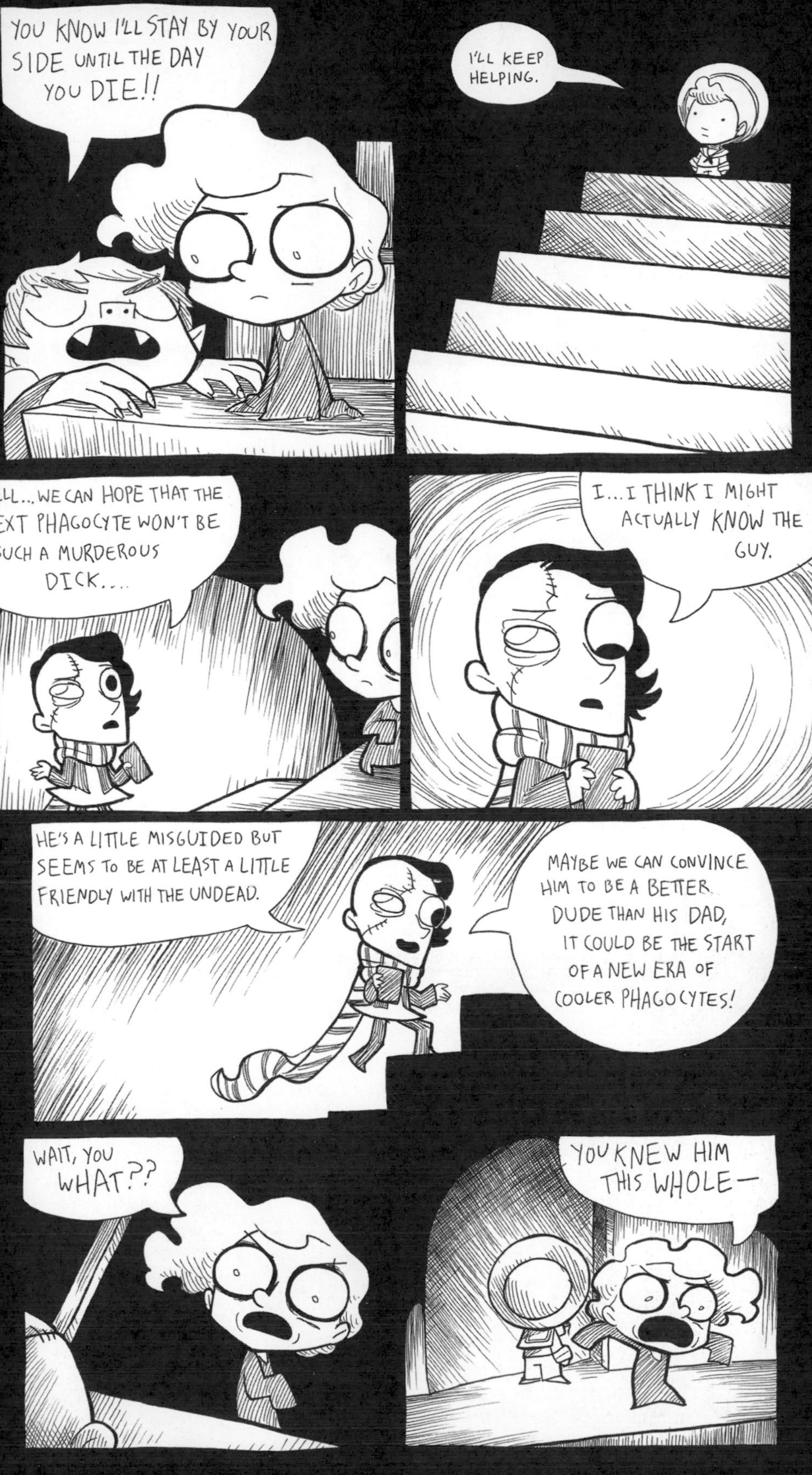
YOU KNOW I'LL STAY BY YOUR SIDE UNTIL THE DAY YOU DIE!!
I'LL KEEP HELPING.
WELL... WE CAN HOPE THAT THE NEXT PHAGOCYTE WON'T BE SUCH A MURDEROUS DICK....
I... I THINK I MIGHT ACTUALLY KNOW THE GUY.
HE'S A LITTLE MISGUIDED BUT SEEMS TO BE AT LEAST A LITTLE FRIENDLY WITH THE UNDEAD.
MAYBE WE CAN CONVINCE HIM TO BE A BETTER DUDE THAN HIS DAD, IT COULD BE THE START OF A NEW ERA OF COOLER PHAGOCYTES!
WAIT, YOU WHAT??
YOU KNEW HIM THIS WHOLE—

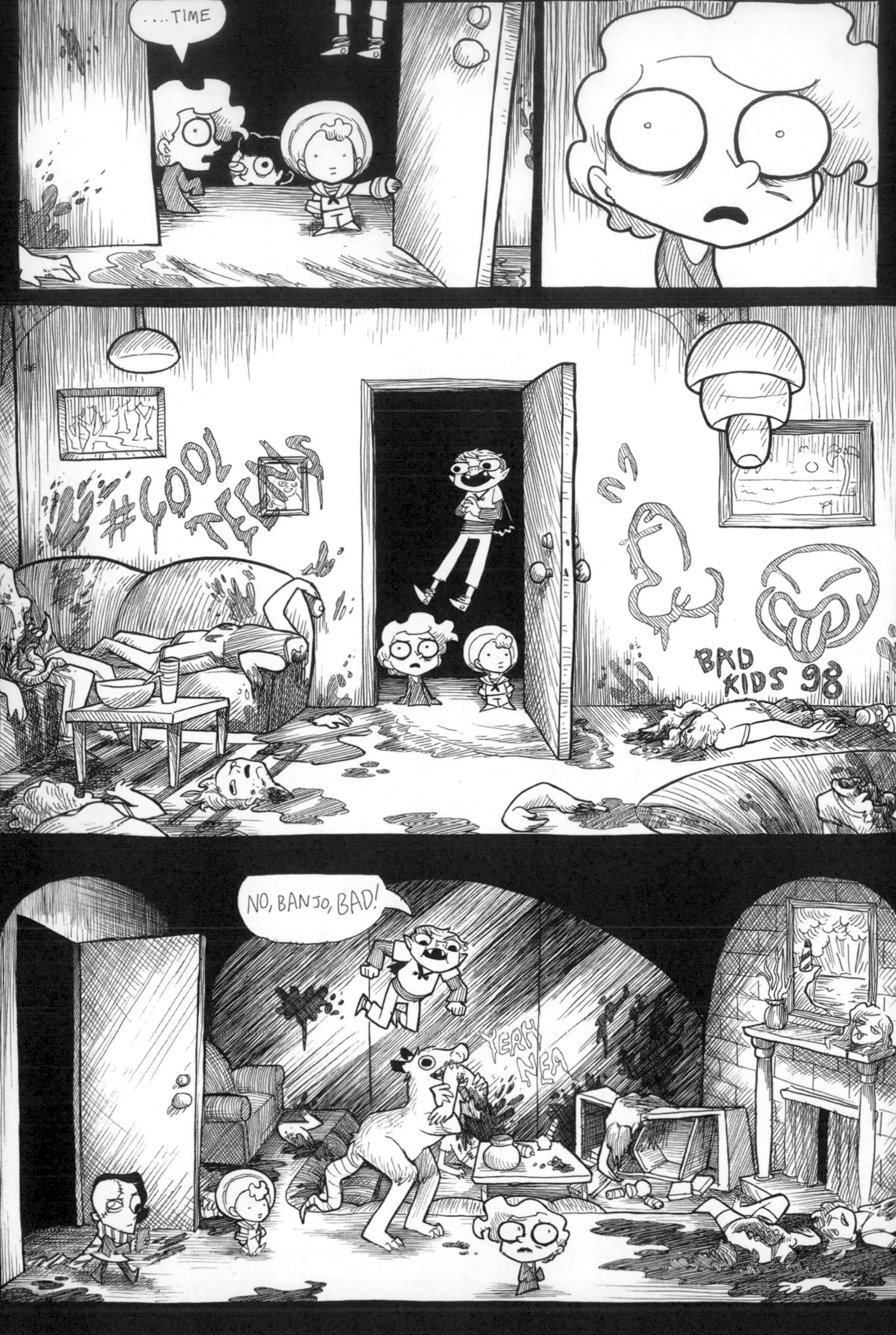

....TIME
BAD KIDS 98
NO, BANJO, BAD!
YEAH

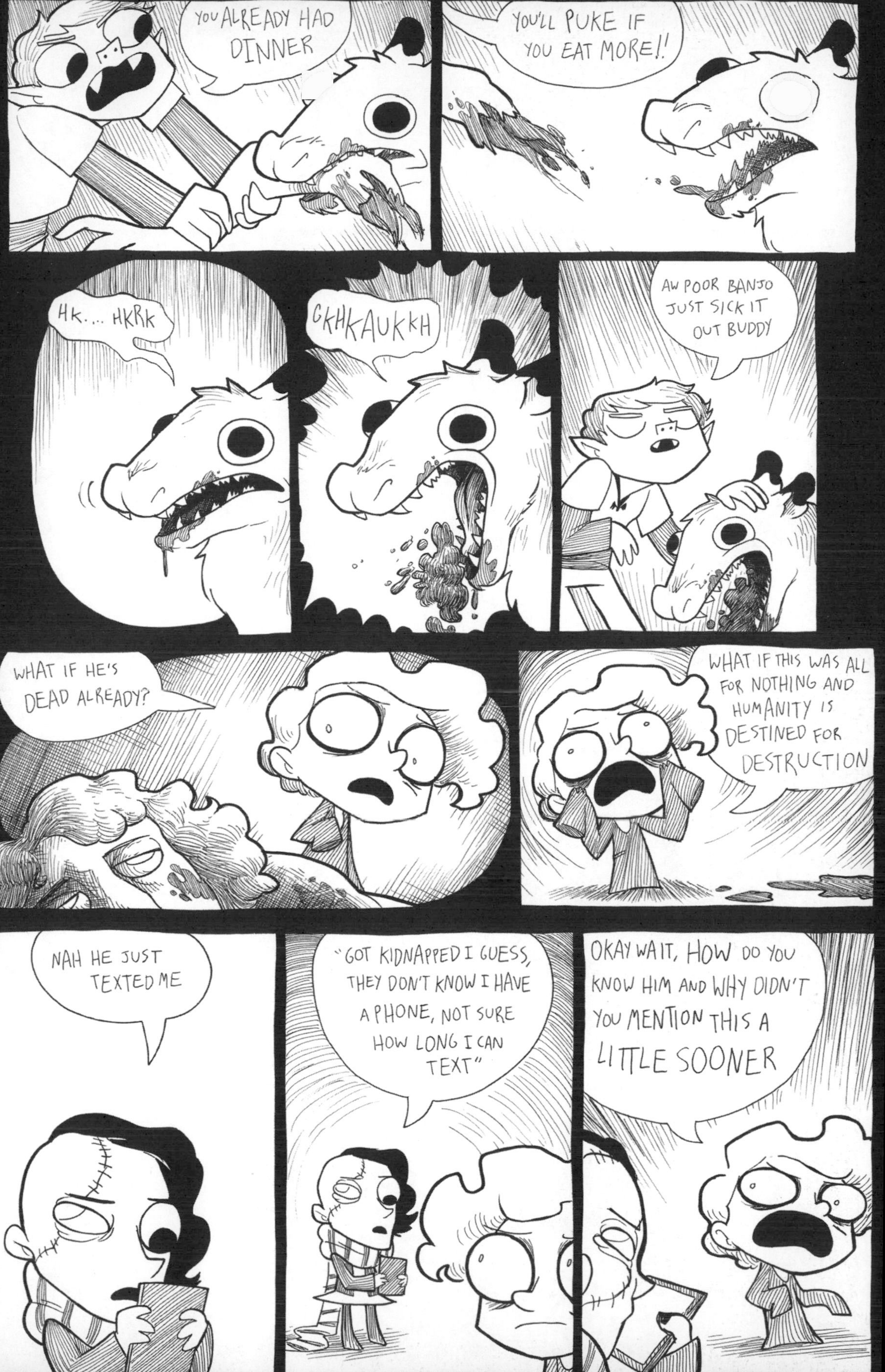
YOU ALREADY HAD DINNER
YOU'LL PUKE IF YOU EAT MORE!!
HK.... HKRK
GKHKAUKKH
AW POOR BANJO JUST SICK IT OUT BUDDY
WHAT IF HE'S DEAD ALREADY?
WHAT IF THIS WAS ALL FOR NOTHING AND HUMANITY IS DESTINED FOR DESTRUCTION
NAH HE JUST TEXTED ME
"GOT KIDNAPPED I GUESS, THEY DON'T KNOW I HAVE A PHONE, NOT SURE HOW LONG I CAN TEXT"
OKAY WAIT, HOW DO YOU KNOW HIM AND WHY DIDN'T YOU MENTION THIS A LITTLE SOONER

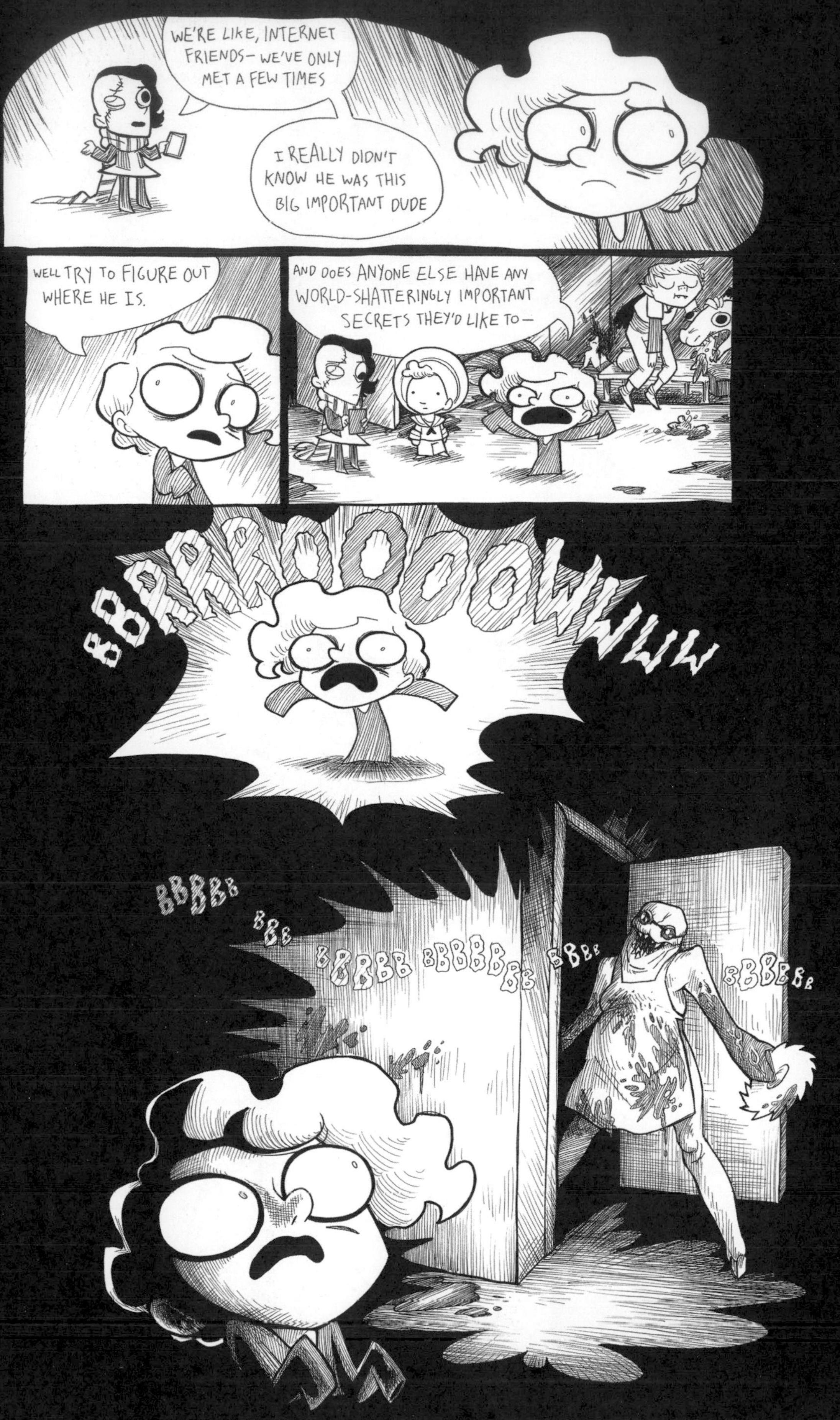
WE'RE LIKE, INTERNET FRIENDS— WE'VE ONLY MET A FEW TIMES
I REALLY DIDN'T KNOW HE WAS THIS BIG IMPORTANT DUDE
WELL TRY TO FIGURE OUT WHERE HE IS.
AND DOES ANYONE ELSE HAVE ANY WORLD-SHATTERINGLY IMPORTANT SECRETS THEY'D LIKE TO—
BBRROOOOOWWW
BBBBB
BBB
BBBBB BBBBBBB BBBB
BBBBBB

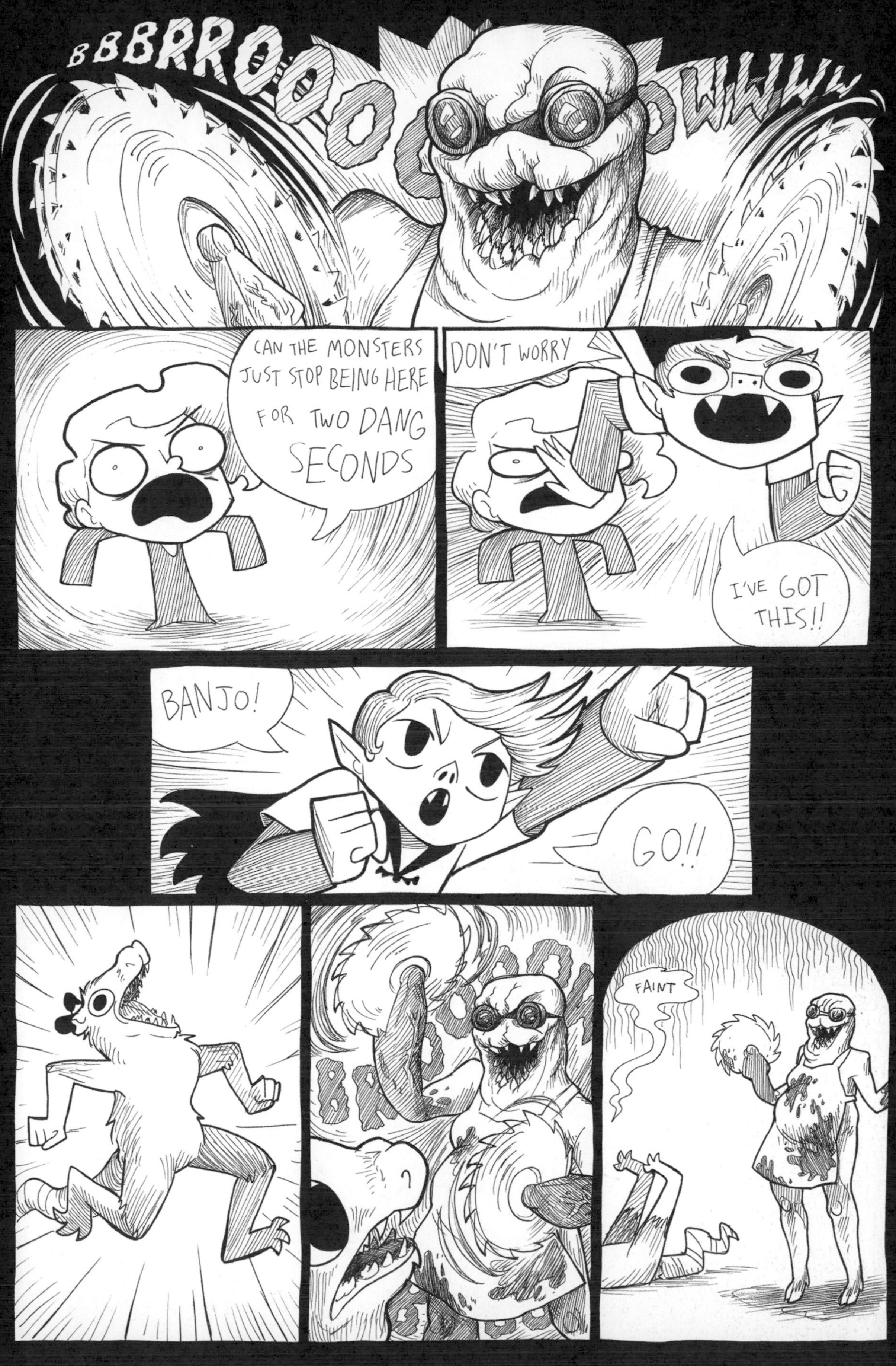
BBBRROOOOOOWWWW
CAN THE MONSTERS JUST STOP BEING HERE FOR TWO DANG SECONDS
DON'T WORRY
I'VE GOT THIS!!
BANJO!
GO!!
FAINT

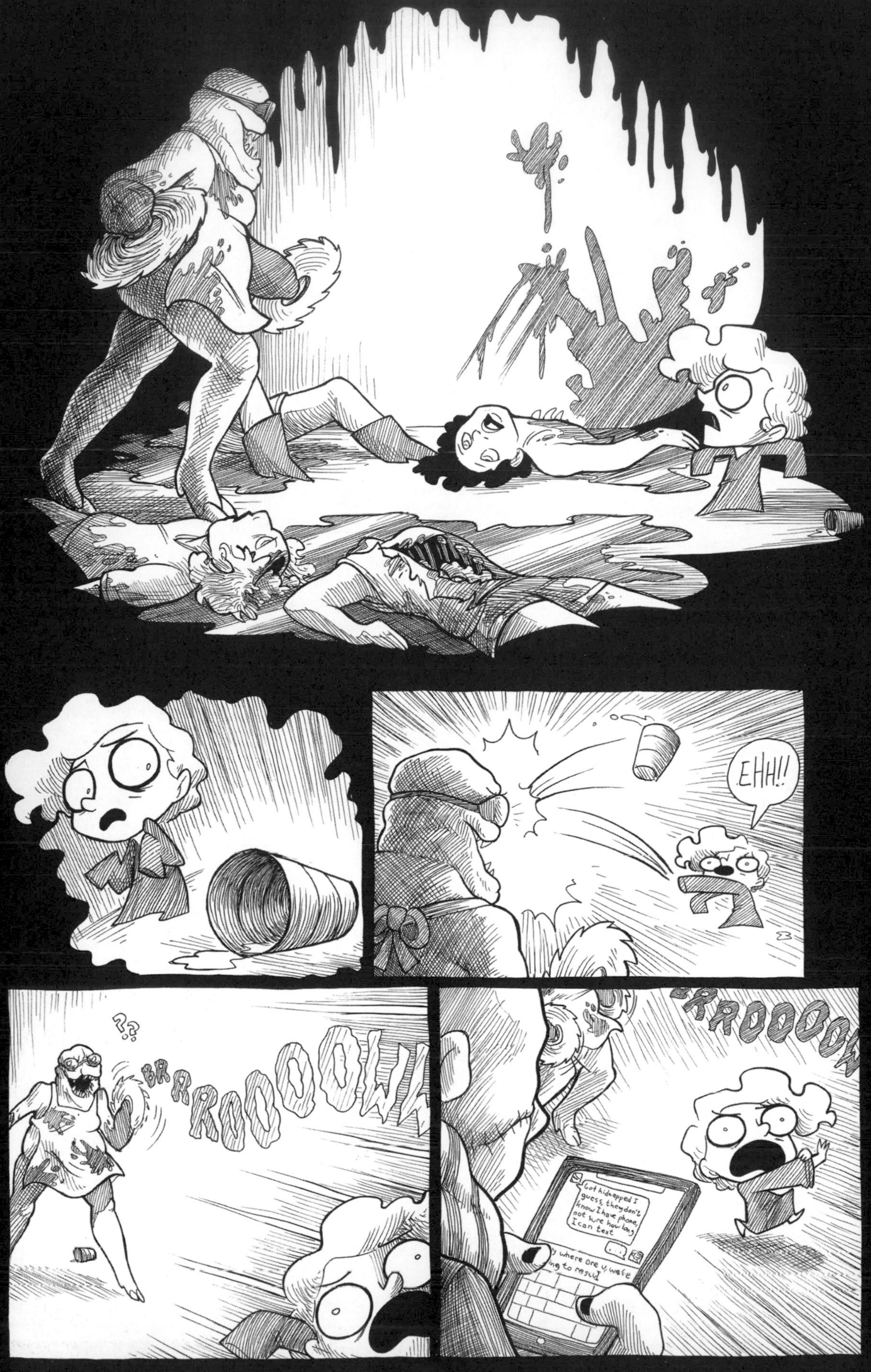
EHH!!
??
BRRROOOOWL
BRRROOOOOW
Got kidnapped I guess, they don't know I have phone, not sure how long I can text

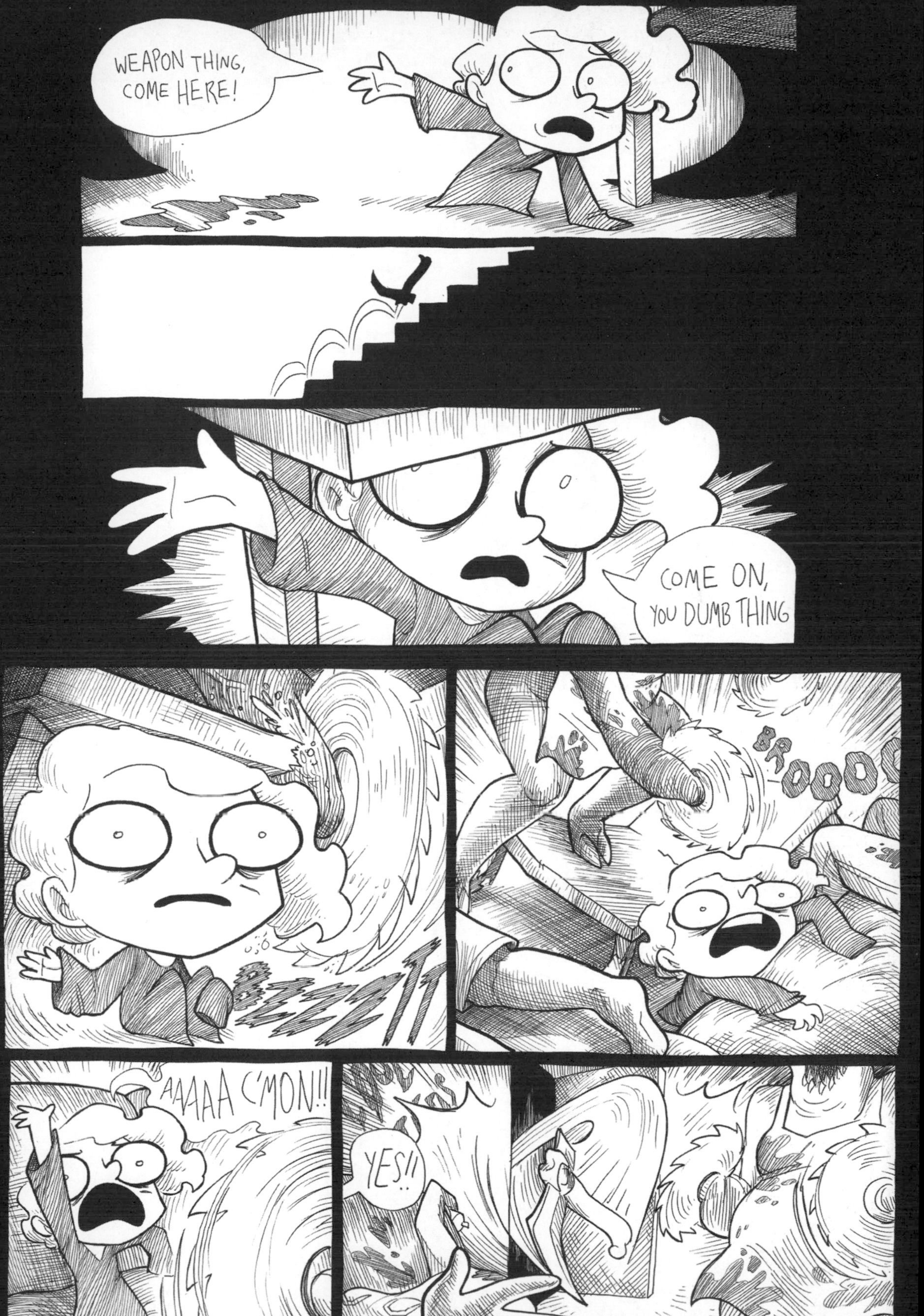
WEAPON THING, COME HERE!
COME ON, YOU DUMB THING
AAAAA C'MON!!
YES!!

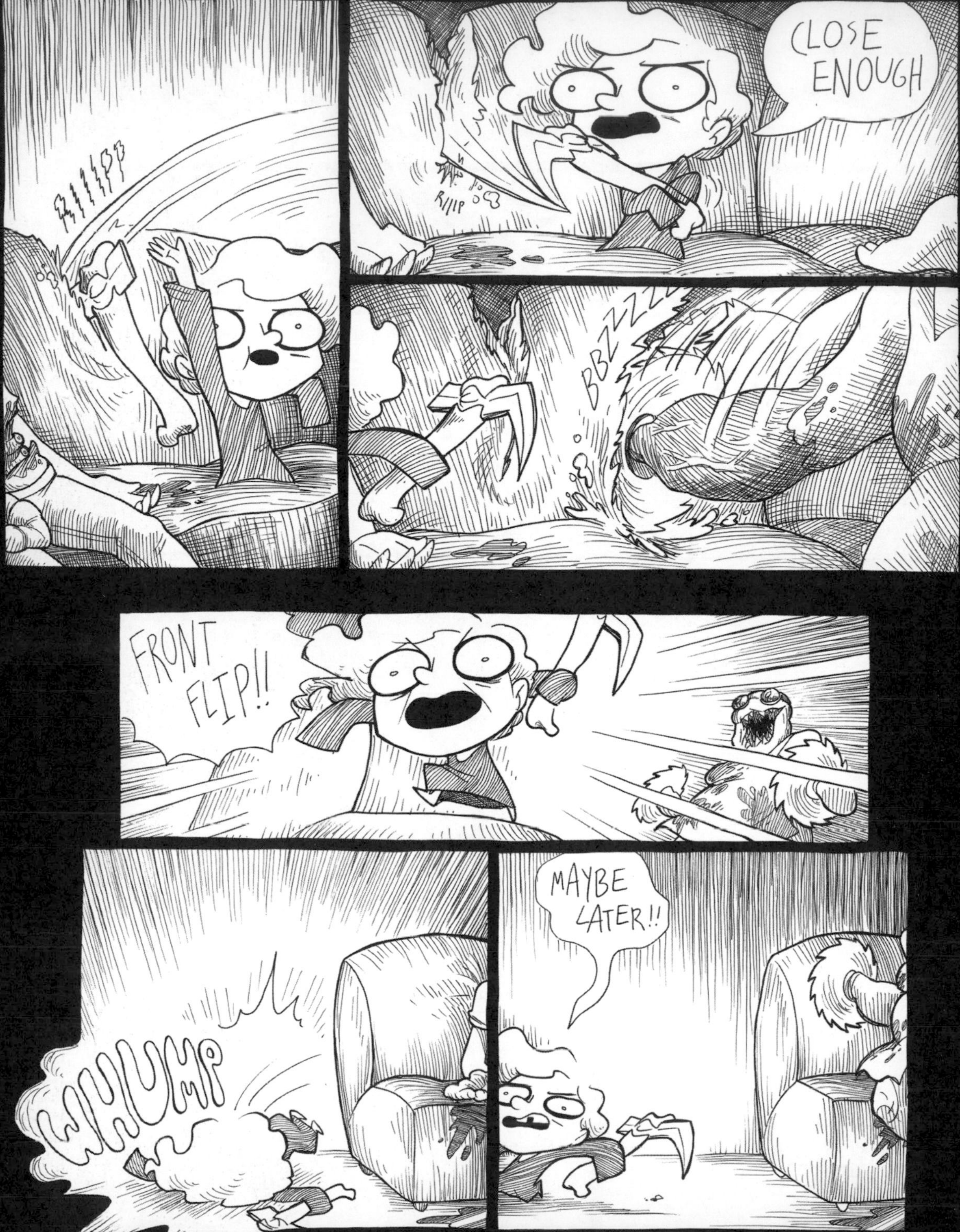
CLOSE ENOUGH
RIIIP
BBZZZZ
FRONT FLIP!!
WHUMP
MAYBE LATER!!

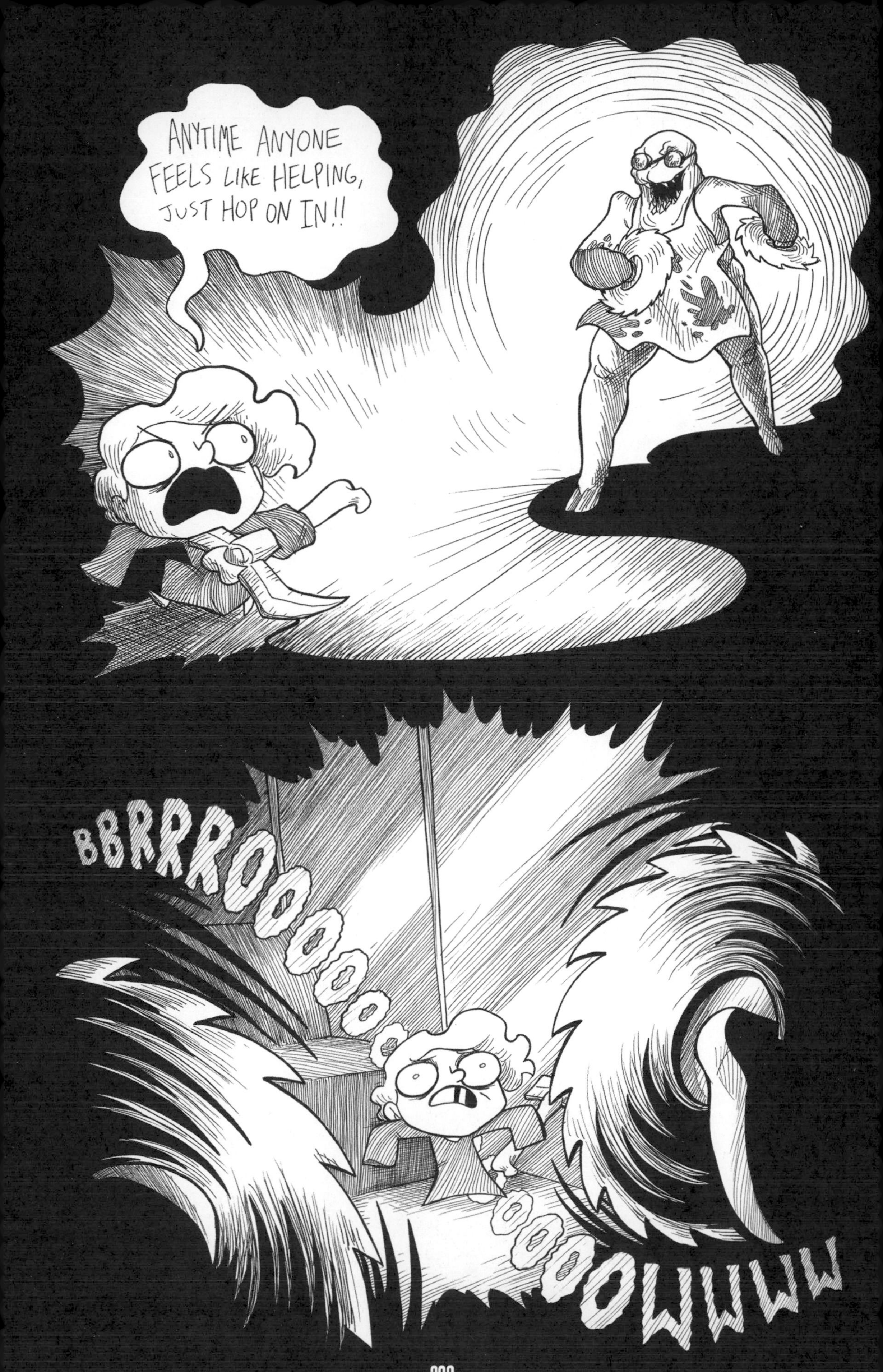
ANYTIME ANYONE FEELS LIKE HELPING, JUST HOP ON IN!!
BBRRROOOOOOOOOOOOOOOWWWW

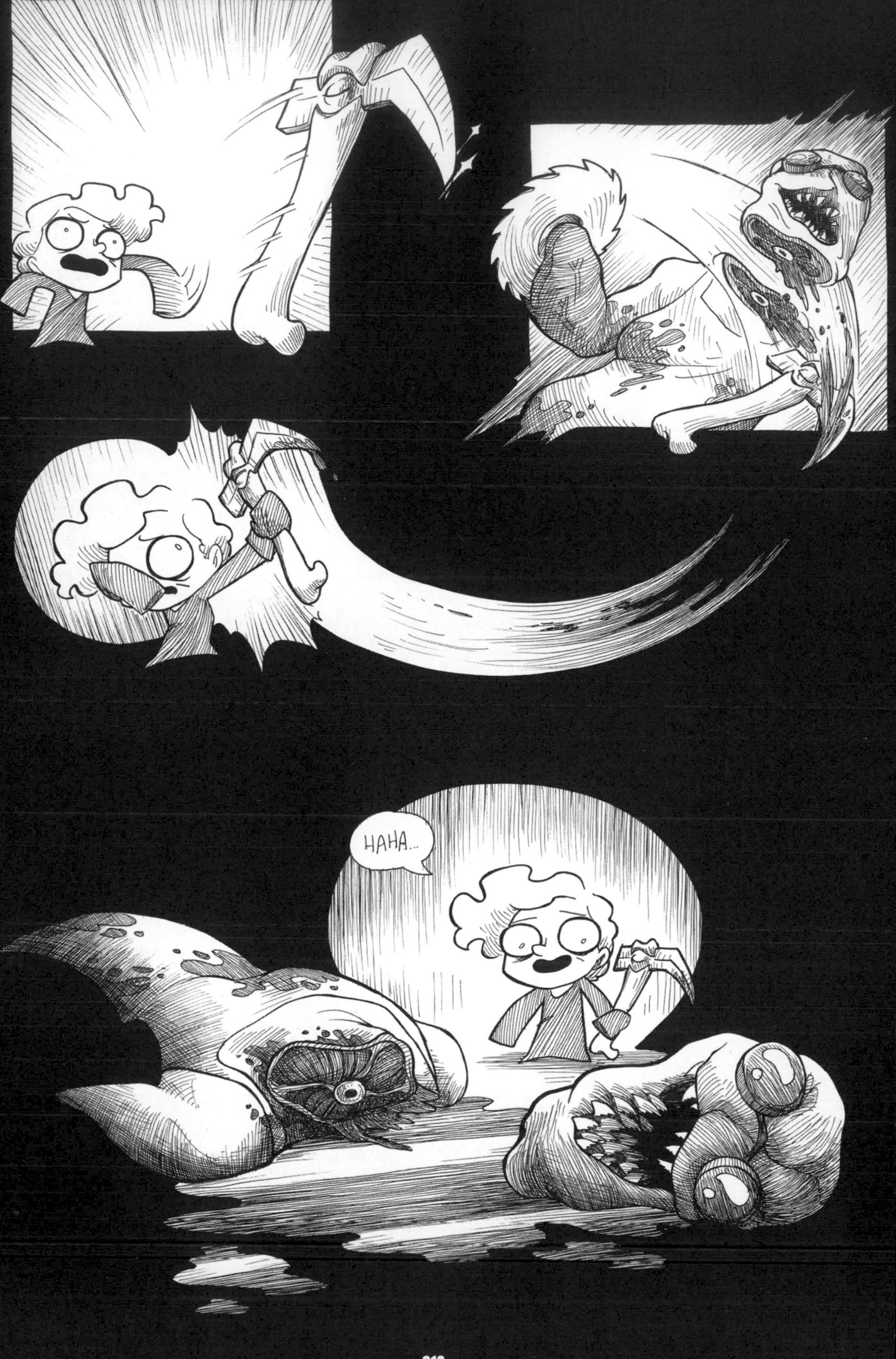
HAHA...

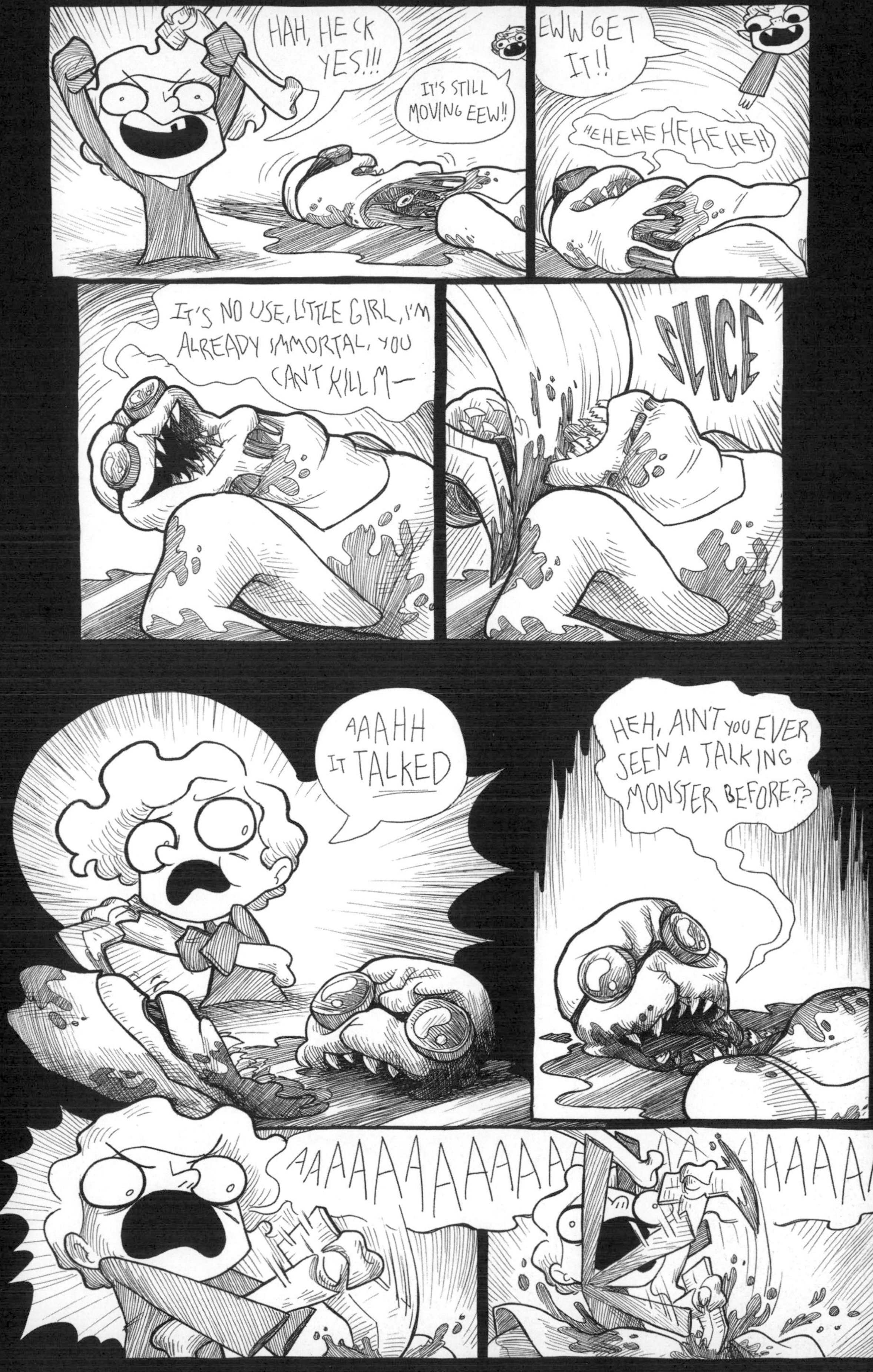
HAH, HECK YES!!!
IT'S STILL MOVING EEW!!
EWW GET IT!!
HEHEHEHEHEHEHEH
IT'S NO USE, LITTLE GIRL, I'M ALREADY IMMORTAL, YOU CAN'T KILL M—
SLICE
AAAHH IT TALKED
HEH, AIN'T YOU EVER SEEN A TALKING MONSTER BEFORE?!
AAAAAAAAAAAAA

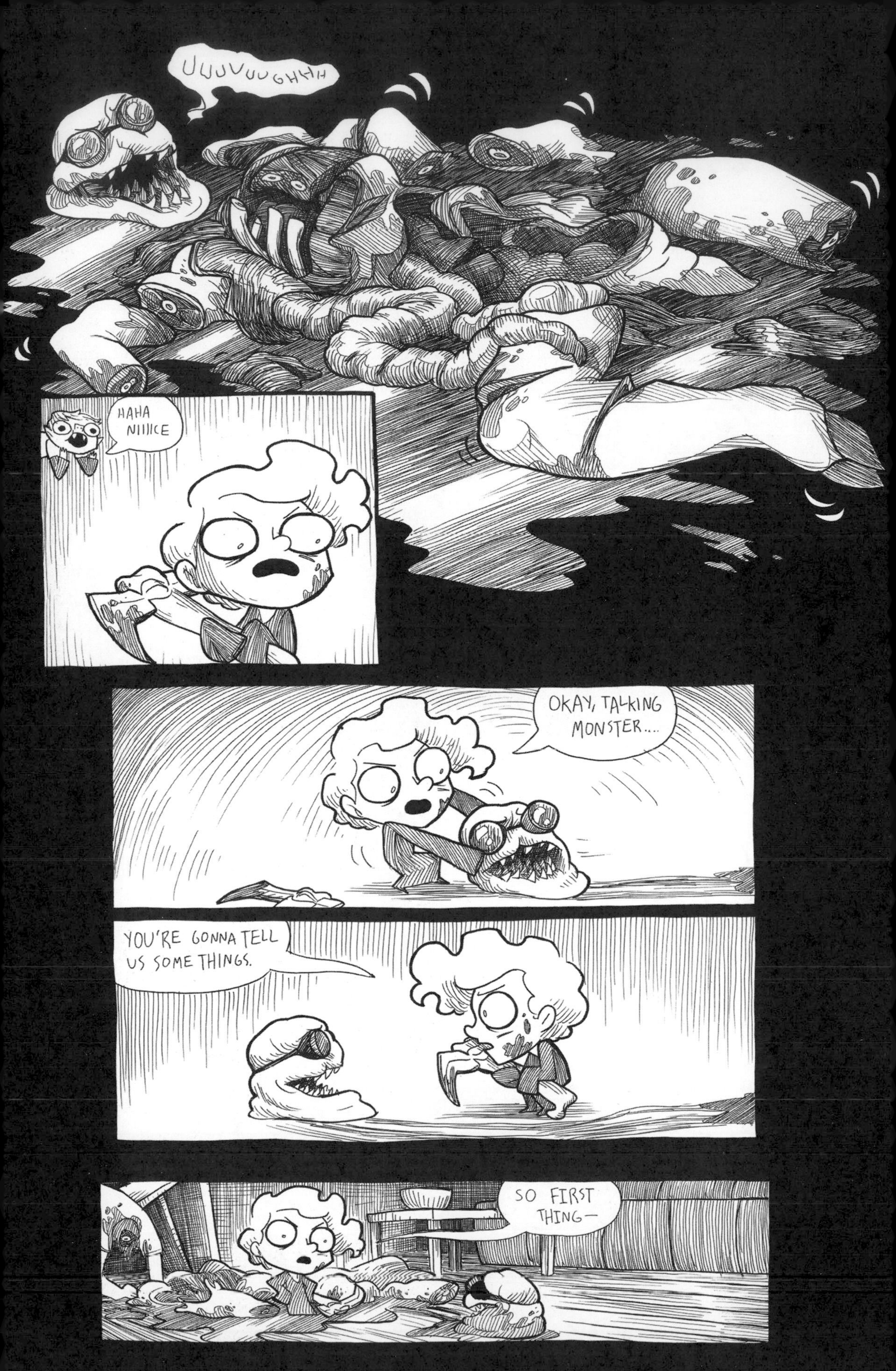
UUUVUUGHHH
HAHA NIIIICE
OKAY, TALKING MONSTER....
YOU'RE GONNA TELL US SOME THINGS.
SO FIRST THING—

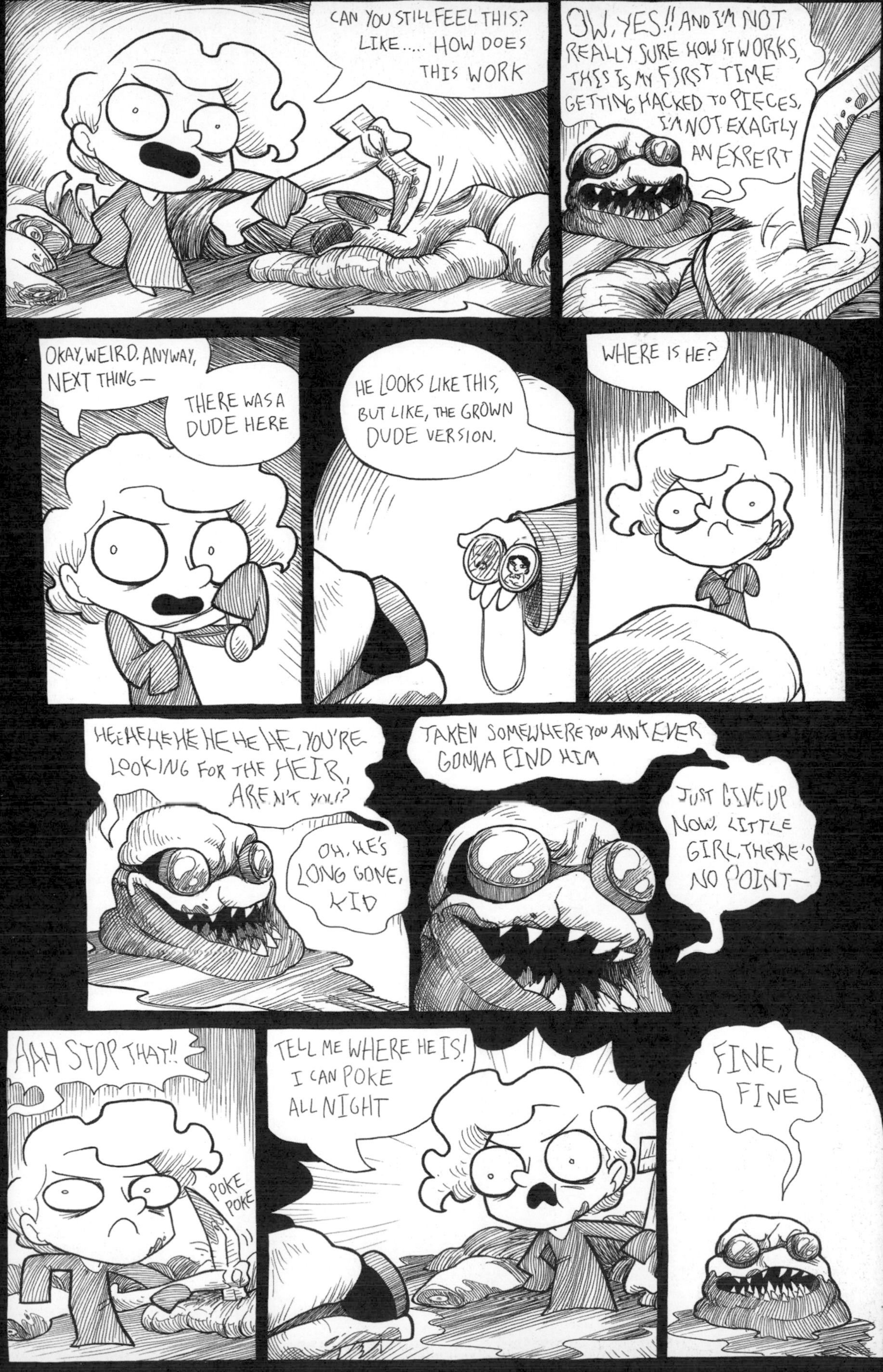
CAN YOU STILL FEEL THIS? LIKE..... HOW DOES THIS WORK
OW, YES!! AND I'M NOT REALLY SURE HOW IT WORKS, THIS IS MY FIRST TIME GETTING HACKED TO PIECES, I'M NOT EXACTLY AN EXPERT
OKAY, WEIRD. ANYWAY, NEXT THING—
THERE WAS A DUDE HERE
HE LOOKS LIKE THIS, BUT LIKE, THE GROWN DUDE VERSION.
WHERE IS HE?
HEEHEHEHEHE HE HE HE HE, YOU'RE LOOKING FOR THE HEIR, AREN'T YOU?
OH, HE'S LONG GONE, KID
TAKEN SOMEWHERE YOU AIN'T EVER GONNA FIND HIM
JUST GIVE UP NOW, LITTLE GIRL, THERE'S NO POINT—
AAH STOP THAT!!
POKE POKE
TELL ME WHERE HE IS! I CAN POKE ALL NIGHT
FINE, FINE

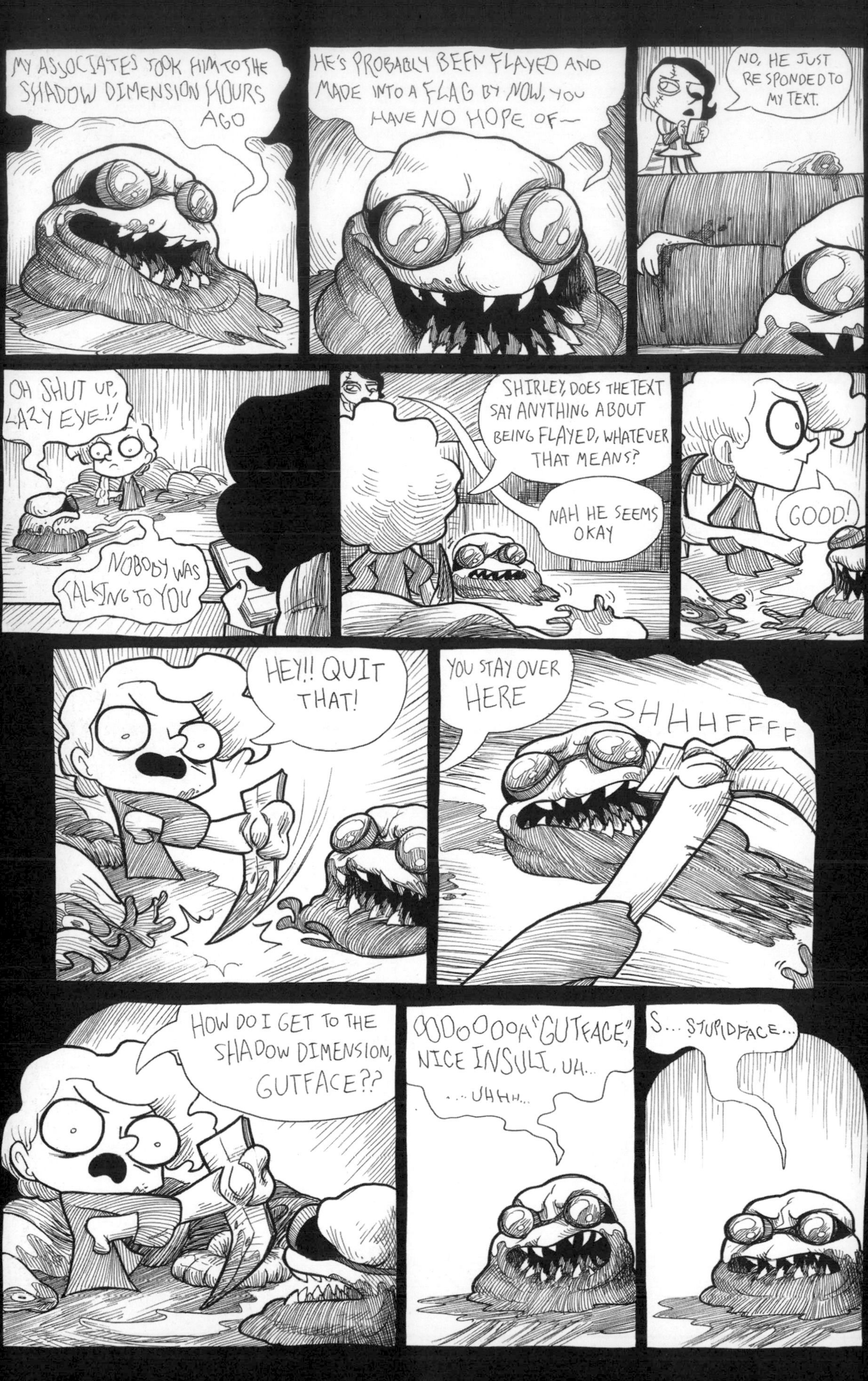

MY ASSOCIATES TOOK HIM TO THE SHADOW DIMENSION HOURS AGO
HE'S PROBABLY BEEN FLAYED AND MADE INTO A FLAG BY NOW, YOU HAVE NO HOPE OF~
NO, HE JUST RESPONDED TO MY TEXT.
OH SHUT UP, LAZY EYE!!
NOBODY WAS TALKING TO YOU
SHIRLEY, DOES THE TEXT SAY ANYTHING ABOUT BEING FLAYED, WHATEVER THAT MEANS?
NAH HE SEEMS OKAY
GOOD!
HEY!! QUIT THAT!
YOU STAY OVER HERE
SSHHHFFFF
HOW DO I GET TO THE SHADOW DIMENSION, GUTFACE??
OOOOOOOOA "GUTFACE," NICE INSULT, UH...
...UHHH...
S... STUPIDFACE...

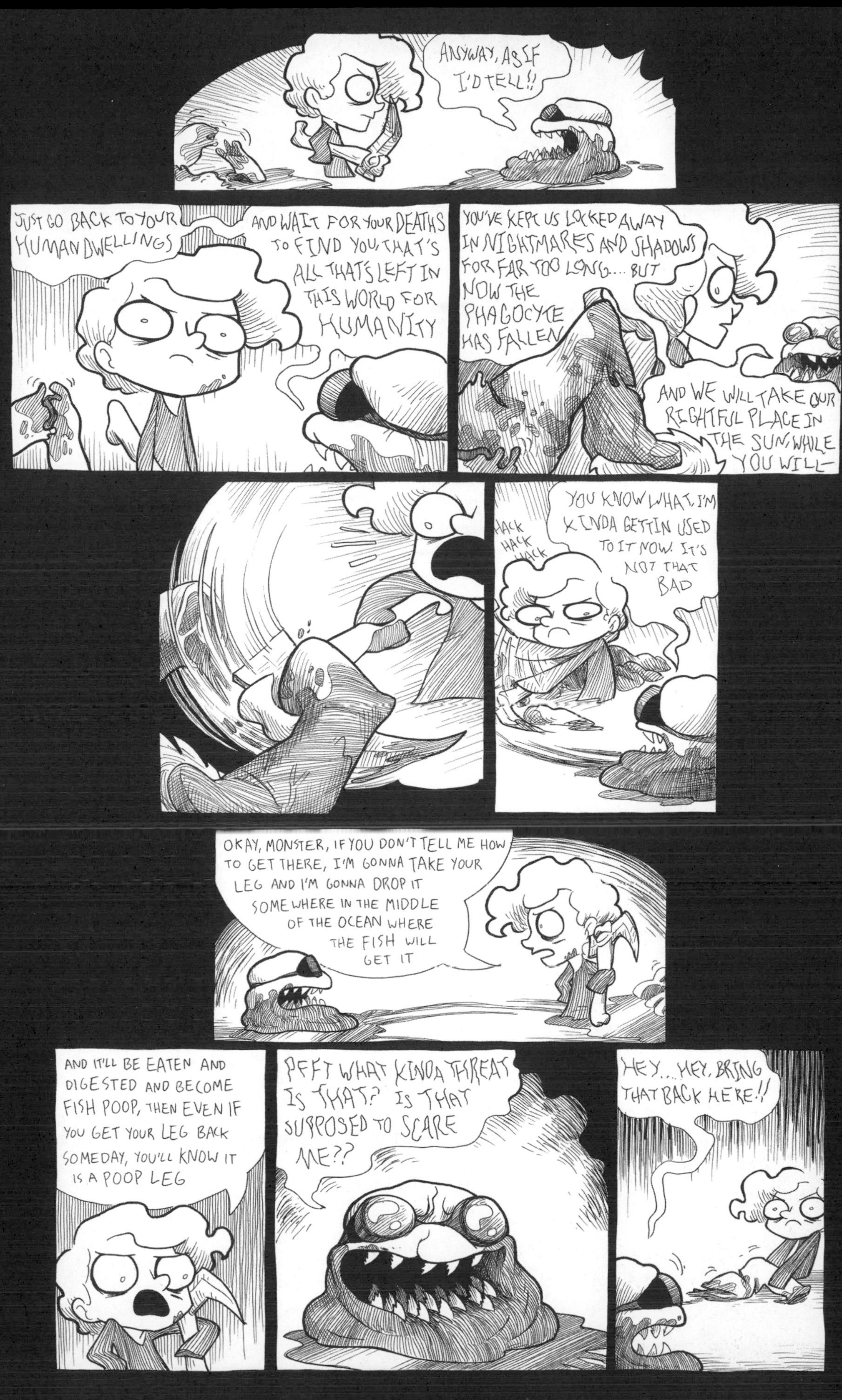
ANYWAY, AS IF I'D TELL!!
JUST GO BACK TO YOUR HUMAN DWELLINGS
AND WAIT FOR YOUR DEATHS TO FIND YOU, THAT'S ALL THAT'S LEFT IN THIS WORLD FOR HUMANITY
YOU'VE KEPT US LOCKED AWAY IN NIGHTMARES AND SHADOWS FOR FAR TOO LONG.... BUT NOW THE PHAGOCYTE HAS FALLEN
AND WE WILL TAKE OUR RIGHTFUL PLACE IN THE SUN, WHILE YOU WILL–
HACK HACK HACK
YOU KNOW WHAT, I'M KINDA GETTIN USED TO IT NOW. IT'S NOT THAT BAD
OKAY, MONSTER, IF YOU DON'T TELL ME HOW TO GET THERE, I'M GONNA TAKE YOUR LEG AND I'M GONNA DROP IT SOMEWHERE IN THE MIDDLE OF THE OCEAN WHERE THE FISH WILL GET IT
AND IT'LL BE EATEN AND DIGESTED AND BECOME FISH POOP, THEN EVEN IF YOU GET YOUR LEG BACK SOMEDAY, YOU'LL KNOW IT IS A POOP LEG
PFFT WHAT KINDA THREAT IS THAT? IS THAT SUPPOSED TO SCARE ME??
HEY... HEY, BRING THAT BACK HERE!!

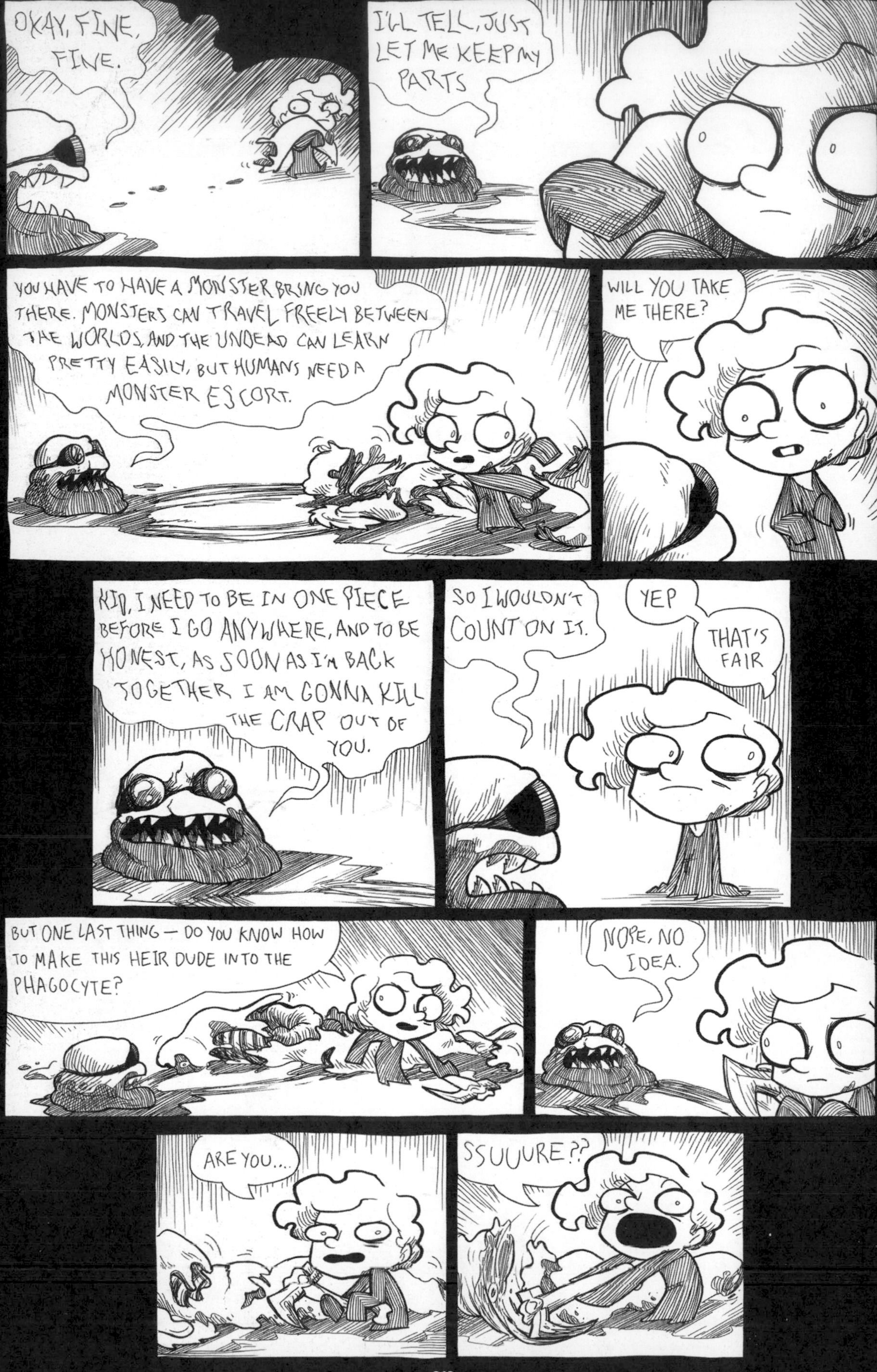
OKAY, FINE, FINE.
I'LL TELL, JUST LET ME KEEP MY PARTS
YOU HAVE TO HAVE A MONSTER BRING YOU THERE. MONSTERS CAN TRAVEL FREELY BETWEEN THE WORLDS, AND THE UNDEAD CAN LEARN PRETTY EASILY, BUT HUMANS NEED A MONSTER ESCORT.
WILL YOU TAKE ME THERE?
KID, I NEED TO BE IN ONE PIECE BEFORE I GO ANYWHERE, AND TO BE HONEST, AS SOON AS I'M BACK TOGETHER I AM GONNA KILL THE CRAP OUT OF YOU.
SO I WOULDN'T COUNT ON IT.
YEP
THAT'S FAIR
BUT ONE LAST THING — DO YOU KNOW HOW TO MAKE THIS HEIR DUDE INTO THE PHAGOCYTE?
NOPE, NO IDEA.
ARE YOU....
SSUUURE??

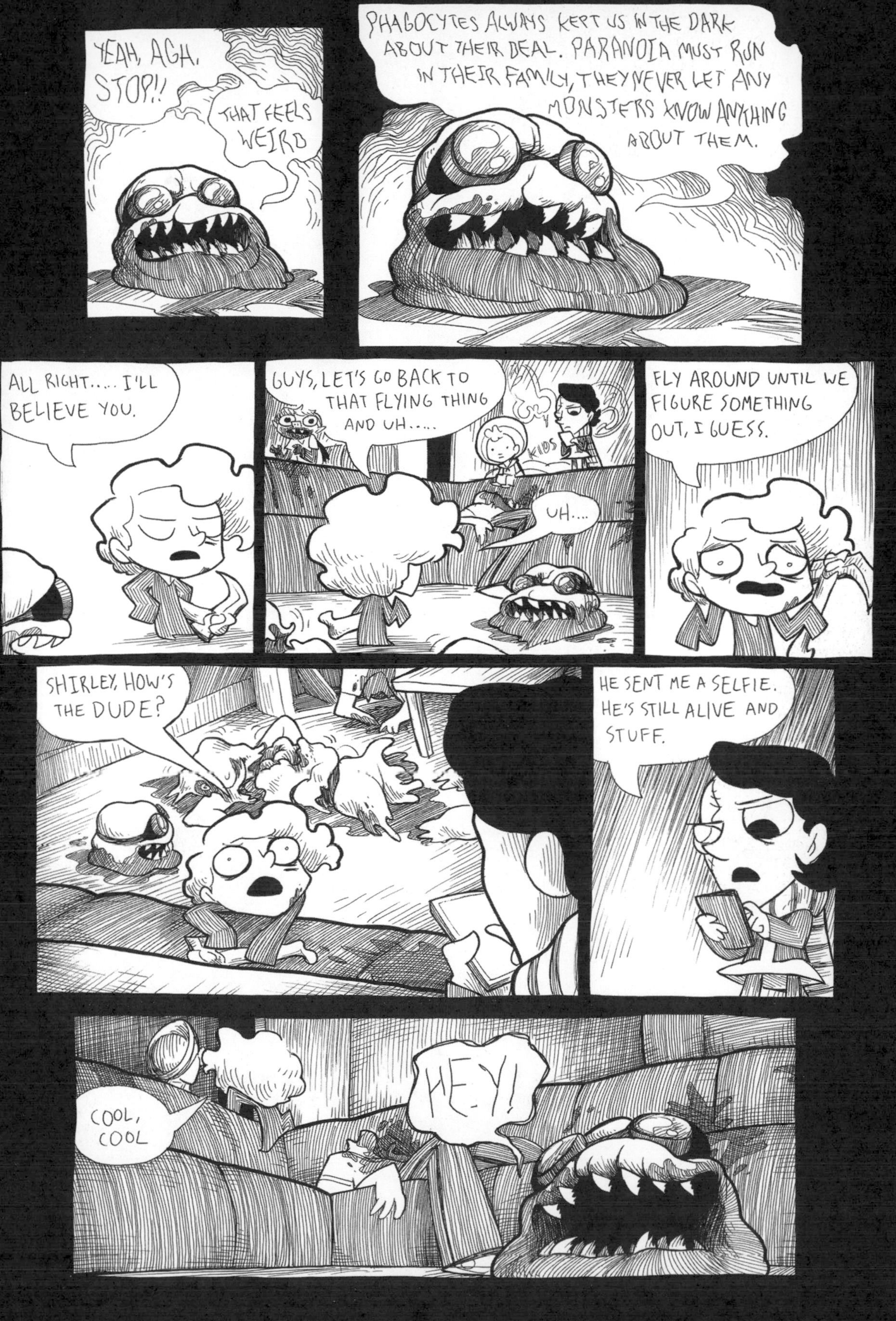
YEAH, AGH, STOP!!
THAT FEELS WEIRD
PHAGOCYTES ALWAYS KEPT US IN THE DARK ABOUT THEIR DEAL. PARANOIA MUST RUN IN THEIR FAMILY, THEY NEVER LET ANY MONSTERS KNOW ANYTHING ABOUT THEM.
ALL RIGHT..... I'LL BELIEVE YOU.
GUYS, LET'S GO BACK TO THAT FLYING THING AND UH.....
UH....
FLY AROUND UNTIL WE FIGURE SOMETHING OUT, I GUESS.
SHIRLEY, HOW'S THE DUDE?
HE SENT ME A SELFIE. HE'S STILL ALIVE AND STUFF.
COOL, COOL
HEY!

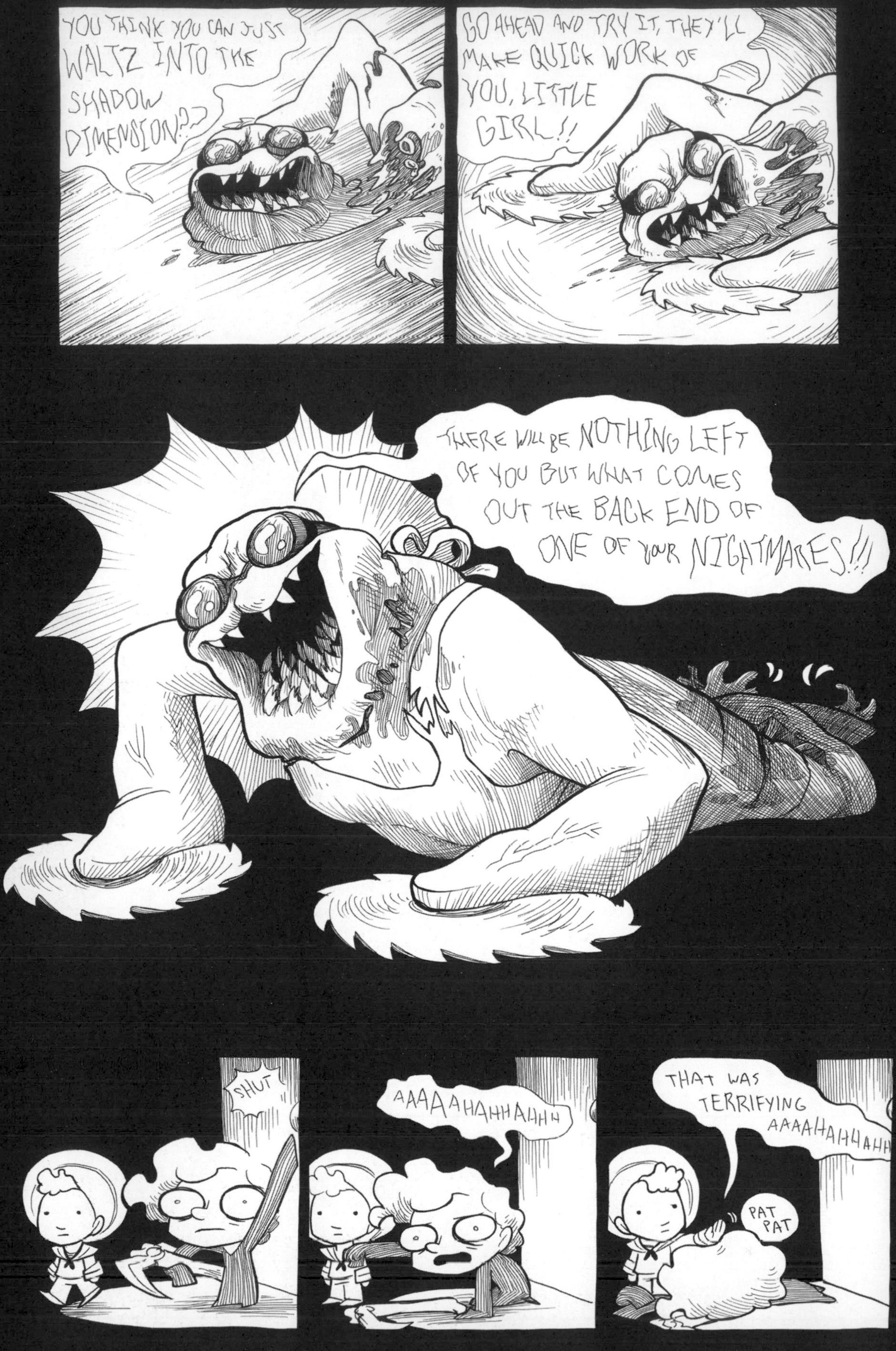
YOU THINK YOU CAN JUST WALTZ INTO THE SHADOW DIMENSION?!?
GO AHEAD AND TRY IT, THEY'LL MAKE QUICK WORK OF YOU, LITTLE GIRL!!
THERE WILL BE NOTHING LEFT OF YOU BUT WHAT COMES OUT THE BACK END OF ONE OF YOUR NIGHTMARES!!!
SHUT
AAAAAHAHHAHHH
THAT WAS TERRIFYING AAAAHAHHAHH
PAT PAT

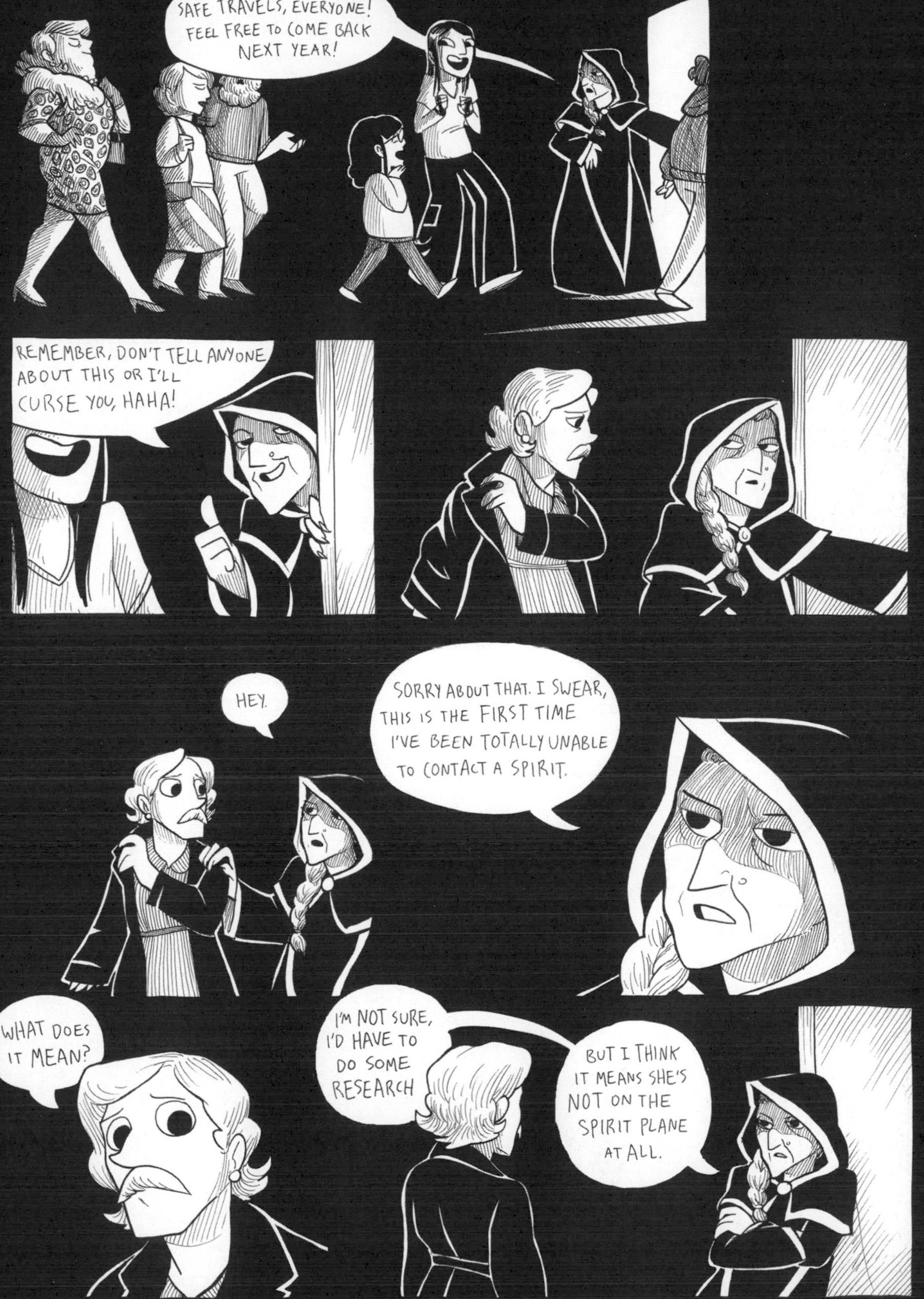
SAFE TRAVELS, EVERYONE! FEEL FREE TO COME BACK NEXT YEAR!
REMEMBER, DON'T TELL ANYONE ABOUT THIS OR I'LL CURSE YOU, HAHA!
HEY.
SORRY ABOUT THAT. I SWEAR, THIS IS THE FIRST TIME I'VE BEEN TOTALLY UNABLE TO CONTACT A SPIRIT.
WHAT DOES IT MEAN?
I'M NOT SURE, I'D HAVE TO DO SOME RESEARCH
BUT I THINK IT MEANS SHE'S NOT ON THE SPIRIT PLANE AT ALL.

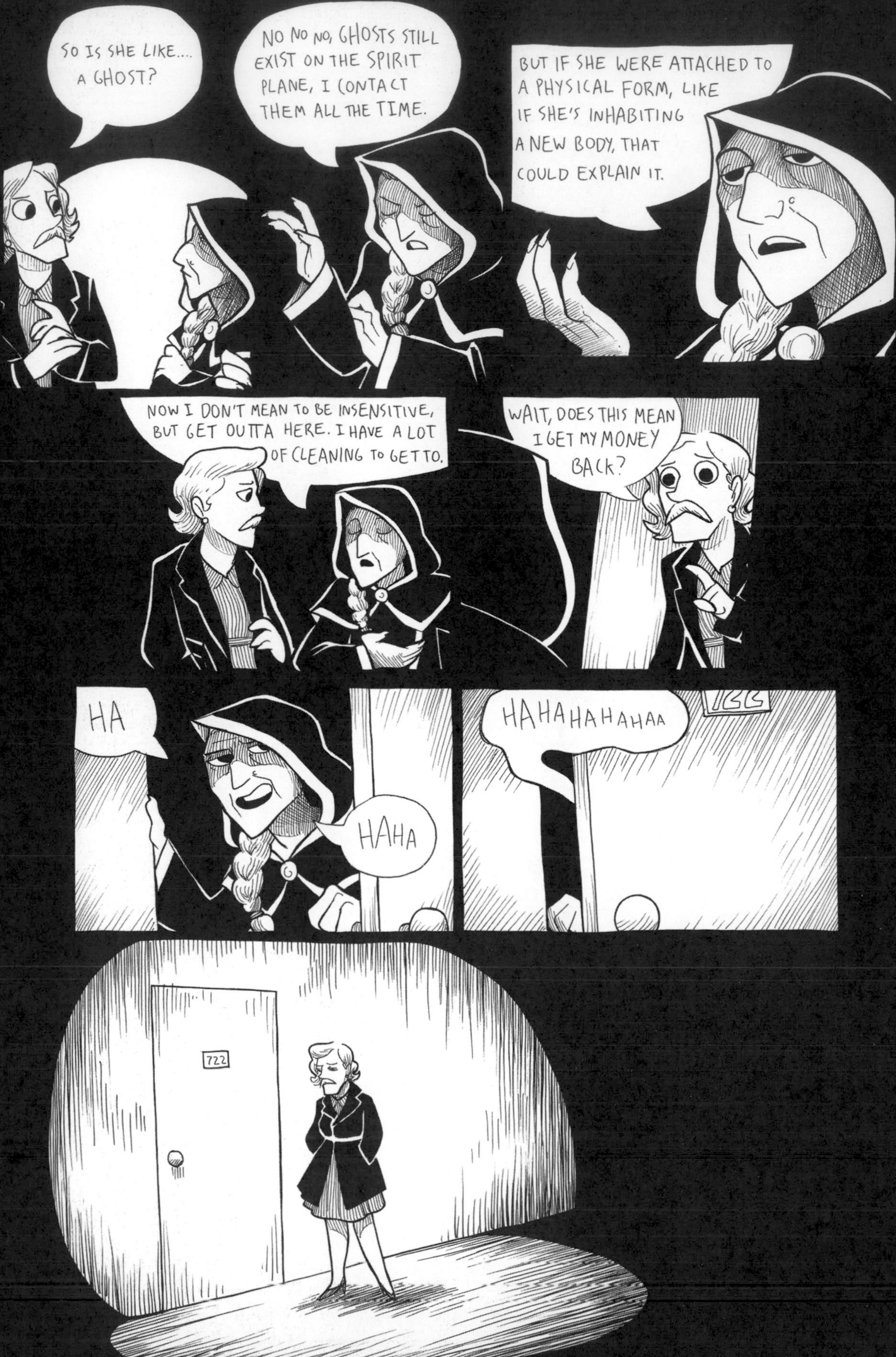
SO IS SHE LIKE.... A GHOST?
NO NO NO, GHOSTS STILL EXIST ON THE SPIRIT PLANE, I CONTACT THEM ALL THE TIME.
BUT IF SHE WERE ATTACHED TO A PHYSICAL FORM, LIKE IF SHE'S INHABITING A NEW BODY, THAT COULD EXPLAIN IT.
NOW I DON'T MEAN TO BE INSENSITIVE, BUT GET OUTTA HERE. I HAVE A LOT OF CLEANING TO GET TO.
WAIT, DOES THIS MEAN I GET MY MONEY BACK?
HA
HAHA
HAHAHAHAHAHAA
722

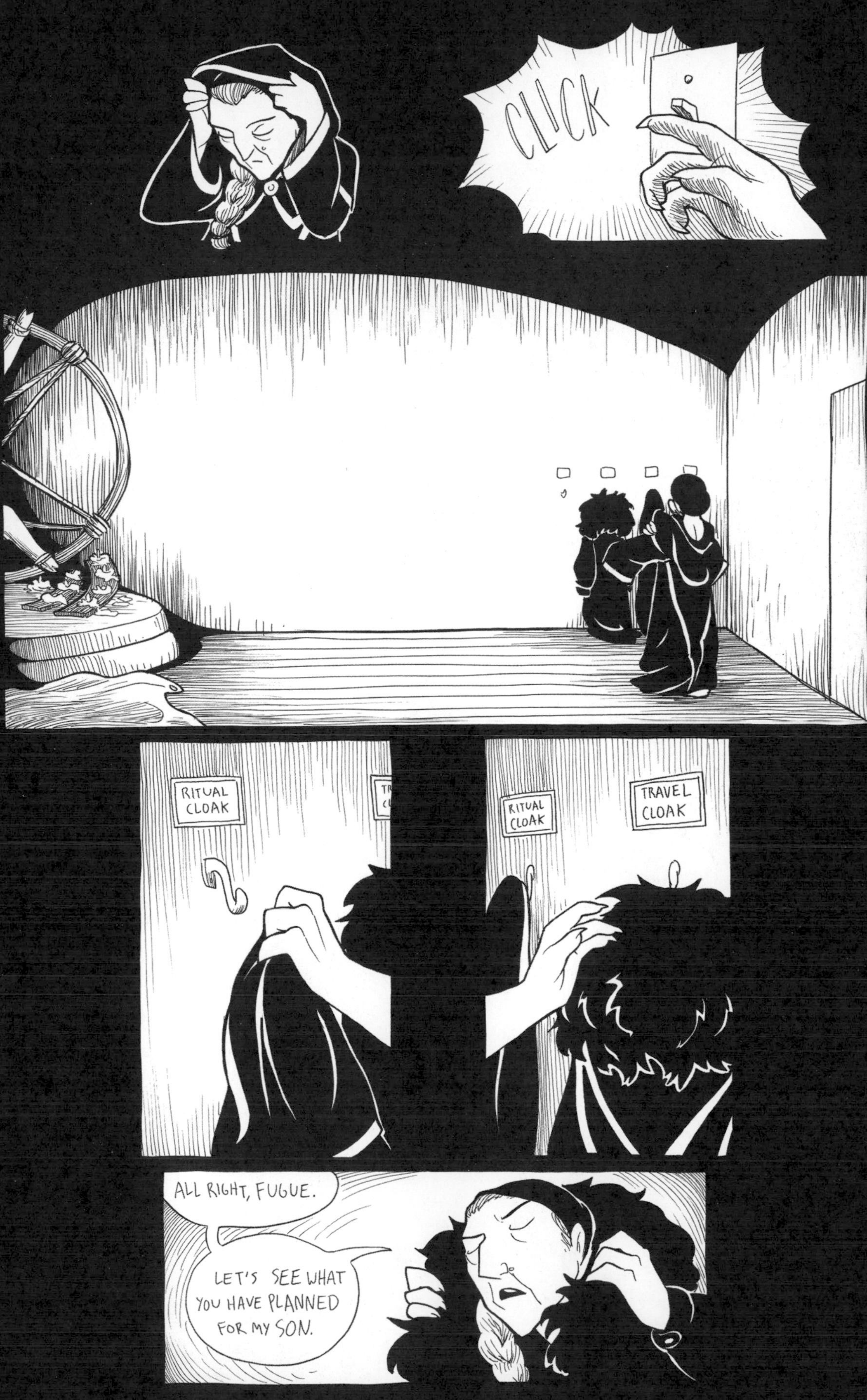
CLICK
RITUAL CLOAK
RITUAL CLOAK
TRAVEL CLOAK
ALL RIGHT, FUGUE.
LET'S SEE WHAT YOU HAVE PLANNED FOR MY SON.

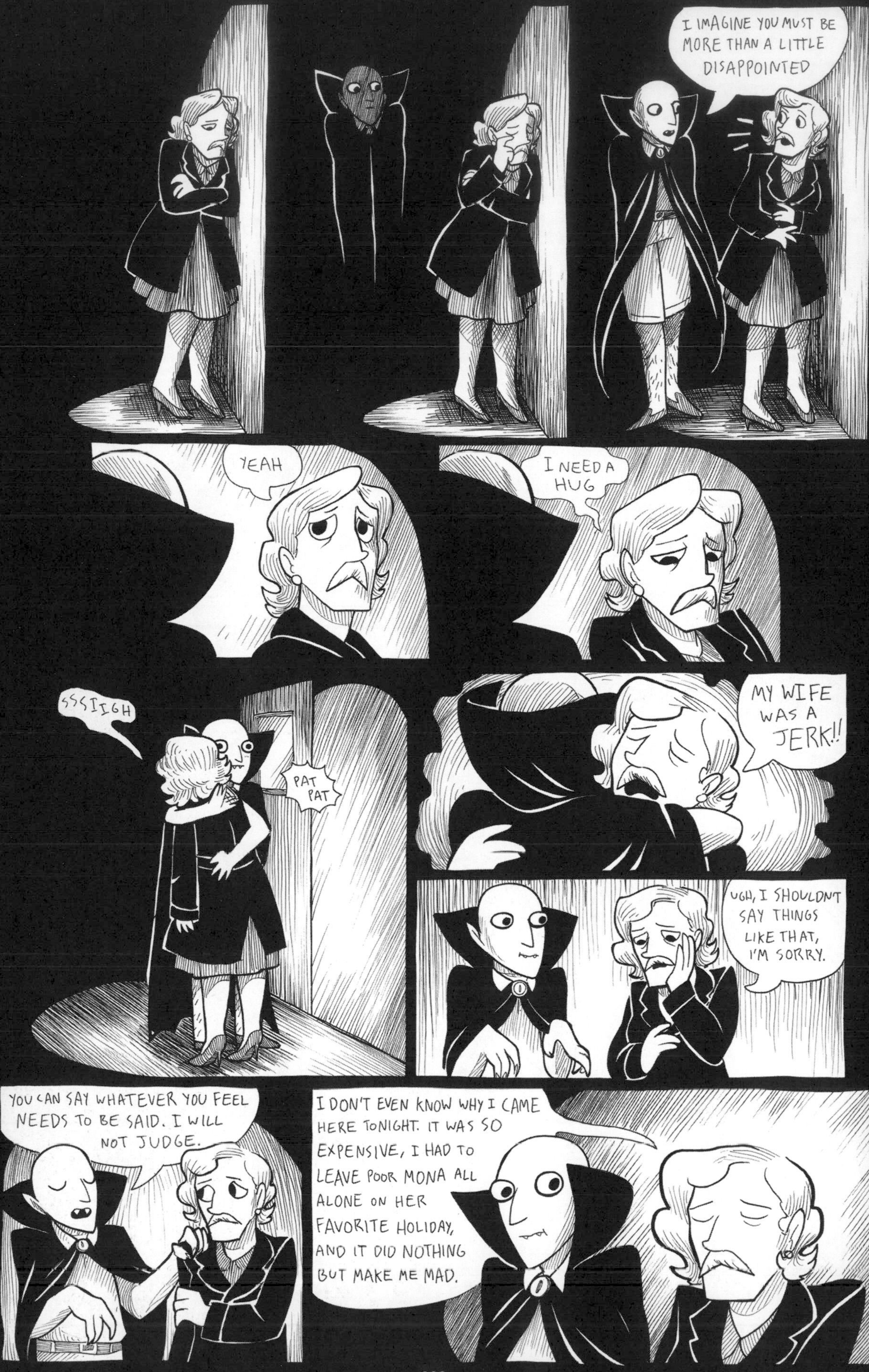
I IMAGINE YOU MUST BE MORE THAN A LITTLE DISAPPOINTED
YEAH
I NEED A HUG
SSSIIGH
PAT PAT
MY WIFE WAS A JERK!!
UGH, I SHOULDNT SAY THINGS LIKE THAT, I'M SORRY.
YOU CAN SAY WHATEVER YOU FEEL NEEDS TO BE SAID. I WILL NOT JUDGE.
I DON'T EVEN KNOW WHY I CAME HERE TONIGHT. IT WAS SO EXPENSIVE, I HAD TO LEAVE POOR MONA ALL ALONE ON HER FAVORITE HOLIDAY, AND IT DID NOTHING BUT MAKE ME MAD.

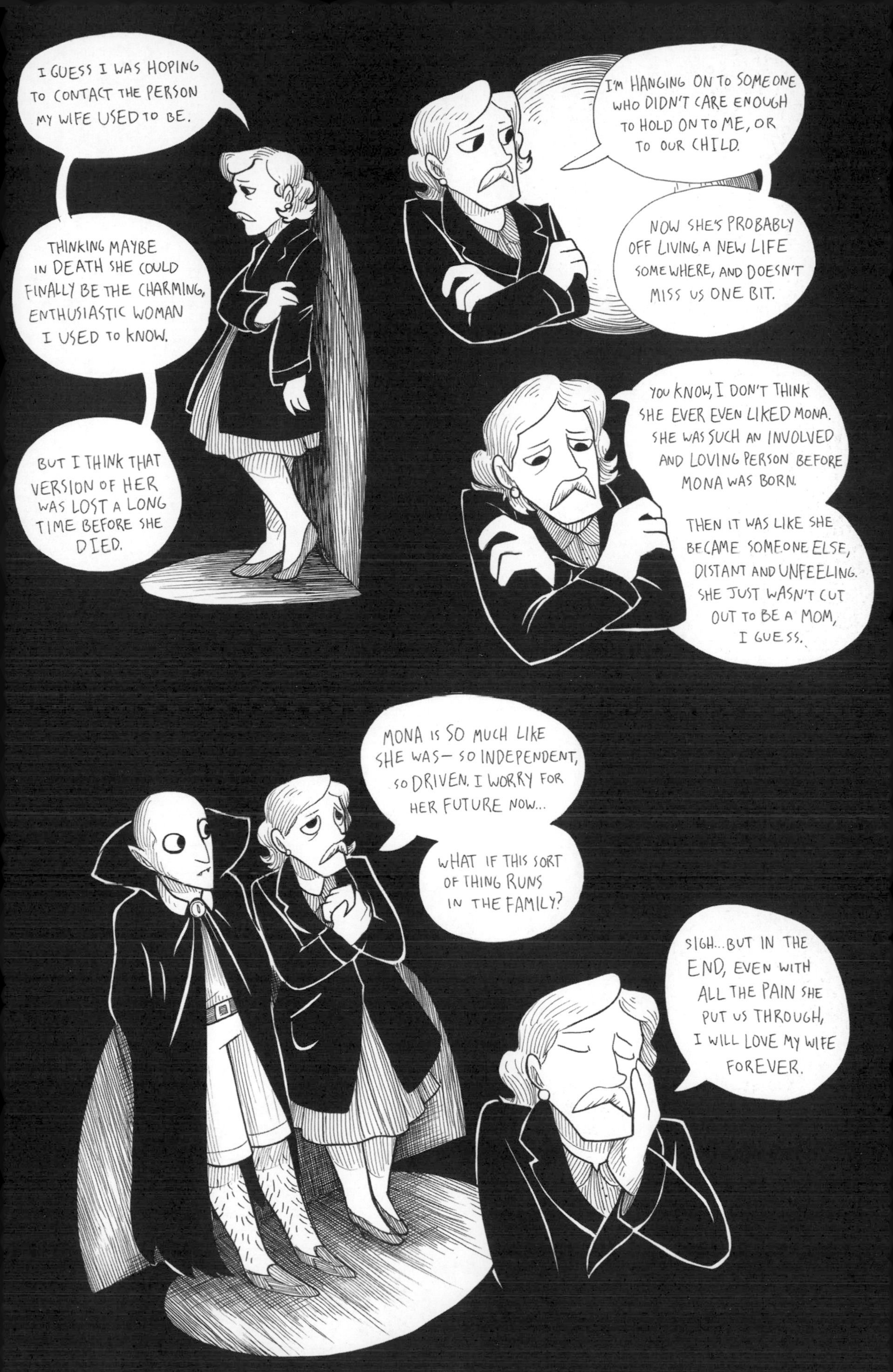
I GUESS I WAS HOPING TO CONTACT THE PERSON MY WIFE USED TO BE.
THINKING MAYBE IN DEATH SHE COULD FINALLY BE THE CHARMING, ENTHUSIASTIC WOMAN I USED TO KNOW.
BUT I THINK THAT VERSION OF HER WAS LOST A LONG TIME BEFORE SHE DIED.
I'M HANGING ON TO SOMEONE WHO DIDN'T CARE ENOUGH TO HOLD ON TO ME, OR TO OUR CHILD.
NOW SHE'S PROBABLY OFF LIVING A NEW LIFE SOMEWHERE, AND DOESN'T MISS US ONE BIT.
YOU KNOW, I DON'T THINK SHE EVER EVEN LIKED MONA. SHE WAS SUCH AN INVOLVED AND LOVING PERSON BEFORE MONA WAS BORN.
THEN IT WAS LIKE SHE BECAME SOMEONE ELSE, DISTANT AND UNFEELING. SHE JUST WASN'T CUT OUT TO BE A MOM, I GUESS.
MONA IS SO MUCH LIKE SHE WAS— SO INDEPENDENT, SO DRIVEN. I WORRY FOR HER FUTURE NOW...
WHAT IF THIS SORT OF THING RUNS IN THE FAMILY?
SIGH... BUT IN THE END, EVEN WITH ALL THE PAIN SHE PUT US THROUGH, I WILL LOVE MY WIFE FOREVER.

"HER DRESSES STILL SMELL LIKE HER. AND IT CAN BE SO COMFORTING TO WEAR THEM SOMETIMES, THOUGH MONA WOULD RATHER I DIDN'T."

"IT HELPS ME HOLD ON TO MY MEMORIES, YOU KNOW?"

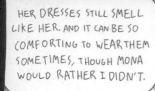

"YES, I ALSO HELD ONTO MY WIFE'S CLOTHES, FOR MANY CENTURIES, EVEN."

"HER BITTERSWEET MEMORY SEEMINGLY LIVING IN THE WEAVE OF THE FABRIC."

"BUT IN TIME THEY MERELY SMELLED OF OLD CLOTHES, AND THEY ROTTED AWAY."

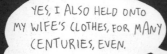

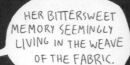

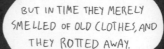

"YET STILL, HUNDREDS OF YEARS AFTER HER DEATH, I HAUNT OUR CASTLE DAY AFTER DAY IN MISERY RATHER THAN GOING OUT AND BEING A PART OF THE WORLD THAT HAS BLOSSOMED SO MARVELLOUSLY SINCE"

"VENTURING OUT A MERE ONCE A YEAR ON HALLOWEEN TO TRY AND CONTACT MY WIFE, ALWAYS UNSUCCESSFULLY."

"I HAVE FOUND THAT A LIFE STEEPED IN MELANCHOLY MEMORIES, OBSESSING OVER WHAT WAS, CAN BE VERY LAME."

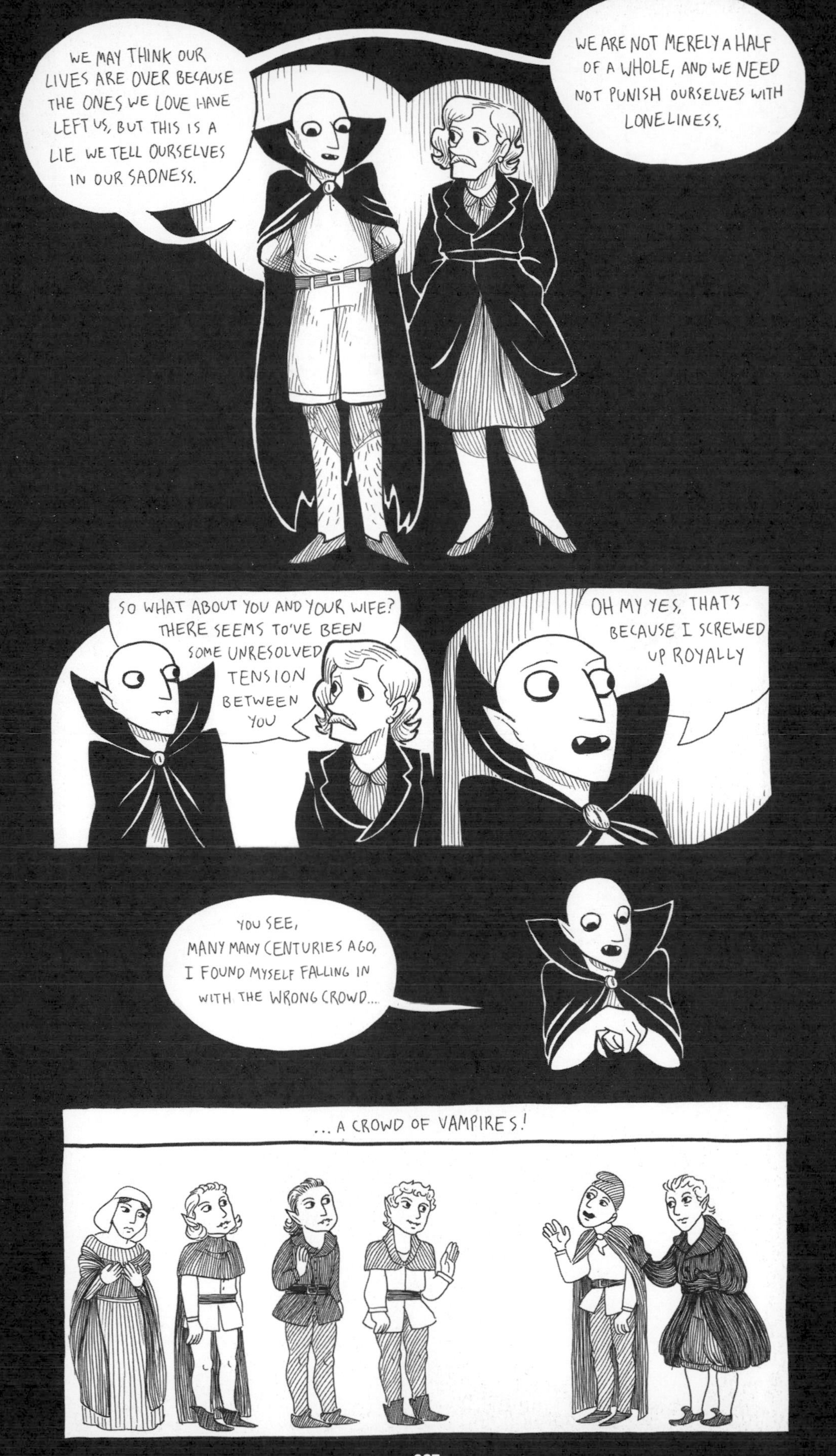
WE MAY THINK OUR LIVES ARE OVER BECAUSE THE ONES WE LOVE HAVE LEFT US, BUT THIS IS A LIE WE TELL OURSELVES IN OUR SADNESS.
WE ARE NOT MERELY A HALF OF A WHOLE, AND WE NEED NOT PUNISH OURSELVES WITH LONELINESS.
SO WHAT ABOUT YOU AND YOUR WIFE? THERE SEEMS TO'VE BEEN SOME UNRESOLVED TENSION BETWEEN YOU
OH MY YES, THAT'S BECAUSE I SCREWED UP ROYALLY
YOU SEE, MANY MANY CENTURIES AGO, I FOUND MYSELF FALLING IN WITH THE WRONG CROWD...
... A CROWD OF VAMPIRES!

AND THEY CONVINCED ME THAT BEING A VAMPIRE WAS THE GREATEST, AND MOST FUN, AND AN EXCELLENT IDEA. IMAGINE: LIVING PAST AGE THIRTY! IT WAS A NOVEL CONCEPT AT THE TIME.

SURE, YOU HAD TO DRINK A LITTLE BLOOD AND STAY INDOORS DURING THE DAY, BUT THAT DIDN'T SOUND SO BAD IN EXCHANGE FOR NEVER HAVING TO FACE THE CRUSHING THREAT OF EVENTUAL NON-EXISTENCE.

SO I LET THEM TURN ME INTO A VAMPIRE, AND AS I HAD COME TO THE CONCLUSION THAT THIS WAS THE HEALTHIEST THING TO DO, I WANTED TO TURN MY WIFE AND CHILD, AS WELL.

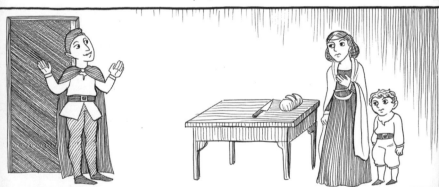

BUT MY WIFE, UPON LEARNING I'D WILLINGLY BECOME AN UNHOLY SERVANT OF DARKNESS, WAS HORRIFIED.

SO SHE KICKED ME OUT OF THE COTTAGE.

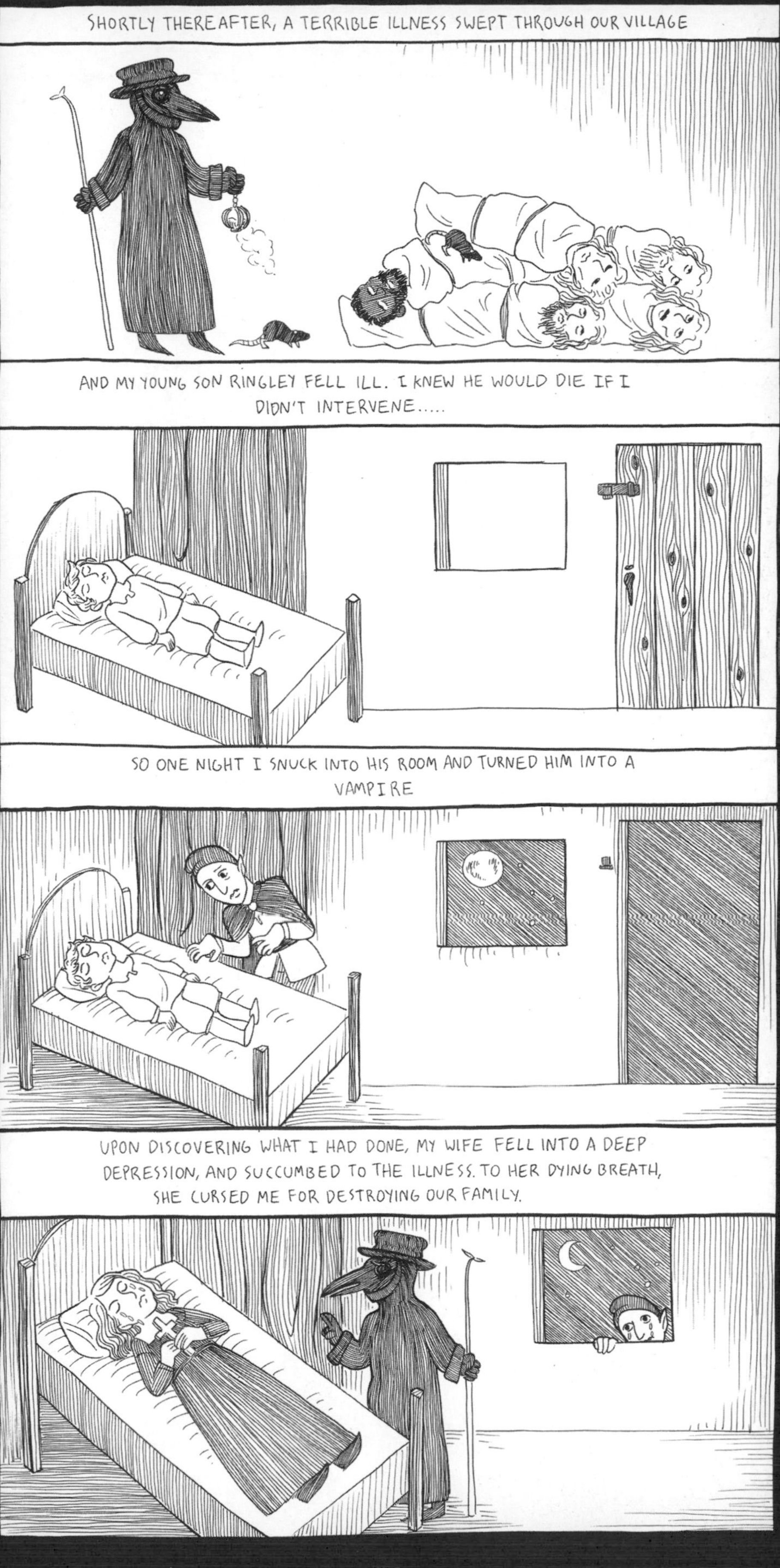
SHORTLY THEREAFTER, A TERRIBLE ILLNESS SWEPT THROUGH OUR VILLAGE
AND MY YOUNG SON RINGLEY FELL ILL. I KNEW HE WOULD DIE IF I DIDN'T INTERVENE.....
SO ONE NIGHT I SNUCK INTO HIS ROOM AND TURNED HIM INTO A VAMPIRE
UPON DISCOVERING WHAT I HAD DONE, MY WIFE FELL INTO A DEEP DEPRESSION, AND SUCCUMBED TO THE ILLNESS. TO HER DYING BREATH, SHE CURSED ME FOR DESTROYING OUR FAMILY.

EVEN THESE COUNTLESS YEARS LATER, SHE REFUSES TO SO MUCH AS SPEAK TO ME, AND RIGHTFULLY SO.

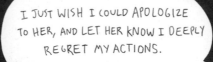

I JUST WISH I COULD APOLOGIZE TO HER, AND LET HER KNOW I DEEPLY REGRET MY ACTIONS.

I NEVER SHOULD HAVE DONE THIS TO RINGLEY, HE'D HAVE BEEN BETTER OFF DYING IN HIS YOUTH THAN SPENDING ETERNITY IN IT. IT'S HAD A DAMAGING EFFECT ON HIM.

HE COULD BE WITH MY WIFE, BUT INSTEAD HE IS HERE, LIVING OUT A CURSED EXISTENCE, DREAMING OF SUNLIGHT AND AN UNINTERRUPTED LIFE.

.....WOW.....

YOU... REALLY TAKE THIS VAMPIRE THING SERIOUSLY

THAT IS BECAUSE I AM A VAMPIRE

WAS THAT NOT CLEAR

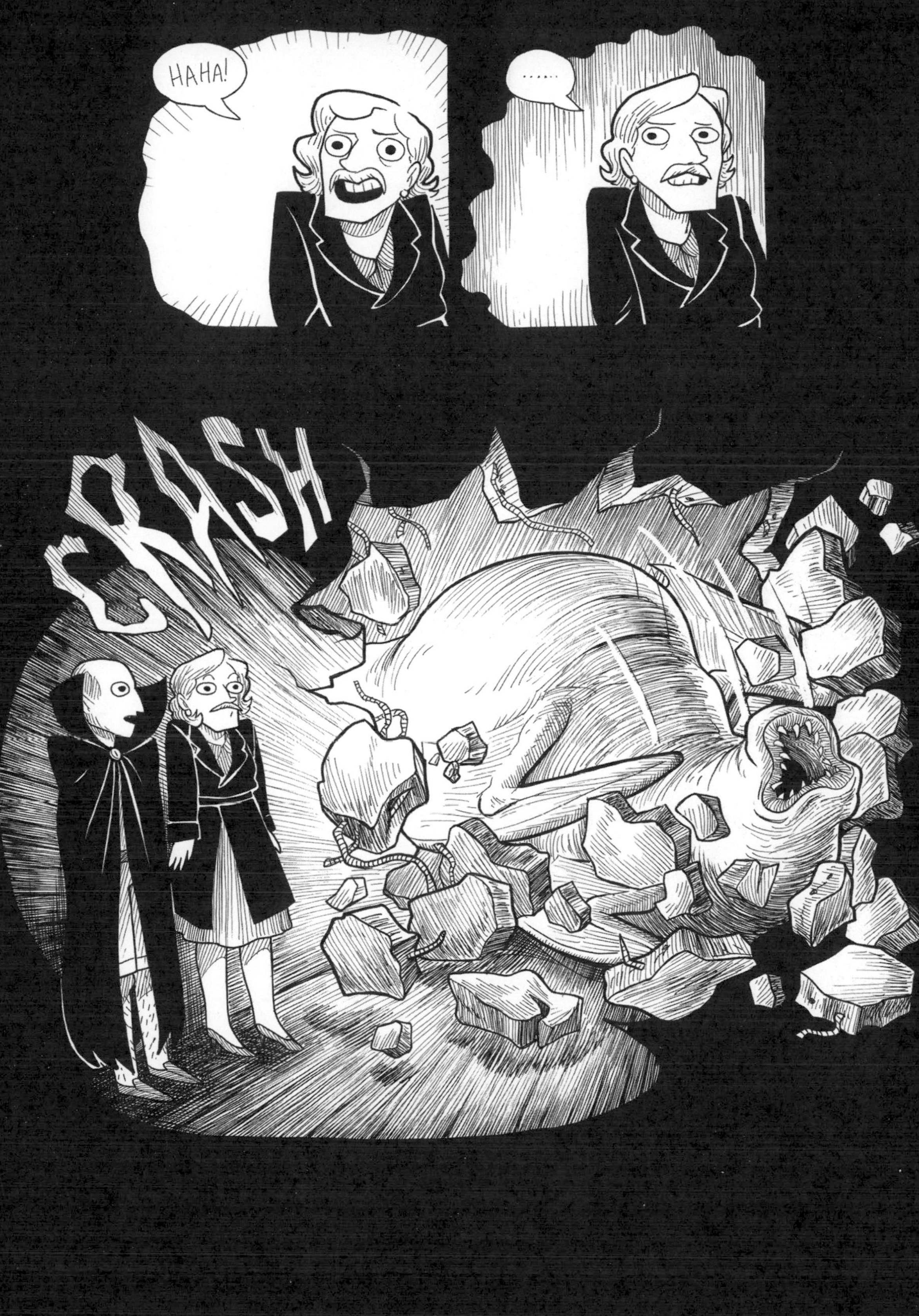
HAHA!
......
CRASH

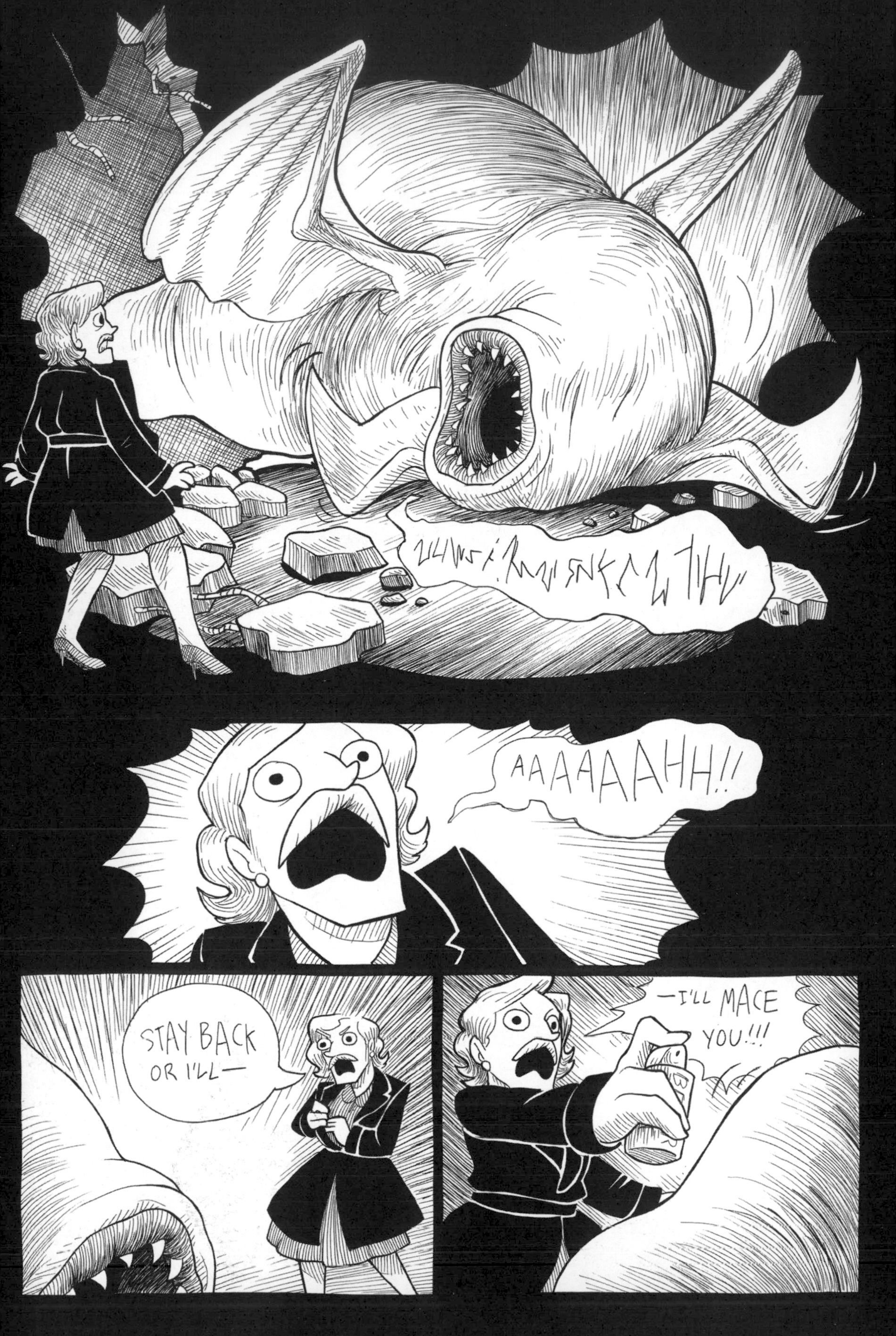
AAAAAAHH!!
STAY BACK OR I'LL—
—I'LL MACE YOU!!!

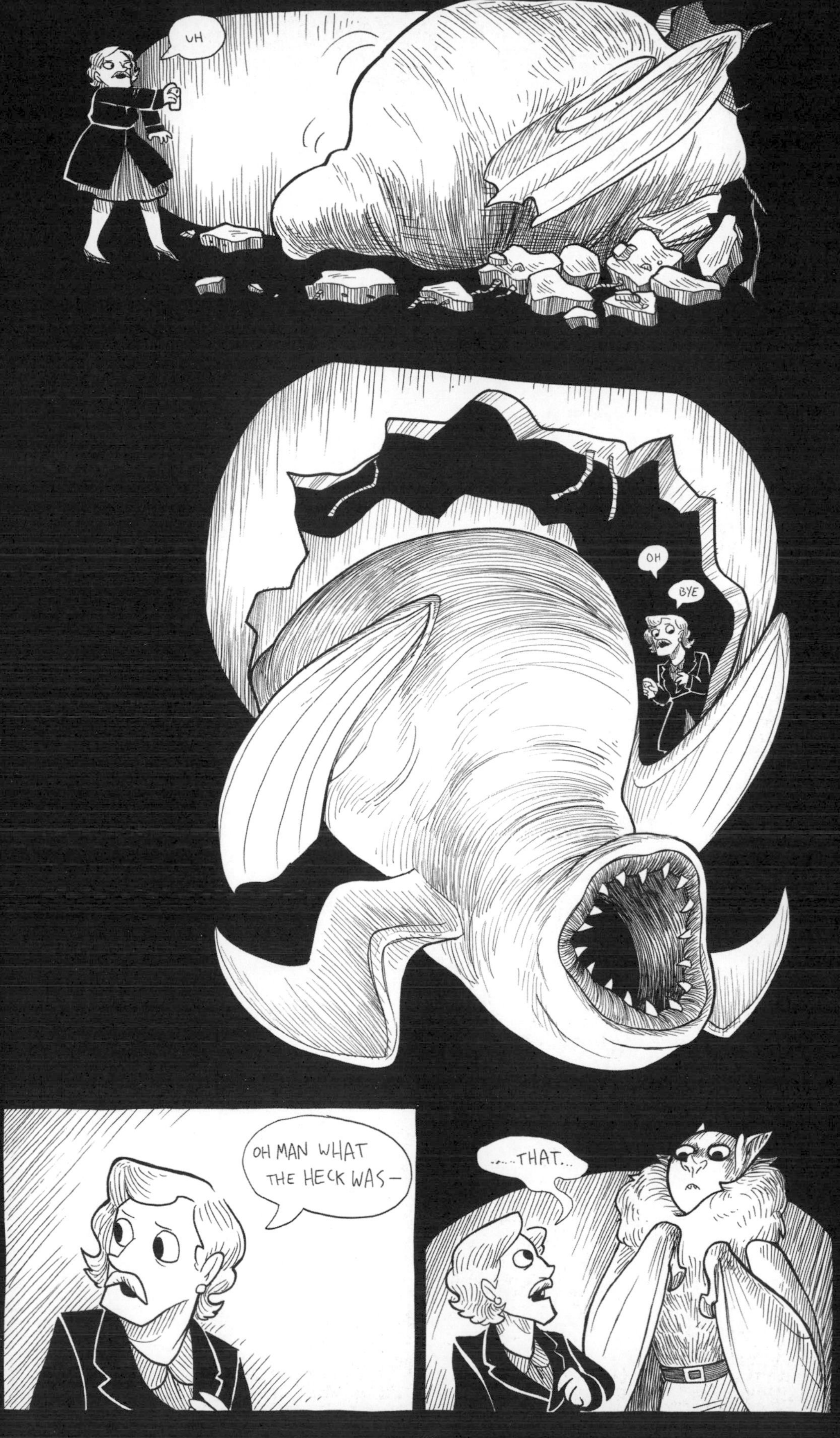
UH
OH
BYE
OH MAN WHAT THE HECK WAS—
...THAT...

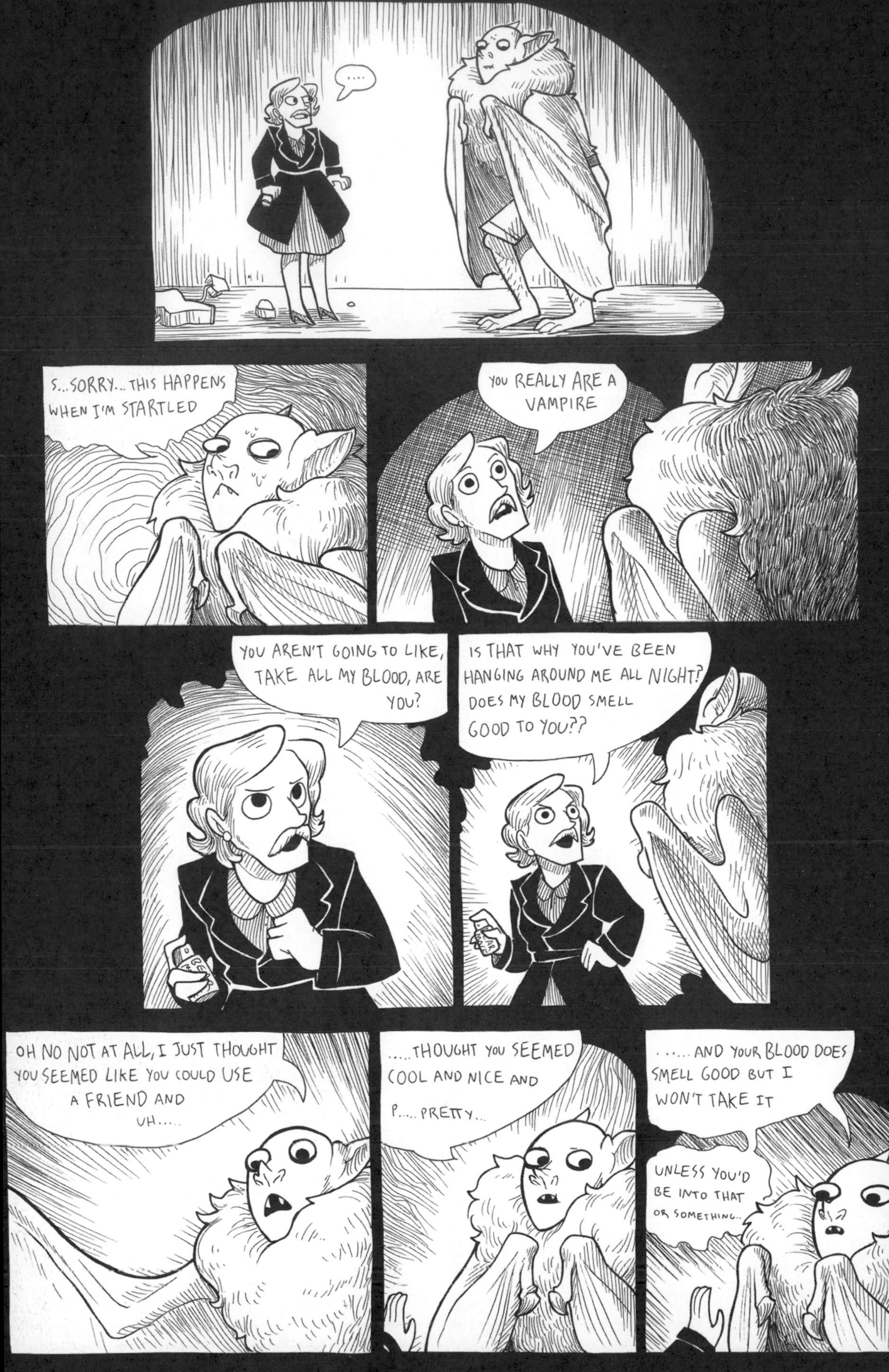

....
S...SORRY... THIS HAPPENS WHEN I'M STARTLED
YOU REALLY ARE A VAMPIRE
YOU AREN'T GOING TO LIKE, TAKE ALL MY BLOOD, ARE YOU?
IS THAT WHY YOU'VE BEEN HANGING AROUND ME ALL NIGHT? DOES MY BLOOD SMELL GOOD TO YOU??
OH NO NOT AT ALL, I JUST THOUGHT YOU SEEMED LIKE YOU COULD USE A FRIEND AND UH.....
.....THOUGHT YOU SEEMED COOL AND NICE AND P..... PRETTY...
......AND YOUR BLOOD DOES SMELL GOOD BUT I WON'T TAKE IT
UNLESS YOU'D BE INTO THAT OR SOMETHING...

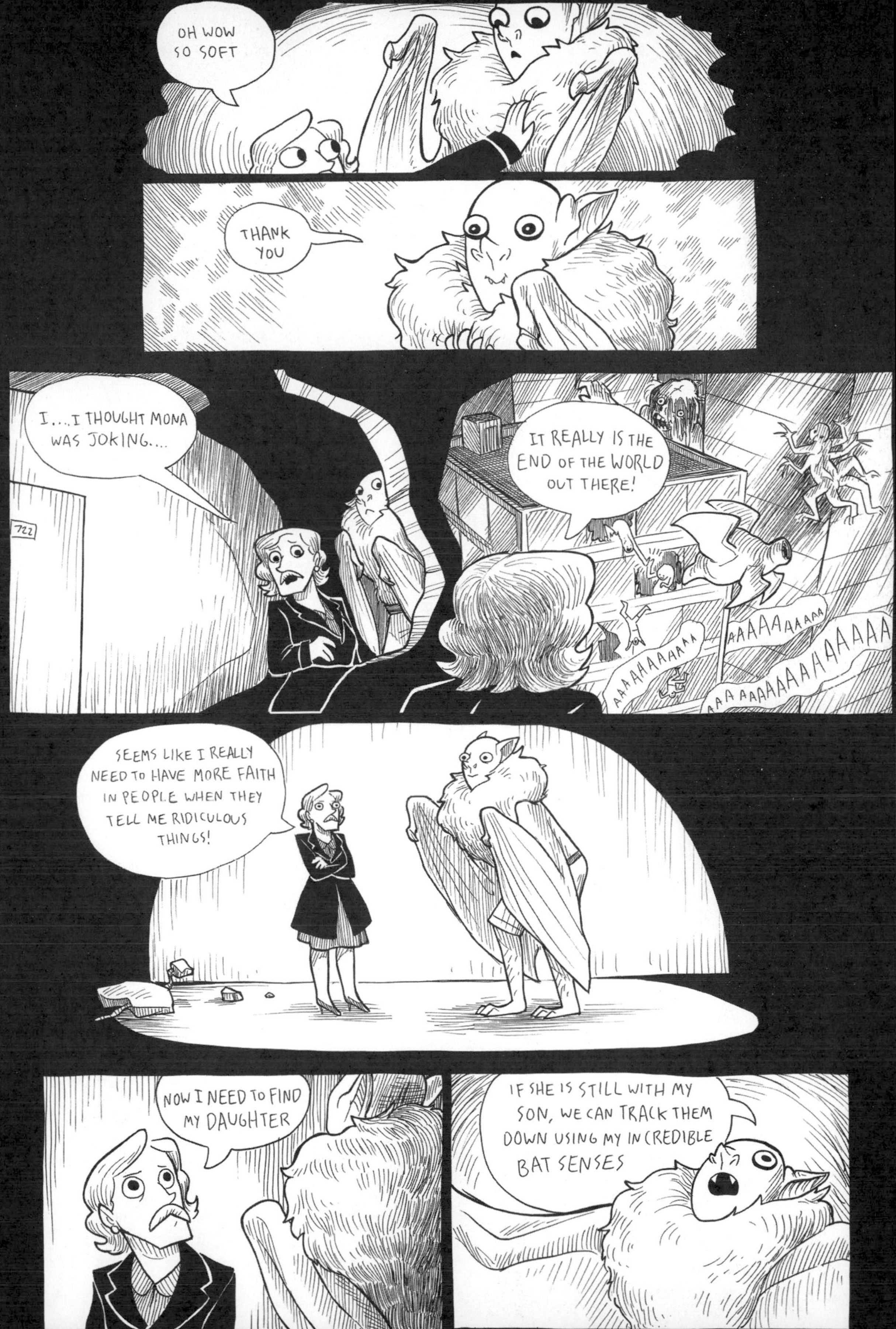
OH WOW SO SOFT
THANK YOU
I....I THOUGHT MONA WAS JOKING....
IT REALLY IS THE END OF THE WORLD OUT THERE!
722
AAAAAAAAAA
AAAAAAAAAAA
AAAAAAAAAAAA
AAAAAAAAAAAAAAA
SEEMS LIKE I REALLY NEED TO HAVE MORE FAITH IN PEOPLE WHEN THEY TELL ME RIDICULOUS THINGS!
NOW I NEED TO FIND MY DAUGHTER
IF SHE IS STILL WITH MY SON, WE CAN TRACK THEM DOWN USING MY INCREDIBLE BAT SENSES

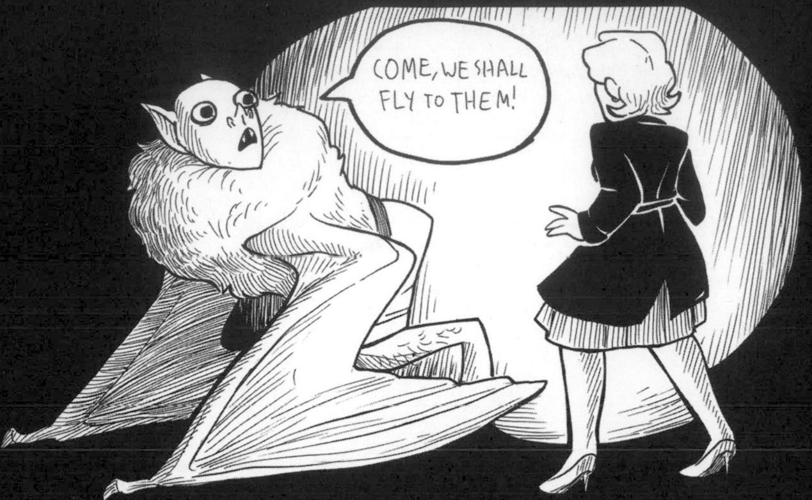
COME, WE SHALL
FLY TO THEM!

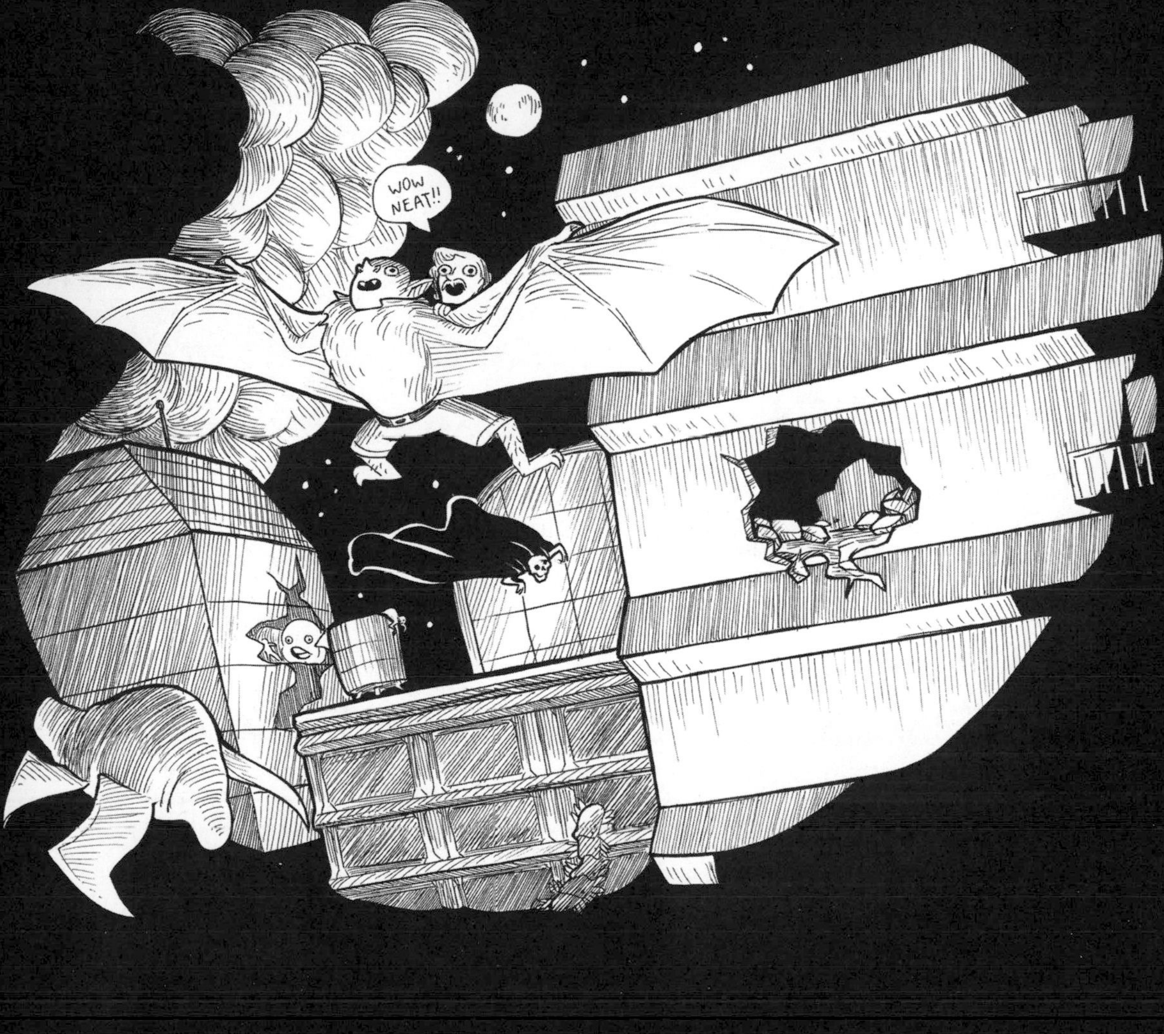
WOW
NEAT!!

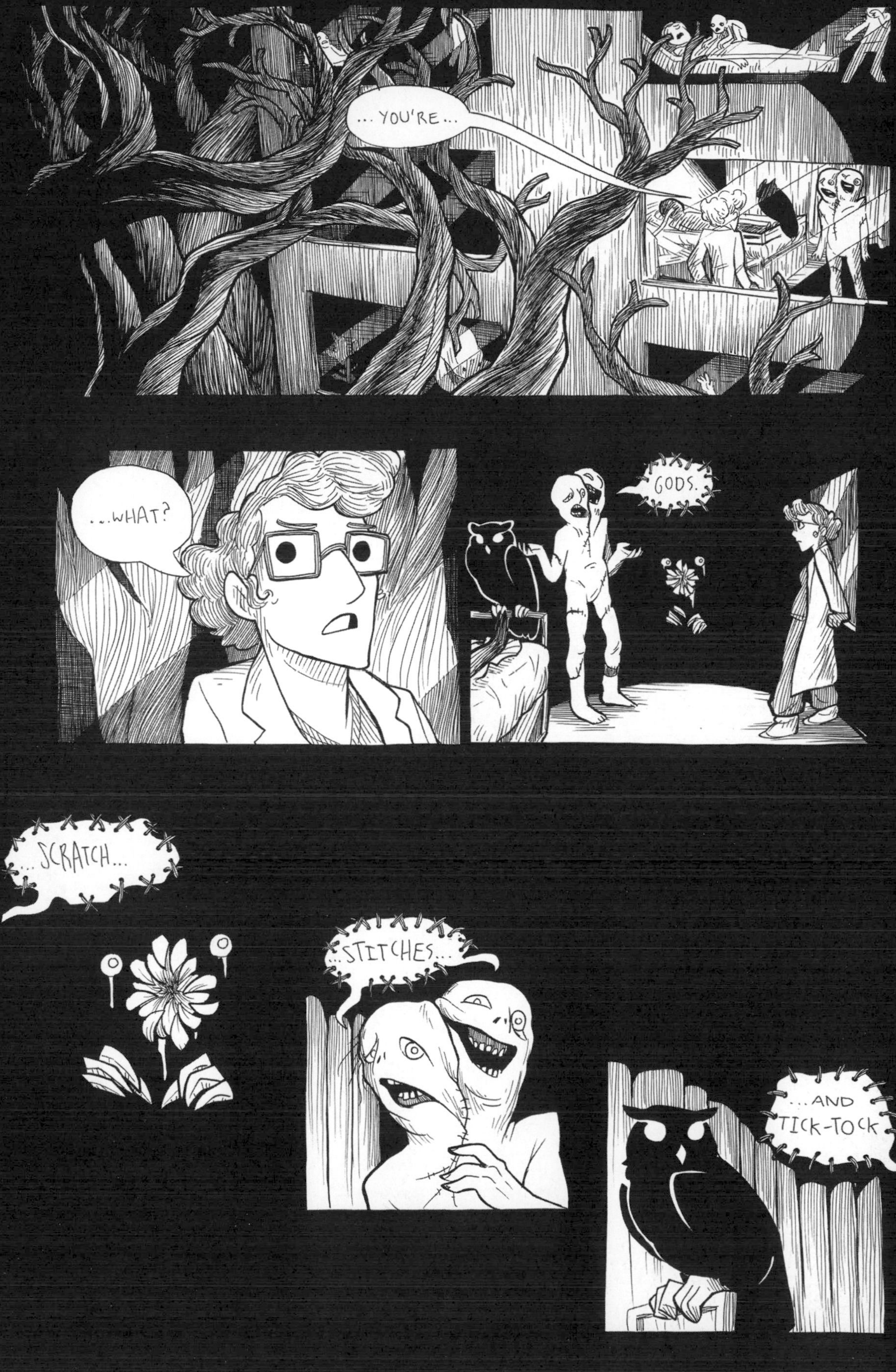
...YOU'RE...
...WHAT?
GODS.
...SCRATCH...
...STITCHES...
...AND TICK-TOCK

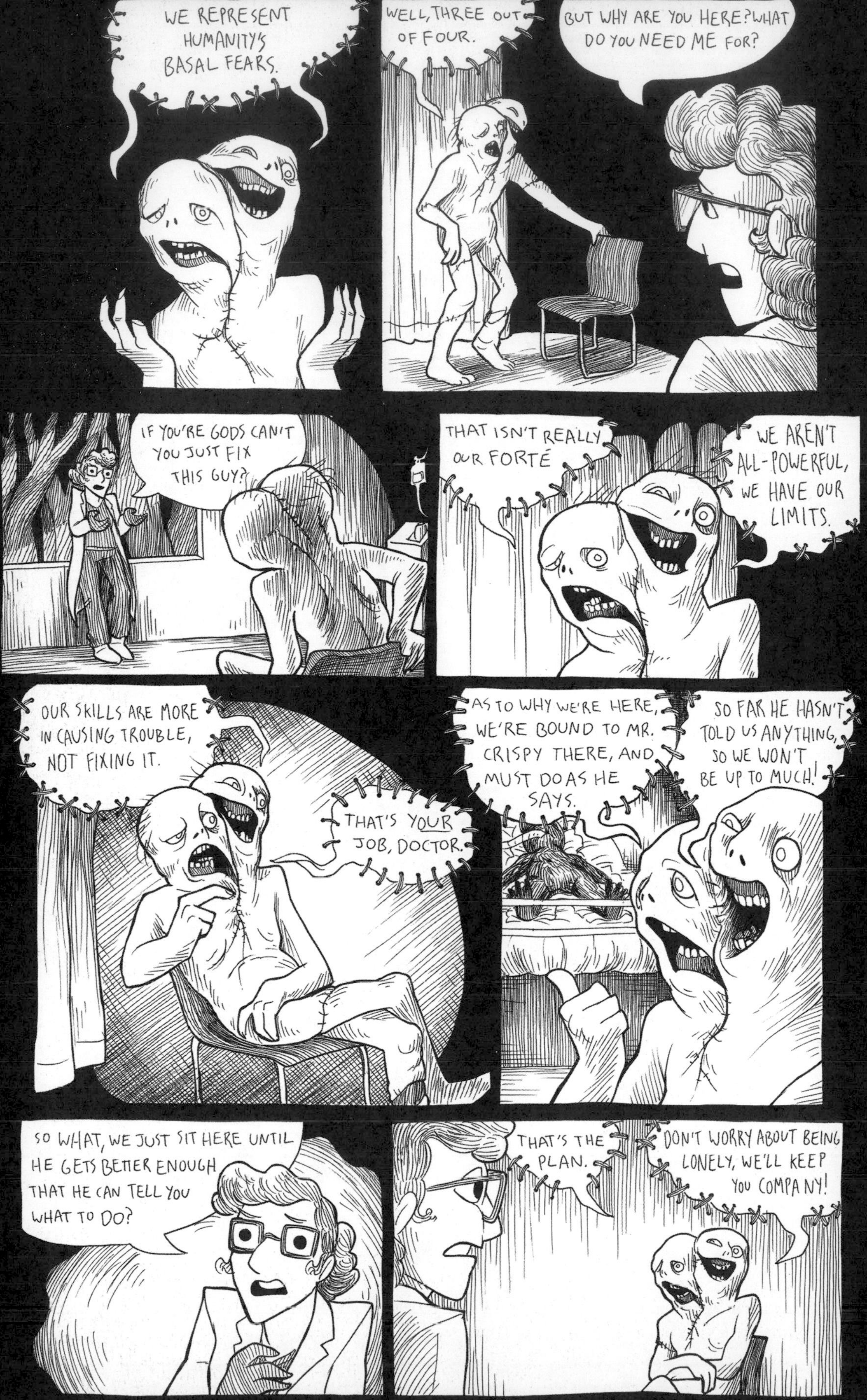
WE REPRESENT HUMANITY'S BASAL FEARS.
WELL, THREE OUT OF FOUR.
BUT WHY ARE YOU HERE? WHAT DO YOU NEED ME FOR?
IF YOU'RE GODS CAN'T YOU JUST FIX THIS GUY?
THAT ISN'T REALLY OUR FORTÉ
WE AREN'T ALL-POWERFUL, WE HAVE OUR LIMITS.
OUR SKILLS ARE MORE IN CAUSING TROUBLE, NOT FIXING IT.
THAT'S YOUR JOB, DOCTOR.
AS TO WHY WE'RE HERE, WE'RE BOUND TO MR. CRISPY THERE, AND MUST DO AS HE SAYS.
SO FAR HE HASN'T TOLD US ANYTHING, SO WE WON'T BE UP TO MUCH!
SO WHAT, WE JUST SIT HERE UNTIL HE GETS BETTER ENOUGH THAT HE CAN TELL YOU WHAT TO DO?
THAT'S THE PLAN.
DON'T WORRY ABOUT BEING LONELY, WE'LL KEEP YOU COMPANY!

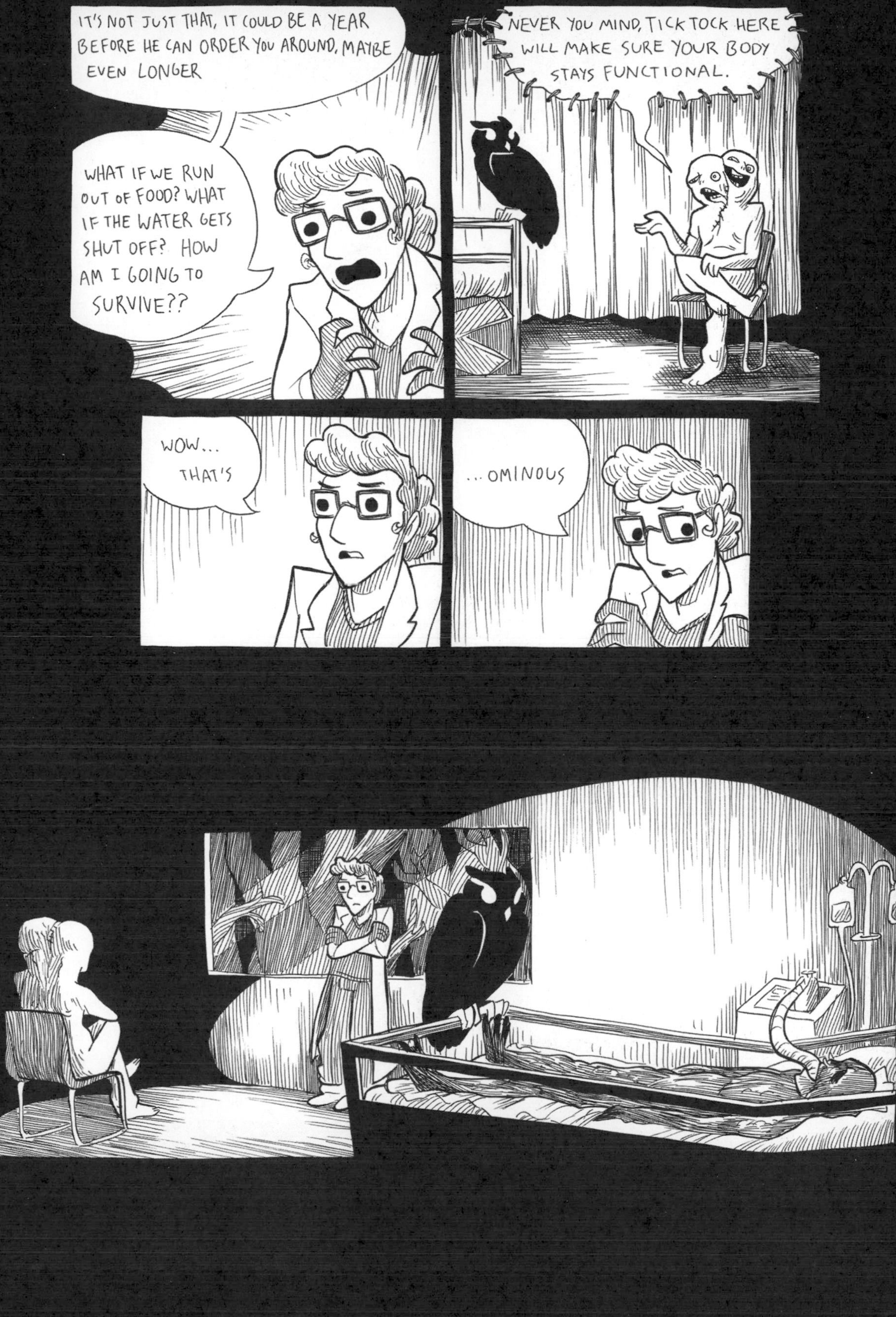
IT'S NOT JUST THAT, IT COULD BE A YEAR BEFORE HE CAN ORDER YOU AROUND, MAYBE EVEN LONGER
WHAT IF WE RUN OUT OF FOOD? WHAT IF THE WATER GETS SHUT OFF? HOW AM I GOING TO SURVIVE??
NEVER YOU MIND, TICK TOCK HERE WILL MAKE SURE YOUR BODY STAYS FUNCTIONAL.
WOW... THAT'S
...OMINOUS

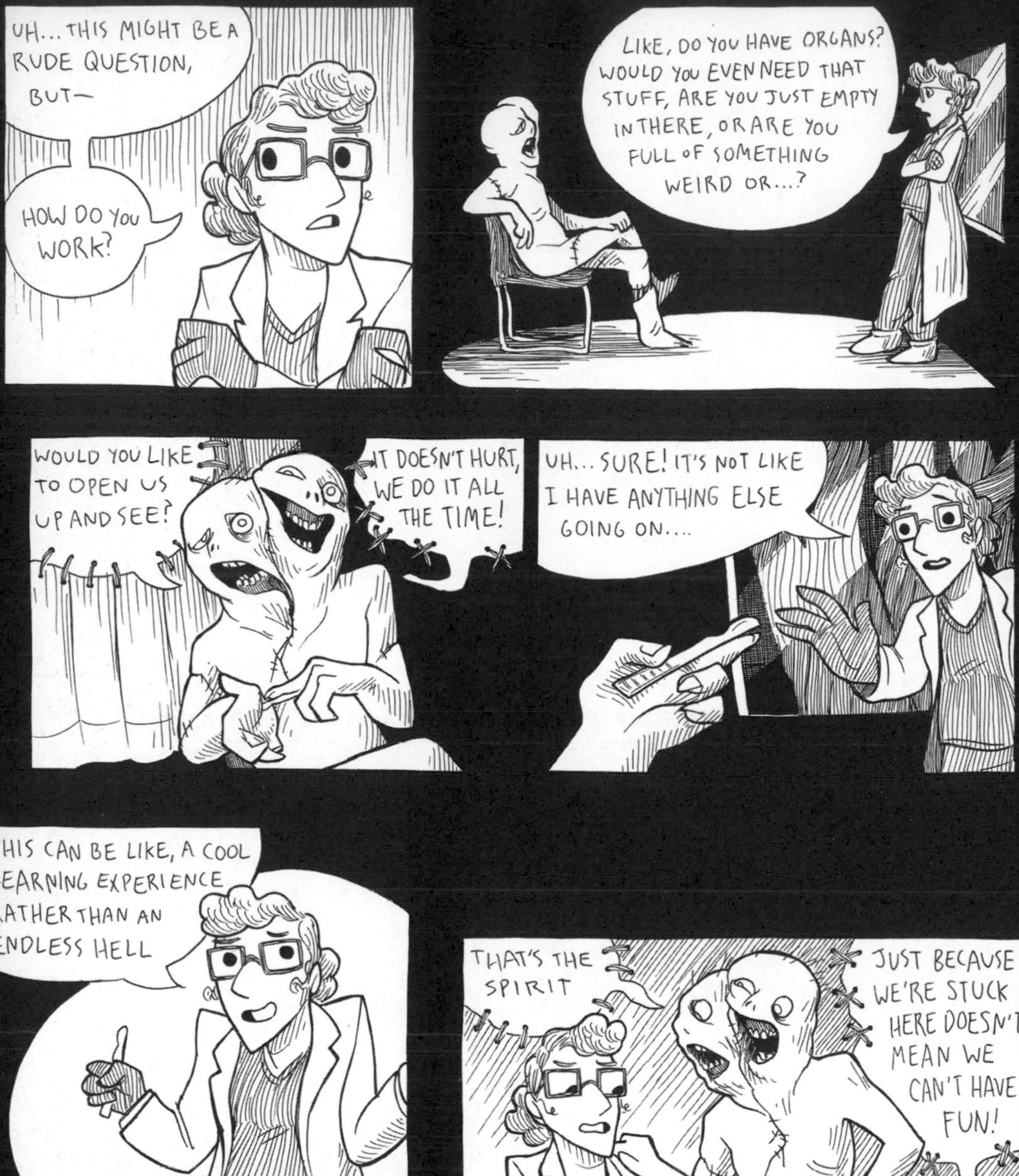
UH... THIS MIGHT BE A RUDE QUESTION, BUT—
HOW DO YOU WORK?
LIKE, DO YOU HAVE ORGANS? WOULD YOU EVEN NEED THAT STUFF, ARE YOU JUST EMPTY IN THERE, OR ARE YOU FULL OF SOMETHING WEIRD OR...?
WOULD YOU LIKE TO OPEN US UP AND SEE?
IT DOESN'T HURT, WE DO IT ALL THE TIME!
UH... SURE! IT'S NOT LIKE I HAVE ANYTHING ELSE GOING ON....
THIS CAN BE LIKE, A COOL LEARNING EXPERIENCE RATHER THAN AN ENDLESS HELL
THAT'S THE SPIRIT
JUST BECAUSE WE'RE STUCK HERE DOESN'T MEAN WE CAN'T HAVE FUN!

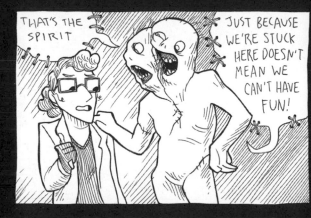

CHAPTER 5

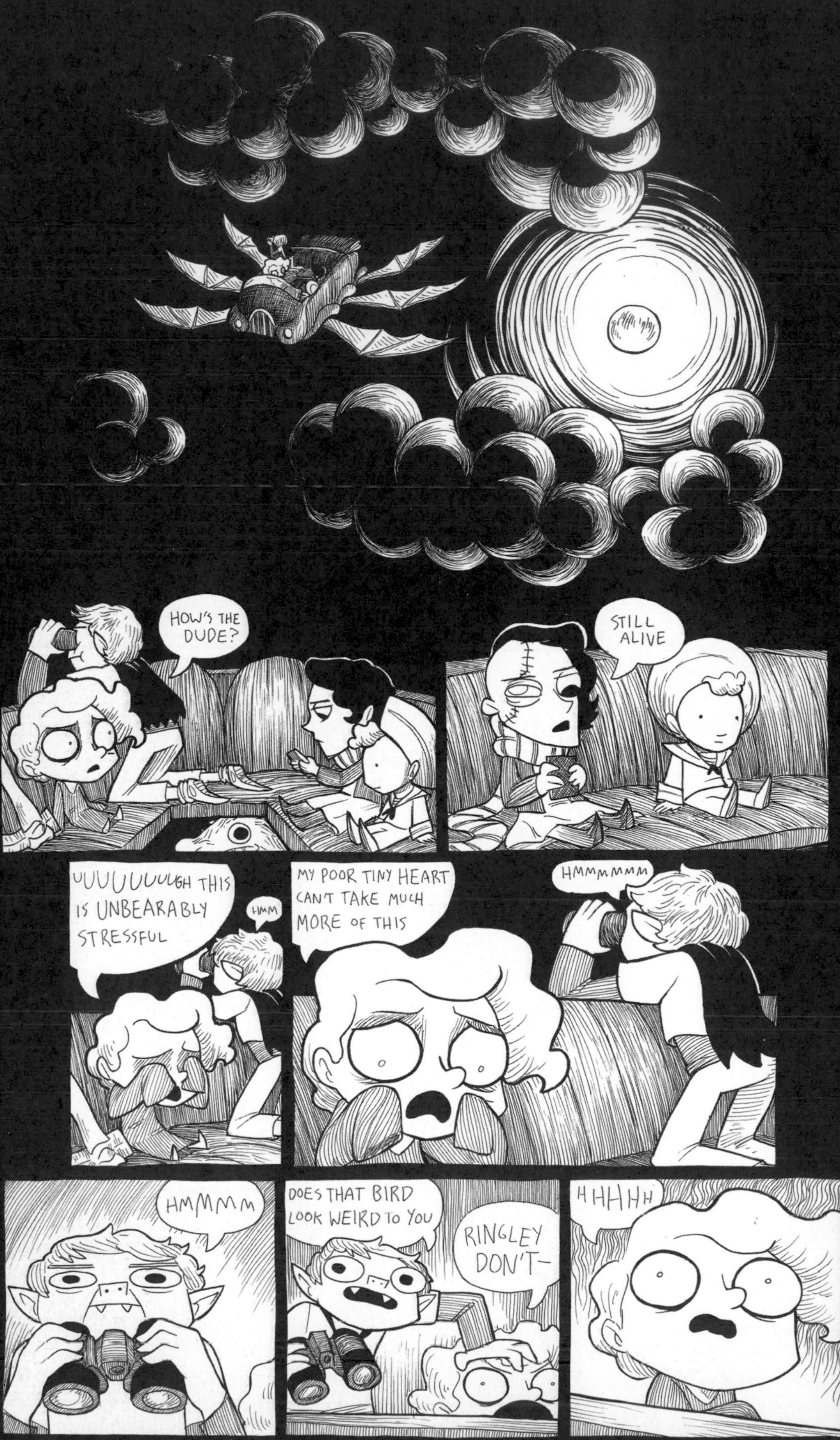
HOW'S THE DUDE?
STILL ALIVE
UUUUUUUGH THIS IS UNBEARABLY STRESSFUL
HMM
MY POOR TINY HEART CAN'T TAKE MUCH MORE OF THIS
HMMMMMM
HMMMM
DOES THAT BIRD LOOK WEIRD TO YOU
RINGLEY DON'T-
HHHHH

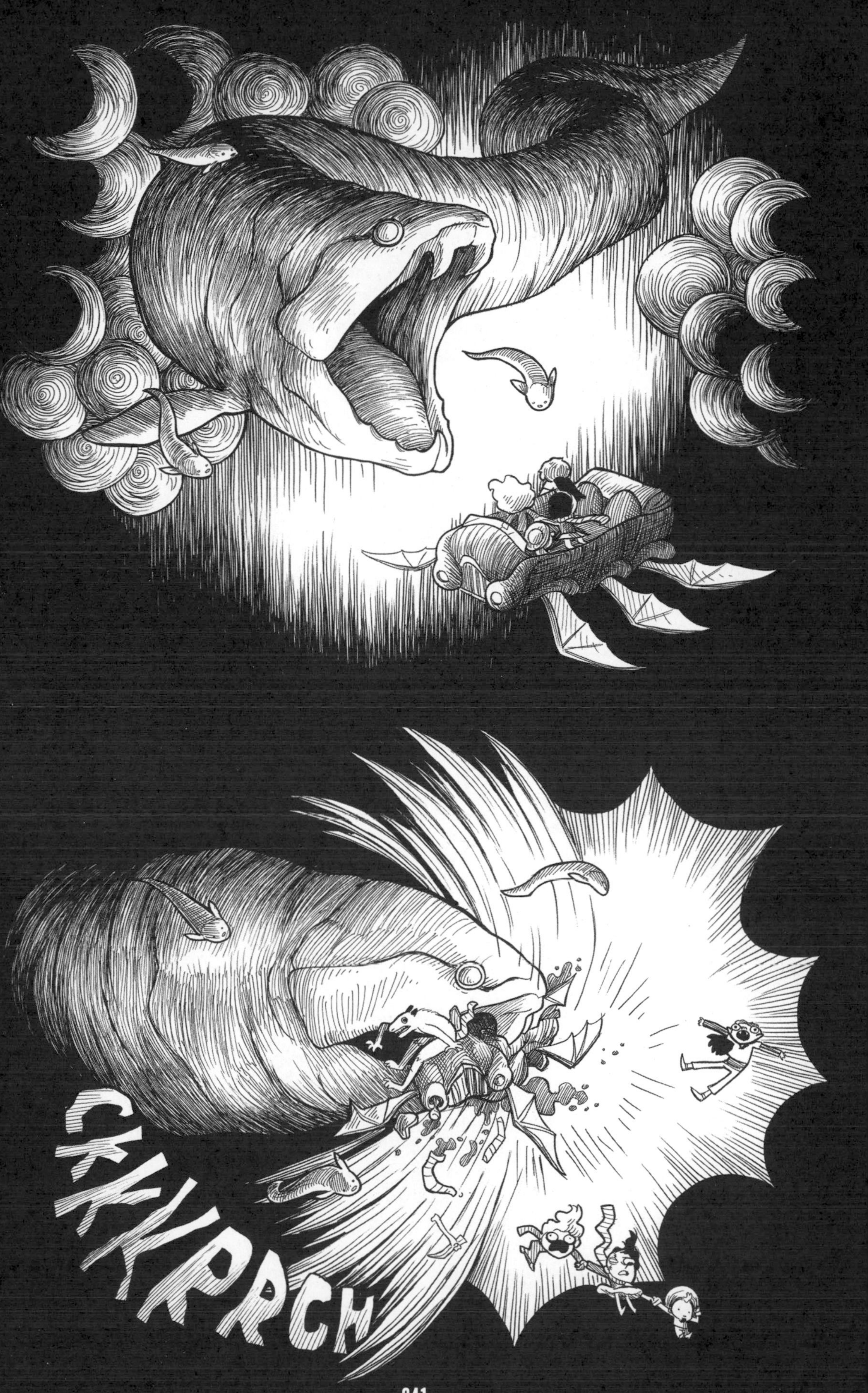
CKKRRCH

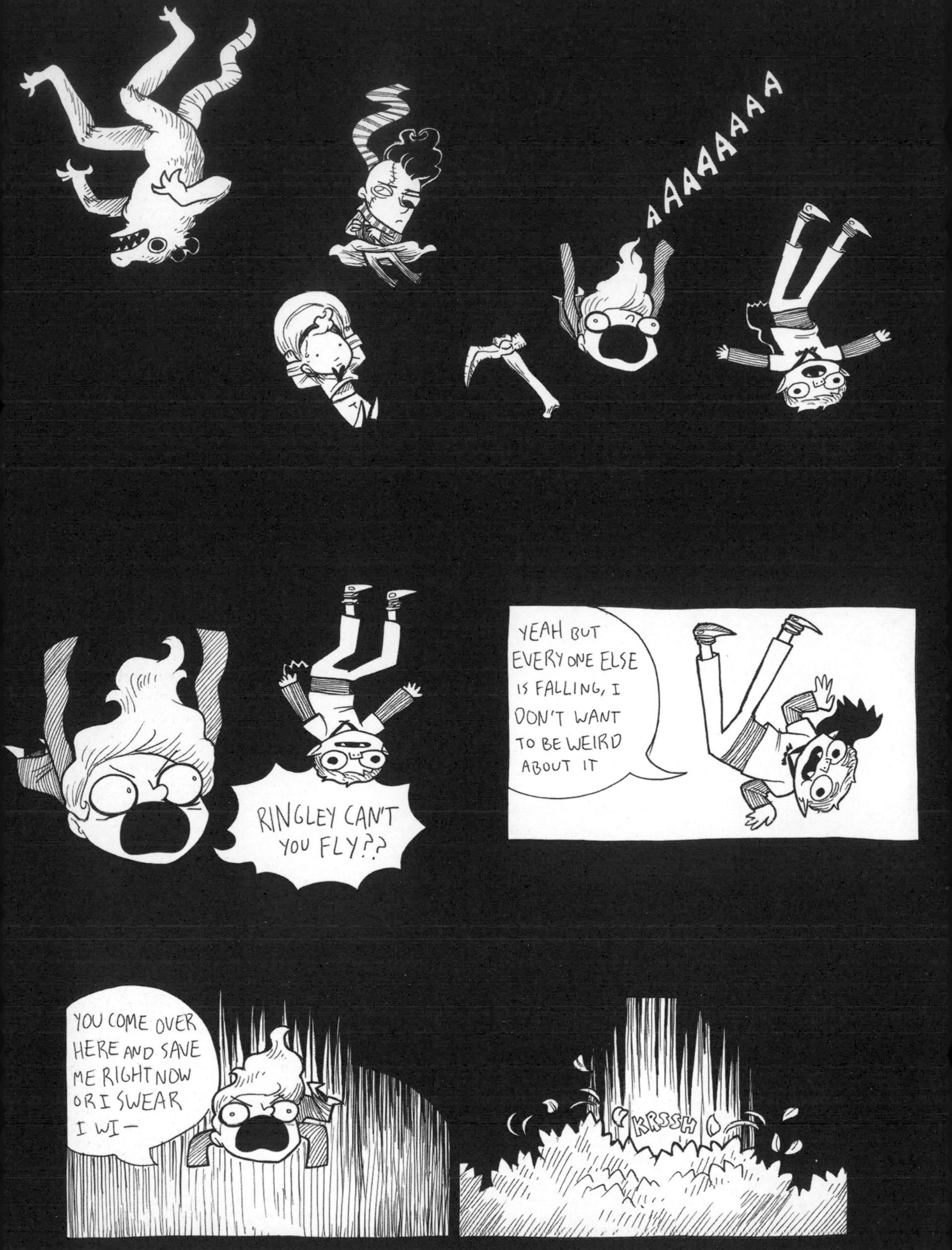
AAAAAAAAA
RINGLEY CAN'T YOU FLY??
YEAH BUT EVERYONE ELSE IS FALLING, I DON'T WANT TO BE WEIRD ABOUT IT
YOU COME OVER HERE AND SAVE ME RIGHT NOW OR I SWEAR I WI—
KRSSH

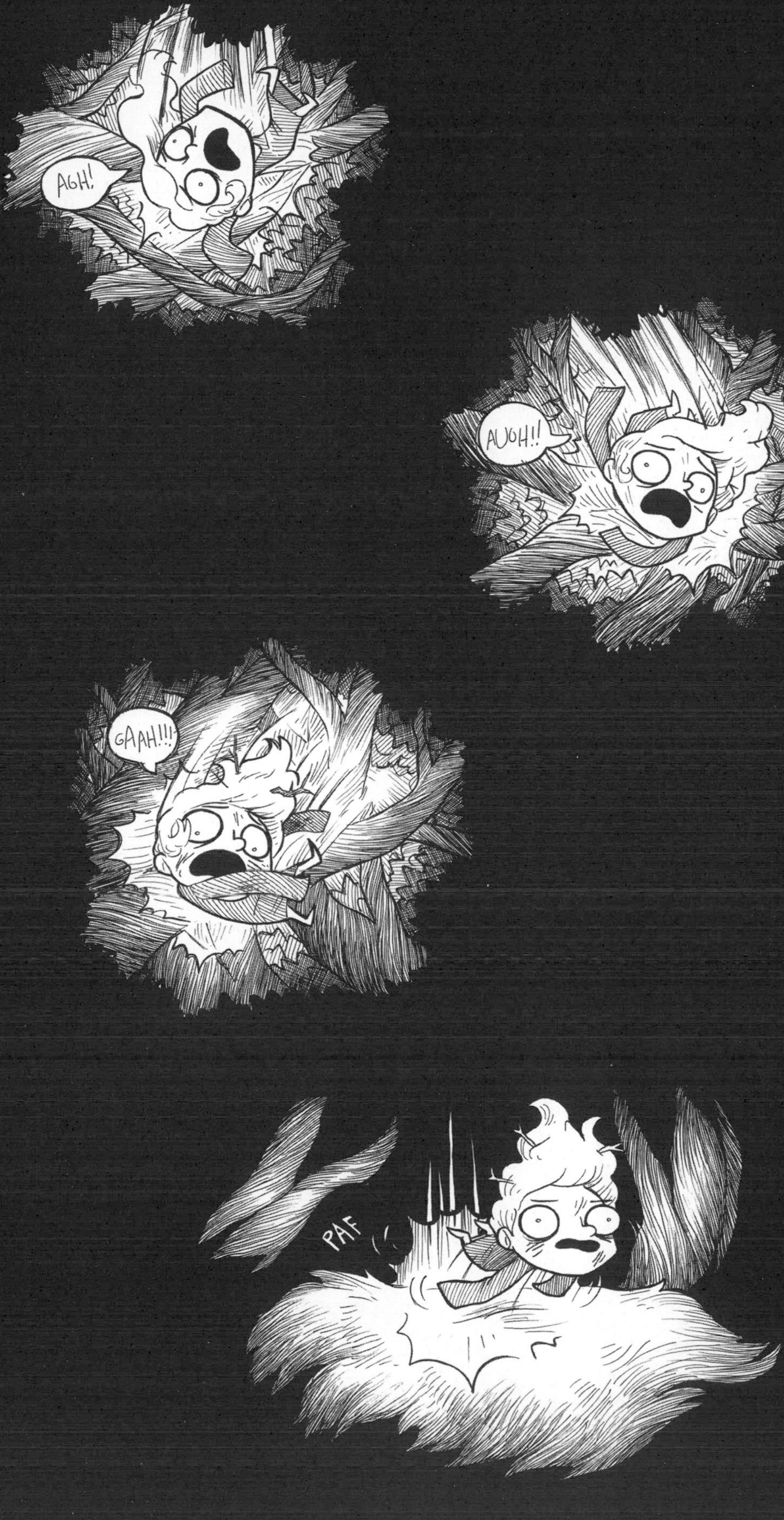
AGH!
AUGH!!
GAAH!!!
PAF

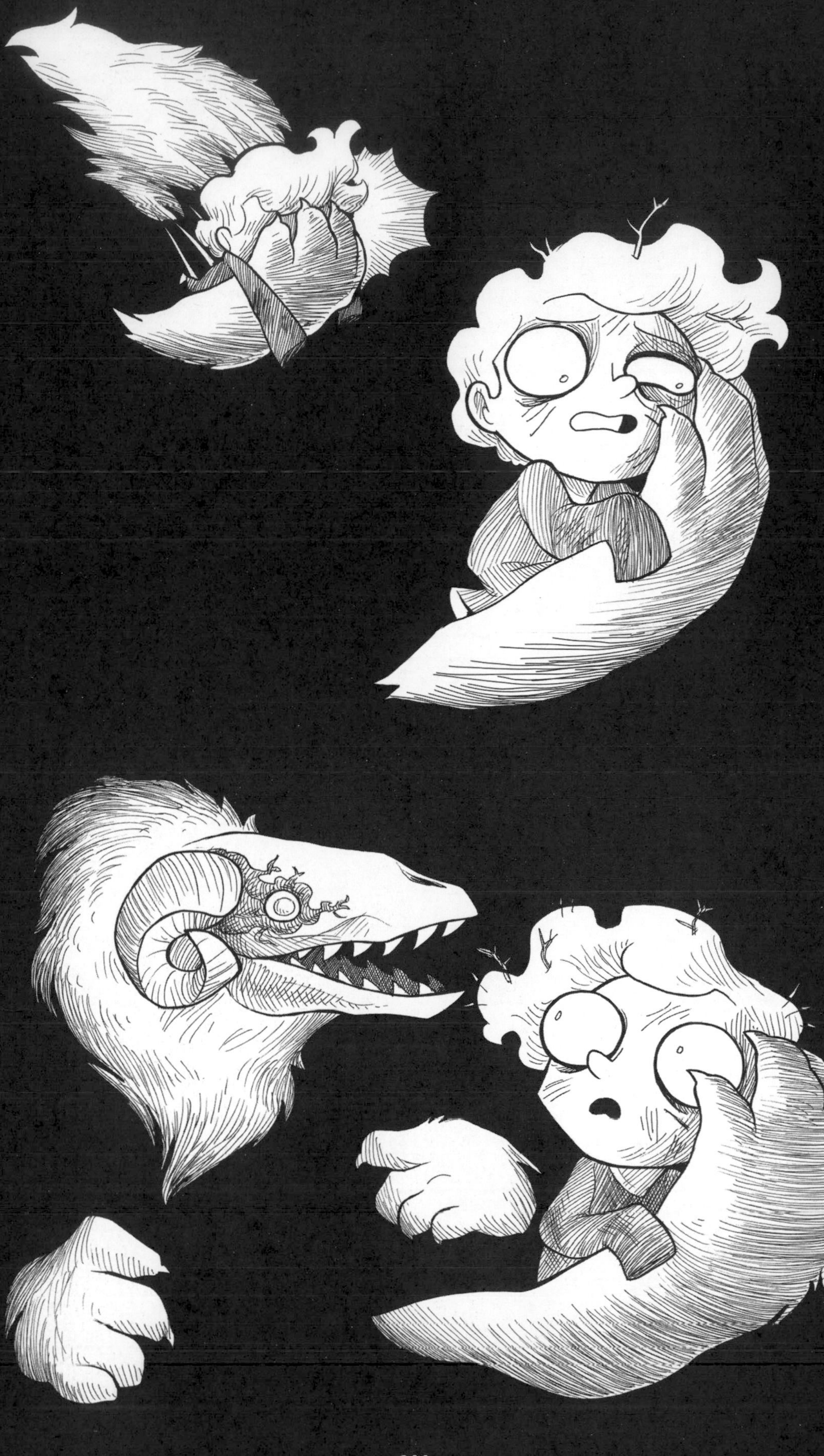

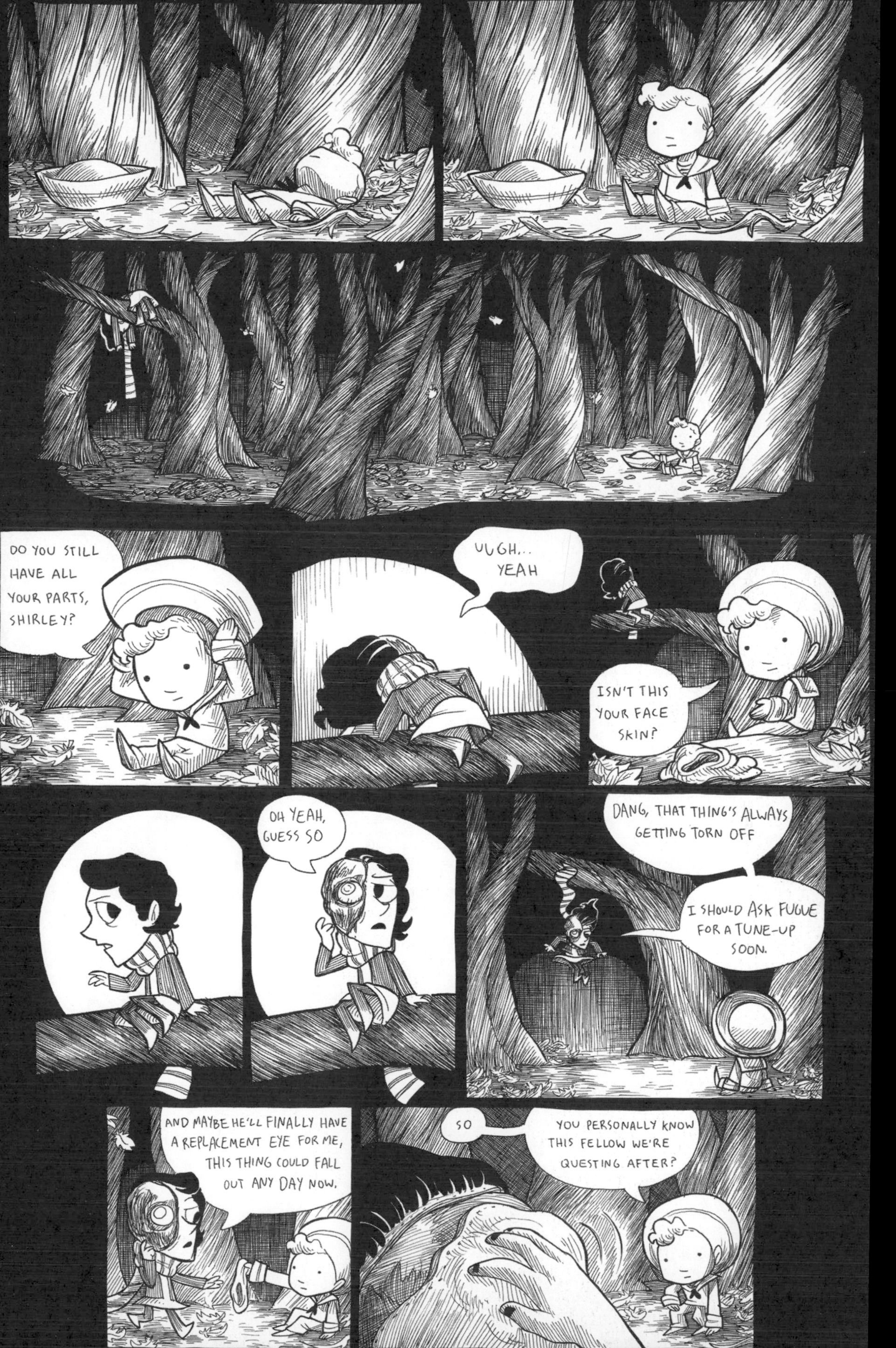
DO YOU STILL HAVE ALL YOUR PARTS, SHIRLEY?
UUGH... YEAH
ISN'T THIS YOUR FACE SKIN?
OH YEAH, GUESS SO
DANG, THAT THING'S ALWAYS GETTING TORN OFF
I SHOULD ASK FUGUE FOR A TUNE-UP SOON.
AND MAYBE HE'LL FINALLY HAVE A REPLACEMENT EYE FOR ME, THIS THING COULD FALL OUT ANY DAY NOW.
SO
YOU PERSONALLY KNOW THIS FELLOW WE'RE QUESTING AFTER?

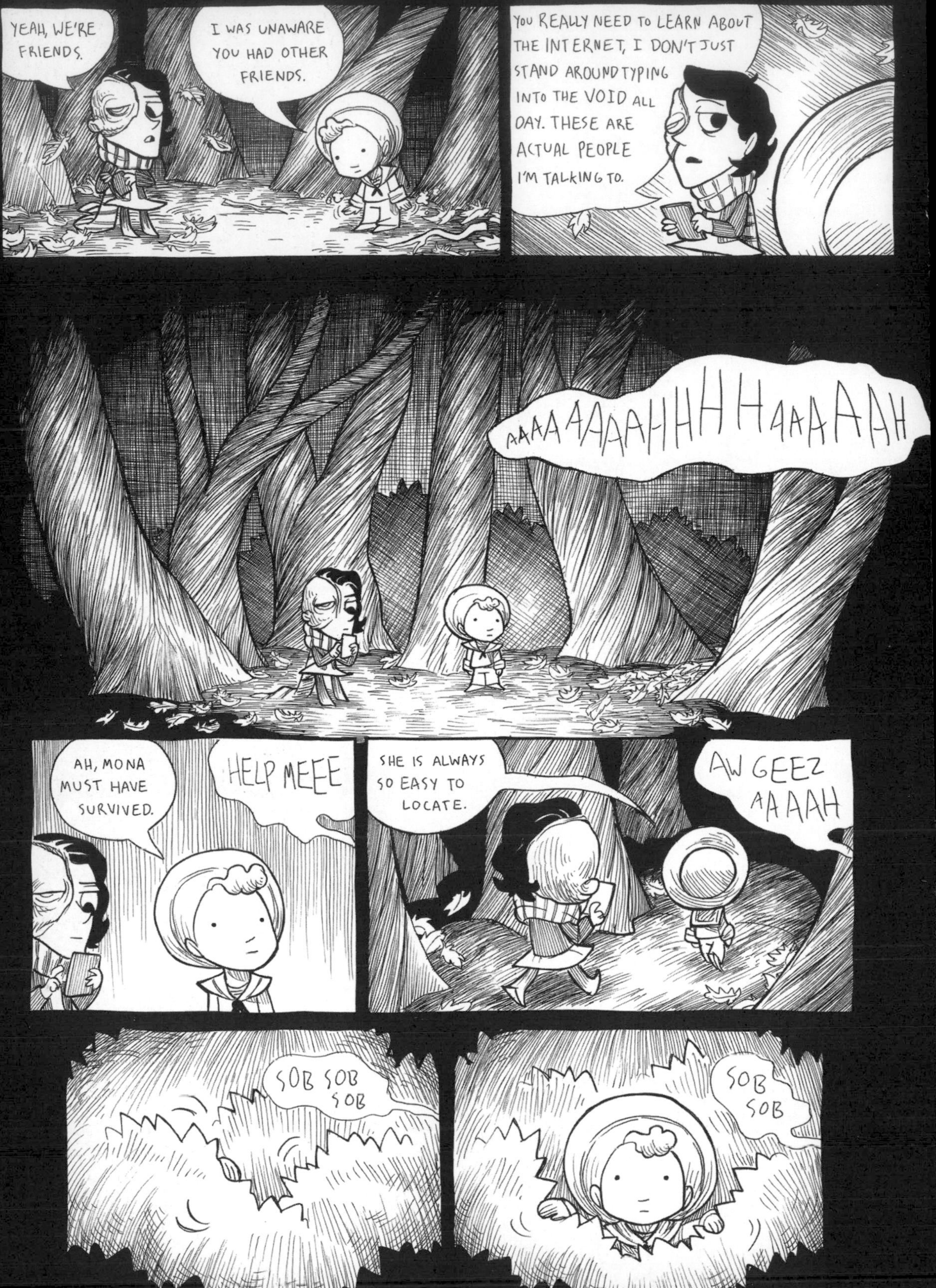
YEAH, WE'RE FRIENDS.
I WAS UNAWARE YOU HAD OTHER FRIENDS.
YOU REALLY NEED TO LEARN ABOUT THE INTERNET, I DON'T JUST STAND AROUND TYPING INTO THE VOID ALL DAY. THESE ARE ACTUAL PEOPLE I'M TALKING TO.
AAAAAAAAHHHHAAAAAH
AH, MONA MUST HAVE SURVIVED.
HELP MEEE
SHE IS ALWAYS SO EASY TO LOCATE.
AW GEEZ AAAAH
SOB SOB SOB
SOB SOB

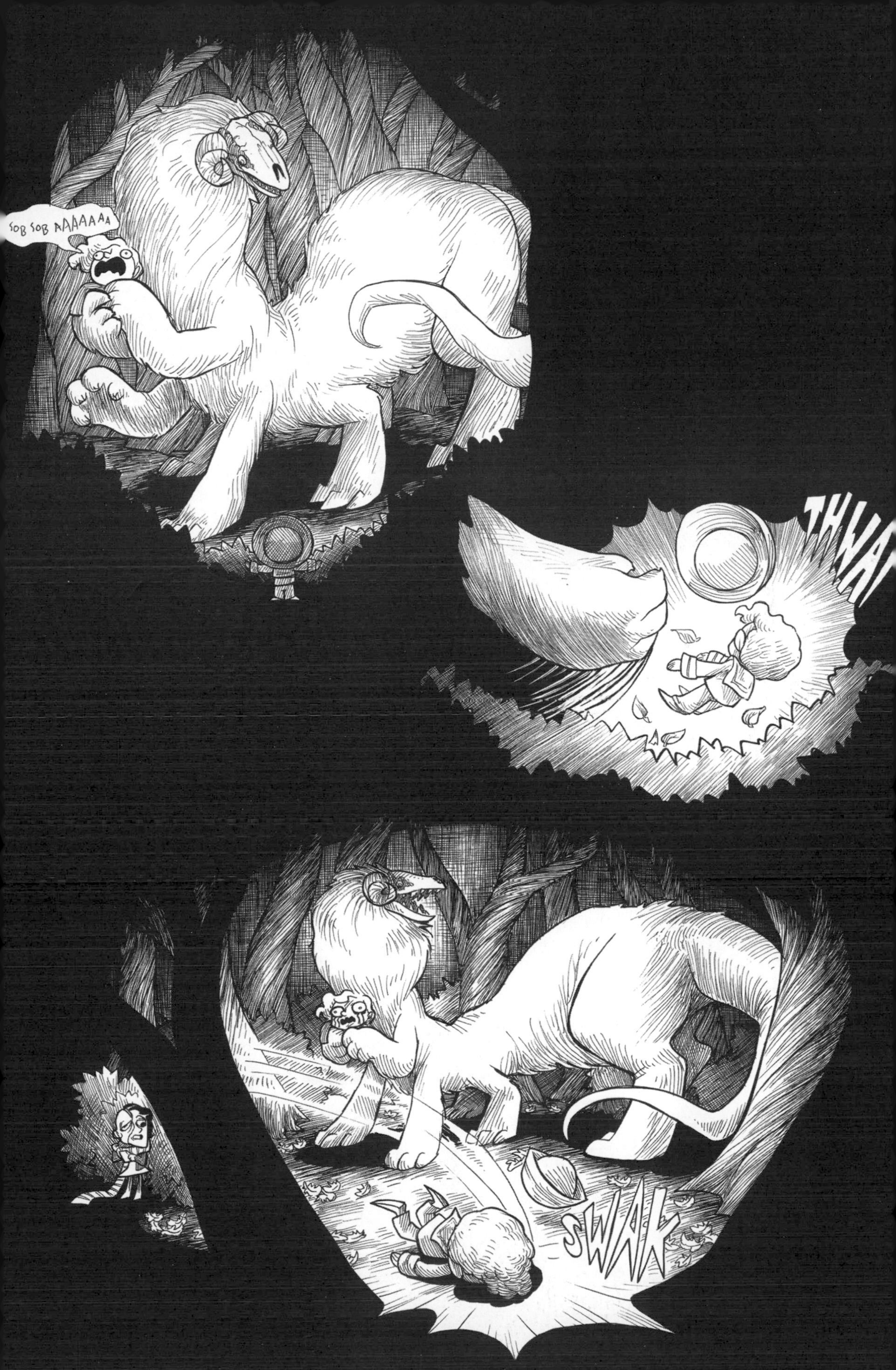
SOB SOB AAAAAAA
THWAP
SWAK

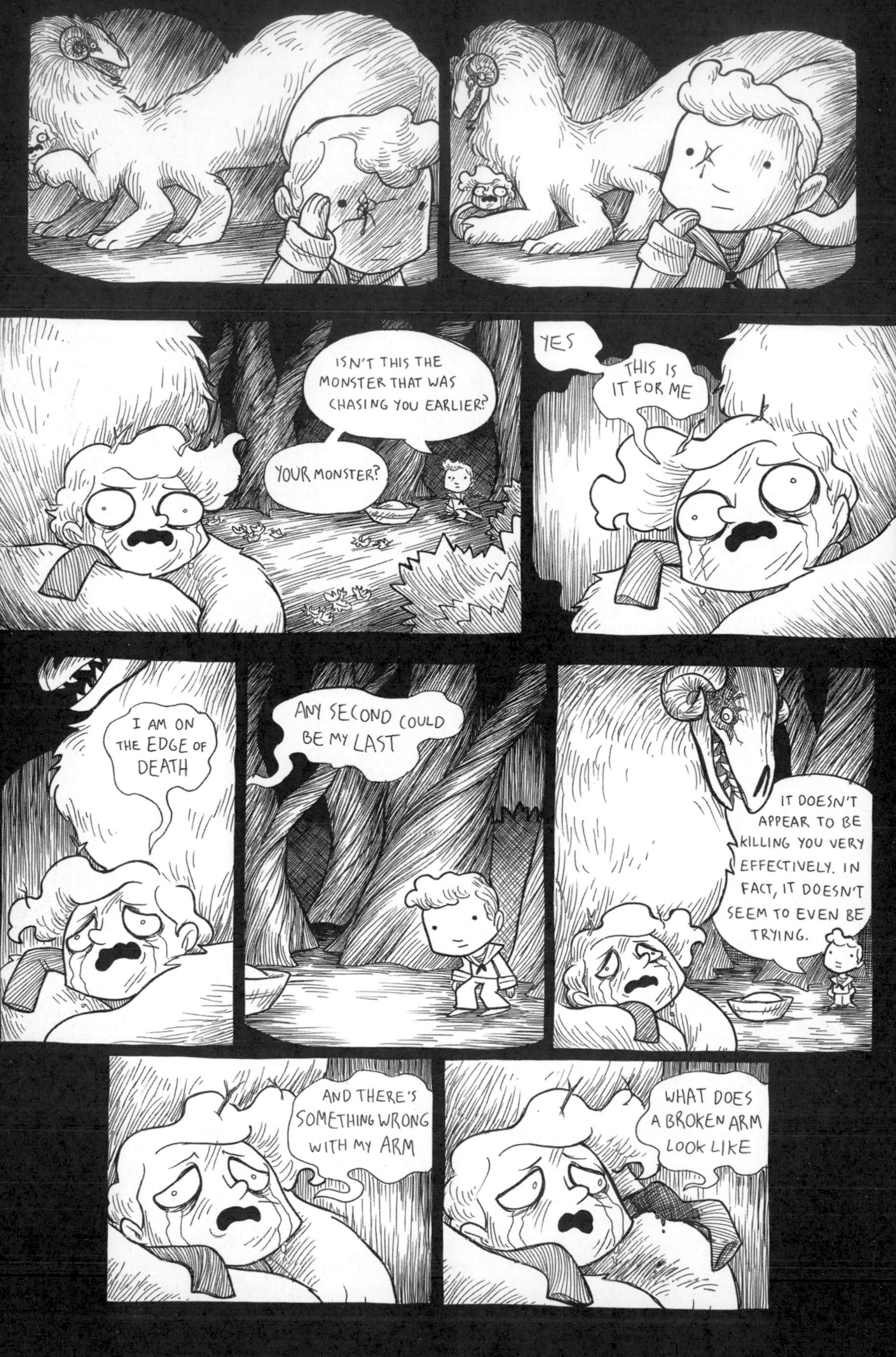
ISN'T THIS THE MONSTER THAT WAS CHASING YOU EARLIER?
YOUR MONSTER?
YES
THIS IS IT FOR ME
I AM ON THE EDGE OF DEATH
ANY SECOND COULD BE MY LAST
IT DOESN'T APPEAR TO BE KILLING YOU VERY EFFECTIVELY. IN FACT, IT DOESN'T SEEM TO EVEN BE TRYING.
AND THERE'S SOMETHING WRONG WITH MY ARM
WHAT DOES A BROKEN ARM LOOK LIKE

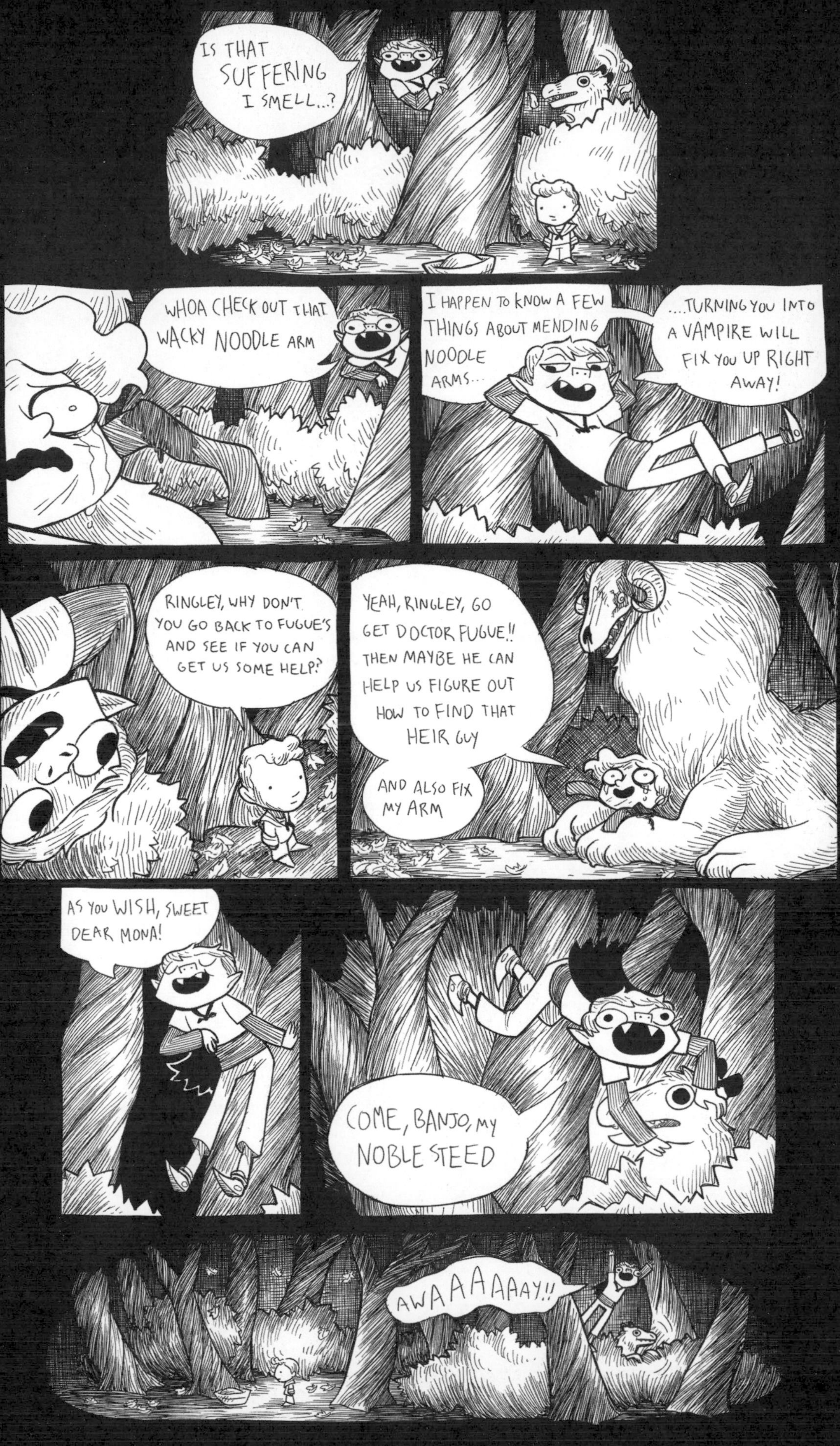
IS THAT SUFFERING I SMELL...?
WHOA CHECK OUT THAT WACKY NOODLE ARM
I HAPPEN TO KNOW A FEW THINGS ABOUT MENDING NOODLE ARMS...
....TURNING YOU INTO A VAMPIRE WILL FIX YOU UP RIGHT AWAY!
RINGLEY, WHY DON'T YOU GO BACK TO FUGUE'S AND SEE IF YOU CAN GET US SOME HELP?
YEAH, RINGLEY, GO GET DOCTOR FUGUE!! THEN MAYBE HE CAN HELP US FIGURE OUT HOW TO FIND THAT HEIR GUY
AND ALSO FIX MY ARM
AS YOU WISH, SWEET DEAR MONA!
COME, BANJO, MY NOBLE STEED
AWAAAAAAAY!!

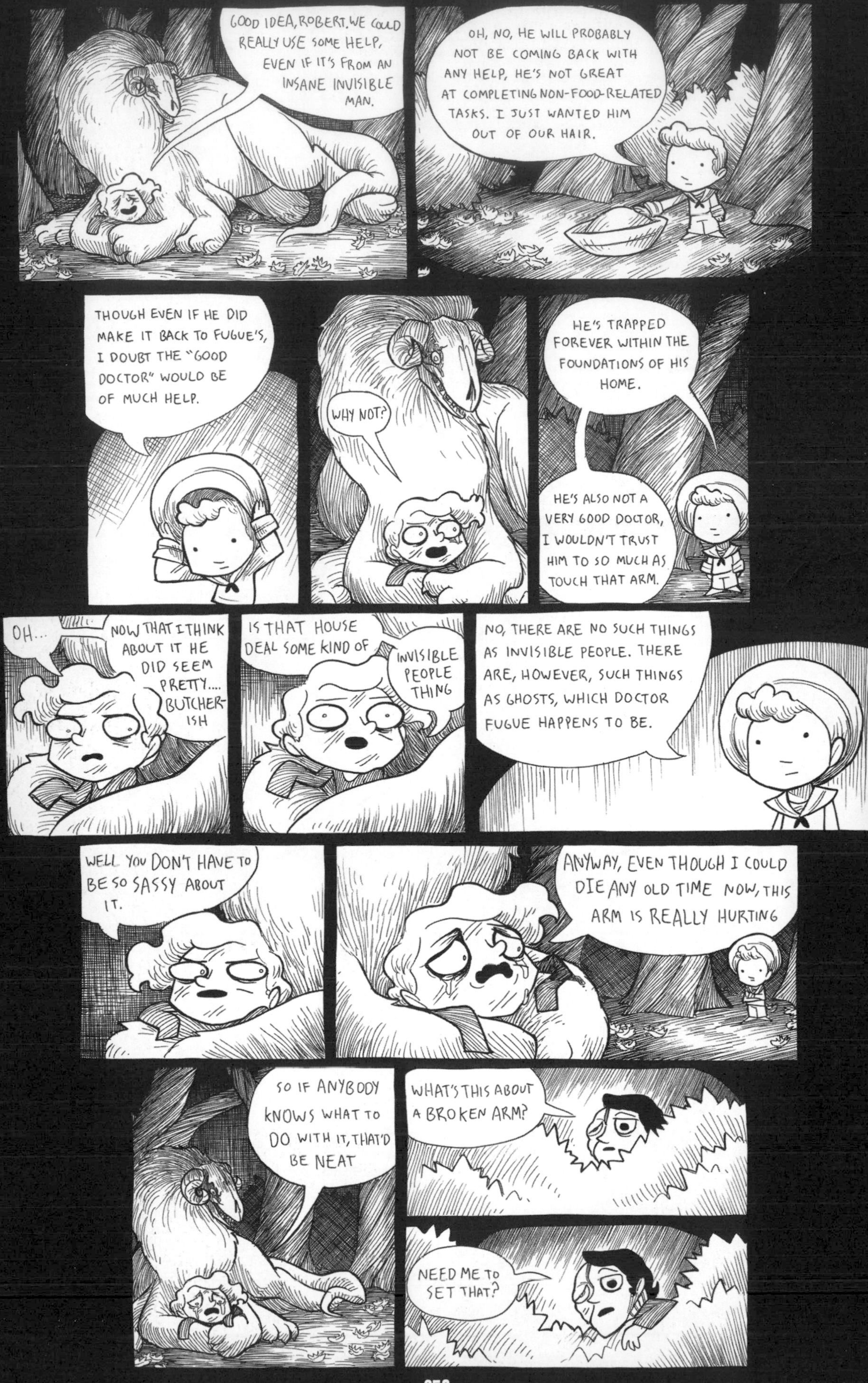
GOOD IDEA, ROBERT. WE COULD REALLY USE SOME HELP, EVEN IF IT'S FROM AN INSANE INVISIBLE MAN.
OH, NO, HE WILL PROBABLY NOT BE COMING BACK WITH ANY HELP, HE'S NOT GREAT AT COMPLETING NON-FOOD-RELATED TASKS. I JUST WANTED HIM OUT OF OUR HAIR.
THOUGH EVEN IF HE DID MAKE IT BACK TO FUGUE'S, I DOUBT THE "GOOD DOCTOR" WOULD BE OF MUCH HELP.
WHY NOT?
HE'S TRAPPED FOREVER WITHIN THE FOUNDATIONS OF HIS HOME.
HE'S ALSO NOT A VERY GOOD DOCTOR, I WOULDN'T TRUST HIM TO SO MUCH AS TOUCH THAT ARM.
OH...
NOW THAT I THINK ABOUT IT HE DID SEEM PRETTY.... BUTCHER-ISH
IS THAT HOUSE DEAL SOME KIND OF
INVISIBLE PEOPLE THING
NO, THERE ARE NO SUCH THINGS AS INVISIBLE PEOPLE. THERE ARE, HOWEVER, SUCH THINGS AS GHOSTS, WHICH DOCTOR FUGUE HAPPENS TO BE.
WELL YOU DON'T HAVE TO BE SO SASSY ABOUT IT.
ANYWAY, EVEN THOUGH I COULD DIE ANY OLD TIME NOW, THIS ARM IS REALLY HURTING
SO IF ANYBODY KNOWS WHAT TO DO WITH IT, THAT'D BE NEAT
WHAT'S THIS ABOUT A BROKEN ARM?
NEED ME TO SET THAT?

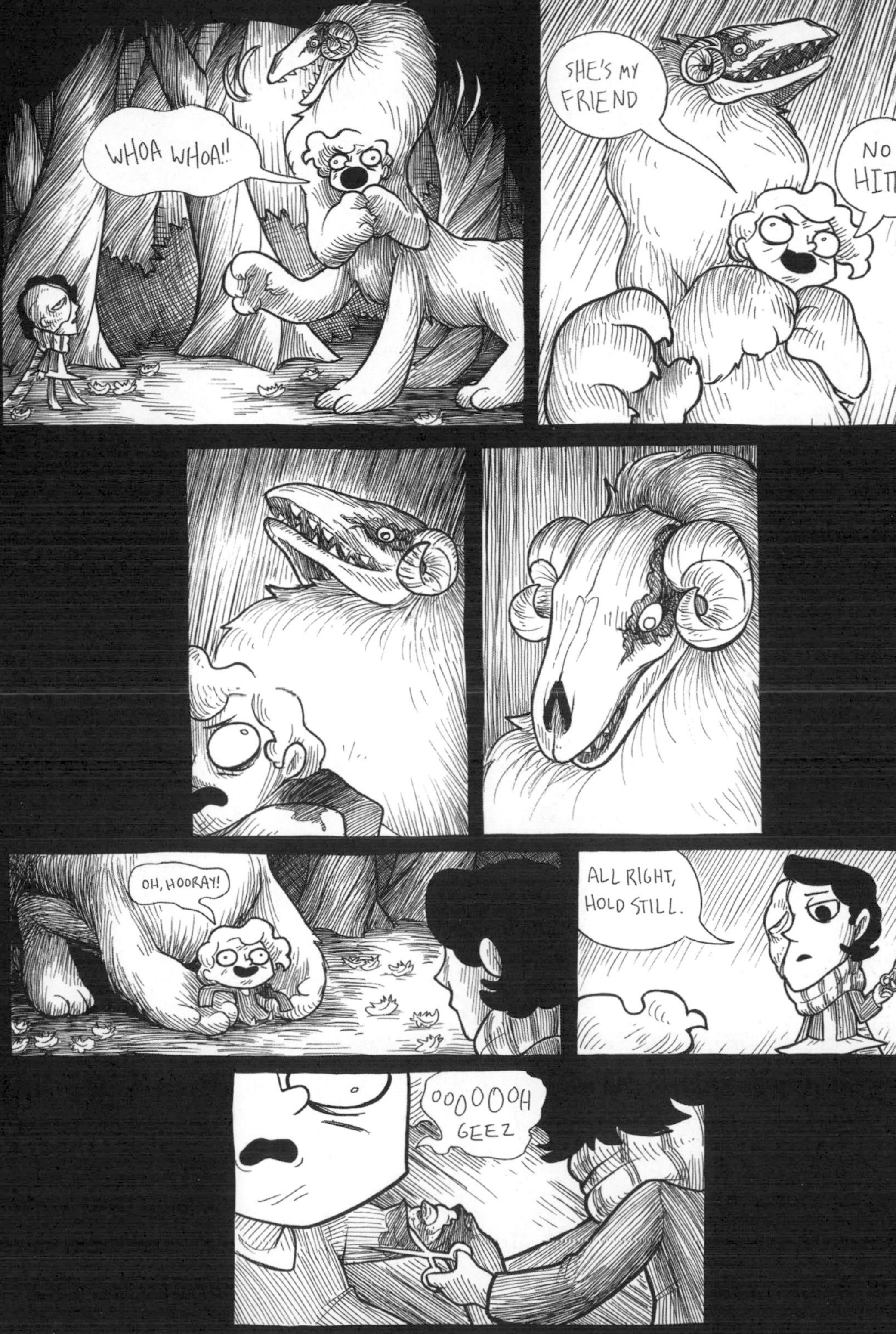
WHOA WHOA!!
SHE'S MY FRIEND
NO HITTING
OH, HOORAY!
ALL RIGHT, HOLD STILL.
OOOOOOH GEEZ

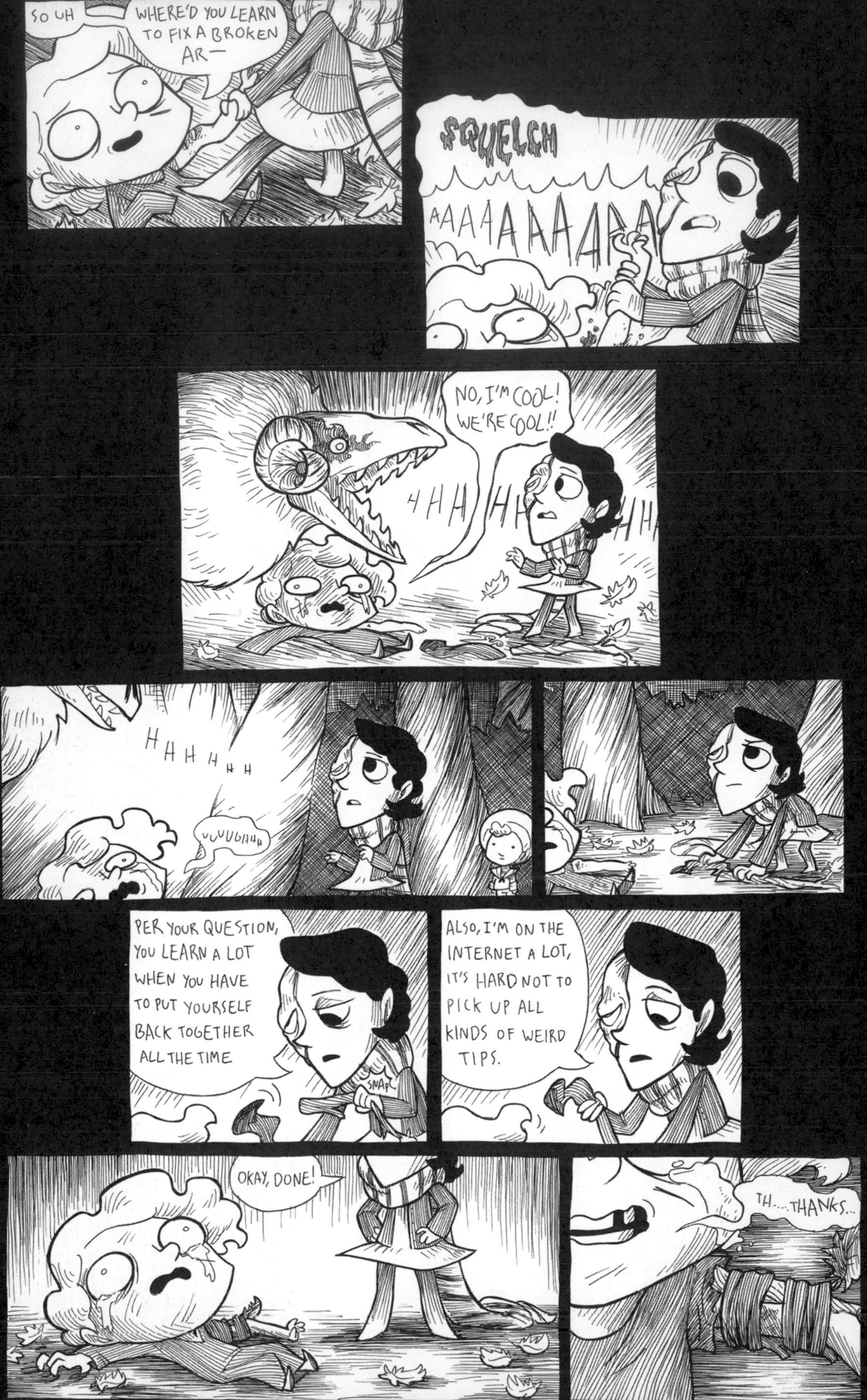
SO UH
WHERE'D YOU LEARN TO FIX A BROKEN AR—
SQUELCH
AAAAAAAAAA
NO, I'M COOL! WE'RE COOL!!
HHHH
HHHHHH
UUUUGHHH
PER YOUR QUESTION, YOU LEARN A LOT WHEN YOU HAVE TO PUT YOURSELF BACK TOGETHER ALL THE TIME
SNAP
ALSO, I'M ON THE INTERNET A LOT, IT'S HARD NOT TO PICK UP ALL KINDS OF WEIRD TIPS.
OKAY, DONE!
TH.....THANKS...

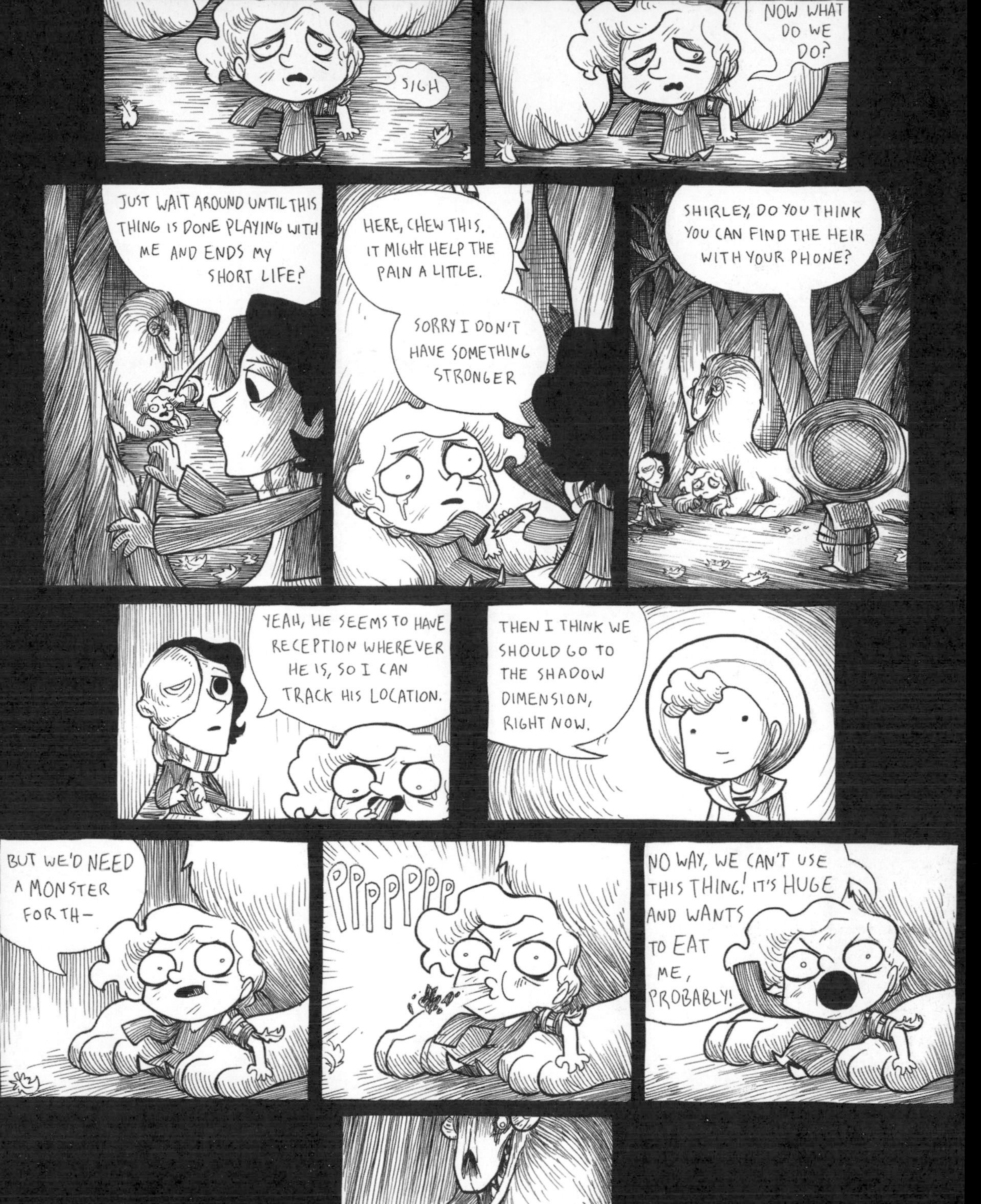
SIGH
NOW WHAT DO WE DO?
JUST WAIT AROUND UNTIL THIS THING IS DONE PLAYING WITH ME AND ENDS MY SHORT LIFE?
HERE, CHEW THIS. IT MIGHT HELP THE PAIN A LITTLE.
SORRY I DON'T HAVE SOMETHING STRONGER
SHIRLEY, DO YOU THINK YOU CAN FIND THE HEIR WITH YOUR PHONE?
YEAH, HE SEEMS TO HAVE RECEPTION WHEREVER HE IS, SO I CAN TRACK HIS LOCATION.
THEN I THINK WE SHOULD GO TO THE SHADOW DIMENSION, RIGHT NOW.
BUT WE'D NEED A MONSTER FOR TH–
PPPPPPP
NO WAY, WE CAN'T USE THIS THING! IT'S HUGE AND WANTS TO EAT ME, PROBABLY!

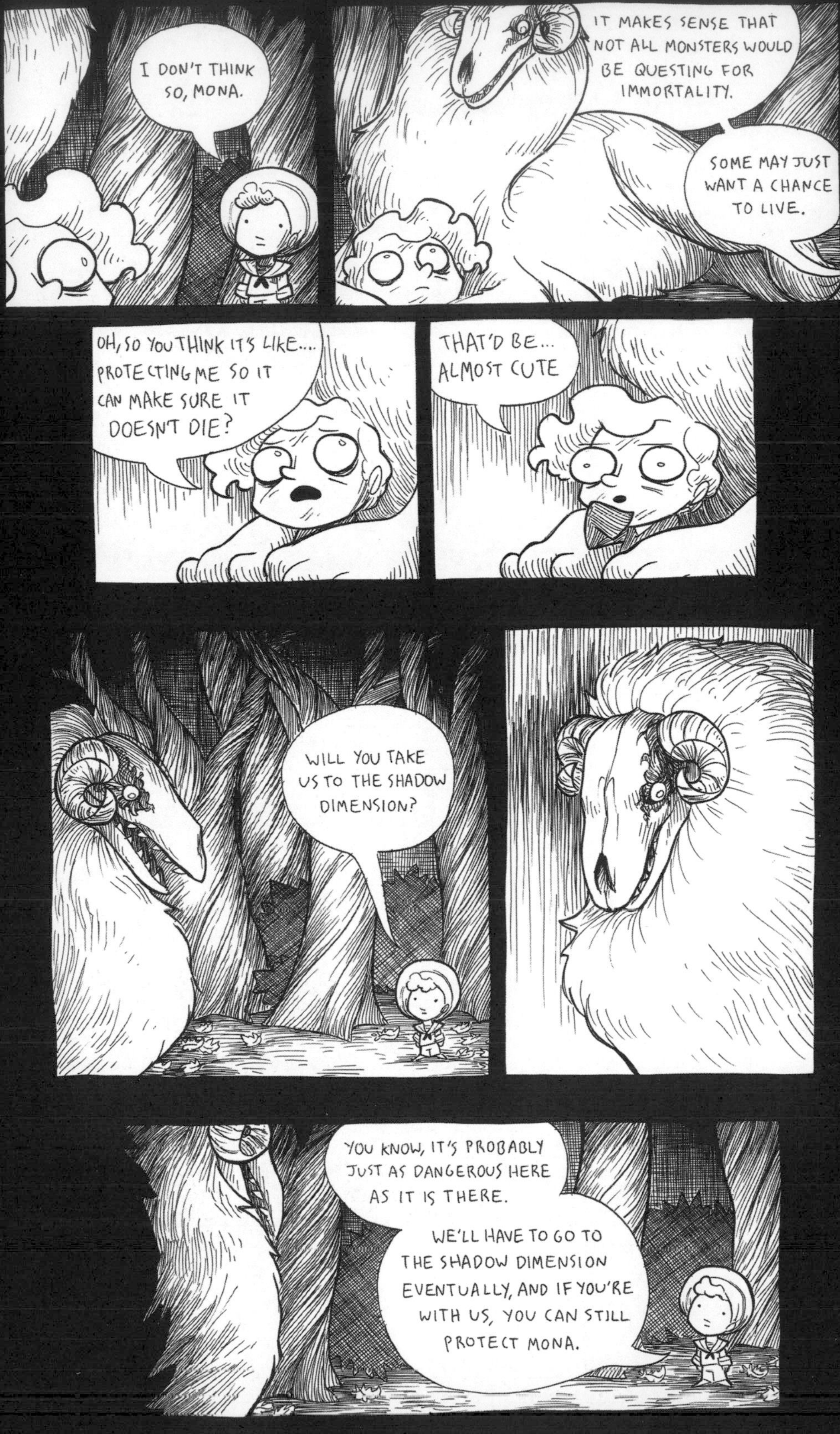
I DON'T THINK SO, MONA.
IT MAKES SENSE THAT NOT ALL MONSTERS WOULD BE QUESTING FOR IMMORTALITY.
SOME MAY JUST WANT A CHANCE TO LIVE.
OH, SO YOU THINK IT'S LIKE... PROTECTING ME SO IT CAN MAKE SURE IT DOESN'T DIE?
THAT'D BE... ALMOST CUTE
WILL YOU TAKE US TO THE SHADOW DIMENSION?
YOU KNOW, IT'S PROBABLY JUST AS DANGEROUS HERE AS IT IS THERE.
WE'LL HAVE TO GO TO THE SHADOW DIMENSION EVENTUALLY, AND IF YOU'RE WITH US, YOU CAN STILL PROTECT MONA.

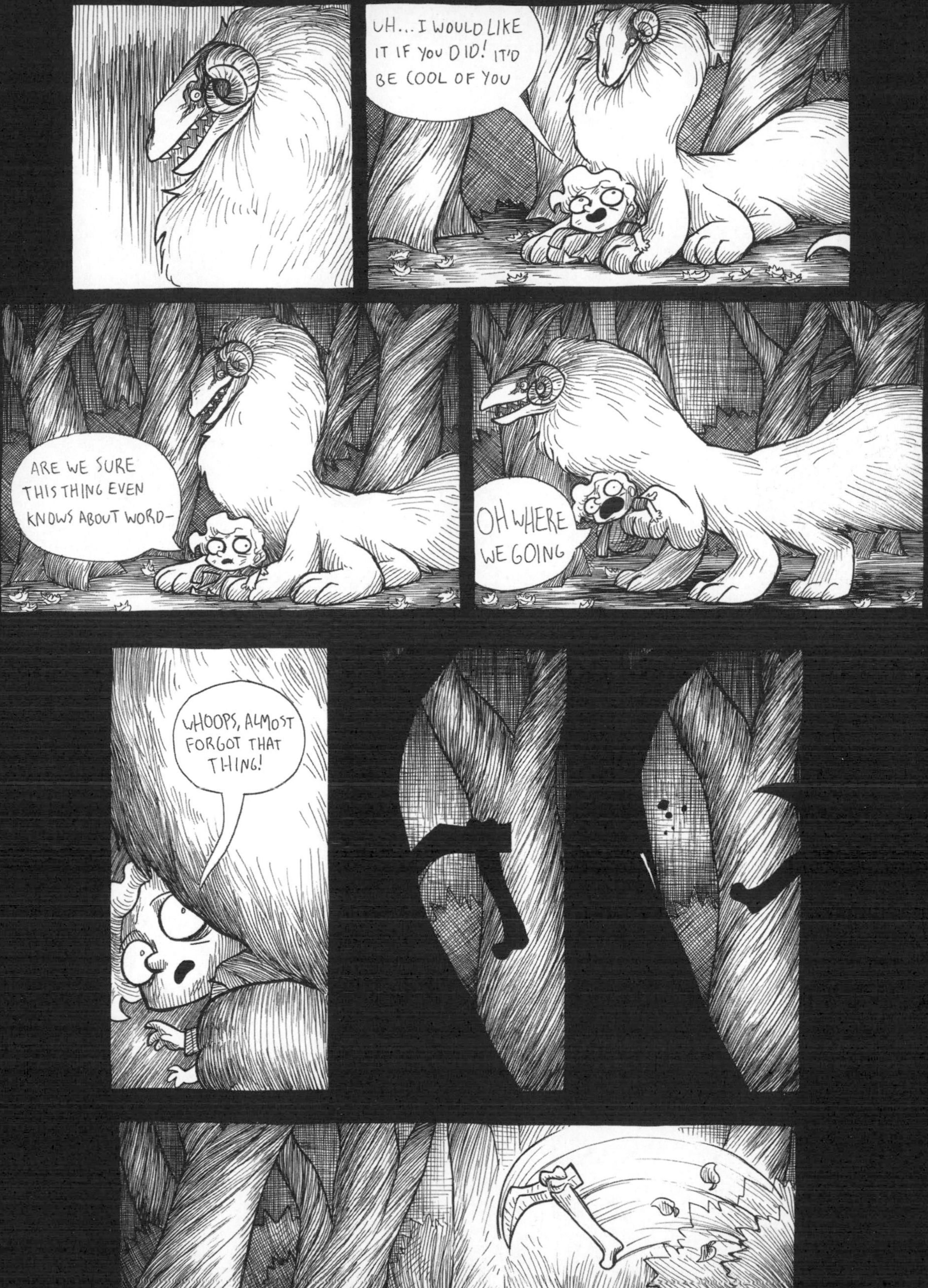
UH... I WOULD LIKE IT IF YOU DID! IT'D BE COOL OF YOU
ARE WE SURE THIS THING EVEN KNOWS ABOUT WORD-
OH WHERE WE GOING
WHOOPS, ALMOST FORGOT THAT THING!

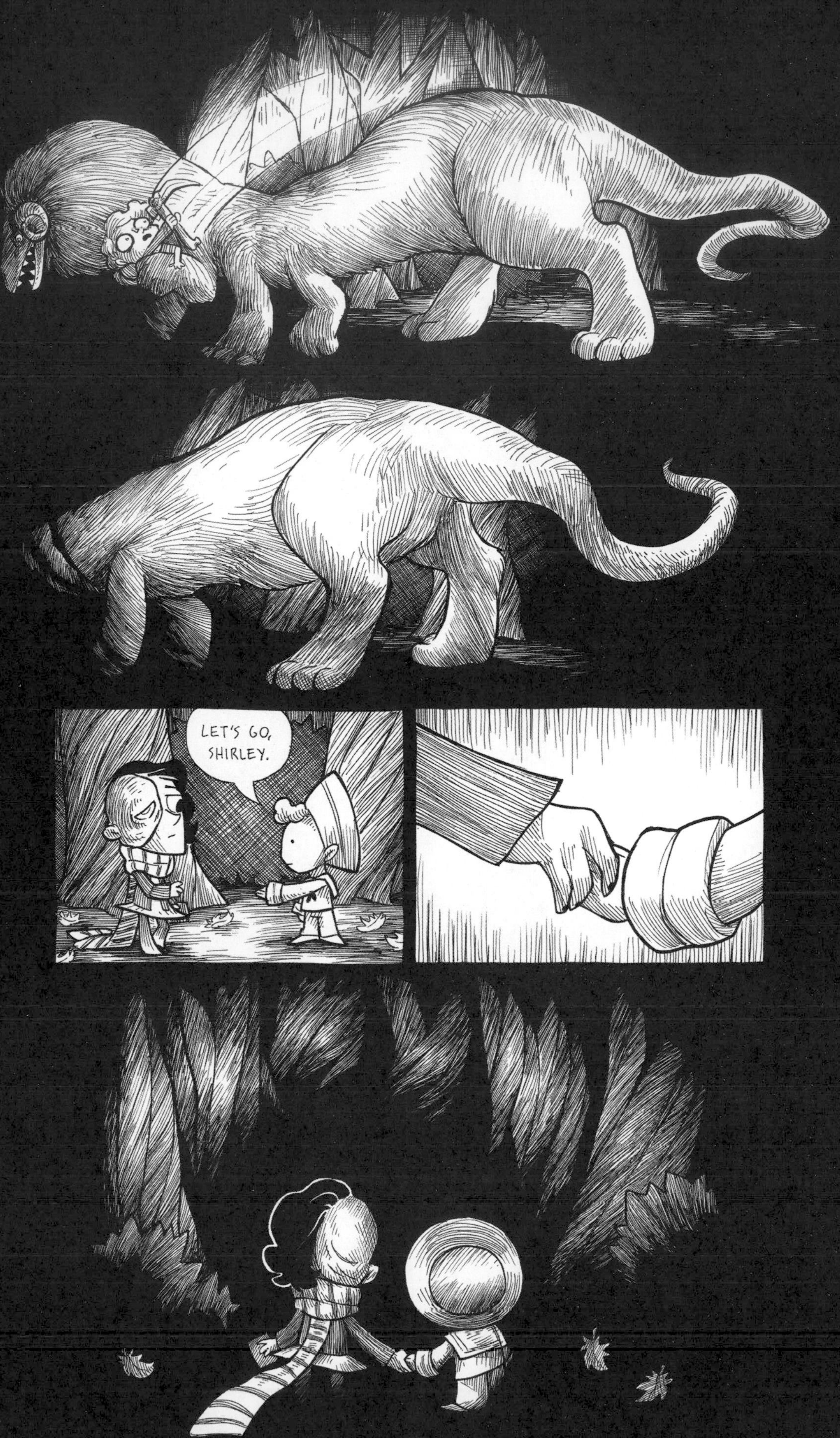
LET'S GO, SHIRLEY.

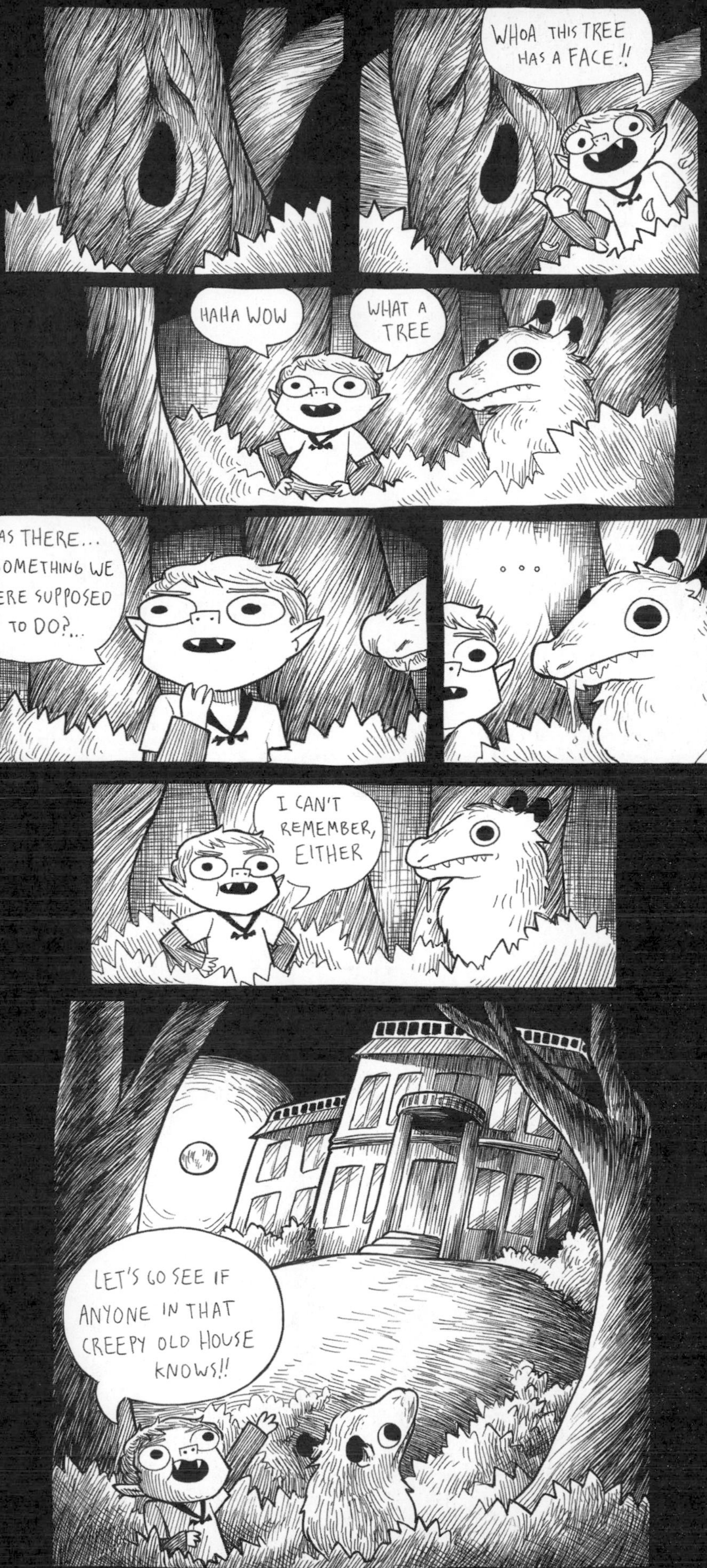
WHOA THIS TREE HAS A FACE!!
HAHA WOW
WHAT A TREE
WAS THERE... SOMETHING WE WERE SUPPOSED TO DO?...
...
I CAN'T REMEMBER, EITHER
LET'S GO SEE IF ANYONE IN THAT CREEPY OLD HOUSE KNOWS!!

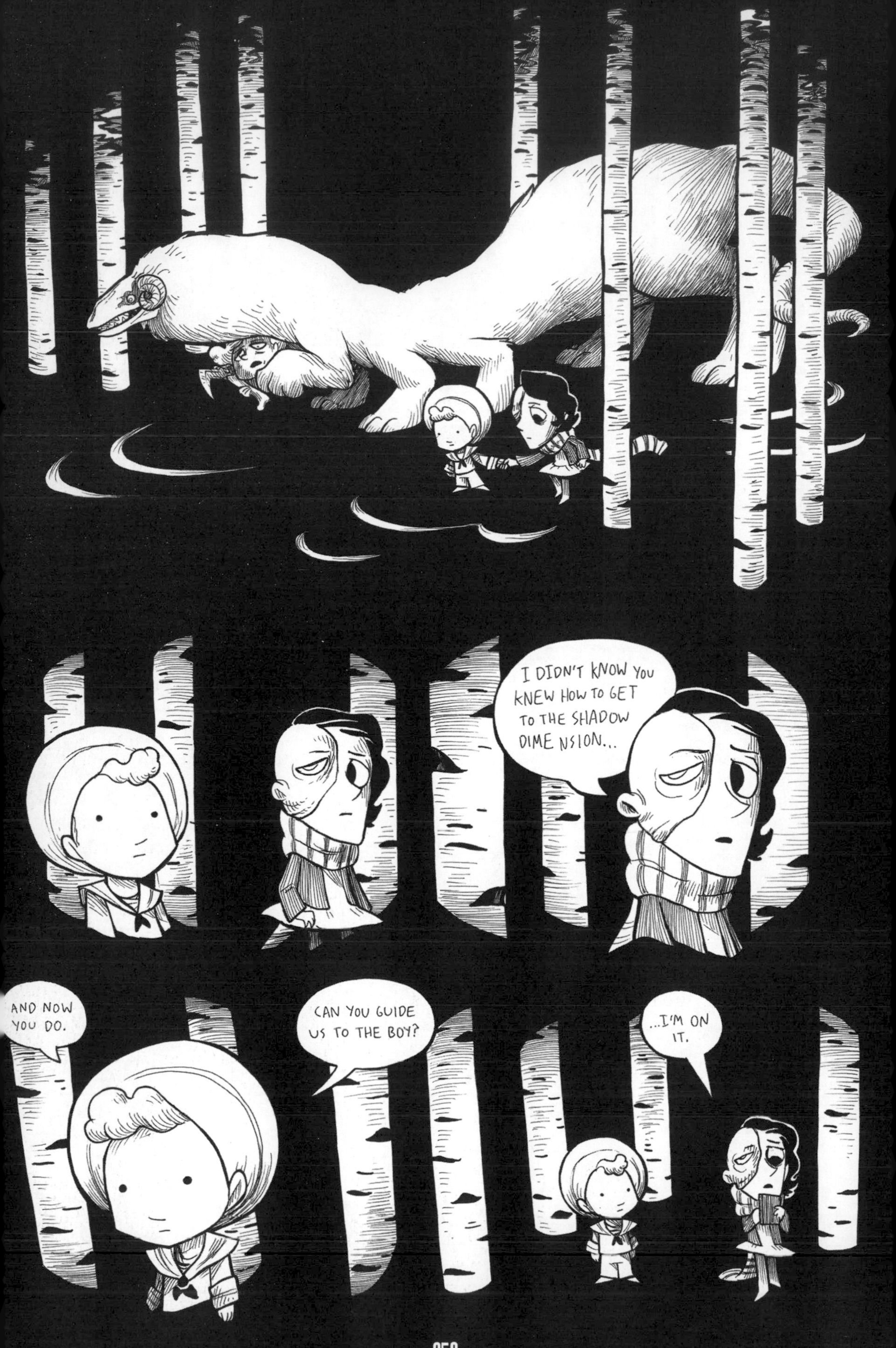
I DIDN'T KNOW YOU KNEW HOW TO GET TO THE SHADOW DIMENSION...
AND NOW YOU DO.
CAN YOU GUIDE US TO THE BOY?
...I'M ON IT.

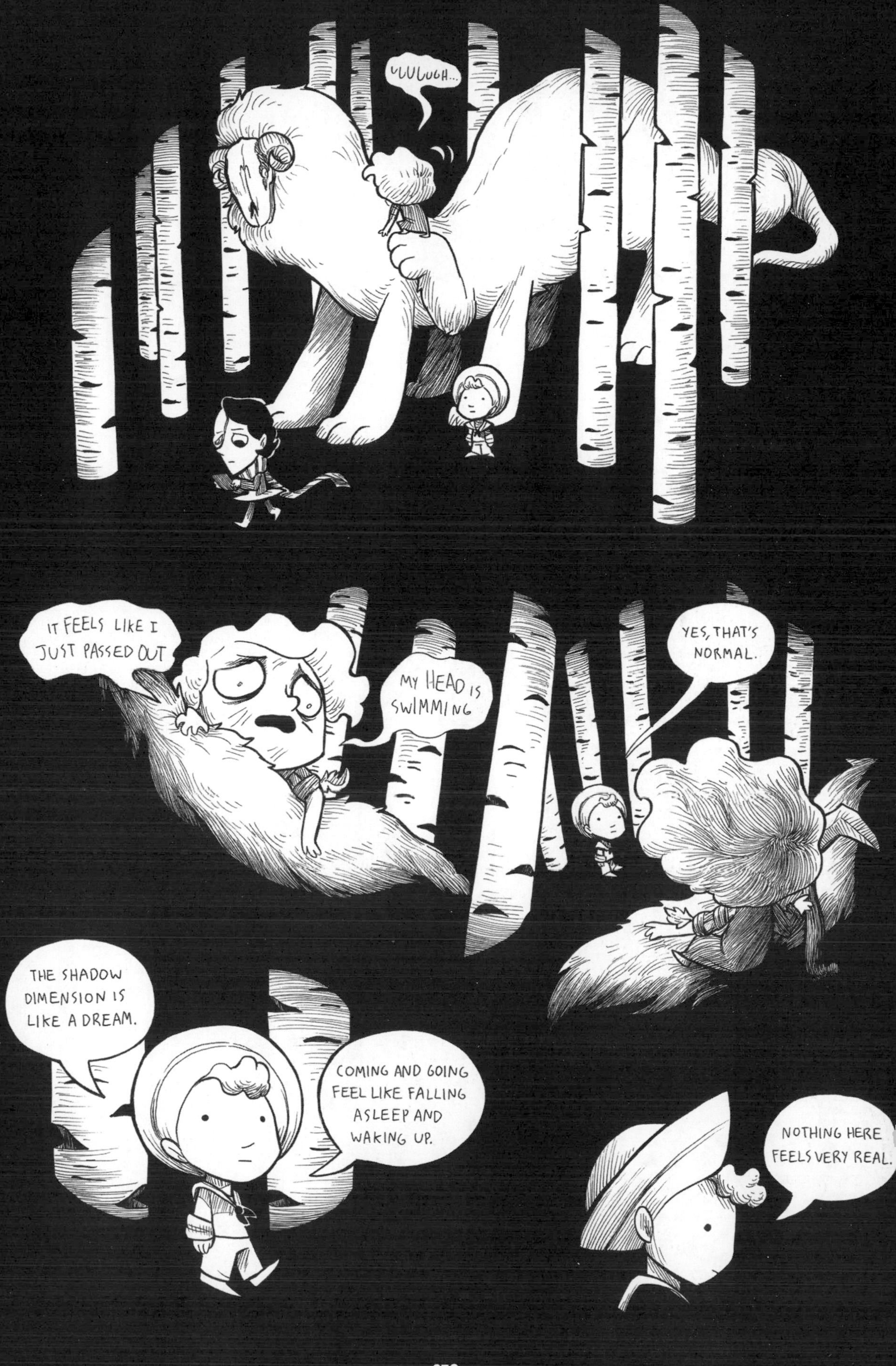
UUUUGH...
IT FEELS LIKE I JUST PASSED OUT
MY HEAD IS SWIMMING
YES, THAT'S NORMAL.
THE SHADOW DIMENSION IS LIKE A DREAM.
COMING AND GOING FEEL LIKE FALLING ASLEEP AND WAKING UP.
NOTHING HERE FEELS VERY REAL.

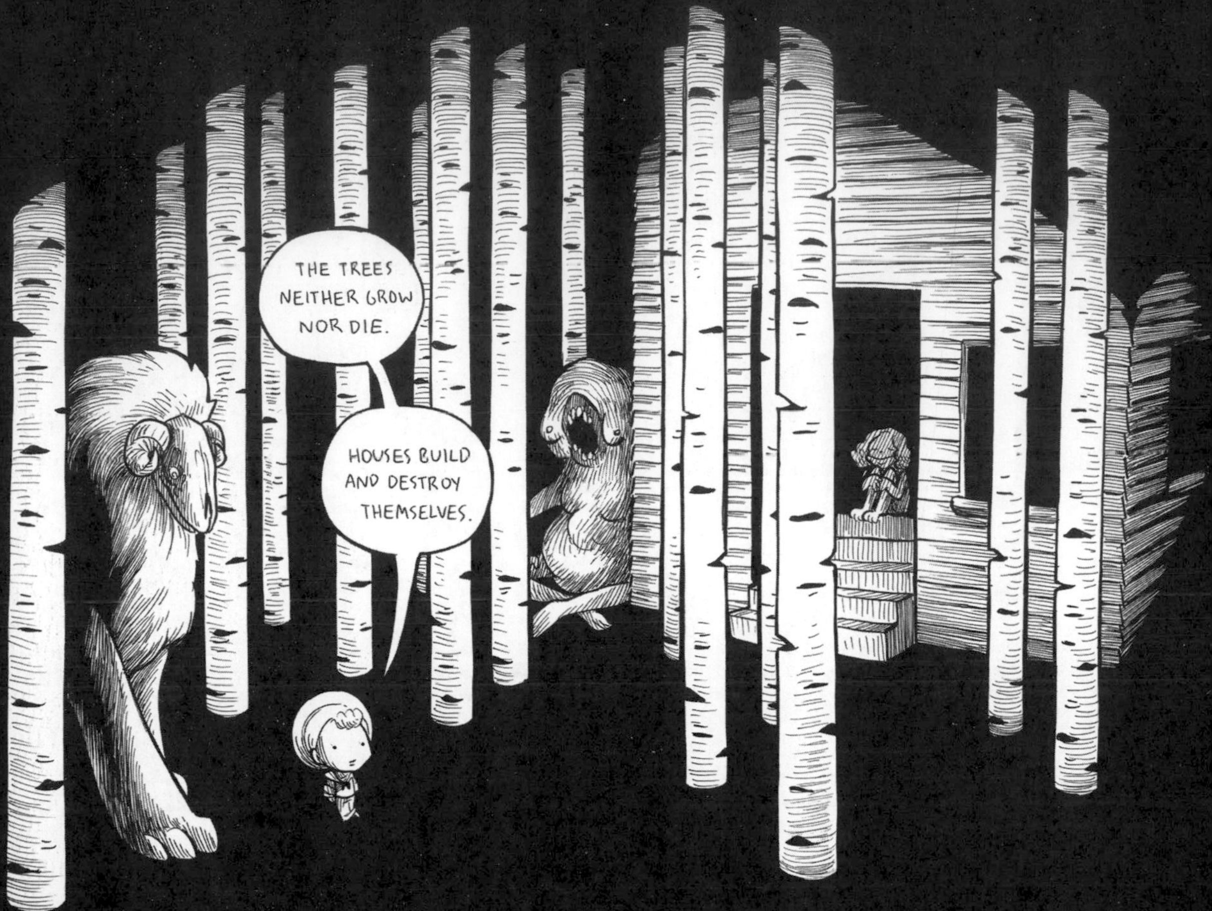
THE TREES NEITHER GROW NOR DIE.
HOUSES BUILD AND DESTROY THEMSELVES.

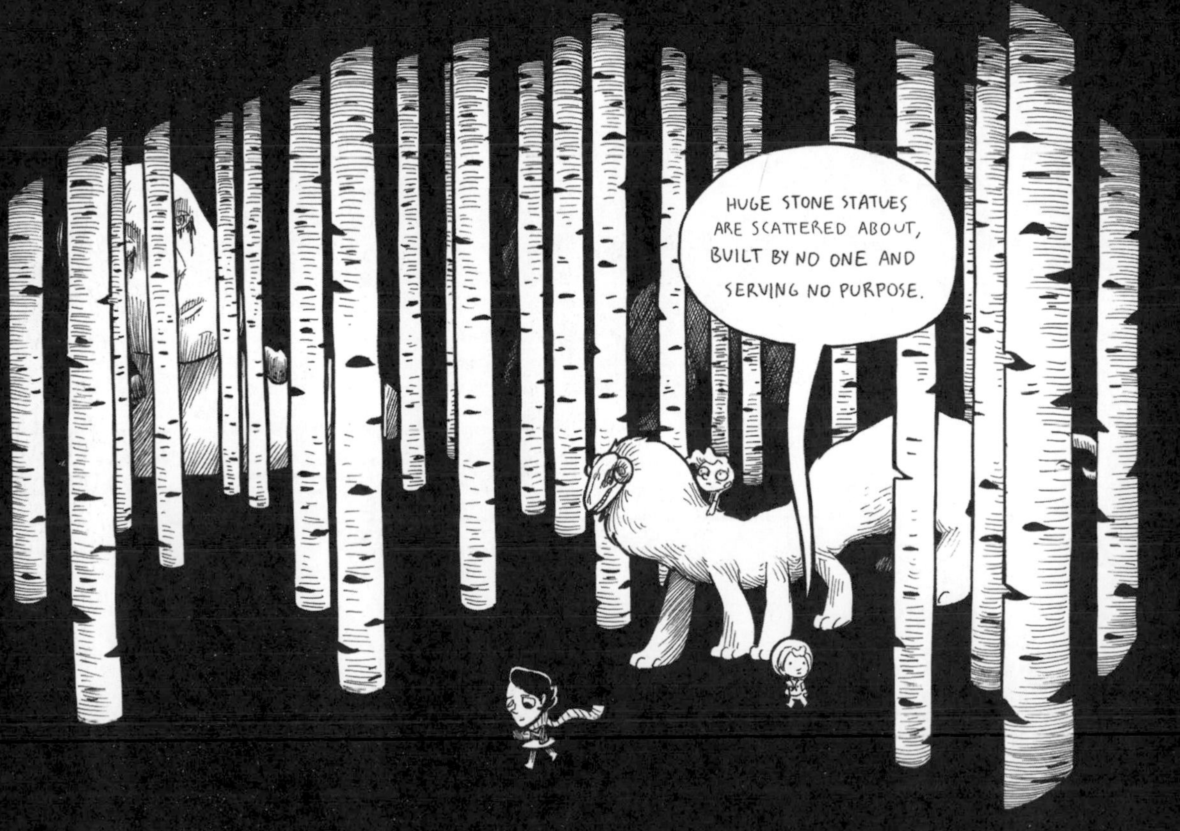
HUGE STONE STATUES ARE SCATTERED ABOUT, BUILT BY NO ONE AND SERVING NO PURPOSE.

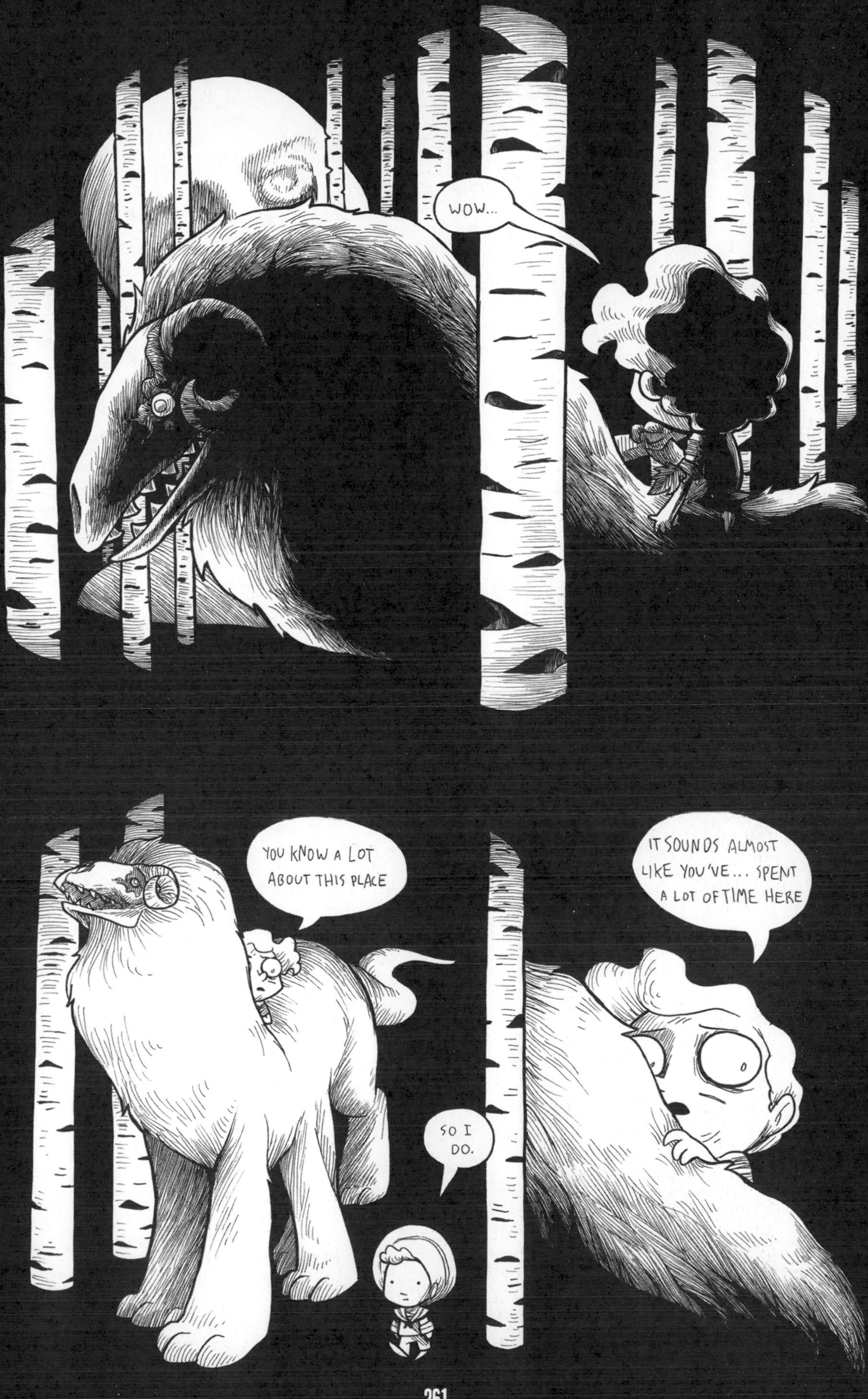
WOW...
YOU KNOW A LOT ABOUT THIS PLACE
SO I DO.
IT SOUNDS ALMOST LIKE YOU'VE... SPENT A LOT OF TIME HERE

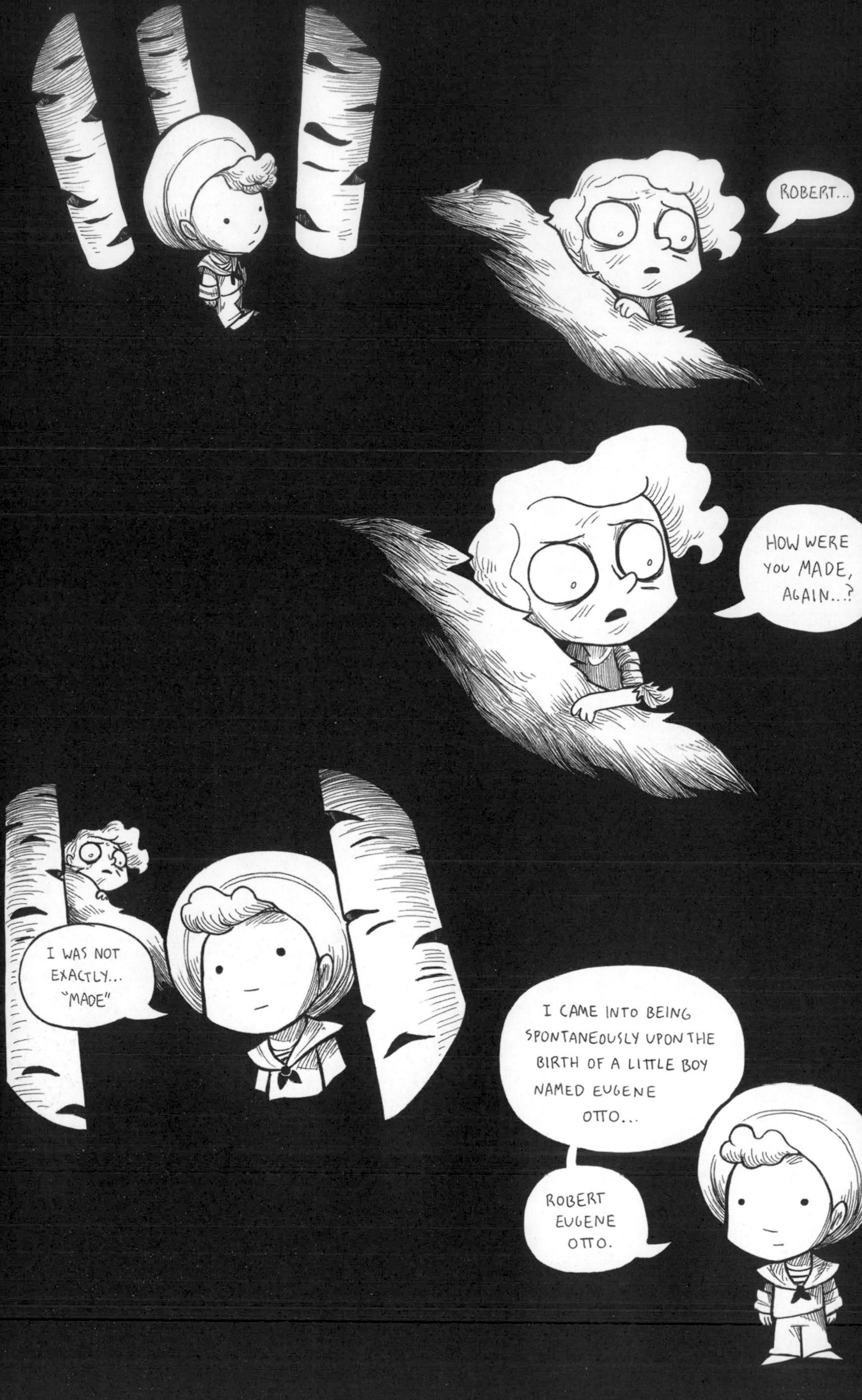
ROBERT...
HOW WERE YOU MADE, AGAIN...?
I WAS NOT EXACTLY... "MADE"
I CAME INTO BEING SPONTANEOUSLY UPON THE BIRTH OF A LITTLE BOY NAMED EUGENE OTTO...
ROBERT EUGENE OTTO.

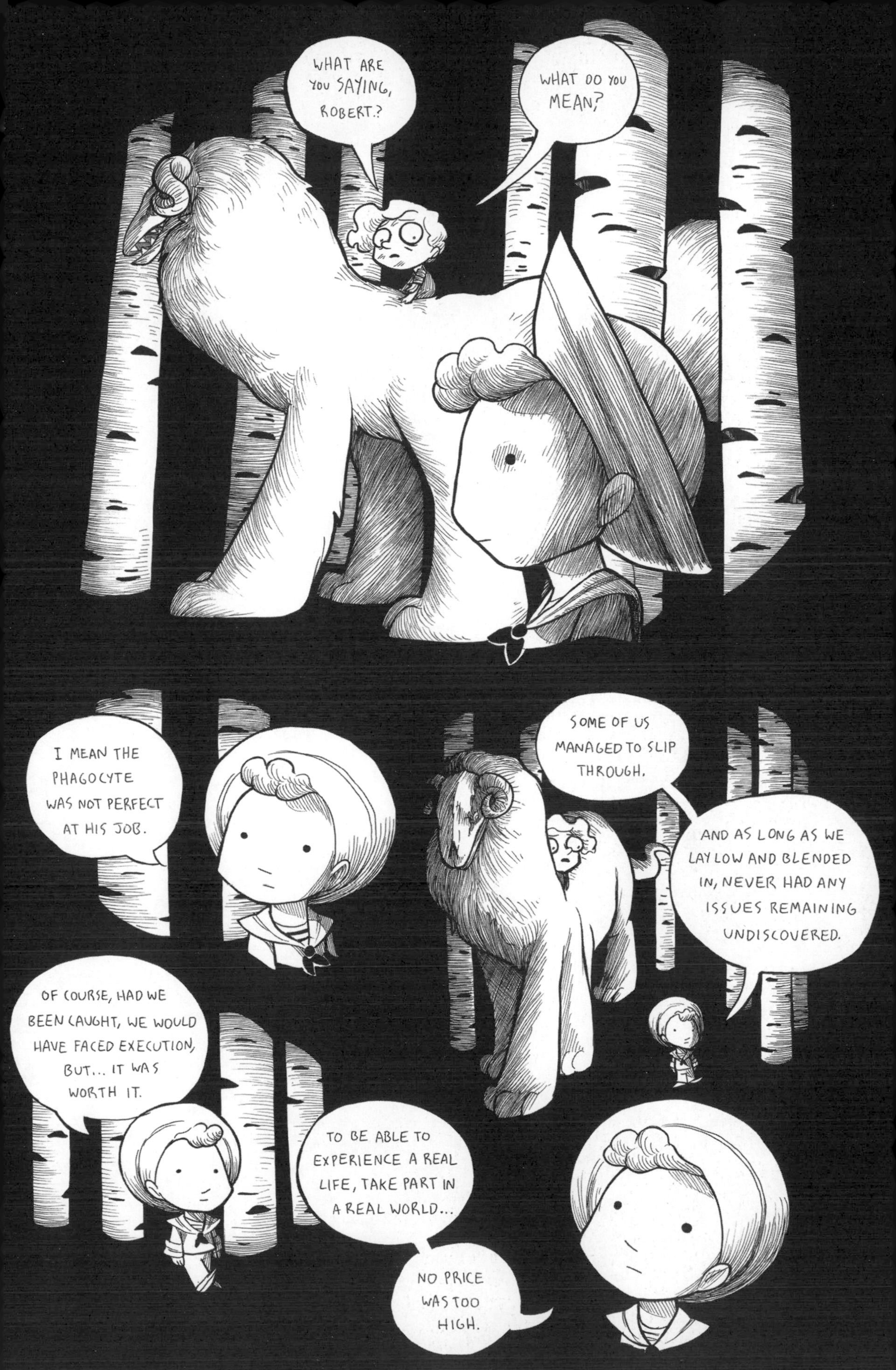
WHAT ARE YOU SAYING, ROBERT.?
WHAT DO YOU MEAN?
I MEAN THE PHAGOCYTE WAS NOT PERFECT AT HIS JOB.
SOME OF US MANAGED TO SLIP THROUGH.
AND AS LONG AS WE LAY LOW AND BLENDED IN, NEVER HAD ANY ISSUES REMAINING UNDISCOVERED.
OF COURSE, HAD WE BEEN CAUGHT, WE WOULD HAVE FACED EXECUTION, BUT... IT WAS WORTH IT.
TO BE ABLE TO EXPERIENCE A REAL LIFE, TAKE PART IN A REAL WORLD...
NO PRICE WAS TOO HIGH.

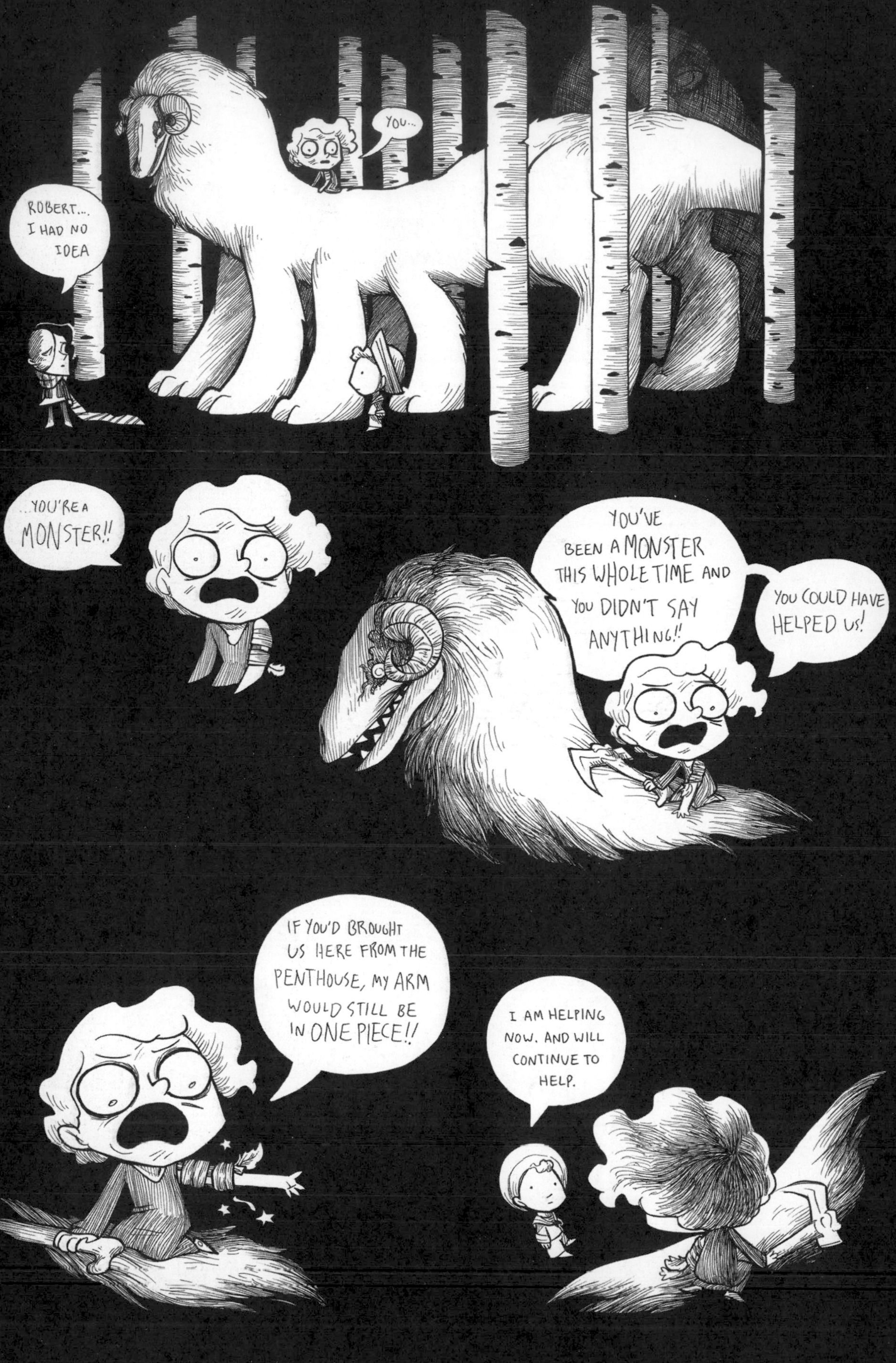
YOU...
ROBERT.... I HAD NO IDEA
...YOU'RE A MONSTER!!
YOU'VE BEEN A MONSTER THIS WHOLE TIME AND YOU DIDN'T SAY ANYTHING!!
YOU COULD HAVE HELPED US!
IF YOU'D BROUGHT US HERE FROM THE PENTHOUSE, MY ARM WOULD STILL BE IN ONE PIECE!!
I AM HELPING NOW. AND WILL CONTINUE TO HELP.

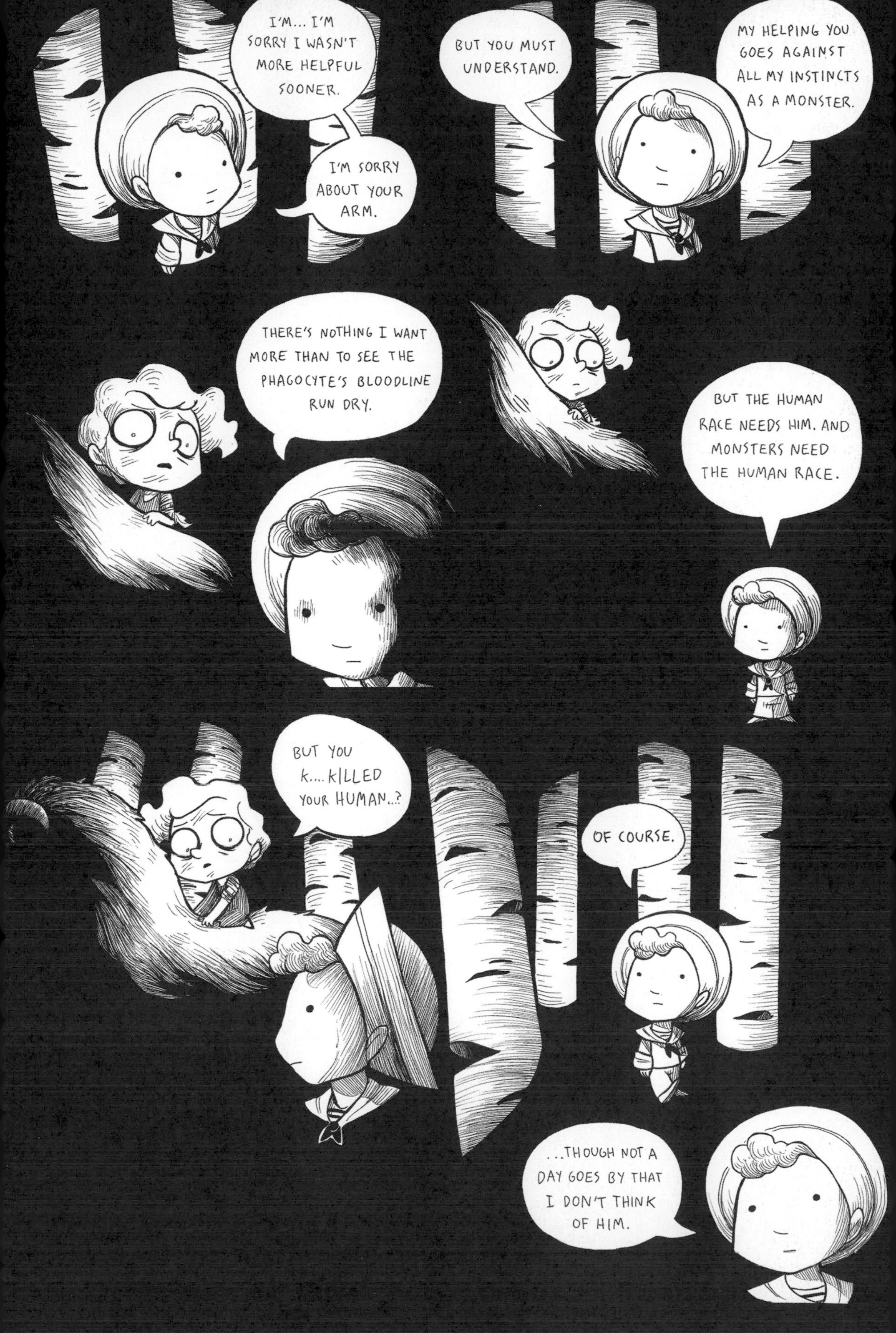
I'M... I'M SORRY I WASN'T MORE HELPFUL SOONER.
I'M SORRY ABOUT YOUR ARM.
BUT YOU MUST UNDERSTAND.
MY HELPING YOU GOES AGAINST ALL MY INSTINCTS AS A MONSTER.
THERE'S NOTHING I WANT MORE THAN TO SEE THE PHAGOCYTE'S BLOODLINE RUN DRY.
BUT THE HUMAN RACE NEEDS HIM. AND MONSTERS NEED THE HUMAN RACE.
BUT YOU K....KILLED YOUR HUMAN..?
OF COURSE.
...THOUGH NOT A DAY GOES BY THAT I DON'T THINK OF HIM.

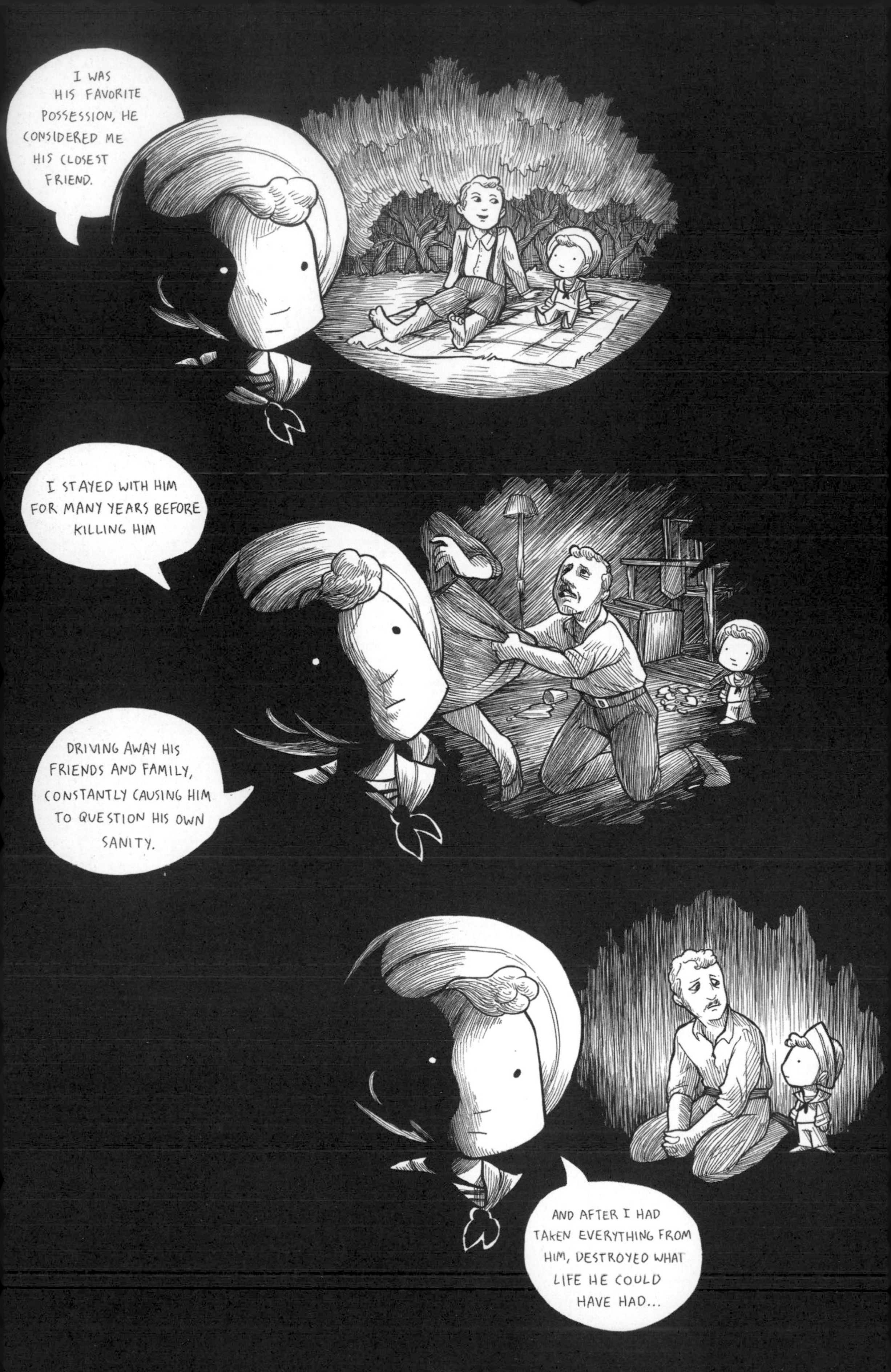
I WAS HIS FAVORITE POSSESSION, HE CONSIDERED ME HIS CLOSEST FRIEND.
I STAYED WITH HIM FOR MANY YEARS BEFORE KILLING HIM
DRIVING AWAY HIS FRIENDS AND FAMILY, CONSTANTLY CAUSING HIM TO QUESTION HIS OWN SANITY.
AND AFTER I HAD TAKEN EVERYTHING FROM HIM, DESTROYED WHAT LIFE HE COULD HAVE HAD...

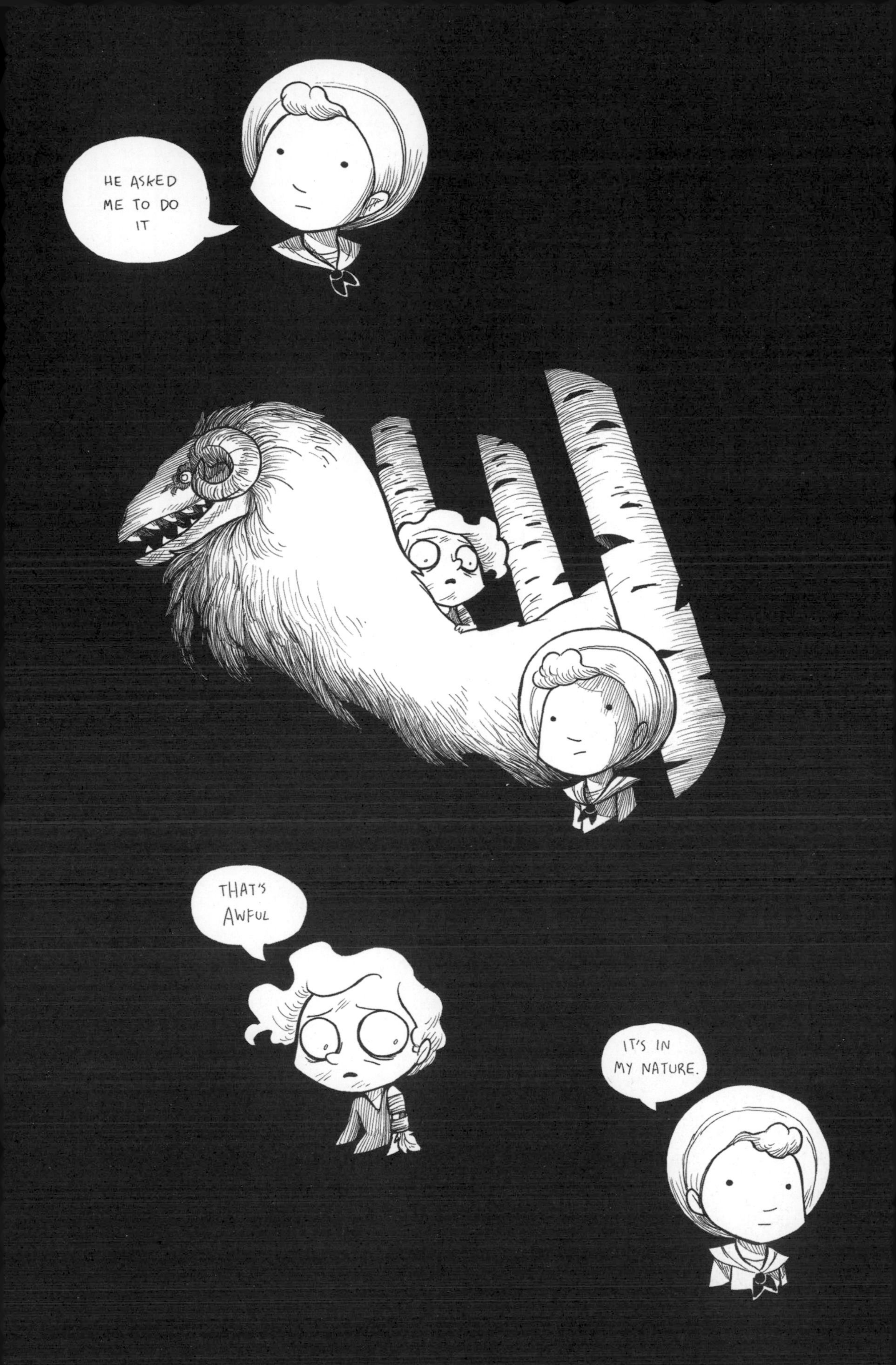
HE ASKED ME TO DO IT
THAT'S AWFUL
IT'S IN MY NATURE.

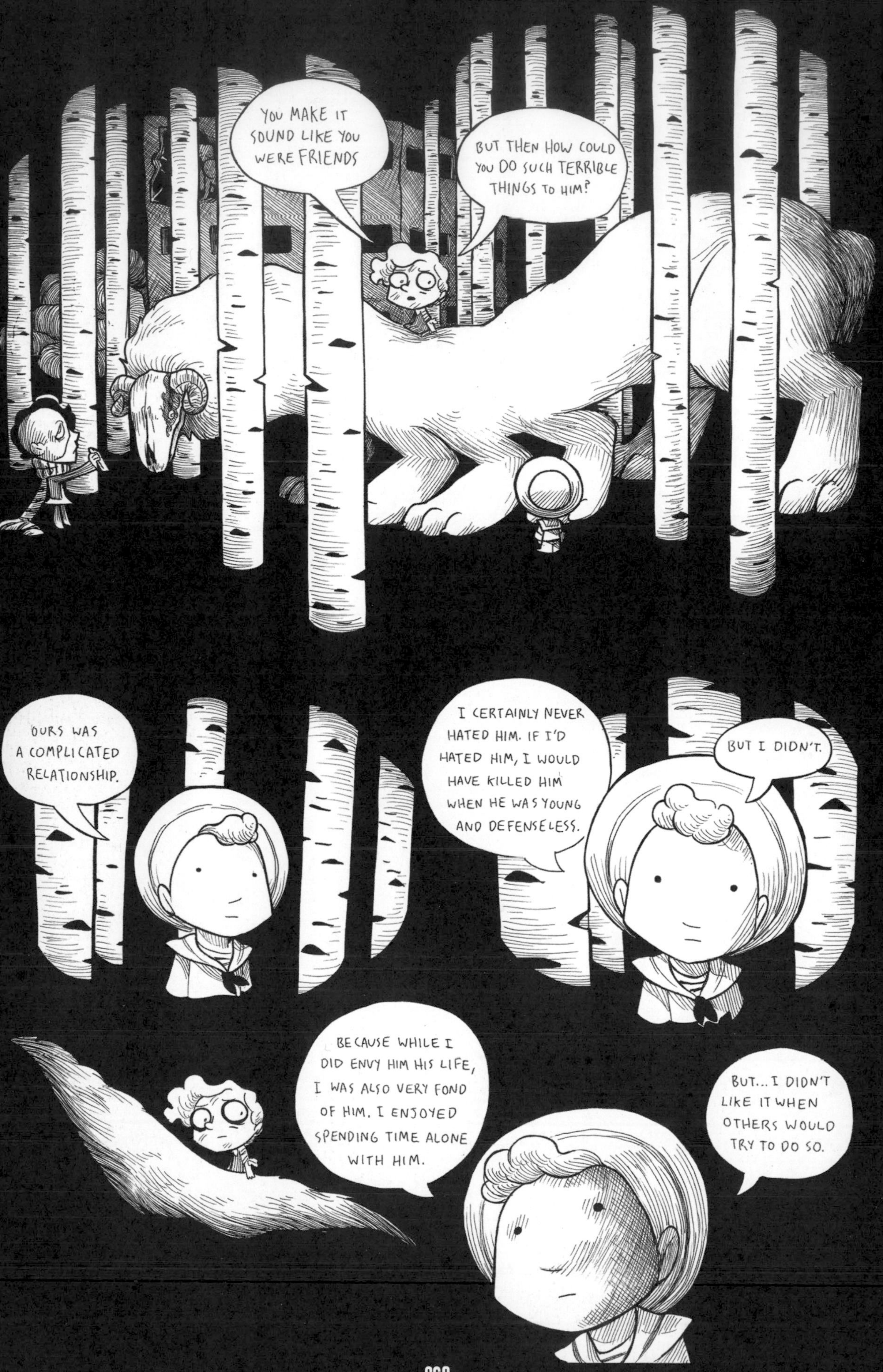
YOU MAKE IT SOUND LIKE YOU WERE FRIENDS
BUT THEN HOW COULD YOU DO SUCH TERRIBLE THINGS TO HIM?
OURS WAS A COMPLICATED RELATIONSHIP.
I CERTAINLY NEVER HATED HIM. IF I'D HATED HIM, I WOULD HAVE KILLED HIM WHEN HE WAS YOUNG AND DEFENSELESS.
BUT I DIDN'T.
BECAUSE WHILE I DID ENVY HIM HIS LIFE, I WAS ALSO VERY FOND OF HIM. I ENJOYED SPENDING TIME ALONE WITH HIM.
BUT... I DIDN'T LIKE IT WHEN OTHERS WOULD TRY TO DO SO.

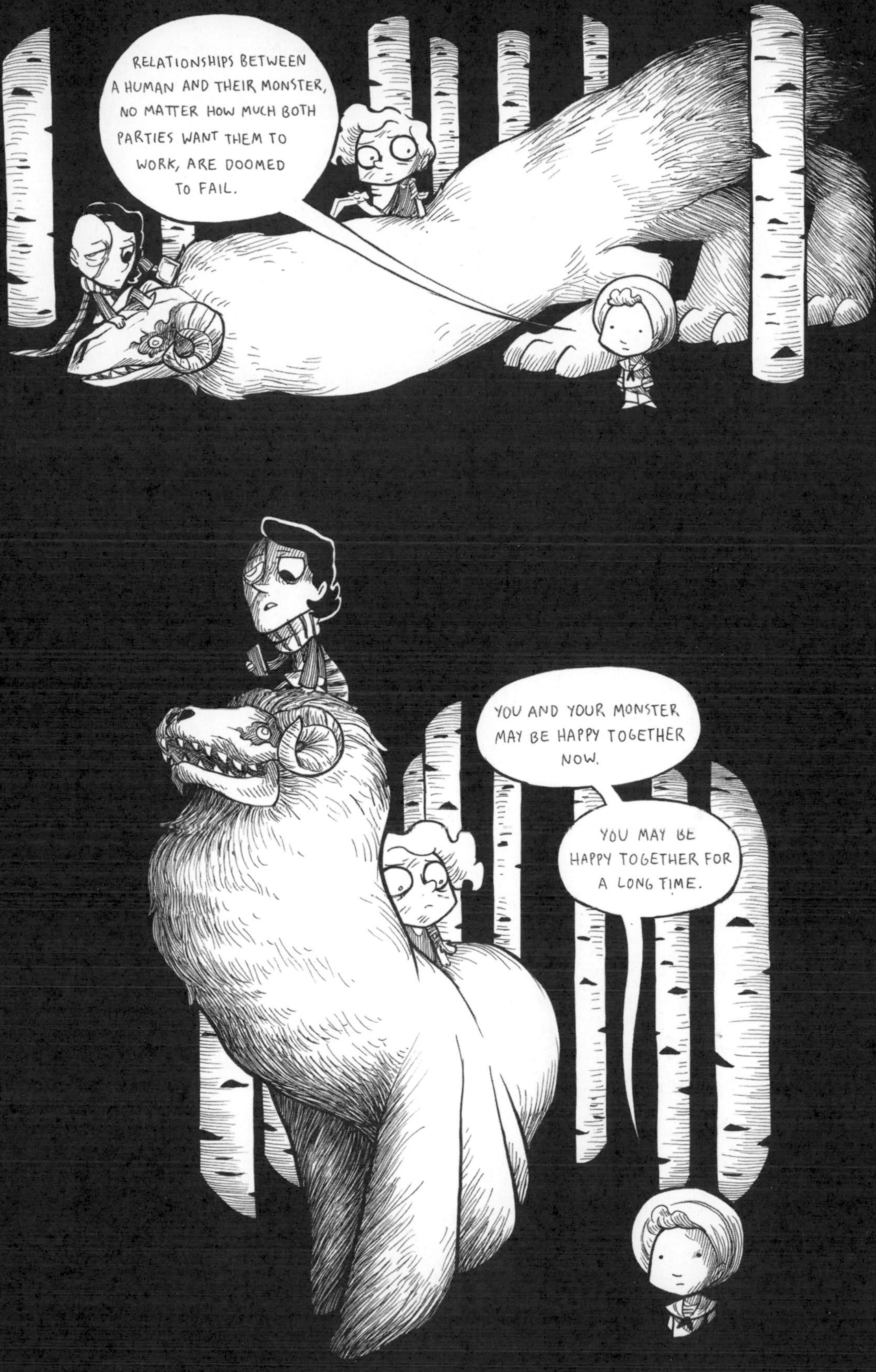
RELATIONSHIPS BETWEEN A HUMAN AND THEIR MONSTER, NO MATTER HOW MUCH BOTH PARTIES WANT THEM TO WORK, ARE DOOMED TO FAIL.
YOU AND YOUR MONSTER MAY BE HAPPY TOGETHER NOW.
YOU MAY BE HAPPY TOGETHER FOR A LONG TIME.

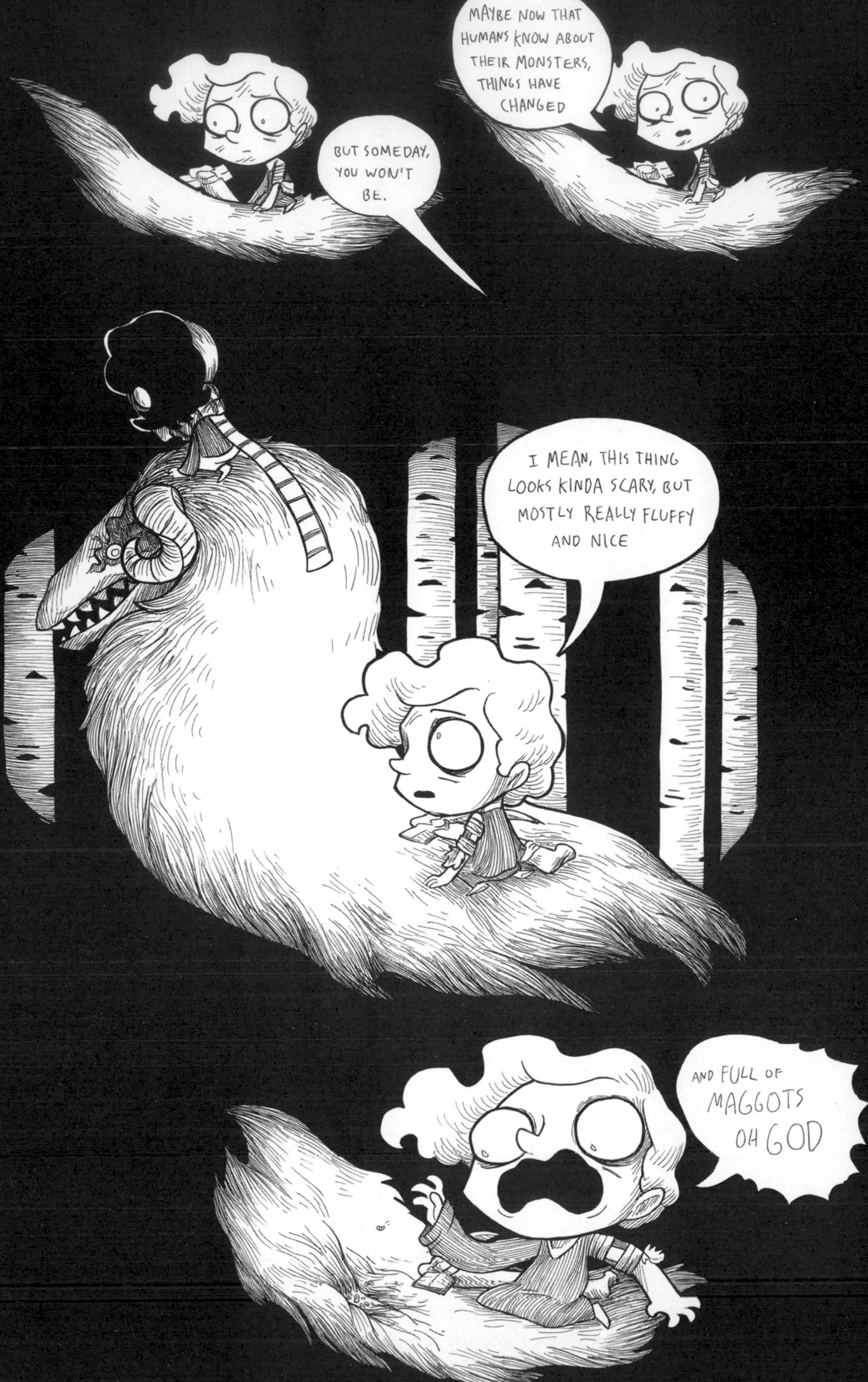
BUT SOMEDAY, YOU WON'T BE.
MAYBE NOW THAT HUMANS KNOW ABOUT THEIR MONSTERS, THINGS HAVE CHANGED
I MEAN, THIS THING LOOKS KINDA SCARY, BUT MOSTLY REALLY FLUFFY AND NICE
AND FULL OF MAGGOTS OH GOD

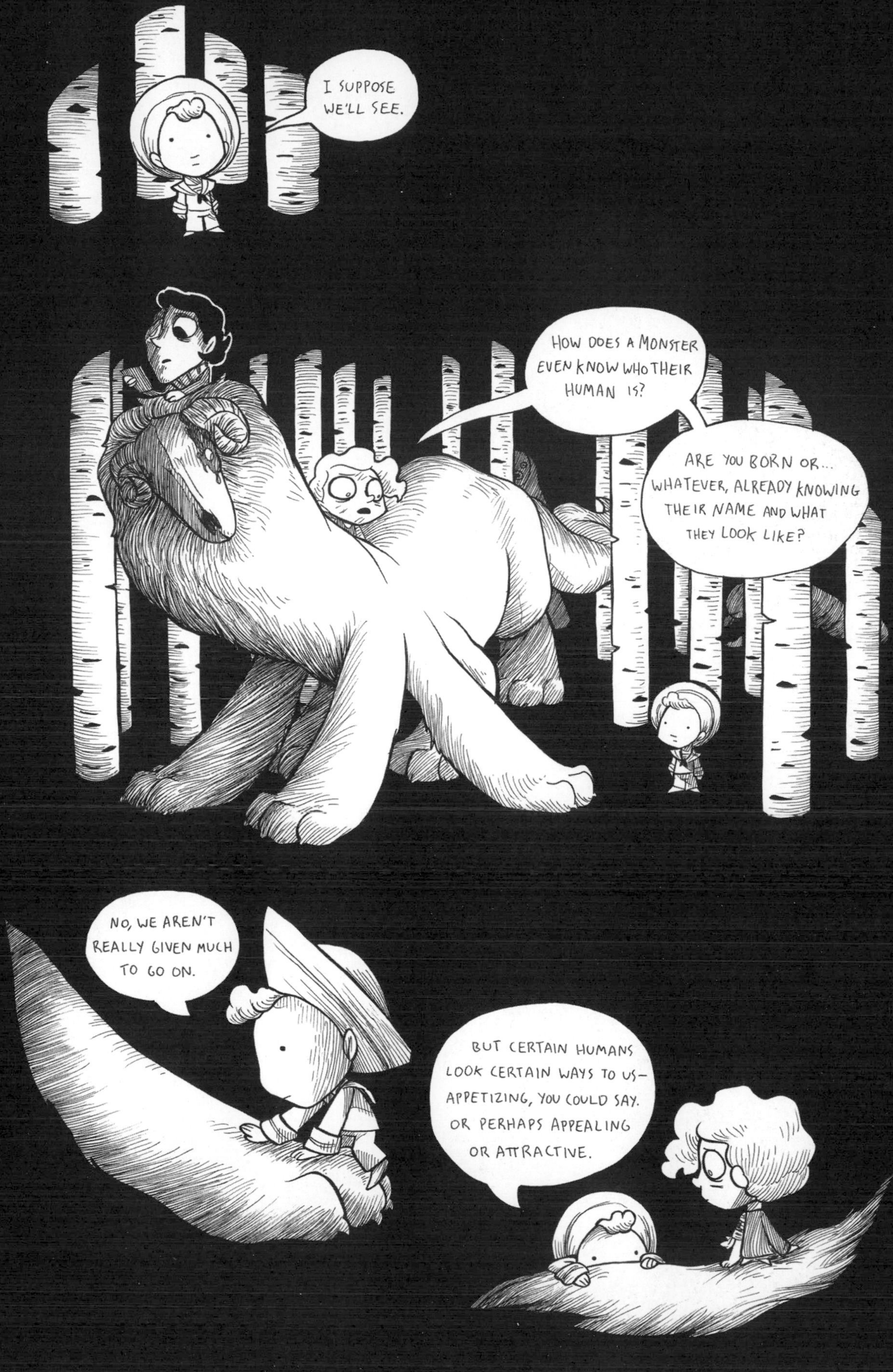
I SUPPOSE WE'LL SEE.
HOW DOES A MONSTER EVEN KNOW WHO THEIR HUMAN IS?
ARE YOU BORN OR... WHATEVER, ALREADY KNOWING THEIR NAME AND WHAT THEY LOOK LIKE?
NO, WE AREN'T REALLY GIVEN MUCH TO GO ON.
BUT CERTAIN HUMANS LOOK CERTAIN WAYS TO US– APPETIZING, YOU COULD SAY. OR PERHAPS APPEALING OR ATTRACTIVE.

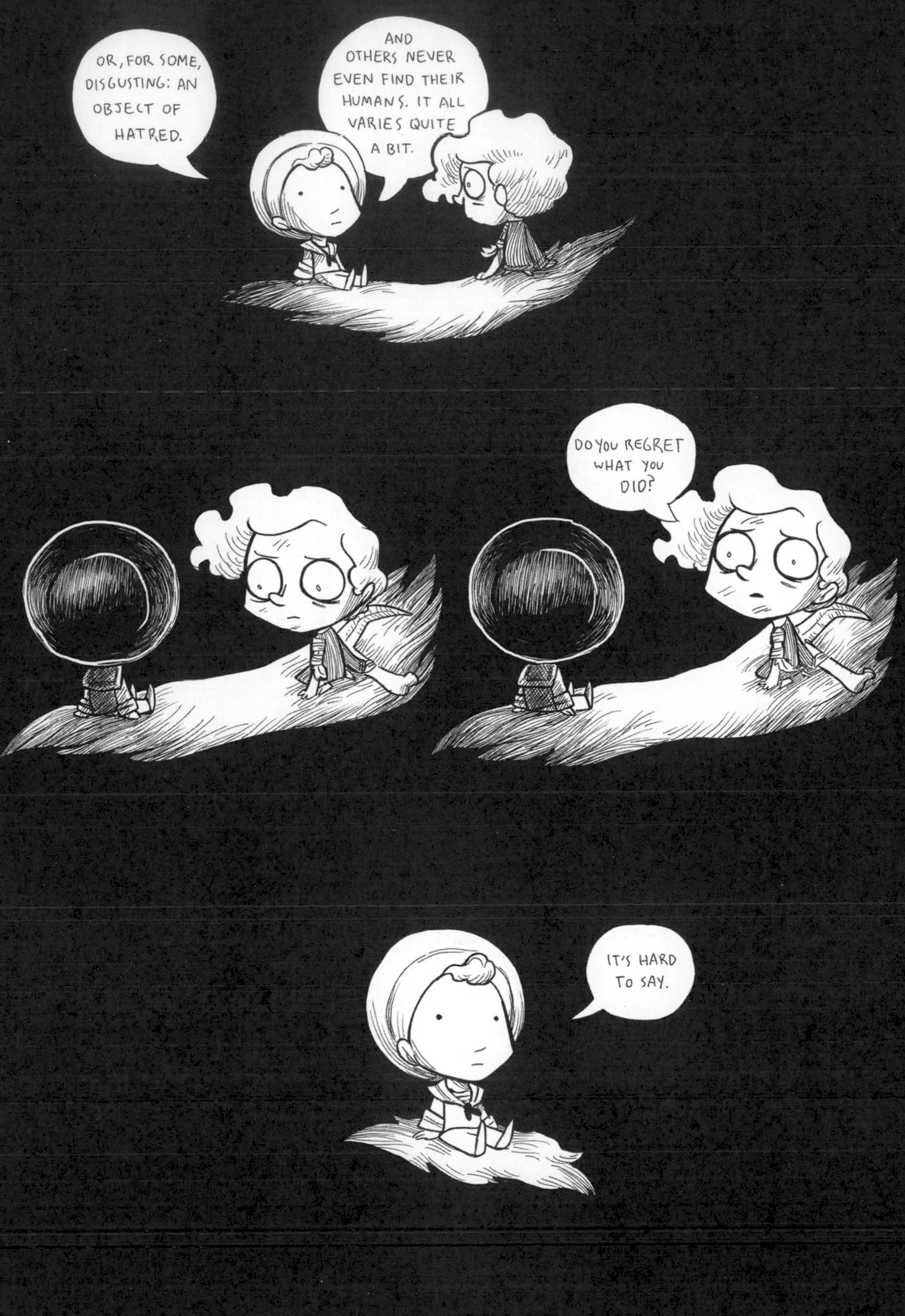

OR, FOR SOME, DISGUSTING: AN OBJECT OF HATRED.
AND OTHERS NEVER EVEN FIND THEIR HUMANS. IT ALL VARIES QUITE A BIT.
DO YOU REGRET WHAT YOU DID?
IT'S HARD TO SAY.

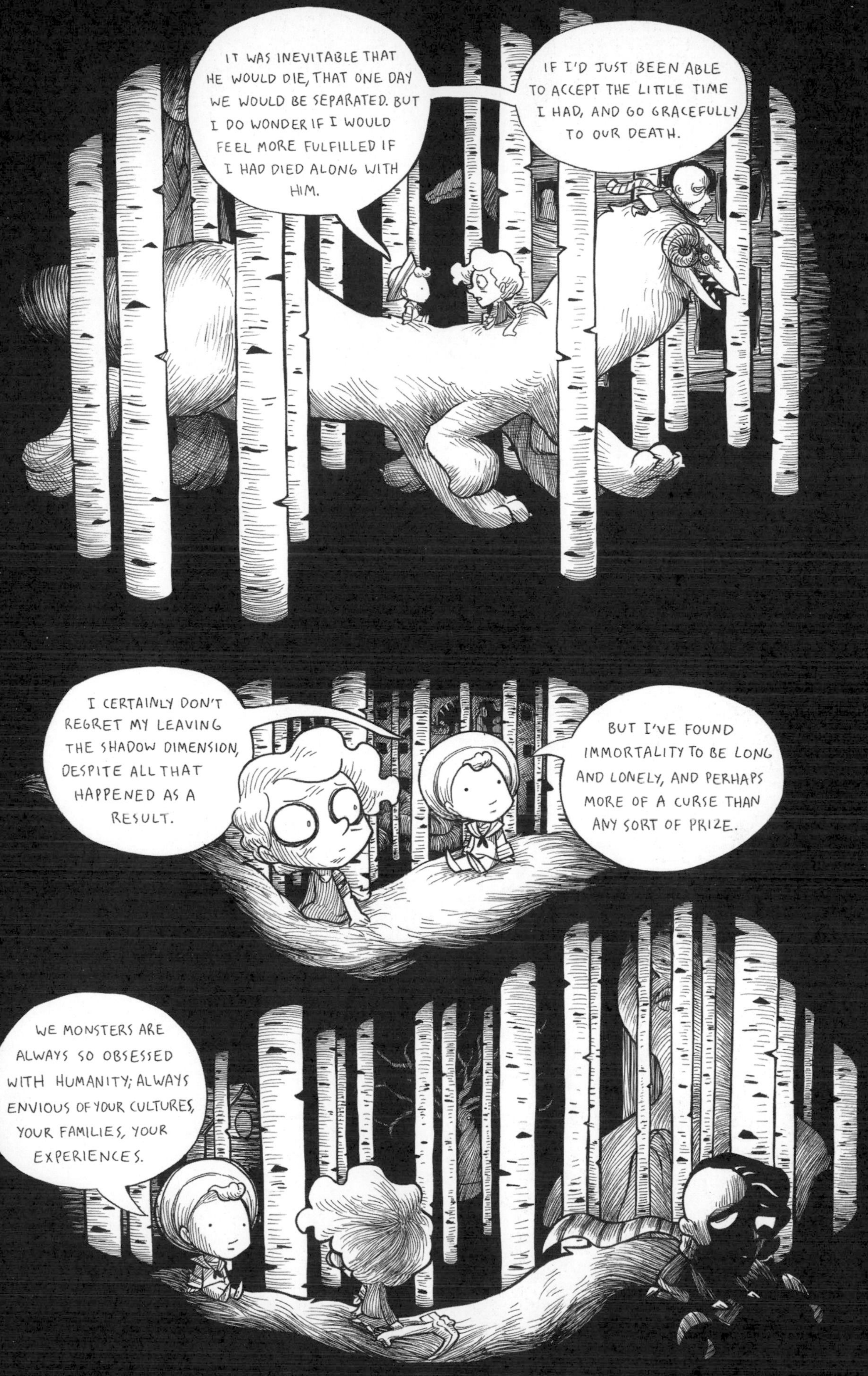
IT WAS INEVITABLE THAT HE WOULD DIE, THAT ONE DAY WE WOULD BE SEPARATED. BUT I DO WONDER IF I WOULD FEEL MORE FULFILLED IF I HAD DIED ALONG WITH HIM.
IF I'D JUST BEEN ABLE TO ACCEPT THE LITTLE TIME I HAD, AND GO GRACEFULLY TO OUR DEATH.
I CERTAINLY DON'T REGRET MY LEAVING THE SHADOW DIMENSION, DESPITE ALL THAT HAPPENED AS A RESULT.
BUT I'VE FOUND IMMORTALITY TO BE LONG AND LONELY, AND PERHAPS MORE OF A CURSE THAN ANY SORT OF PRIZE.
WE MONSTERS ARE ALWAYS SO OBSESSED WITH HUMANITY; ALWAYS ENVIOUS OF YOUR CULTURES, YOUR FAMILIES, YOUR EXPERIENCES.

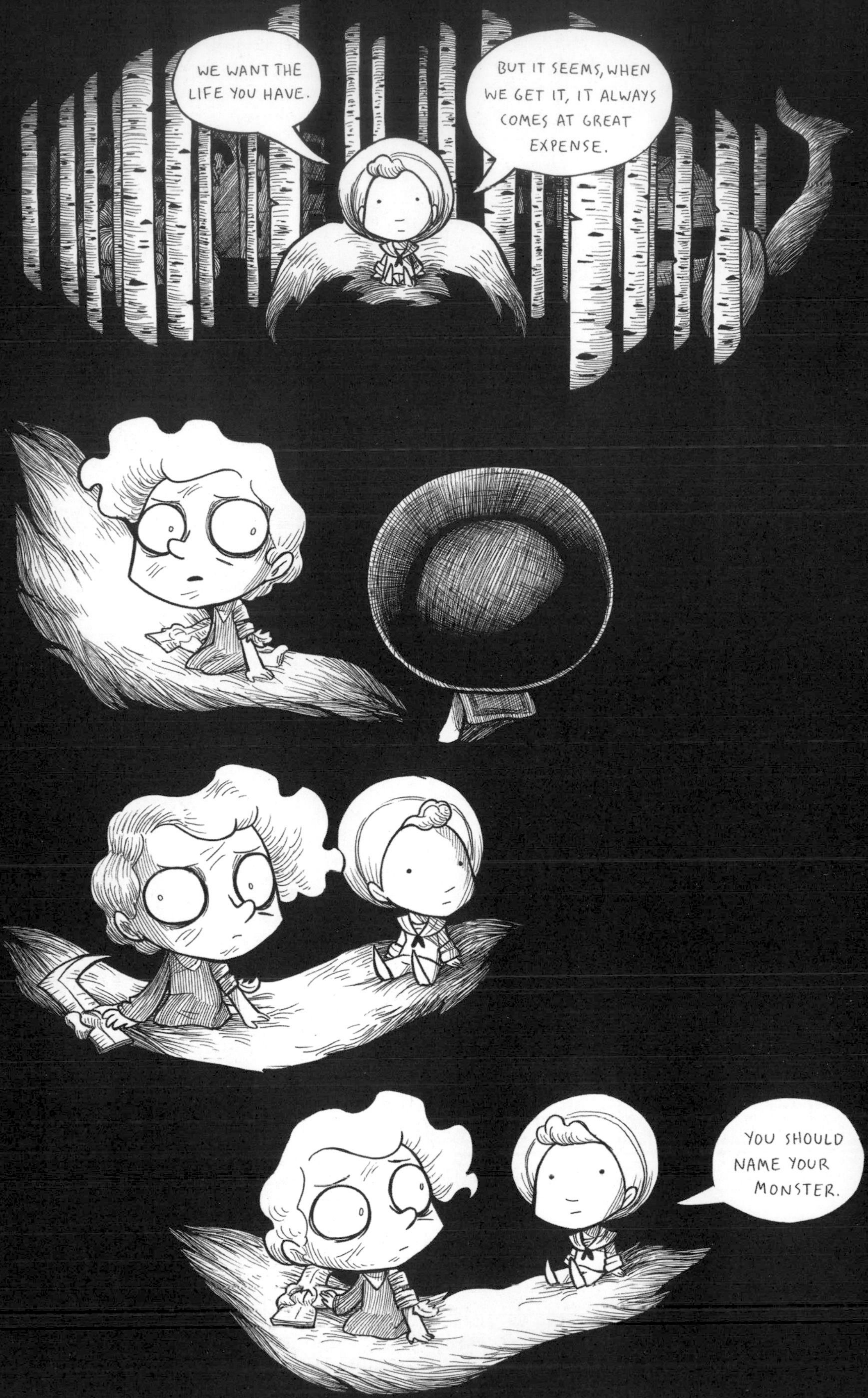
WE WANT THE LIFE YOU HAVE.
BUT IT SEEMS, WHEN WE GET IT, IT ALWAYS COMES AT GREAT EXPENSE.
YOU SHOULD NAME YOUR MONSTER.

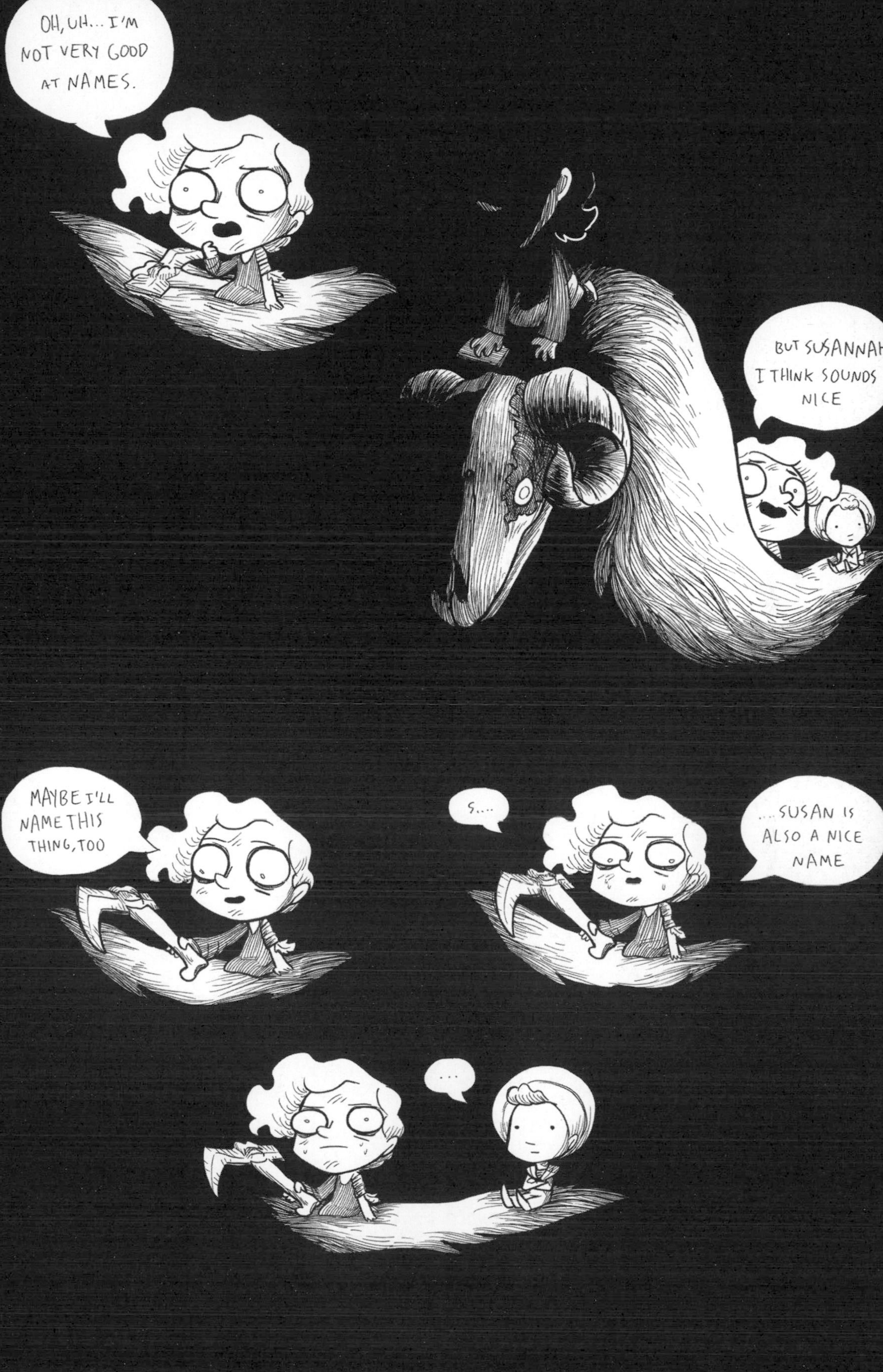
OH, UH... I'M NOT VERY GOOD AT NAMES.
BUT SUSANNAH I THINK SOUNDS NICE
MAYBE I'LL NAME THIS THING, TOO
S....
...SUSAN IS ALSO A NICE NAME
...

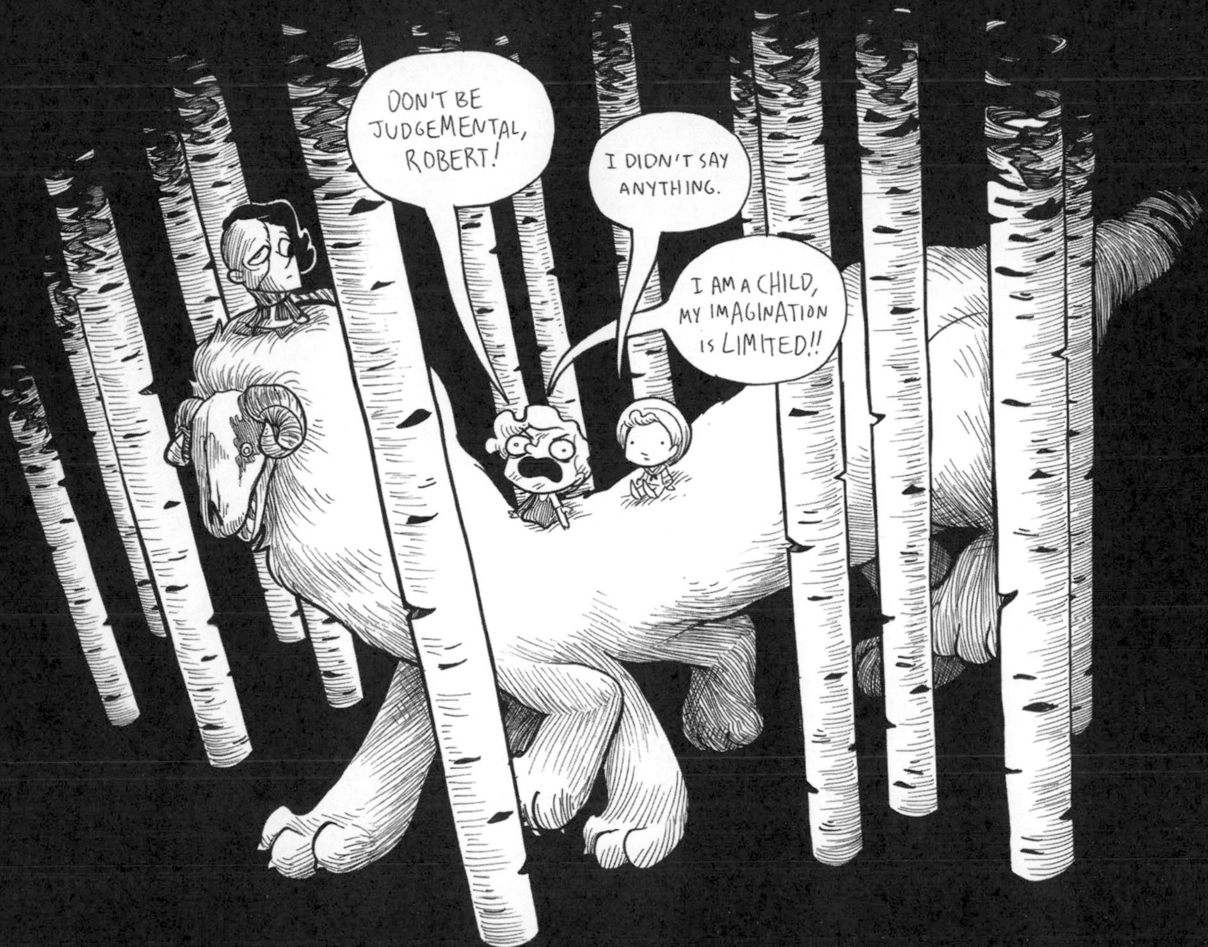
DON'T BE JUDGEMENTAL, ROBERT!
I DIDN'T SAY ANYTHING.
I AM A CHILD, MY IMAGINATION IS LIMITED!!

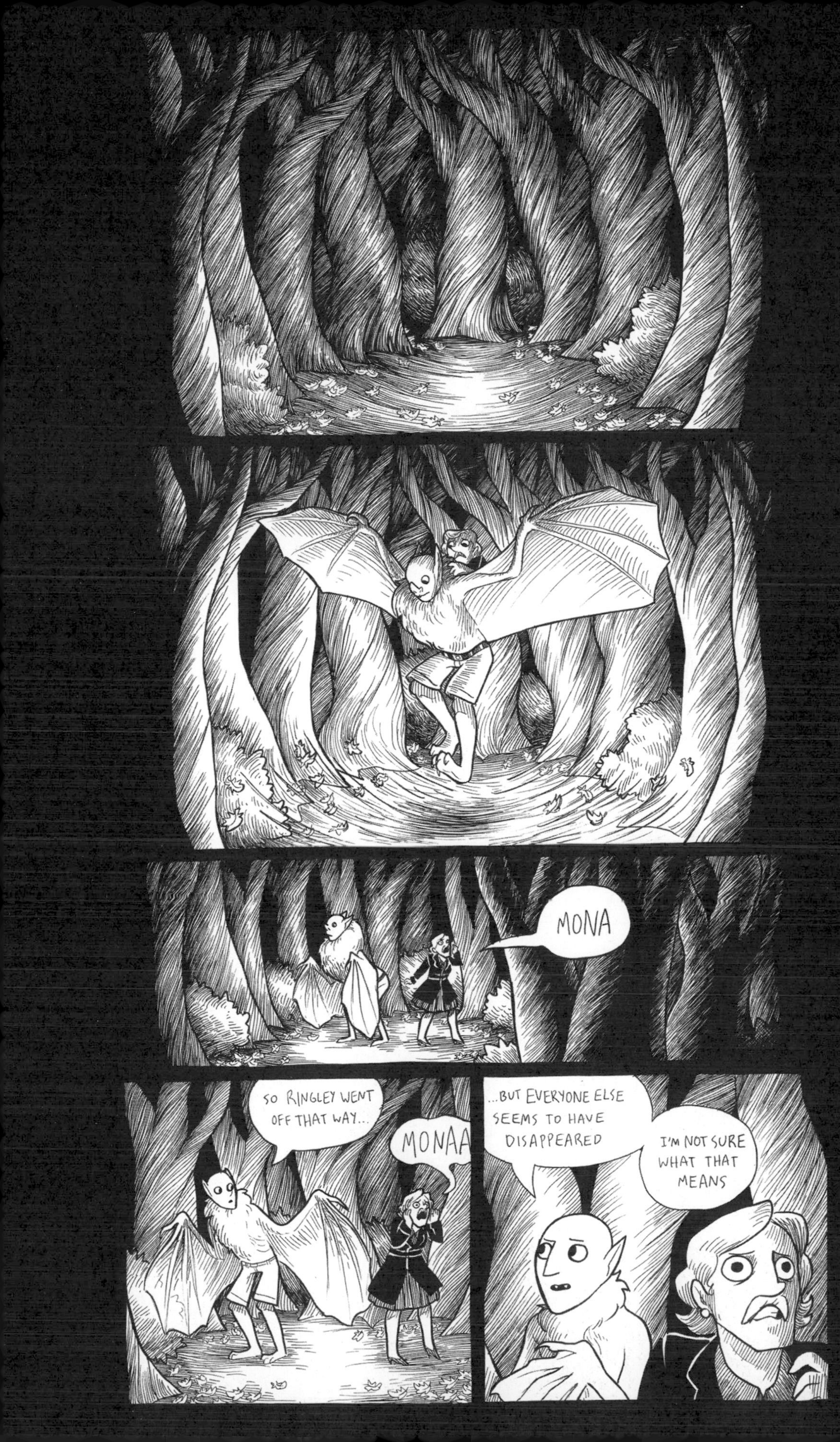
MONA
SO RINGLEY WENT OFF THAT WAY...
MONAA
...BUT EVERYONE ELSE SEEMS TO HAVE DISAPPEARED
I'M NOT SURE WHAT THAT MEANS

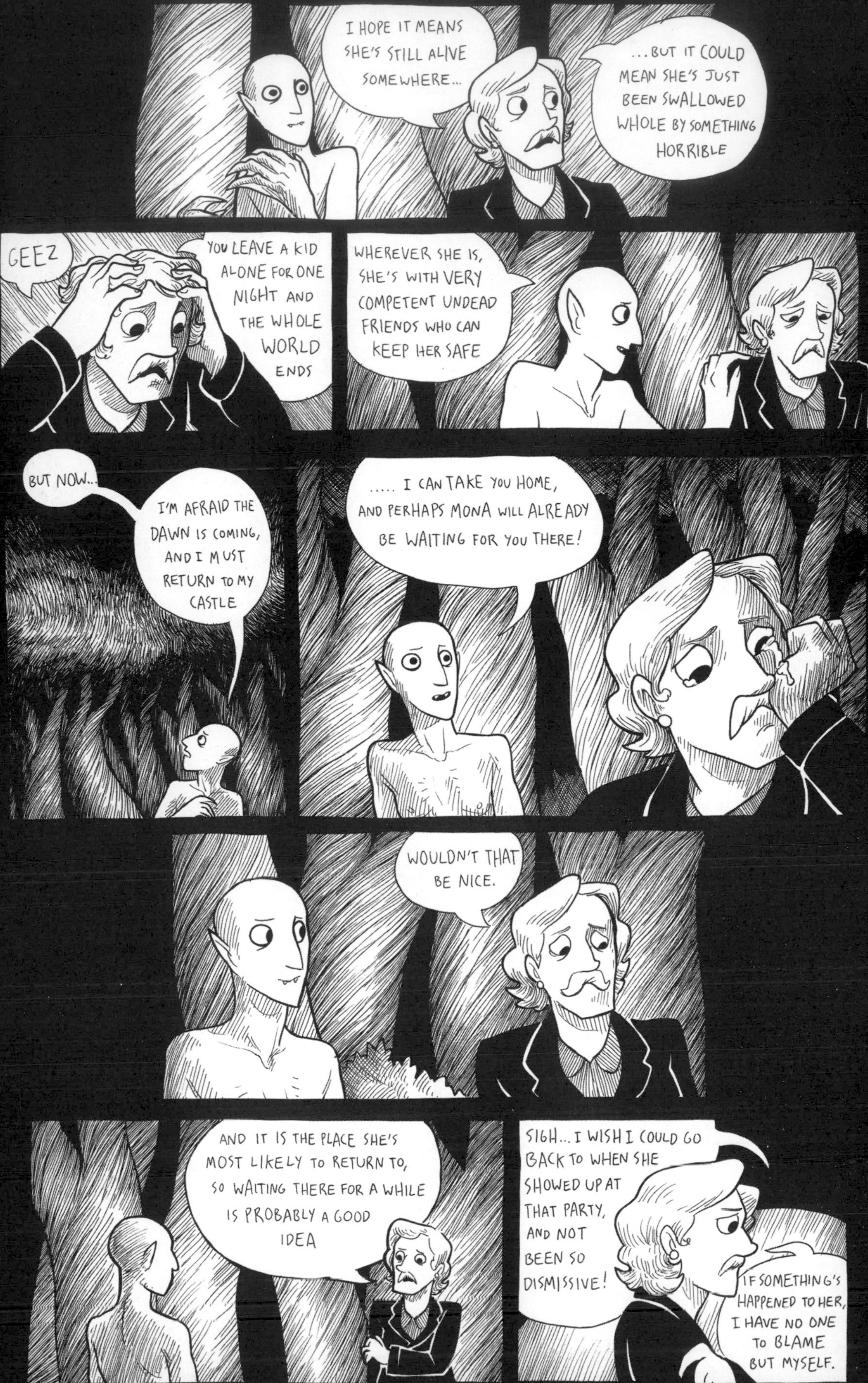
I HOPE IT MEANS SHE'S STILL ALIVE SOMEWHERE...
...BUT IT COULD MEAN SHE'S JUST BEEN SWALLOWED WHOLE BY SOMETHING HORRIBLE
GEEZ
YOU LEAVE A KID ALONE FOR ONE NIGHT AND THE WHOLE WORLD ENDS
WHEREVER SHE IS, SHE'S WITH VERY COMPETENT UNDEAD FRIENDS WHO CAN KEEP HER SAFE
BUT NOW...
I'M AFRAID THE DAWN IS COMING, AND I MUST RETURN TO MY CASTLE
..... I CAN TAKE YOU HOME, AND PERHAPS MONA WILL ALREADY BE WAITING FOR YOU THERE!
WOULDN'T THAT BE NICE.
AND IT IS THE PLACE SHE'S MOST LIKELY TO RETURN TO, SO WAITING THERE FOR A WHILE IS PROBABLY A GOOD IDEA
SIGH... I WISH I COULD GO BACK TO WHEN SHE SHOWED UP AT THAT PARTY, AND NOT BEEN SO DISMISSIVE!
IF SOMETHING'S HAPPENED TO HER, I HAVE NO ONE TO BLAME BUT MYSELF.

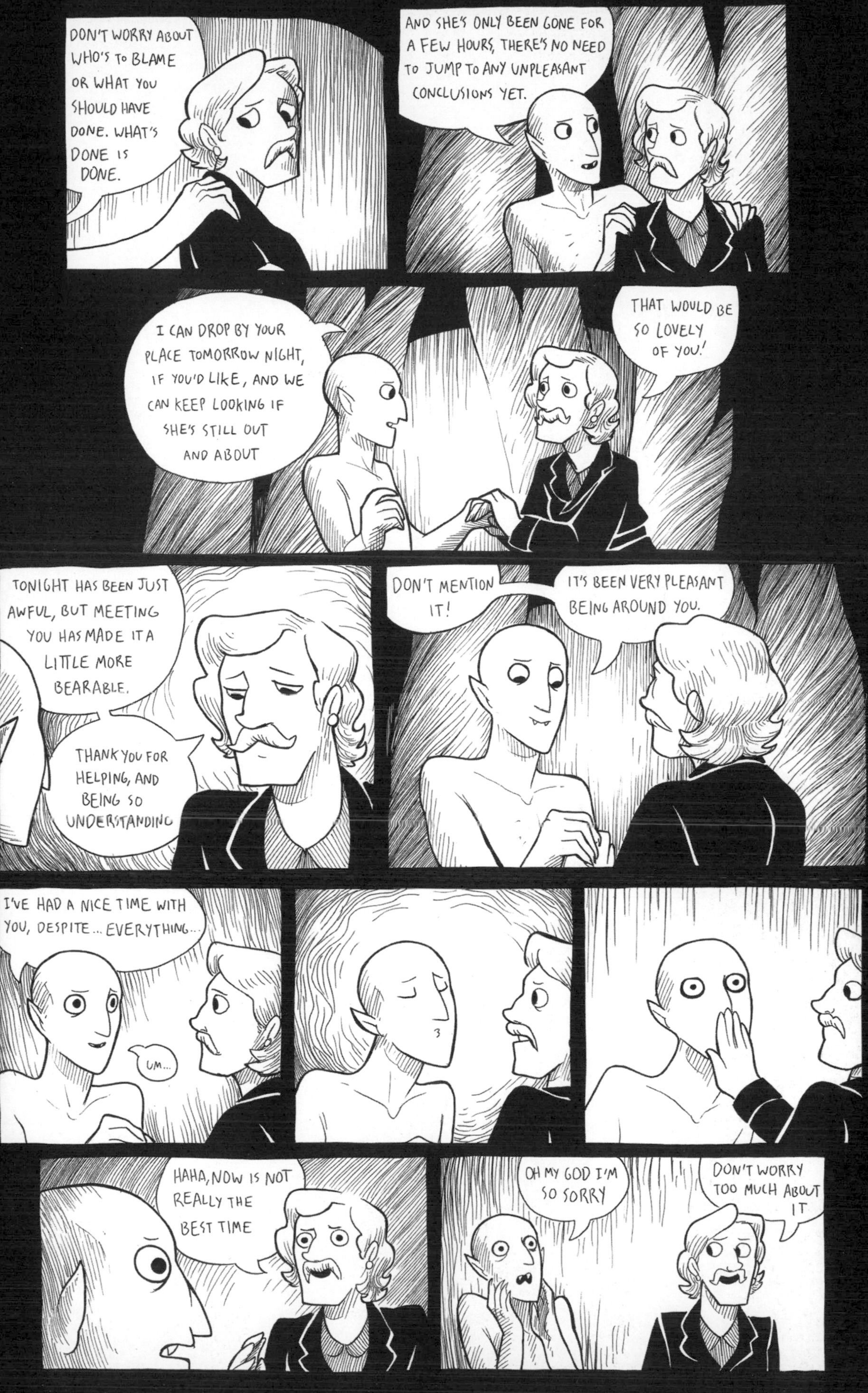
DON'T WORRY ABOUT WHO'S TO BLAME OR WHAT YOU SHOULD HAVE DONE. WHAT'S DONE IS DONE.
AND SHE'S ONLY BEEN GONE FOR A FEW HOURS, THERE'S NO NEED TO JUMP TO ANY UNPLEASANT CONCLUSIONS YET.
I CAN DROP BY YOUR PLACE TOMORROW NIGHT, IF YOU'D LIKE, AND WE CAN KEEP LOOKING IF SHE'S STILL OUT AND ABOUT
THAT WOULD BE SO LOVELY OF YOU!
TONIGHT HAS BEEN JUST AWFUL, BUT MEETING YOU HAS MADE IT A LITTLE MORE BEARABLE.
THANK YOU FOR HELPING, AND BEING SO UNDERSTANDING
DON'T MENTION IT!
IT'S BEEN VERY PLEASANT BEING AROUND YOU.
I'VE HAD A NICE TIME WITH YOU, DESPITE... EVERYTHING...
UM...
HAHA, NOW IS NOT REALLY THE BEST TIME
OH MY GOD I'M SO SORRY
DON'T WORRY TOO MUCH ABOUT IT

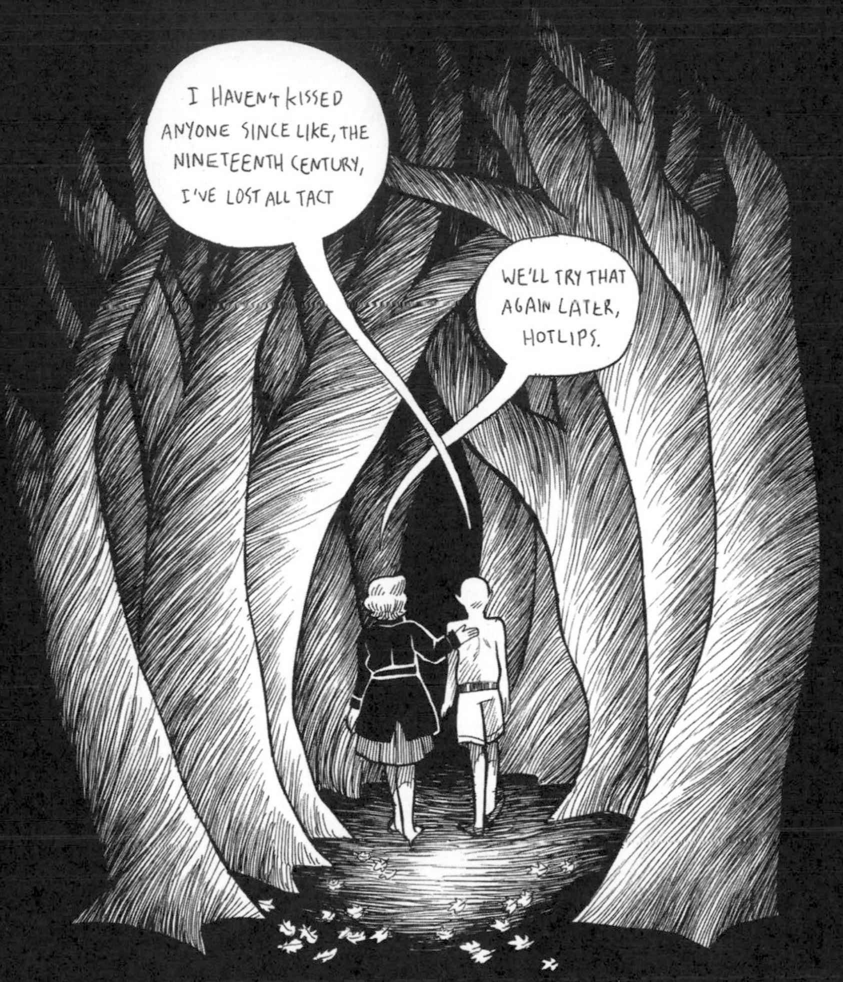
I HAVEN'T KISSED ANYONE SINCE LIKE, THE NINETEENTH CENTURY, I'VE LOST ALL TACT
WE'LL TRY THAT AGAIN LATER, HOTLIPS.

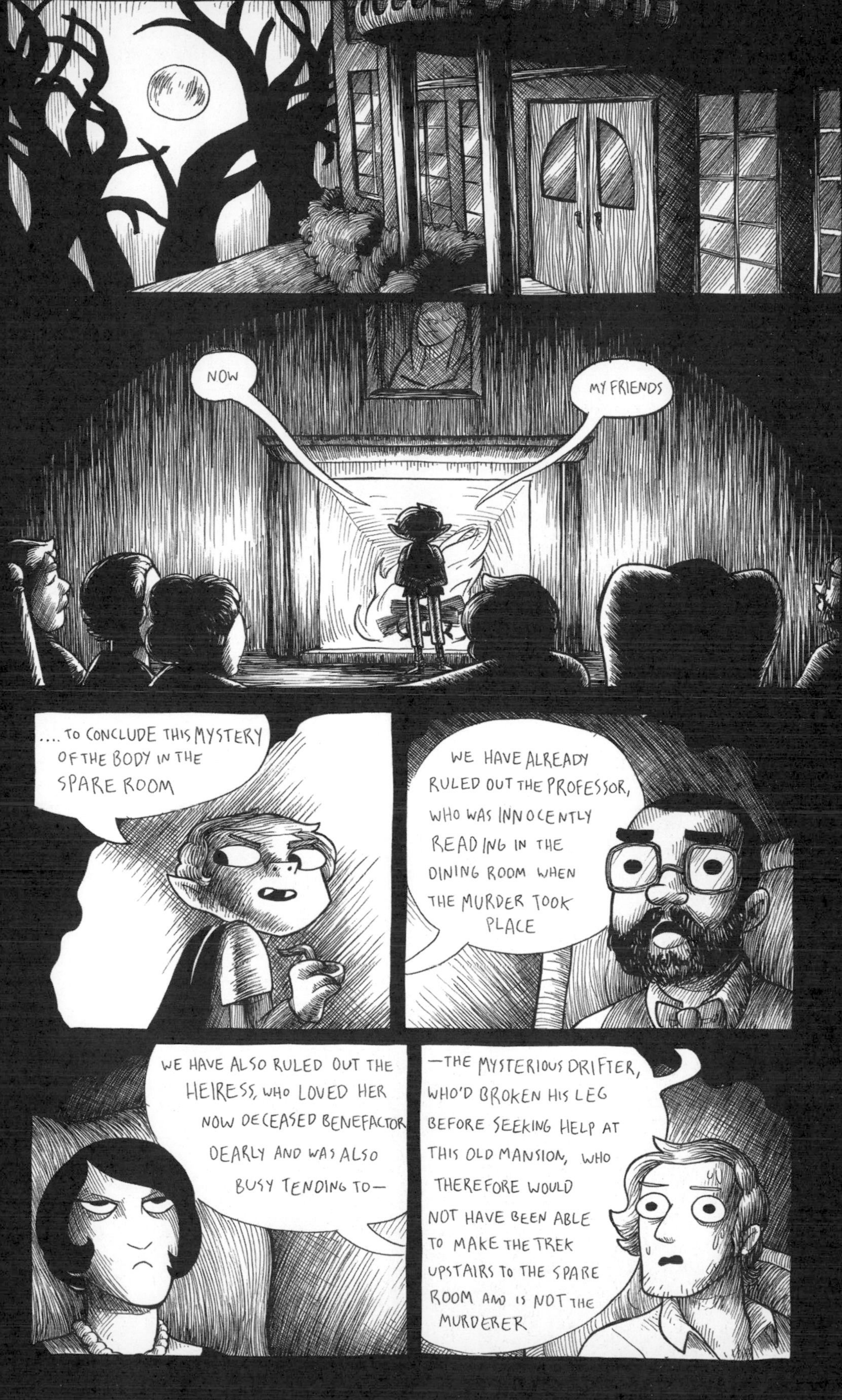
NOW
MY FRIENDS
....TO CONCLUDE THIS MYSTERY OF THE BODY IN THE SPARE ROOM
WE HAVE ALREADY RULED OUT THE PROFESSOR, WHO WAS INNOCENTLY READING IN THE DINING ROOM WHEN THE MURDER TOOK PLACE
WE HAVE ALSO RULED OUT THE HEIRESS, WHO LOVED HER NOW DECEASED BENEFACTOR DEARLY AND WAS ALSO BUSY TENDING TO—
—THE MYSTERIOUS DRIFTER, WHO'D BROKEN HIS LEG BEFORE SEEKING HELP AT THIS OLD MANSION, WHO THEREFORE WOULD NOT HAVE BEEN ABLE TO MAKE THE TREK UPSTAIRS TO THE SPARE ROOM AND IS NOT THE MURDERER

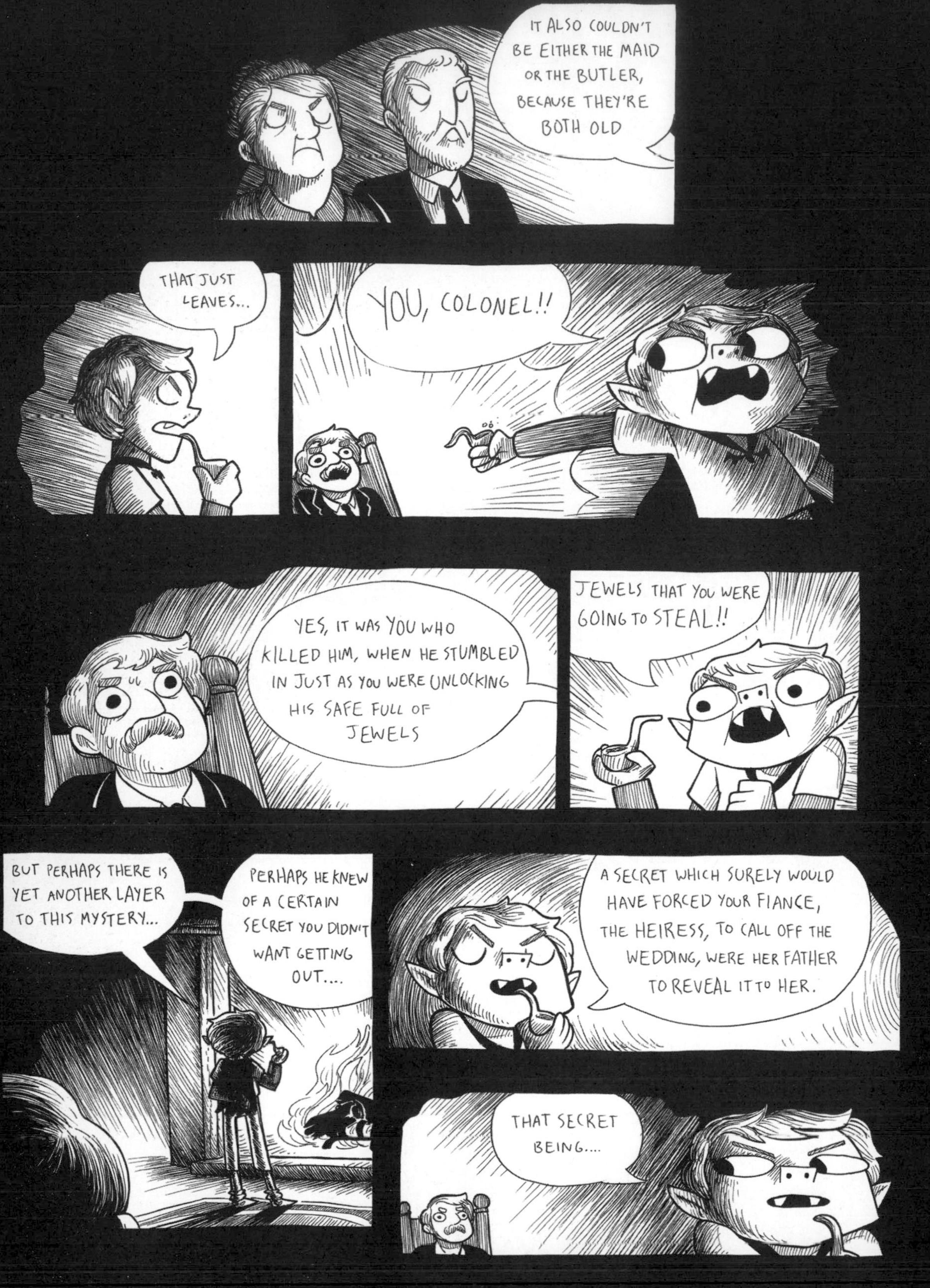
IT ALSO COULDN'T BE EITHER THE MAID OR THE BUTLER, BECAUSE THEY'RE BOTH OLD
THAT JUST LEAVES...
YOU, COLONEL!!
YES, IT WAS YOU WHO KILLED HIM, WHEN HE STUMBLED IN JUST AS YOU WERE UNLOCKING HIS SAFE FULL OF JEWELS
JEWELS THAT YOU WERE GOING TO STEAL!!
BUT PERHAPS THERE IS YET ANOTHER LAYER TO THIS MYSTERY...
PERHAPS HE KNEW OF A CERTAIN SECRET YOU DIDN'T WANT GETTING OUT....
A SECRET WHICH SURELY WOULD HAVE FORCED YOUR FIANCE, THE HEIRESS, TO CALL OFF THE WEDDING, WERE HER FATHER TO REVEAL IT TO HER.
THAT SECRET BEING....

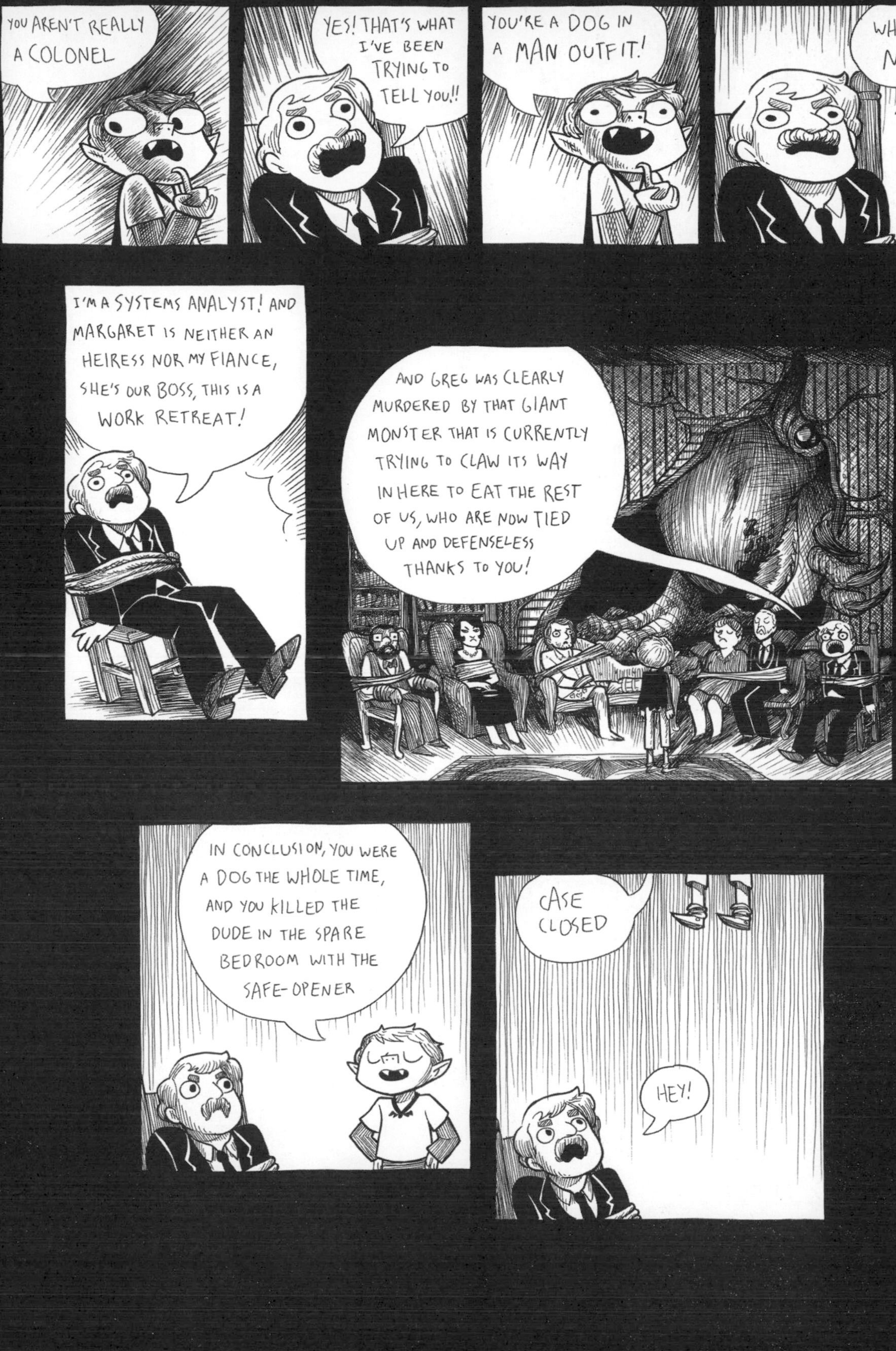
YOU AREN'T REALLY A COLONEL
YES! THAT'S WHAT I'VE BEEN TRYING TO TELL YOU!!
YOU'RE A DOG IN A MAN OUTFIT!
WHAT, NO
I'M A SYSTEMS ANALYST! AND MARGARET IS NEITHER AN HEIRESS NOR MY FIANCE, SHE'S OUR BOSS, THIS IS A WORK RETREAT!
AND GREG WAS CLEARLY MURDERED BY THAT GIANT MONSTER THAT IS CURRENTLY TRYING TO CLAW ITS WAY IN HERE TO EAT THE REST OF US, WHO ARE NOW TIED UP AND DEFENSELESS THANKS TO YOU!
IN CONCLUSION, YOU WERE A DOG THE WHOLE TIME, AND YOU KILLED THE DUDE IN THE SPARE BEDROOM WITH THE SAFE-OPENER
CASE CLOSED
HEY!

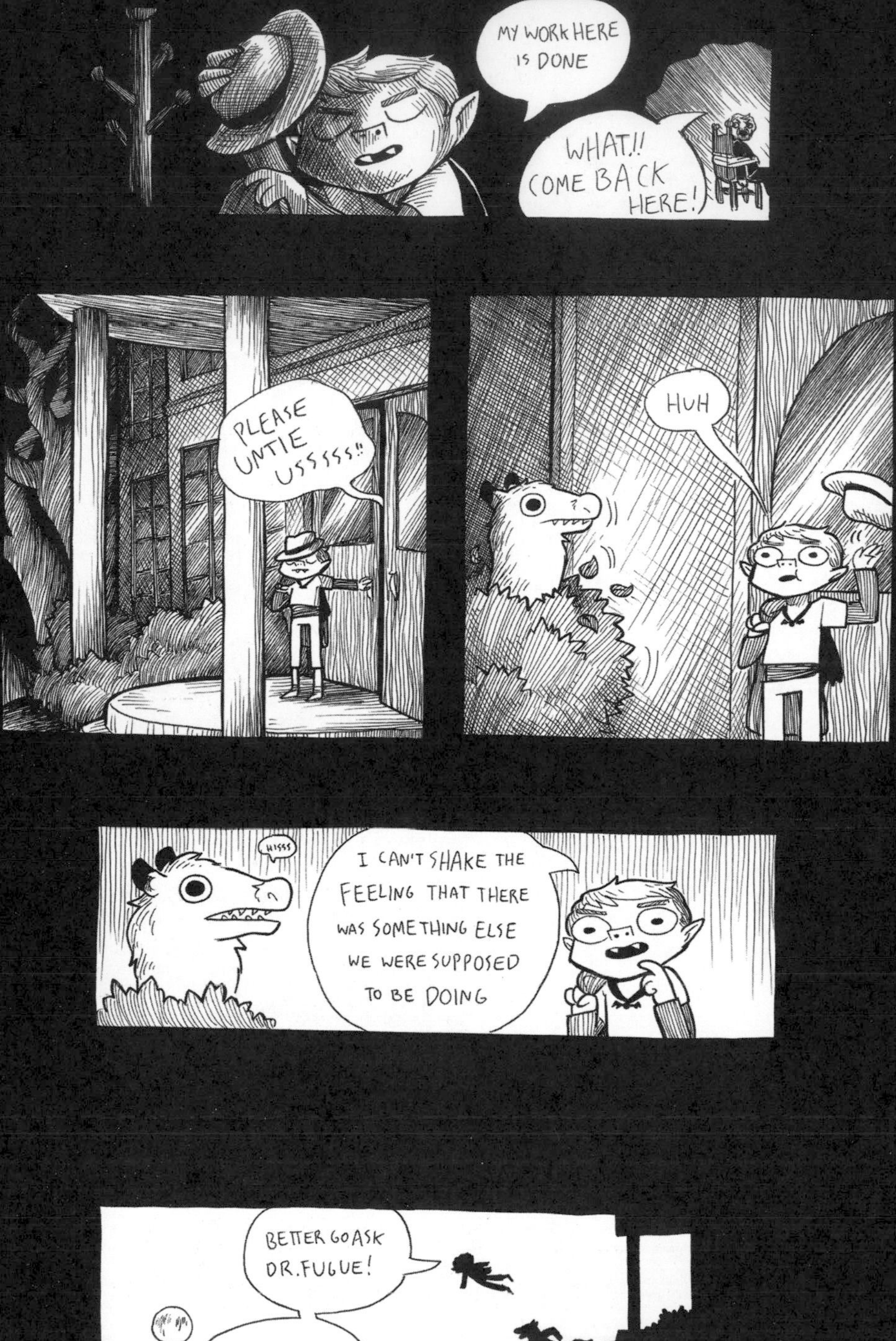
MY WORK HERE IS DONE
WHAT!! COME BACK HERE!
PLEASE UNTIE USSSSS!!
HUH
HISSS
I CAN'T SHAKE THE FEELING THAT THERE WAS SOMETHING ELSE WE WERE SUPPOSED TO BE DOING
BETTER GO ASK DR. FUGUE!
THAT DUDE KNOWS EVERYTHING

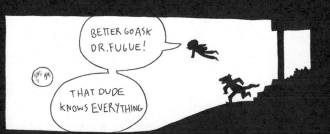

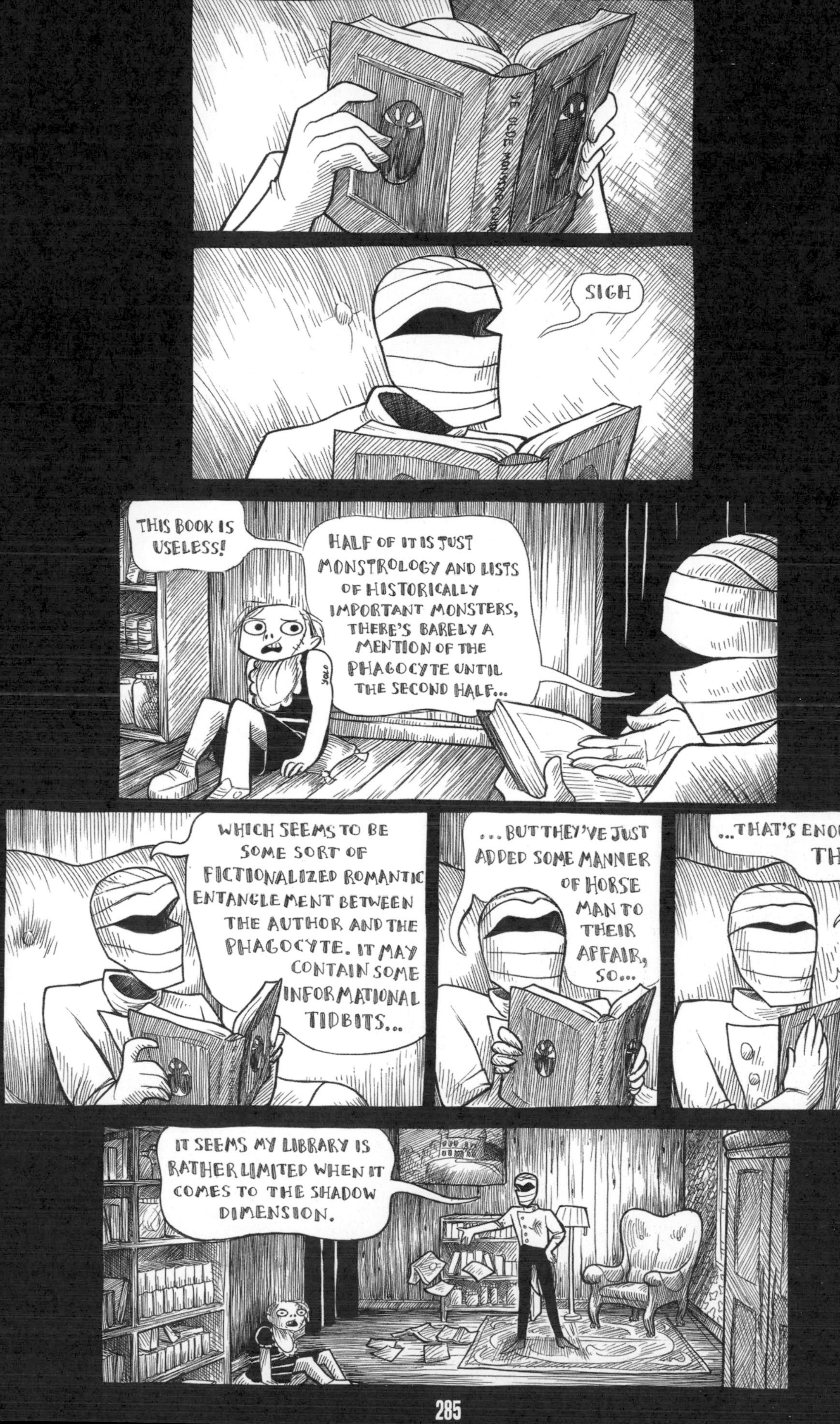

YE OLDE MONSTER GUIDE
SIGH
THIS BOOK IS USELESS!
HALF OF IT IS JUST MONSTROLOGY AND LISTS OF HISTORICALLY IMPORTANT MONSTERS, THERE'S BARELY A MENTION OF THE PHAGOCYTE UNTIL THE SECOND HALF...
YOLO
WHICH SEEMS TO BE SOME SORT OF FICTIONALIZED ROMANTIC ENTANGLEMENT BETWEEN THE AUTHOR AND THE PHAGOCYTE. IT MAY CONTAIN SOME INFORMATIONAL TIDBITS...
...BUT THEY'VE JUST ADDED SOME MANNER OF HORSE MAN TO THEIR AFFAIR, SO...
...THAT'S ENOUGH OF THAT
IT SEEMS MY LIBRARY IS RATHER LIMITED WHEN IT COMES TO THE SHADOW DIMENSION.

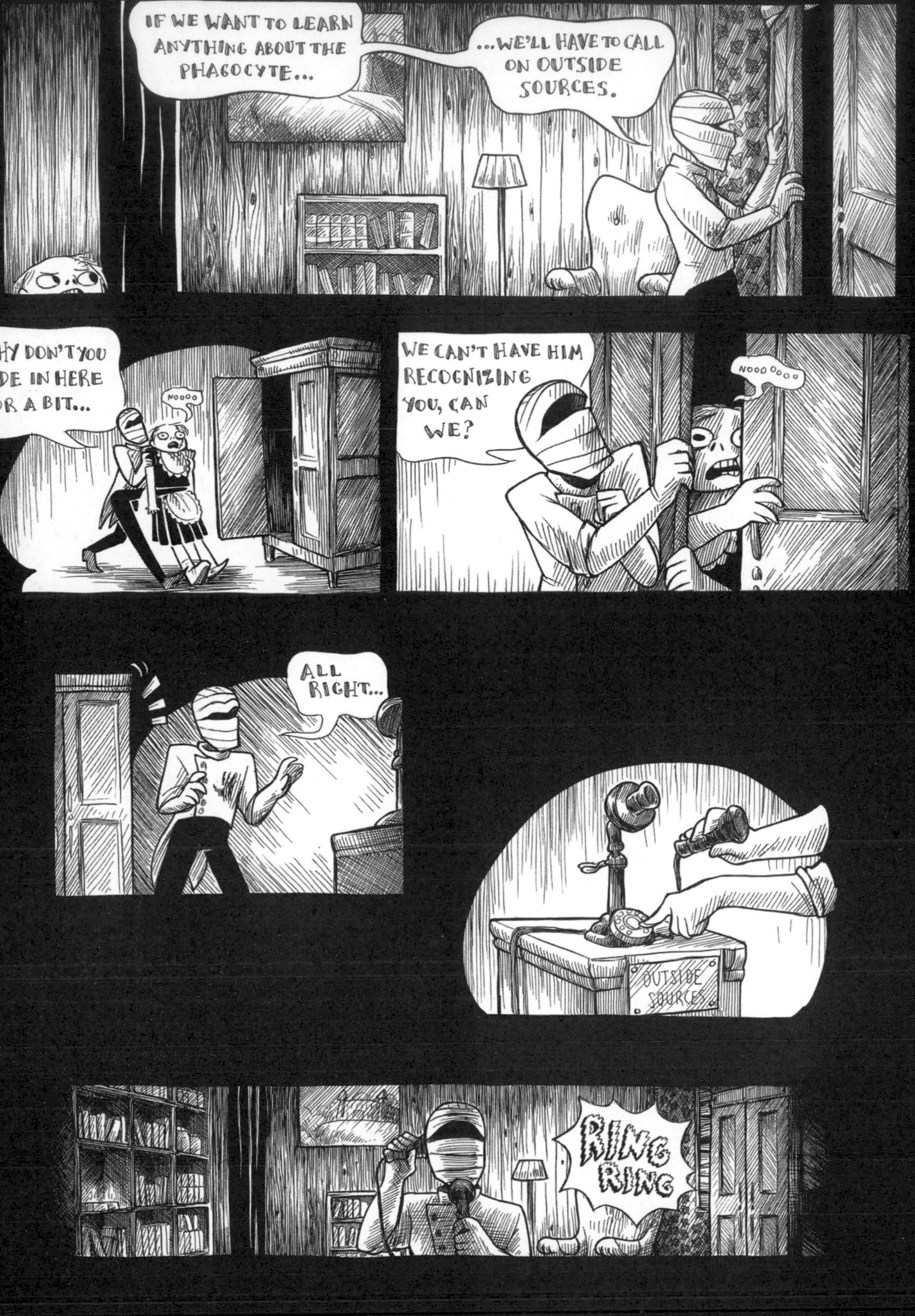
IF WE WANT TO LEARN ANYTHING ABOUT THE PHAGOCYTE...
...WE'LL HAVE TO CALL ON OUTSIDE SOURCES.
WHY DON'T YOU HIDE IN HERE FOR A BIT...
NOOOO
WE CAN'T HAVE HIM RECOGNIZING YOU, CAN WE?
NOOOOOOO
ALL RIGHT...
OUTSIDE SOURCES
RING RING

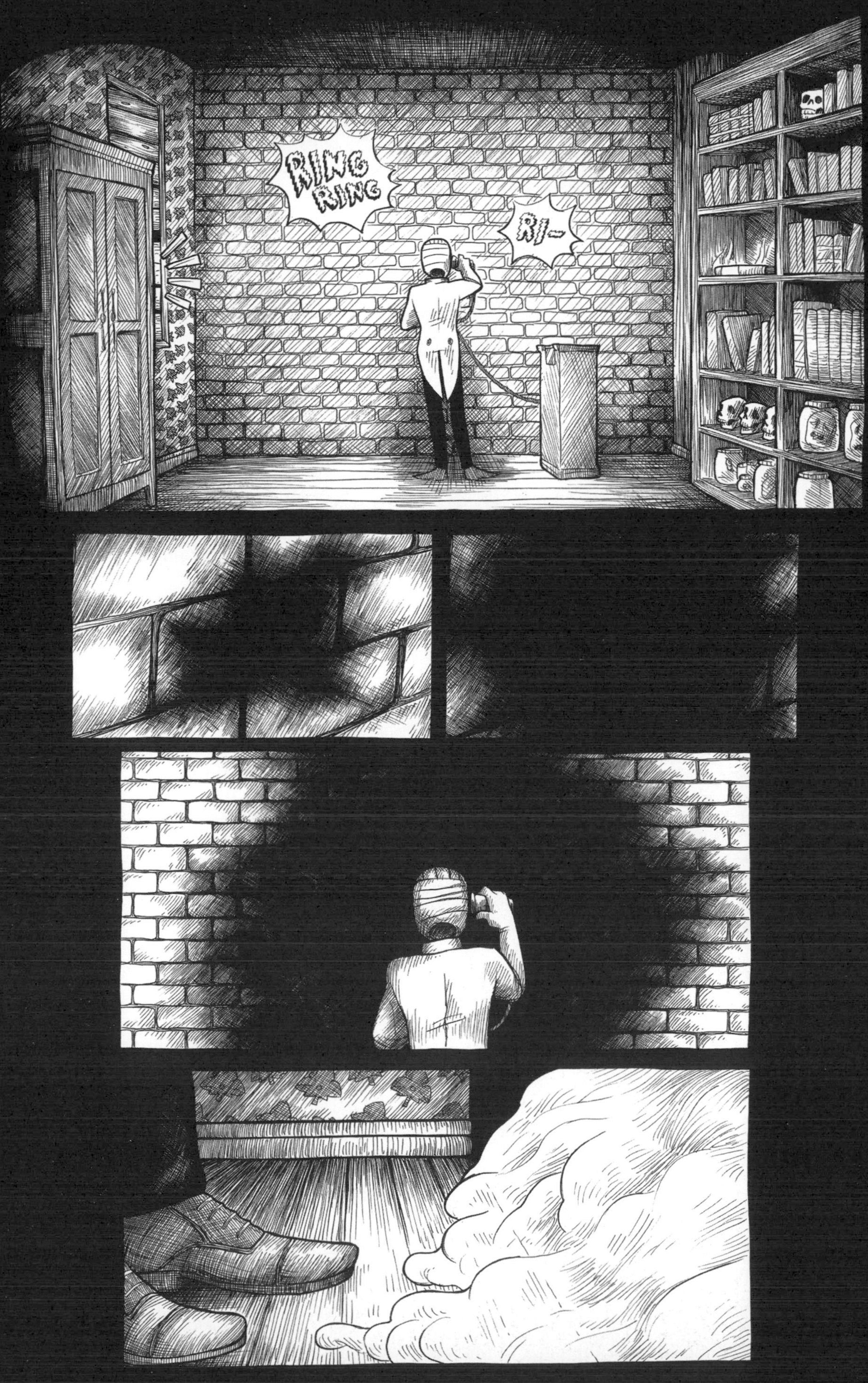
RING RING
RI-

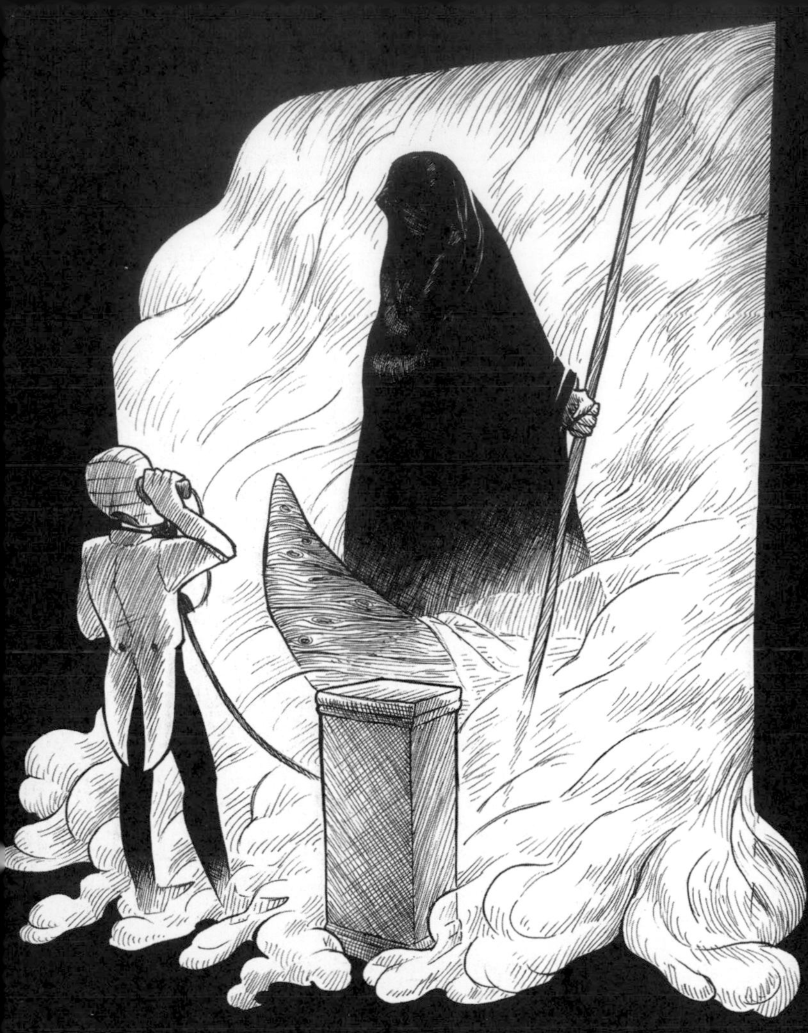

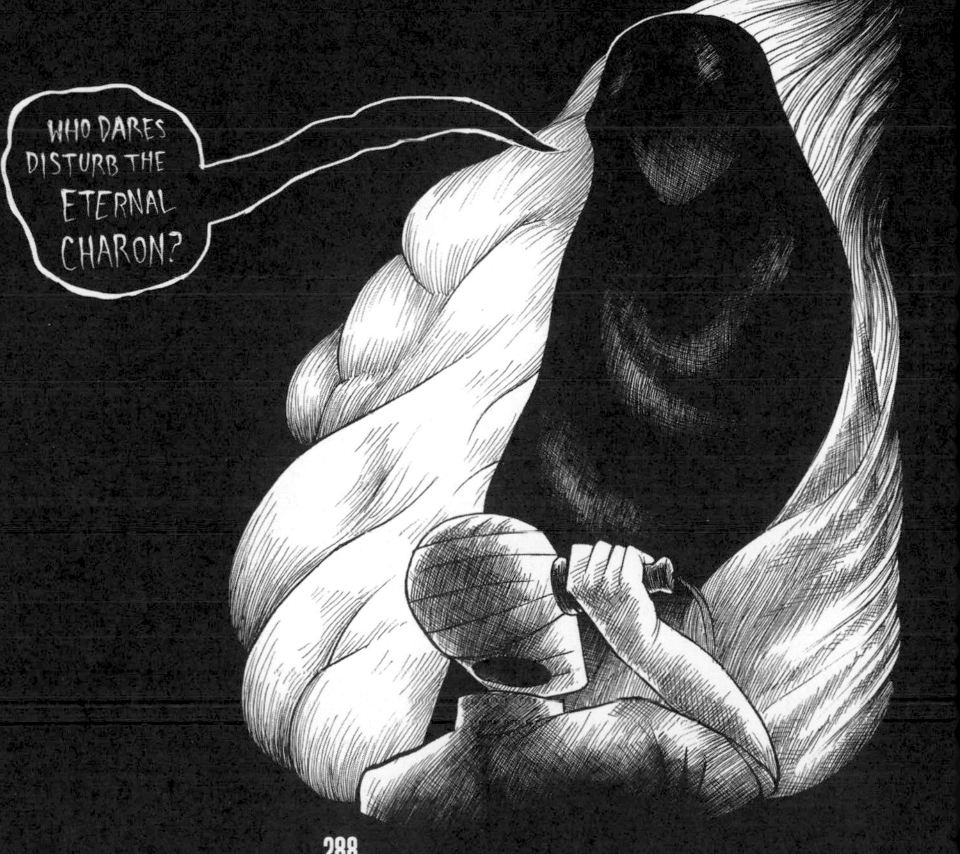
WHO DARES DISTURB THE ETERNAL CHARON?

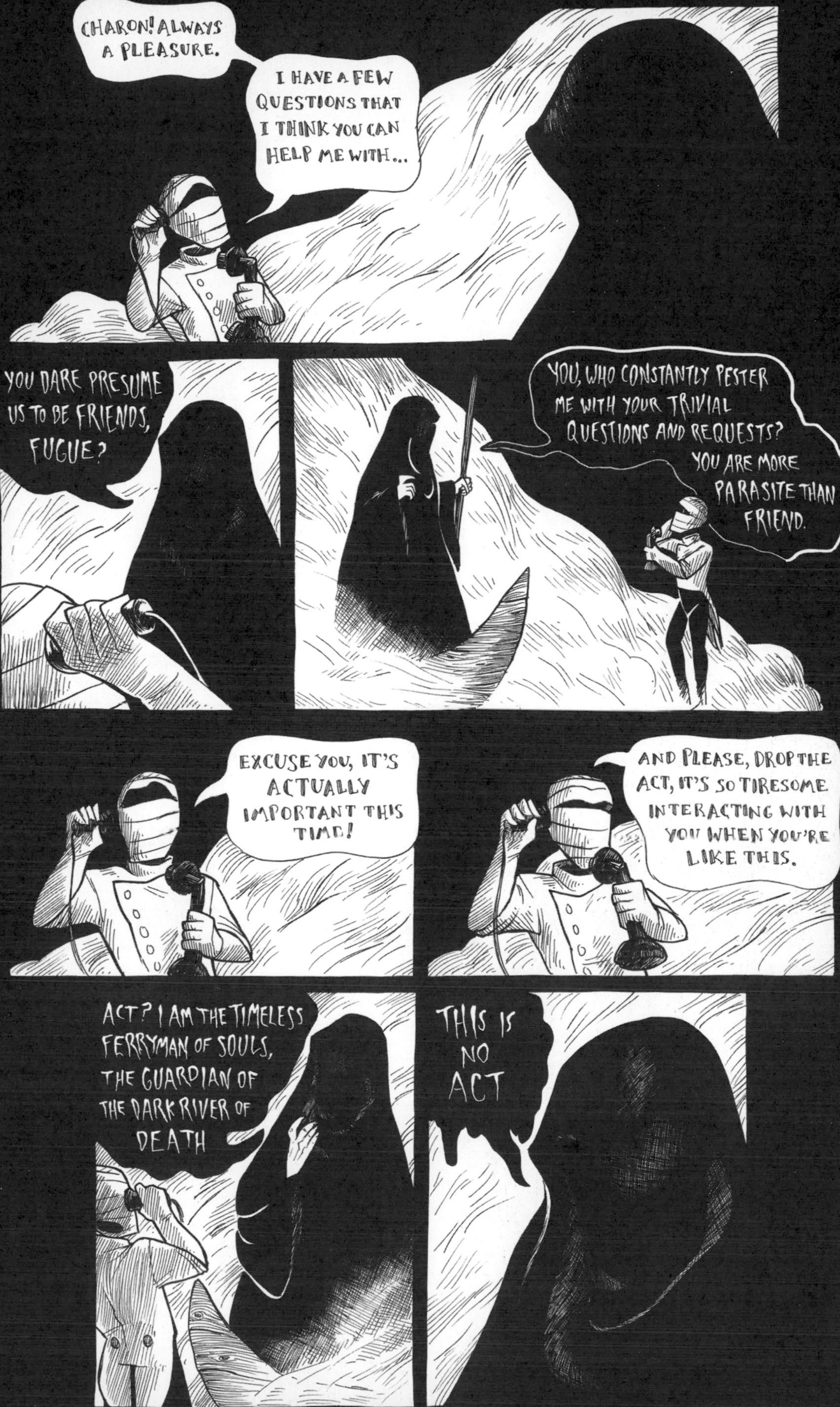
CHARON! ALWAYS A PLEASURE.
I HAVE A FEW QUESTIONS THAT I THINK YOU CAN HELP ME WITH...
YOU DARE PRESUME US TO BE FRIENDS, FUGUE?
YOU, WHO CONSTANTLY PESTER ME WITH YOUR TRIVIAL QUESTIONS AND REQUESTS? YOU ARE MORE PARASITE THAN FRIEND.
EXCUSE YOU, IT'S ACTUALLY IMPORTANT THIS TIME!
AND PLEASE, DROP THE ACT, IT'S SO TIRESOME INTERACTING WITH YOU WHEN YOU'RE LIKE THIS.
ACT? I AM THE TIMELESS FERRYMAN OF SOULS, THE GUARDIAN OF THE DARK RIVER OF DEATH
THIS IS NO ACT

COME ON, CHARON, THIS IS URGENT!

UGGHH FINE

JUST TAKE ALL THE FUN OUT OF MY JOB, WHY DON'T YOU?

IF ANYBODY ASKS, TELL THEM I SHOOK YOU TO YOUR VERY CORE. I HAVE A REPUTATION TO UPHOLD, YOU KNOW.

NOW WHAT IS SO IMPORTANT THAT YOU HAD TO INTERRUPT MY IMMORTAL SUFFERING?

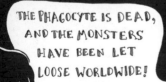

THE PHAGOCYTE IS DEAD, AND THE MONSTERS HAVE BEEN LET LOOSE WORLDWIDE!

HUMANITY IS IN GRAVE PERIL.

I CURRENTLY HAVE A TEAM TRACKING DOWN THE HEIR, BUT I DON'T KNOW HOW TO—

OKAY, NO, HE'S NOT DEAD.

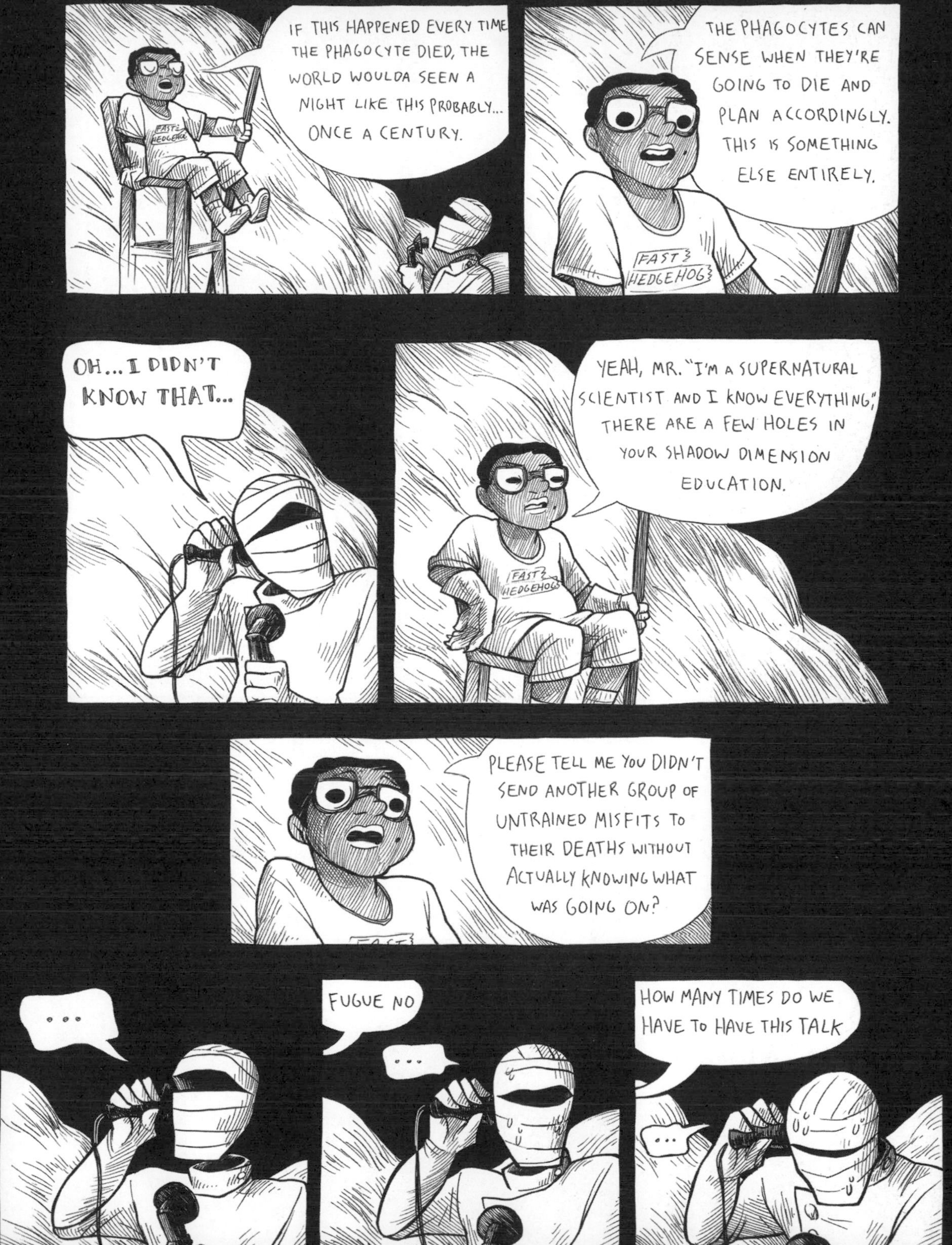
IF THIS HAPPENED EVERY TIME THE PHAGOCYTE DIED, THE WORLD WOULDA SEEN A NIGHT LIKE THIS PROBABLY... ONCE A CENTURY.
FAST HEDGEHOG
THE PHAGOCYTES CAN SENSE WHEN THEY'RE GOING TO DIE AND PLAN ACCORDINGLY. THIS IS SOMETHING ELSE ENTIRELY.
FAST HEDGEHOG
OH... I DIDN'T KNOW THAT...
YEAH, MR. "I'M A SUPERNATURAL SCIENTIST AND I KNOW EVERYTHING," THERE ARE A FEW HOLES IN YOUR SHADOW DIMENSION EDUCATION.
FAST HEDGEHOG
PLEASE TELL ME YOU DIDN'T SEND ANOTHER GROUP OF UNTRAINED MISFITS TO THEIR DEATHS WITHOUT ACTUALLY KNOWING WHAT WAS GOING ON?
...
FUGUE NO
...
HOW MANY TIMES DO WE HAVE TO HAVE THIS TALK
...

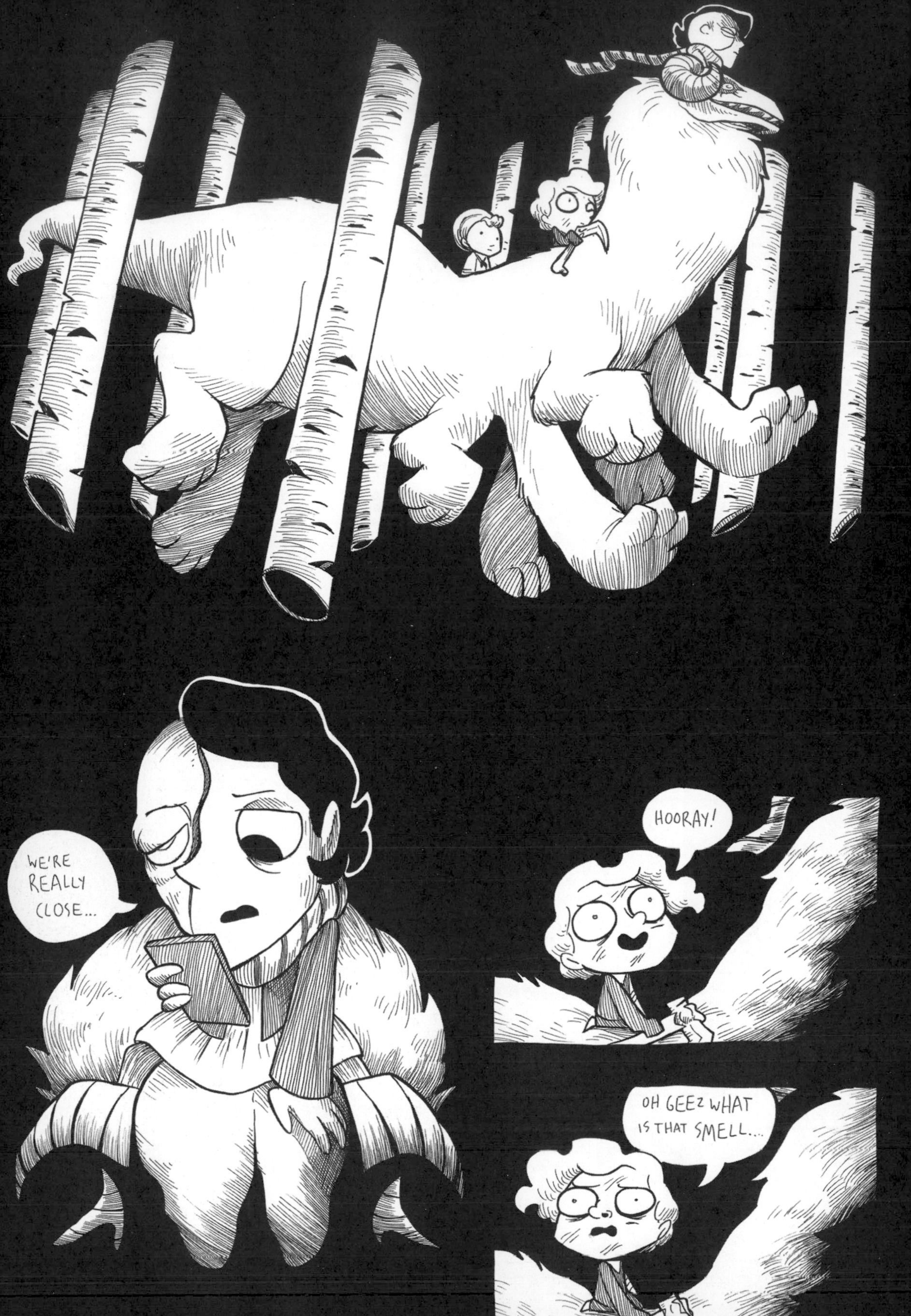
WE'RE REALLY CLOSE...
HOORAY!
OH GEEZ WHAT IS THAT SMELL...

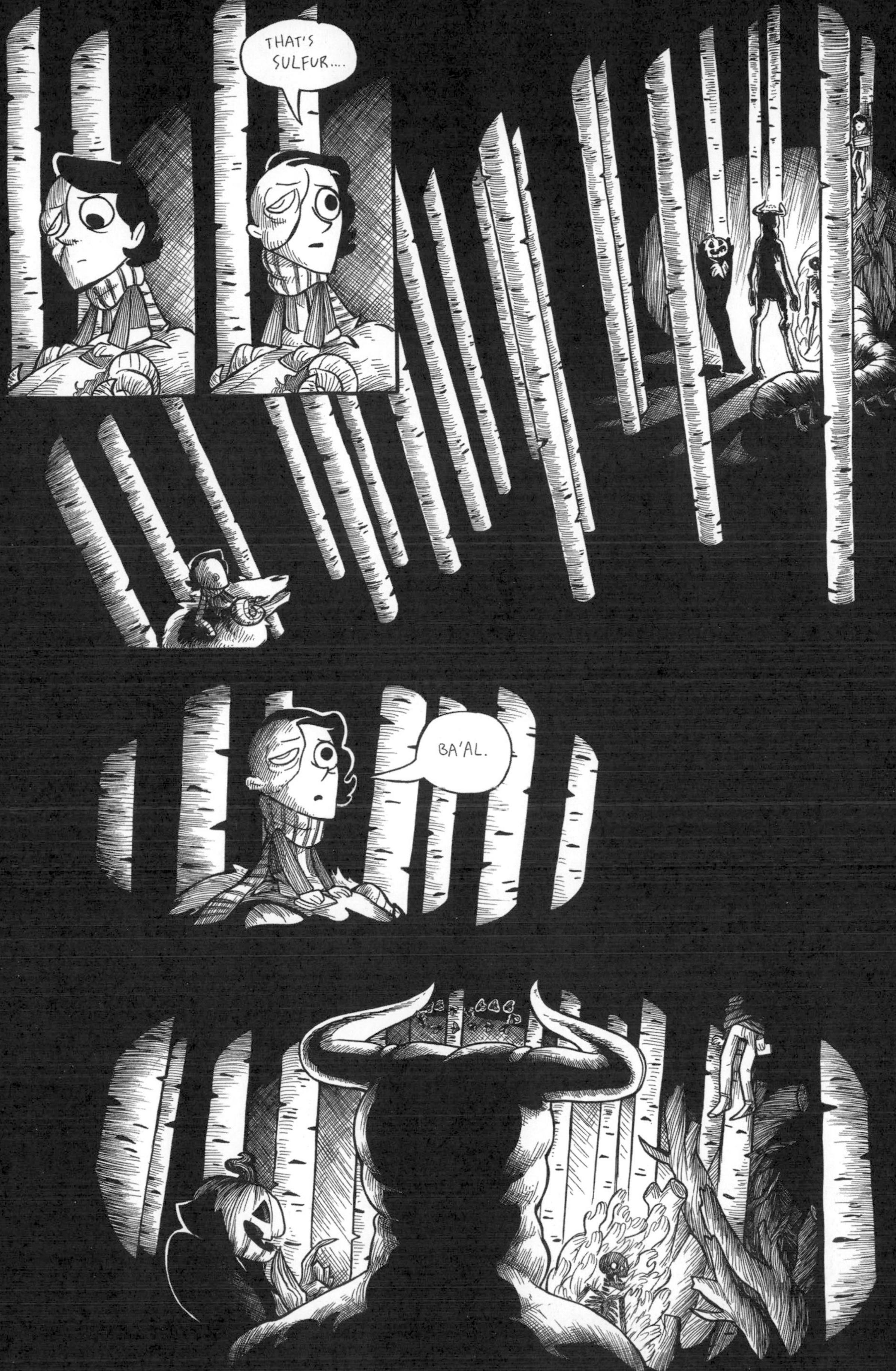
THAT'S SULFUR....
BA'AL.

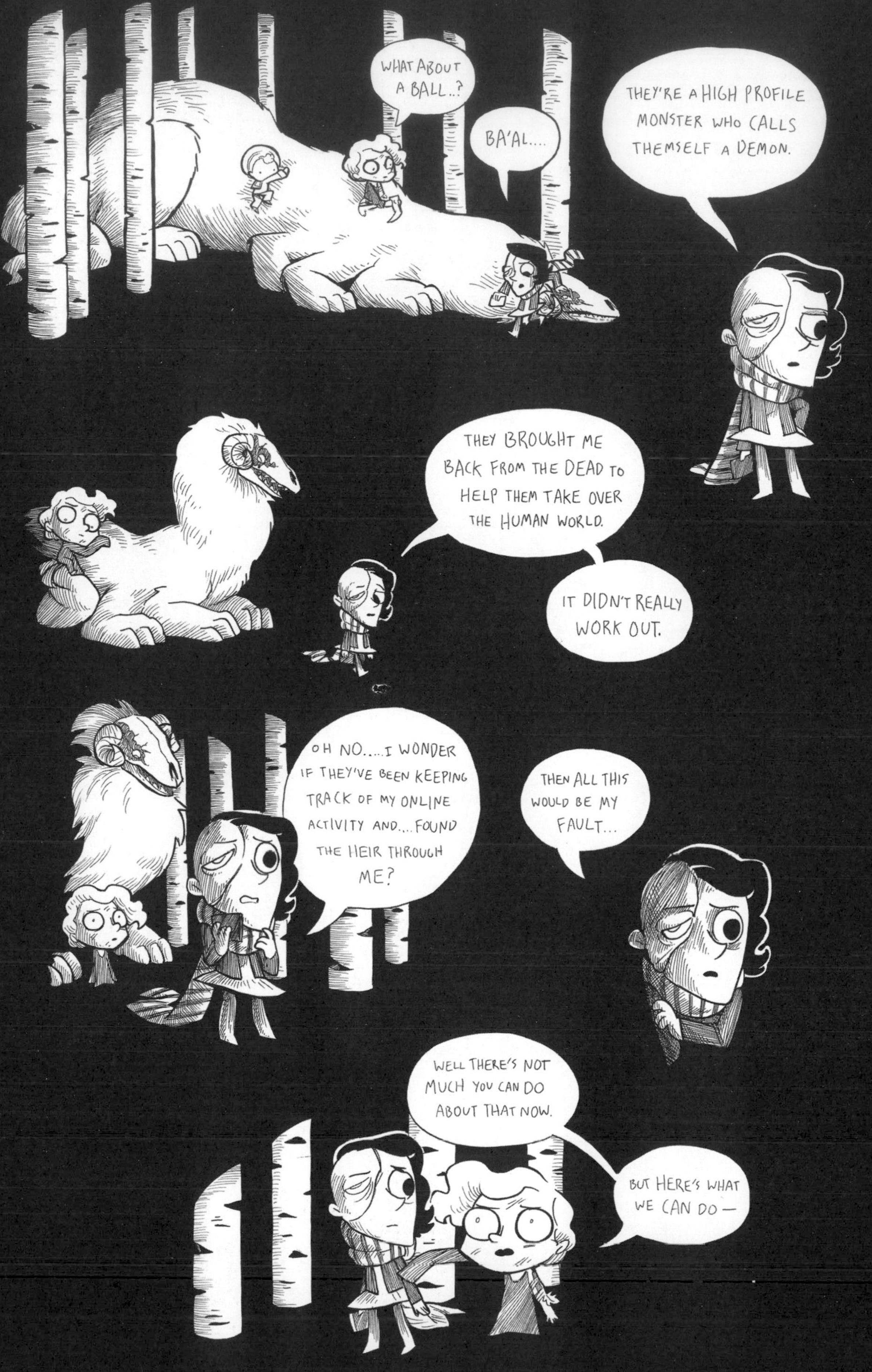
WHAT ABOUT A BALL..?
BA'AL....
THEY'RE A HIGH PROFILE MONSTER WHO CALLS THEMSELF A DEMON.
THEY BROUGHT ME BACK FROM THE DEAD TO HELP THEM TAKE OVER THE HUMAN WORLD.
IT DIDN'T REALLY WORK OUT.
OH NO.....I WONDER IF THEY'VE BEEN KEEPING TRACK OF MY ONLINE ACTIVITY AND....FOUND THE HEIR THROUGH ME?
THEN ALL THIS WOULD BE MY FAULT...
WELL THERE'S NOT MUCH YOU CAN DO ABOUT THAT NOW.
BUT HERE'S WHAT WE CAN DO—

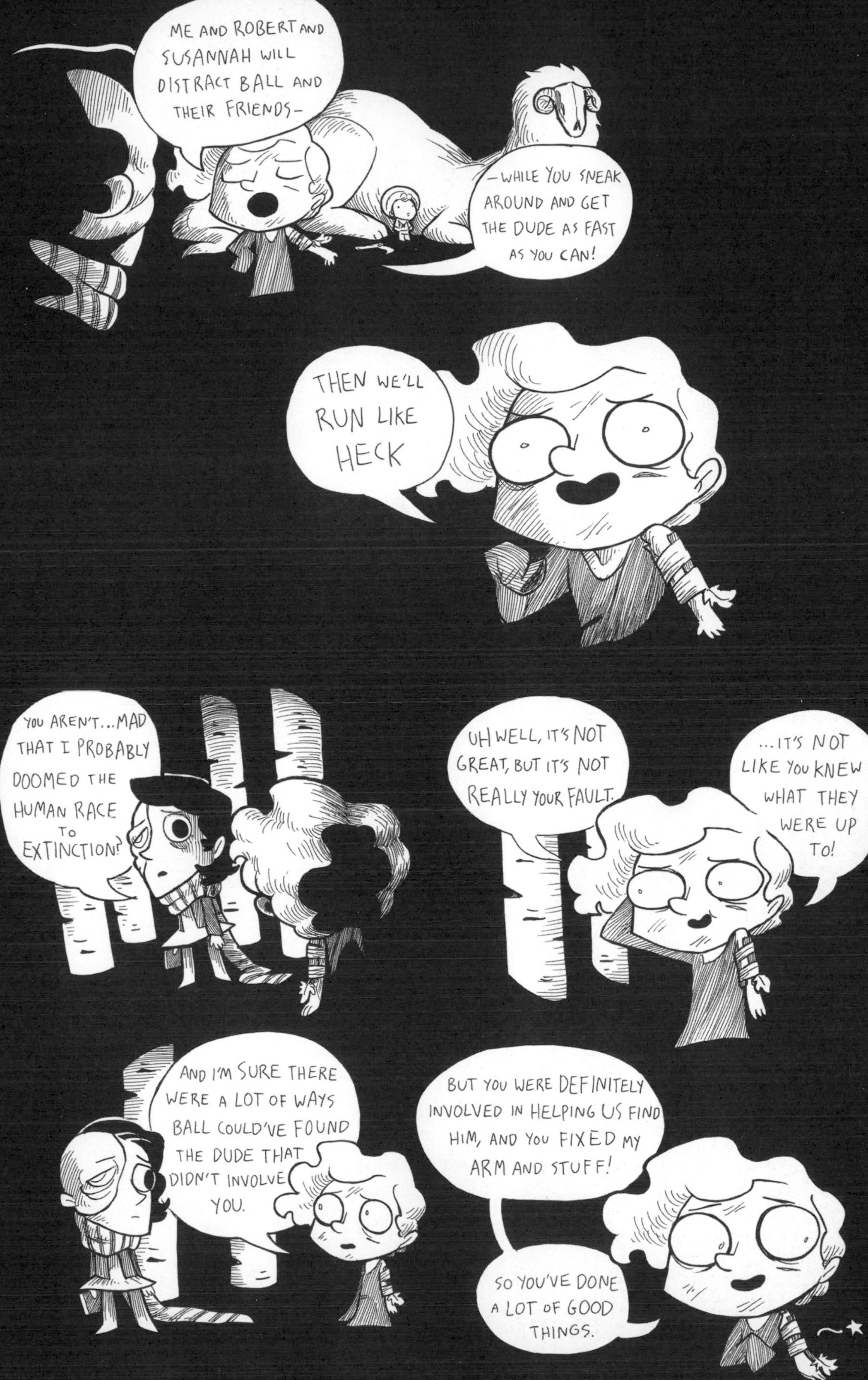

ME AND ROBERT AND SUSANNAH WILL DISTRACT BALL AND THEIR FRIENDS–
–WHILE YOU SNEAK AROUND AND GET THE DUDE AS FAST AS YOU CAN!
THEN WE'LL RUN LIKE HECK
YOU AREN'T...MAD THAT I PROBABLY DOOMED THE HUMAN RACE TO EXTINCTION?
UH WELL, IT'S NOT GREAT, BUT IT'S NOT REALLY YOUR FAULT.
...IT'S NOT LIKE YOU KNEW WHAT THEY WERE UP TO!
AND I'M SURE THERE WERE A LOT OF WAYS BALL COULD'VE FOUND THE DUDE THAT DIDN'T INVOLVE YOU.
BUT YOU WERE DEFINITELY INVOLVED IN HELPING US FIND HIM, AND YOU FIXED MY ARM AND STUFF!
SO YOU'VE DONE A LOT OF GOOD THINGS.

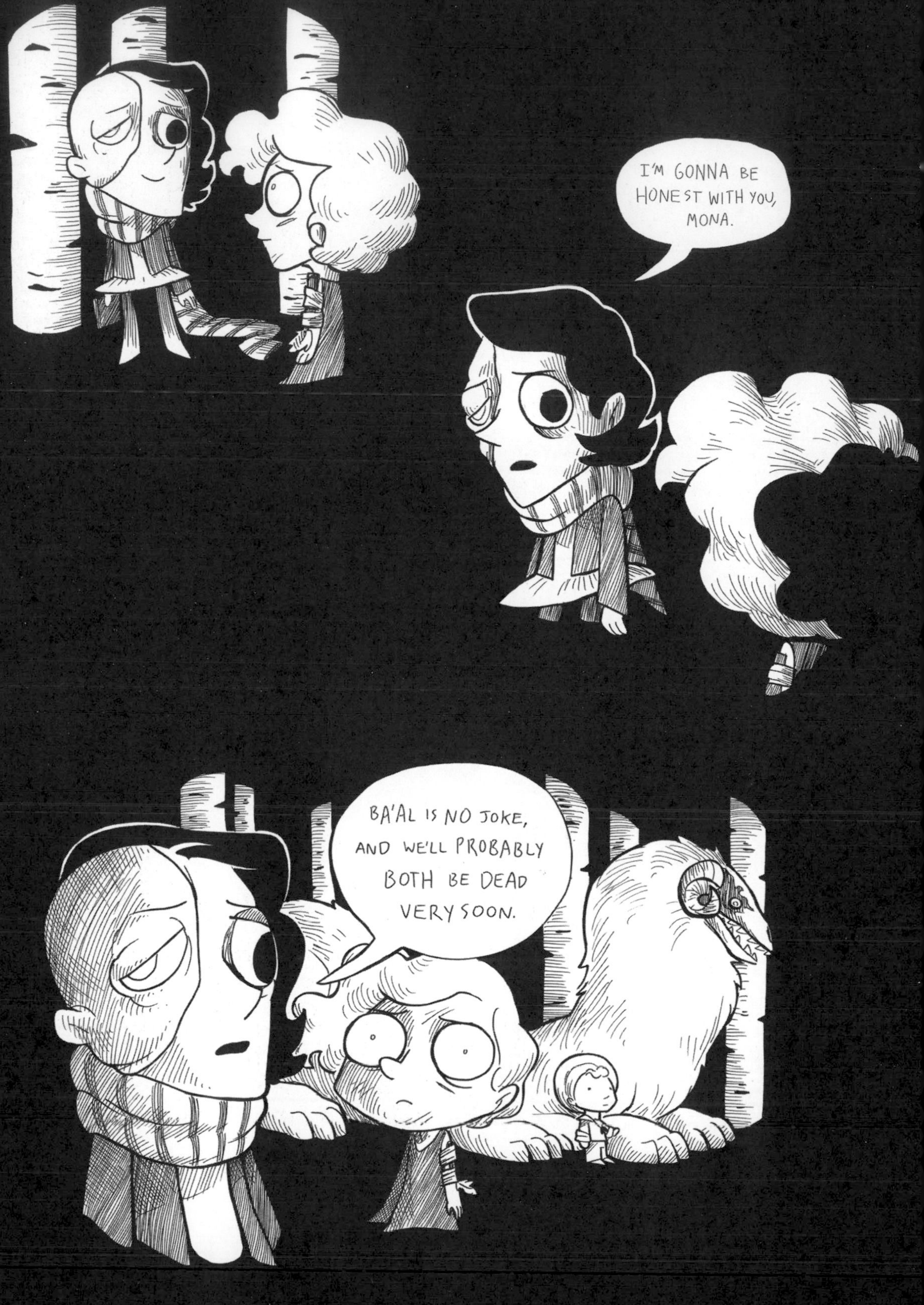
I'M GONNA BE HONEST WITH YOU, MONA.
BA'AL IS NO JOKE, AND WE'LL PROBABLY BOTH BE DEAD VERY SOON.

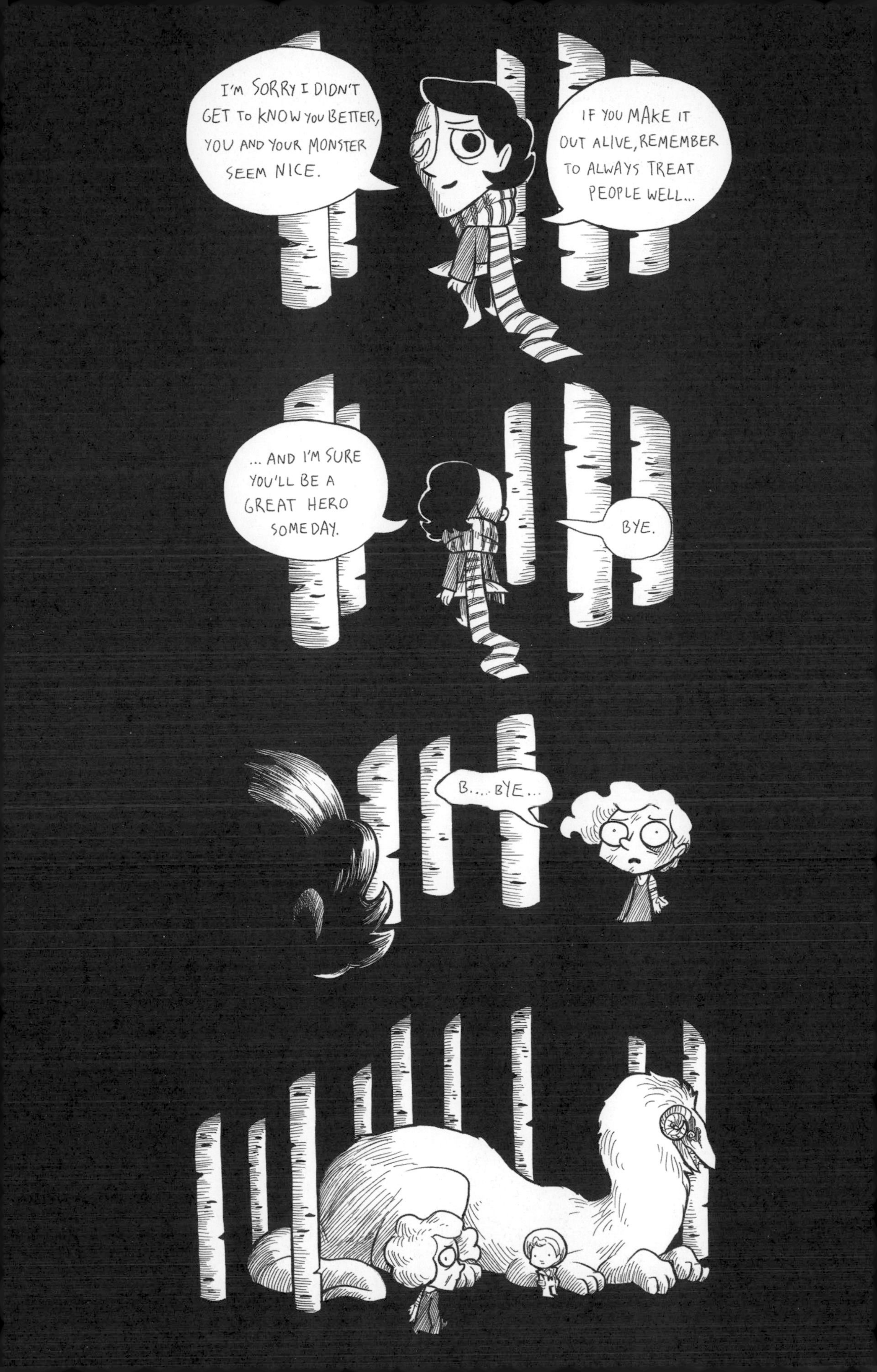
I'M SORRY I DIDN'T GET TO KNOW YOU BETTER, YOU AND YOUR MONSTER SEEM NICE.
IF YOU MAKE IT OUT ALIVE, REMEMBER TO ALWAYS TREAT PEOPLE WELL...
... AND I'M SURE YOU'LL BE A GREAT HERO SOMEDAY.
BYE.
B.... BYE...

HAVE WE COME THIS FAR JUST TO DIE?

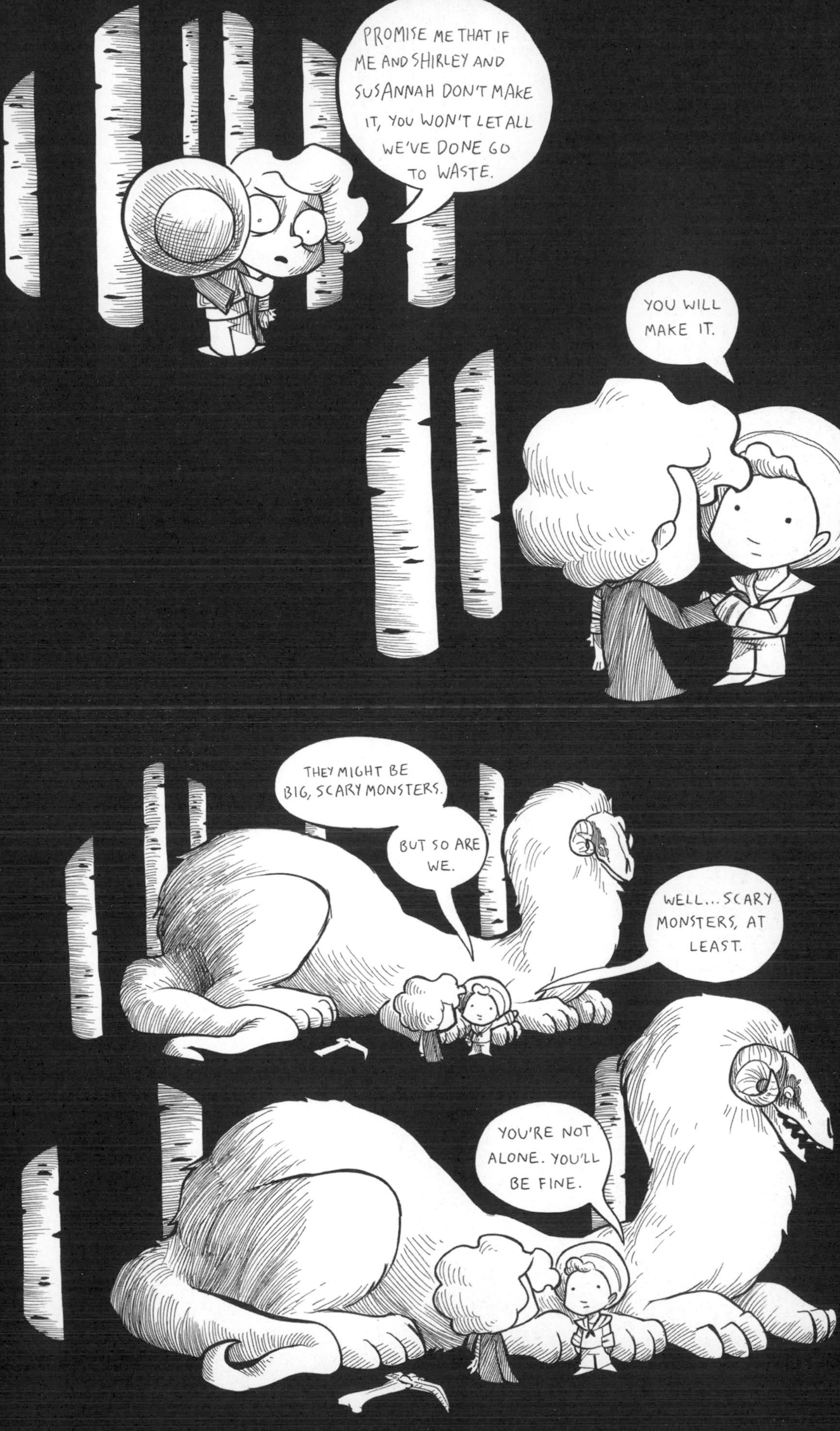
PROMISE ME THAT IF ME AND SHIRLEY AND SUSANNAH DON'T MAKE IT, YOU WON'T LET ALL WE'VE DONE GO TO WASTE.
YOU WILL MAKE IT.
THEY MIGHT BE BIG, SCARY MONSTERS.
BUT SO ARE WE.
WELL... SCARY MONSTERS, AT LEAST.
YOU'RE NOT ALONE. YOU'LL BE FINE.

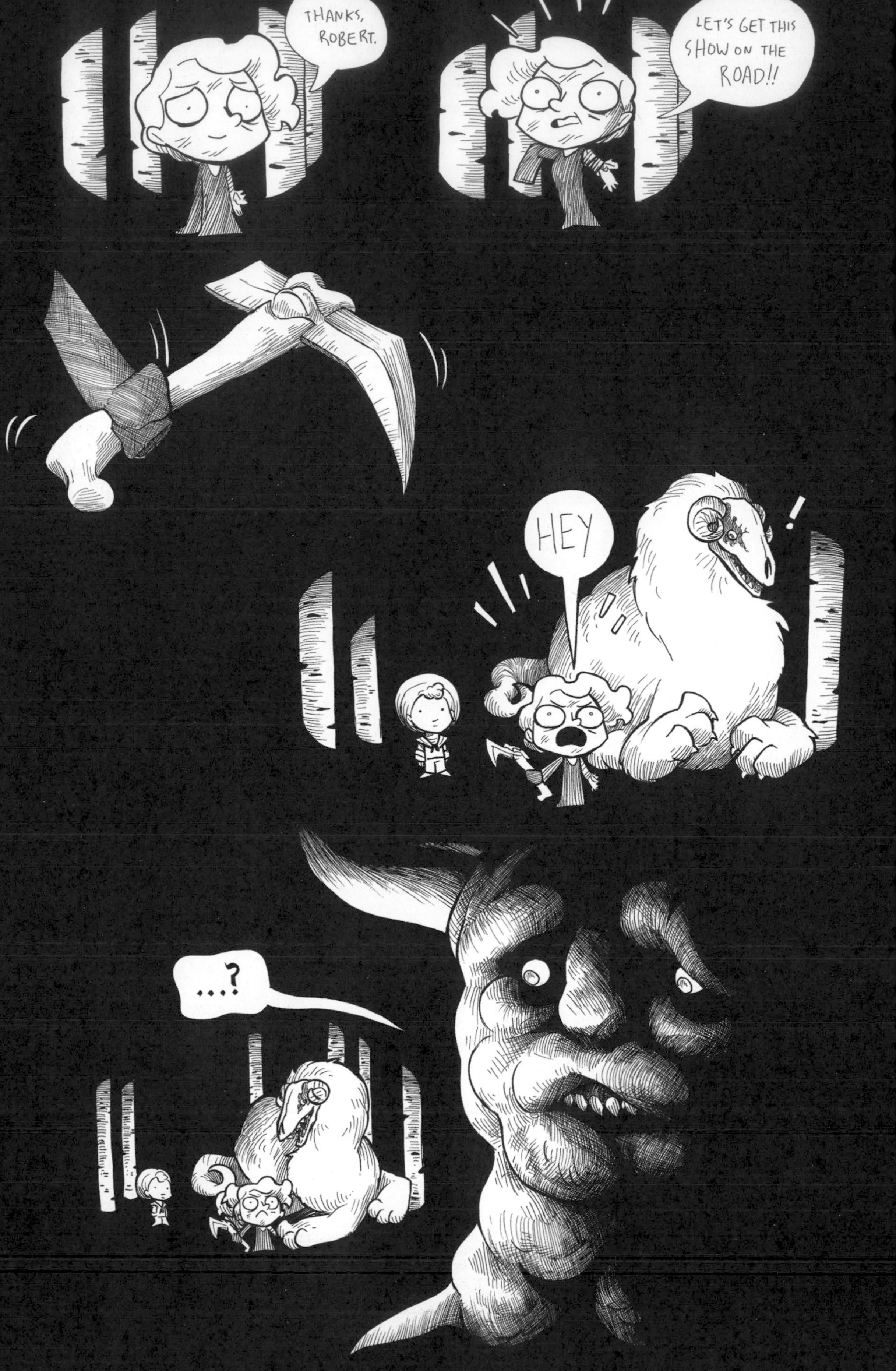
THANKS, ROBERT.
LET'S GET THIS SHOW ON THE ROAD!!
HEY
!
...?

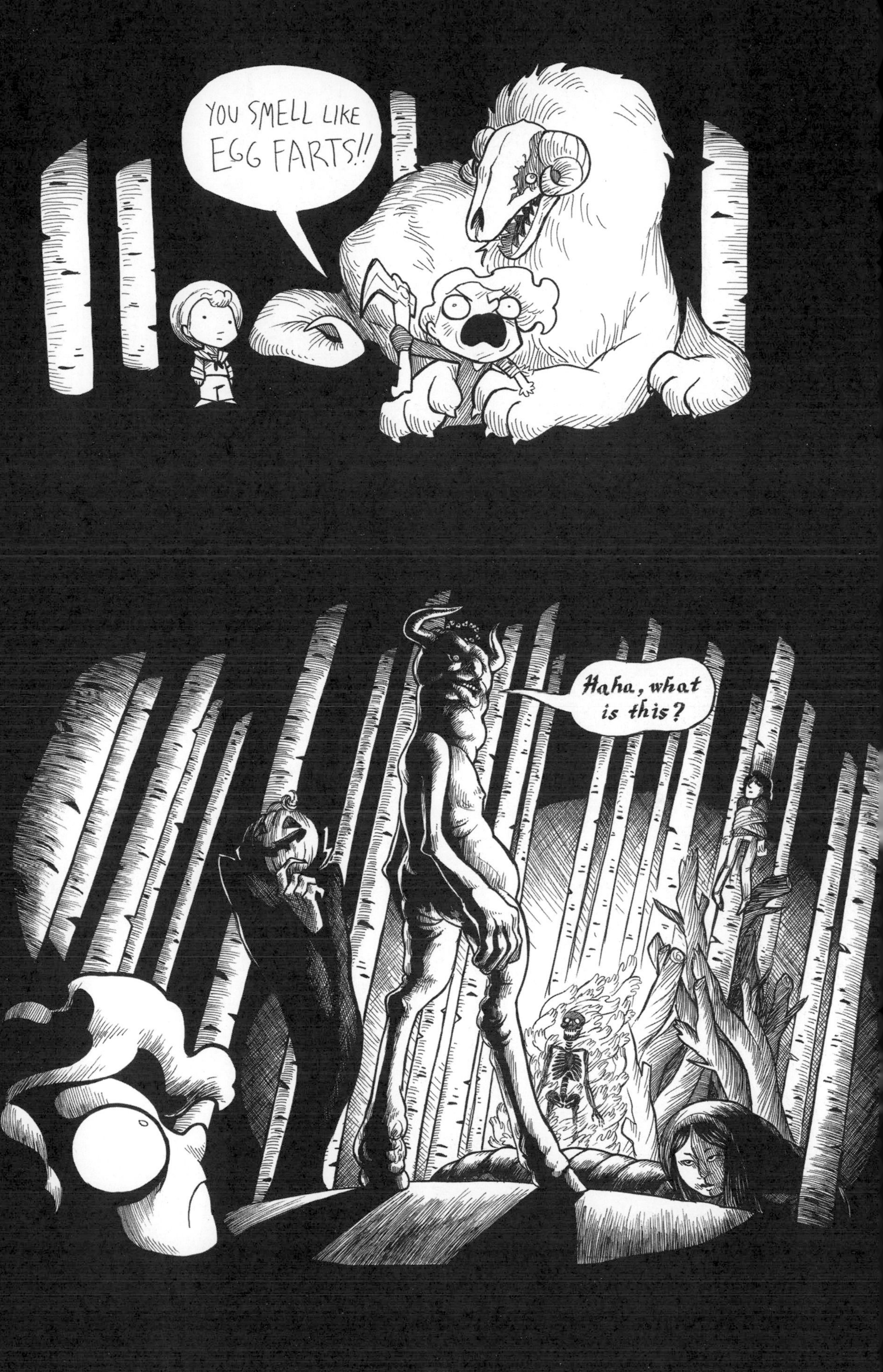
YOU SMELL LIKE EGG FARTS!!
Haha, what is this?

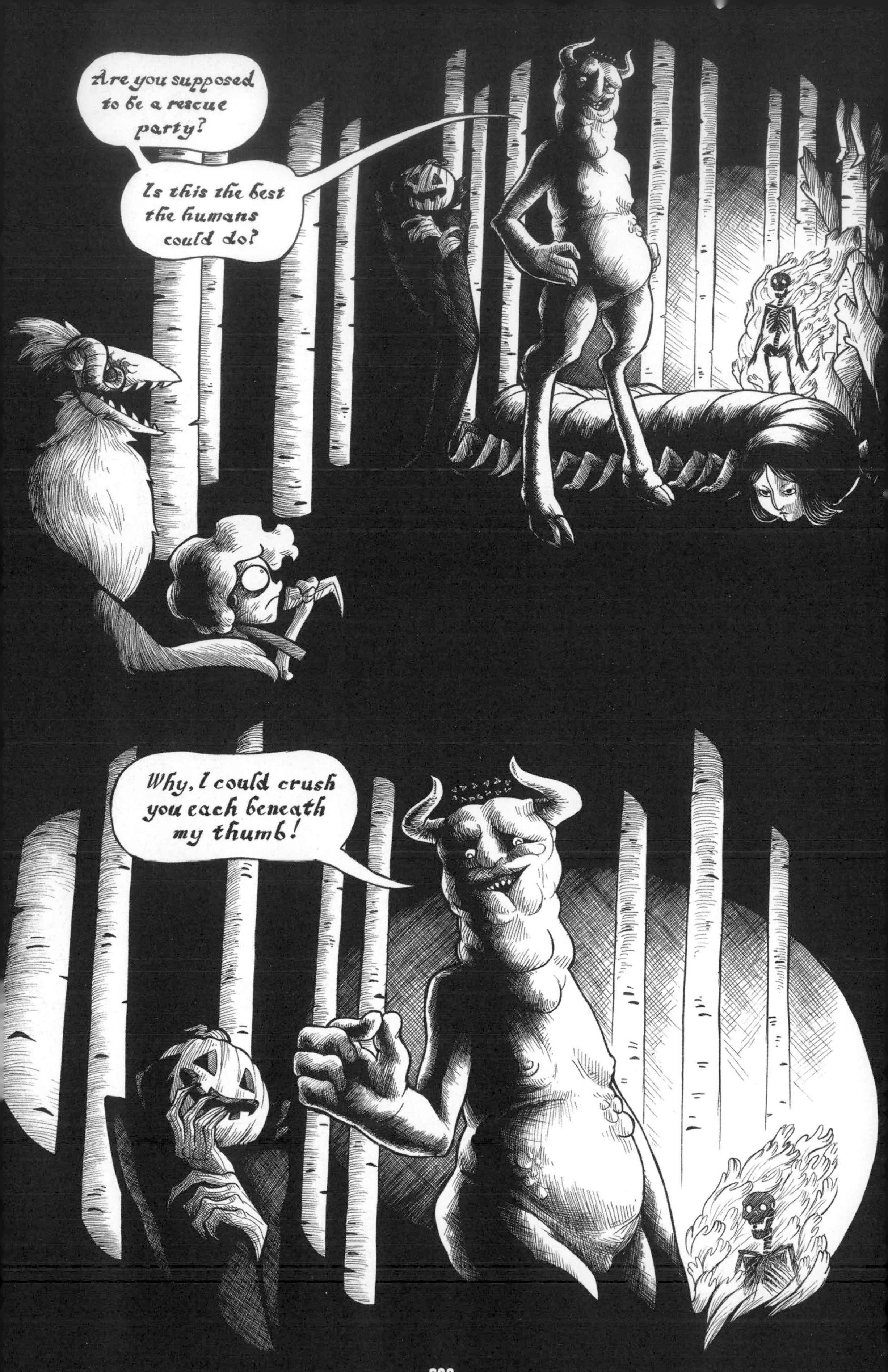
Are you supposed to be a rescue party?
Is this the best the humans could do?
Why, I could crush you each beneath my thumb!

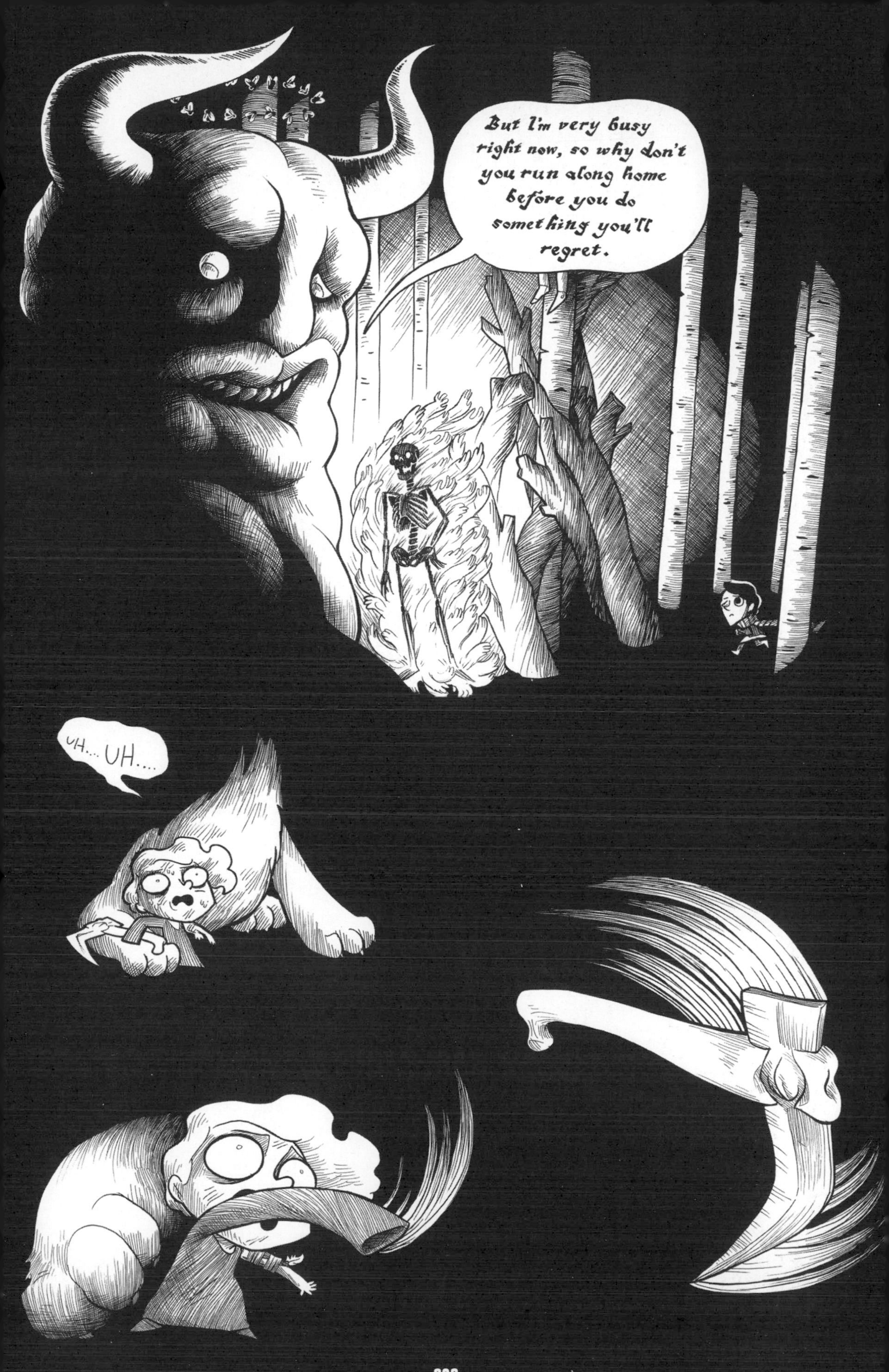
But I'm very busy right now, so why don't you run along home before you do something you'll regret.
UH.... UH....

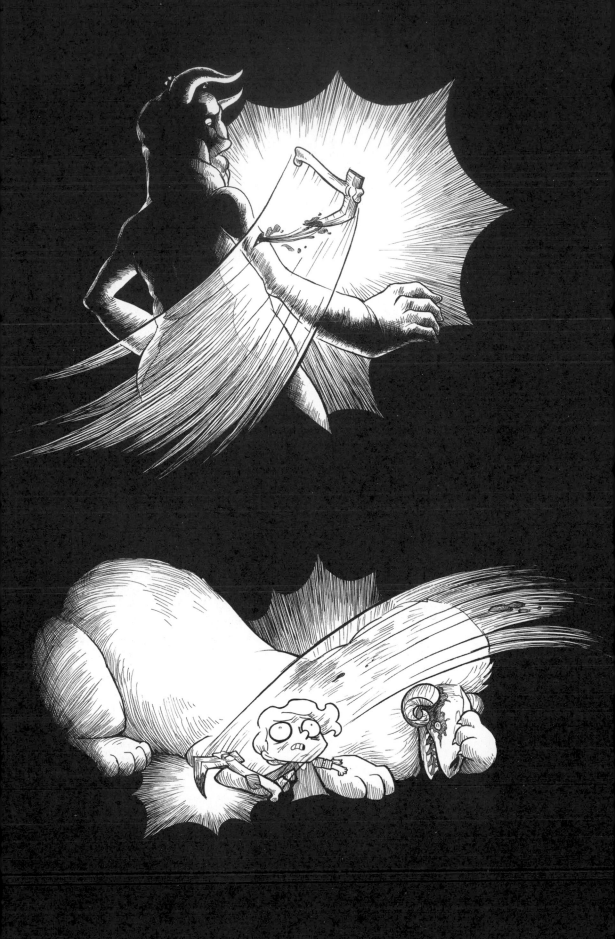

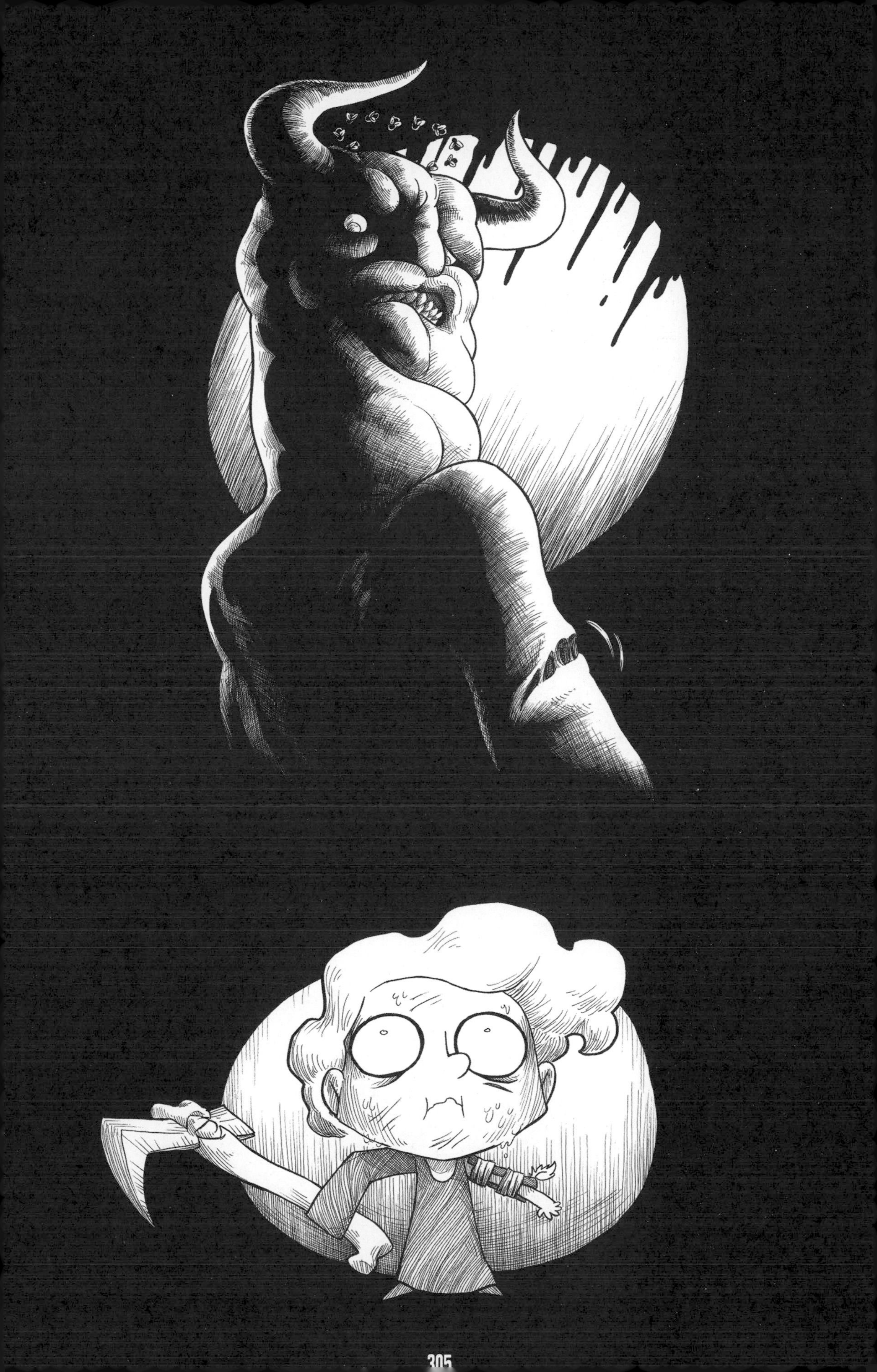

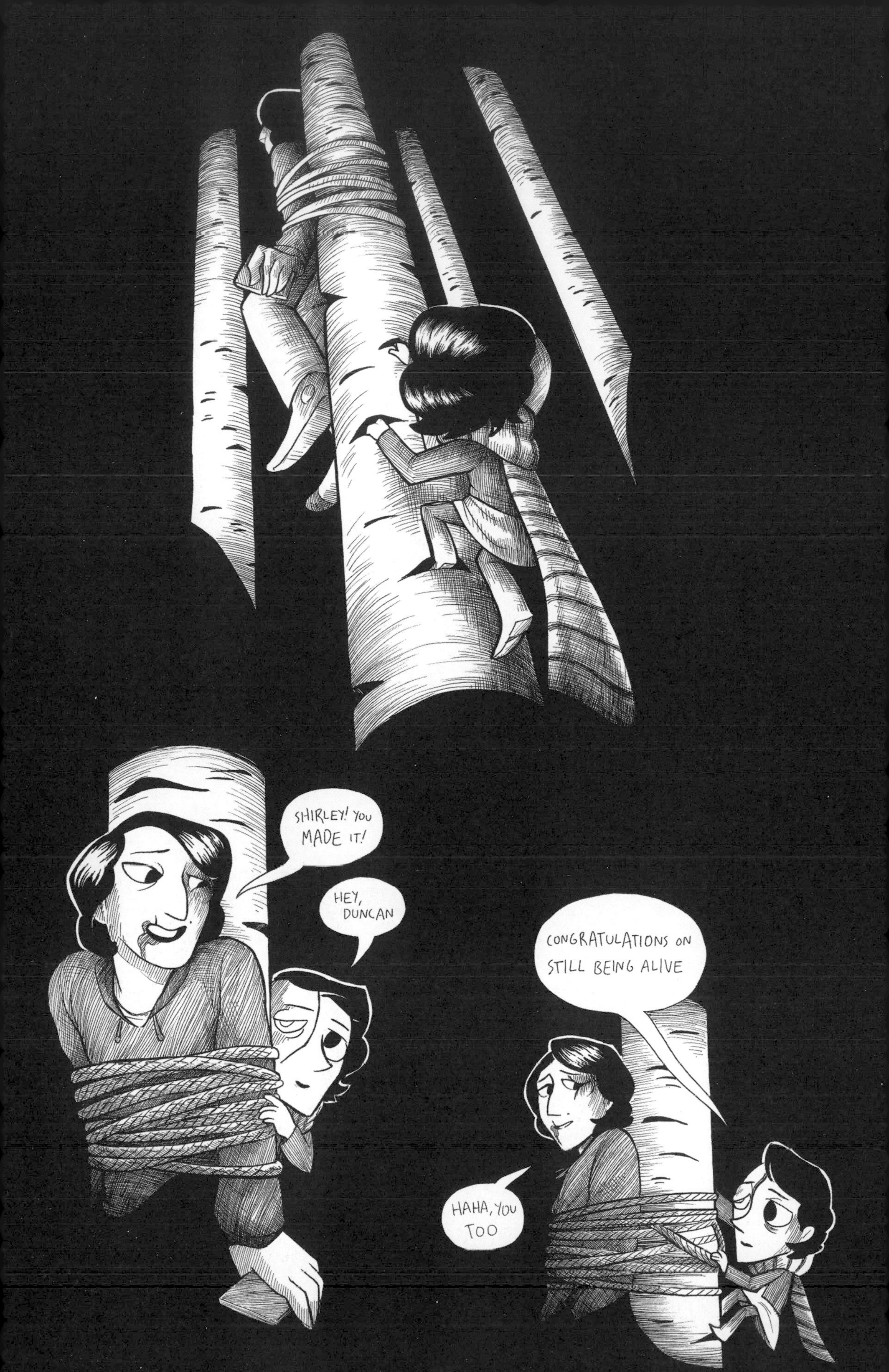
SHIRLEY! YOU MADE IT!
HEY, DUNCAN
CONGRATULATIONS ON STILL BEING ALIVE
HAHA, YOU TOO

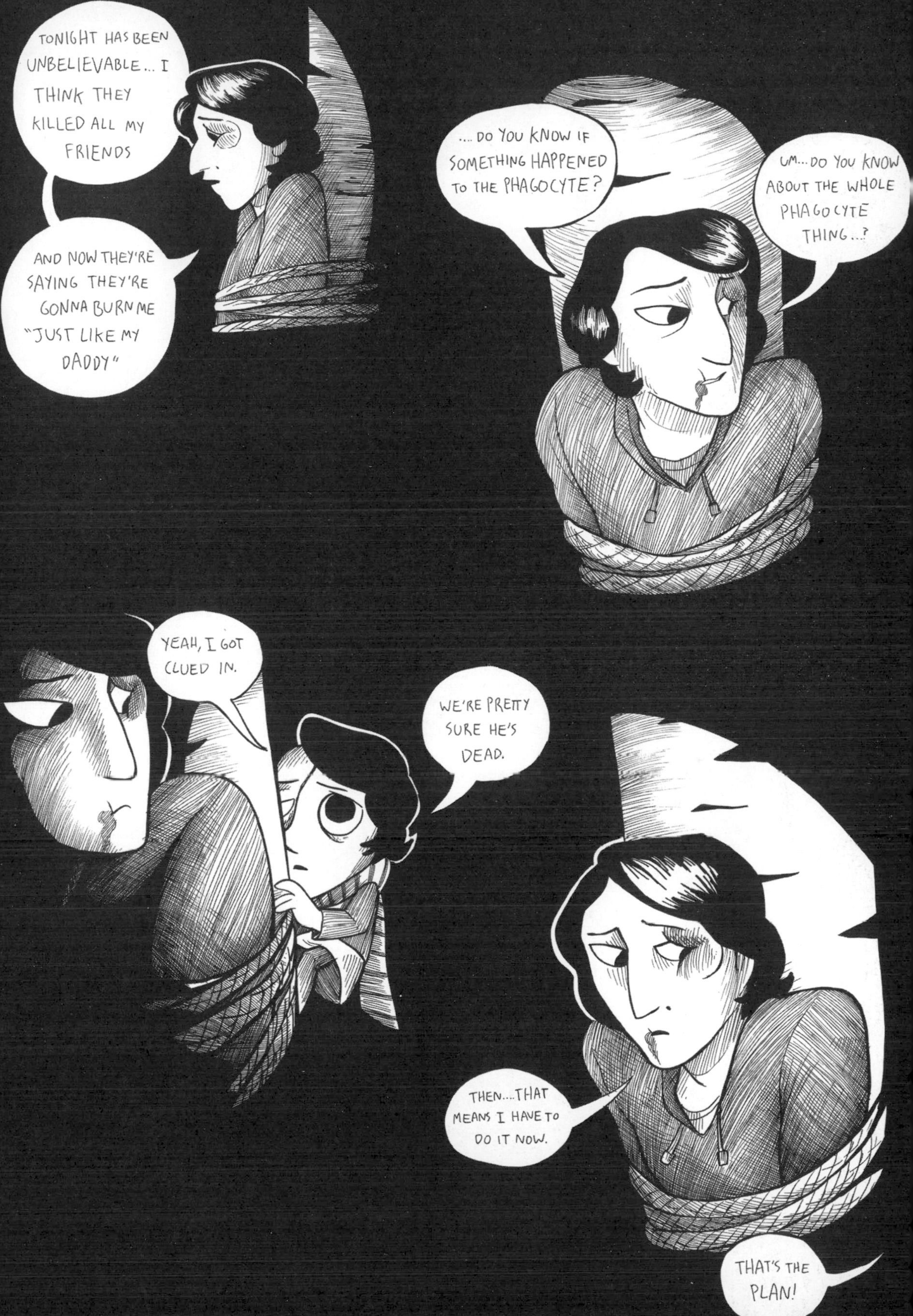

TONIGHT HAS BEEN UNBELIEVABLE... I THINK THEY KILLED ALL MY FRIENDS
AND NOW THEY'RE SAYING THEY'RE GONNA BURN ME "JUST LIKE MY DADDY"
...DO YOU KNOW IF SOMETHING HAPPENED TO THE PHAGOCYTE?
UM...DO YOU KNOW ABOUT THE WHOLE PHAGOCYTE THING...?
YEAH, I GOT CLUED IN.
WE'RE PRETTY SURE HE'S DEAD.
THEN....THAT MEANS I HAVE TO DO IT NOW.
THAT'S THE PLAN!

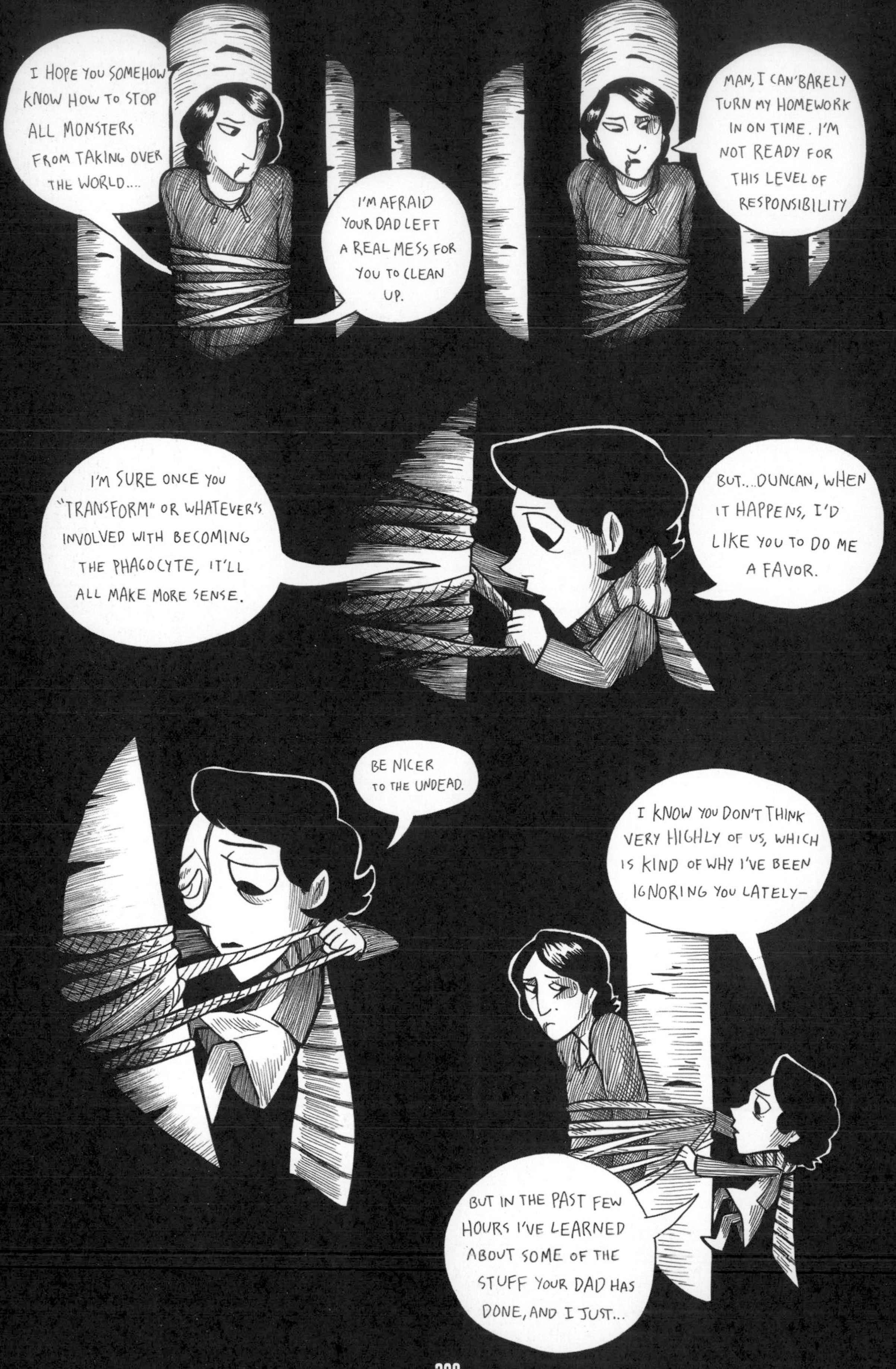
I HOPE YOU SOMEHOW KNOW HOW TO STOP ALL MONSTERS FROM TAKING OVER THE WORLD....
I'M AFRAID YOUR DAD LEFT A REAL MESS FOR YOU TO CLEAN UP.
MAN, I CAN'BARELY TURN MY HOMEWORK IN ON TIME. I'M NOT READY FOR THIS LEVEL OF RESPONSIBILITY
I'M SURE ONCE YOU "TRANSFORM" OR WHATEVER'S INVOLVED WITH BECOMING THE PHAGOCYTE, IT'LL ALL MAKE MORE SENSE.
BUT....DUNCAN, WHEN IT HAPPENS, I'D LIKE YOU TO DO ME A FAVOR.
BE NICER TO THE UNDEAD.
I KNOW YOU DON'T THINK VERY HIGHLY OF US, WHICH IS KIND OF WHY I'VE BEEN IGNORING YOU LATELY-
BUT IN THE PAST FEW HOURS I'VE LEARNED ABOUT SOME OF THE STUFF YOUR DAD HAS DONE, AND I JUST...

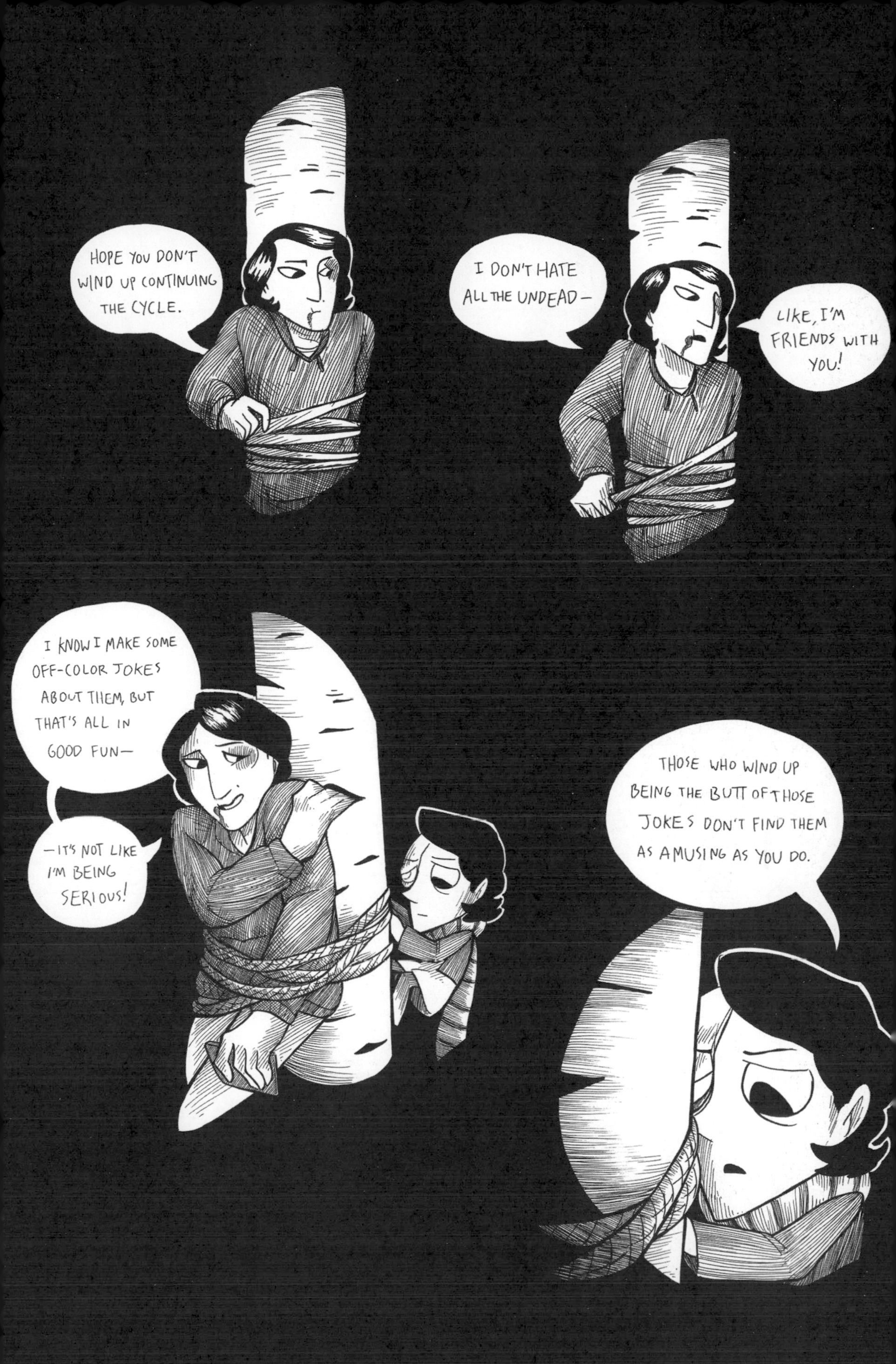
HOPE YOU DON'T WIND UP CONTINUING THE CYCLE.
I DON'T HATE ALL THE UNDEAD—
LIKE, I'M FRIENDS WITH YOU!
I KNOW I MAKE SOME OFF-COLOR JOKES ABOUT THEM, BUT THAT'S ALL IN GOOD FUN—
—IT'S NOT LIKE I'M BEING SERIOUS!
THOSE WHO WIND UP BEING THE BUTT OF THOSE JOKES DON'T FIND THEM AS AMUSING AS YOU DO.

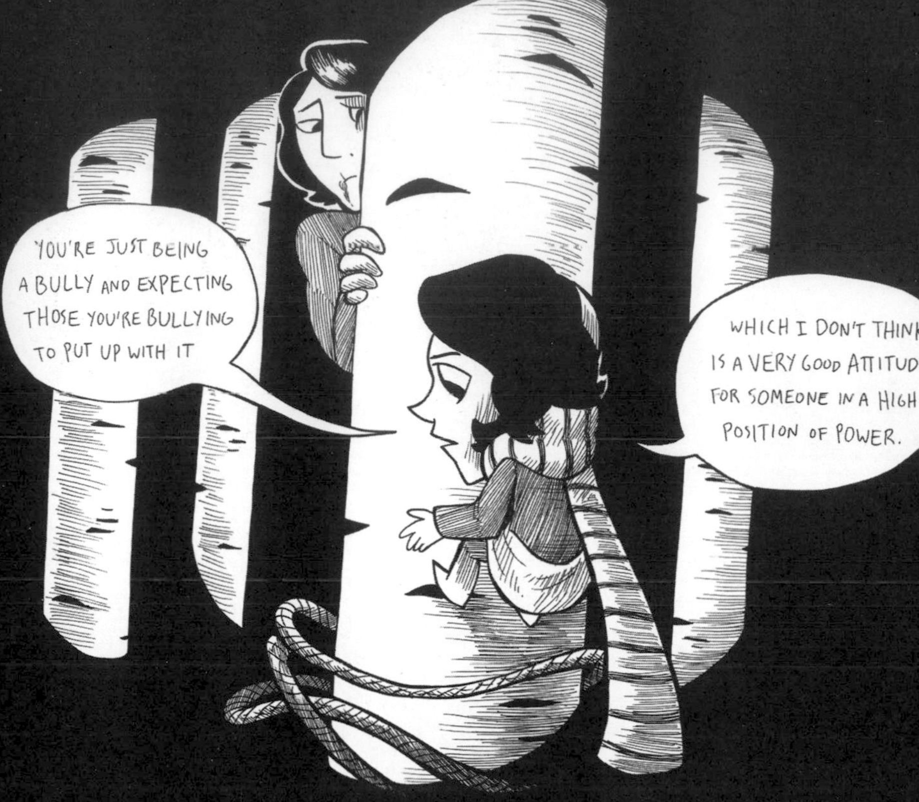
YOU'RE JUST BEING A BULLY AND EXPECTING THOSE YOU'RE BULLYING TO PUT UP WITH IT
WHICH I DON'T THINK IS A VERY GOOD ATTITUDE FOR SOMEONE IN A HIGH POSITION OF POWER.

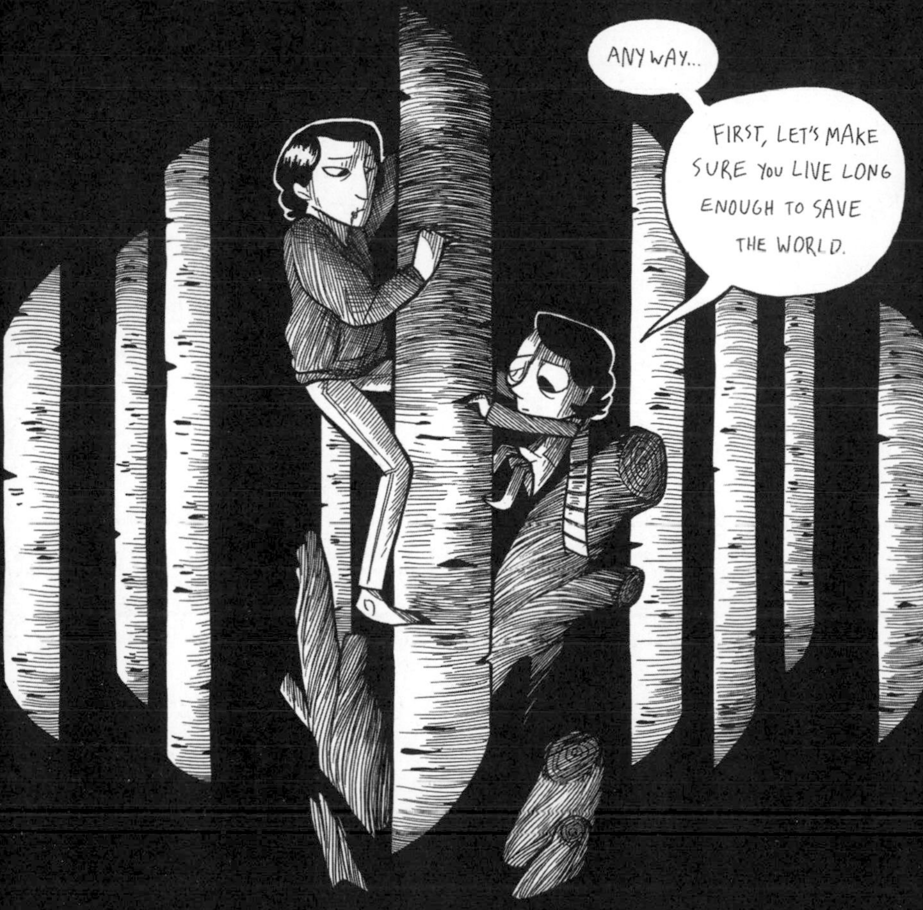
ANYWAY...
FIRST, LET'S MAKE SURE YOU LIVE LONG ENOUGH TO SAVE THE WORLD.

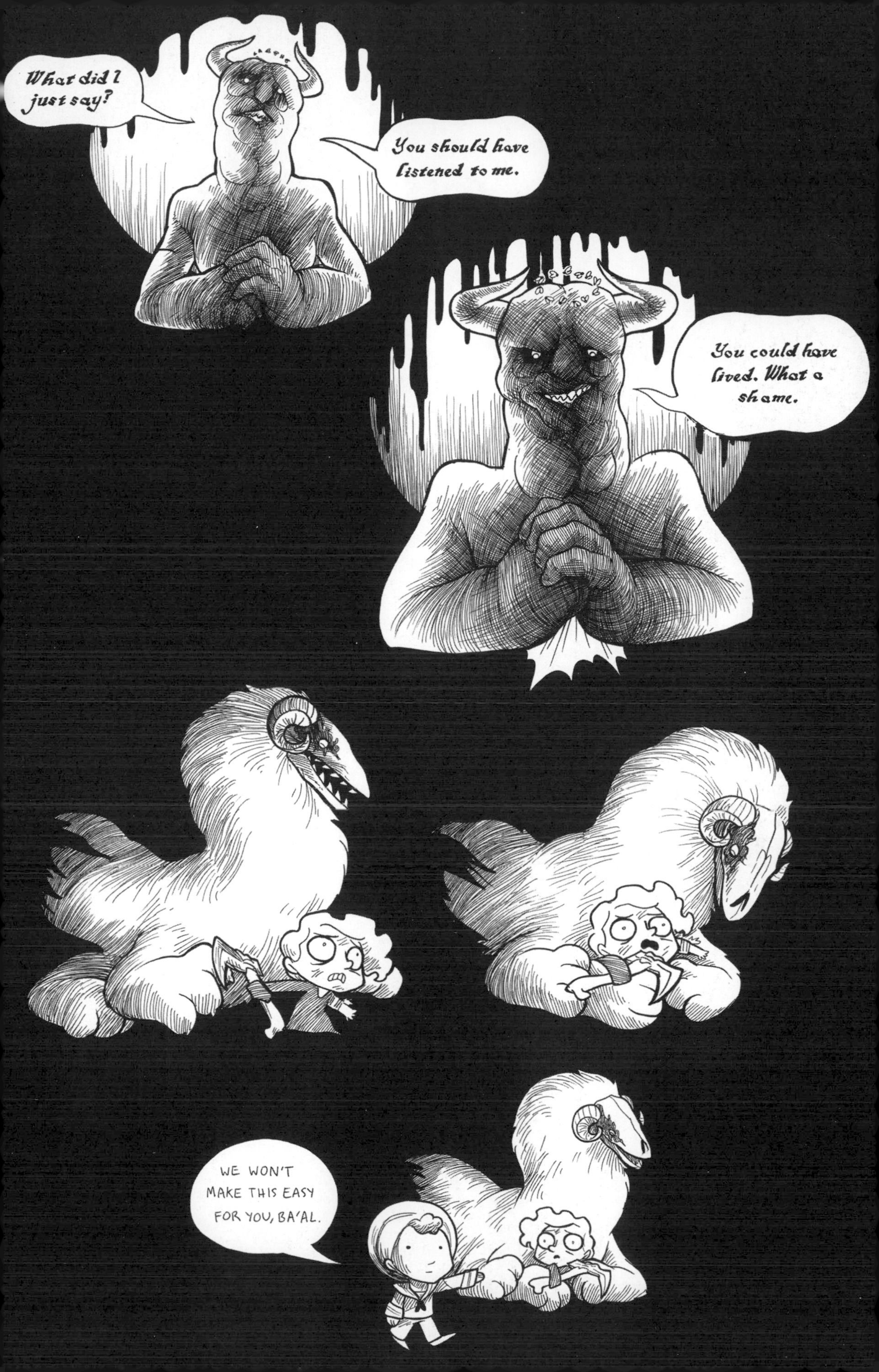
What did I just say?
You should have listened to me.
You could have lived. What a shame.
WE WON'T MAKE THIS EASY FOR YOU, BA'AL.

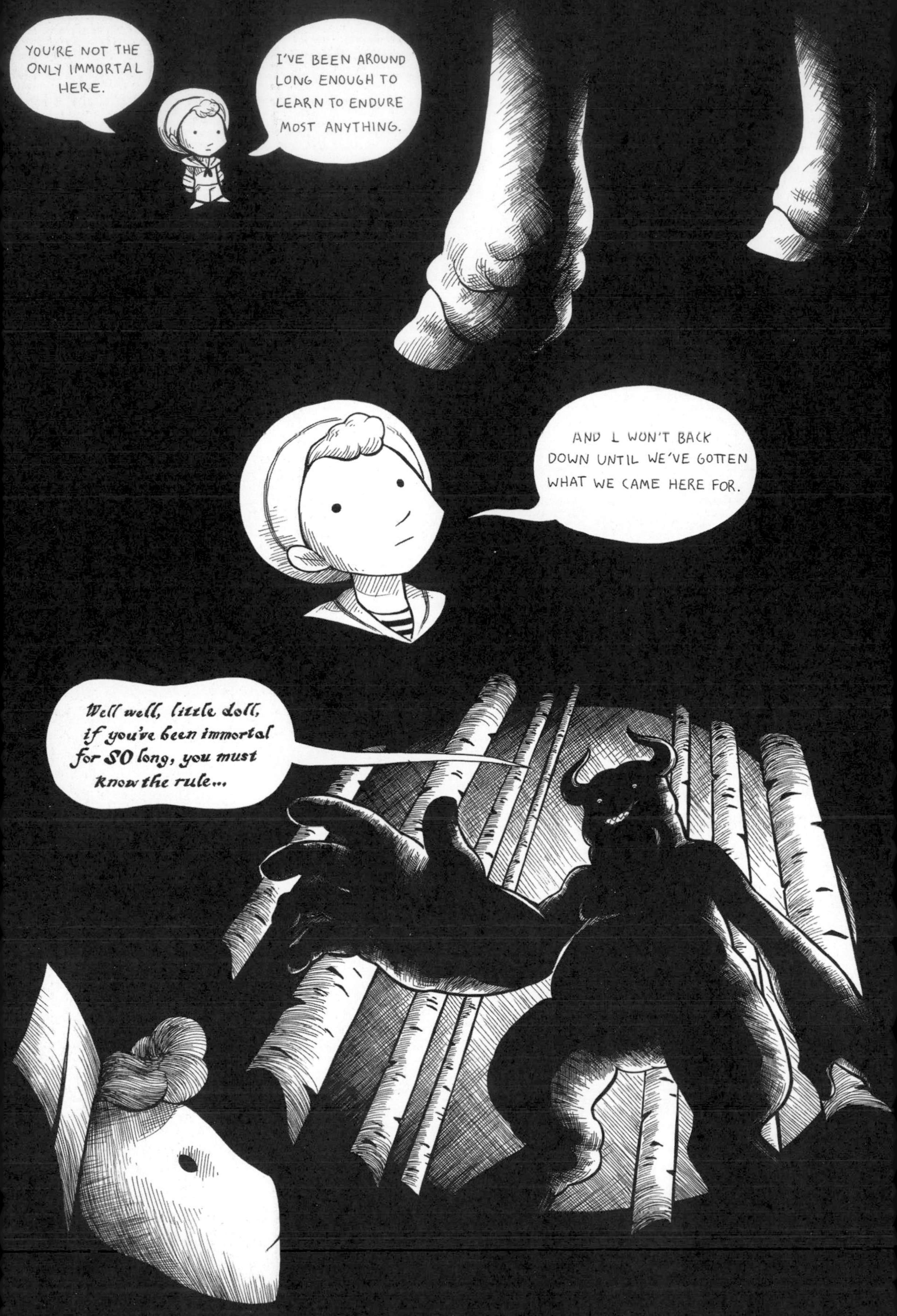
YOU'RE NOT THE ONLY IMMORTAL HERE.
I'VE BEEN AROUND LONG ENOUGH TO LEARN TO ENDURE MOST ANYTHING.
AND I WON'T BACK DOWN UNTIL WE'VE GOTTEN WHAT WE CAME HERE FOR.
Well well, little doll, if you've been immortal for SO long, you must know the rule...

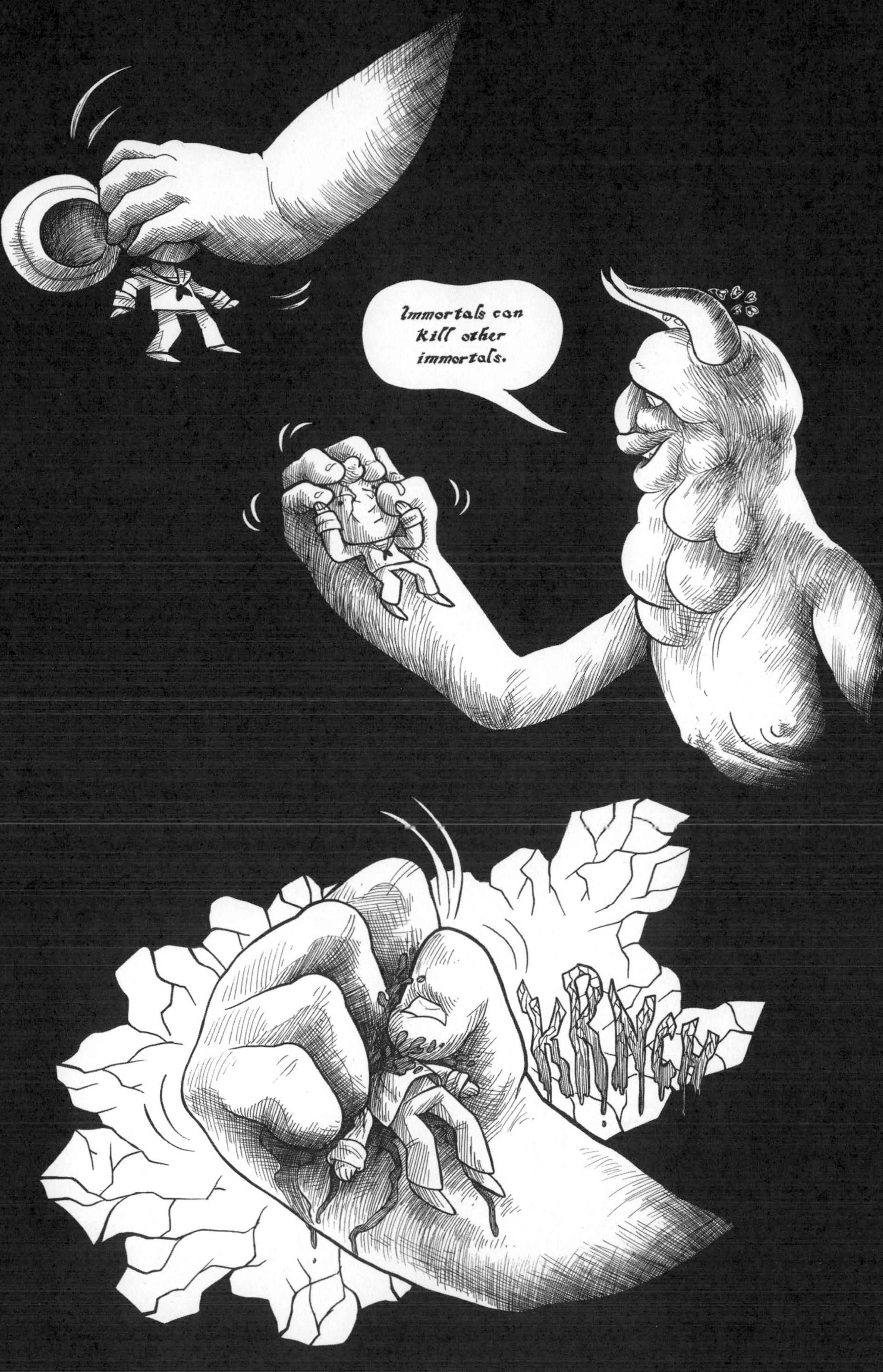
Immortals can kill other immortals.
KRNCH

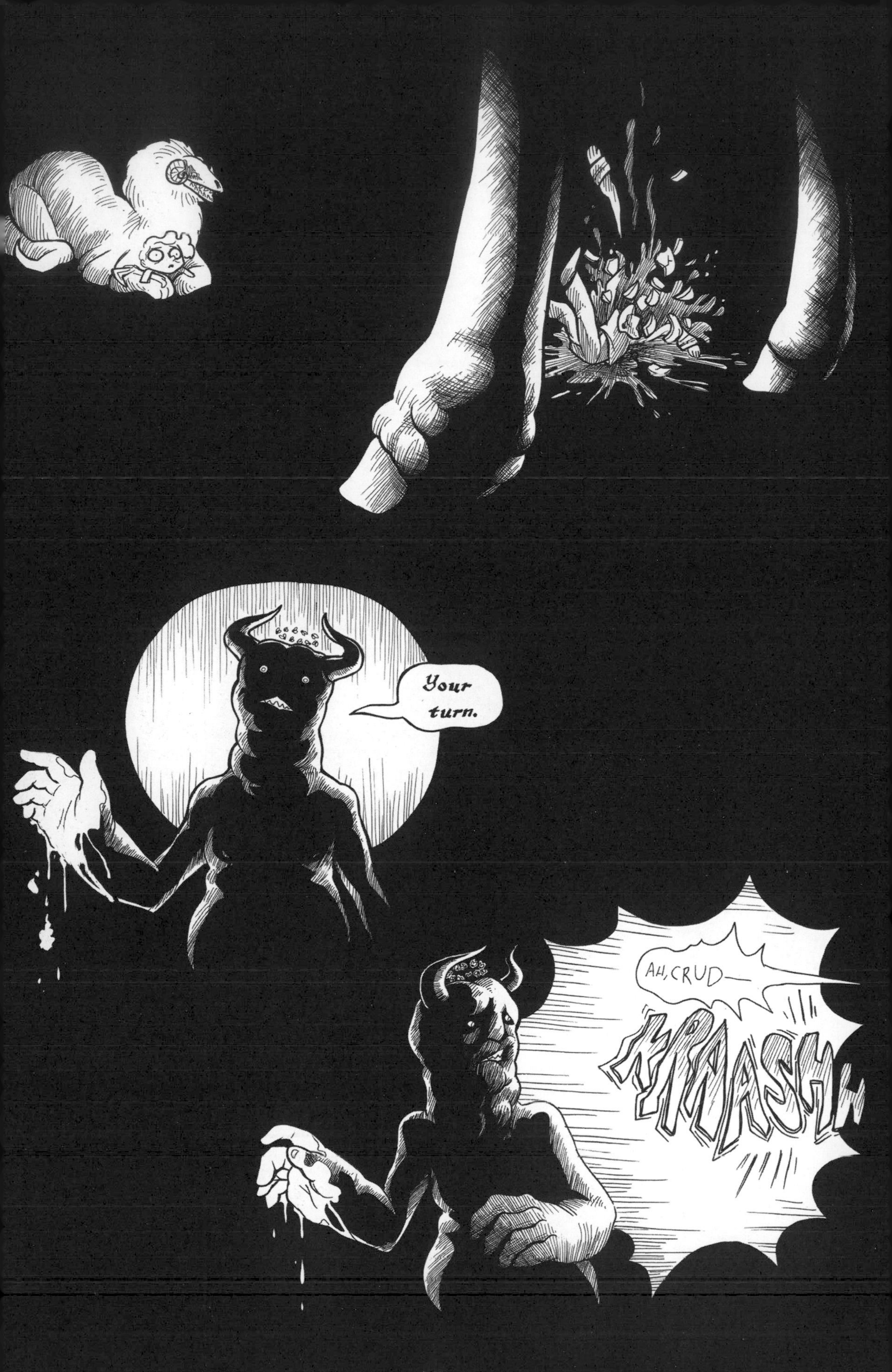
Your turn.
AH, CRUD—
KRASH

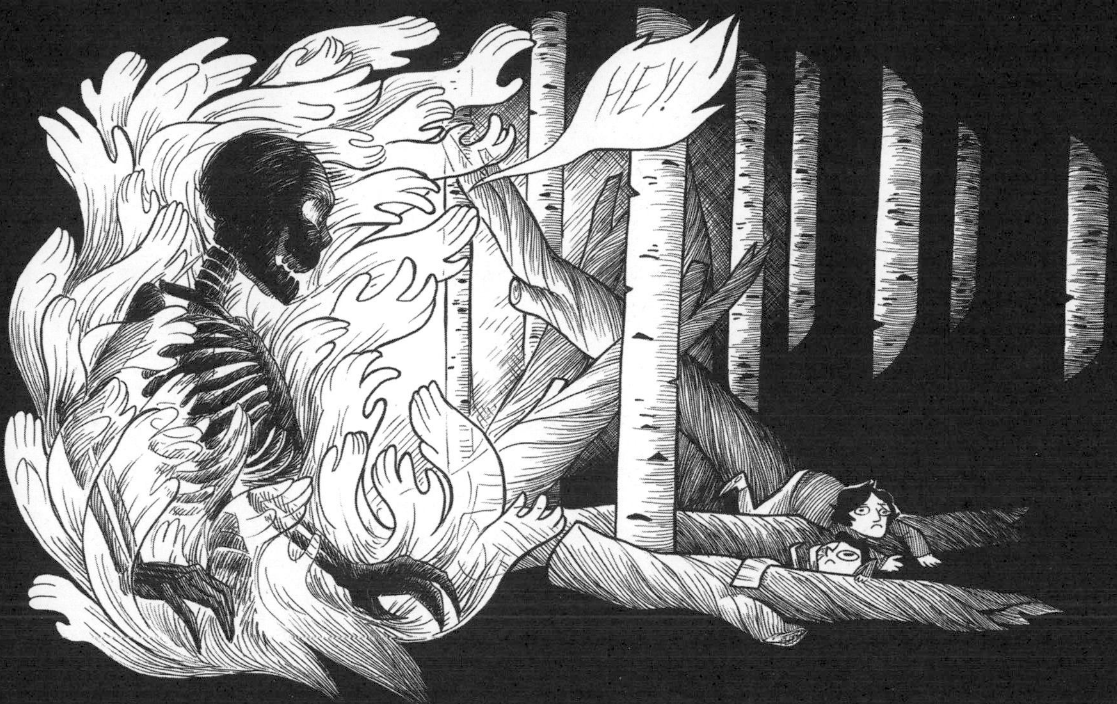
HEY!

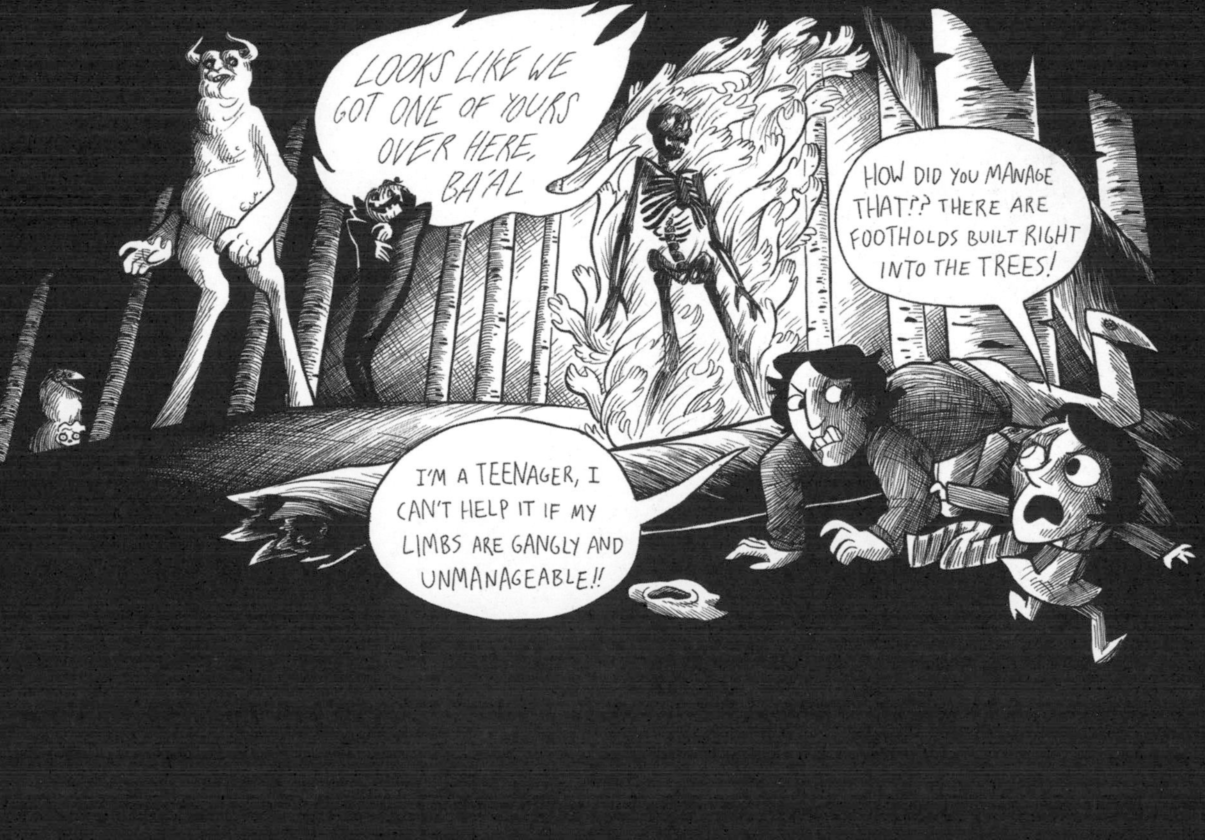
LOOKS LIKE WE GOT ONE OF YOURS OVER HERE, BA'AL
HOW DID YOU MANAGE THAT!?? THERE ARE FOOTHOLDS BUILT RIGHT INTO THE TREES!
I'M A TEENAGER, I CAN'T HELP IT IF MY LIMBS ARE GANGLY AND UNMANAGEABLE!!

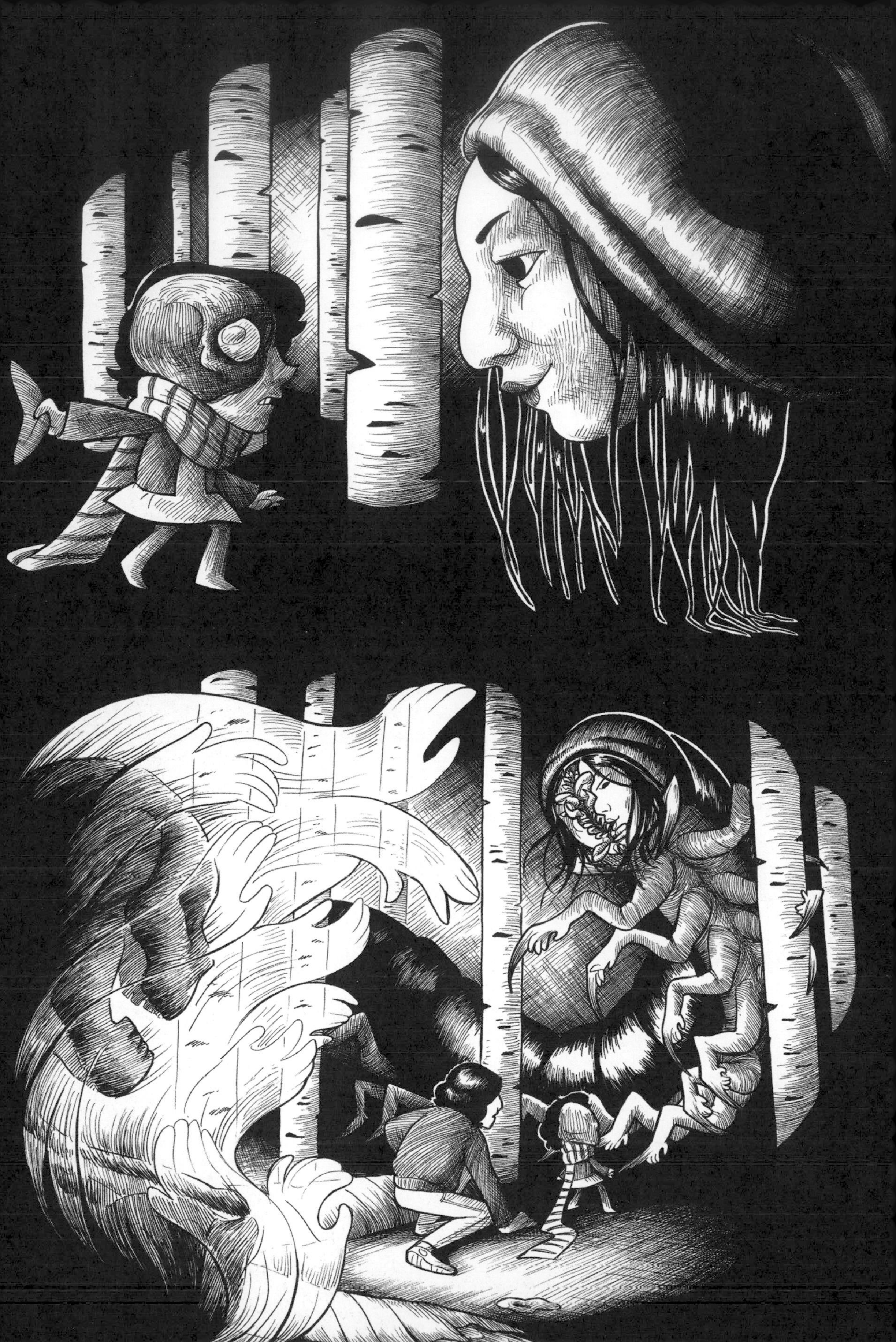

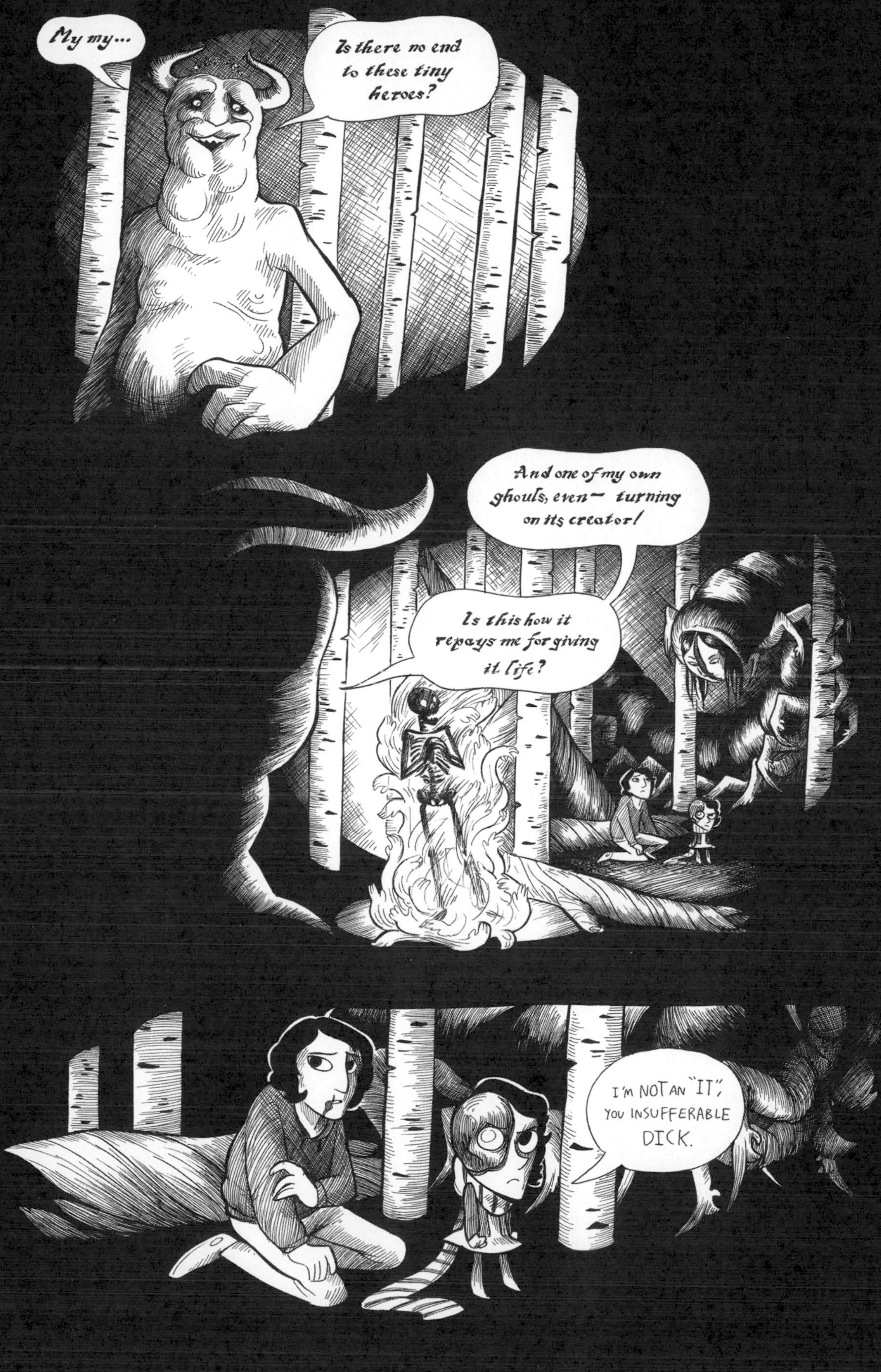
My my...
Is there no end to these tiny heroes?
And one of my own ghouls, even— turning on its creator!
Is this how it repays me for giving it life?
I'M NOT AN "IT", YOU INSUFFERABLE DICK.

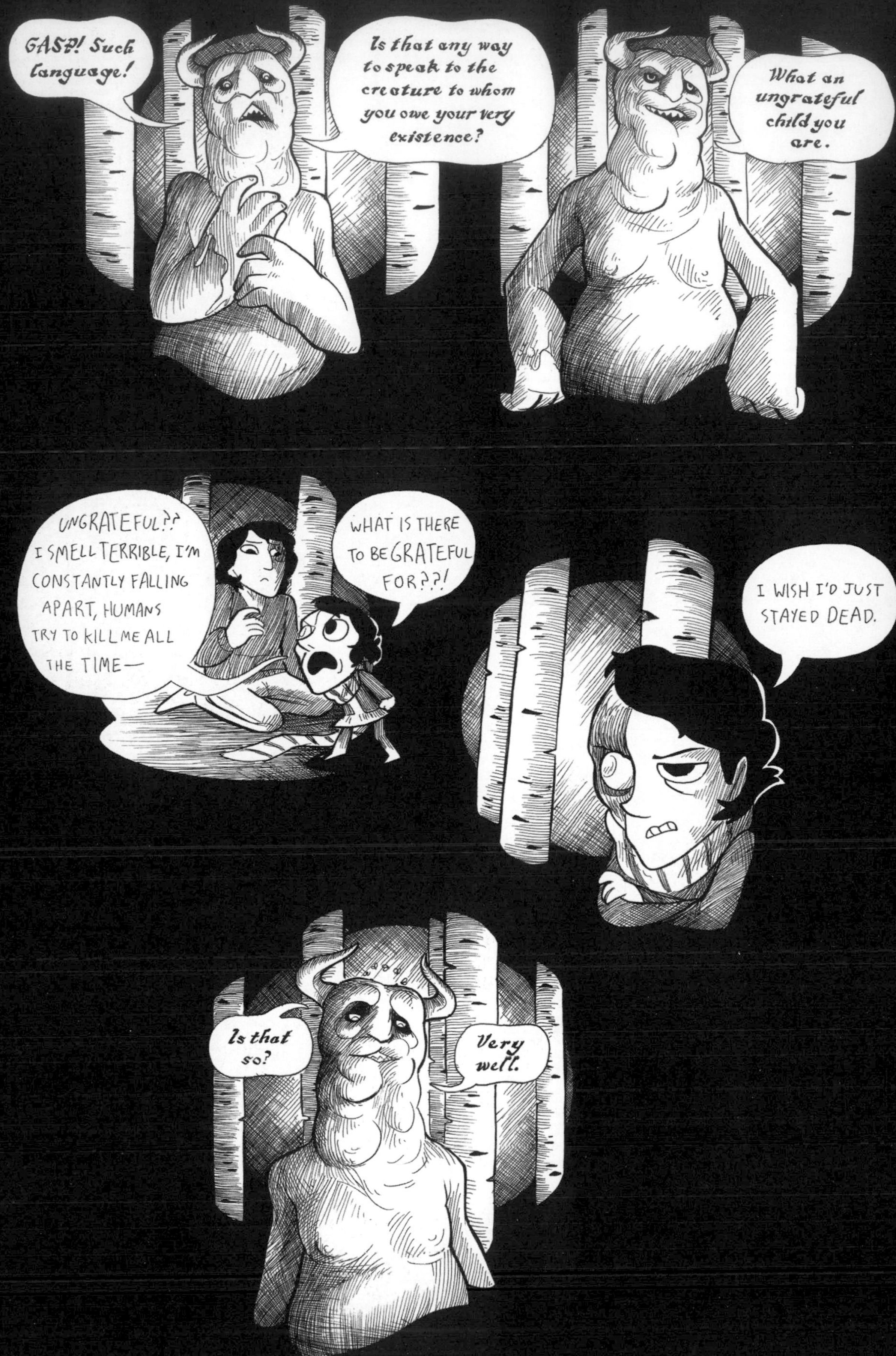
GASP! Such language!
Is that any way to speak to the creature to whom you owe your very existence?
What an ungrateful child you are.
UNGRATEFUL?!? I SMELL TERRIBLE, I'M CONSTANTLY FALLING APART, HUMANS TRY TO KILL ME ALL THE TIME—
WHAT IS THERE TO BE GRATEFUL FOR??!
I WISH I'D JUST STAYED DEAD.
Is that so?
Very well.

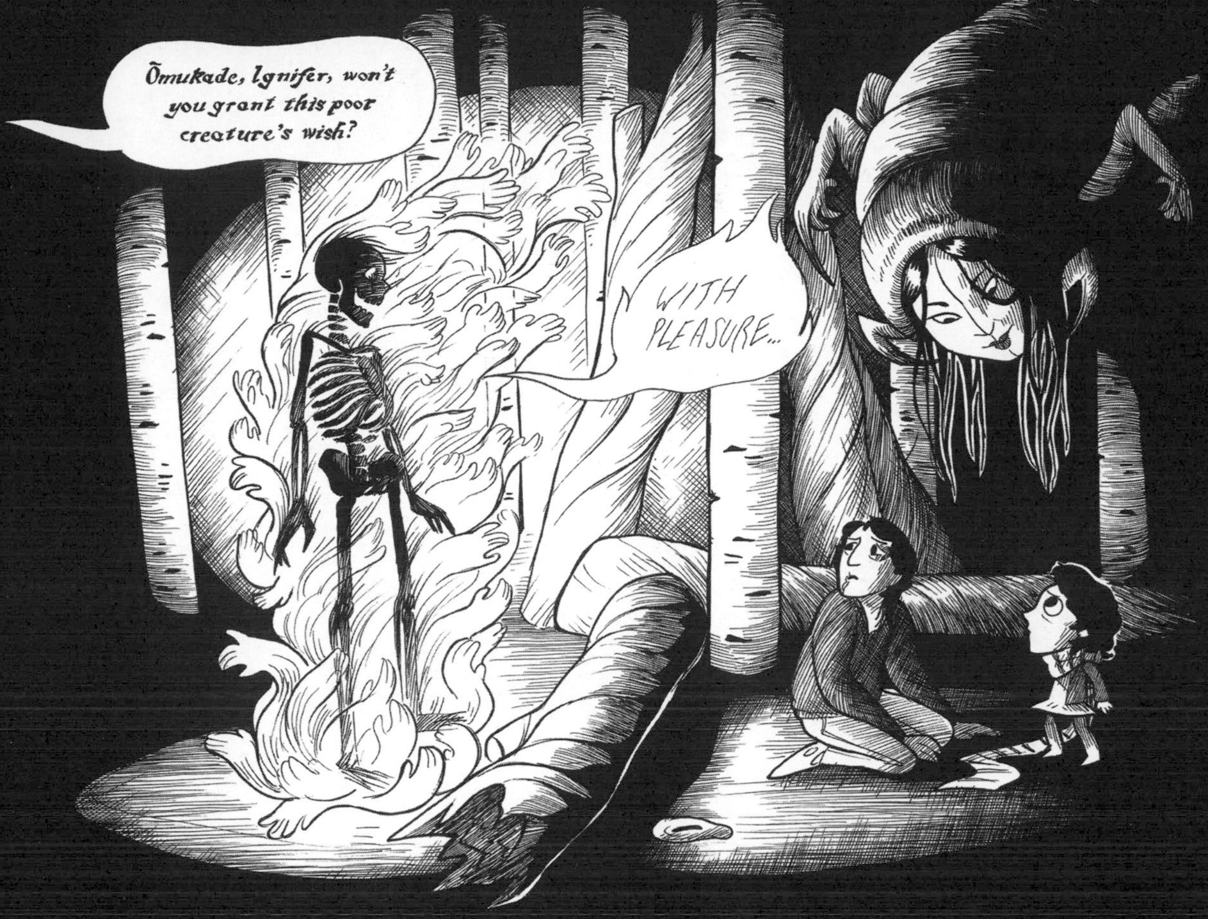
Ōmukade, Ignifer, won't you grant this poor creature's wish?
WITH PLEASURE...

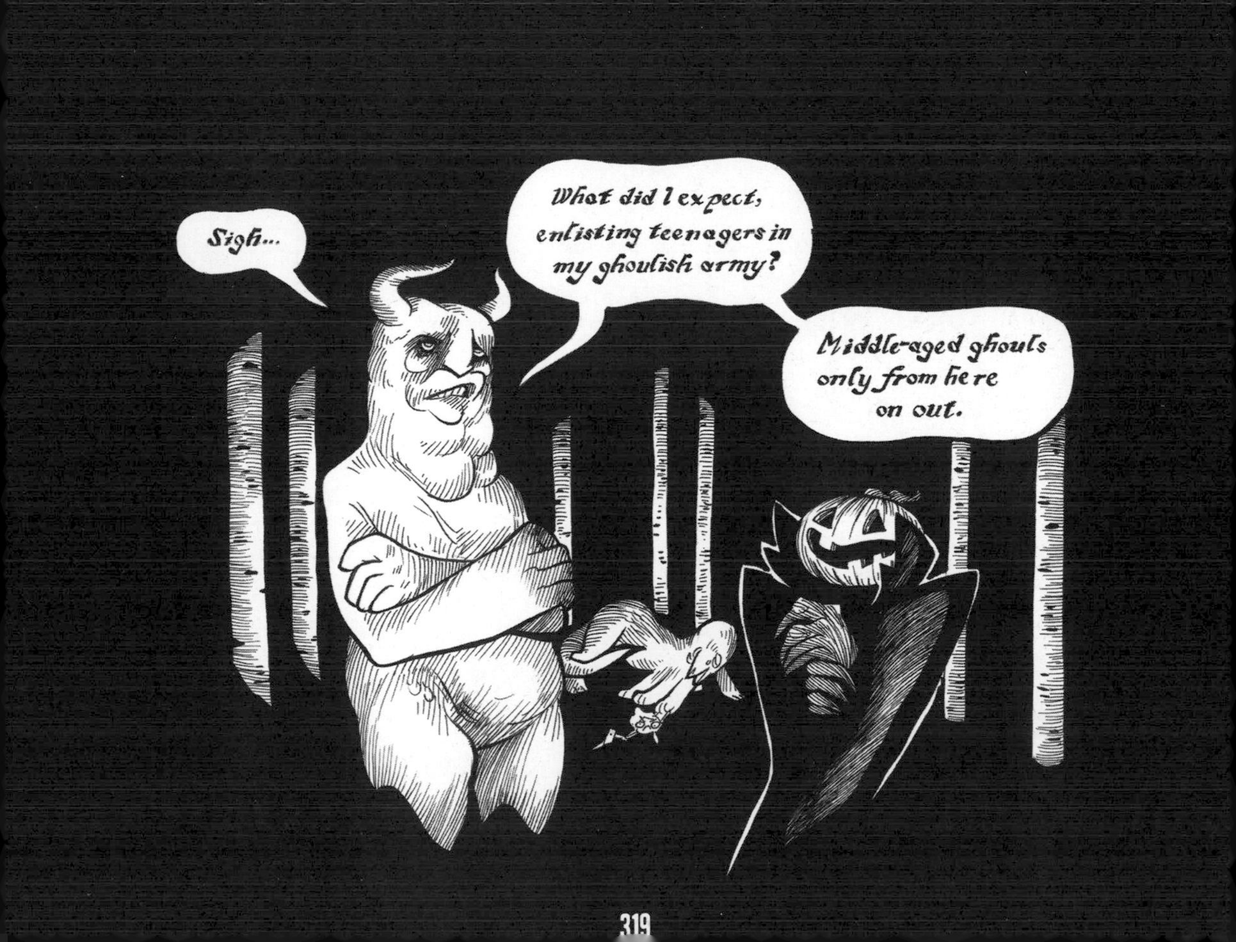
Sigh...
What did I expect, enlisting teenagers in my ghoulish army?
Middle-aged ghouls only from here on out.

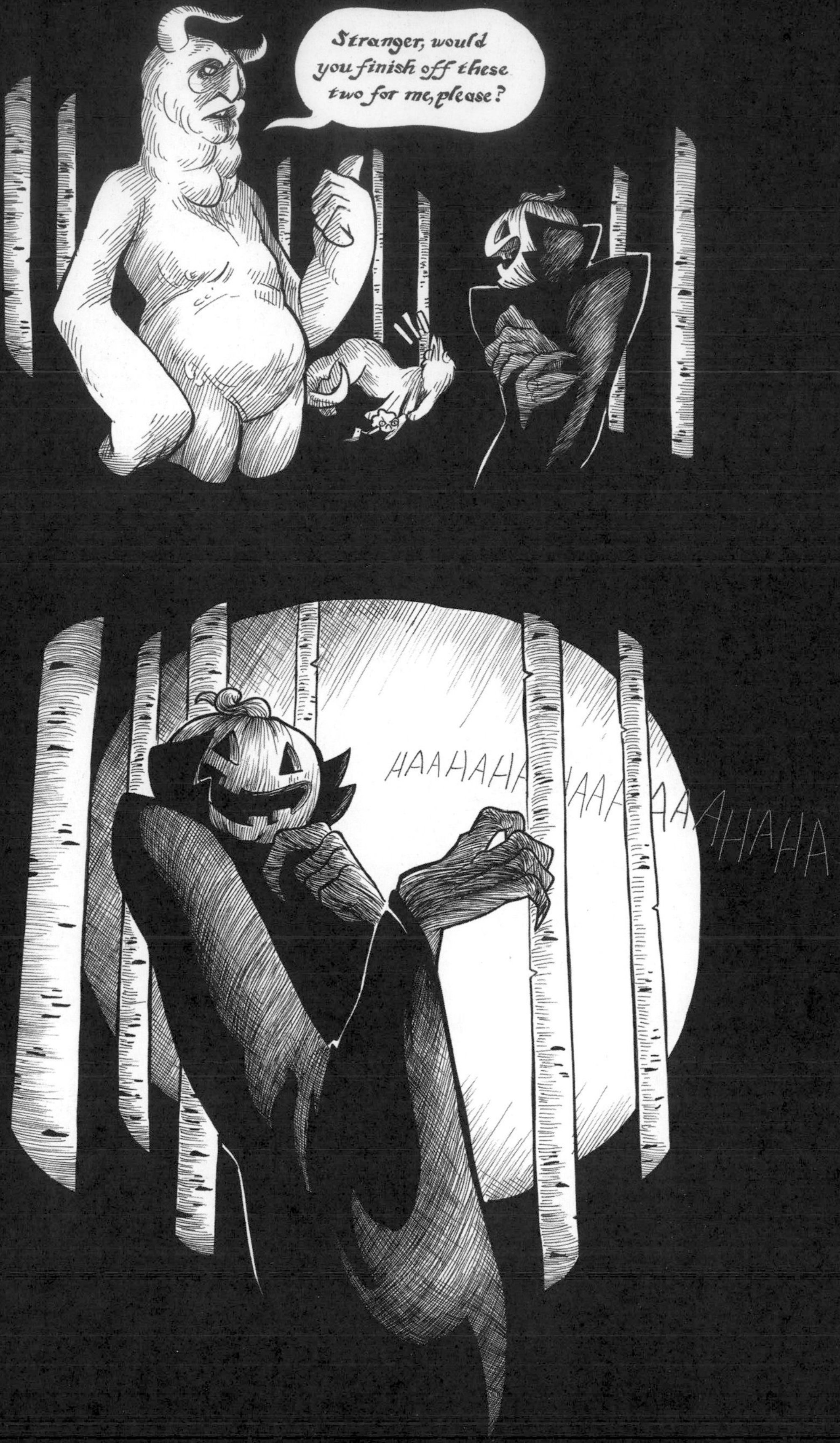
Stranger, would you finish off these two for me, please?
HAAAHAHAHAAAHAAAHAHAHA

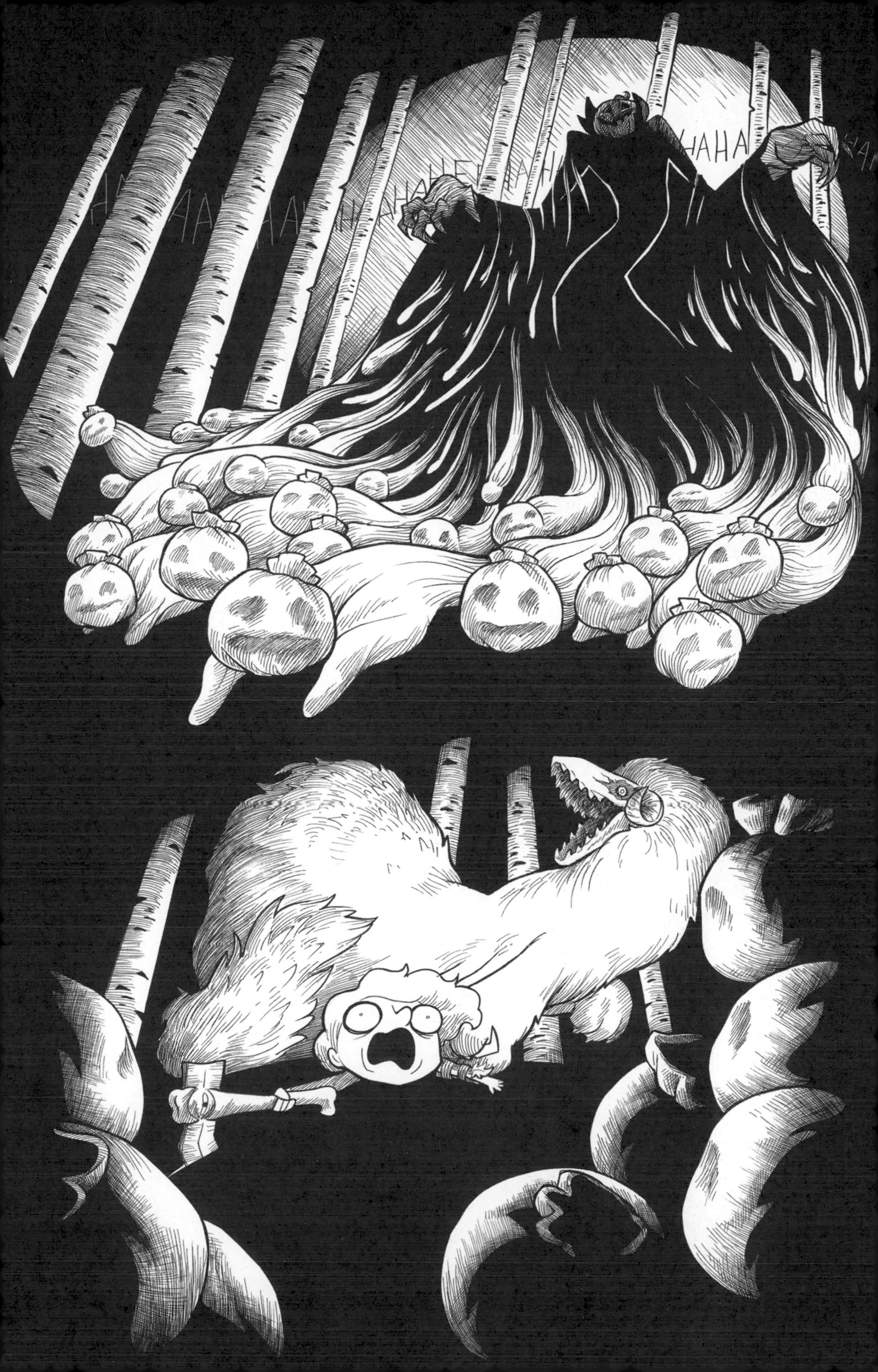
HAHA

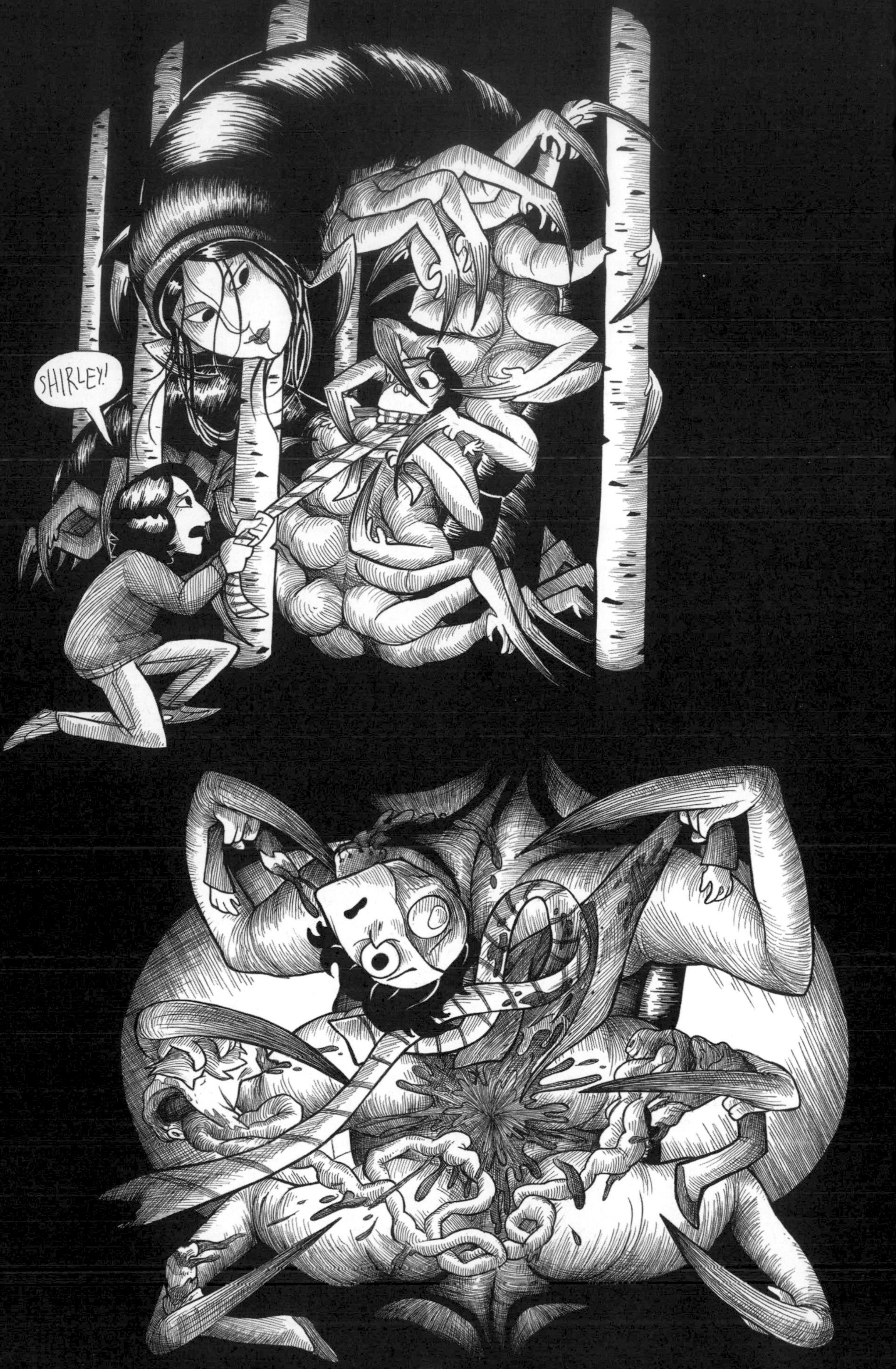
SHIRLEY!

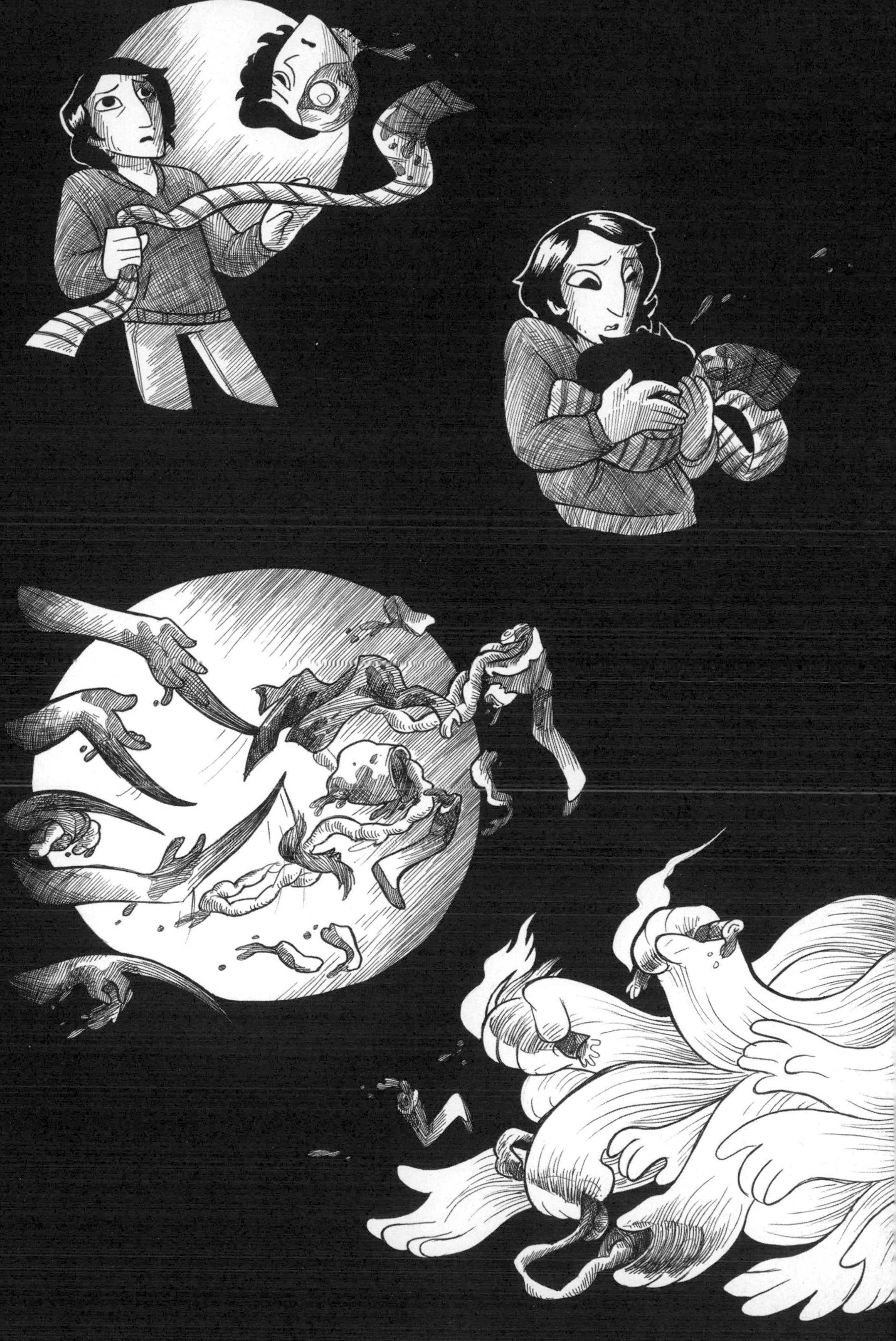

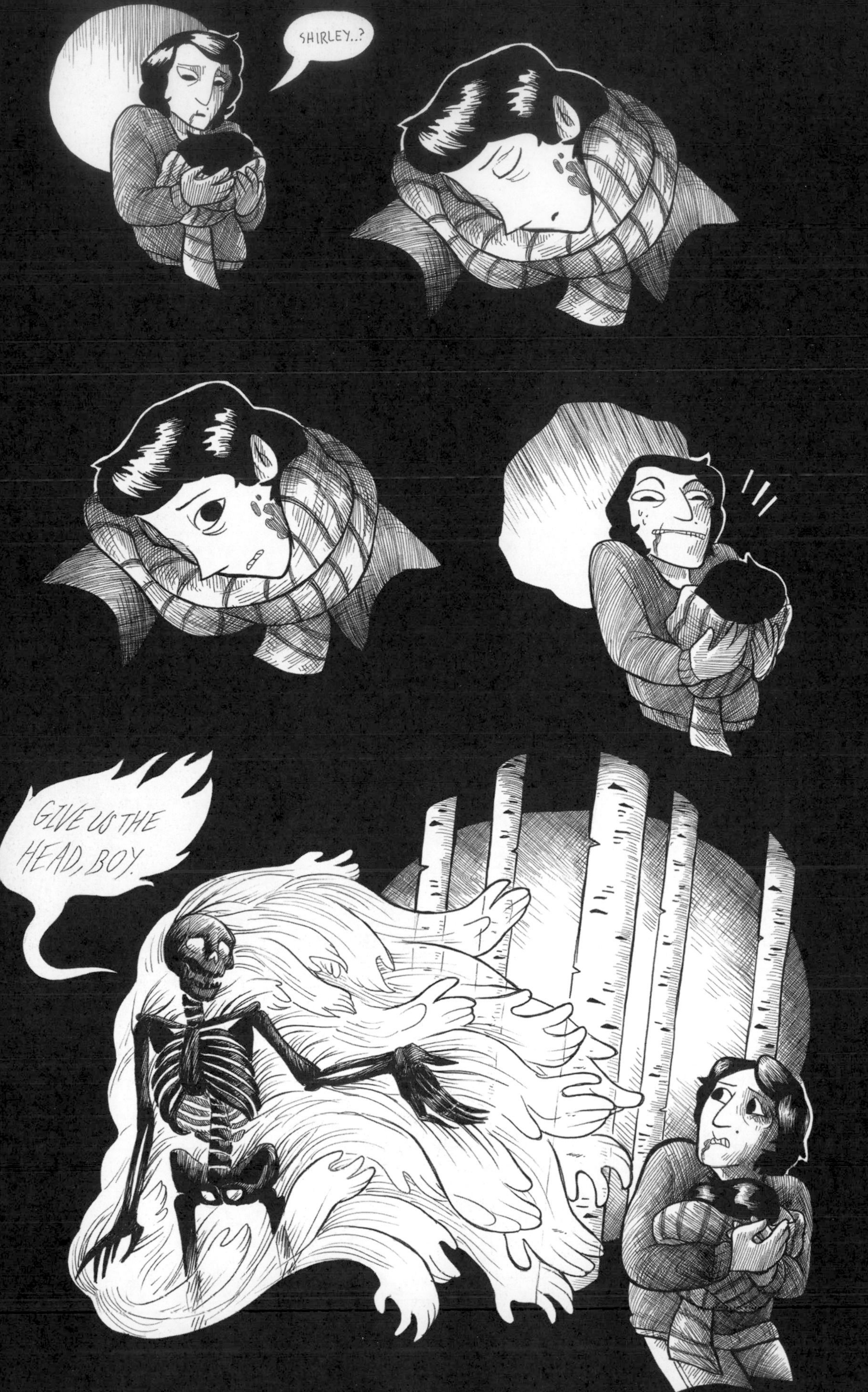
SHIRLEY..?
GIVE US THE HEAD, BOY.

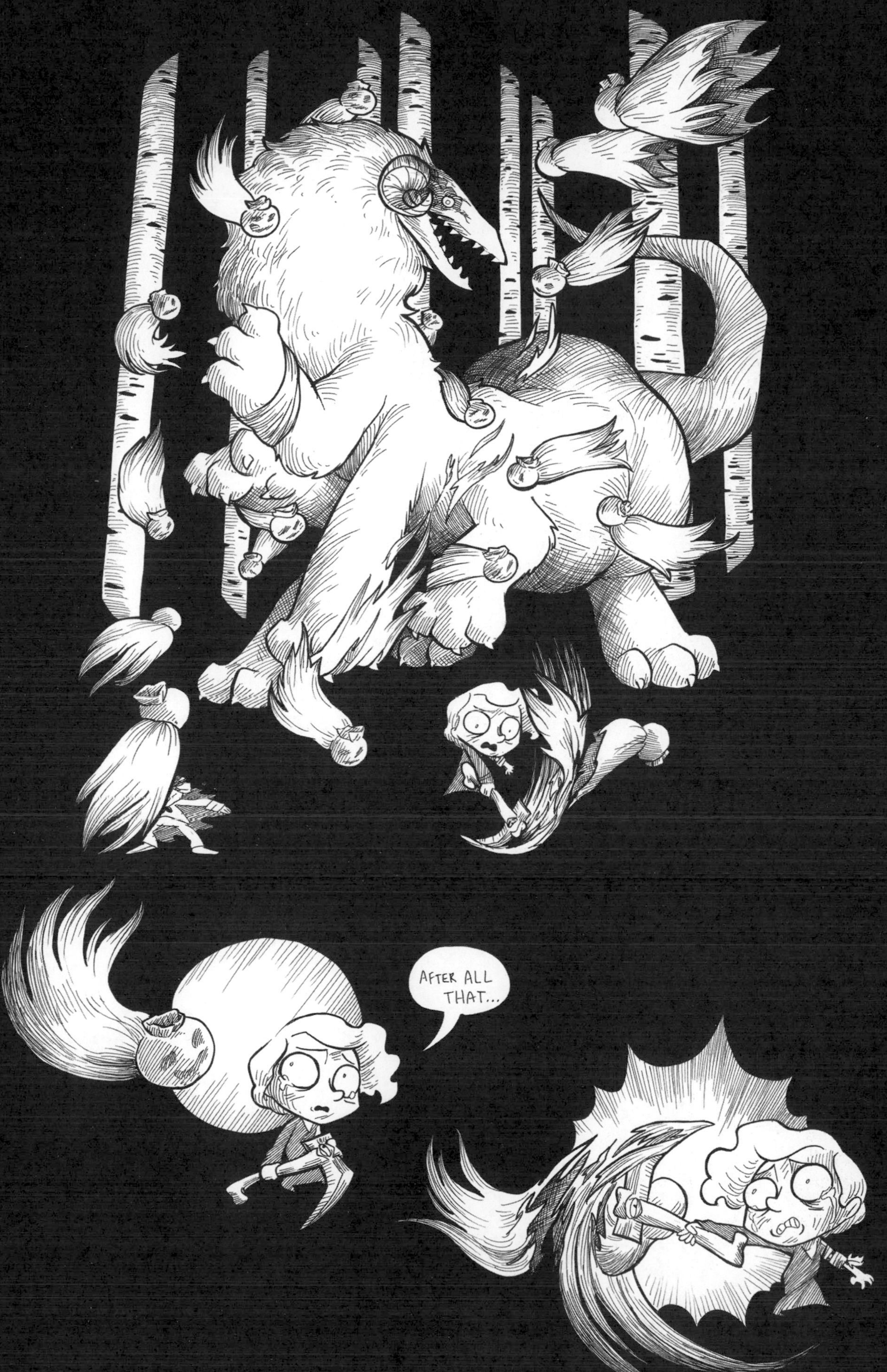
AFTER ALL THAT...

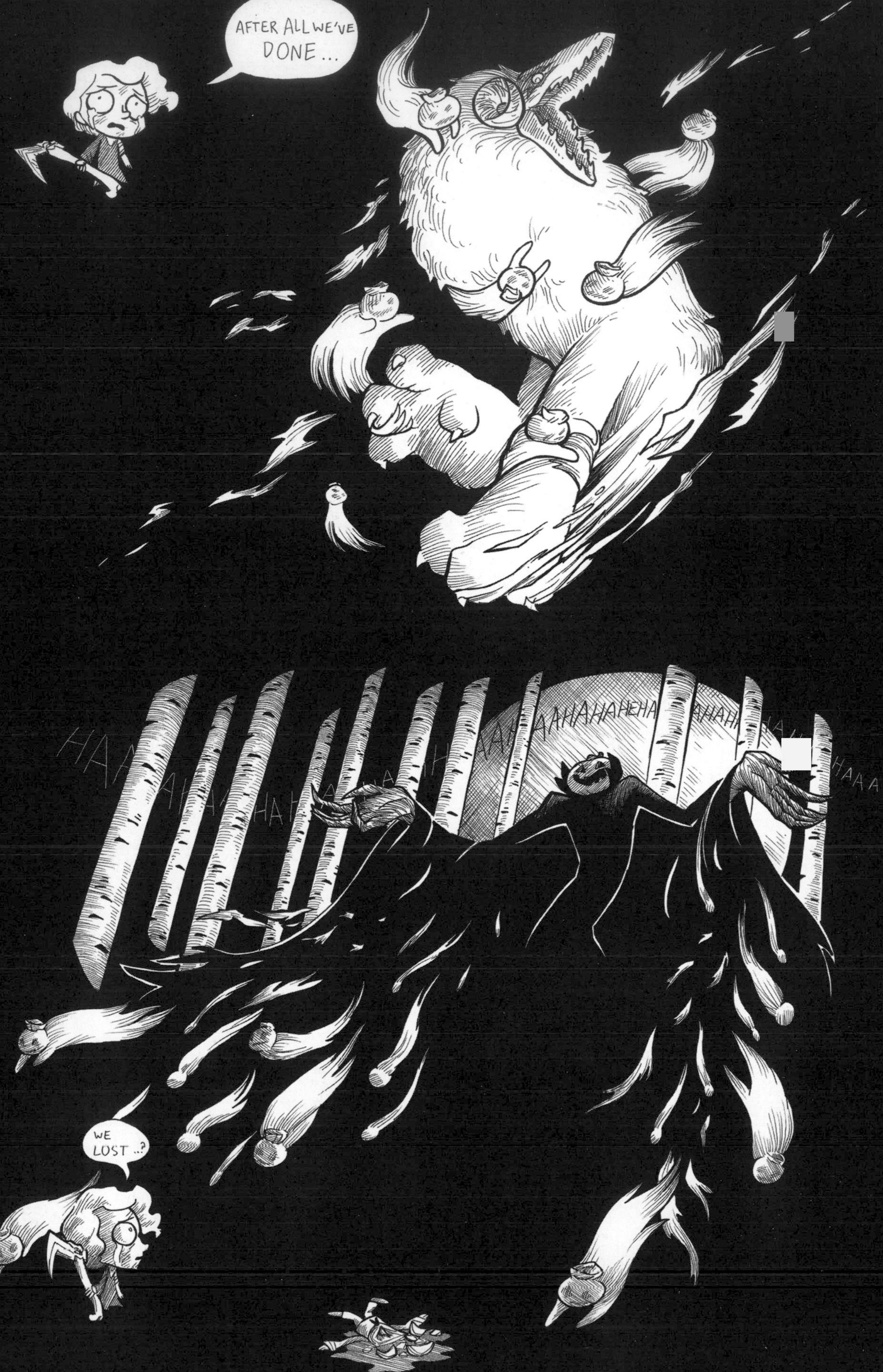
AFTER ALL WE'VE DONE...
WE LOST ..?

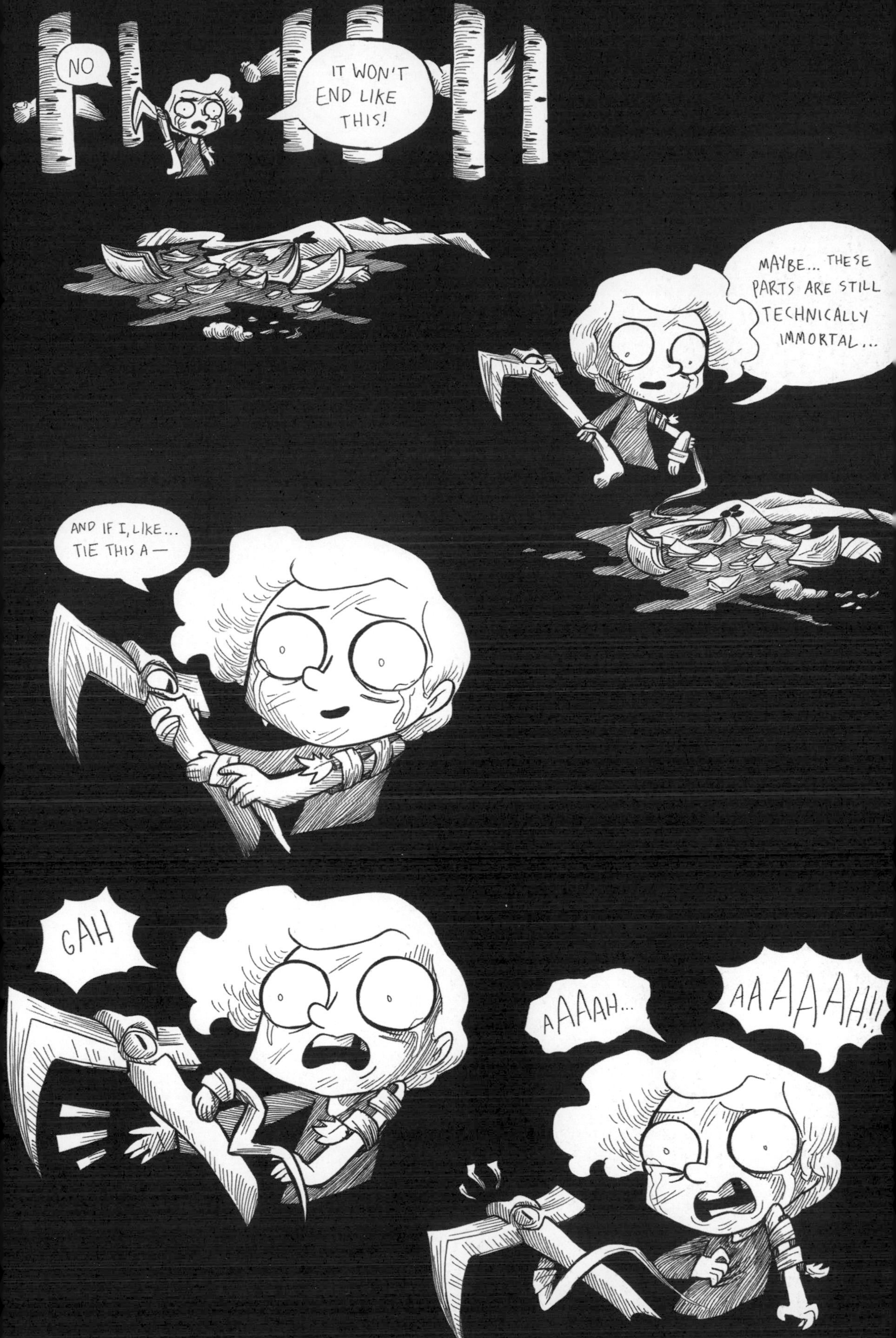
NO
IT WON'T END LIKE THIS!
MAYBE... THESE PARTS ARE STILL TECHNICALLY IMMORTAL...
AND IF I, LIKE... TIE THIS A—
GAH
AAAAH...
AAAAAH!!

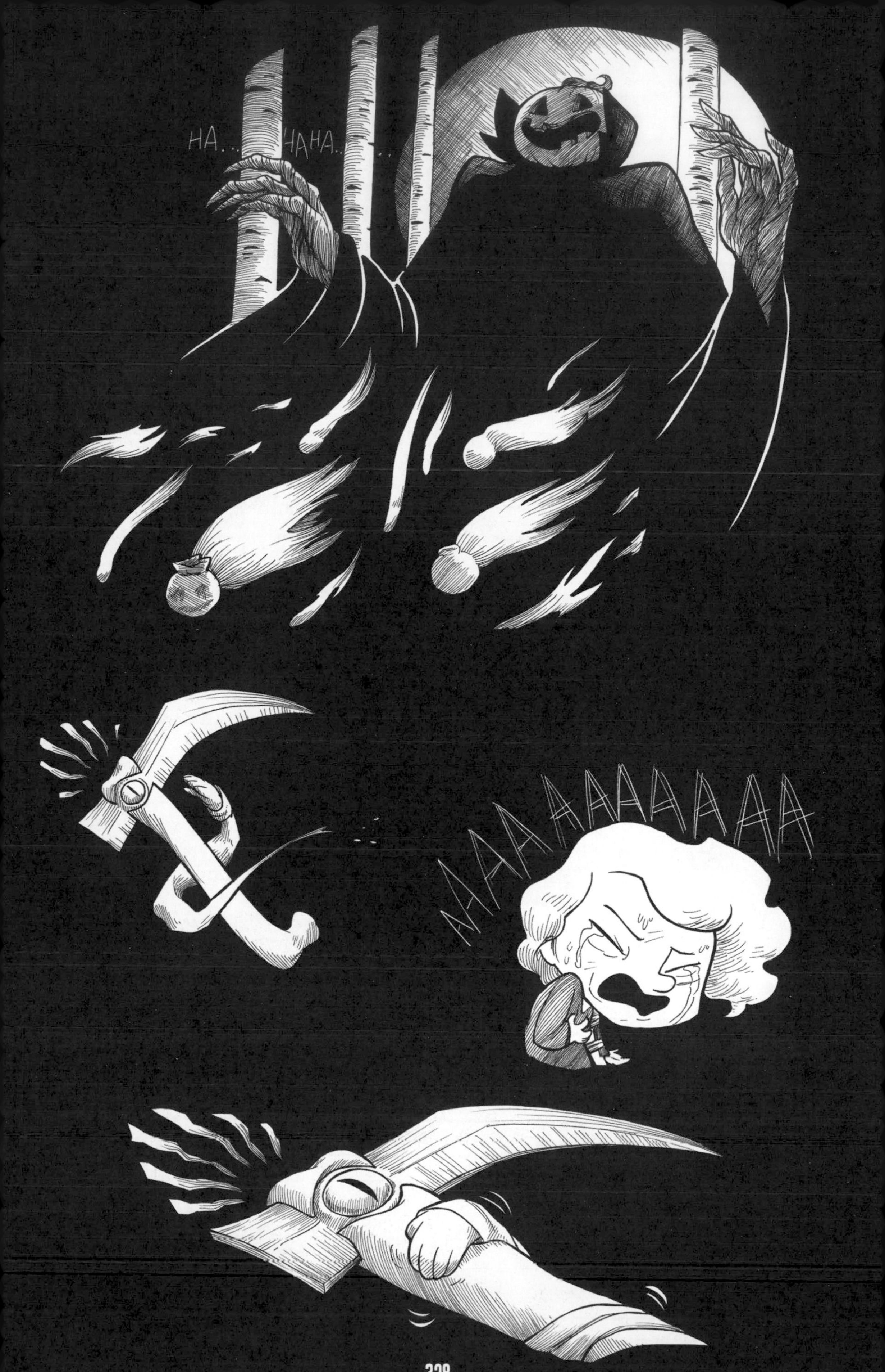
HA... HAHA...
AAAAAAAAAAAA

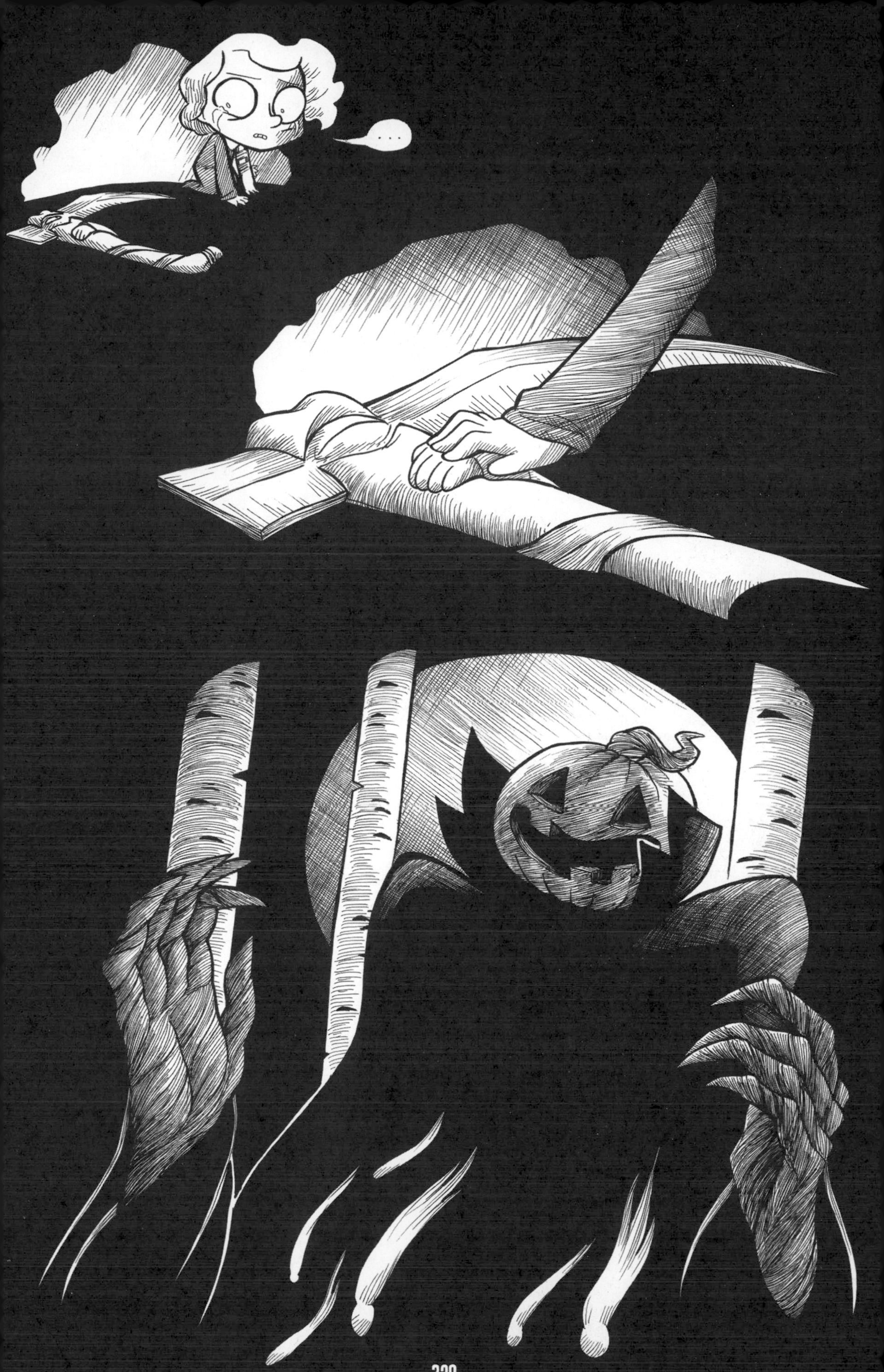
...

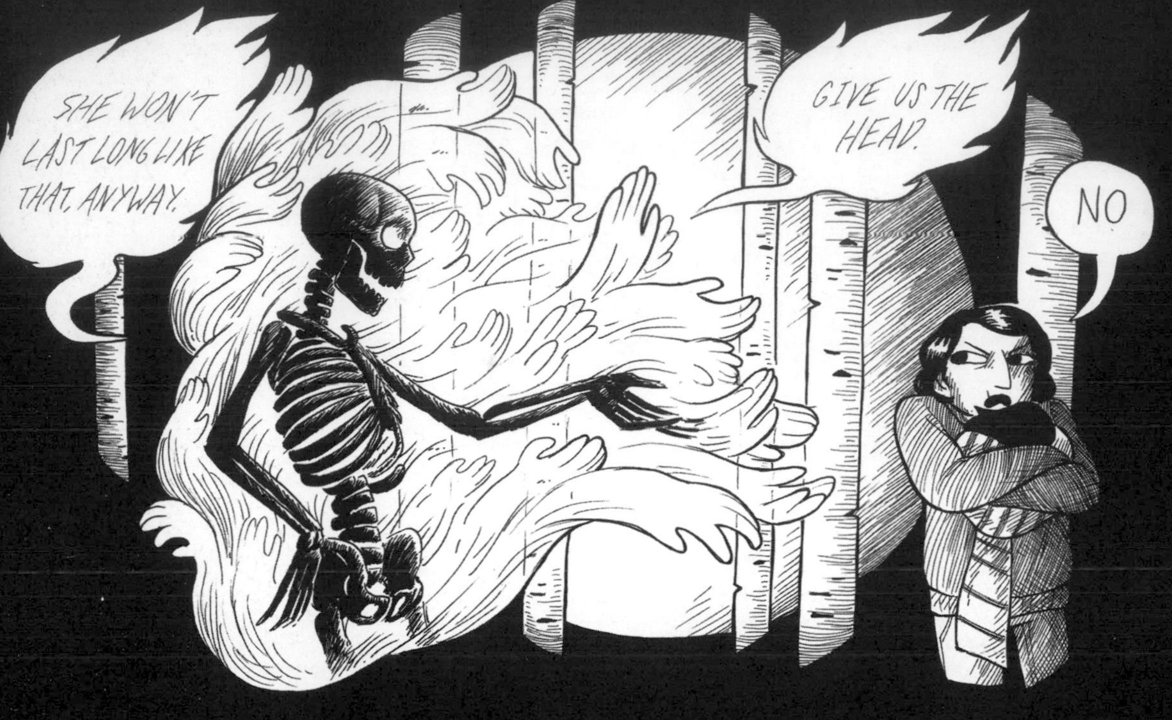
SHE WON'T LAST LONG LIKE THAT, ANYWAY.
GIVE US THE HEAD.
NO

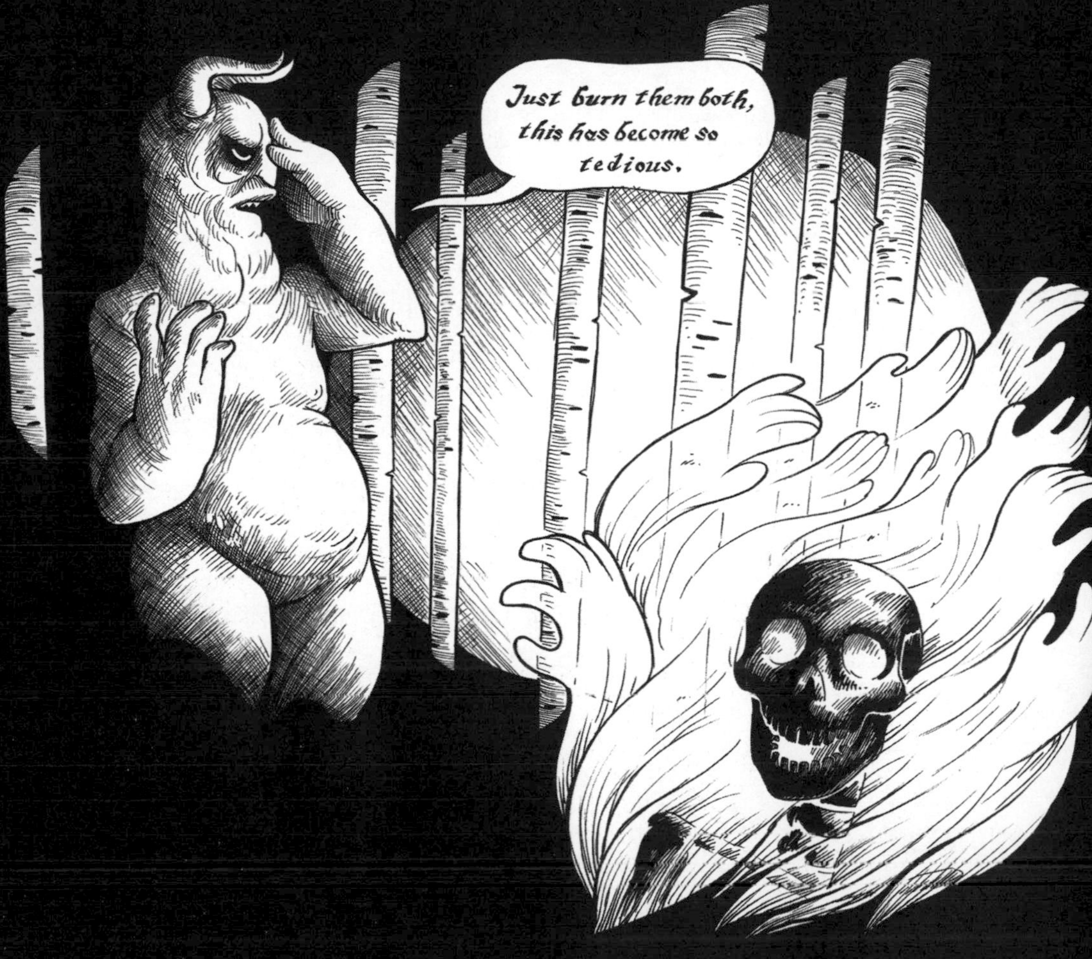
Just burn them both, this has become so tedious.

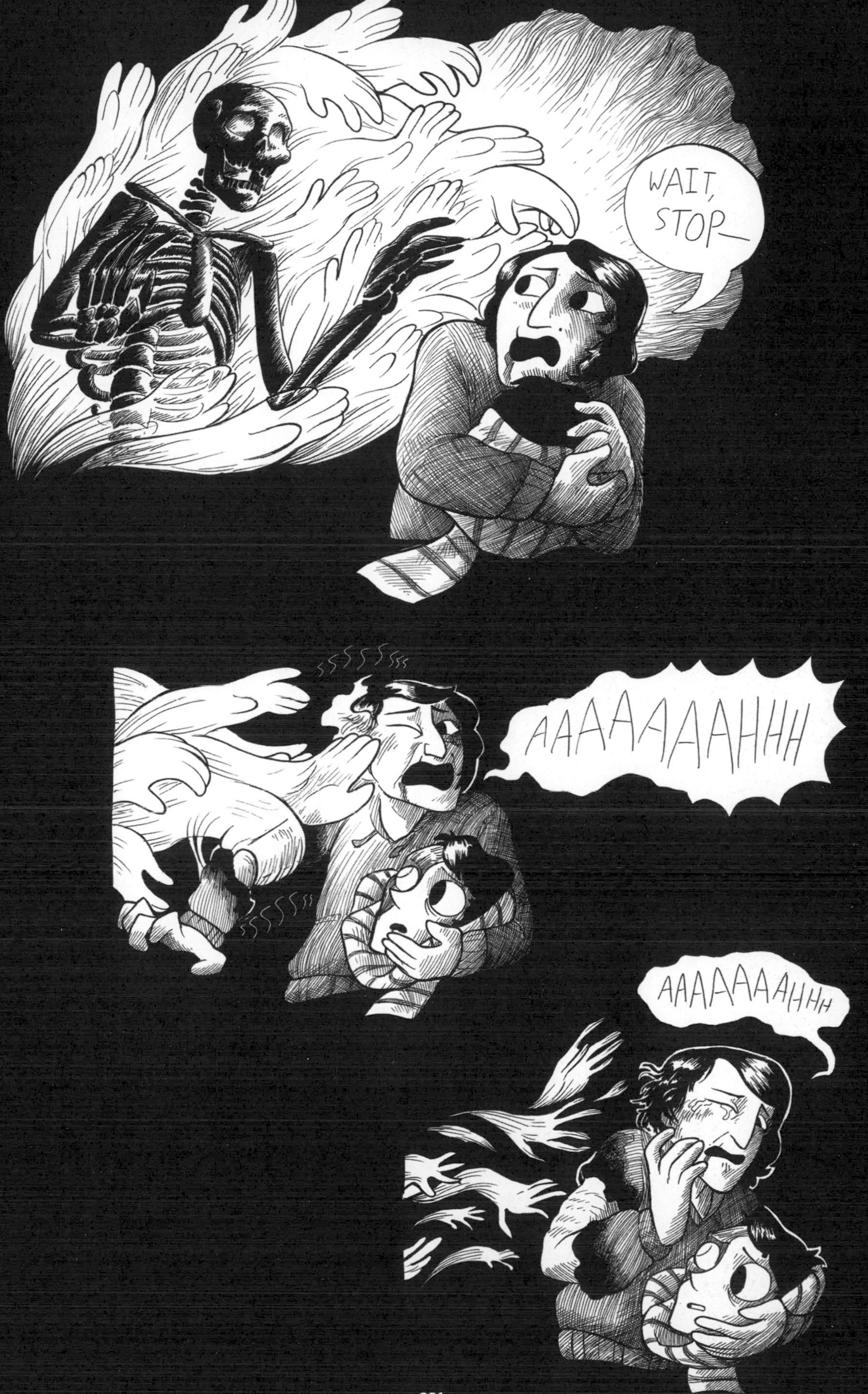
WAIT, STOP—
AAAAAAAAHHH
AAAAAAAHHH

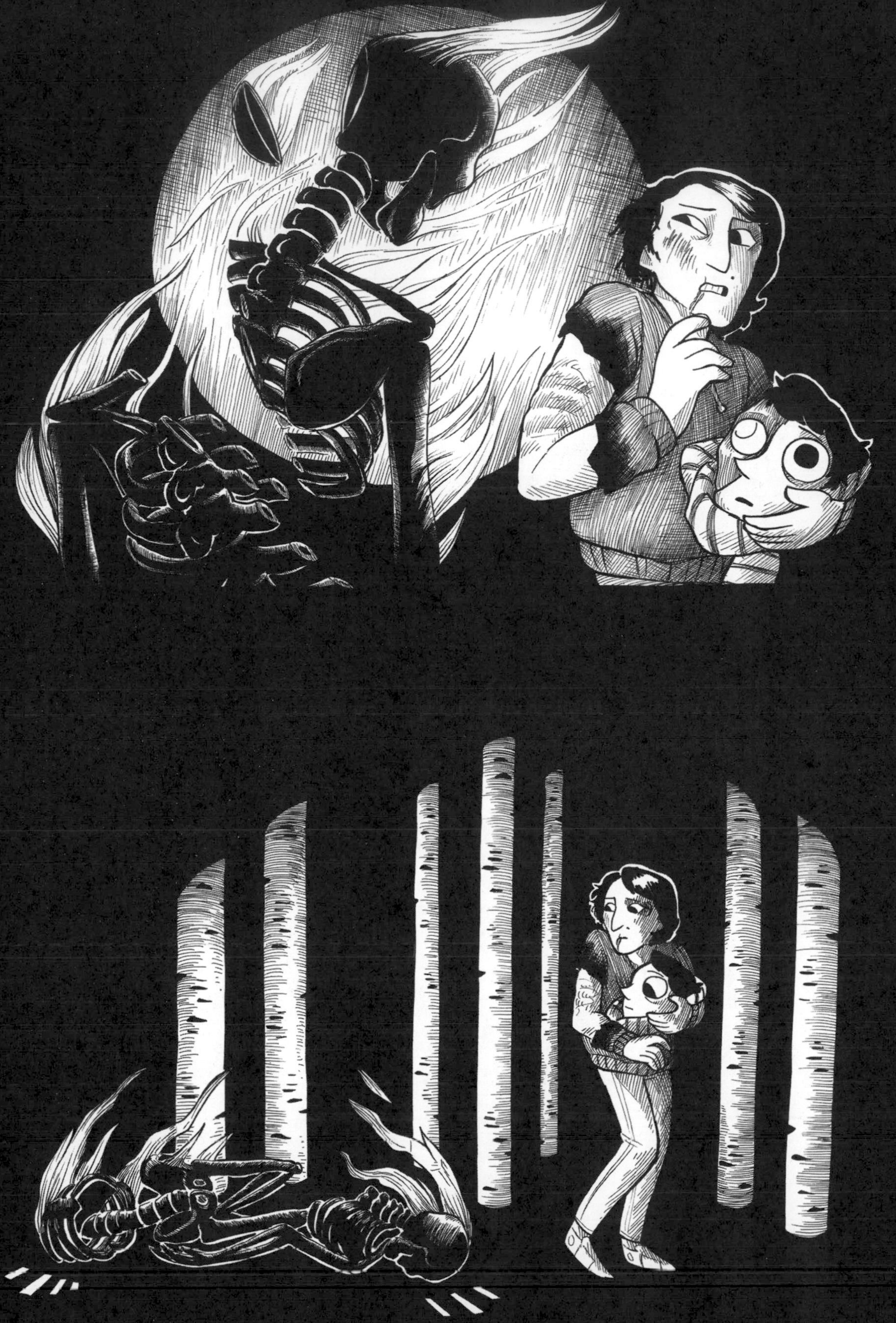

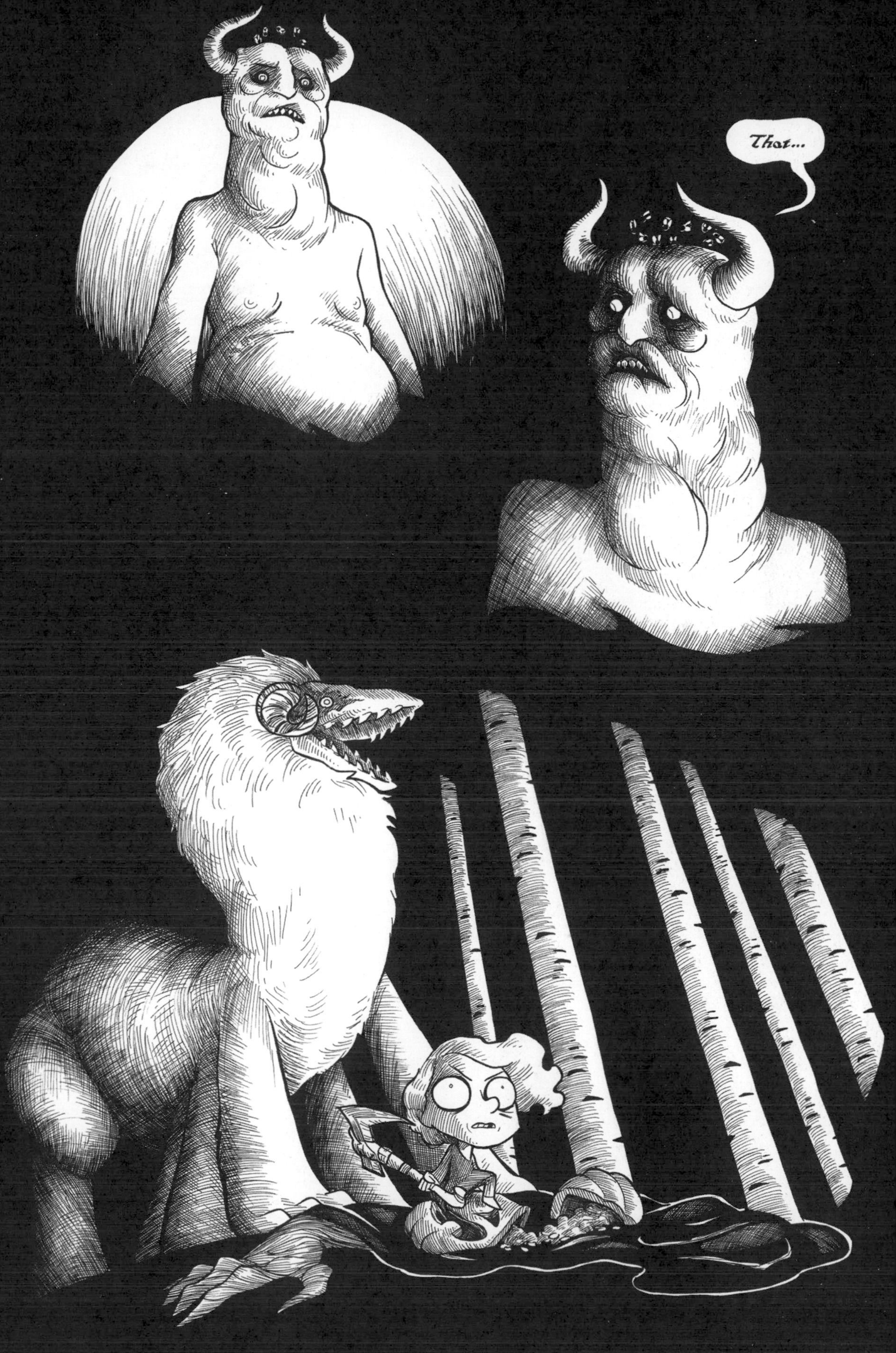
That...

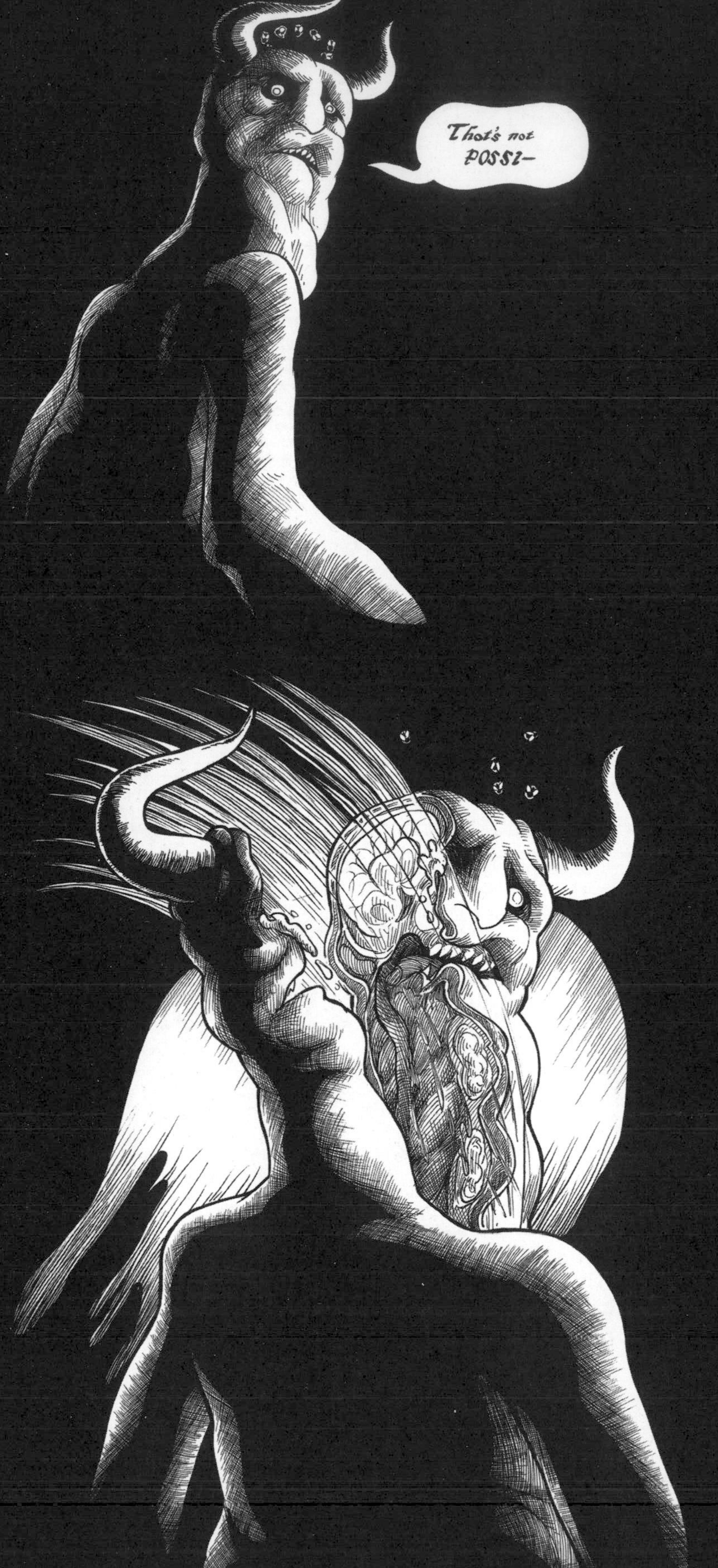
That's not POSSI-

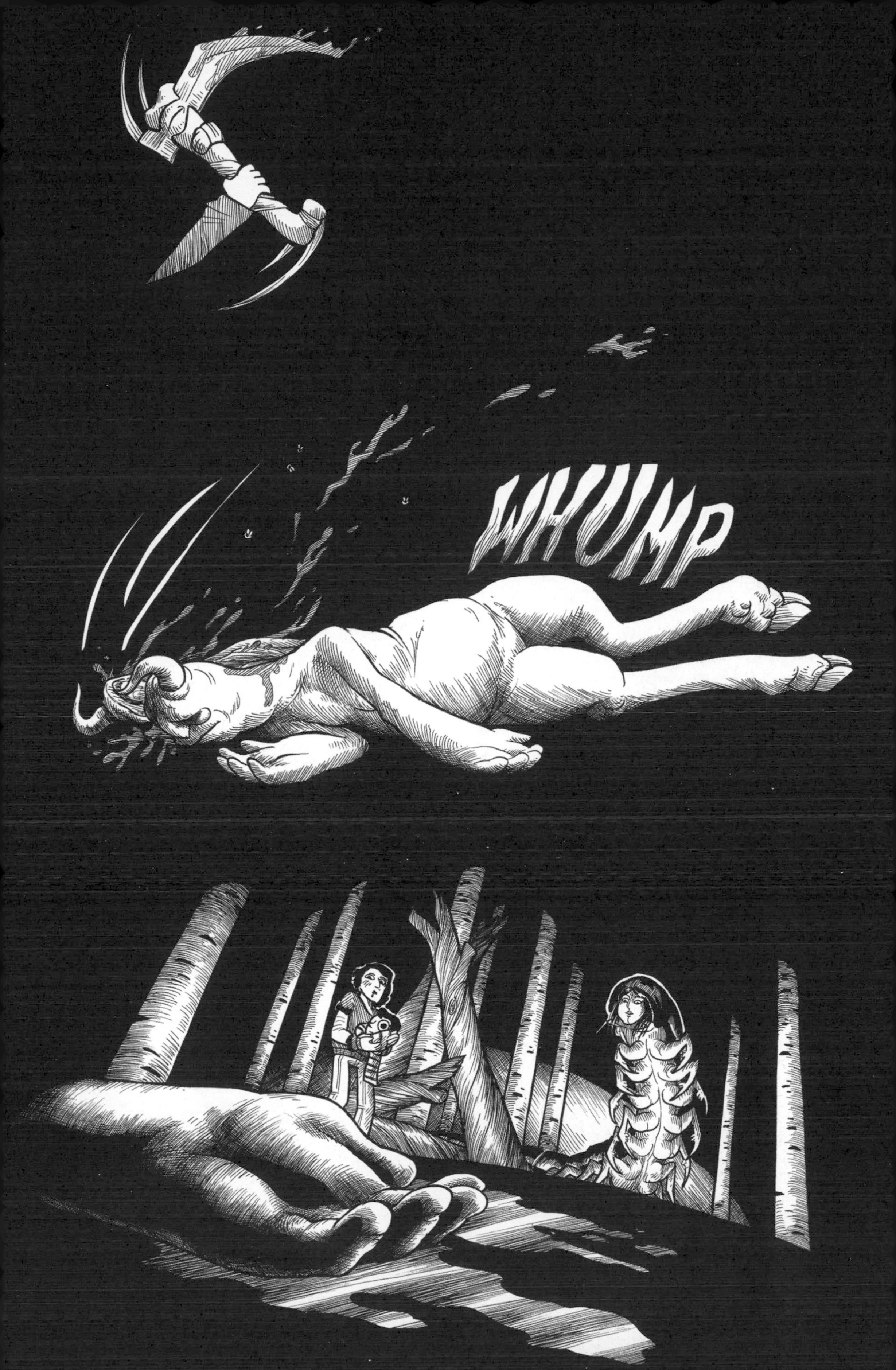
WHUMP

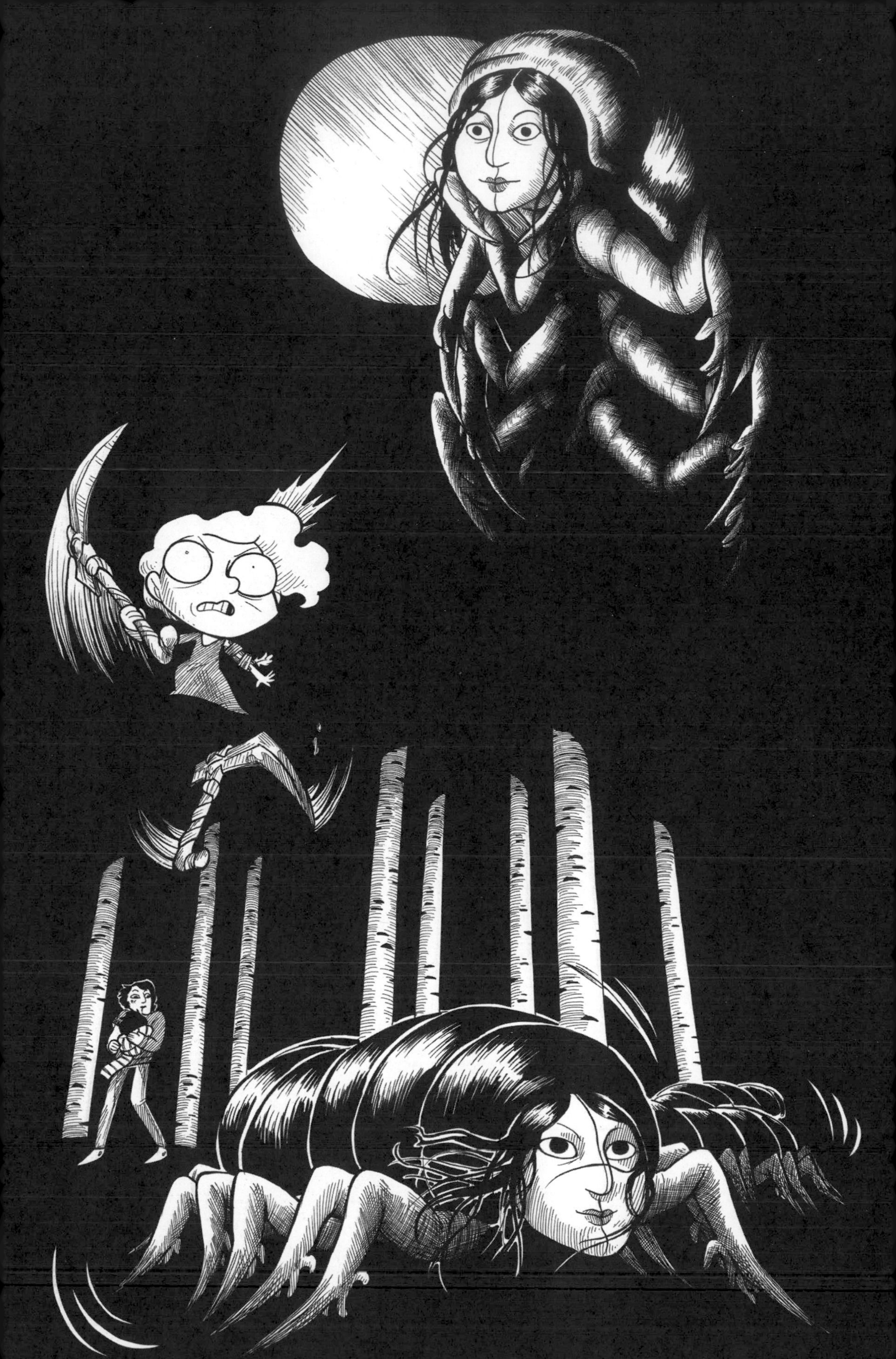

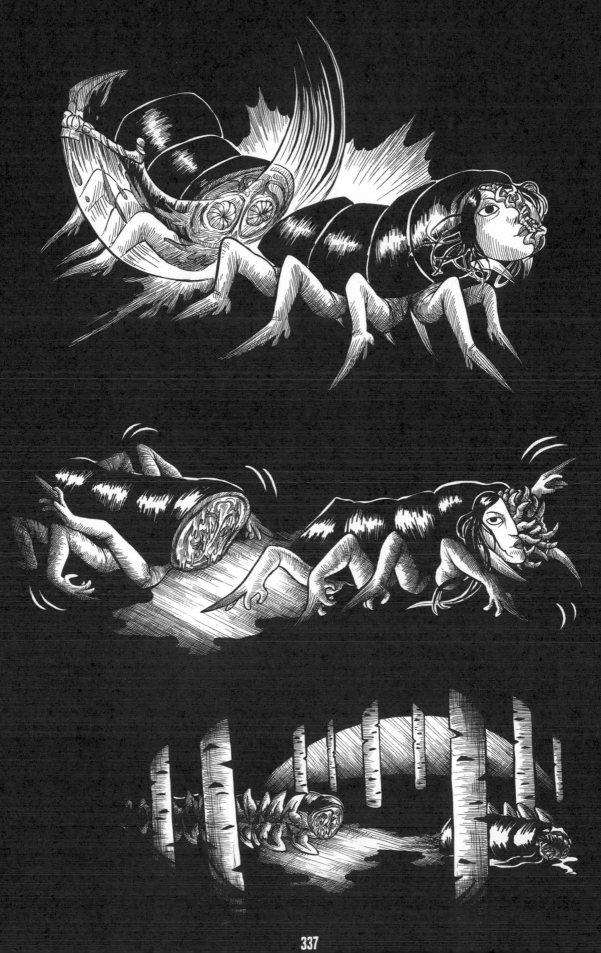

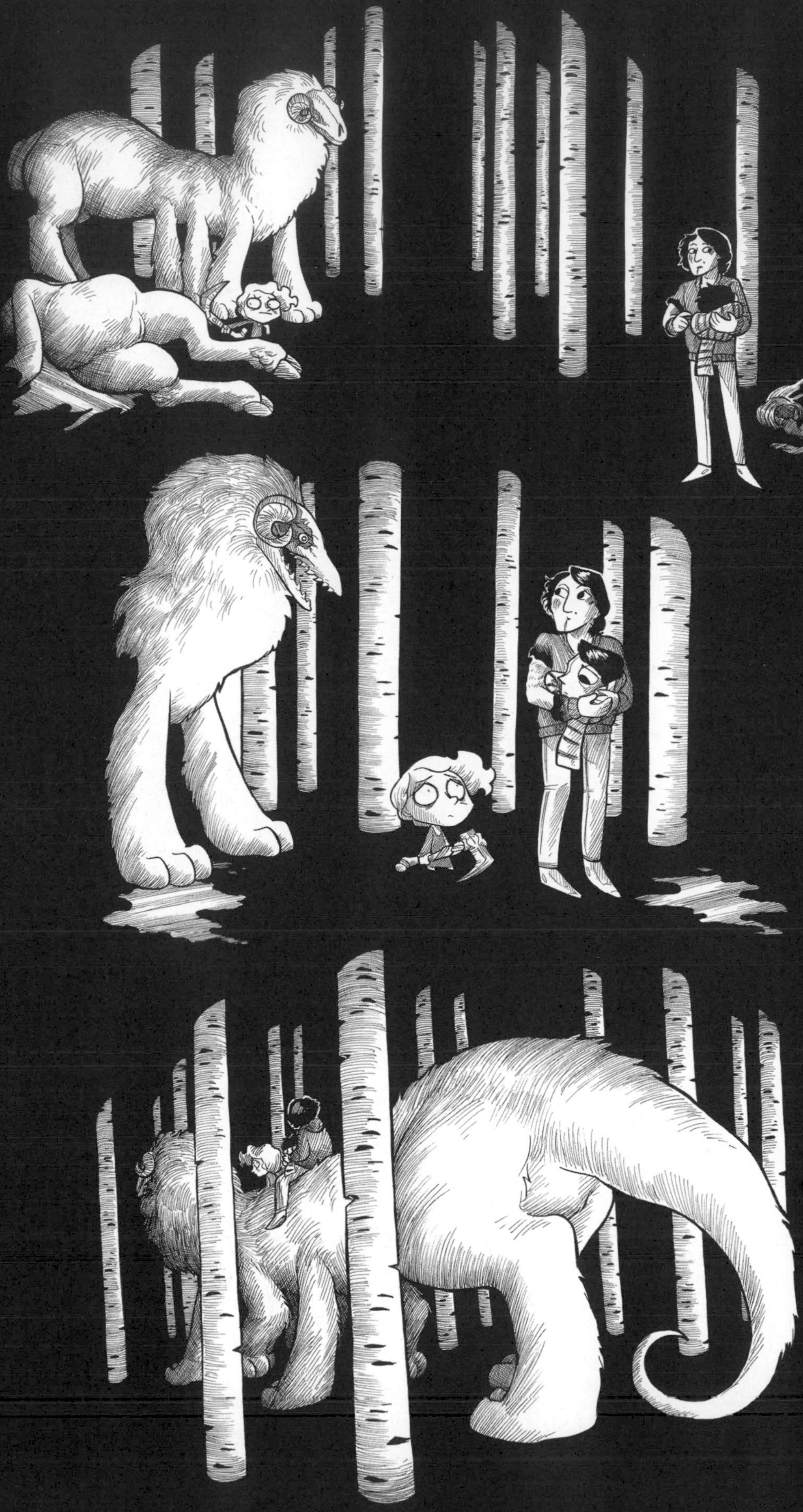

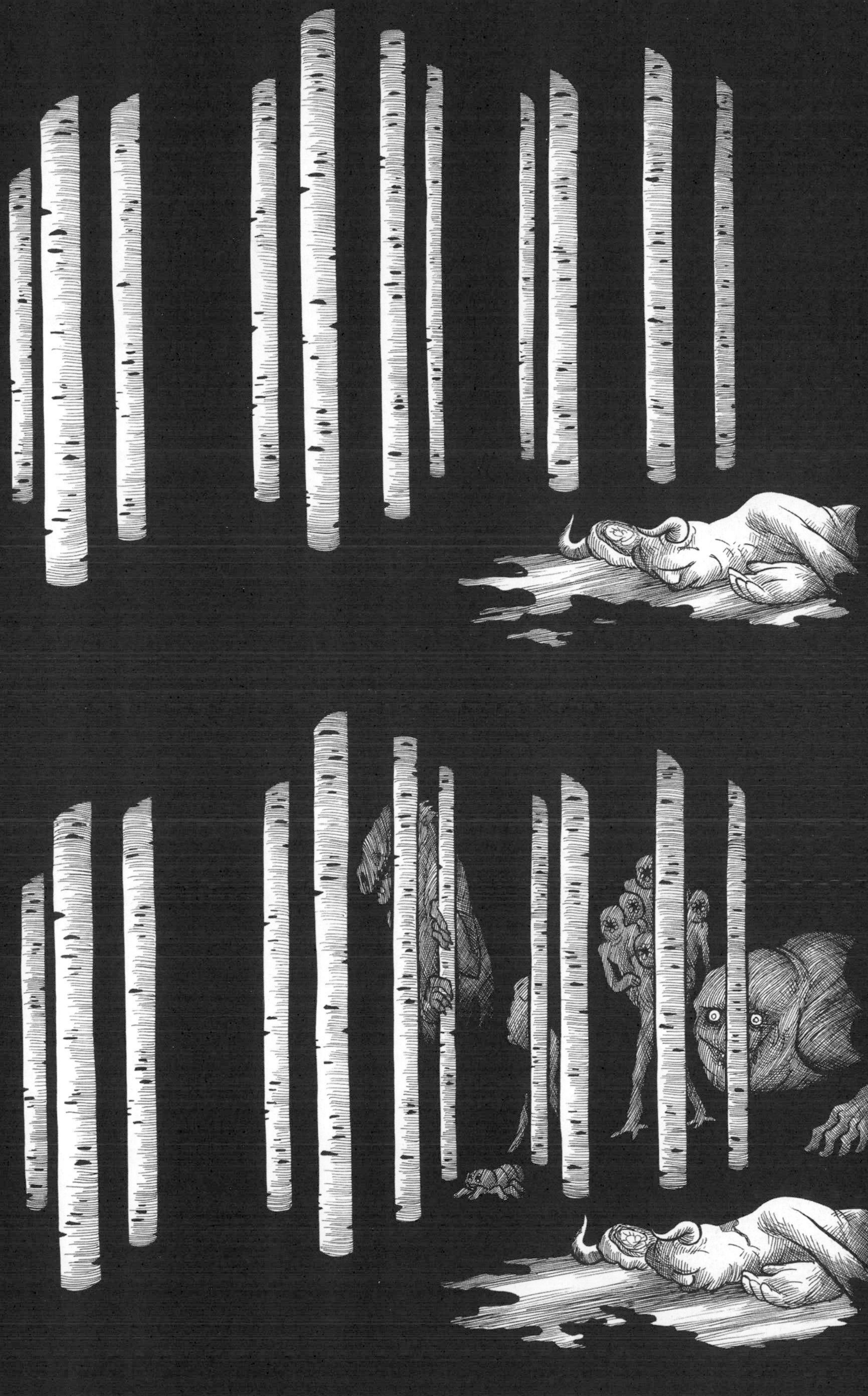

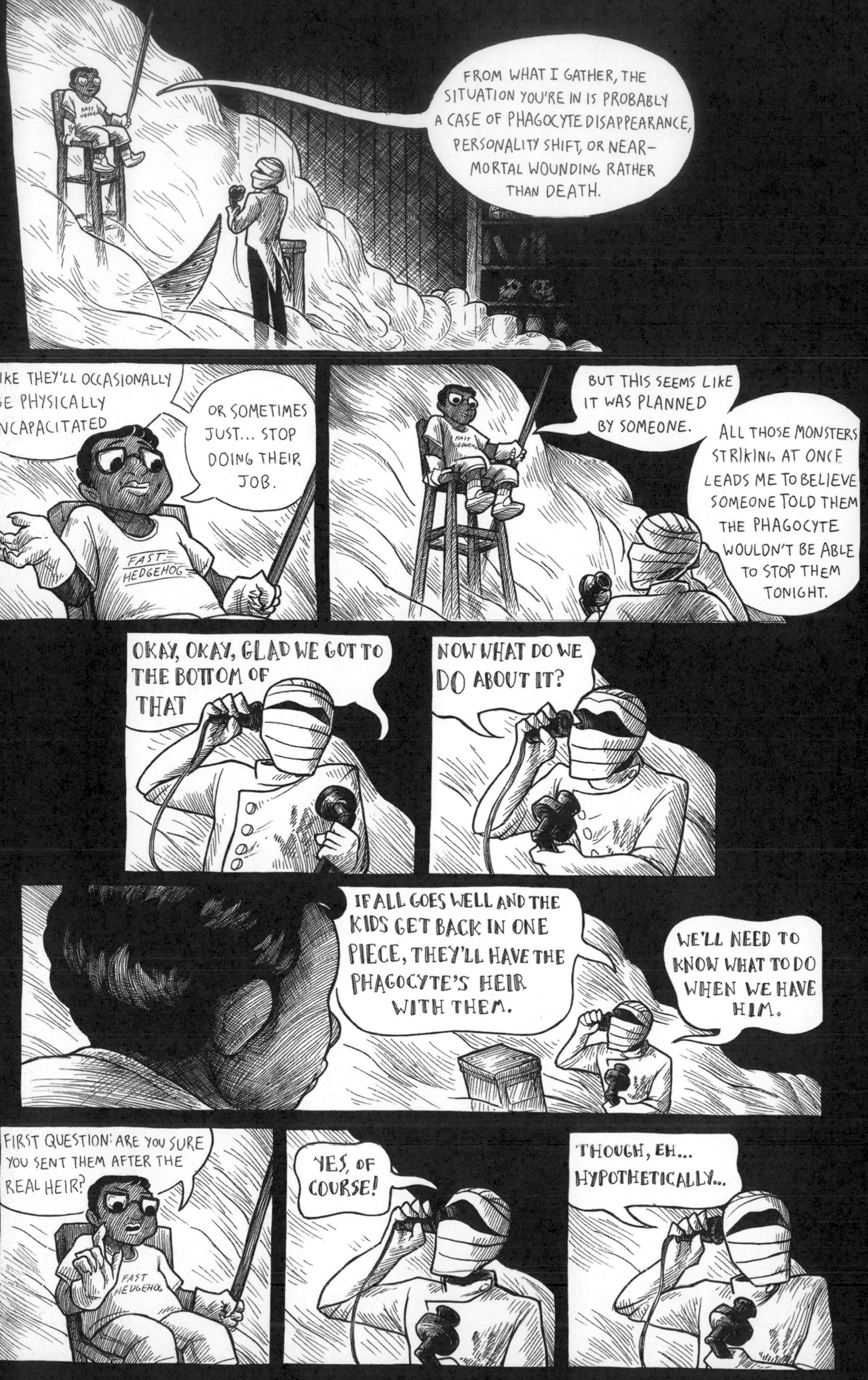
FROM WHAT I GATHER, THE SITUATION YOU'RE IN IS PROBABLY A CASE OF PHAGOCYTE DISAPPEARANCE, PERSONALITY SHIFT, OR NEAR-MORTAL WOUNDING RATHER THAN DEATH.
LIKE THEY'LL OCCASIONALLY BE PHYSICALLY INCAPACITATED
OR SOMETIMES JUST... STOP DOING THEIR JOB.
FAST HEDGEHOG
BUT THIS SEEMS LIKE IT WAS PLANNED BY SOMEONE.
ALL THOSE MONSTERS STRIKING AT ONCE LEADS ME TO BELIEVE SOMEONE TOLD THEM THE PHAGOCYTE WOULDN'T BE ABLE TO STOP THEM TONIGHT.
OKAY, OKAY, GLAD WE GOT TO THE BOTTOM OF THAT
NOW WHAT DO WE DO ABOUT IT?
IF ALL GOES WELL AND THE KIDS GET BACK IN ONE PIECE, THEY'LL HAVE THE PHAGOCYTE'S HEIR WITH THEM.
WE'LL NEED TO KNOW WHAT TO DO WHEN WE HAVE HIM.
FIRST QUESTION: ARE YOU SURE YOU SENT THEM AFTER THE REAL HEIR?
FAST HEDGEHOG
YES, OF COURSE!
THOUGH, EH... HYPOTHETICALLY...

Panel 1: HOW WOULD WE HAVE NOT... GONE AFTER THE REAL ONE...?

Panel 2: BY GOING AFTER, PERHAPS—

A SIBLING OF THEIRS?

Panel 3: ONLY ONE KID INHERITS THE PHAGOCYTE'S QUALITIES

SUCH AS BEING MONSTERLESS AND BEING ABLE TO HANDLE LARGE MAGIC LOADS, WHICH KEEPS THEM FROM DISSOLVING FROM THE INSIDE OUT IF THEY BECOME THE PHAGOCYTE.

Panel 4: THAT'S A LOT OF MAGIC FOR PEOPLE TO DEAL WITH, IT'D KILL MOST HUMANS.

Panel 5: I WAS PRETTY SURE HE ONLY HAD THE ONE KID....

Panel 6: WELL.

SORRY. NO.

Panel 7: LET'S HOPE YOU GOT THE RIGHT ONE, I GUESS!!

Panel 8: THOUGH TO BE HONEST, DUDE.... AND I HATE TO SAY THIS....

Panel 9: IT'S NOT GONNA DO YOU MUCH GOOD, ANYWAY.

Panel 10: THERE CAN ONLY BE ONE PHAGOCYTE AT A TIME—

THE CURRENT PHAGOCYTE IS STILL ALIVE OUT THERE SOMEWHERE.

SO YOU'D HAVE TO FIND THE CURRENT PHAGOCYTE AND FINISH EM OFF, WHICH IS PROBABLY EXTREMELY DIFFICULT AND DANGEROUS, AND THERE'S LIKE THIS WHOLE THING ABOUT HOW NEITHER MONSTER NOR MAN CAN KILL THEM, IT'S A HUGE HASSLE.

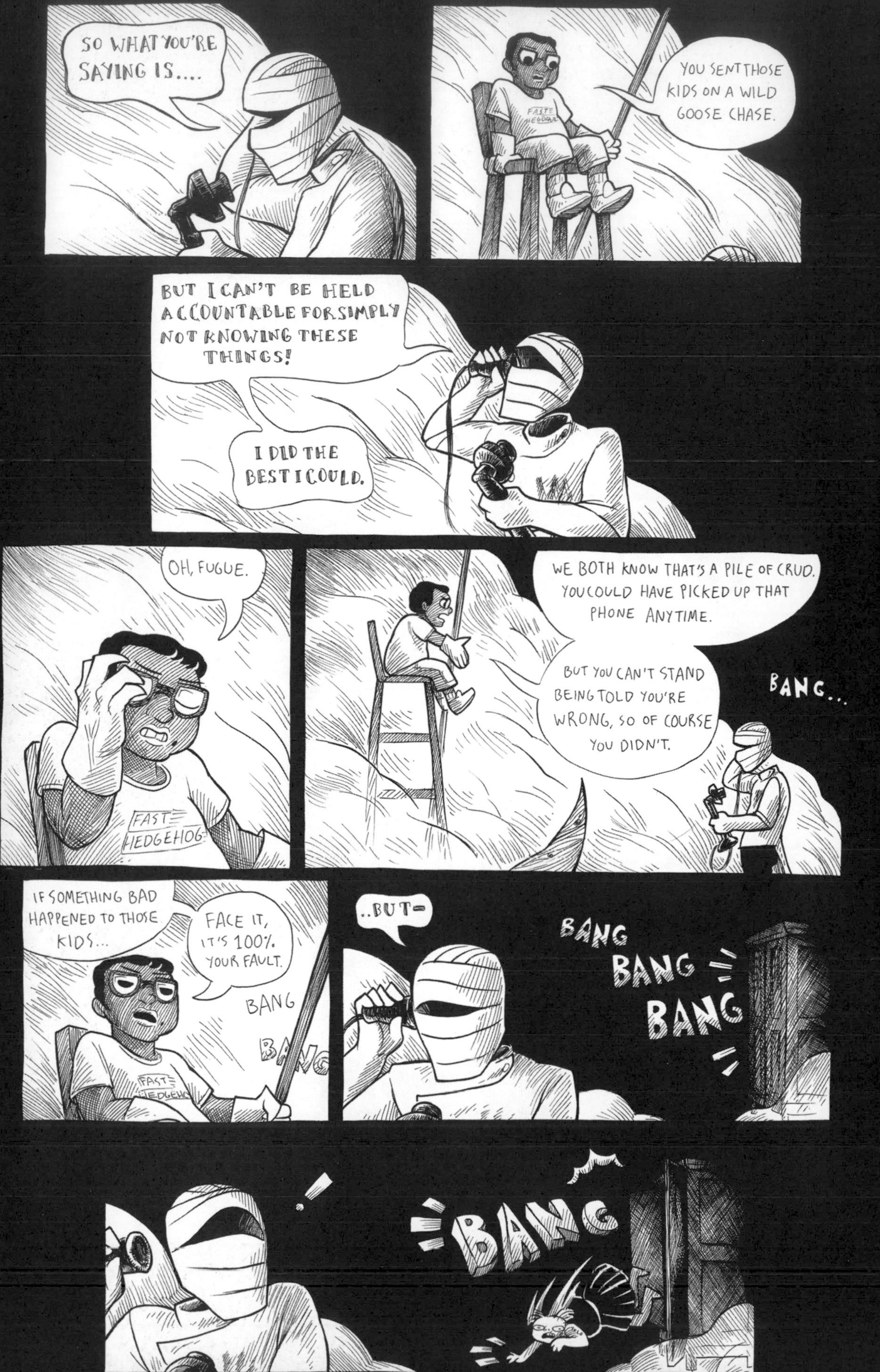

SO WHAT YOU'RE SAYING IS....
YOU SENT THOSE KIDS ON A WILD GOOSE CHASE.
FAST HEDGEHOG
BUT I CAN'T BE HELD ACCOUNTABLE FOR SIMPLY NOT KNOWING THESE THINGS!
I DID THE BEST I COULD.
OH, FUGUE.
FAST HEDGEHOG
WE BOTH KNOW THAT'S A PILE OF CRUD. YOU COULD HAVE PICKED UP THAT PHONE ANYTIME.
BUT YOU CAN'T STAND BEING TOLD YOU'RE WRONG, SO OF COURSE YOU DIDN'T.
BANG...
IF SOMETHING BAD HAPPENED TO THOSE KIDS...
FACE IT, IT'S 100%. YOUR FAULT.
BANG
BANG
FAST HEDGEHO
..BUT–
BANG
BANG
BANG
!
BANG

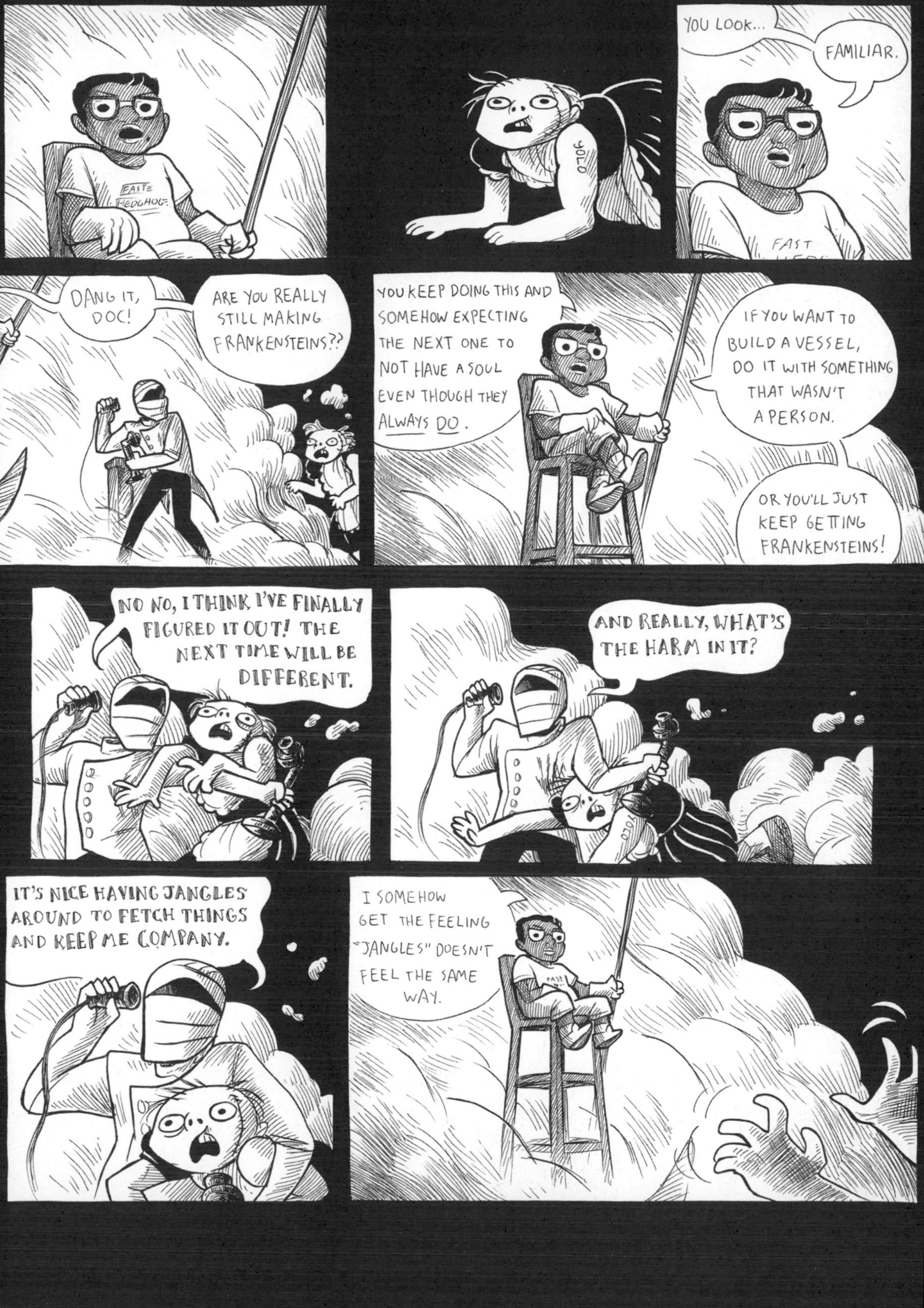
FAST HEDGHOG
YOLO
YOU LOOK...
FAMILIAR.
DANG IT, DOC!
ARE YOU REALLY STILL MAKING FRANKENSTEINS??
YOU KEEP DOING THIS AND SOMEHOW EXPECTING THE NEXT ONE TO NOT HAVE A SOUL EVEN THOUGH THEY ALWAYS DO.
IF YOU WANT TO BUILD A VESSEL, DO IT WITH SOMETHING THAT WASN'T A PERSON.
OR YOU'LL JUST KEEP GETTING FRANKENSTEINS!
NO NO, I THINK I'VE FINALLY FIGURED IT OUT! THE NEXT TIME WILL BE DIFFERENT.
AND REALLY, WHAT'S THE HARM IN IT?
IT'S NICE HAVING JANGLES AROUND TO FETCH THINGS AND KEEP ME COMPANY.
I SOMEHOW GET THE FEELING "JANGLES" DOESN'T FEEL THE SAME WAY.

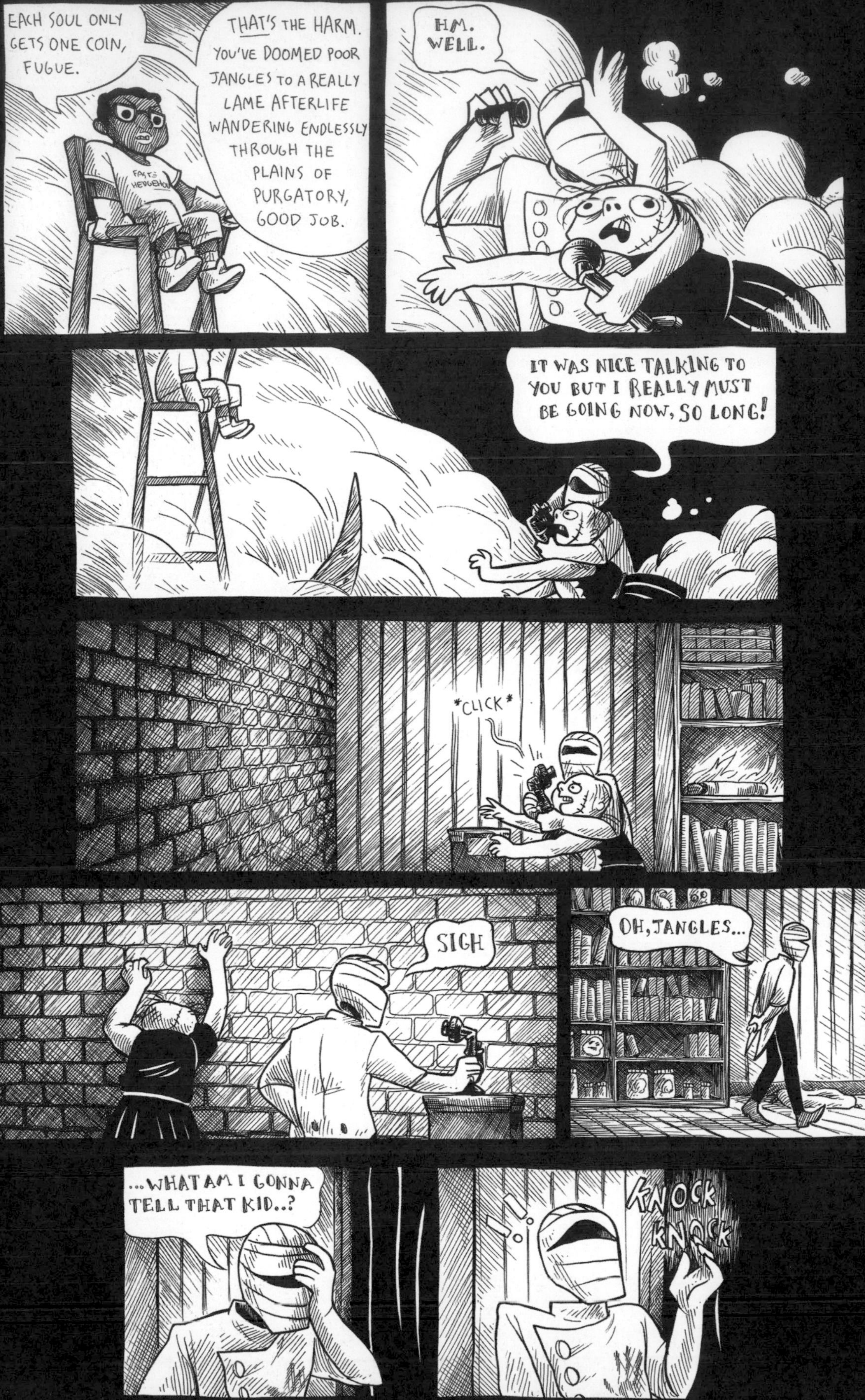
EACH SOUL ONLY GETS ONE COIN, FUGUE.
THAT'S THE HARM. YOU'VE DOOMED POOR JANGLES TO A REALLY LAME AFTERLIFE WANDERING ENDLESSLY THROUGH THE PLAINS OF PURGATORY, GOOD JOB.
HM. WELL.
IT WAS NICE TALKING TO YOU BUT I REALLY MUST BE GOING NOW, SO LONG!
CLICK
SIGH
OH, JANGLES...
...WHAT AM I GONNA TELL THAT KID..?
KNOCK KNOCK

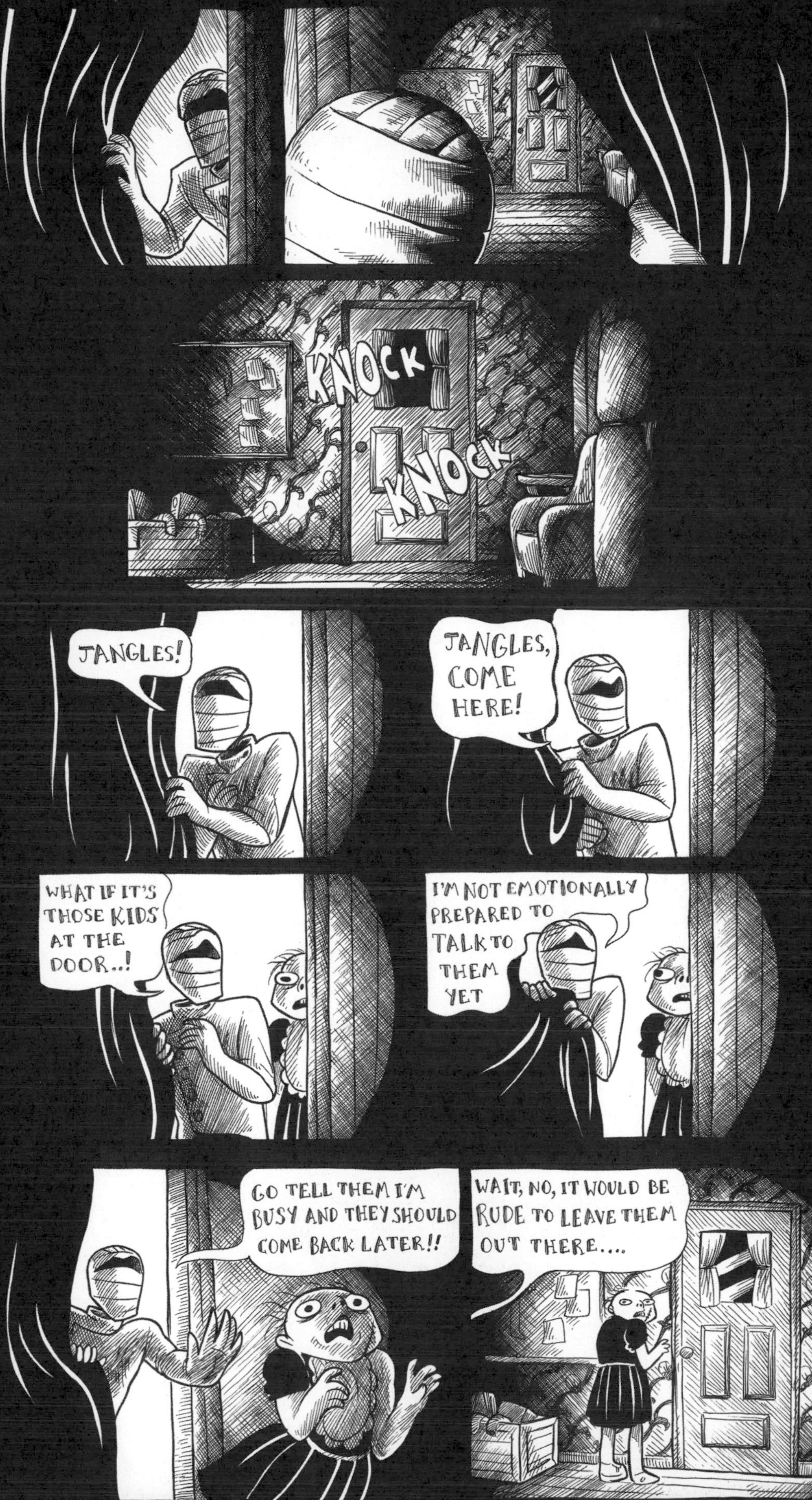
KNOCK
KNOCK
JANGLES!
JANGLES, COME HERE!
WHAT IF IT'S THOSE KIDS AT THE DOOR...!
I'M NOT EMOTIONALLY PREPARED TO TALK TO THEM YET
GO TELL THEM I'M BUSY AND THEY SHOULD COME BACK LATER!!
WAIT, NO, IT WOULD BE RUDE TO LEAVE THEM OUT THERE....

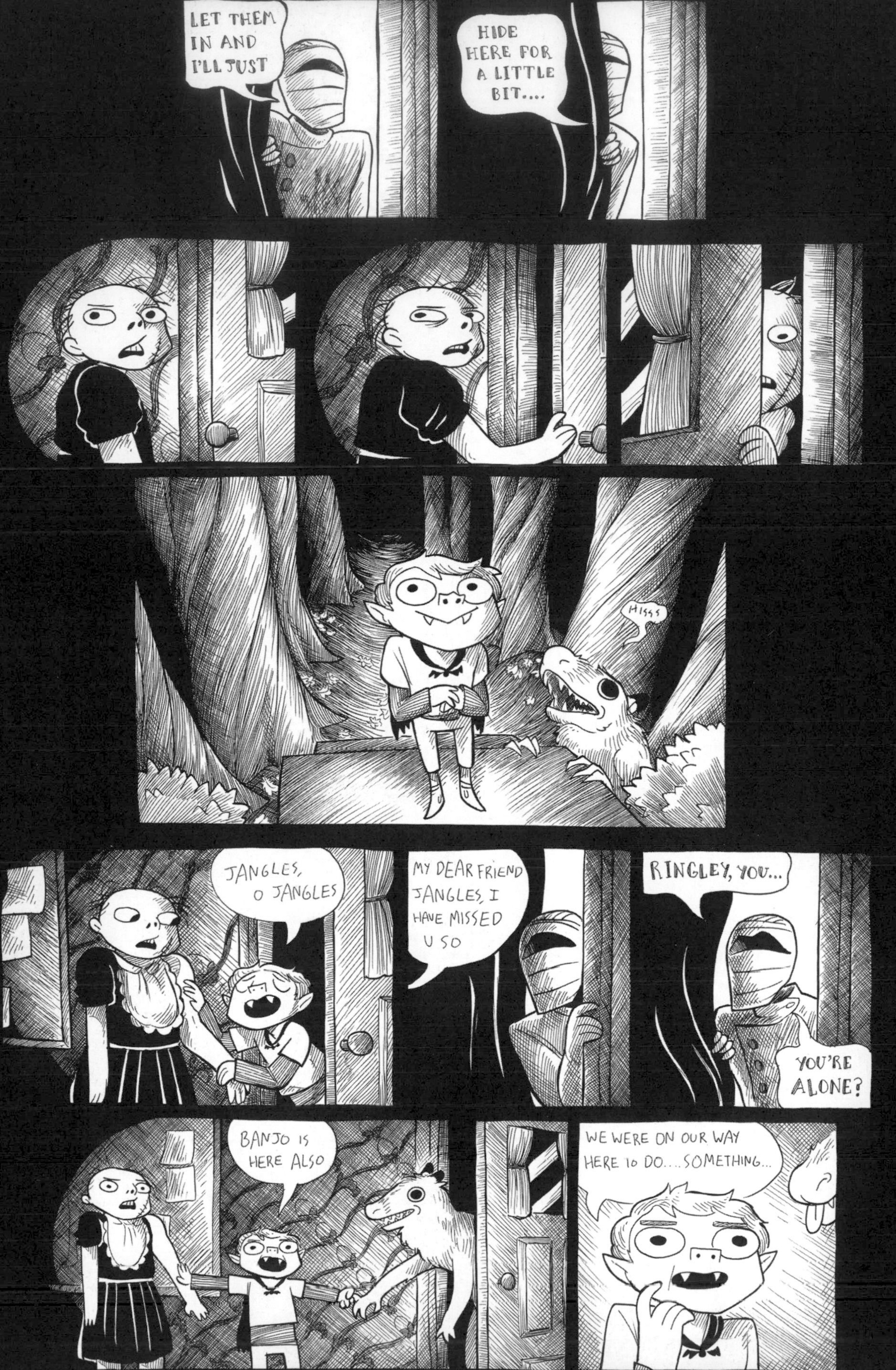
LET THEM IN AND I'LL JUST
HIDE HERE FOR A LITTLE BIT....
HISSS
JANGLES, O JANGLES
MY DEAR FRIEND JANGLES, I HAVE MISSED U SO
RINGLEY, YOU...
YOU'RE ALONE?
BANJO IS HERE ALSO
WE WERE ON OUR WAY HERE TO DO.... SOMETHING...

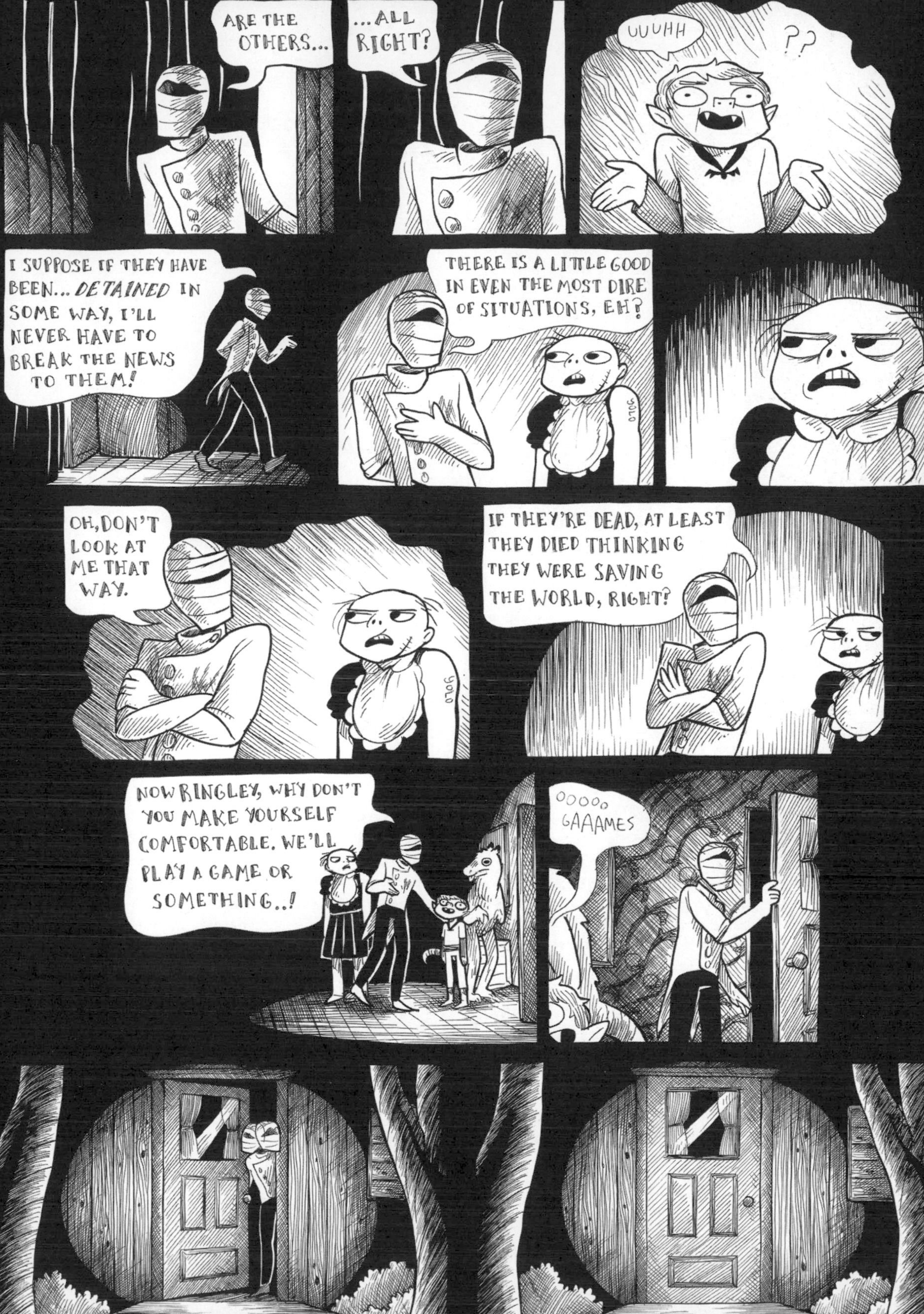
ARE THE OTHERS...
...ALL RIGHT?
UUUHH
??
I SUPPOSE IF THEY HAVE BEEN... *DETAINED* IN SOME WAY, I'LL NEVER HAVE TO BREAK THE NEWS TO THEM!
THERE IS A LITTLE GOOD IN EVEN THE MOST DIRE OF SITUATIONS, EH?
YOLO
OH, DON'T LOOK AT ME THAT WAY.
YOLO
IF THEY'RE DEAD, AT LEAST THEY DIED THINKING THEY WERE SAVING THE WORLD, RIGHT?
NOW RINGLEY, WHY DON'T YOU MAKE YOURSELF COMFORTABLE. WE'LL PLAY A GAME OR SOMETHING..!
OOOOO GAAAMES

CHAPTER 6

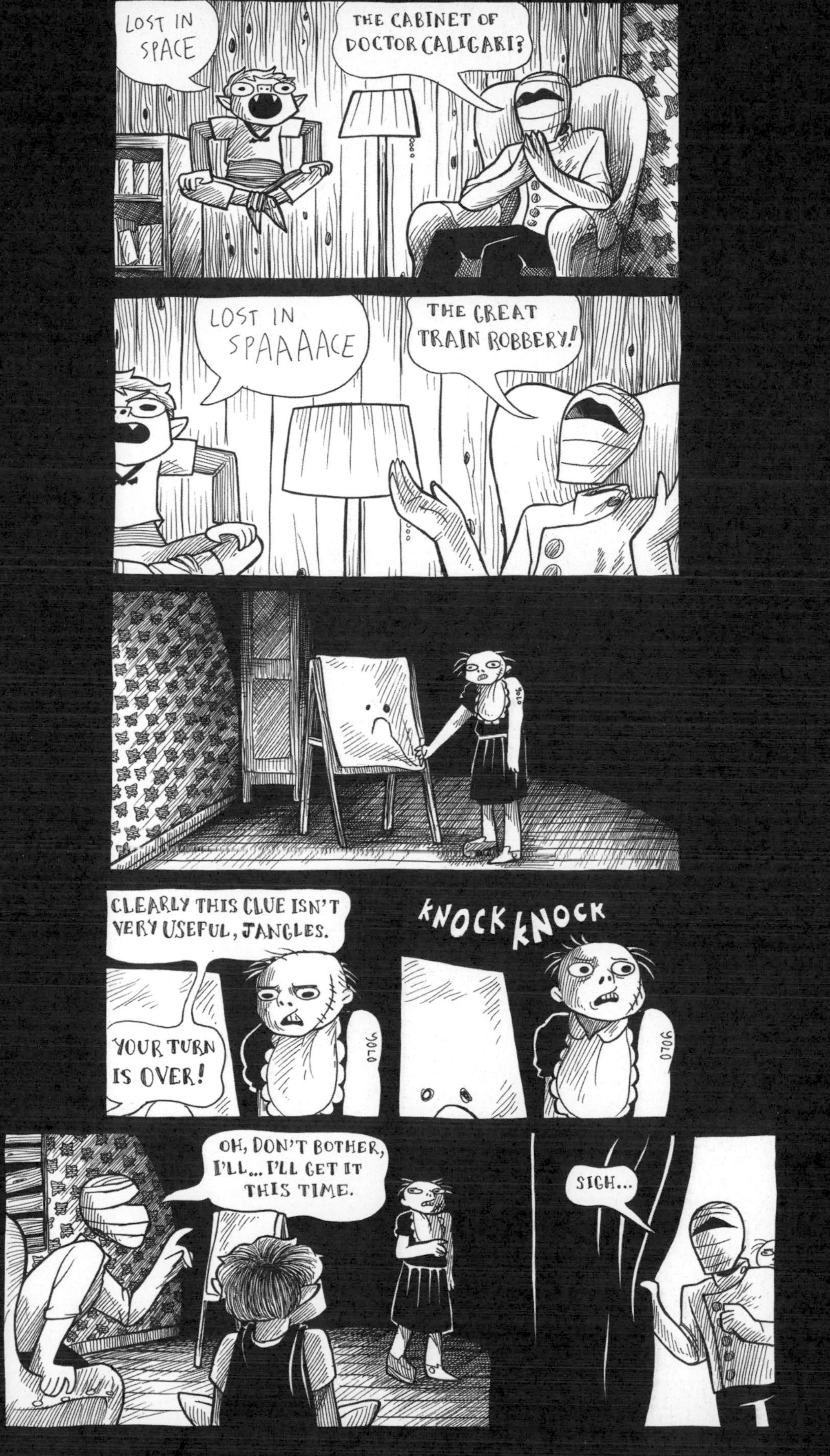
LOST IN SPACE
THE CABINET OF DOCTOR CALIGARI?
LOST IN SPAAAACE
THE GREAT TRAIN ROBBERY!
CLEARLY THIS CLUE ISN'T VERY USEFUL, JANGLES.
YOUR TURN IS OVER!
KNOCK KNOCK
OH, DON'T BOTHER, I'LL... I'LL GET IT THIS TIME.
SIGH...

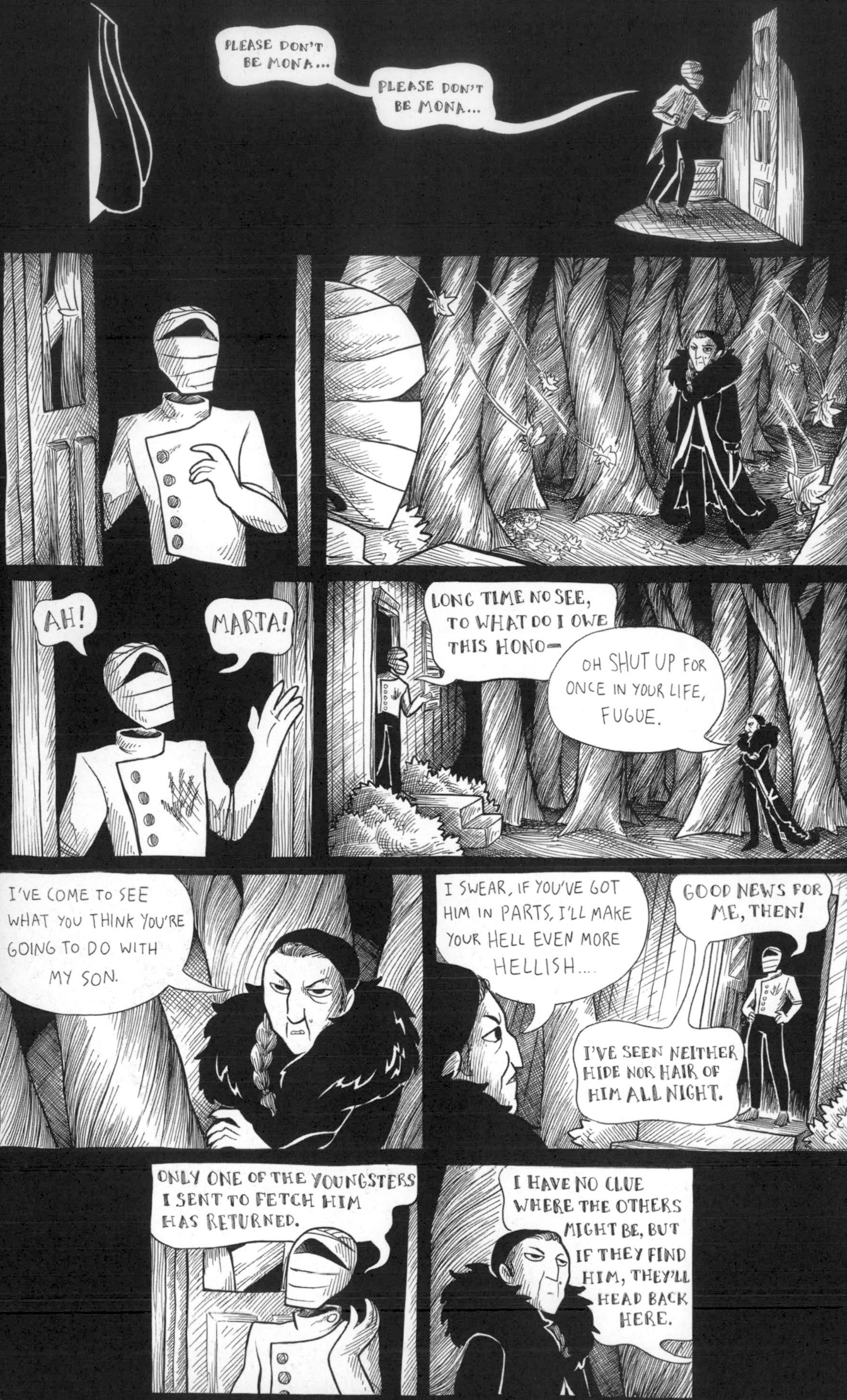
PLEASE DON'T BE MONA...
PLEASE DON'T BE MONA...
AH!
MARTA!
LONG TIME NO SEE, TO WHAT DO I OWE THIS HONO—
OH SHUT UP FOR ONCE IN YOUR LIFE, FUGUE.
I'VE COME TO SEE WHAT YOU THINK YOU'RE GOING TO DO WITH MY SON.
I SWEAR, IF YOU'VE GOT HIM IN PARTS, I'LL MAKE YOUR HELL EVEN MORE HELLISH....
GOOD NEWS FOR ME, THEN!
I'VE SEEN NEITHER HIDE NOR HAIR OF HIM ALL NIGHT.
ONLY ONE OF THE YOUNGSTERS I SENT TO FETCH HIM HAS RETURNED.
I HAVE NO CLUE WHERE THE OTHERS MIGHT BE, BUT IF THEY FIND HIM, THEY'LL HEAD BACK HERE.

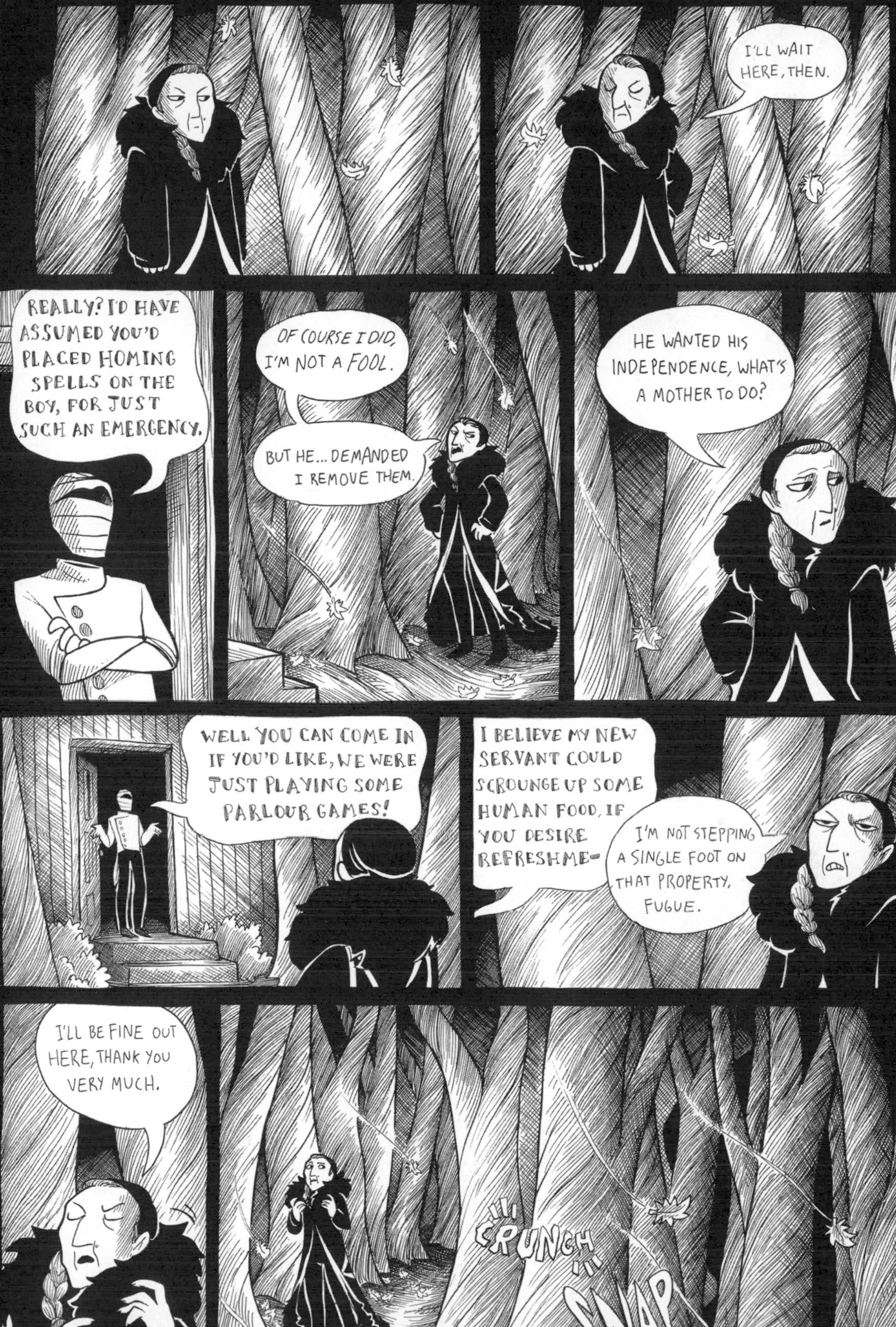
I'LL WAIT HERE, THEN.
REALLY? I'D HAVE ASSUMED YOU'D PLACED HOMING SPELLS ON THE BOY, FOR JUST SUCH AN EMERGENCY.
OF COURSE I DID, I'M NOT A FOOL.
BUT HE... DEMANDED I REMOVE THEM.
HE WANTED HIS INDEPENDENCE, WHAT'S A MOTHER TO DO?
WELL YOU CAN COME IN IF YOU'D LIKE, WE WERE JUST PLAYING SOME PARLOUR GAMES!
I BELIEVE MY NEW SERVANT COULD SCROUNGE UP SOME HUMAN FOOD, IF YOU DESIRE REFRESHME-
I'M NOT STEPPING A SINGLE FOOT ON THAT PROPERTY, FUGUE.
I'LL BE FINE OUT HERE, THANK YOU VERY MUCH.
CRUNCH
SNAP

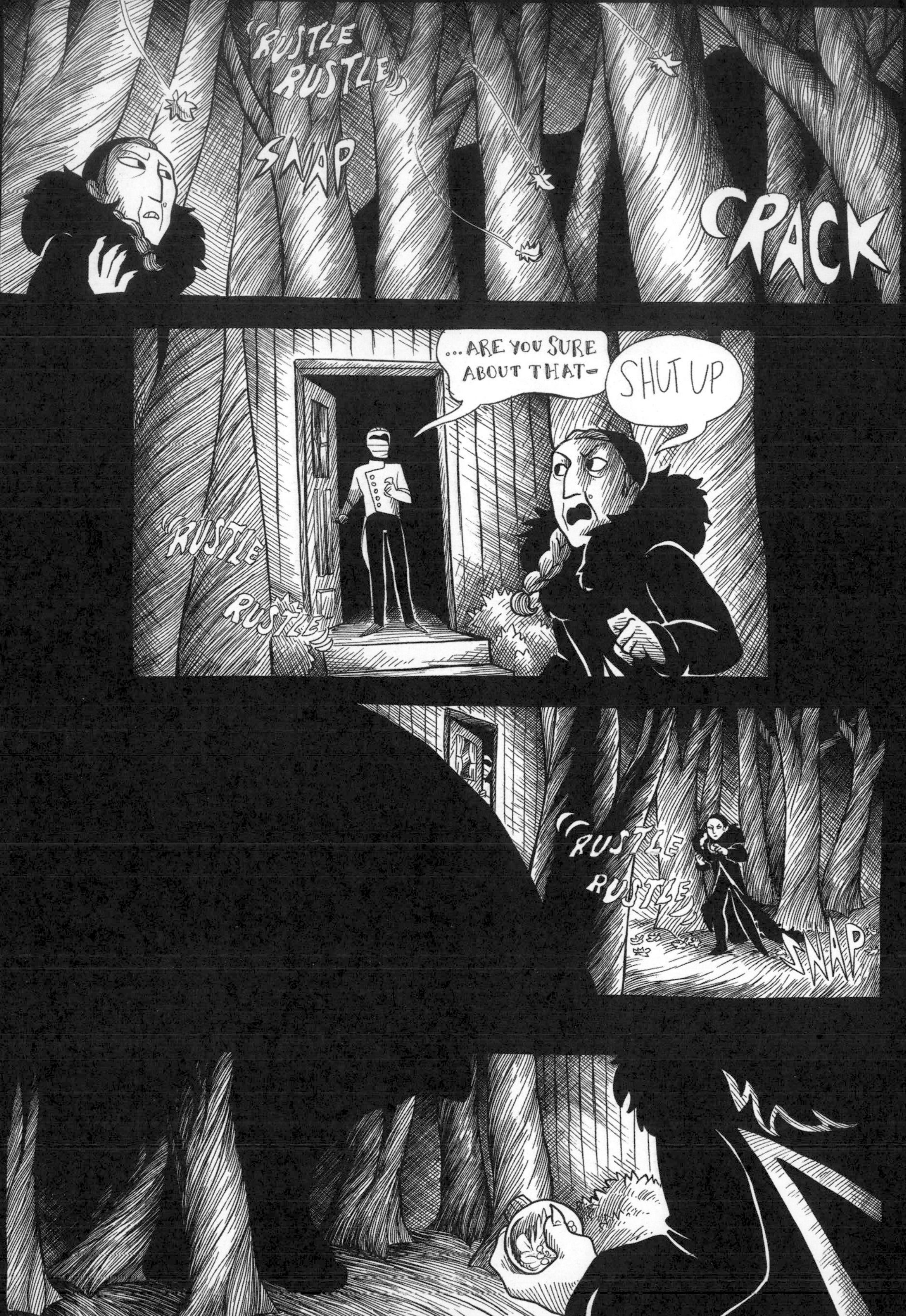
RUSTLE
RUSTLE
SNAP
CRACK
...ARE YOU SURE ABOUT THAT-
SHUT UP
RUSTLE
RUSTLE
RUSTLE
RUSTLE
SNAP

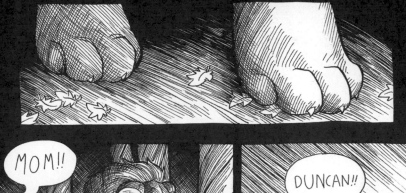

MOM!!

DUNCAN!!

I WAS WORRIED THEY'D MADE MINCEMEAT OUT OF YOU!

BET YOU WISH YOU STILL HAD THAT HOMING SPELL ON YOU, HHM?

AWW, MOM...

I'M GLAD TO SEE YOU.

WHAT IS... THIS?

OH, THIS IS MY FRIEND, SHIRLEY!

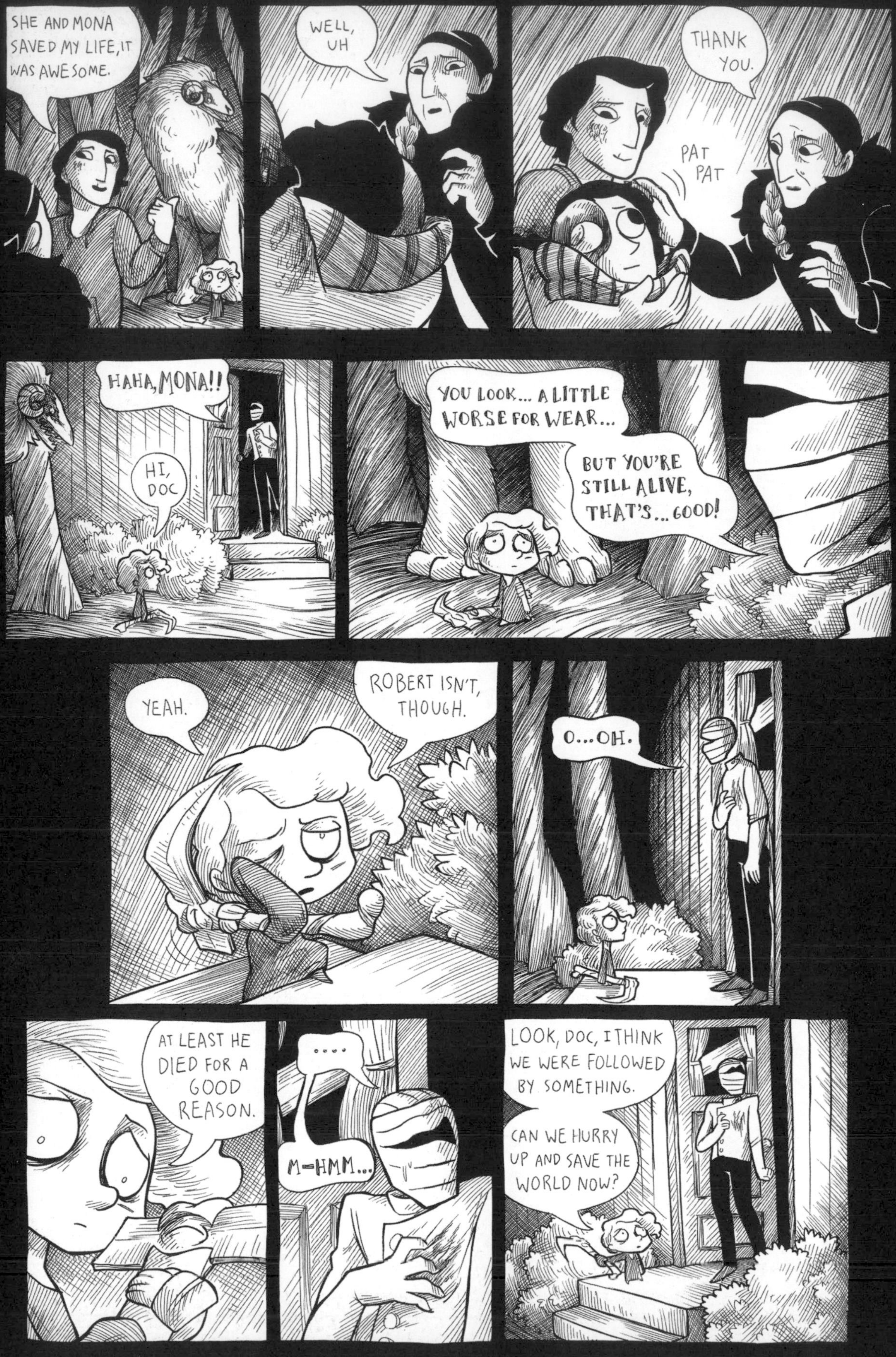
SHE AND MONA SAVED MY LIFE, IT WAS AWESOME.
WELL, UH
THANK YOU.
PAT PAT
HAHA, MONA!!
HI, DOC
YOU LOOK... A LITTLE WORSE FOR WEAR...
BUT YOU'RE STILL ALIVE, THAT'S... GOOD!
YEAH.
ROBERT ISN'T, THOUGH.
O...OH.
AT LEAST HE DIED FOR A GOOD REASON.
....
M-HMM...
LOOK, DOC, I THINK WE WERE FOLLOWED BY SOMETHING.
CAN WE HURRY UP AND SAVE THE WORLD NOW?

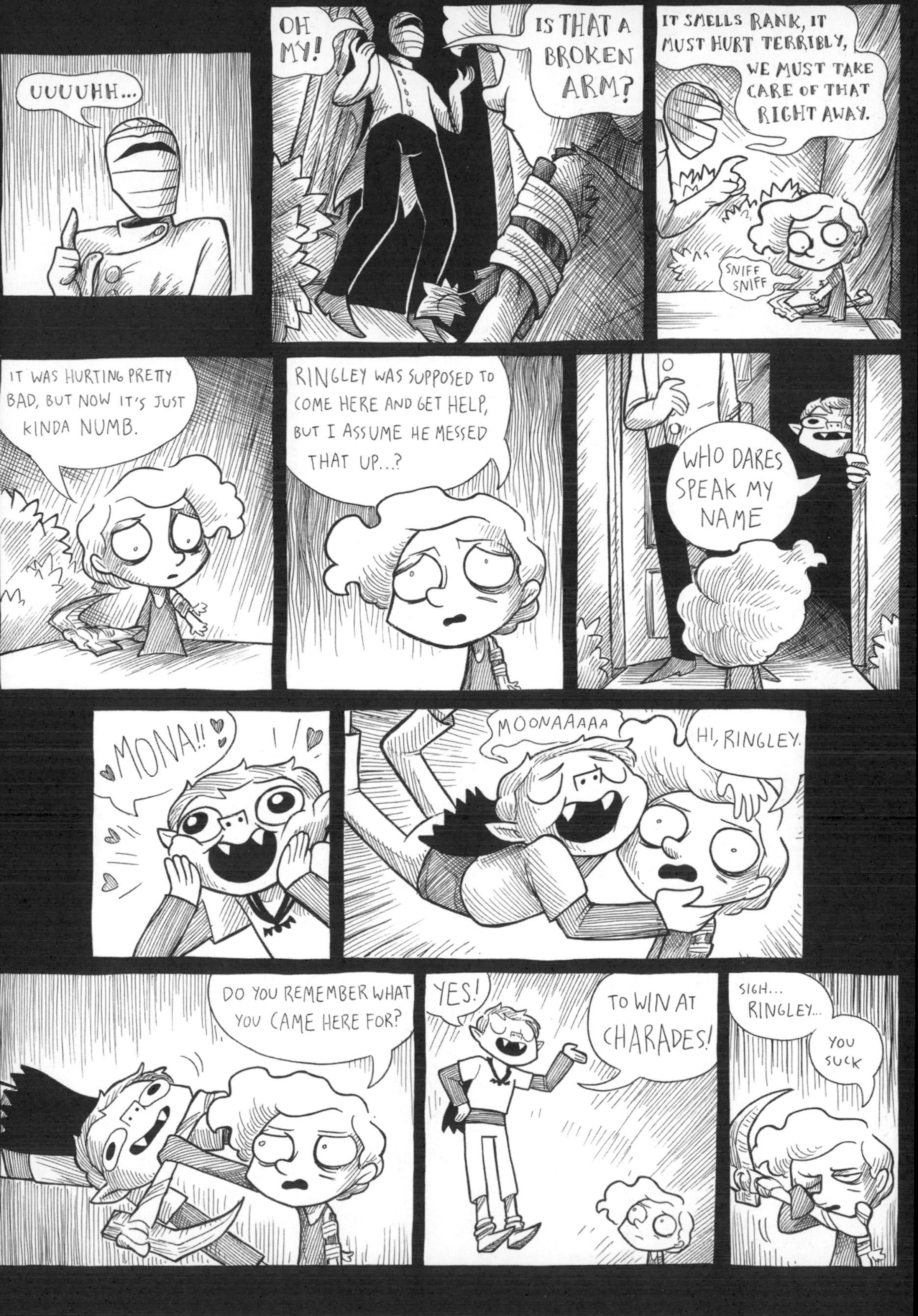
UUUUHH...
OH MY!
IS THAT A BROKEN ARM?
IT SMELLS RANK, IT MUST HURT TERRIBLY,
WE MUST TAKE CARE OF THAT RIGHT AWAY.
SNIFF SNIFF
IT WAS HURTING PRETTY BAD, BUT NOW IT'S JUST KINDA NUMB.
RINGLEY WAS SUPPOSED TO COME HERE AND GET HELP, BUT I ASSUME HE MESSED THAT UP...?
WHO DARES SPEAK MY NAME
MONA!!
MOONAAAAA
HI, RINGLEY.
DO YOU REMEMBER WHAT YOU CAME HERE FOR?
YES!
TO WIN AT CHARADES!
SIGH... RINGLEY...
YOU SUCK

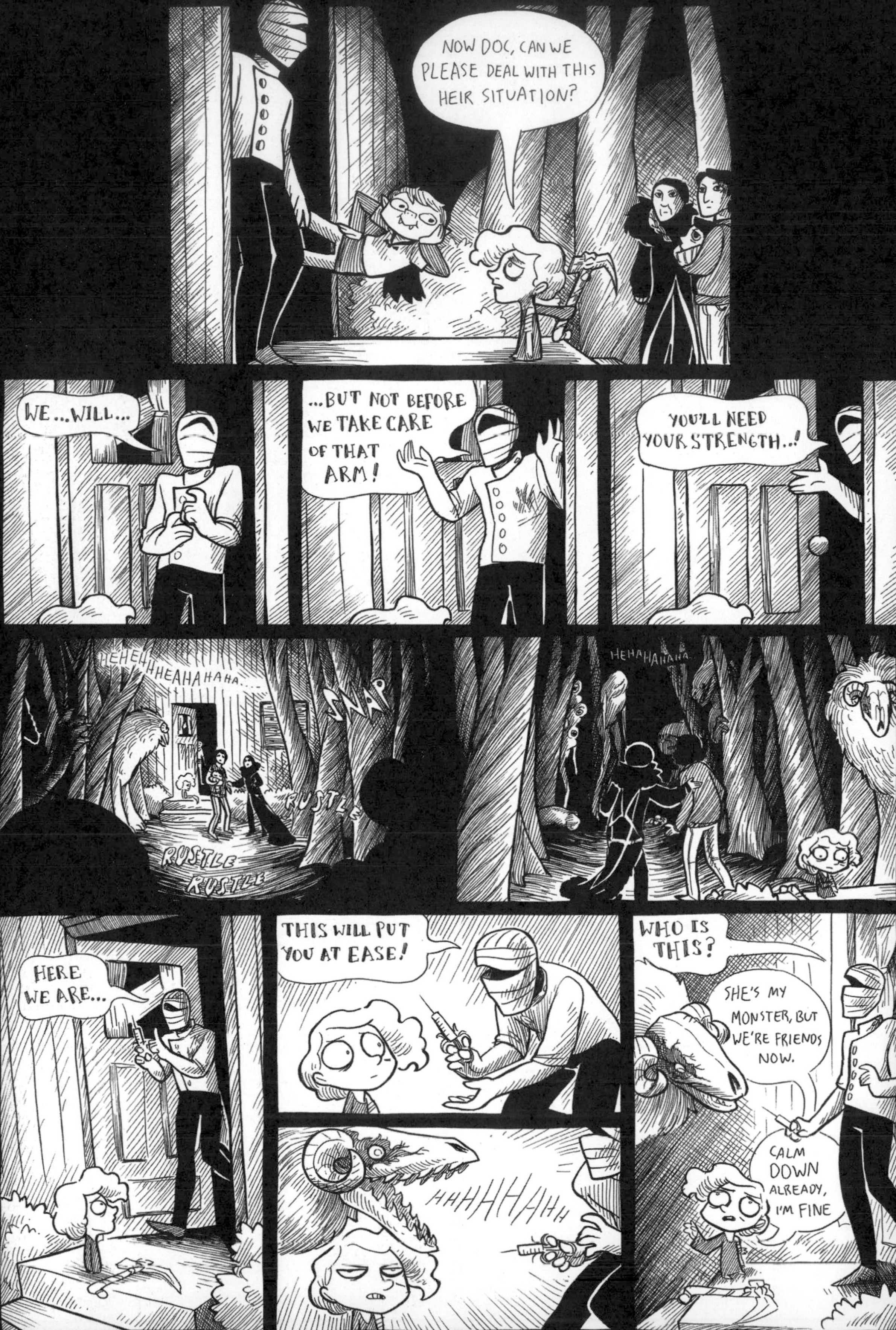
NOW DOC, CAN WE PLEASE DEAL WITH THIS HEIR SITUATION?
WE... WILL...
...BUT NOT BEFORE WE TAKE CARE OF THAT ARM!
YOU'LL NEED YOUR STRENGTH...!
HEHEHHHEAHAHAHA...
SNAP
RUSTLE
RUSTLE
RUSTLE
HEHAHAHAHA...
HERE WE ARE...
THIS WILL PUT YOU AT EASE!
AHHHHHAHH
WHO IS THIS?
SHE'S MY MONSTER, BUT WE'RE FRIENDS NOW.
CALM DOWN ALREADY, I'M FINE

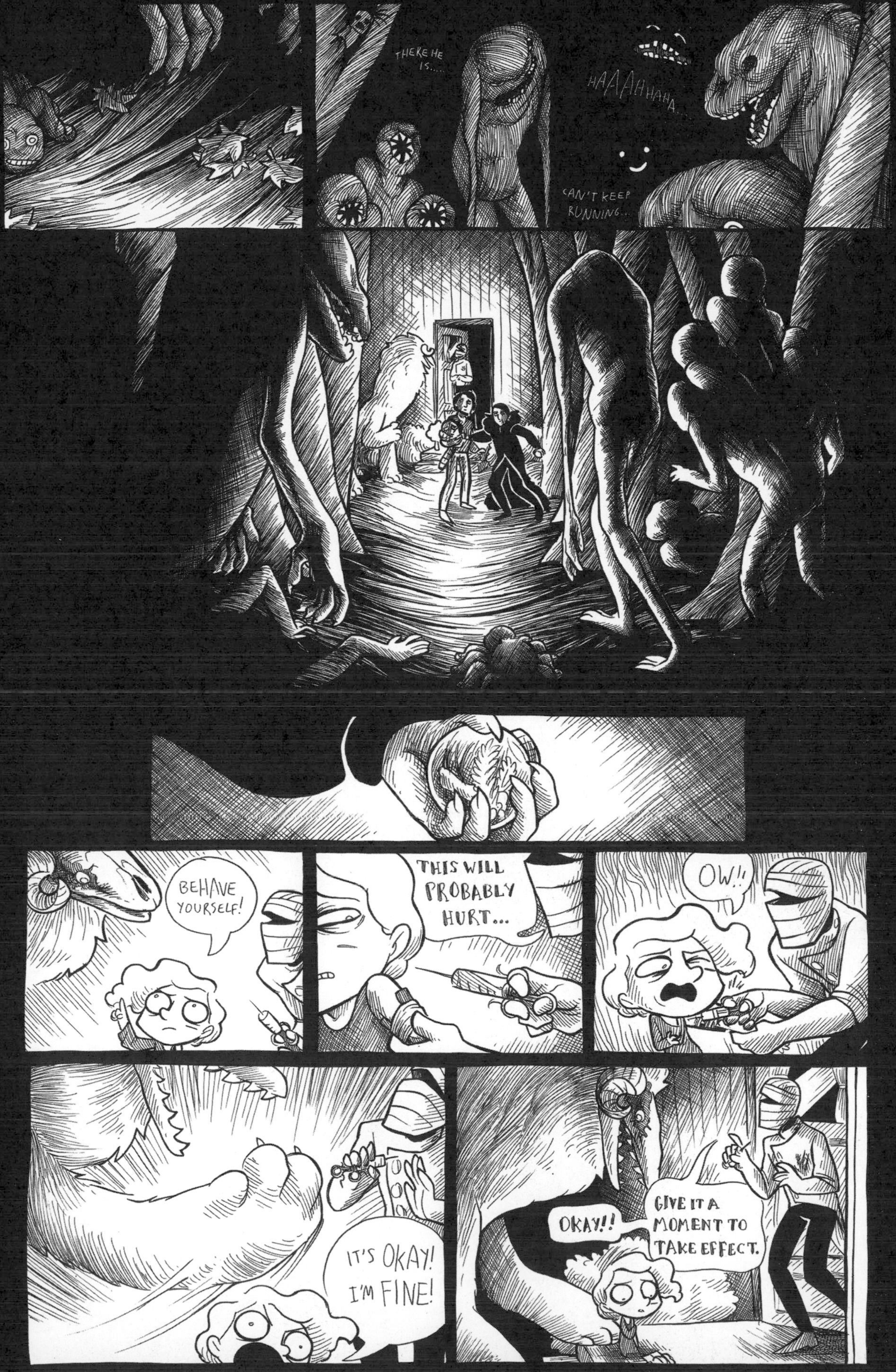
THERE HE IS...
HAAAHHAHA...
CAN'T KEEP RUNNING...
BEHAVE YOURSELF!
THIS WILL PROBABLY HURT...
OW!!
IT'S OKAY! I'M FINE!
OKAY!!
GIVE IT A MOMENT TO TAKE EFFECT.

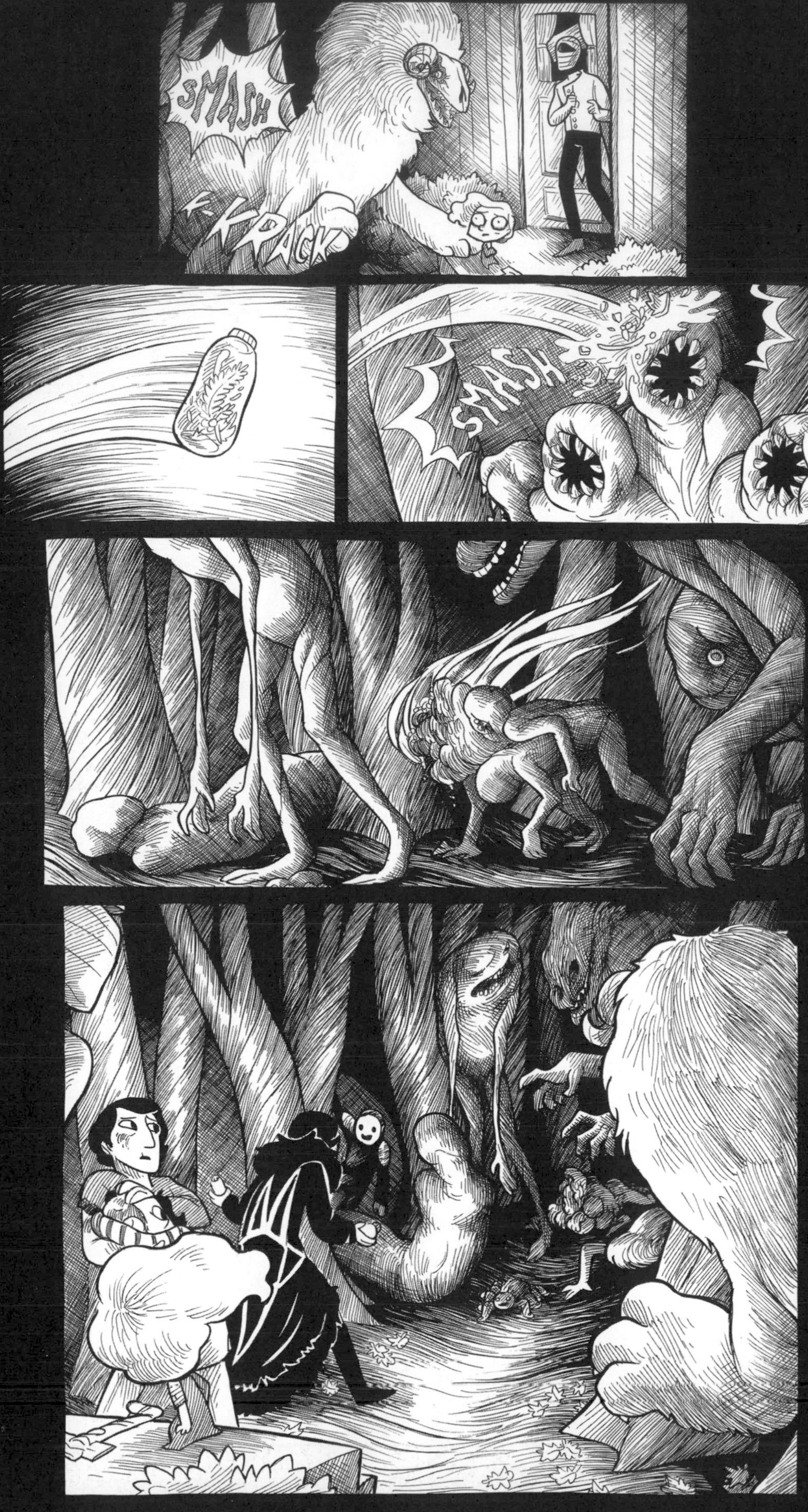
SMASH
K-KRACK
SMASH

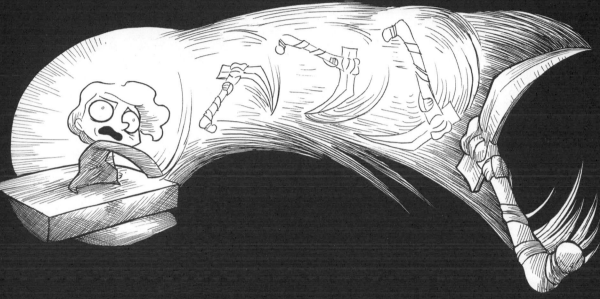

THOK

AAAAAHH STUPID TREES

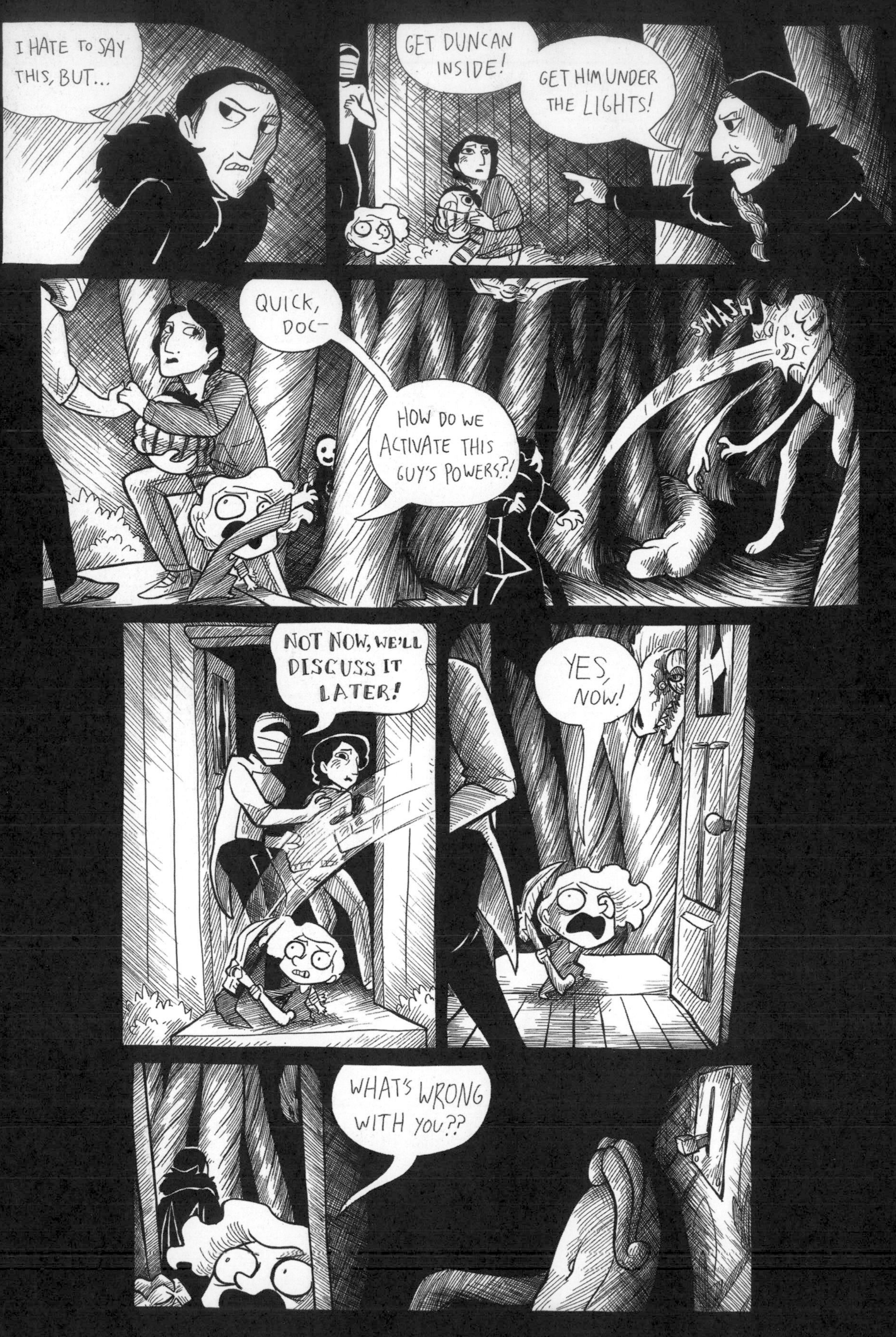
I HATE TO SAY THIS, BUT...
GET DUNCAN INSIDE!
GET HIM UNDER THE LIGHTS!
QUICK, DOC-
HOW DO WE ACTIVATE THIS GUY'S POWERS?!
SMASH
NOT NOW, WE'LL DISCUSS IT LATER!
YES, NOW!
WHAT'S WRONG WITH YOU??

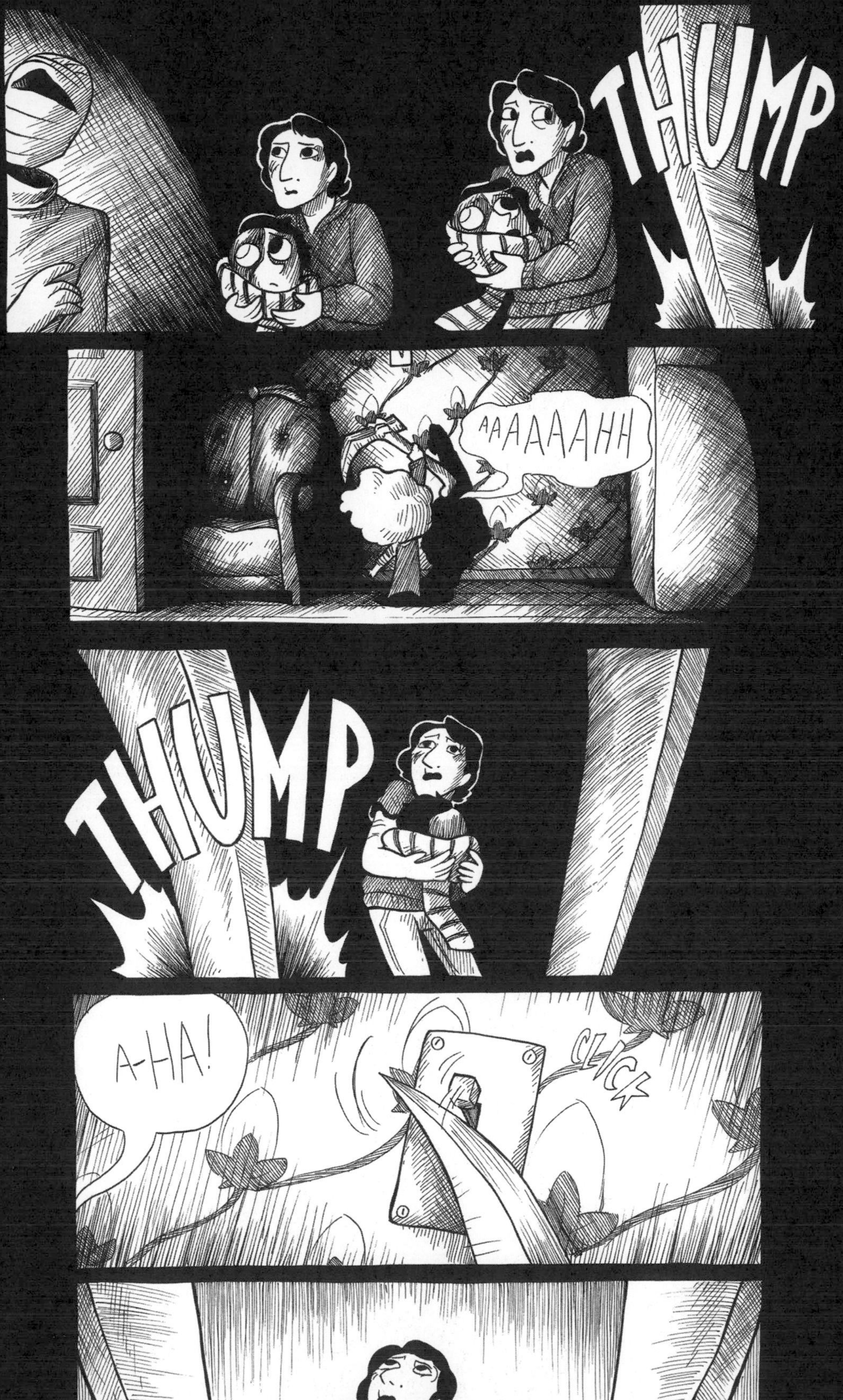
THUMP
AAAAAAHH
THUMP
A-HA!
CLICK

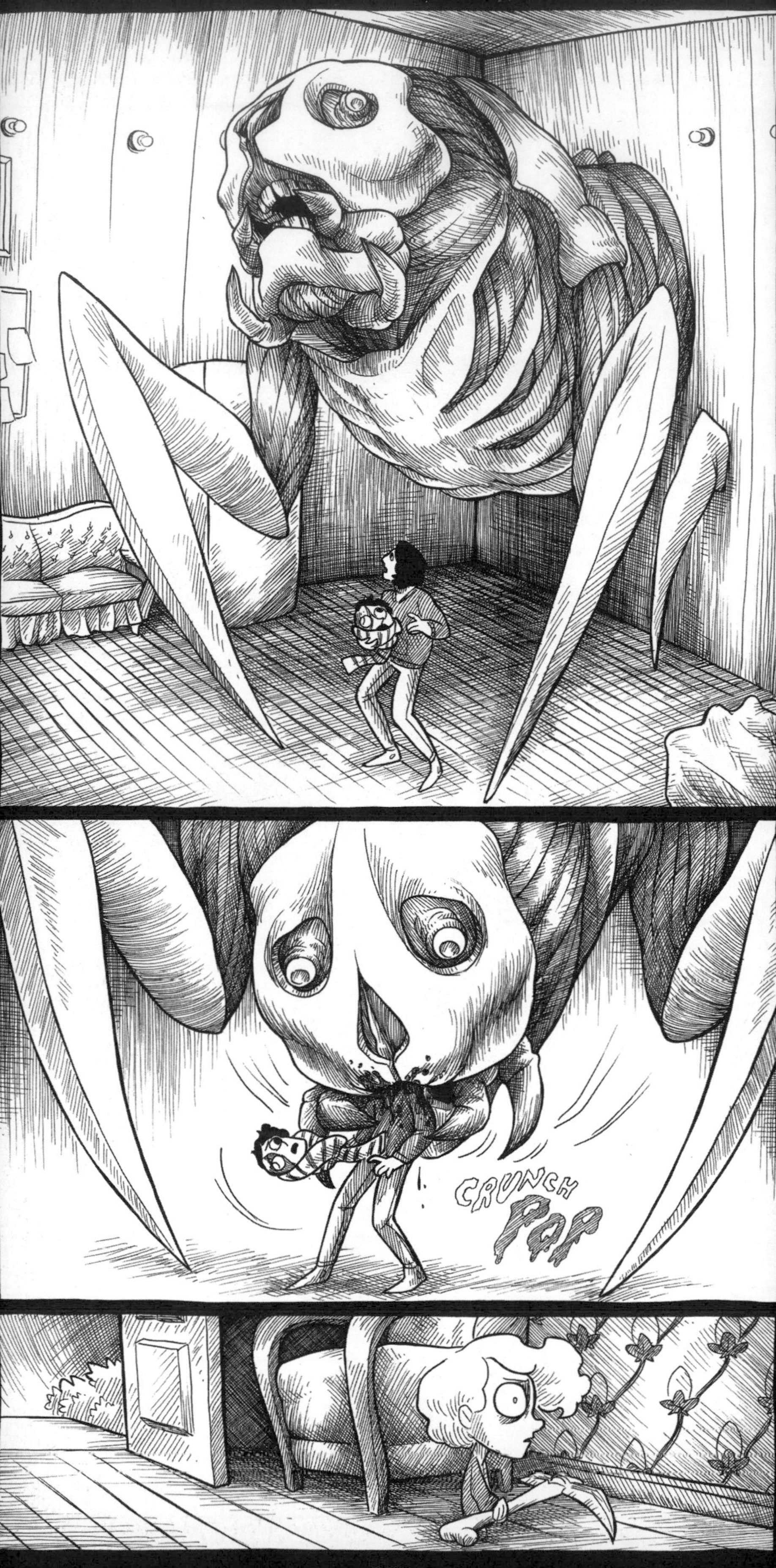
CRUNCH
POP

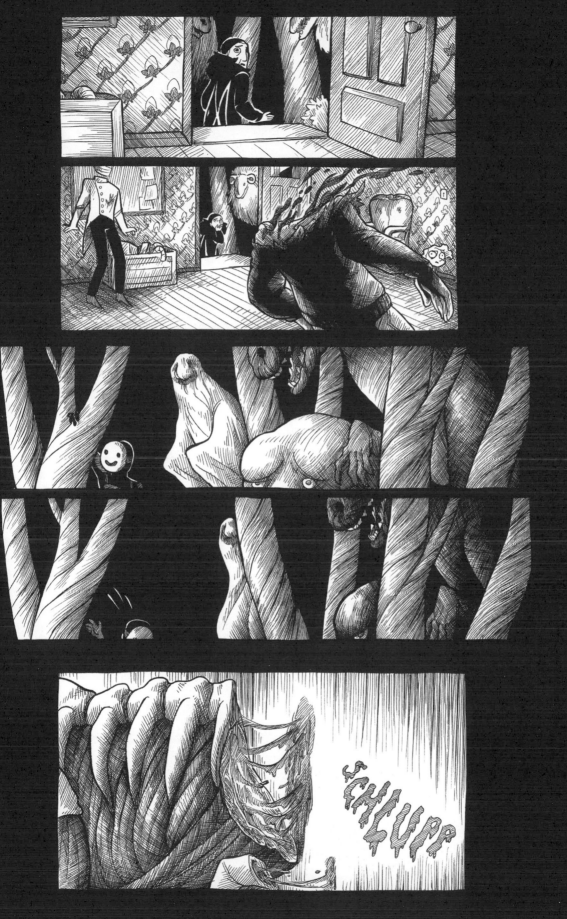

SCHLURP

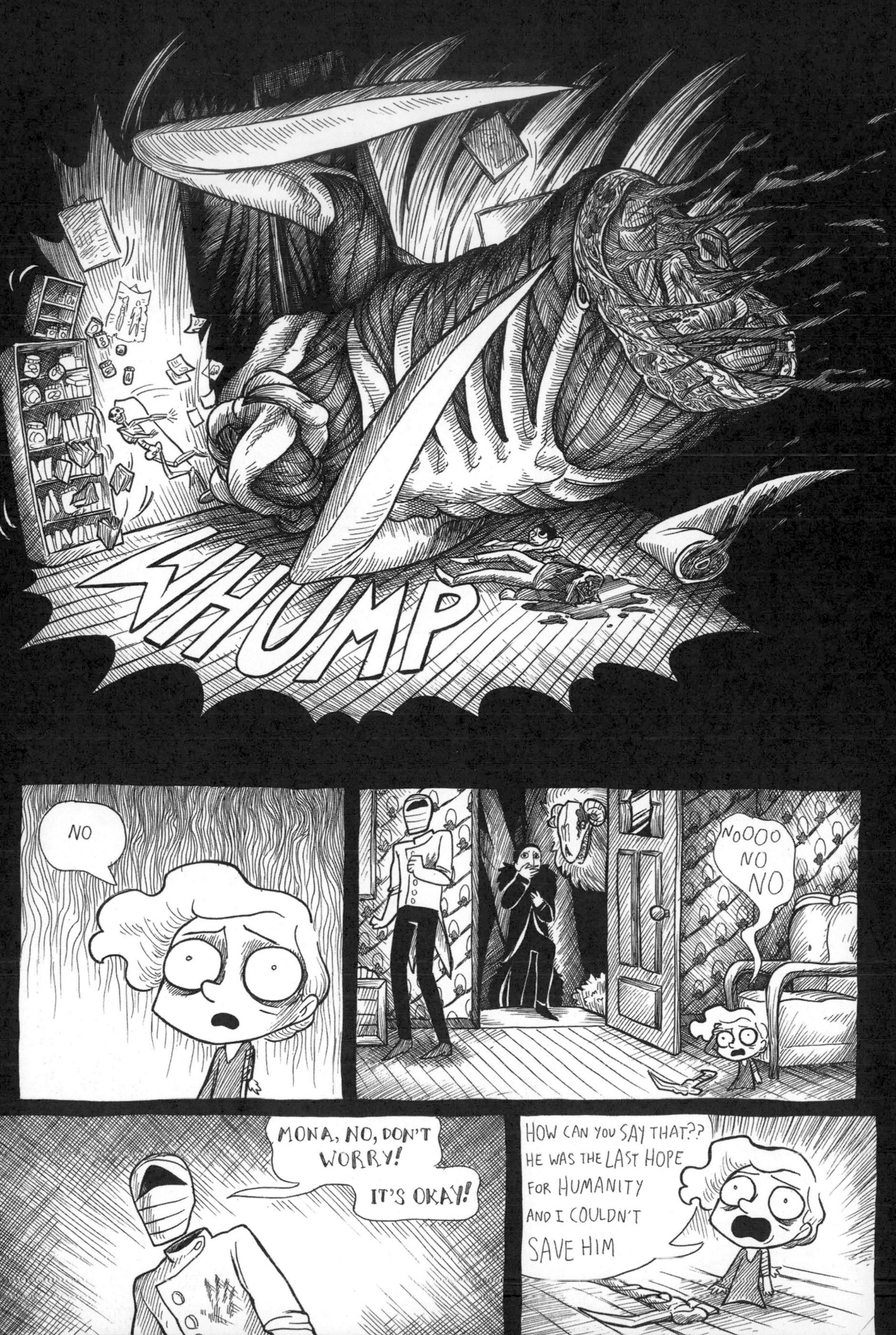
WHUMP
NO
NOOOO NO NO
MONA, NO, DON'T WORRY!
IT'S OKAY!
HOW CAN YOU SAY THAT?? HE WAS THE LAST HOPE FOR HUMANITY AND I COULDN'T SAVE HIM

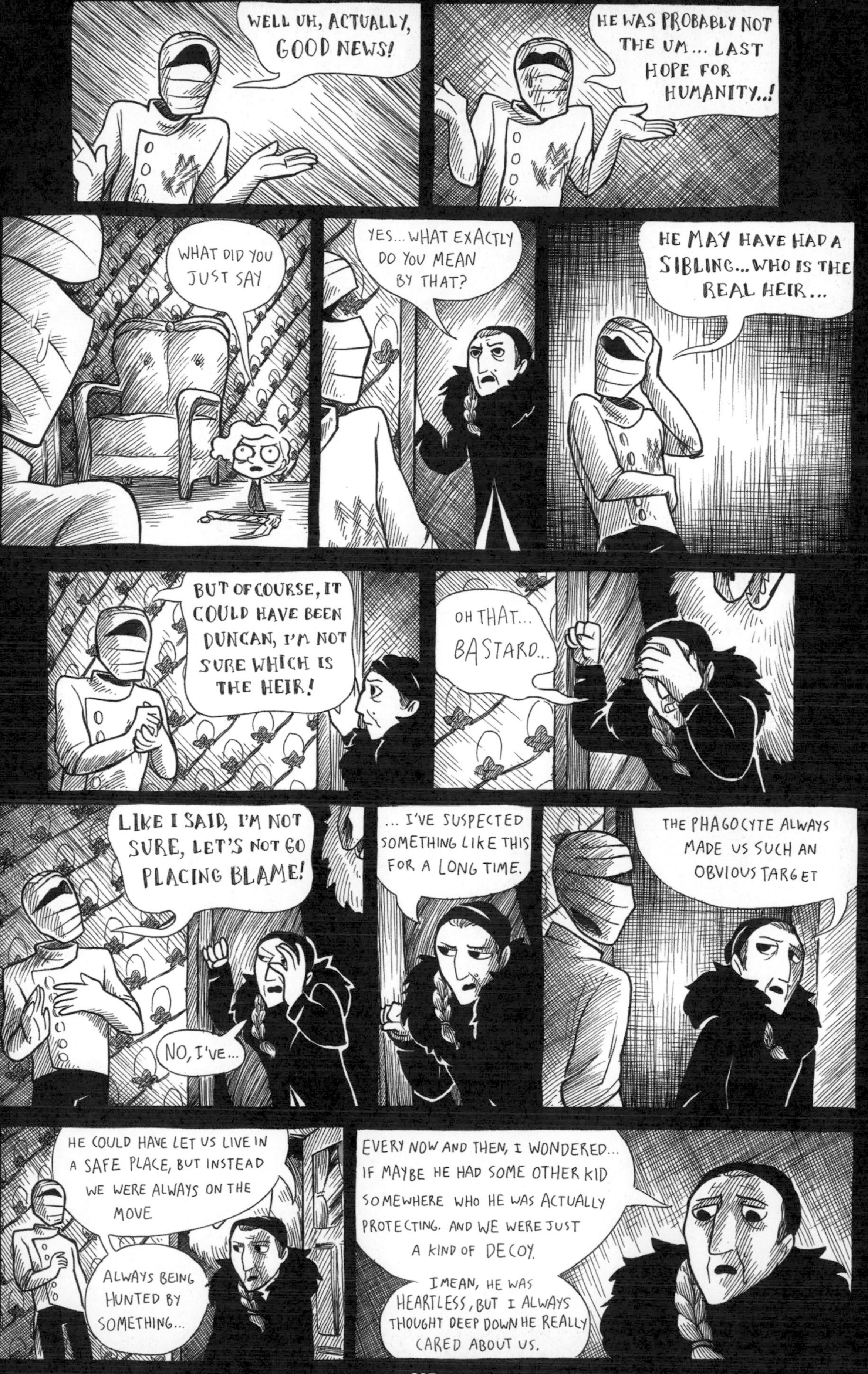
WELL UH, ACTUALLY, GOOD NEWS!
HE WAS PROBABLY NOT THE UM... LAST HOPE FOR HUMANITY..!
WHAT DID YOU JUST SAY
YES... WHAT EXACTLY DO YOU MEAN BY THAT?
HE MAY HAVE HAD A SIBLING... WHO IS THE REAL HEIR...
BUT OF COURSE, IT COULD HAVE BEEN DUNCAN, I'M NOT SURE WHICH IS THE HEIR!
OH THAT... BASTARD...
LIKE I SAID, I'M NOT SURE, LET'S NOT GO PLACING BLAME!
NO, I'VE...
... I'VE SUSPECTED SOMETHING LIKE THIS FOR A LONG TIME.
THE PHAGOCYTE ALWAYS MADE US SUCH AN OBVIOUS TARGET
HE COULD HAVE LET US LIVE IN A SAFE PLACE, BUT INSTEAD WE WERE ALWAYS ON THE MOVE
ALWAYS BEING HUNTED BY SOMETHING...
EVERY NOW AND THEN, I WONDERED... IF MAYBE HE HAD SOME OTHER KID SOMEWHERE WHO HE WAS ACTUALLY PROTECTING. AND WE WERE JUST A KIND OF DECOY.
I MEAN, HE WAS HEARTLESS, BUT I ALWAYS THOUGHT DEEP DOWN HE REALLY CARED ABOUT US.

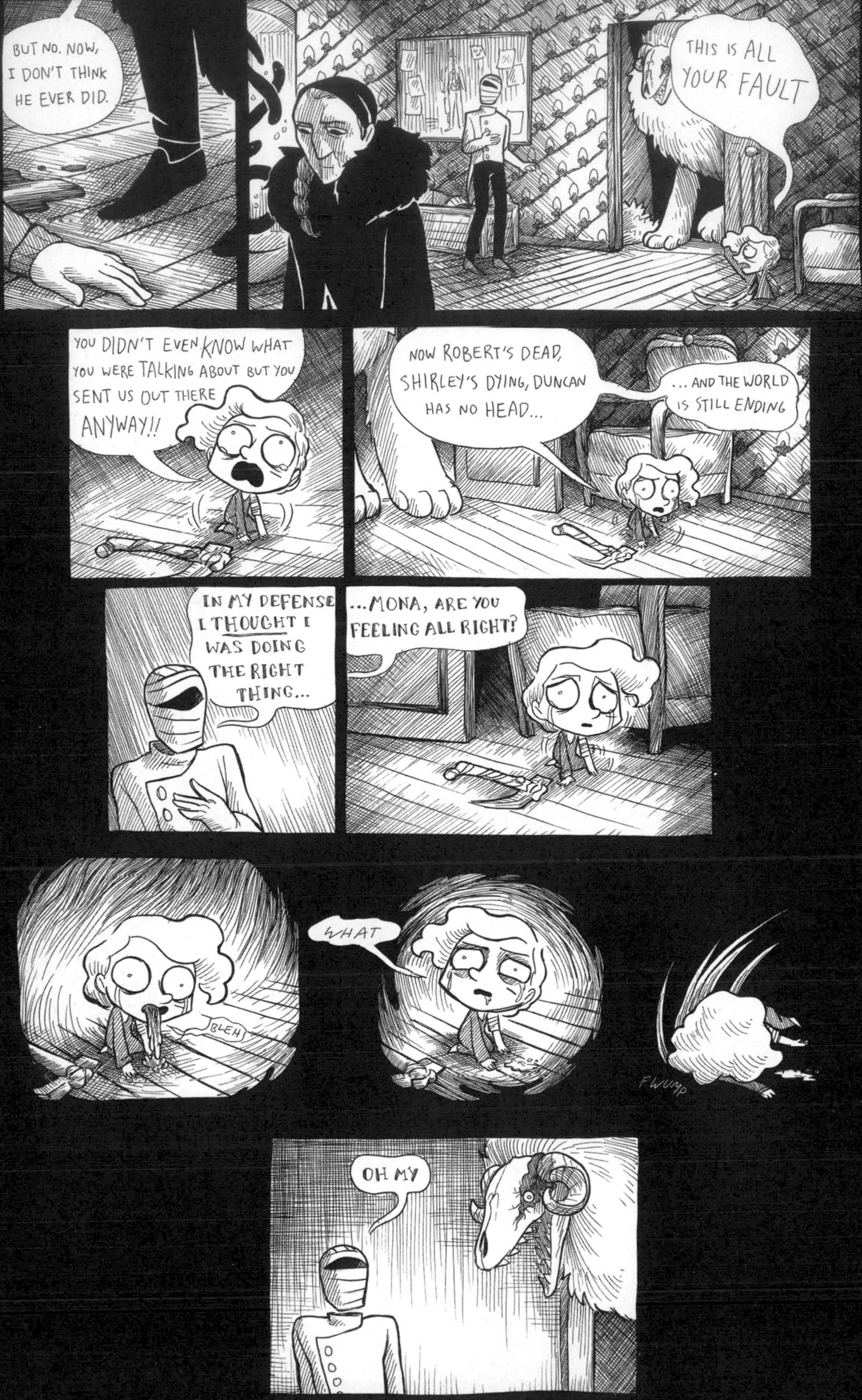
BUT NO. NOW, I DON'T THINK HE EVER DID.
THIS IS ALL YOUR FAULT
YOU DIDN'T EVEN KNOW WHAT YOU WERE TALKING ABOUT BUT YOU SENT US OUT THERE ANYWAY!!
NOW ROBERT'S DEAD, SHIRLEY'S DYING, DUNCAN HAS NO HEAD...
...AND THE WORLD IS STILL ENDING
IN MY DEFENSE I THOUGHT I WAS DOING THE RIGHT THING...
...MONA, ARE YOU FEELING ALL RIGHT?
BLEH
WHAT
FWUMP
OH MY

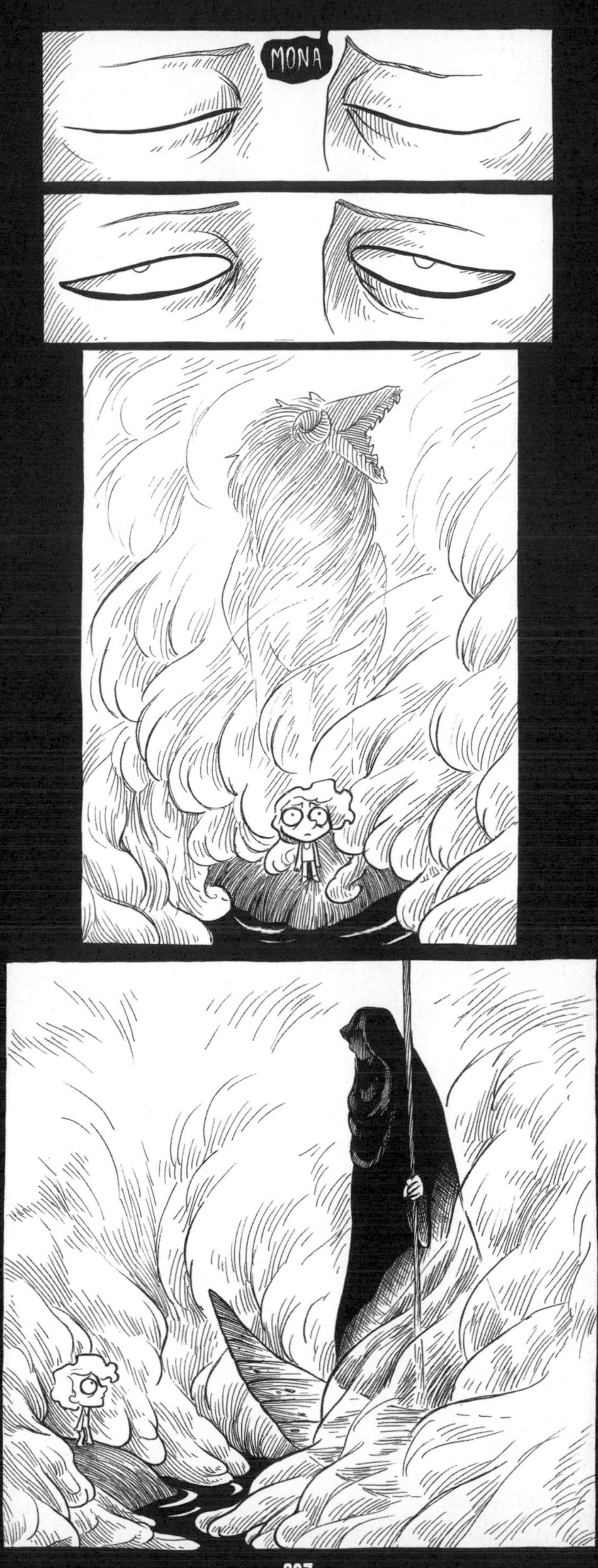
MONA

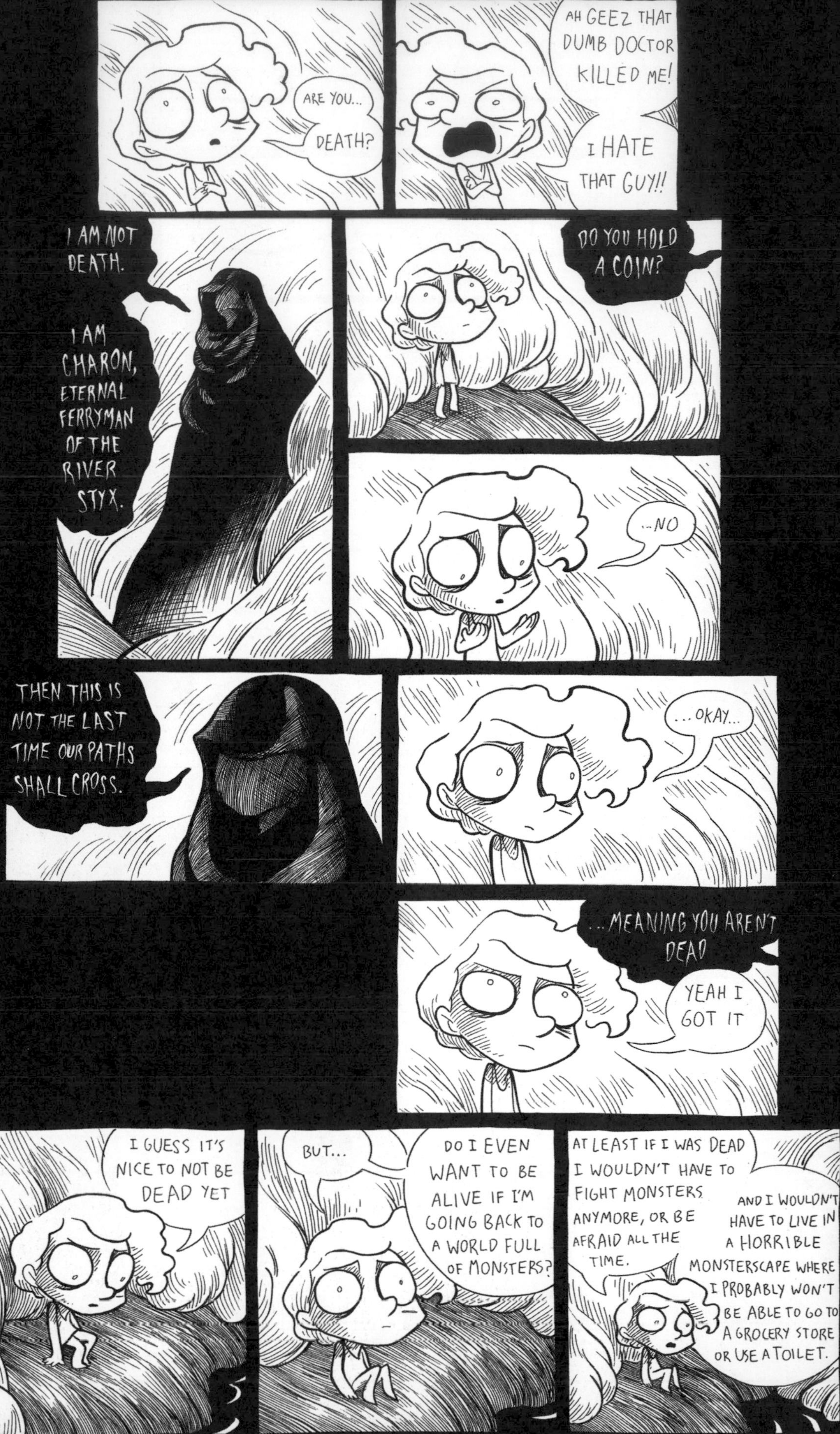

ARE YOU...
DEATH?
AH GEEZ THAT DUMB DOCTOR KILLED ME!
I HATE THAT GUY!!
I AM NOT DEATH.
I AM CHARON, ETERNAL FERRYMAN OF THE RIVER STYX.
DO YOU HOLD A COIN?
...NO
THEN THIS IS NOT THE LAST TIME OUR PATHS SHALL CROSS.
...OKAY...
...MEANING YOU AREN'T DEAD
YEAH I GOT IT
I GUESS IT'S NICE TO NOT BE DEAD YET
BUT...
DO I EVEN WANT TO BE ALIVE IF I'M GOING BACK TO A WORLD FULL OF MONSTERS?
AT LEAST IF I WAS DEAD I WOULDN'T HAVE TO FIGHT MONSTERS ANYMORE, OR BE AFRAID ALL THE TIME.
AND I WOULDN'T HAVE TO LIVE IN A HORRIBLE MONSTERSCAPE WHERE I PROBABLY WON'T BE ABLE TO GO TO A GROCERY STORE OR USE A TOILET.

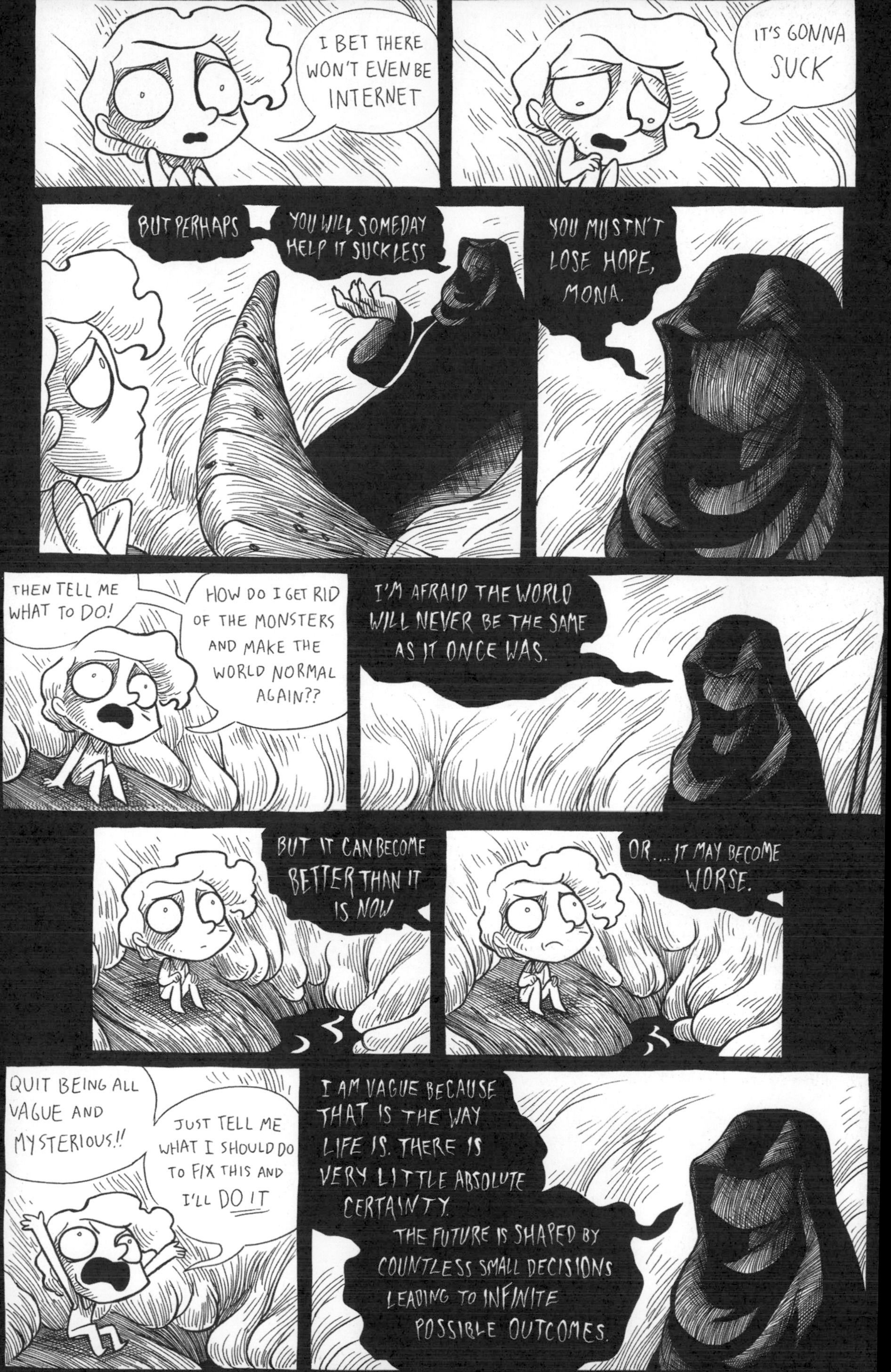
I BET THERE WON'T EVEN BE INTERNET
IT'S GONNA SUCK
BUT PERHAPS
YOU WILL SOMEDAY HELP IT SUCK LESS
YOU MUSTN'T LOSE HOPE, MONA.
THEN TELL ME WHAT TO DO!
HOW DO I GET RID OF THE MONSTERS AND MAKE THE WORLD NORMAL AGAIN??
I'M AFRAID THE WORLD WILL NEVER BE THE SAME AS IT ONCE WAS.
BUT IT CAN BECOME BETTER THAN IT IS NOW
OR.... IT MAY BECOME WORSE.
QUIT BEING ALL VAGUE AND MYSTERIOUS!!
JUST TELL ME WHAT I SHOULD DO TO FIX THIS AND I'LL DO IT
I AM VAGUE BECAUSE THAT IS THE WAY LIFE IS. THERE IS VERY LITTLE ABSOLUTE CERTAINTY.
THE FUTURE IS SHAPED BY COUNTLESS SMALL DECISIONS LEADING TO INFINITE POSSIBLE OUTCOMES.

THAT'S STUPID

EVERYTHING IS STUPID

I'M TIRED AND I WANT TO GO HOME

THEN I SHALL RETURN YOU TO YOUR REALM.

BUT MONA, KNOW THIS AND REMEMBER.

YOU WERE NOT BORN A HERO, BUT THIS DOES NOT PREVENT YOU FROM BECOMING ONE.

IT IS NOT YOUR GOAL ITSELF BUT THE CHOICES YOU SHALL MAKE ALONG THE WAY THAT DETERMINE YOUR FATE

AND THE FATE OF THE WORLD.

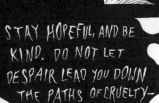

STAY HOPEFUL, AND BE KIND. DO NOT LET DESPAIR LEAD YOU DOWN THE PATHS OF CRUELTY—

SO CAN I GO NOW

... OKAY, SURE, FINE

NOT LIKE THIS IS IMPORTANT INFO OR ANYTHING

WHEN YOU AWAKEN, FUGUE WILL TELL YOU WHAT TO DO. YOU CAN TRUST HIM NOW.

GOODBYE, MONA...

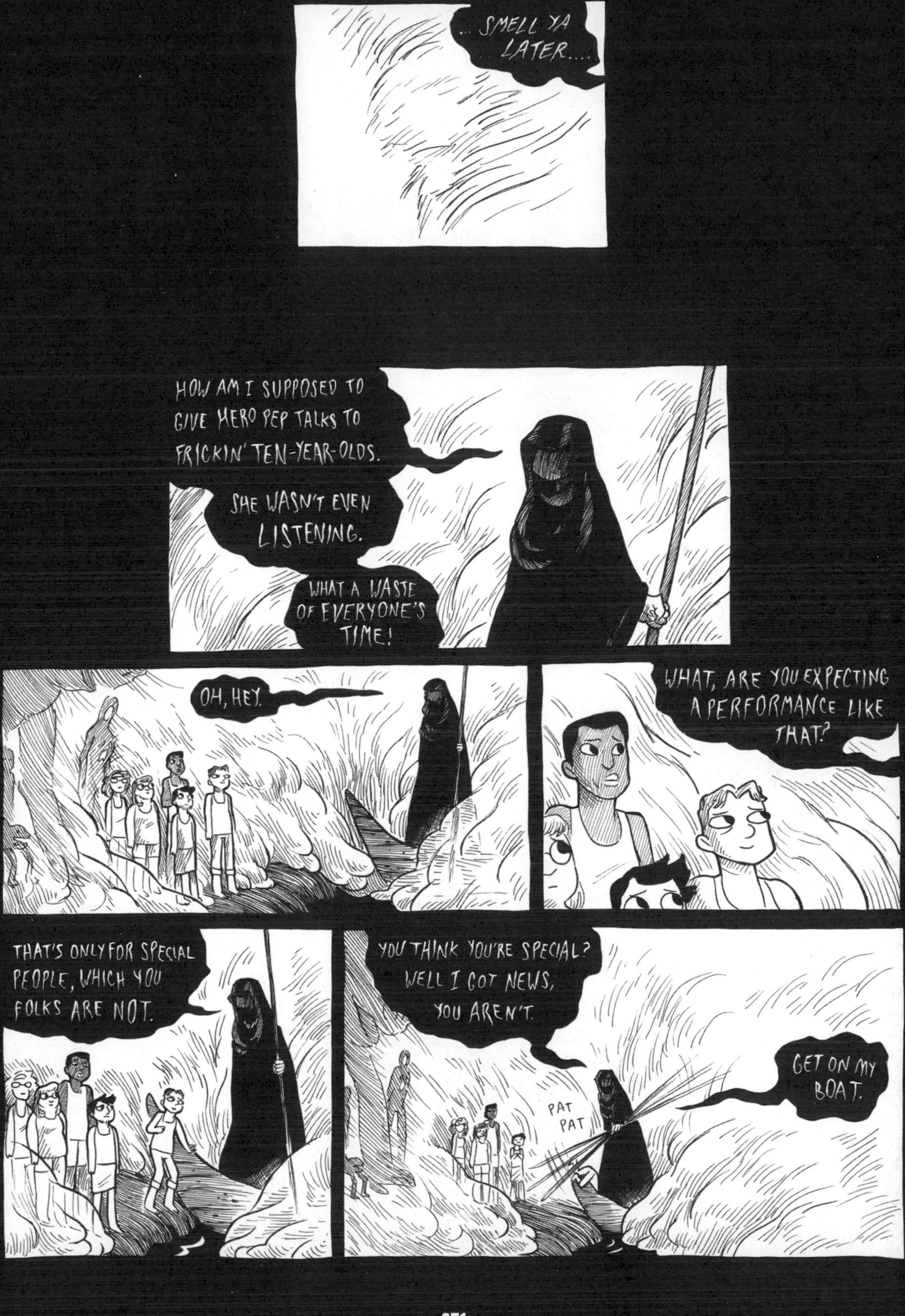

... SMELL YA LATER.....
HOW AM I SUPPOSED TO GIVE HERO PEP TALKS TO FRICKIN' TEN-YEAR-OLDS.
SHE WASN'T EVEN LISTENING.
WHAT A WASTE OF EVERYONE'S TIME!
OH, HEY.
WHAT, ARE YOU EXPECTING A PERFORMANCE LIKE THAT?
THAT'S ONLY FOR SPECIAL PEOPLE, WHICH YOU FOLKS ARE NOT.
YOU THINK YOU'RE SPECIAL? WELL I GOT NEWS, YOU AREN'T.
PAT PAT
GET ON MY BOAT.

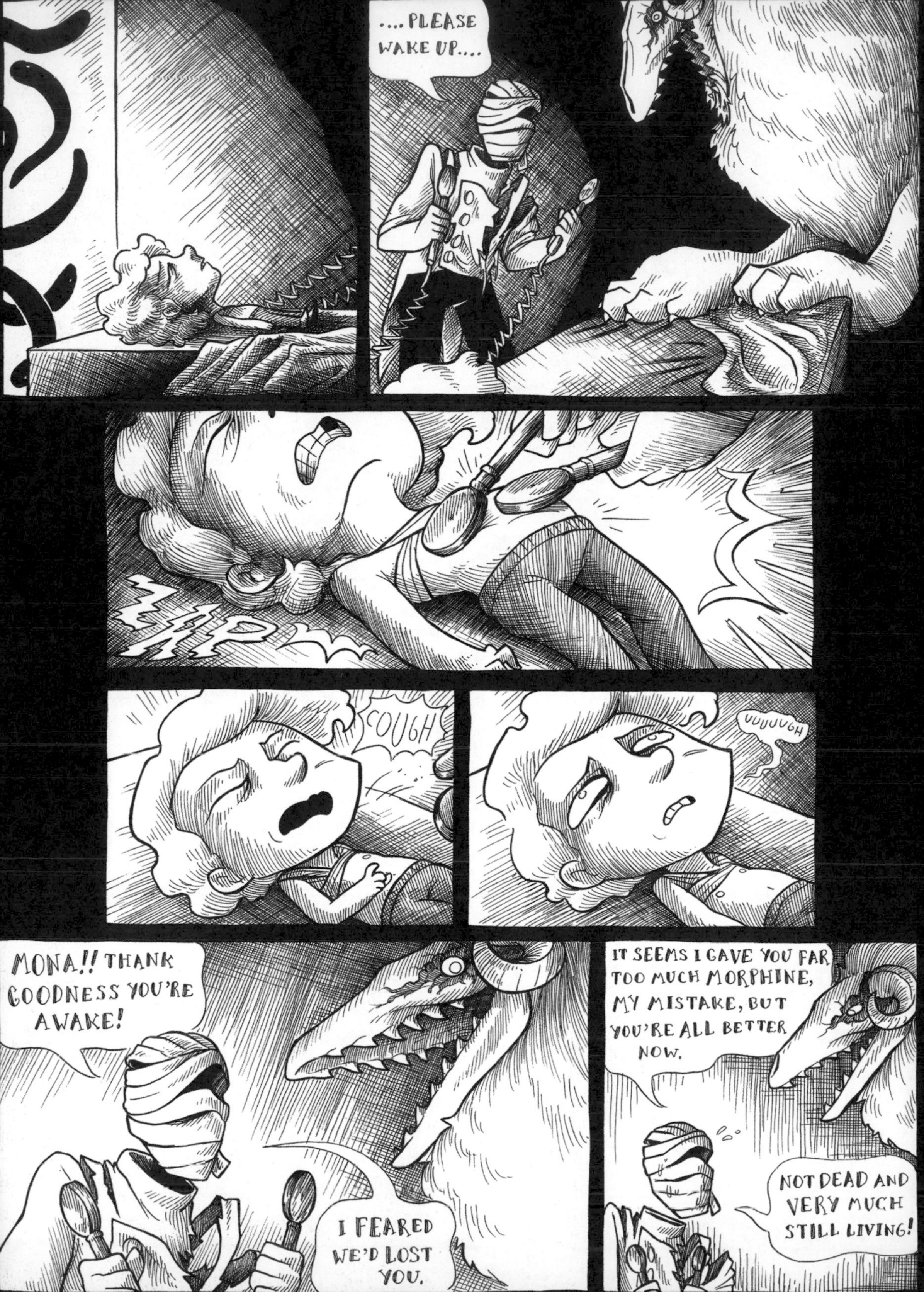
....PLEASE WAKE UP....
WHP
COUGH
UUUUUGH
MONA!! THANK GOODNESS YOU'RE AWAKE!
I FEARED WE'D LOST YOU.
IT SEEMS I GAVE YOU FAR TOO MUCH MORPHINE, MY MISTAKE, BUT YOU'RE ALL BETTER NOW.
NOT DEAD AND VERY MUCH STILL LIVING!

I'M...SORRY, FOR ALL YOU'VE BEEN THROUGH TONIGHT.

I CAN BE SOMEWHAT HEADSTRONG, AND YOU SHOULDN'T HAVE HAD TO SUFFER FOR IT.

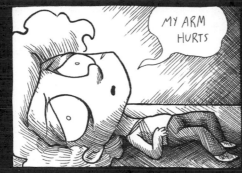
MY ARM HURTS

WH...WHERE...

WHAT DID YOU DO

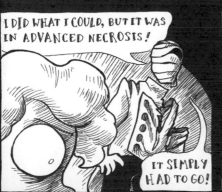
I DID WHAT I COULD, BUT IT WAS IN ADVANCED NECROSIS!

IT SIMPLY HAD TO GO!

EVEN WITH THE FINEST MODERN EQUIPMENT IT COULDN'T HAVE BEEN SAVED

IT WAS FOR THE BEST, REALLY!

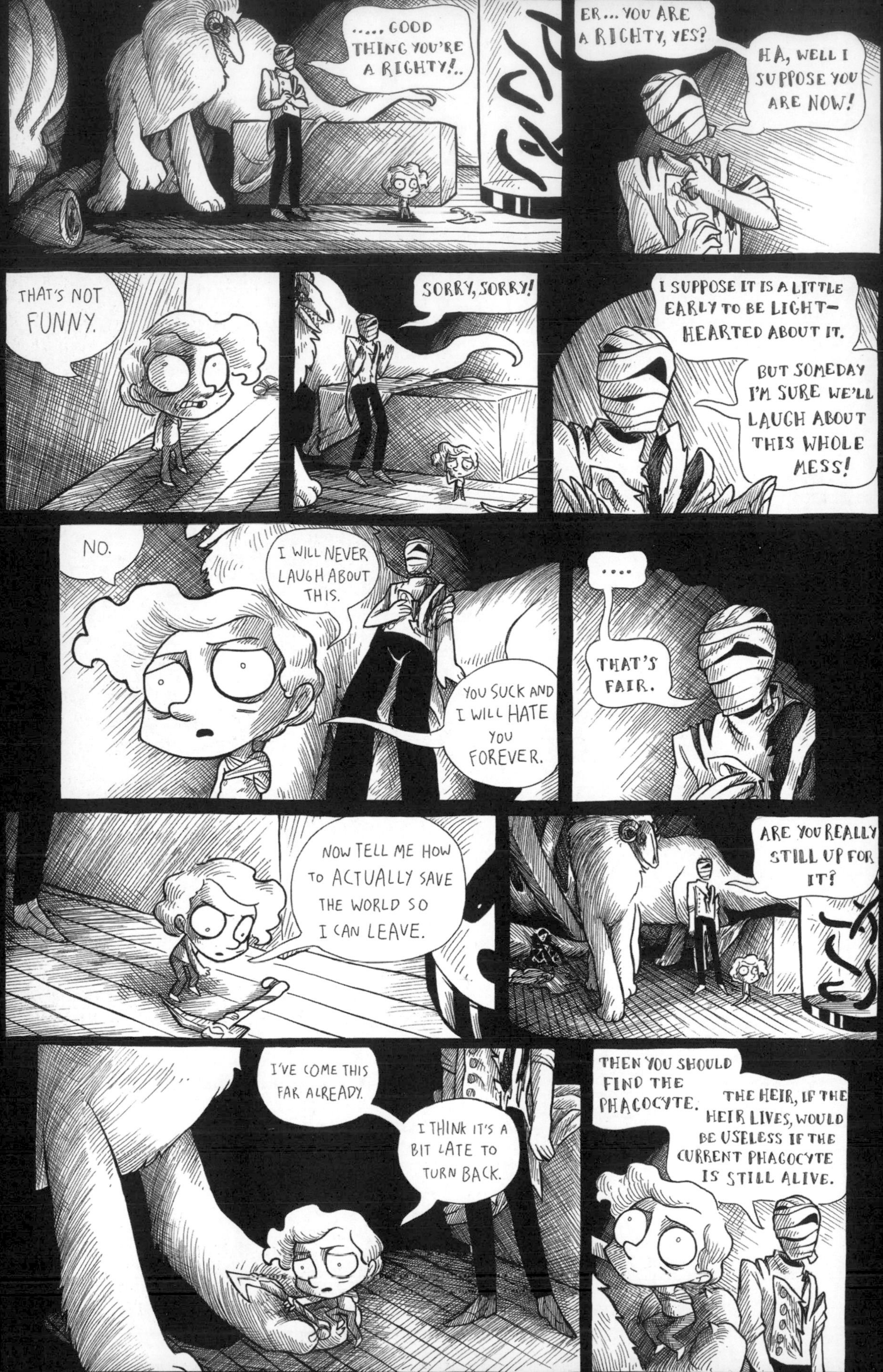

....., GOOD THING YOU'RE A RIGHTY!..
ER... YOU ARE A RIGHTY, YES?
HA, WELL I SUPPOSE YOU ARE NOW!
THAT'S NOT FUNNY.
SORRY, SORRY!
I SUPPOSE IT IS A LITTLE EARLY TO BE LIGHT-HEARTED ABOUT IT.
BUT SOMEDAY I'M SURE WE'LL LAUGH ABOUT THIS WHOLE MESS!
NO.
I WILL NEVER LAUGH ABOUT THIS.
YOU SUCK AND I WILL HATE YOU FOREVER.
....
THAT'S FAIR.
NOW TELL ME HOW TO ACTUALLY SAVE THE WORLD SO I CAN LEAVE.
ARE YOU REALLY STILL UP FOR IT?
I'VE COME THIS FAR ALREADY.
I THINK IT'S A BIT LATE TO TURN BACK.
THEN YOU SHOULD FIND THE PHAGOCYTE.
THE HEIR, IF THE HEIR LIVES, WOULD BE USELESS IF THE CURRENT PHAGOCYTE IS STILL ALIVE.

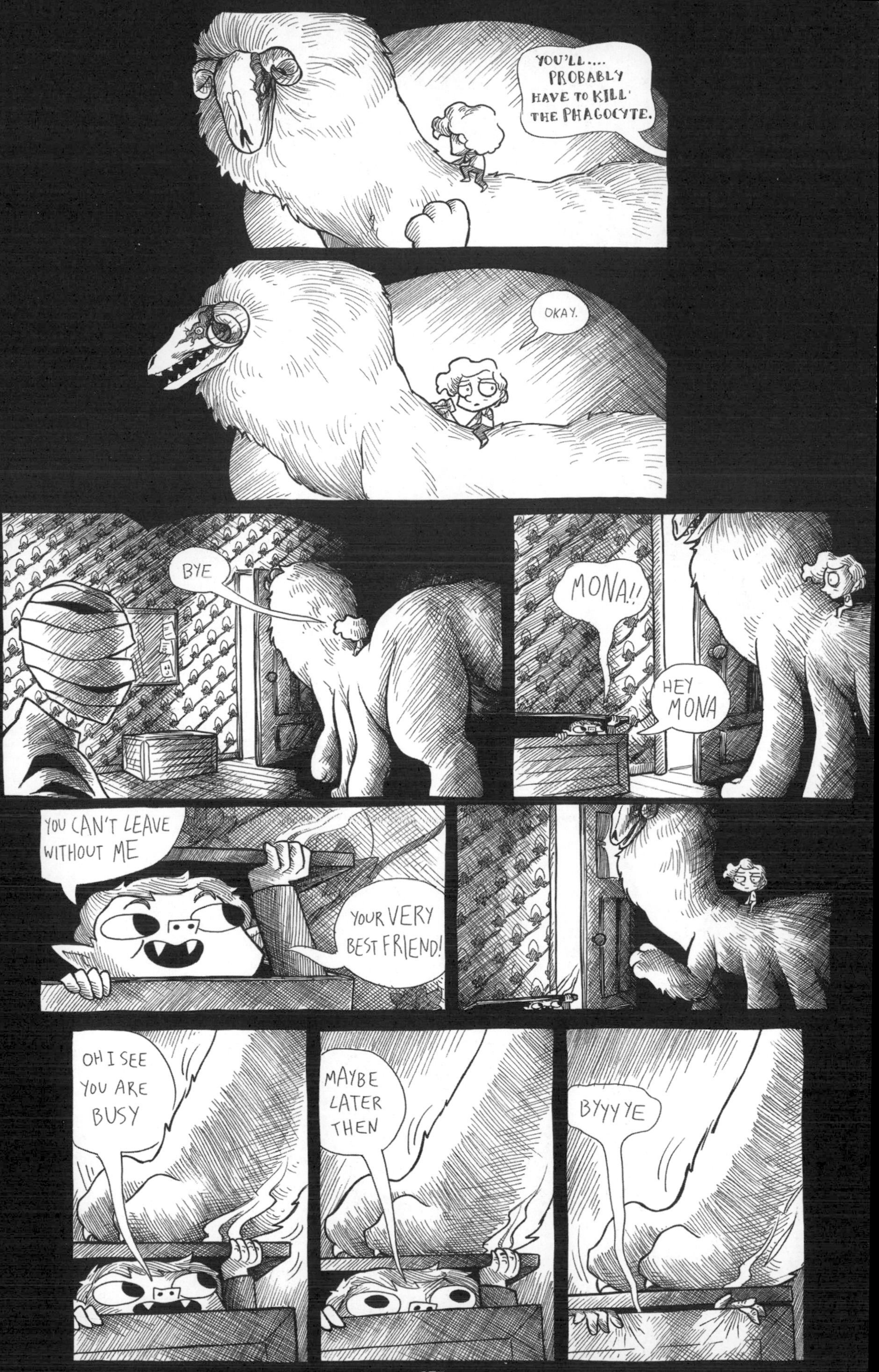
YOU'LL.... PROBABLY HAVE TO KILL THE PHAGOCYTE.
OKAY.
BYE
MONA!!
HEY MONA
YOU CAN'T LEAVE WITHOUT ME
YOUR VERY BEST FRIEND!
OH I SEE YOU ARE BUSY
MAYBE LATER THEN
BYYYYE

NOW THAT ALL THAT'S TAKEN CARE OF...

WHAT ARE WE GOING TO DO ABOUT MY SON?

WELL... HIS HEAD WAS CRUSHED.

YOU AND I BOTH KNOW THAT'S AN ISSUE.

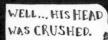

YOU'RE SURE THERE AREN'T ANY SPELLS YOU KEPT SECRET FROM ME THAT CAN BRING BACK A HEADLESS PERSON?

EVEN IF HE'S SOME REPULSIVE, SHAMBLING MESS, HE'S MY SON.

WE'D MAKE IT WORK.

I'M AFRAID NOT. I TAUGHT YOU ALL I KNOW ABOUT THESE THINGS.

IT SEEMS LIKE ONCE THE HEAD IS GONE, THERE'S NOTHING TO BE DONE.

...ALTHOUGH...

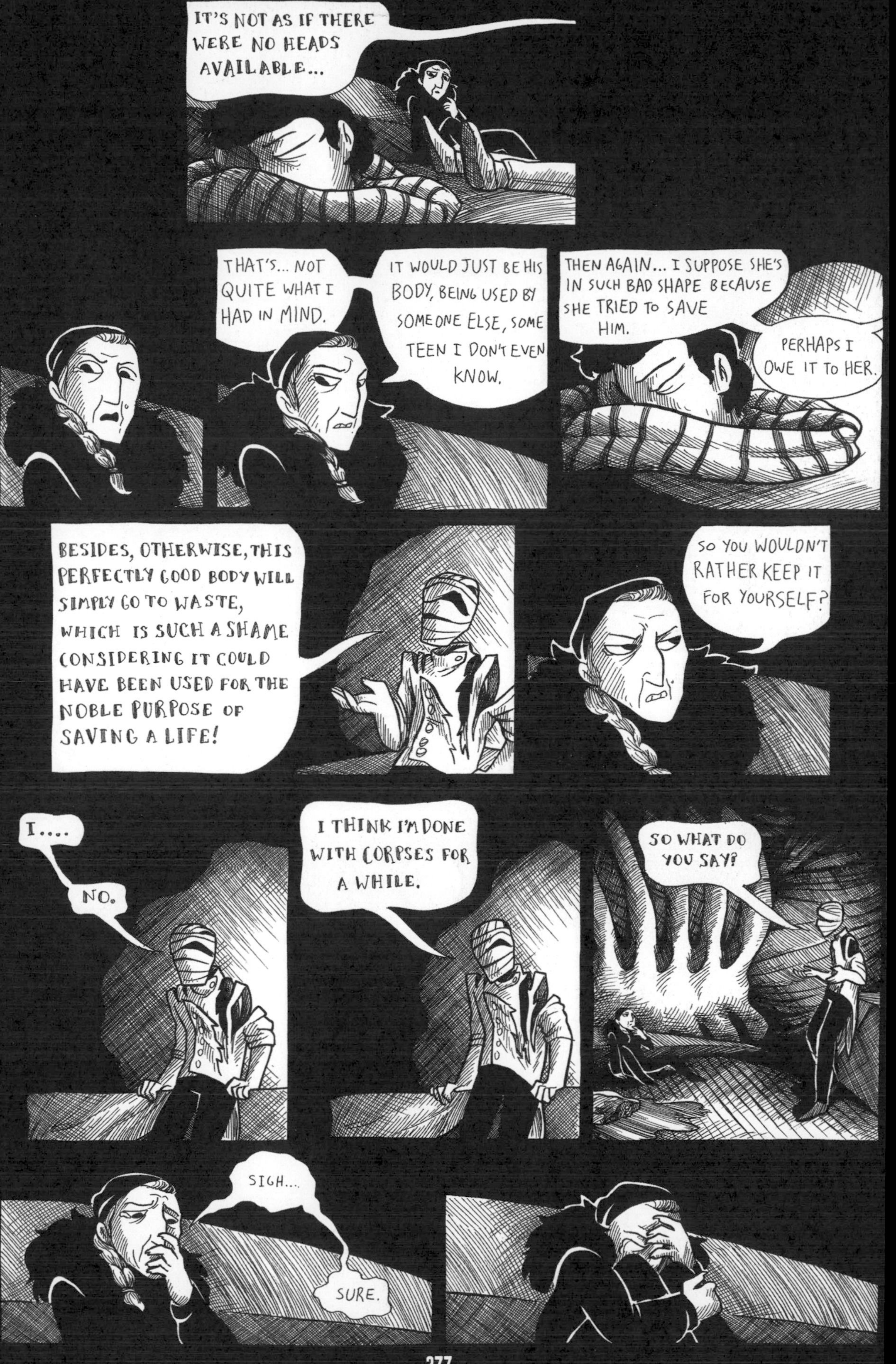
IT'S NOT AS IF THERE WERE NO HEADS AVAILABLE...
THAT'S... NOT QUITE WHAT I HAD IN MIND.
IT WOULD JUST BE HIS BODY, BEING USED BY SOMEONE ELSE, SOME TEEN I DON'T EVEN KNOW.
THEN AGAIN... I SUPPOSE SHE'S IN SUCH BAD SHAPE BECAUSE SHE TRIED TO SAVE HIM.
PERHAPS I OWE IT TO HER.
BESIDES, OTHERWISE, THIS PERFECTLY GOOD BODY WILL SIMPLY GO TO WASTE, WHICH IS SUCH A SHAME CONSIDERING IT COULD HAVE BEEN USED FOR THE NOBLE PURPOSE OF SAVING A LIFE!
SO YOU WOULDN'T RATHER KEEP IT FOR YOURSELF?
I....
NO.
I THINK I'M DONE WITH CORPSES FOR A WHILE.
SO WHAT DO YOU SAY?
SIGH....
SURE.

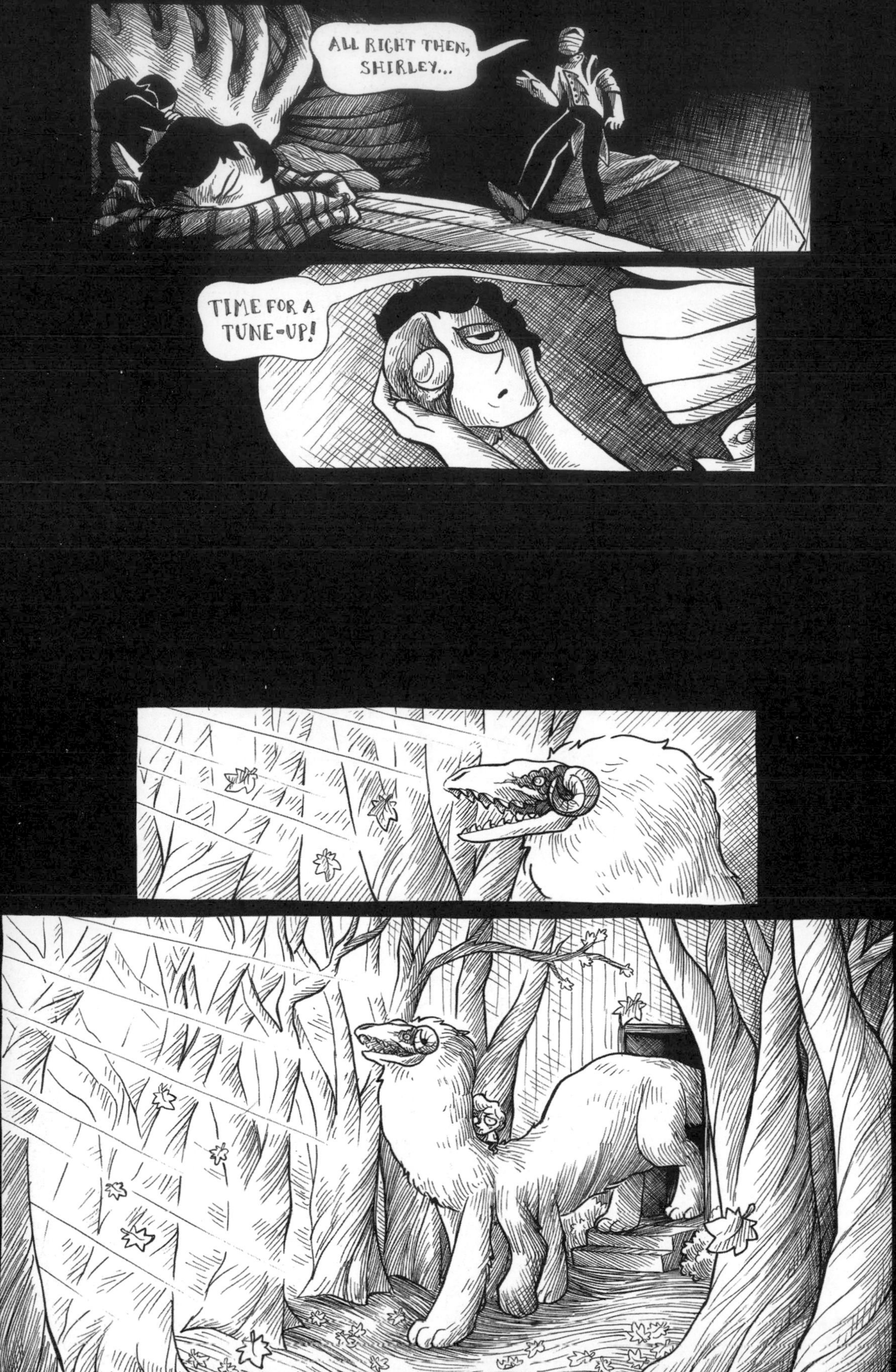
ALL RIGHT THEN, SHIRLEY...
TIME FOR A TUNE-UP!

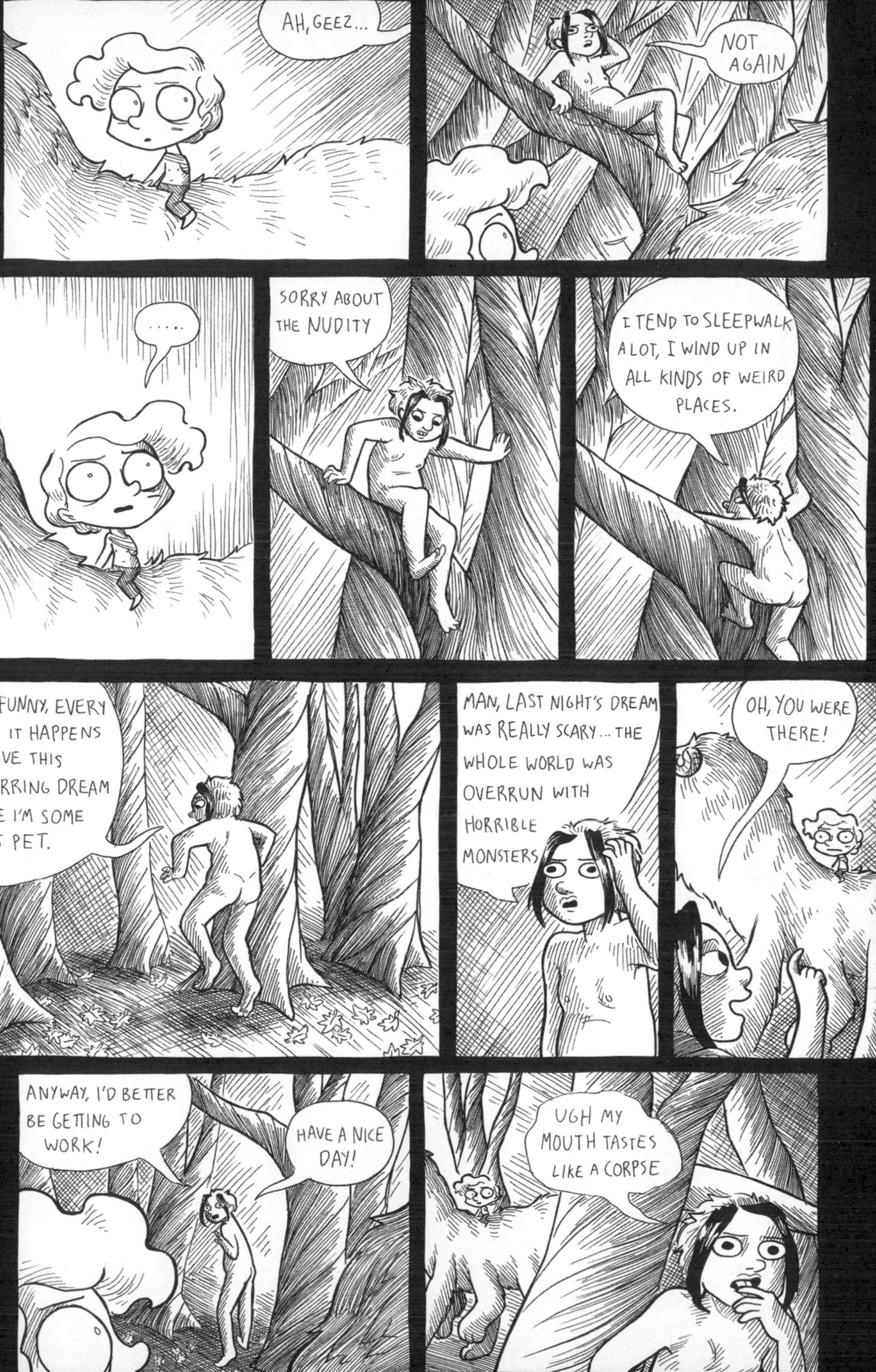
AH, GEEZ...
NOT AGAIN
.....
SORRY ABOUT THE NUDITY
I TEND TO SLEEPWALK A LOT, I WIND UP IN ALL KINDS OF WEIRD PLACES.
IT'S FUNNY, EVERY TIME IT HAPPENS I HAVE THIS RECURRING DREAM WHERE I'M SOME KID'S PET.
MAN, LAST NIGHT'S DREAM WAS REALLY SCARY... THE WHOLE WORLD WAS OVERRUN WITH HORRIBLE MONSTERS
OH, YOU WERE THERE!
ANYWAY, I'D BETTER BE GETTING TO WORK!
HAVE A NICE DAY!
UGH MY MOUTH TASTES LIKE A CORPSE

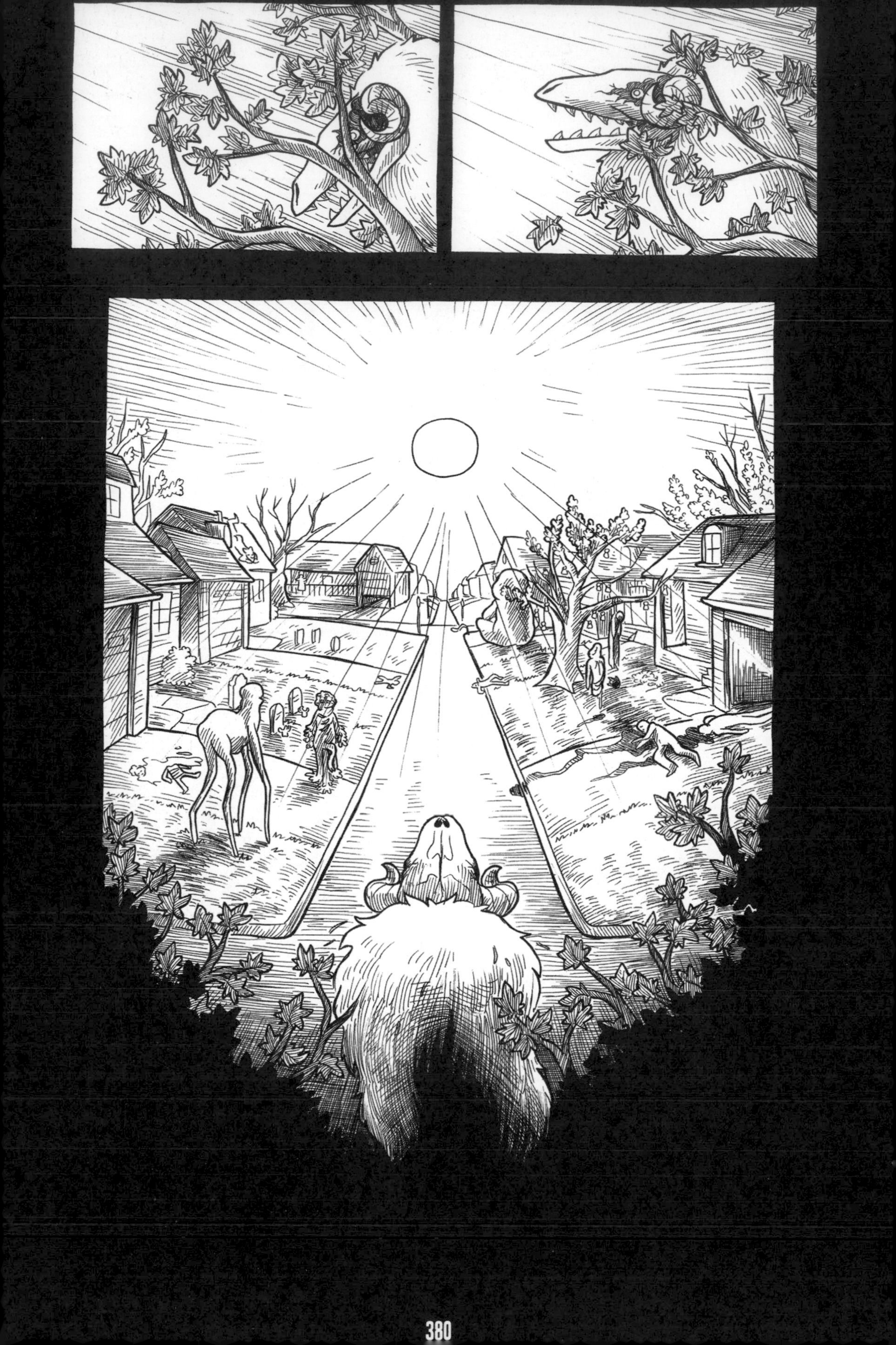

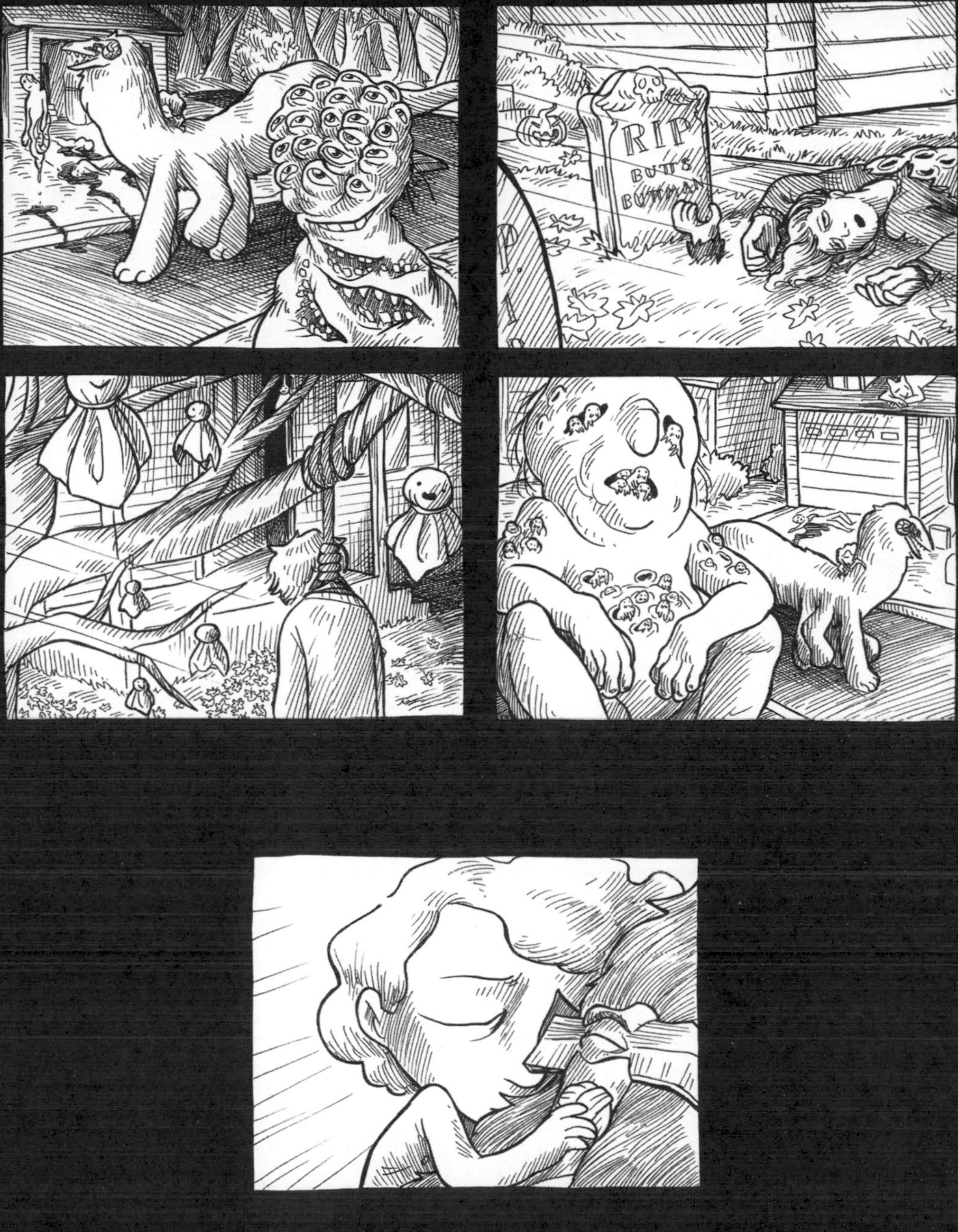
RIP
BUTTS

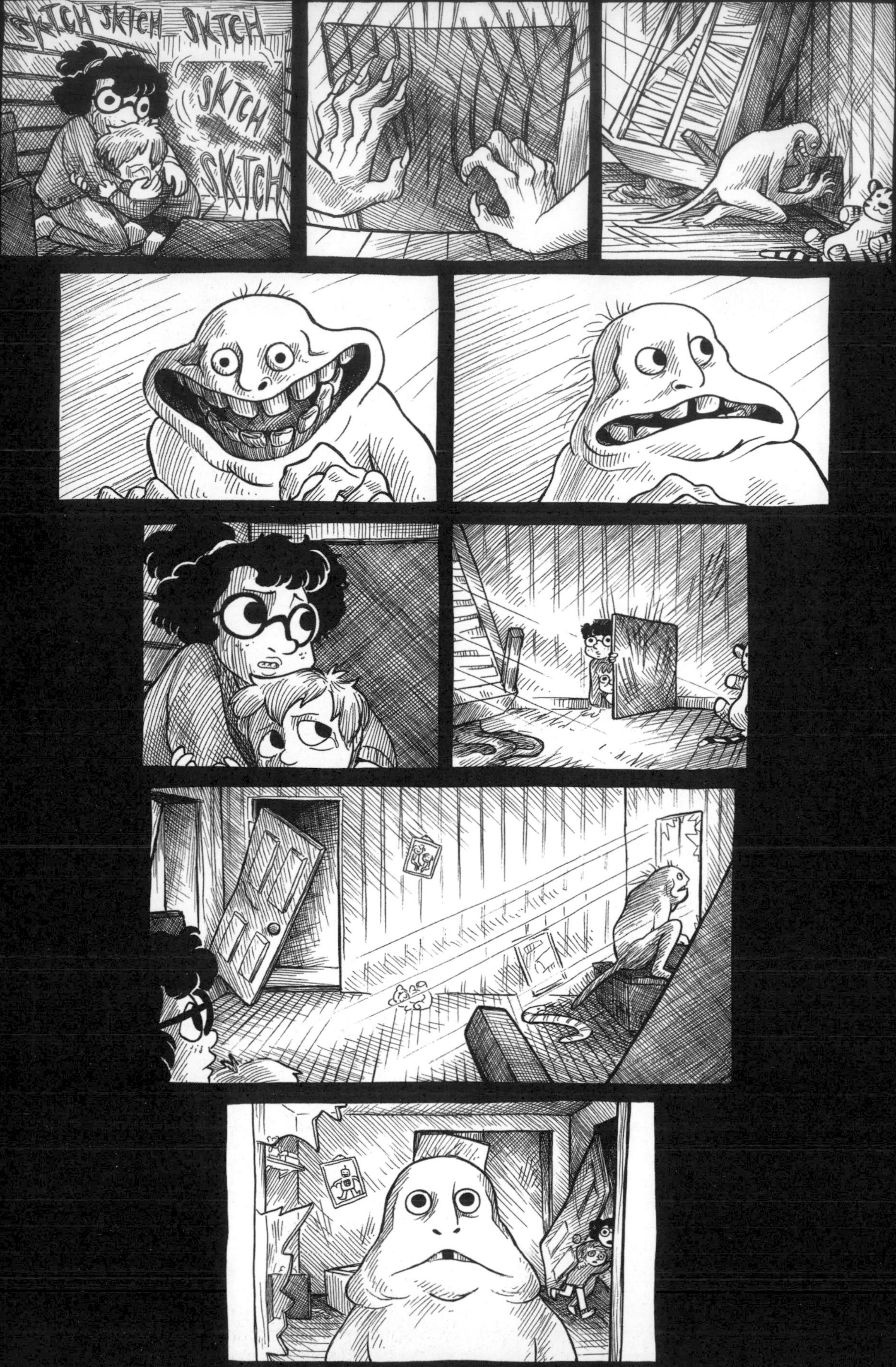
SKTCH SKTCH SKTCH
SKTCH
SKTCH

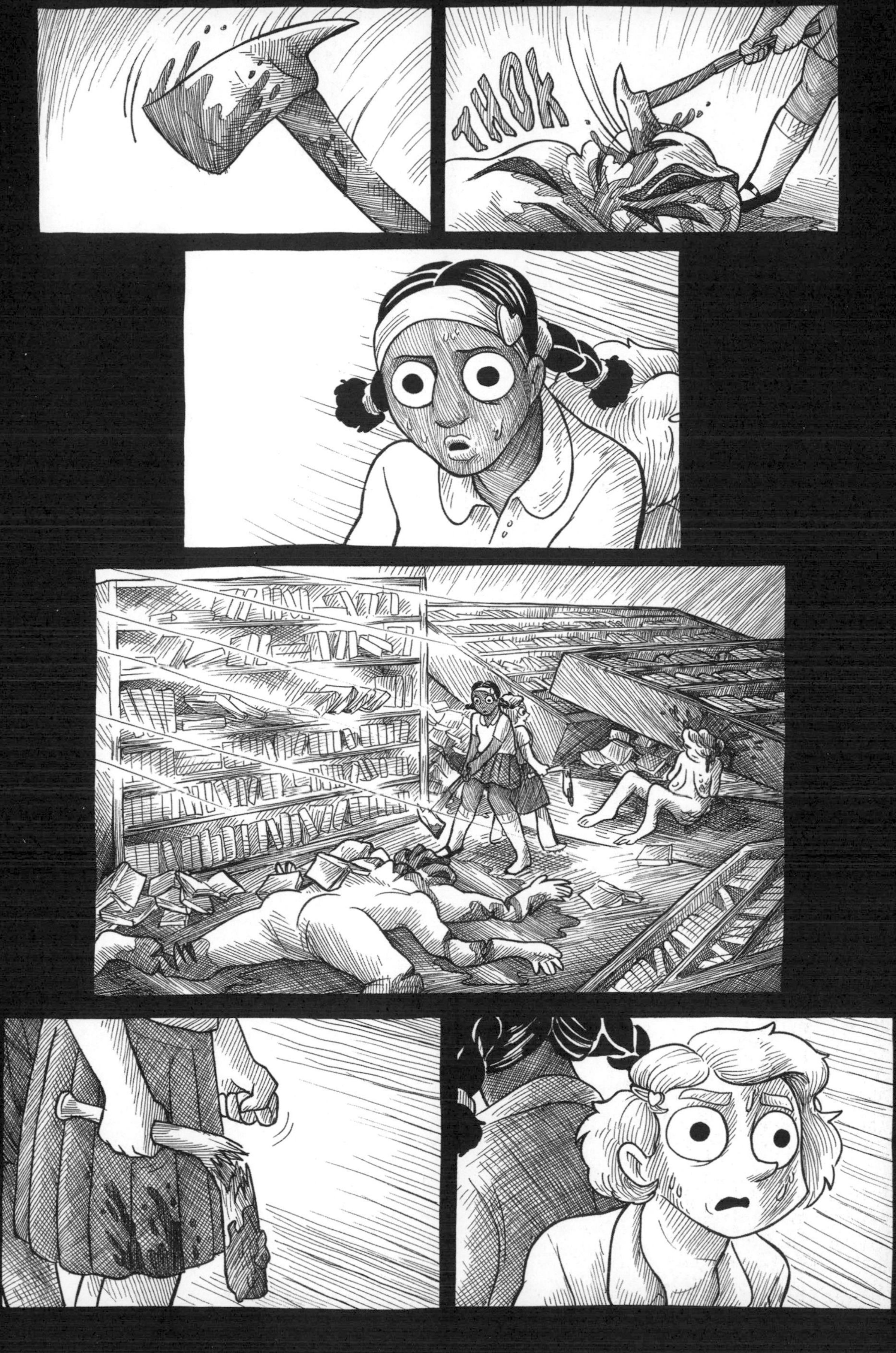
THOK

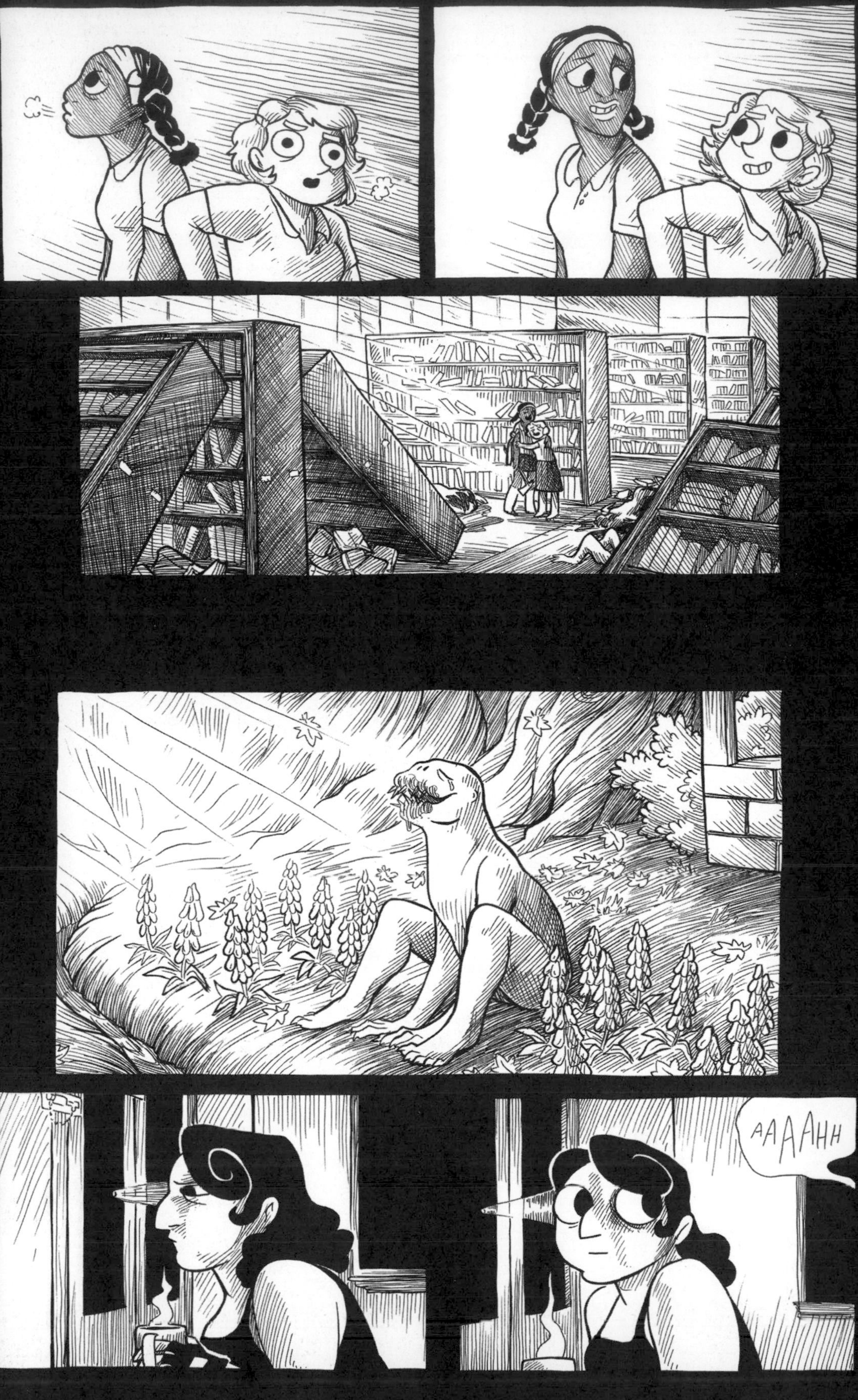
AAAAHH

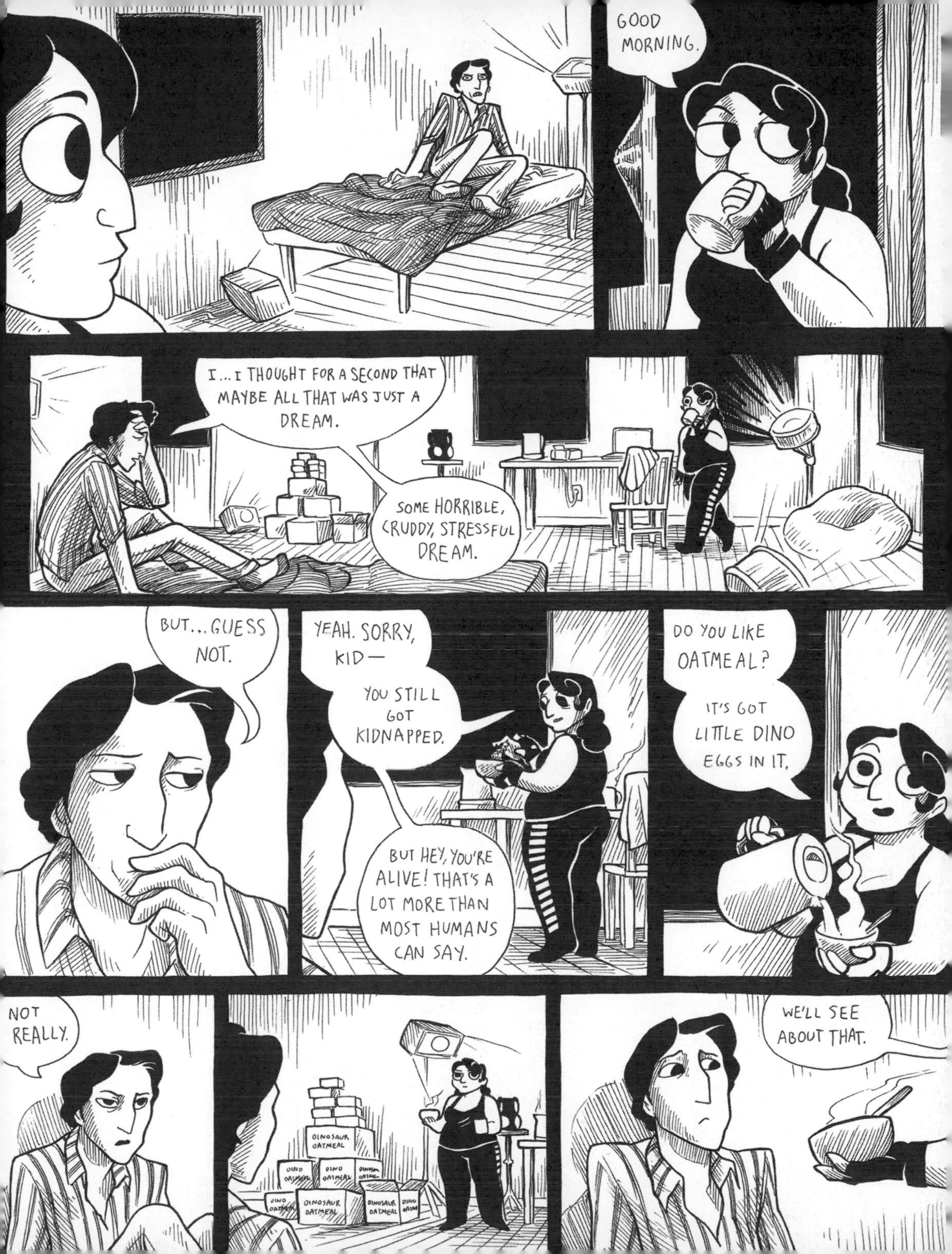
GOOD MORNING.
I... I THOUGHT FOR A SECOND THAT MAYBE ALL THAT WAS JUST A DREAM.
SOME HORRIBLE, CRUDDY, STRESSFUL DREAM.
BUT... GUESS NOT.
YEAH. SORRY, KID—
YOU STILL GOT KIDNAPPED.
BUT HEY, YOU'RE ALIVE! THAT'S A LOT MORE THAN MOST HUMANS CAN SAY.
DO YOU LIKE OATMEAL?
IT'S GOT LITTLE DINO EGGS IN IT.
NOT REALLY.
DINOSAUR OATMEAL
DINO OATMEAL
DINO OATMEAL
DINOSAUR OATMEAL
DINOSAUR OATMEAL
WE'LL SEE ABOUT THAT.

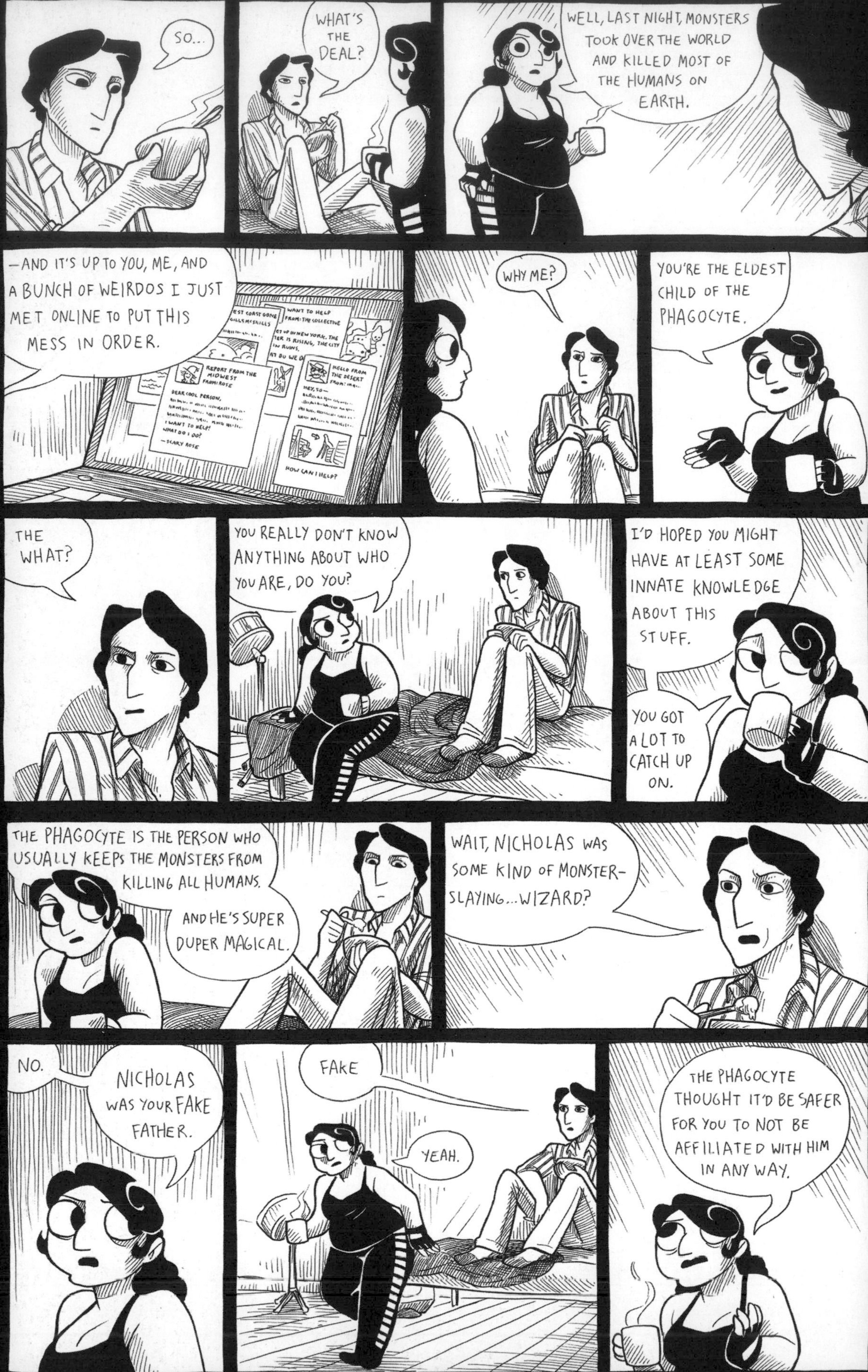
SO...
WHAT'S THE DEAL?
WELL, LAST NIGHT, MONSTERS TOOK OVER THE WORLD AND KILLED MOST OF THE HUMANS ON EARTH.
—AND IT'S UP TO YOU, ME, AND A BUNCH OF WEIRDOS I JUST MET ONLINE TO PUT THIS MESS IN ORDER.
WANT TO HELP FROM: THE COLLECTIVE
REPORT FROM THE MIDWEST FROM: ROSE
DEAR COOL PERSON,
I WANT TO HELP! WHAT DO I DO?
—SCARY ROSE
HELLO FROM THE DESERT
HEY, SO—
HOW CAN I HELP?
WHY ME?
YOU'RE THE ELDEST CHILD OF THE PHAGOCYTE.
THE WHAT?
YOU REALLY DON'T KNOW ANYTHING ABOUT WHO YOU ARE, DO YOU?
I'D HOPED YOU MIGHT HAVE AT LEAST SOME INNATE KNOWLEDGE ABOUT THIS STUFF.
YOU GOT A LOT TO CATCH UP ON.
THE PHAGOCYTE IS THE PERSON WHO USUALLY KEEPS THE MONSTERS FROM KILLING ALL HUMANS.
AND HE'S SUPER DUPER MAGICAL.
WAIT, NICHOLAS WAS SOME KIND OF MONSTER-SLAYING...WIZARD?
NO.
NICHOLAS WAS YOUR FAKE FATHER.
FAKE
YEAH.
THE PHAGOCYTE THOUGHT IT'D BE SAFER FOR YOU TO NOT BE AFFILIATED WITH HIM IN ANY WAY.

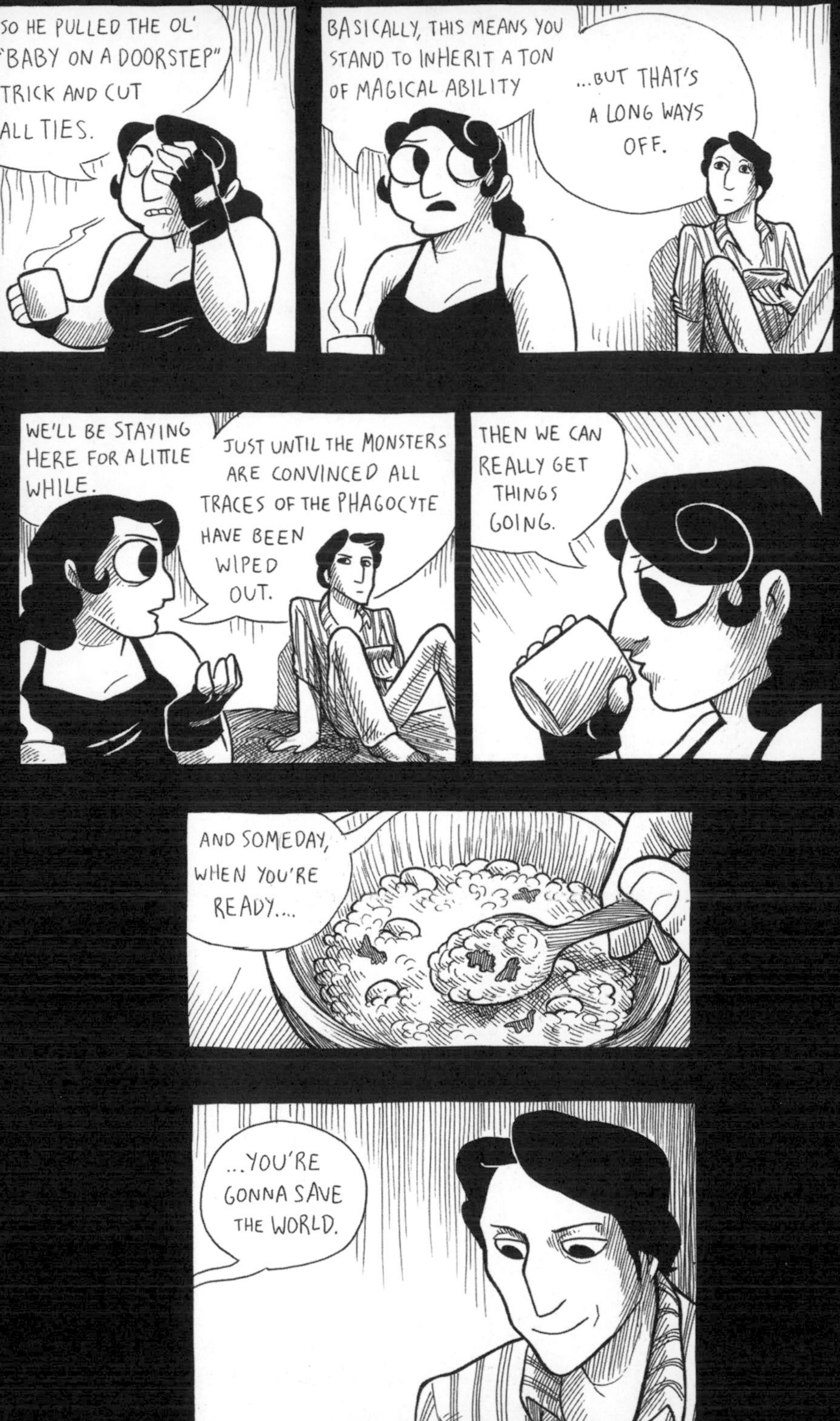
SO HE PULLED THE OL' "BABY ON A DOORSTEP" TRICK AND CUT ALL TIES.
BASICALLY, THIS MEANS YOU STAND TO INHERIT A TON OF MAGICAL ABILITY
...BUT THAT'S A LONG WAYS OFF.
WE'LL BE STAYING HERE FOR A LITTLE WHILE.
JUST UNTIL THE MONSTERS ARE CONVINCED ALL TRACES OF THE PHAGOCYTE HAVE BEEN WIPED OUT.
THEN WE CAN REALLY GET THINGS GOING.
AND SOMEDAY, WHEN YOU'RE READY....
...YOU'RE GONNA SAVE THE WORLD.

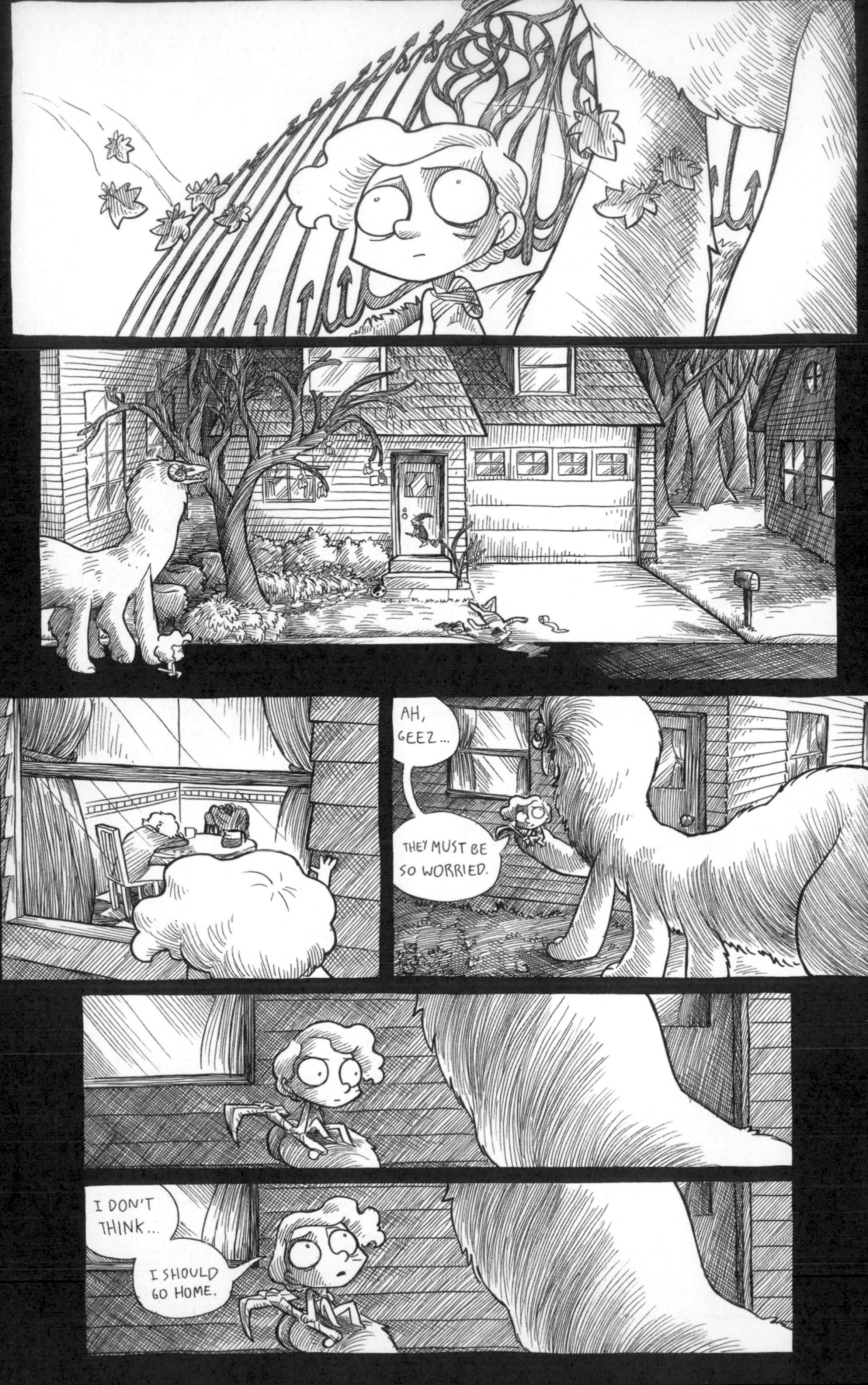
AH, GEEZ...
THEY MUST BE SO WORRIED.
I DON'T THINK...
I SHOULD GO HOME.

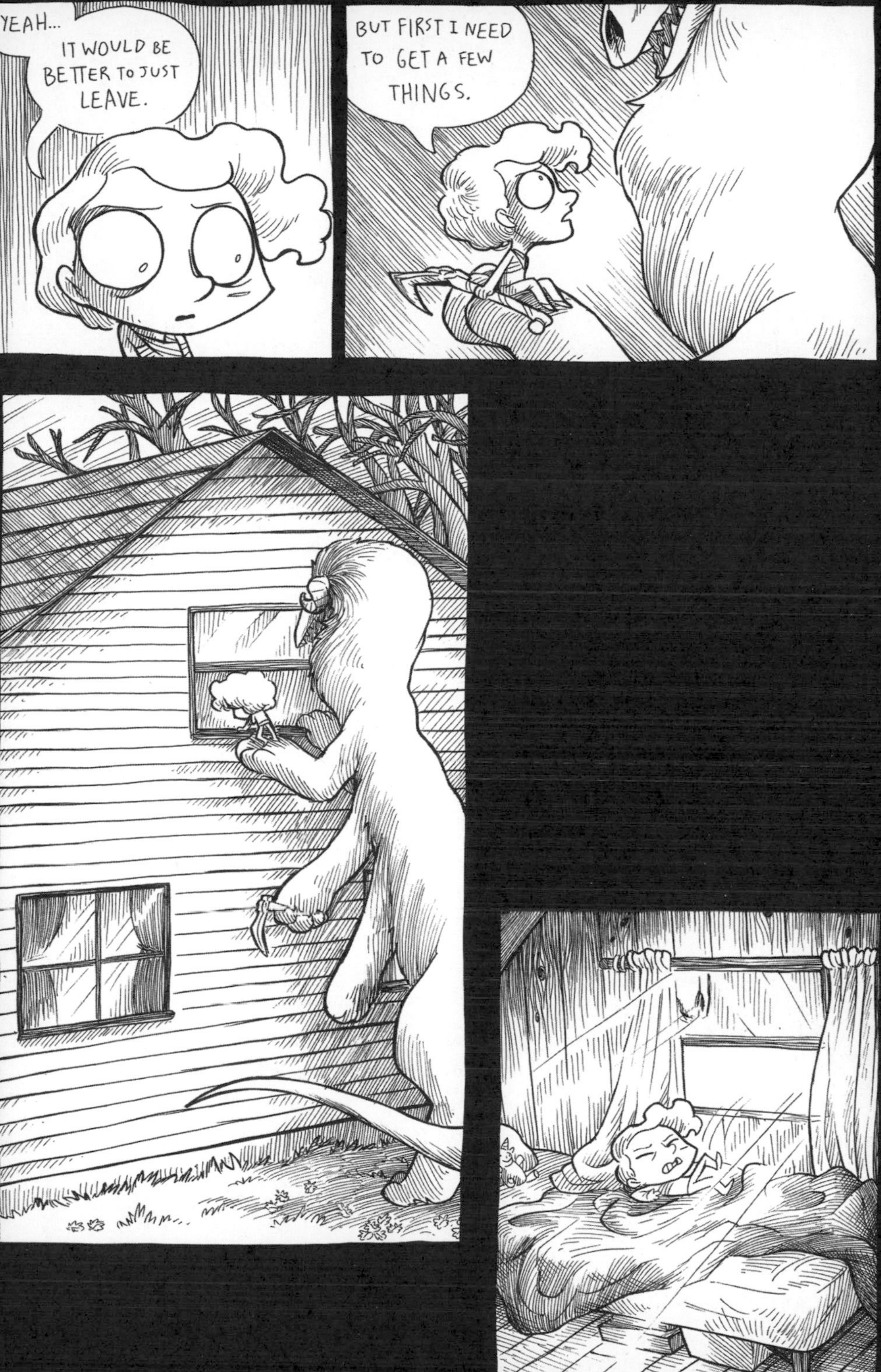
YEAH...
IT WOULD BE BETTER TO JUST LEAVE.
BUT FIRST I NEED TO GET A FEW THINGS.

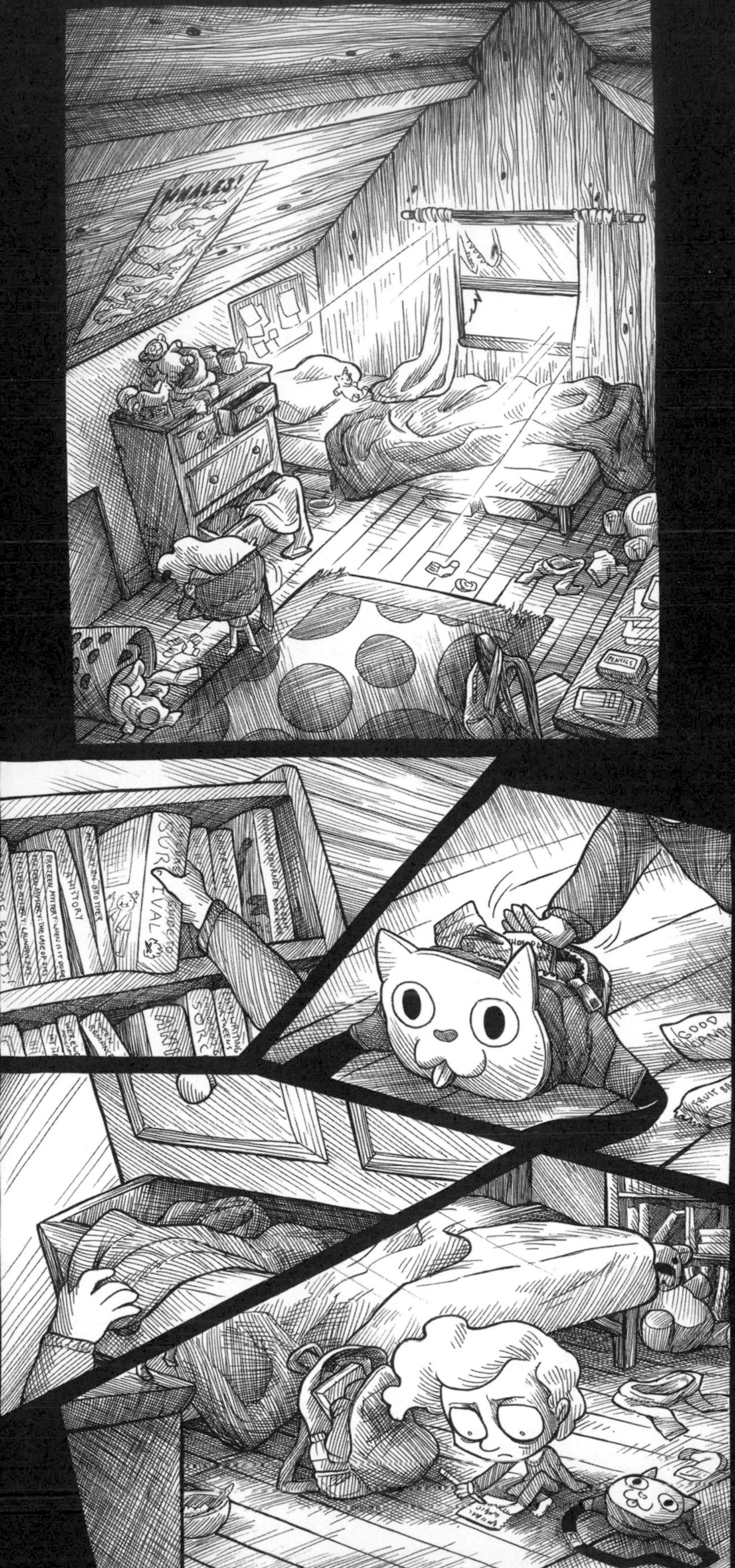
WHALES!
PENCILS
PRETEEN MYSTERY: WHEN IS IT DONE
PRETEEN MYSTERY: THE CASE OF ZITS
PRETEEN MYSTERY: LAUNDRY DAY
A HISTORY
MY HAIRY BIG BROTHER
GUIDE TO SURVIVAL
A JOURNEY
SONGWRITING FOR TWEENS

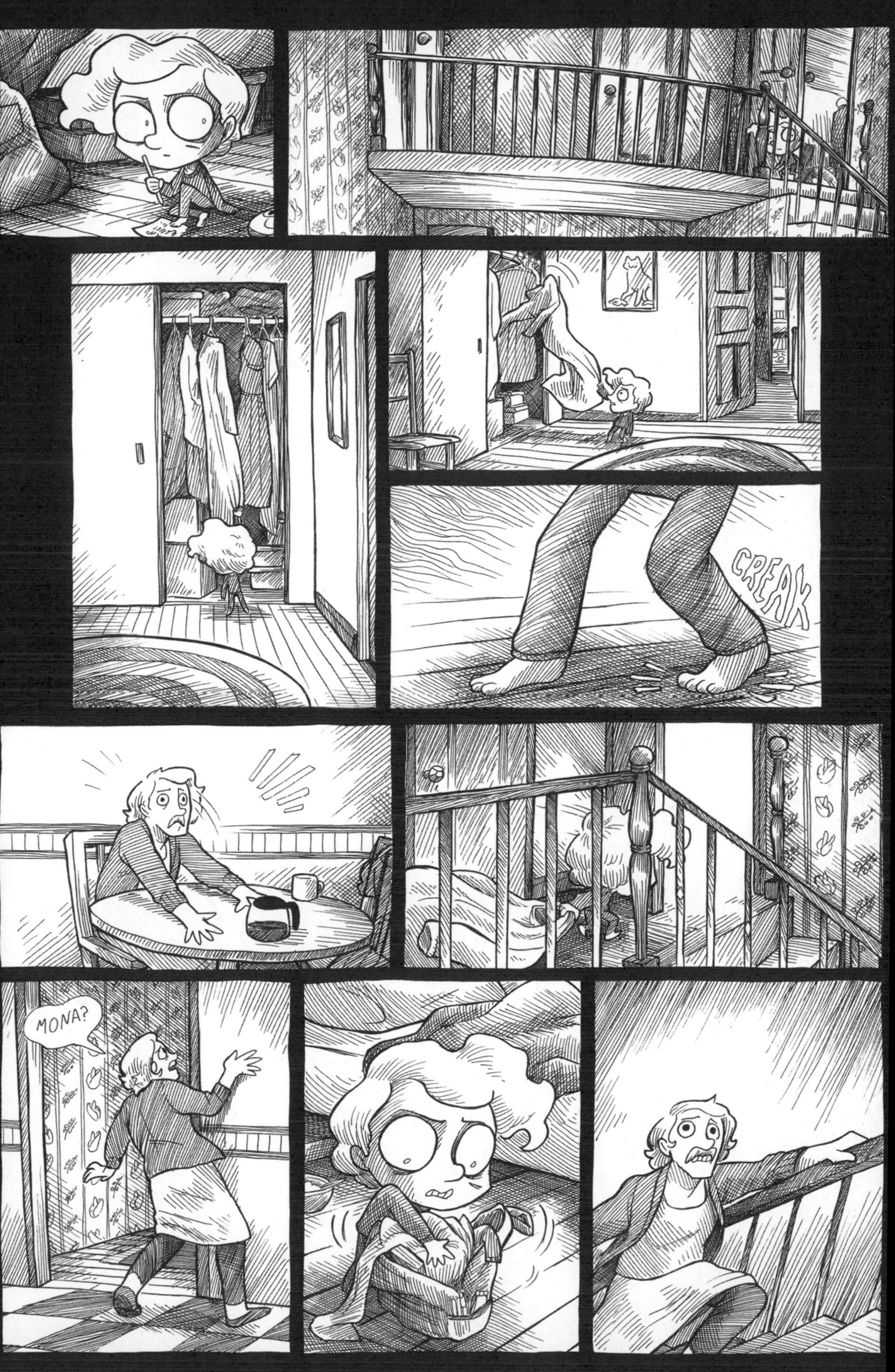
CREAK
MONA?

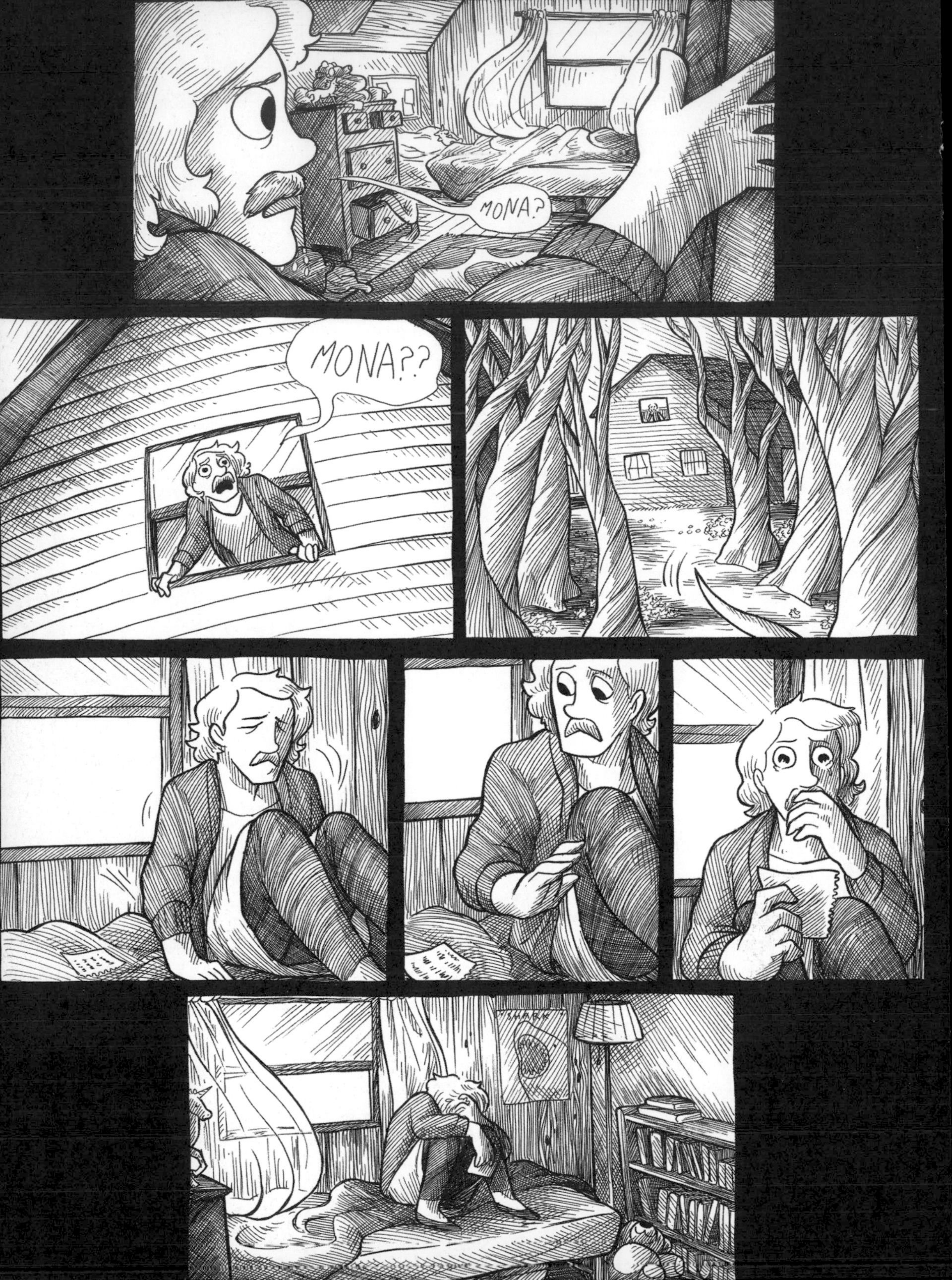
MONA?
MONA??

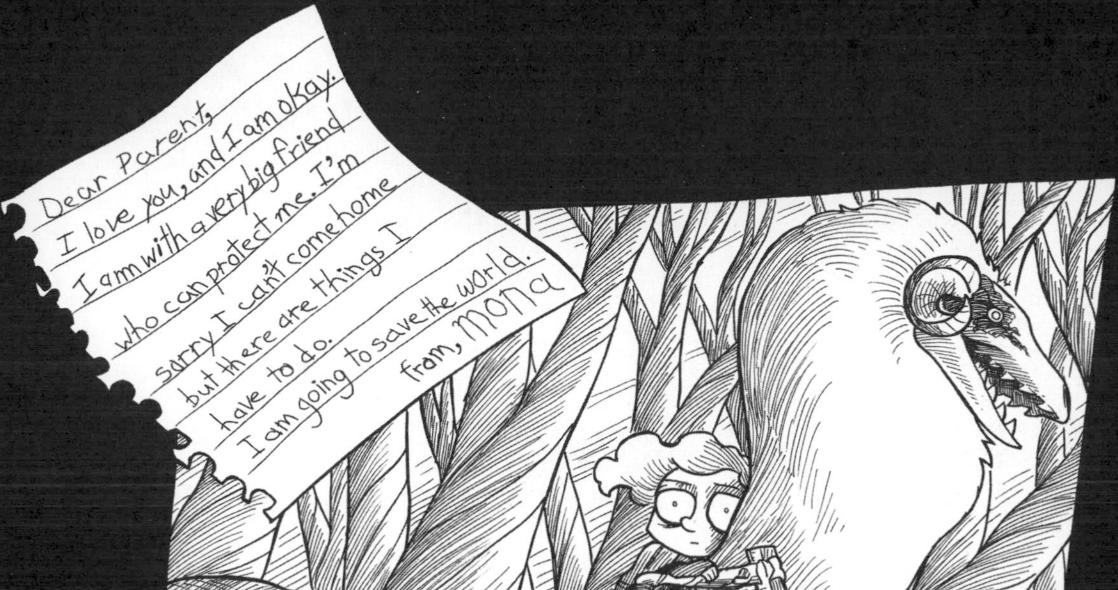
Dear Parent,
I love you, and I am okay.
I am with a very big friend
who can protect me. I'm
sorry I can't come home
but there are things I
have to do.
I am going to save the world.
from, mona

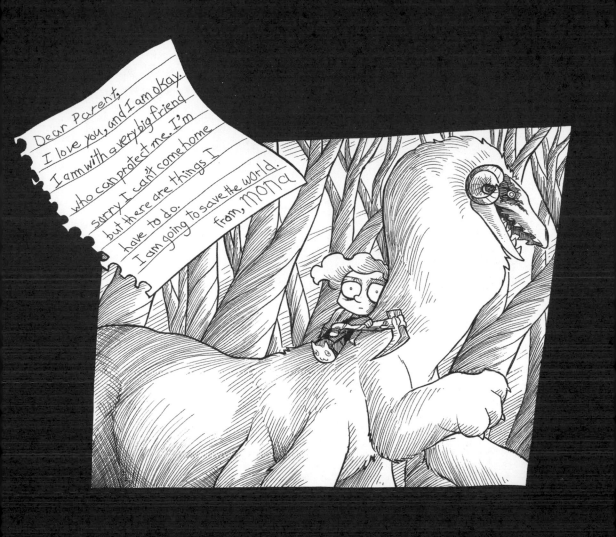

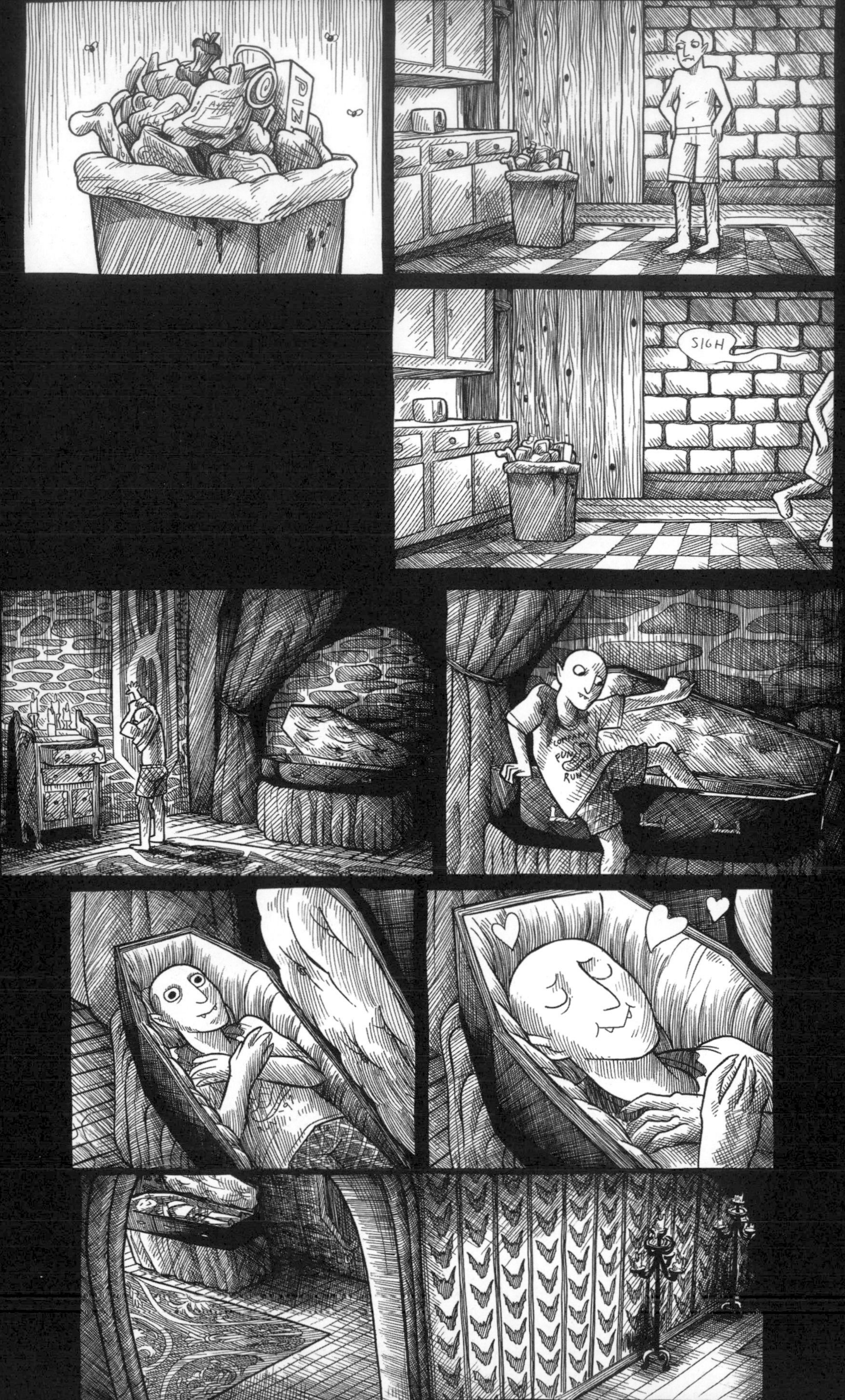
SIGH

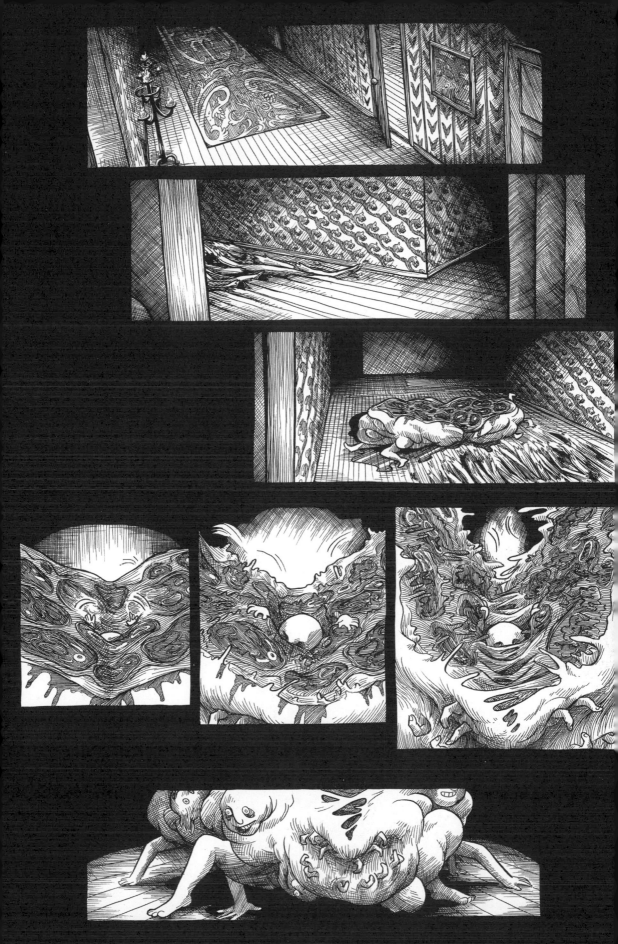

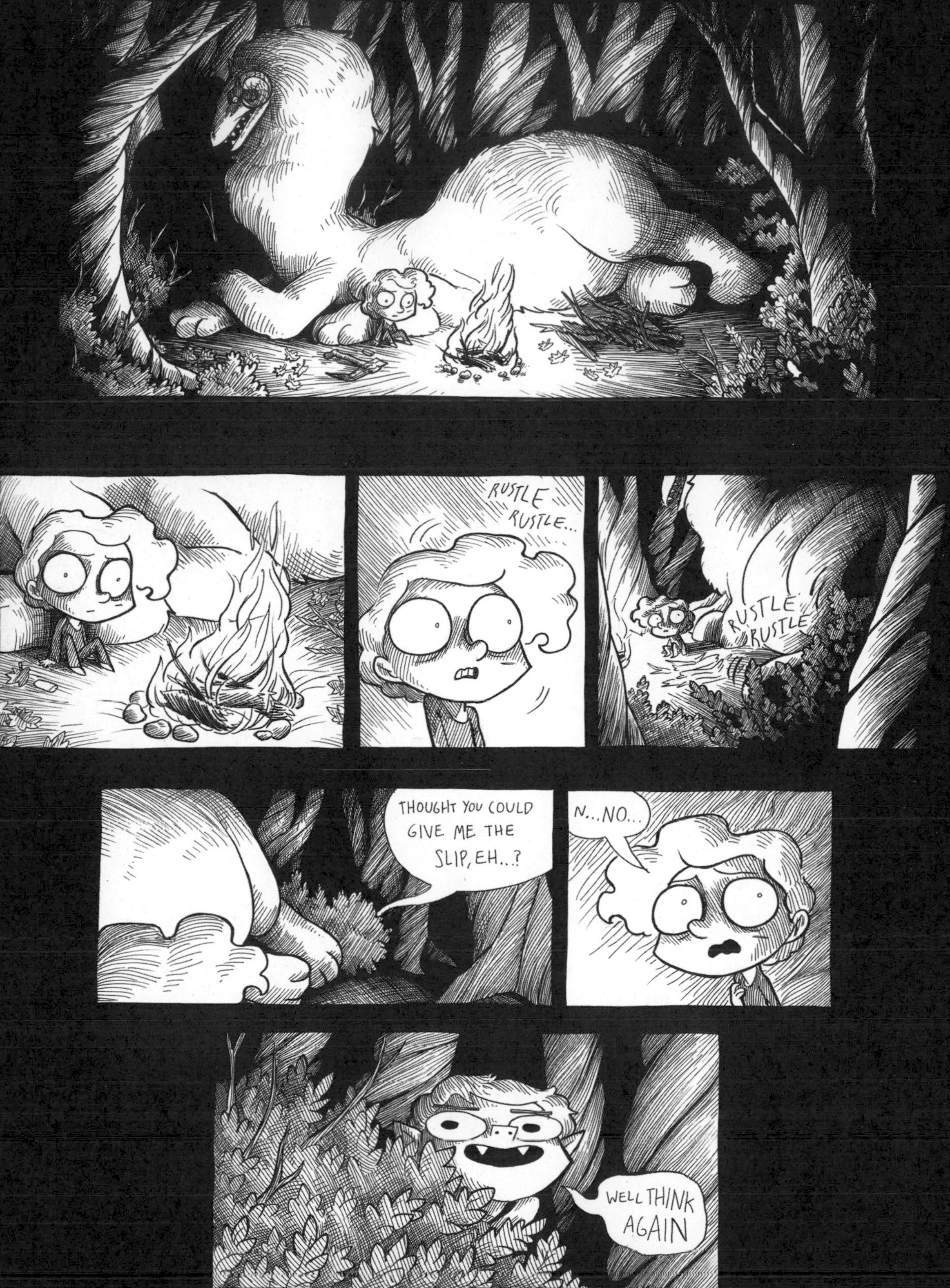
RUSTLE RUSTLE...
RUSTLE RUSTLE
THOUGHT YOU COULD GIVE ME THE SLIP, EH...?
N...NO...
WELL THINK AGAIN

YOU CAN NEVER ESCAPE MY FRIENDSHIP, MONA
WE ARE BEST FRIENDS FOREVER!!
NO
NOOOOOOOOo

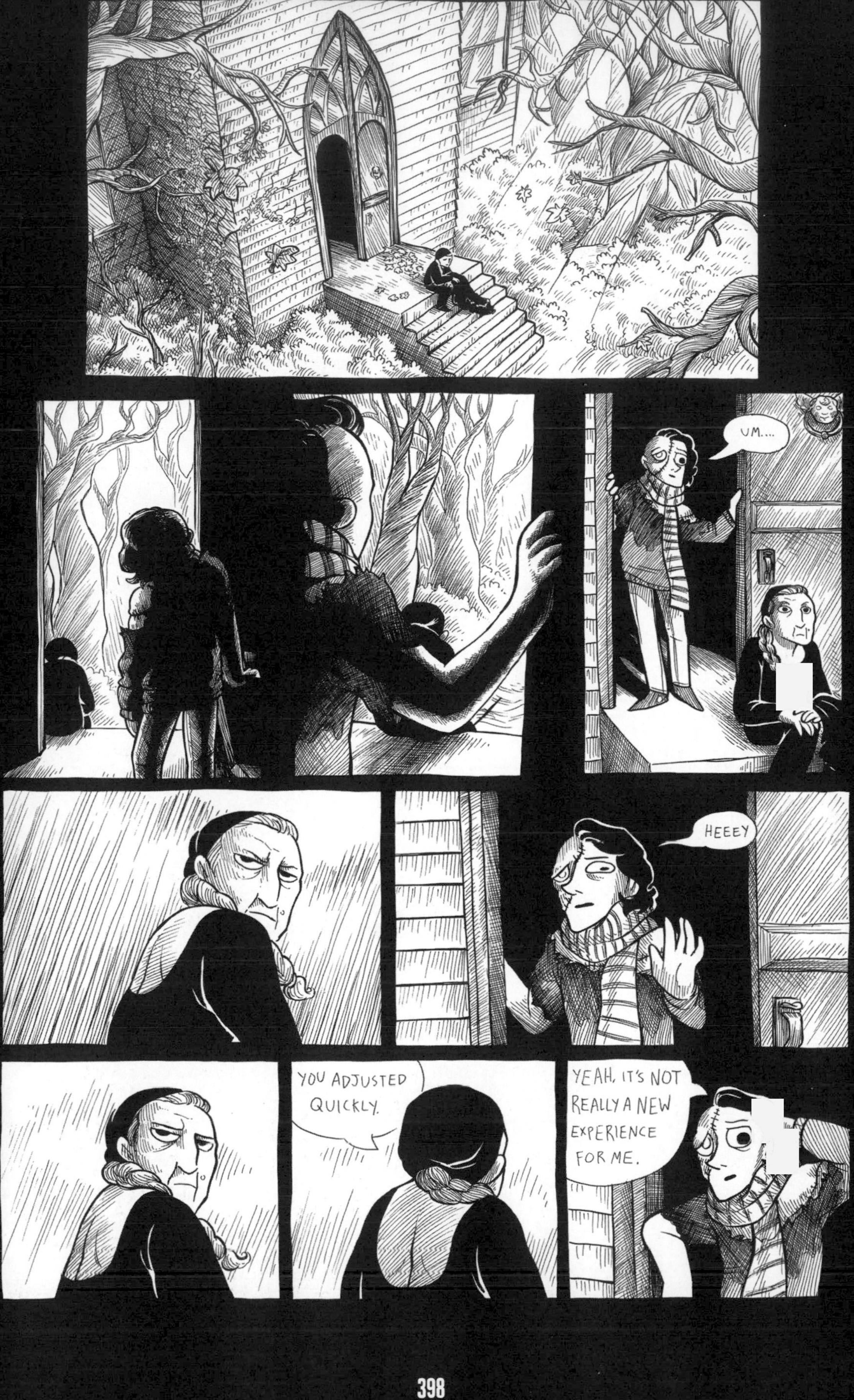
UM....
HEEEY
YOU ADJUSTED QUICKLY.
YEAH, IT'S NOT REALLY A NEW EXPERIENCE FOR ME.

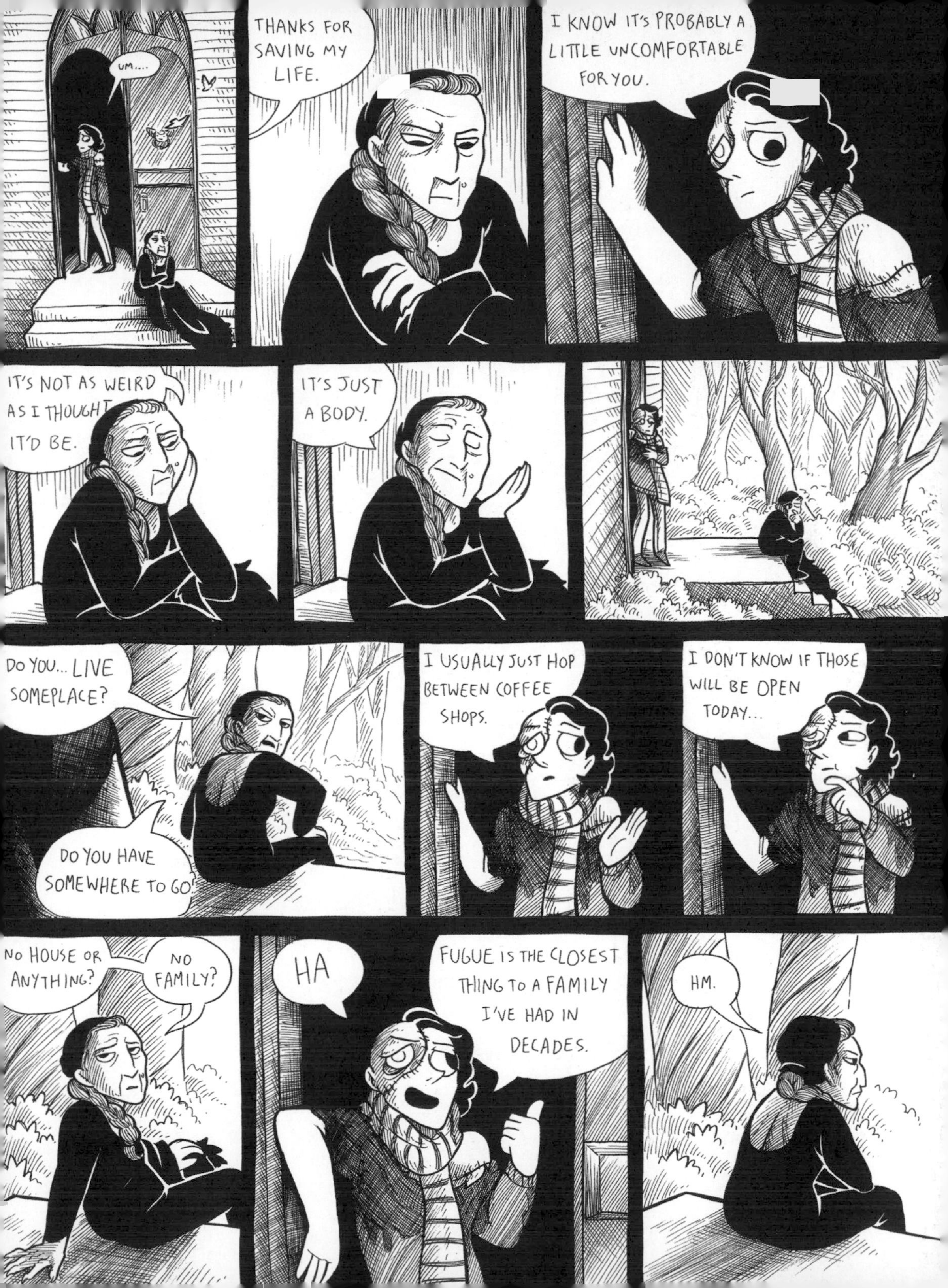
UM....
THANKS FOR SAVING MY LIFE.
I KNOW IT'S PROBABLY A LITTLE UNCOMFORTABLE FOR YOU.
IT'S NOT AS WEIRD AS I THOUGHT IT'D BE.
IT'S JUST A BODY.
DO YOU... LIVE SOMEPLACE?
DO YOU HAVE SOMEWHERE TO GO?
I USUALLY JUST HOP BETWEEN COFFEE SHOPS.
I DON'T KNOW IF THOSE WILL BE OPEN TODAY...
NO HOUSE OR ANYTHING?
NO FAMILY?
HA
FUGUE IS THE CLOSEST THING TO A FAMILY I'VE HAD IN DECADES.
HM.

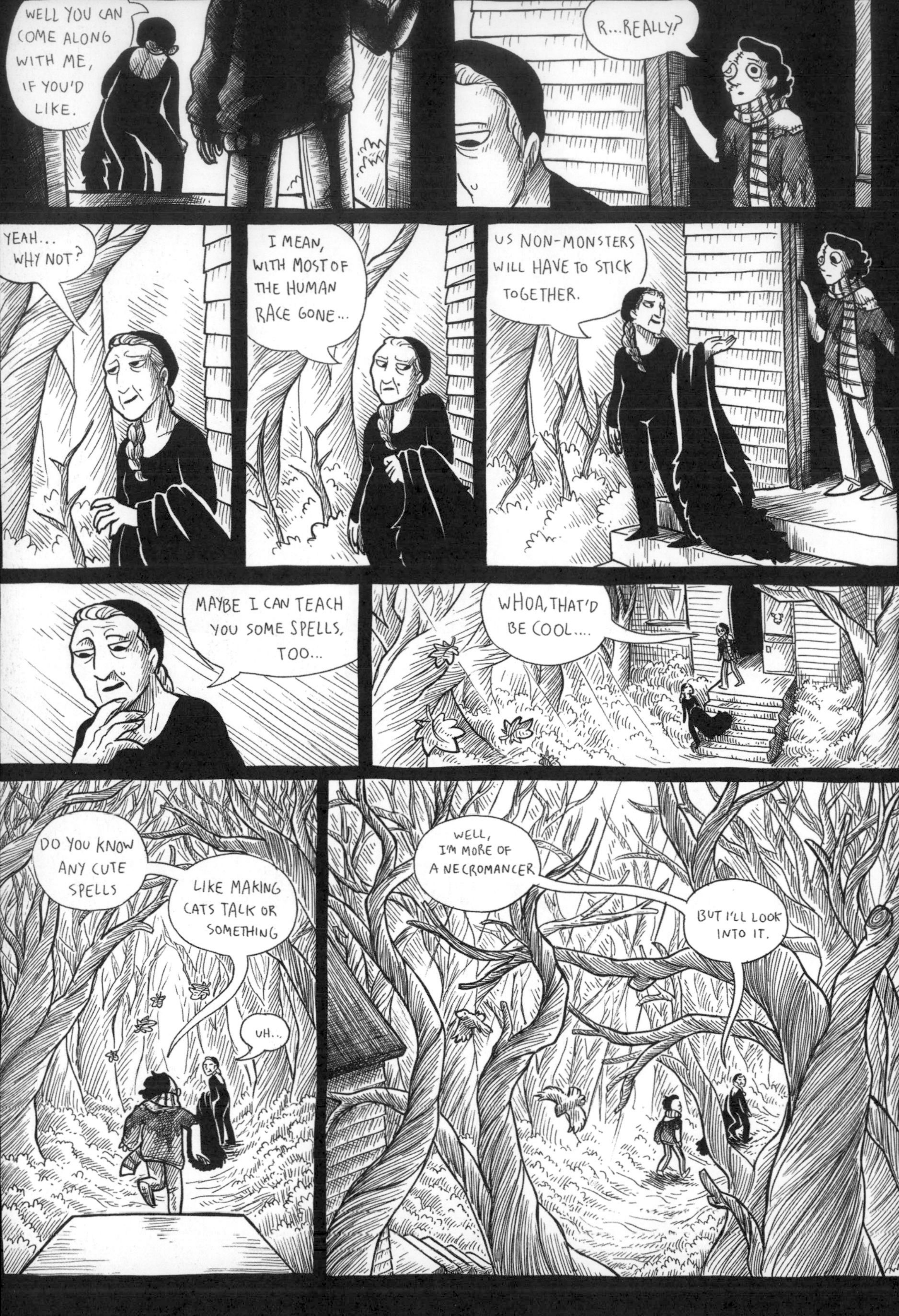
WELL YOU CAN COME ALONG WITH ME, IF YOU'D LIKE.
R...REALLY?
YEAH... WHY NOT?
I MEAN, WITH MOST OF THE HUMAN RACE GONE...
US NON-MONSTERS WILL HAVE TO STICK TOGETHER.
MAYBE I CAN TEACH YOU SOME SPELLS, TOO...
WHOA, THAT'D BE COOL....
DO YOU KNOW ANY CUTE SPELLS
LIKE MAKING CATS TALK OR SOMETHING
UH...
WELL, I'M MORE OF A NECROMANCER
BUT I'LL LOOK INTO IT.

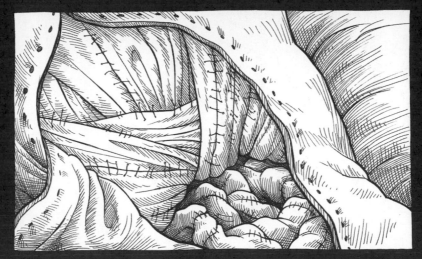

WOW.

SO YOU'RE BASICALLY JUST... SKIN ALL THE WAY DOWN, HUH?

INDEED.

WE'RE JUST SKIN AND BONES, AS YOU HUMANS WOULD SAY!

THAT DOESN'T MAKE ANY SENSE...

OF COURSE NOT.

WERE YOU REALLY EXPECTING IT TO?

SO...

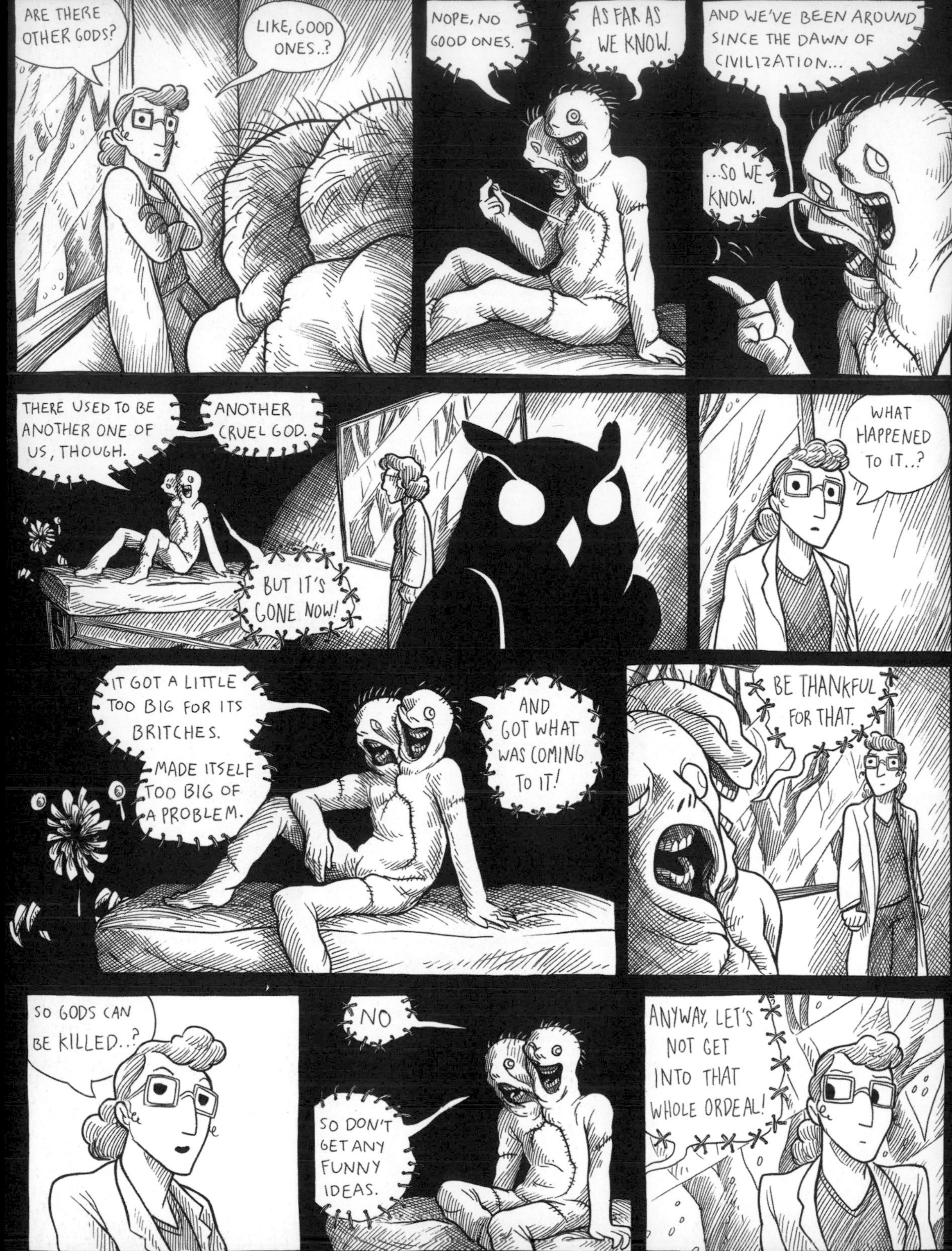
ARE THERE OTHER GODS?
LIKE, GOOD ONES..?
NOPE, NO GOOD ONES.
AS FAR AS WE KNOW.
AND WE'VE BEEN AROUND SINCE THE DAWN OF CIVILIZATION...
...SO WE KNOW.
THERE USED TO BE ANOTHER ONE OF US, THOUGH.
ANOTHER CRUEL GOD.
BUT IT'S GONE NOW!
WHAT HAPPENED TO IT..?
IT GOT A LITTLE TOO BIG FOR ITS BRITCHES.
MADE ITSELF TOO BIG OF A PROBLEM.
AND GOT WHAT WAS COMING TO IT!
BE THANKFUL FOR THAT.
SO GODS CAN BE KILLED..?
NO
SO DON'T GET ANY FUNNY IDEAS.
ANYWAY, LET'S NOT GET INTO THAT WHOLE ORDEAL!

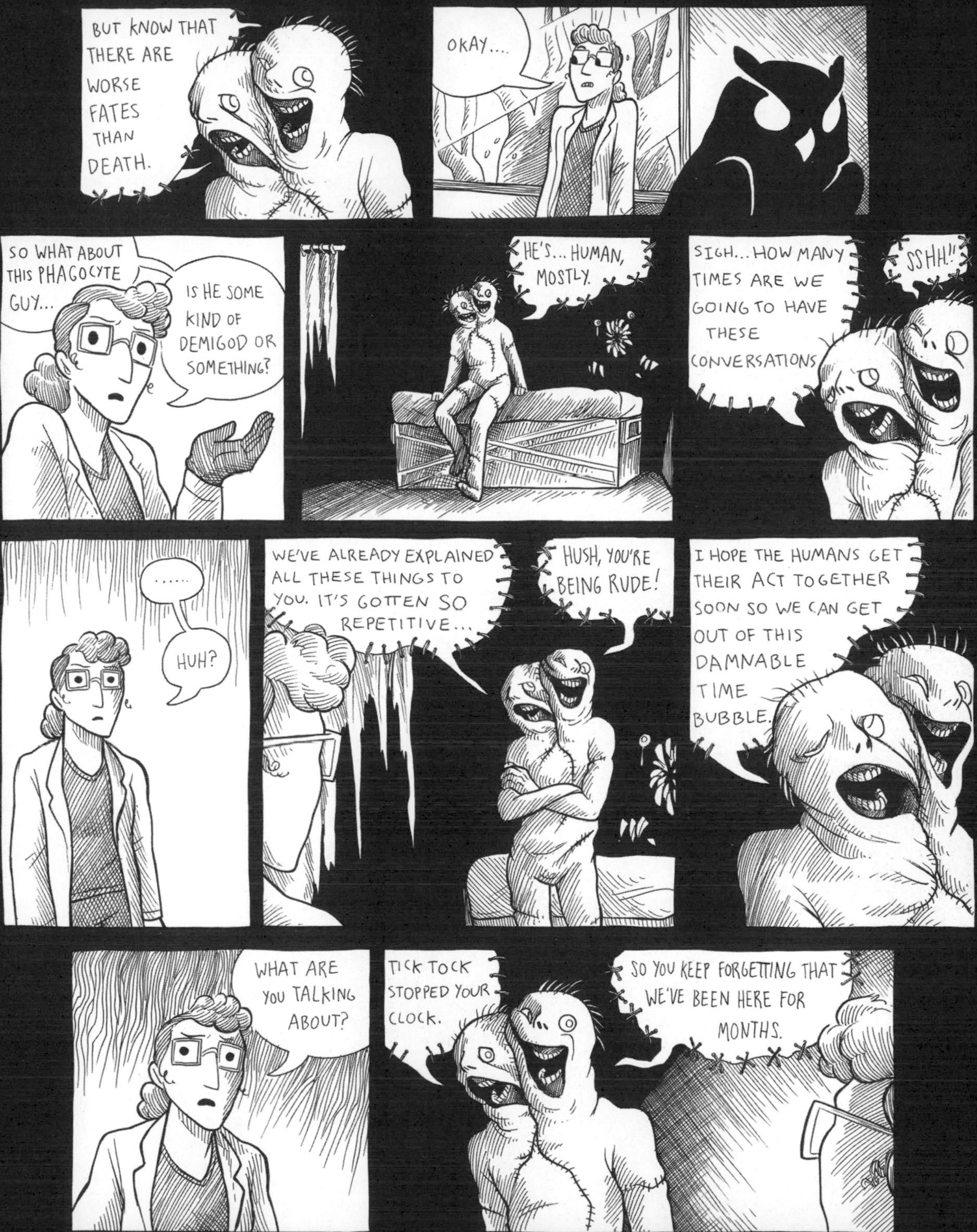
BUT KNOW THAT THERE ARE WORSE FATES THAN DEATH.
OKAY....
SO WHAT ABOUT THIS PHAGOCYTE GUY...
IS HE SOME KIND OF DEMIGOD OR SOMETHING?
HE'S... HUMAN, MOSTLY.
SIGH... HOW MANY TIMES ARE WE GOING TO HAVE THESE CONVERSATIONS
SSHH!!
......
HUH?
WE'VE ALREADY EXPLAINED ALL THESE THINGS TO YOU. IT'S GOTTEN SO REPETITIVE...
HUSH, YOU'RE BEING RUDE!
I HOPE THE HUMANS GET THEIR ACT TOGETHER SOON SO WE CAN GET OUT OF THIS DAMNABLE TIME BUBBLE.
WHAT ARE YOU TALKING ABOUT?
TICK TOCK STOPPED YOUR CLOCK.
SO YOU KEEP FORGETTING THAT WE'VE BEEN HERE FOR MONTHS.

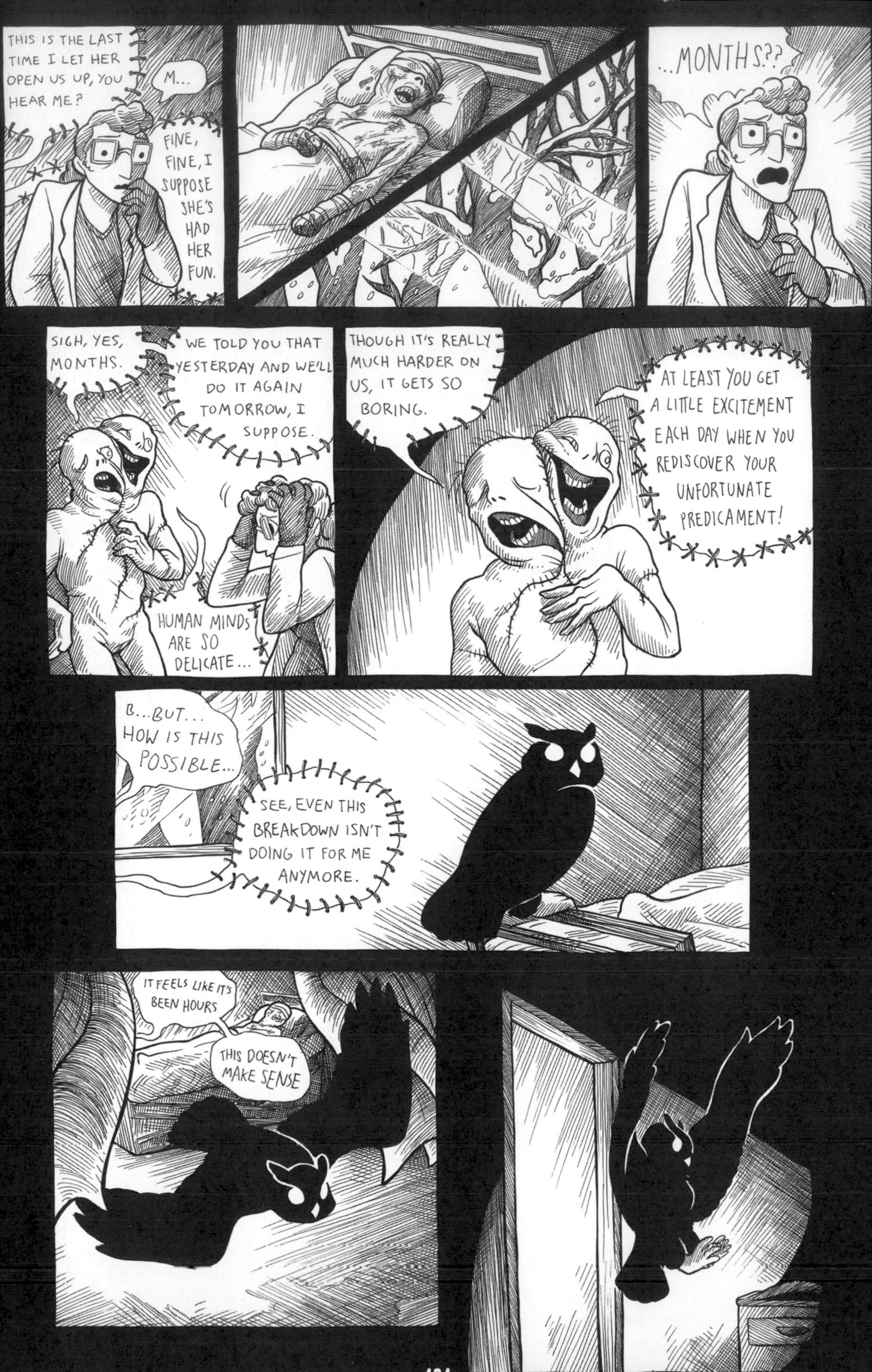
THIS IS THE LAST TIME I LET HER OPEN US UP, YOU HEAR ME?
M...
FINE, FINE, I SUPPOSE SHE'S HAD HER FUN.
...MONTHS??
SIGH, YES, MONTHS.
WE TOLD YOU THAT YESTERDAY AND WE'LL DO IT AGAIN TOMORROW, I SUPPOSE.
HUMAN MINDS ARE SO DELICATE...
THOUGH IT'S REALLY MUCH HARDER ON US, IT GETS SO BORING.
AT LEAST YOU GET A LITTLE EXCITEMENT EACH DAY WHEN YOU REDISCOVER YOUR UNFORTUNATE PREDICAMENT!
B...BUT... HOW IS THIS POSSIBLE...
SEE, EVEN THIS BREAKDOWN ISN'T DOING IT FOR ME ANYMORE.
IT FEELS LIKE IT'S BEEN HOURS
THIS DOESN'T MAKE SENSE

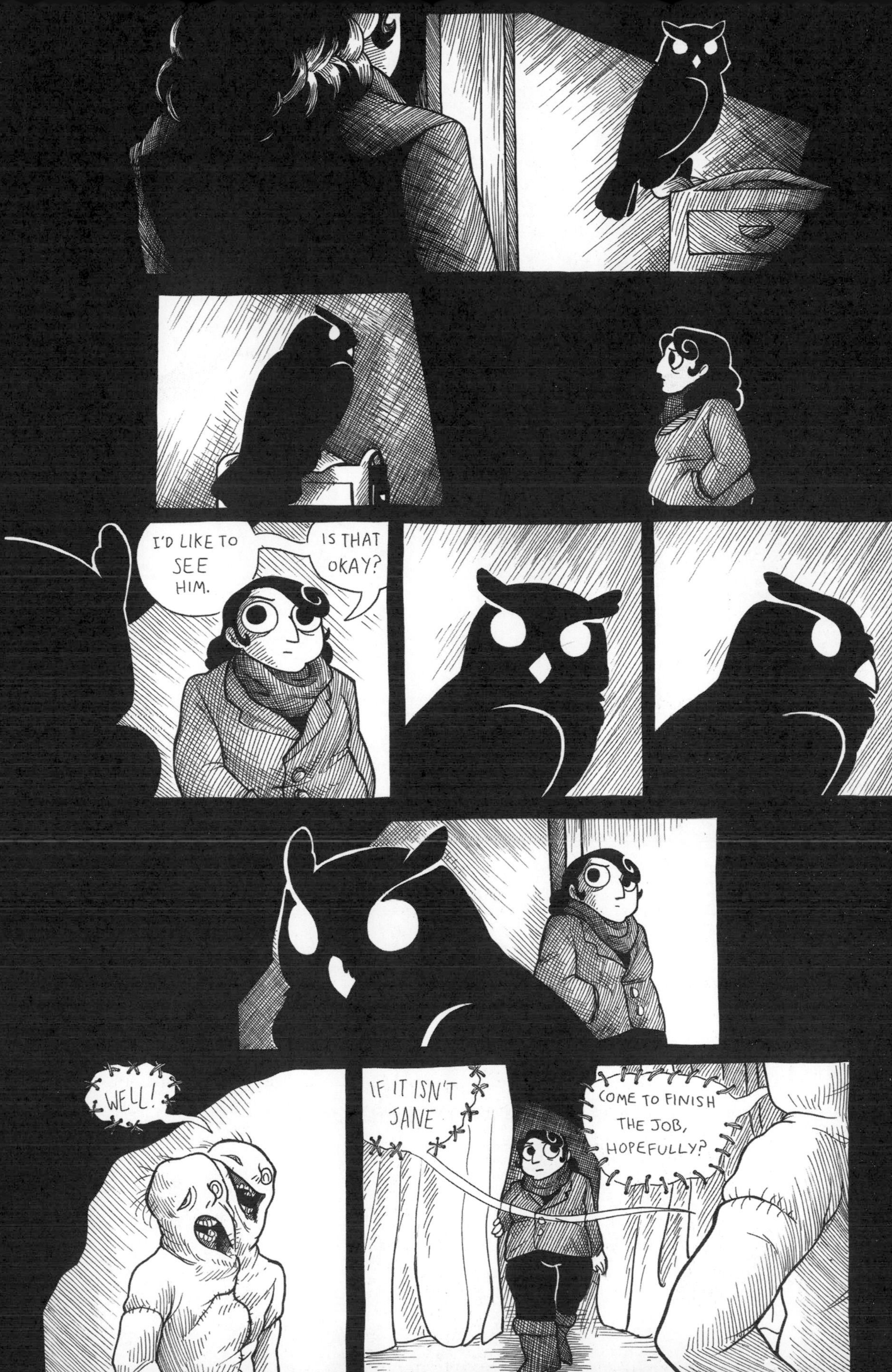
I'D LIKE TO SEE HIM.
IS THAT OKAY?
WELL!
IF IT ISN'T JANE
COME TO FINISH THE JOB, HOPEFULLY?

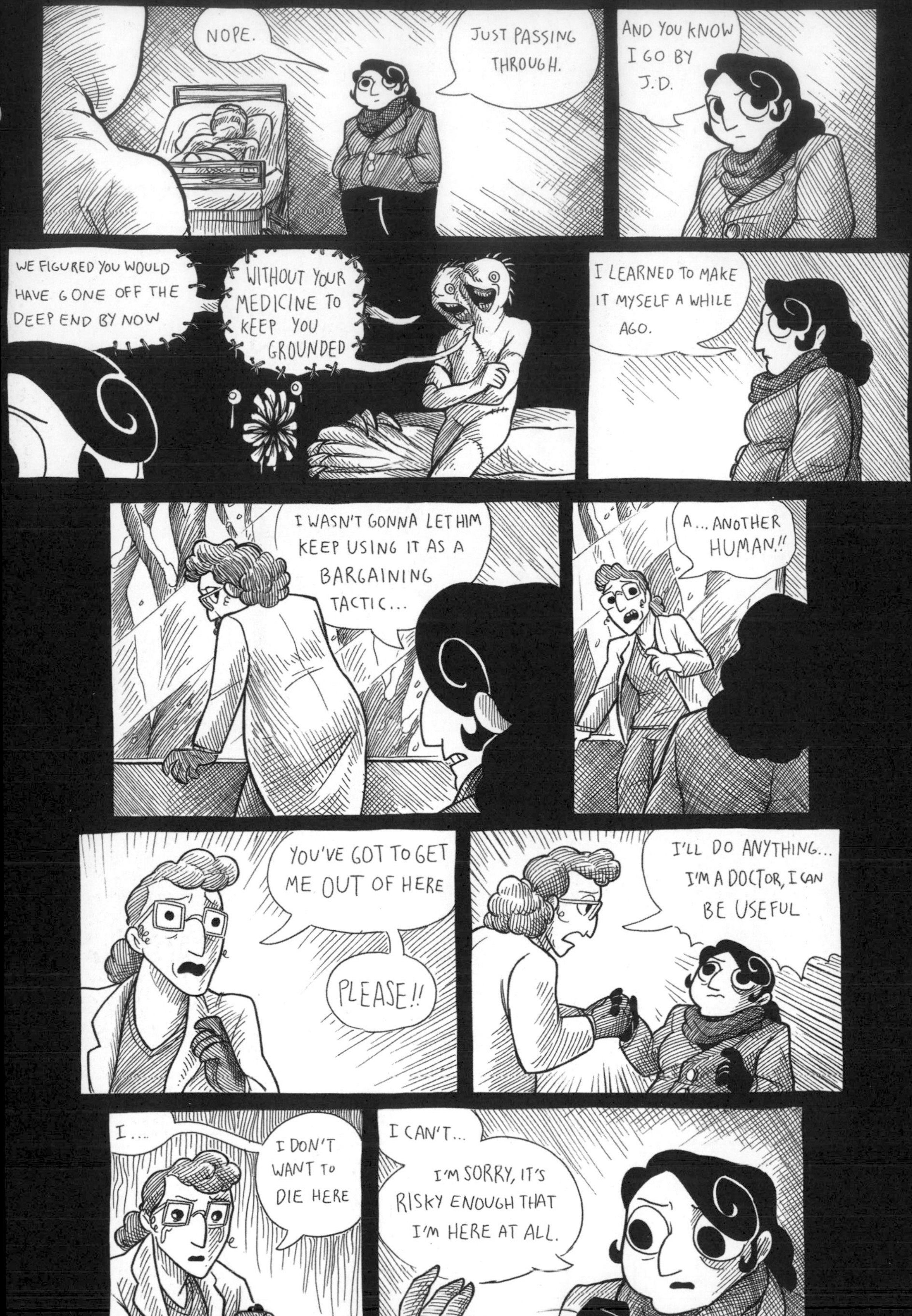
NOPE.
JUST PASSING THROUGH.
AND YOU KNOW I GO BY J.D.
WE FIGURED YOU WOULD HAVE GONE OFF THE DEEP END BY NOW
WITHOUT YOUR MEDICINE TO KEEP YOU GROUNDED
I LEARNED TO MAKE IT MYSELF A WHILE AGO.
I WASN'T GONNA LET HIM KEEP USING IT AS A BARGAINING TACTIC...
A... ANOTHER HUMAN!!
YOU'VE GOT TO GET ME OUT OF HERE
PLEASE!!
I'LL DO ANYTHING... I'M A DOCTOR, I CAN BE USEFUL
I...
I DON'T WANT TO DIE HERE
I CAN'T...
I'M SORRY, IT'S RISKY ENOUGH THAT I'M HERE AT ALL.

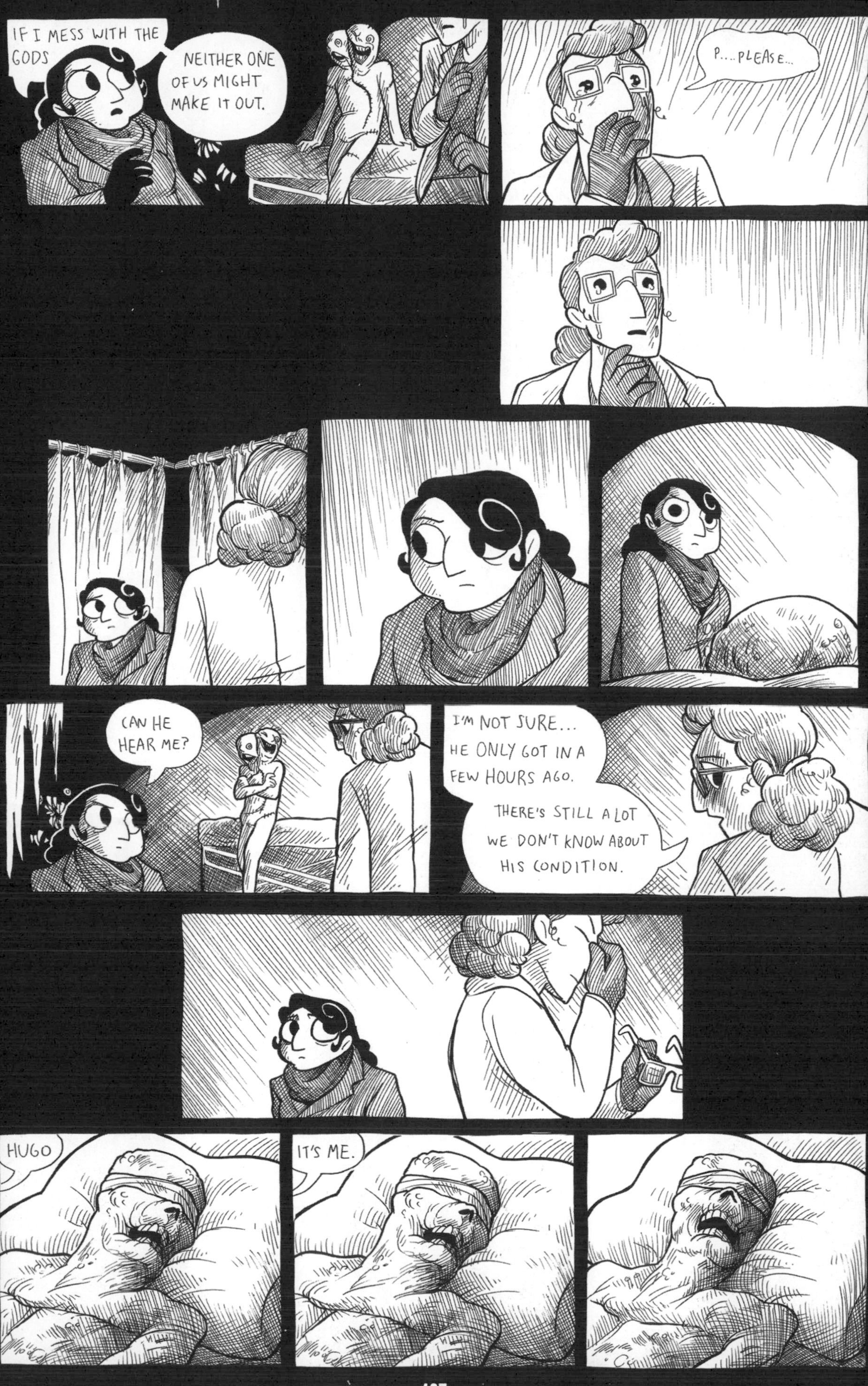
IF I MESS WITH THE GODS
NEITHER ONE OF US MIGHT MAKE IT OUT.
P....PLEASE...
CAN HE HEAR ME?
I'M NOT SURE... HE ONLY GOT IN A FEW HOURS AGO.
THERE'S STILL A LOT WE DON'T KNOW ABOUT HIS CONDITION.
HUGO
IT'S ME.

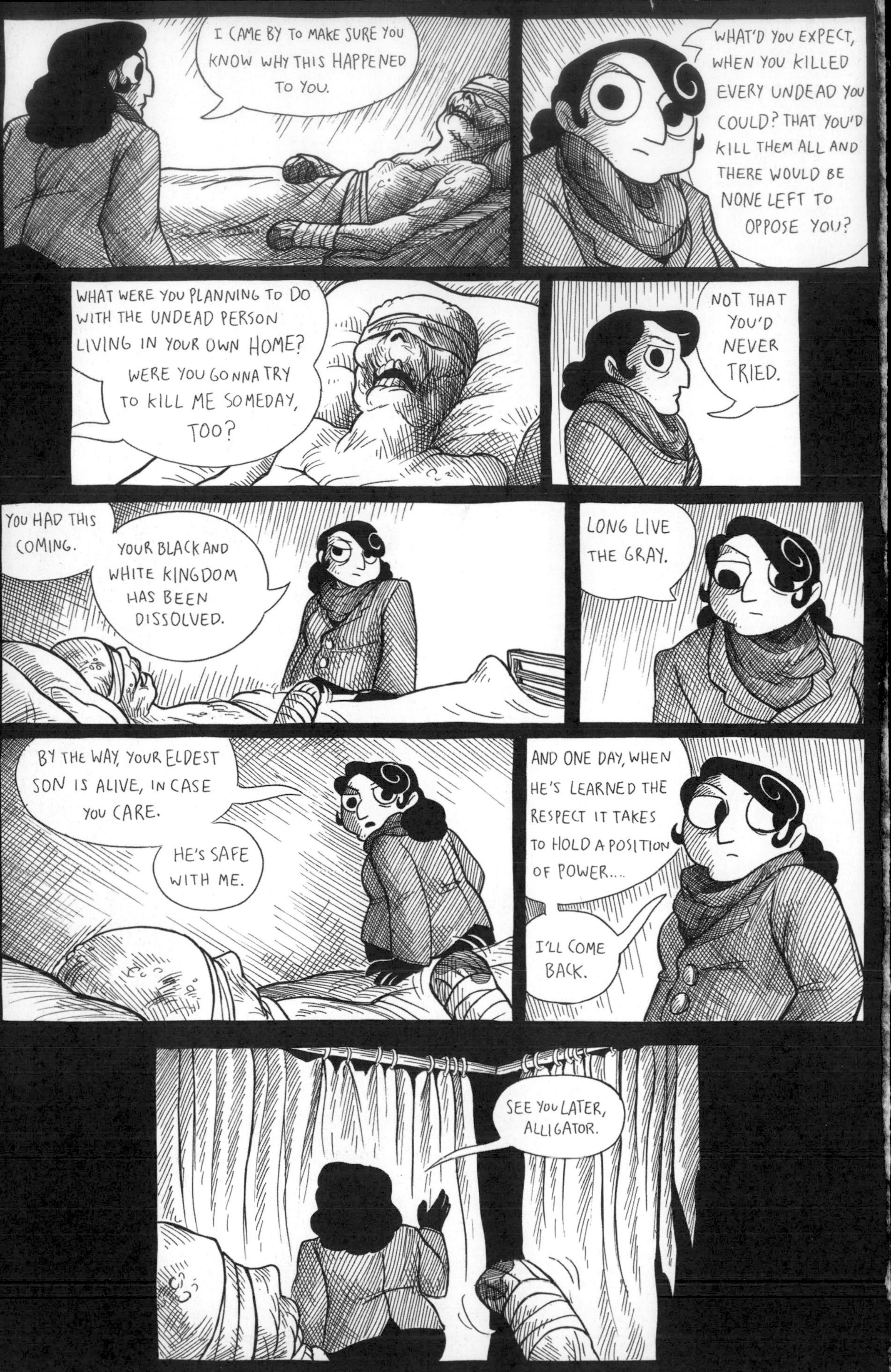
I CAME BY TO MAKE SURE YOU KNOW WHY THIS HAPPENED TO YOU.
WHAT'D YOU EXPECT, WHEN YOU KILLED EVERY UNDEAD YOU COULD? THAT YOU'D KILL THEM ALL AND THERE WOULD BE NONE LEFT TO OPPOSE YOU?
WHAT WERE YOU PLANNING TO DO WITH THE UNDEAD PERSON LIVING IN YOUR OWN HOME? WERE YOU GONNA TRY TO KILL ME SOMEDAY, TOO?
NOT THAT YOU'D NEVER TRIED.
YOU HAD THIS COMING.
YOUR BLACK AND WHITE KINGDOM HAS BEEN DISSOLVED.
LONG LIVE THE GRAY.
BY THE WAY, YOUR ELDEST SON IS ALIVE, IN CASE YOU CARE.
HE'S SAFE WITH ME.
AND ONE DAY, WHEN HE'S LEARNED THE RESPECT IT TAKES TO HOLD A POSITION OF POWER...
I'LL COME BACK.
SEE YOU LATER, ALLIGATOR.

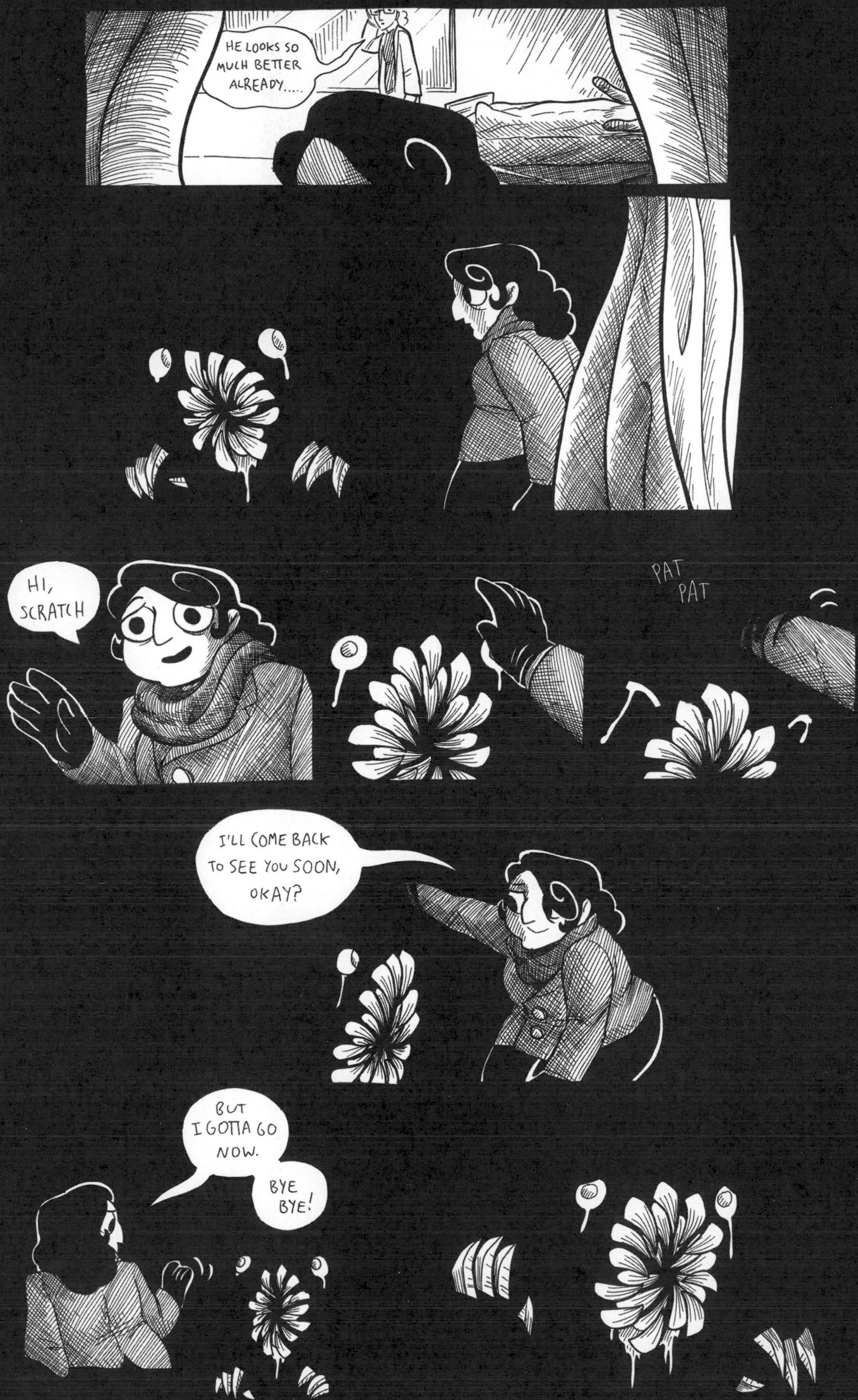
HE LOOKS SO MUCH BETTER ALREADY.....
HI, SCRATCH
PAT PAT
I'LL COME BACK TO SEE YOU SOON, OKAY?
BUT I GOTTA GO NOW.
BYE BYE!

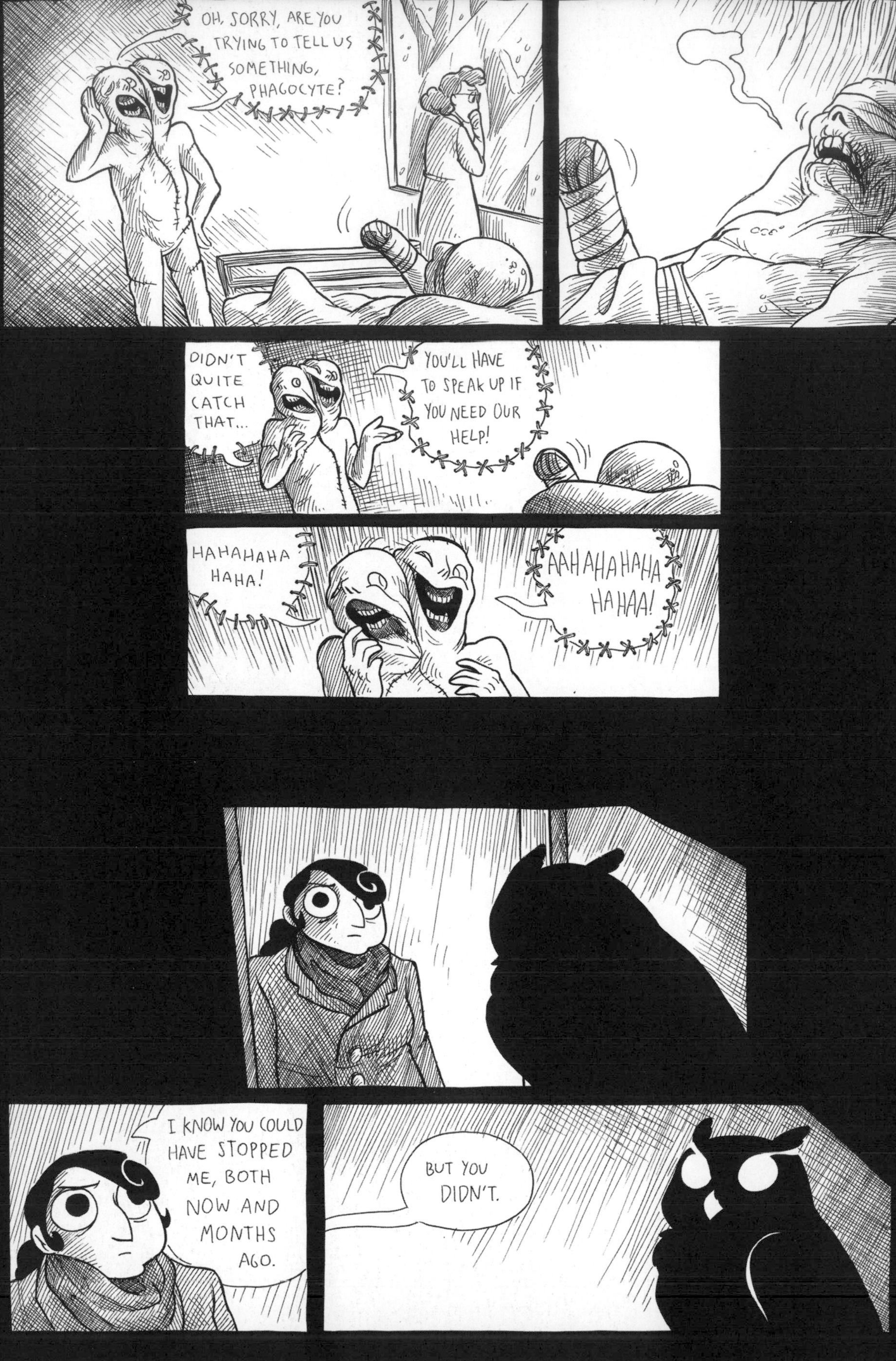
OH, SORRY, ARE YOU TRYING TO TELL US SOMETHING, PHAGOCYTE?
DIDN'T QUITE CATCH THAT...
YOU'LL HAVE TO SPEAK UP IF YOU NEED OUR HELP!
HAHAHAHA HAHA!
AAHAHAHAHA HAHAA!
I KNOW YOU COULD HAVE STOPPED ME, BOTH NOW AND MONTHS AGO.
BUT YOU DIDN'T.

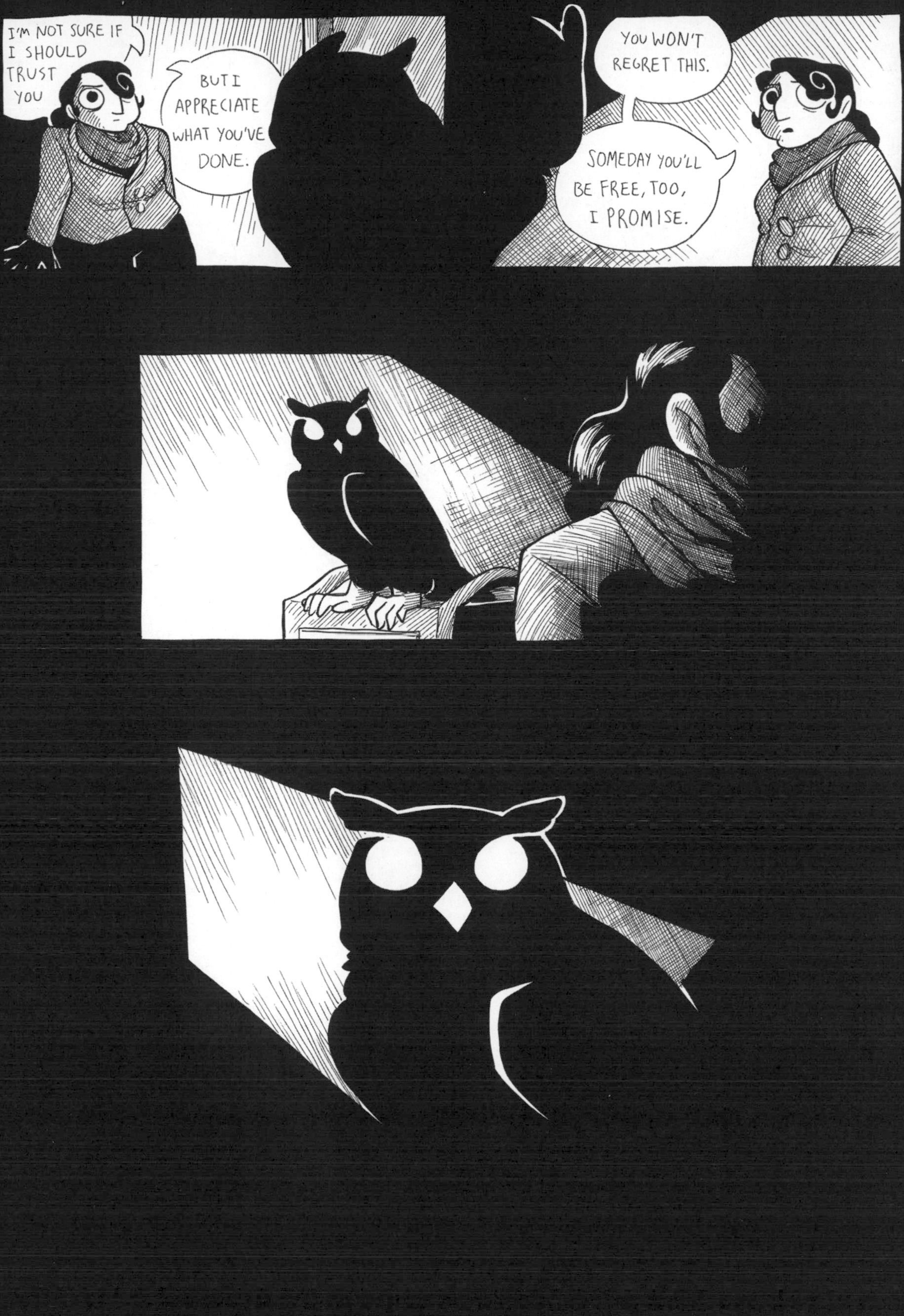
I'M NOT SURE IF I SHOULD TRUST YOU
BUT I APPRECIATE WHAT YOU'VE DONE.
YOU WON'T REGRET THIS.
SOMEDAY YOU'LL BE FREE, TOO, I PROMISE.

END OF
BOOK 1

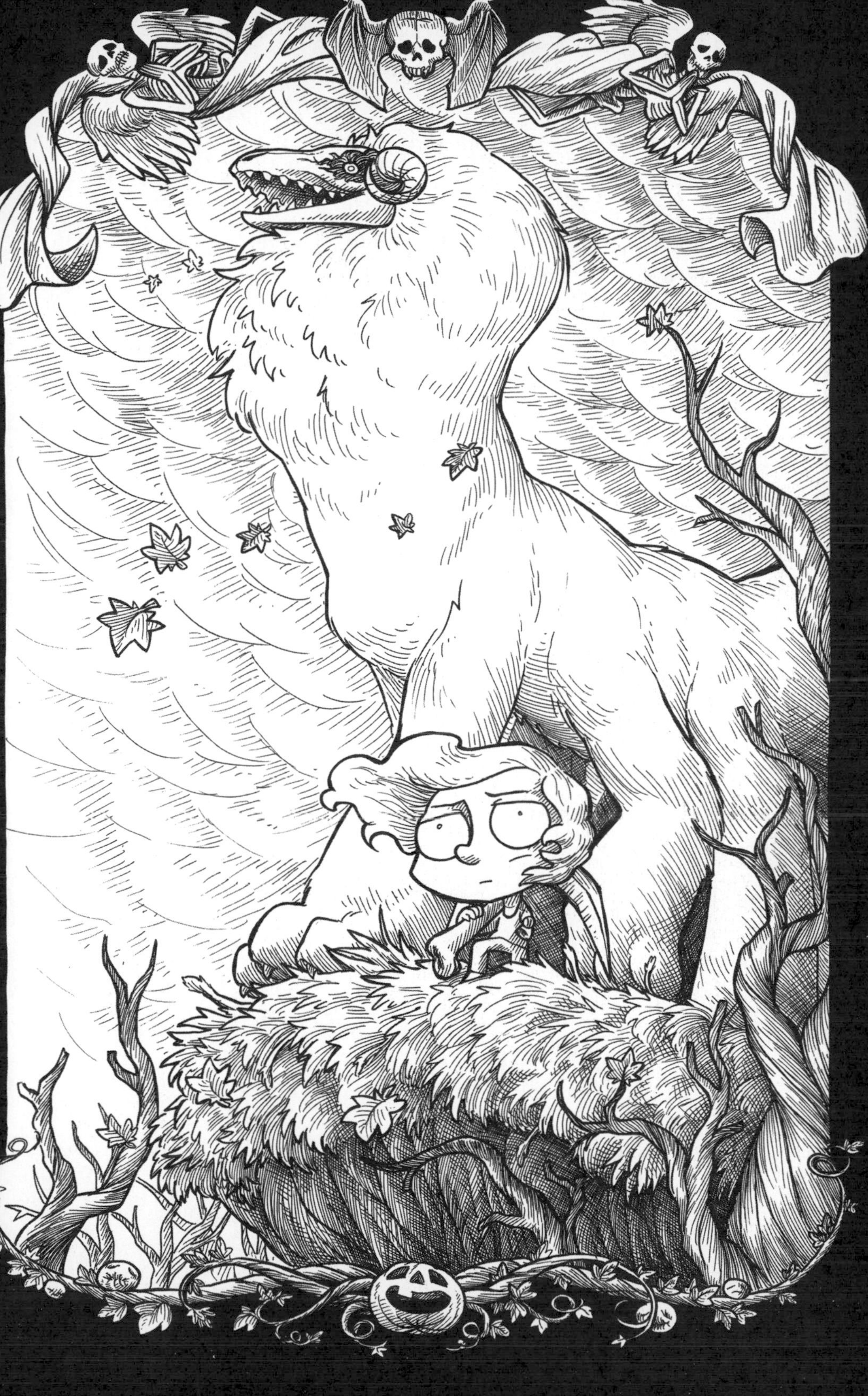

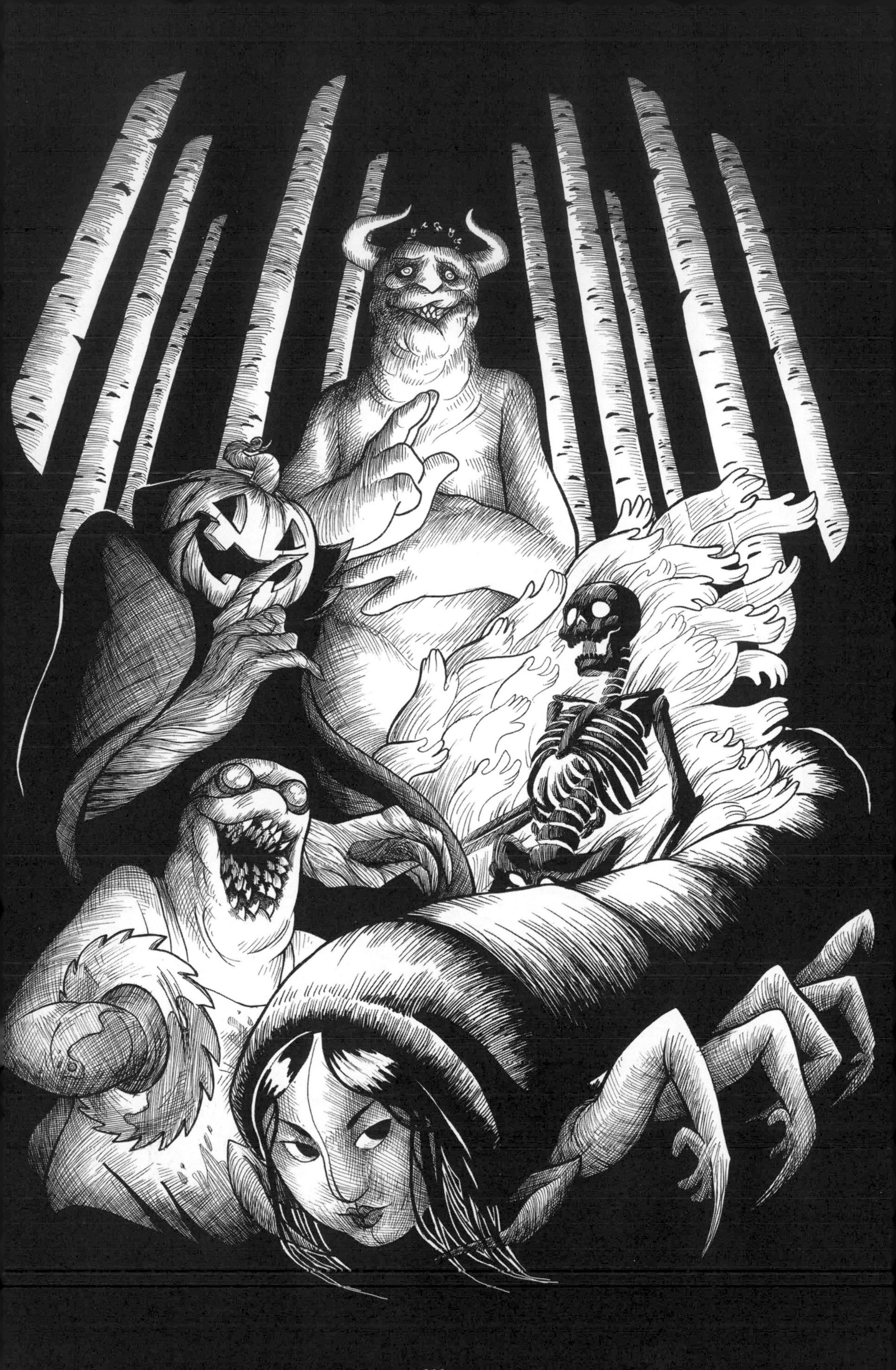

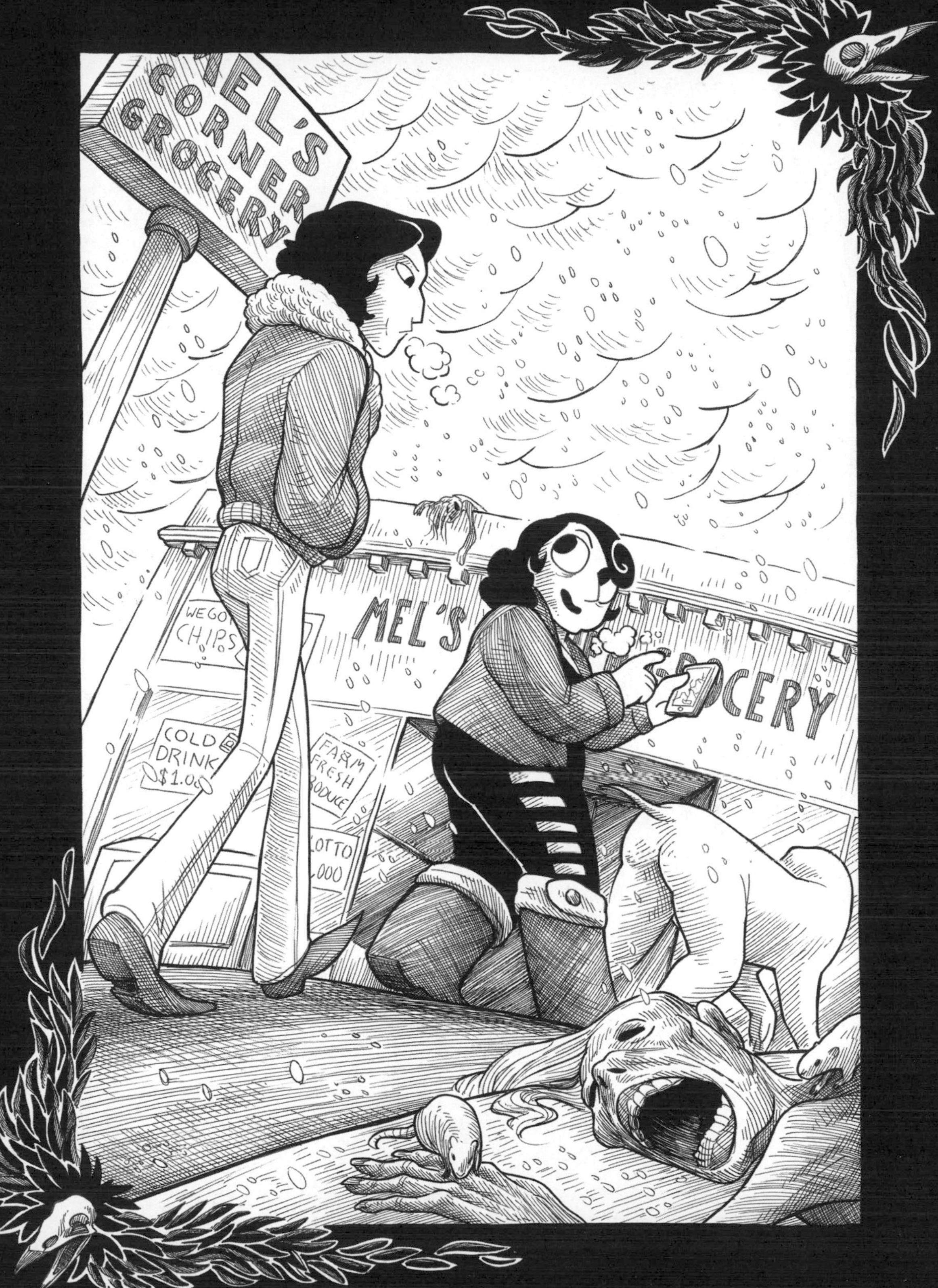
MEL'S CORNER GROCERY
WE GOT CHIPS
MEL'S
OCERY
COLD DRINK $1.0
FARM FRESH RODUCE
LOTTO ,000

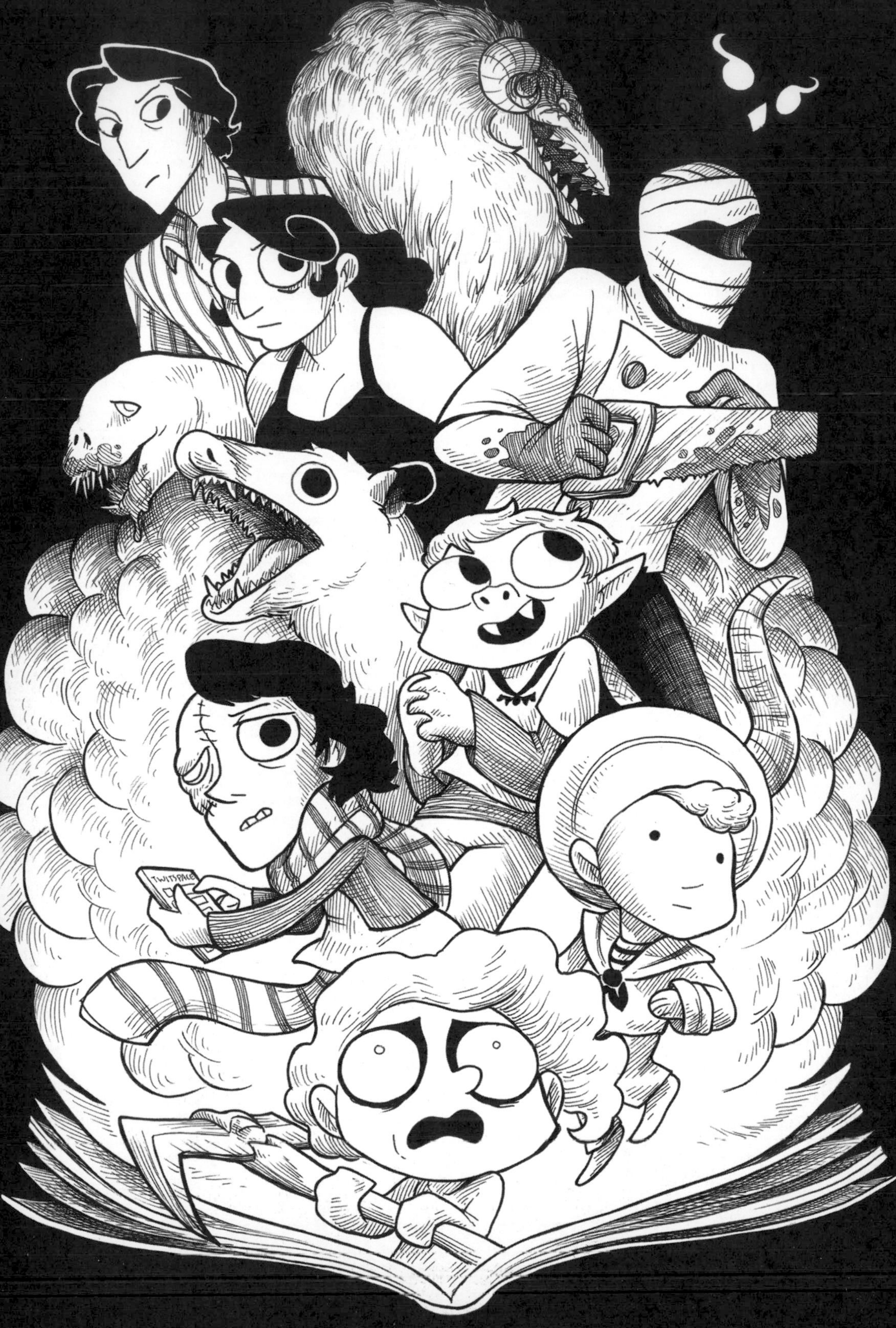
TWITSPACE

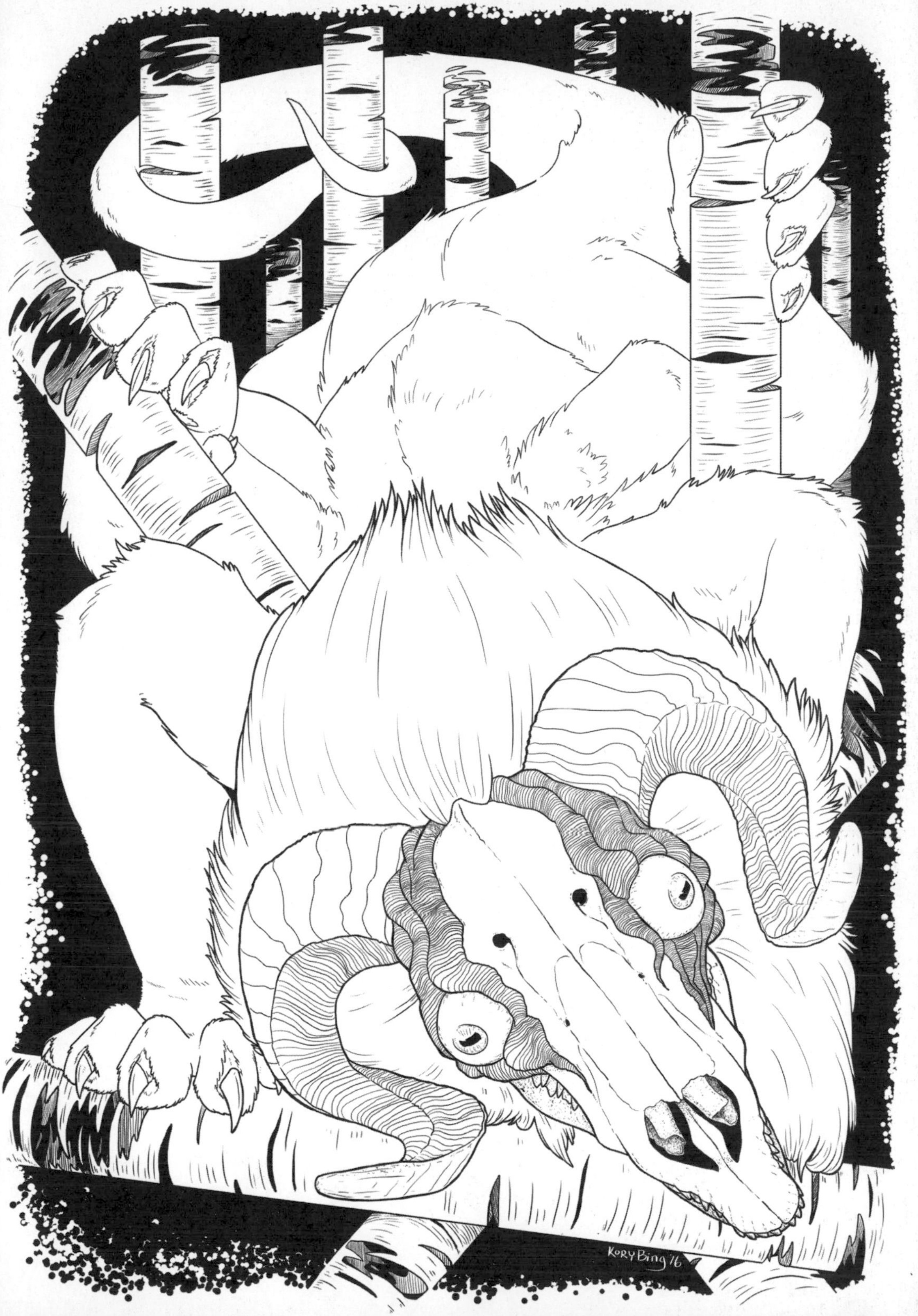
KORY Bing '16

Art by **Kory Bing**
Creator of the comic Skin Deep

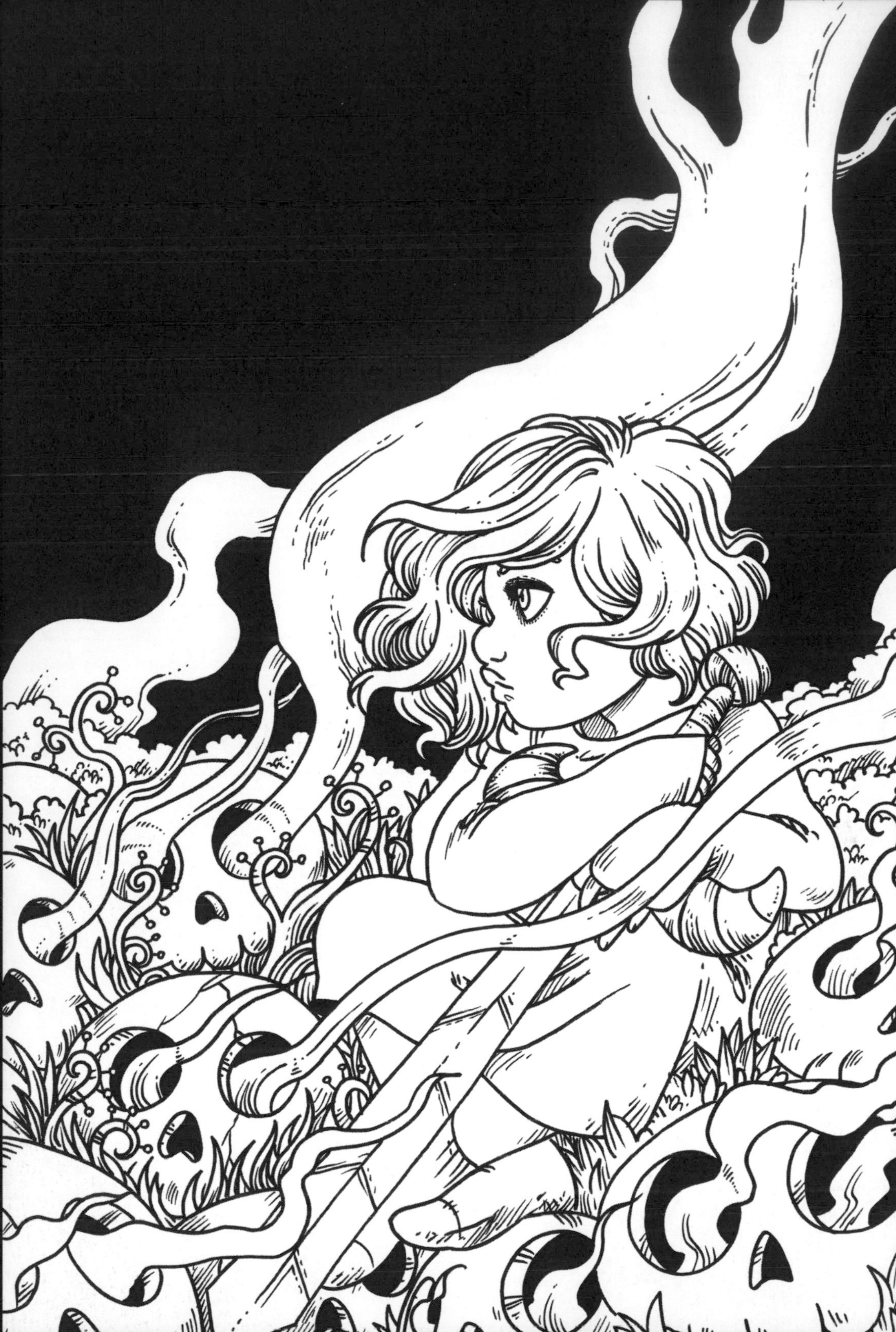

Art by **Isabelle Melançon**
Artist of the comic Namesake

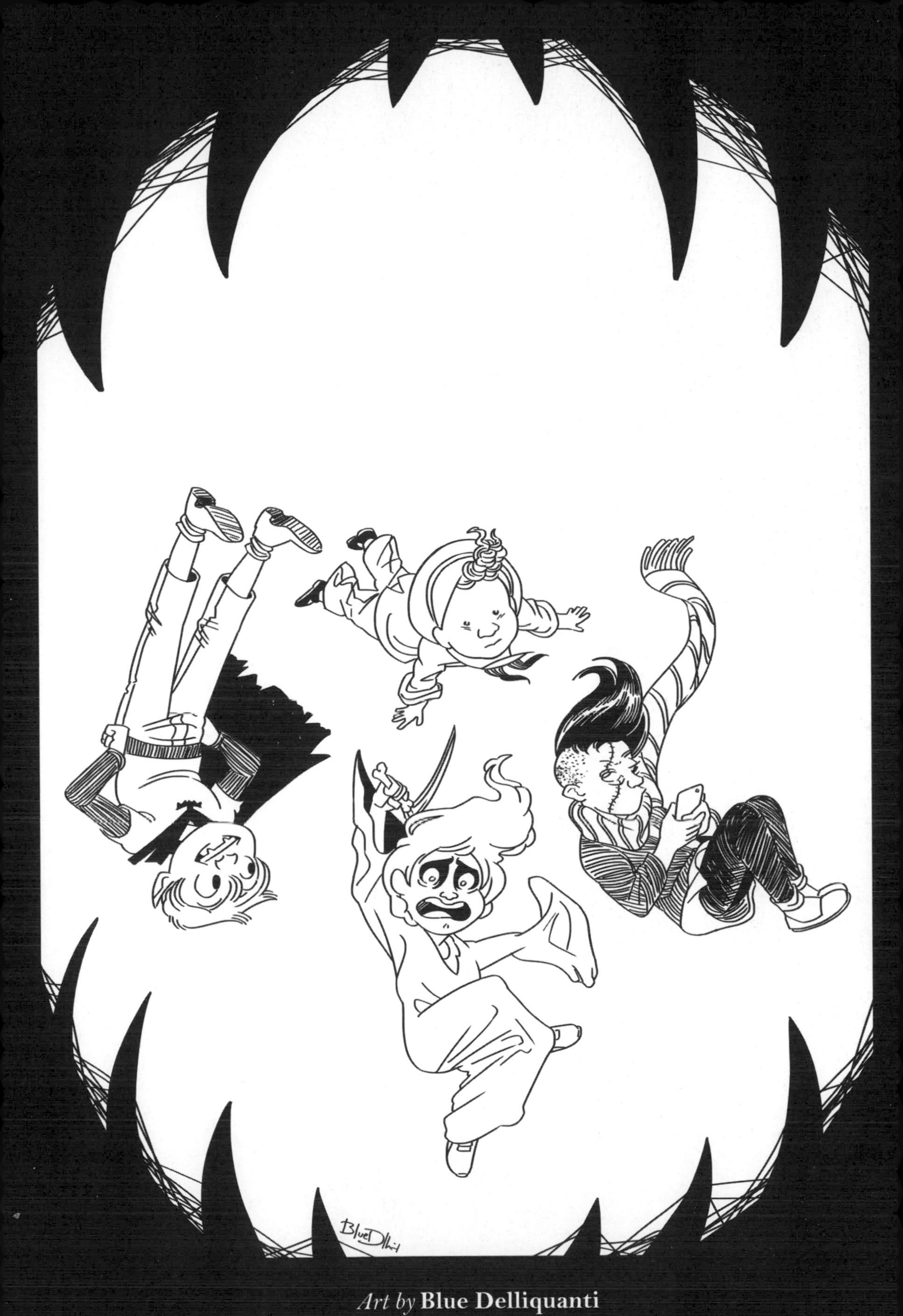
BlueDlhi

Art by **Blue Delliquanti**
Creator of the comic O Human Star

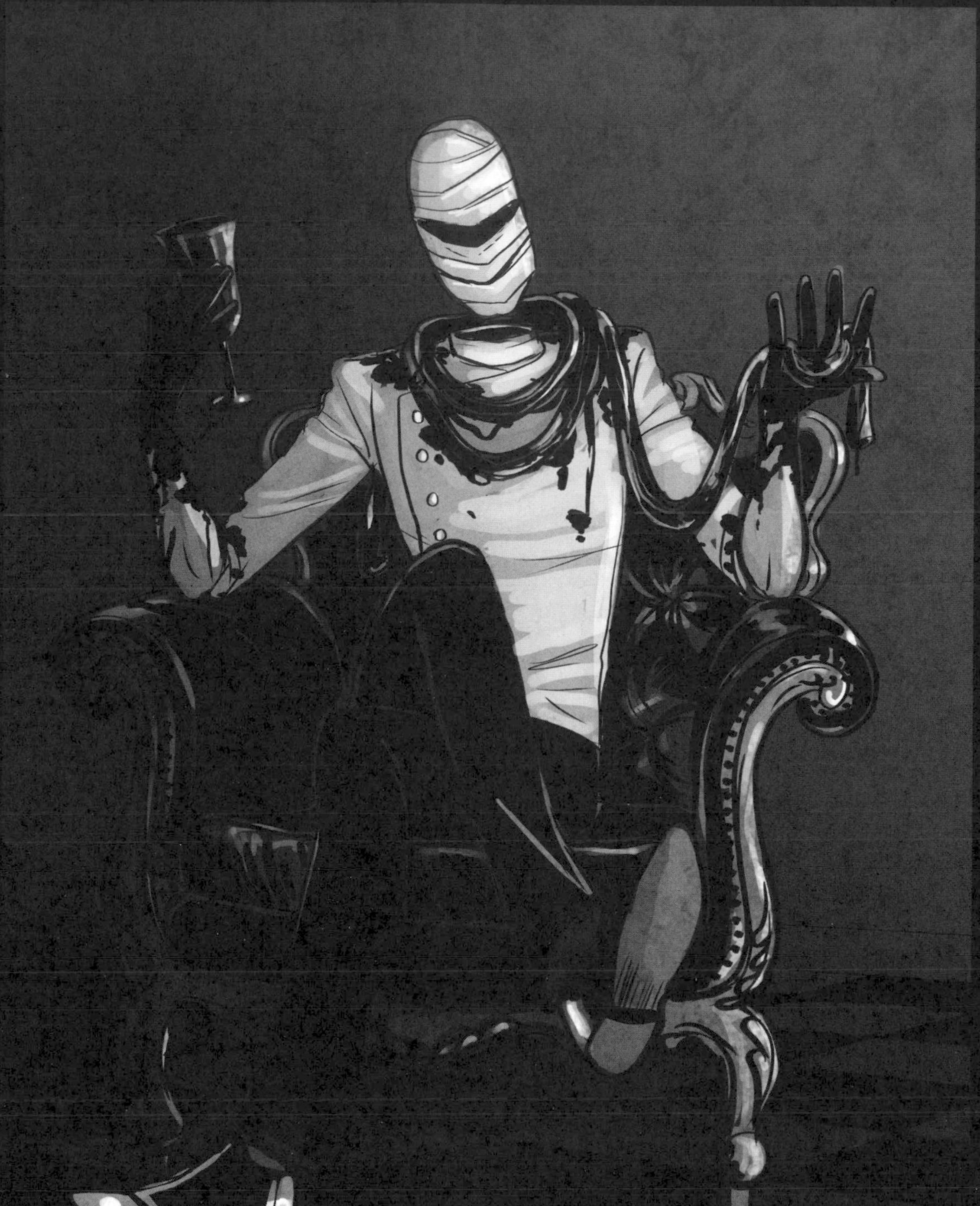

Art by **Pascalle Lepas**
Creator of the comic Wilde Life

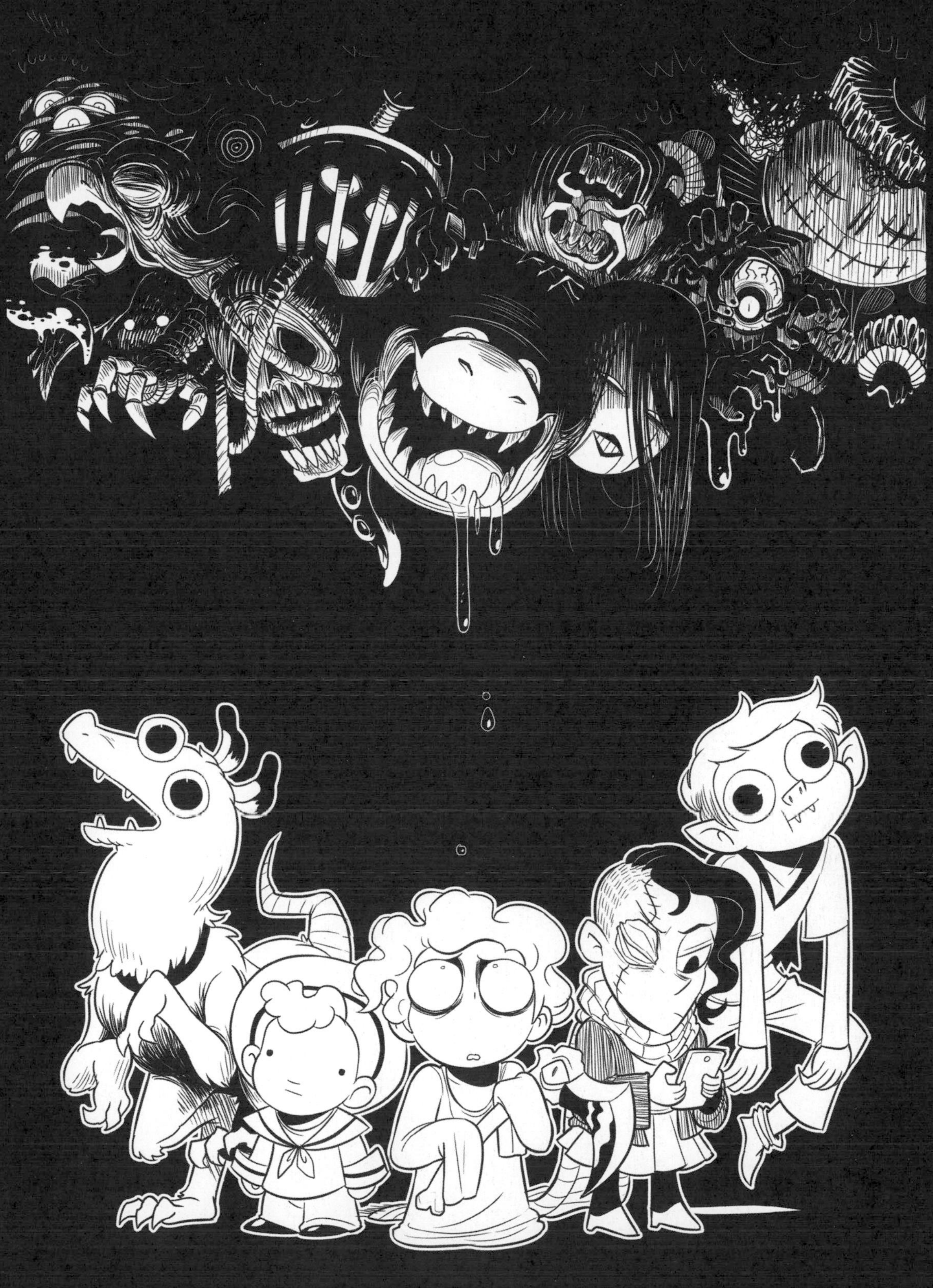

Art by **Zack Morrison**
Creator of the comic Paranatural

CHARACTERS

MONA – NORMAL HUMAN, AGE 10

PRONOUNS: SHE/HER

ABILITIES: SCREAM, RUN, THROW THE THING

MONA ASKS SO LITTLE OF THIS WORLD, YET THE WORLD ASKS SO MUCH OF HER. SOMEBODY GET THIS KID SOME HALLOWEEN CANDY ALREADY.

STATUS: TRAUMATIZED BUT ALIVE

SUSANNAH – MONA'S MONSTER, AGE 10

PRONOUNS: SHE/HER

ABILITIES: SWIPE, SLASH, GET REAL BIG, CHOMP

SUSANNAH WANTS NOTHING MORE THAN TO MAKE SURE MONA IS OKAY. IT COULD MERELY BE FOR SELF-PRESERVATION, OR SHE MAY GENUINELY LOVE MONA. SHE ALSO SMELLS LIKE A CORPSE.

STATUS: ALIVE

RINGLEY – HORRIBLE VAMPIRE CHILD, PERPETUAL TWEEN

PRONOUNS: HE/HIM

ABILITIES: BEING THE WORST, BUT ALSO THE FAVORITE? BITE, FLOAT

RINGLEY IS JUST TERRIBLE. BUT WHEN HE HAS A GOAL IN MIND, HE WILL DO WHATEVER IT TAKES TO GET IT DONE. UNFORTUNATELY, MOST OF THE TIME HIS GOALS ARE "BE BEST FRIENDS WITH ___"

STATUS: ALIVE, UNFORTUNATELY

SHIRLEY – GHOUL, ETERNALLY AGE 13

PRONOUNS: SHE/HER

ABILITIES: SCOFF, GOOGLE

SHIRLEY IS JUST AN UNDEAD TEEN TRYING TO FIND HER PLACE IN THE WORLD, DESPITE BEING A CORPSE IN A CONSTANT STATE OF FALLING APART. SHE CARES ABOUT SOCIAL ISSUES AND DOES NOT HAVE TIME FOR YOU.

STATUS: ALIVE-ISH, AND WITH A SWEET NEW BOD

BANJO – WEREOPOSSUM, AGE 20-SOMETHING

PRONOUNS: MAYBE HE/HIM, ACCORDING TO RINGLEY

ABILITIES: EAT, HISS, PLAY DEAD

BANJO IS VERY NICE, BUT NOT VERY HELPFUL. KIND OF LIKE A DOG IF DOGS SMELLED WORSE AND WISHED YOU WOULD LEAVE THEM ALONE.

STATUS: ALIVE AND PROBABLY VERY CONFUSED

ROBERT – LIVING DOLL, AGE 116

PRONOUNS: HE/HIM

ABILITIES: STARE, CREEP

ROBERT IS A VERY SAD BOY WHO SAYS MEAN THINGS BUT DEEP DOWN WISHES HE HAD SOME FRIENDS. THAT AREN'T RINGLEY, OF COURSE.

STATUS: DECEASED (SAVE FOR ONE ARM)

DOCTOR FUGUE – GHOST, VERY OLD

PRONOUNS: HE/HIM

ABILITIES: MUTILATE, RESURRECT, LIE

"DOCTOR" FUGUE MAY NEVER HAVE BEEN A LICENSED DOCTOR, BUT HE'S SURE HE KNOWS HOW TO FIX WHATEVER AILS YOU. BURNS EVERY BRIDGE HE COMES ACROSS, ALL WHILE BLAMING THE OTHER PARTY TO KEEP FROM FACING HIS OWN FAULTS. KNOWS A FAIR BIT OF UNSPEAKABLE MAGIC. TRAPPED WITHIN THE FOUNDATION OF THE HOUSE HE DIED IN.

STATUS: GHOST

J.D. – UNDEAD, AGE LOST TO TIME

PRONOUNS: SHE/HER

ABILITIES: DRIVE, STAB, OUTLAST

J.D. REALLY DIDN'T SET OUT TO KILL MOST OF HUMANITY, BUT THAT'S KINDA HOW IT TURNED OUT. BUT SHE WILL MAKE THE BEST OF IT AND DO WHAT SHE CAN TO HELP THE UNDEAD, MONSTERS, AND HUMANS ALIKE.

STATUS: ALIVE-ISH

DOGMAN – IMMORTAL MONSTER, AGE UNKNOWN

PRONOUNS: HE/HIM

ABILITIES: BITE, IGNITE

DOGMAN IS J.D.'S FRIEND AND ACCOMPLICE, THOUGH THEY ARE CURRENTLY ON ROCKY FOOTING AFTER DOGMAN CAUSED THE DEATHS OF COUNTLESS HUMANS WHEN HE SPILLED THE BEANS ABOUT THE PHAGOCYTE'S PREDICAMENT TO CERTAIN DANGEROUS MONSTERS. THOUGH HE MAY HAVE HAD AN AGENDA, HE CARES DEEPLY FOR THE FATE OF THE WORLD AND OF HIS FRIEND, EVEN IF SHE ASKS HIM TO BLOW HIMSELF UP A LITTLE MORE OFTEN THAN HE'D LIKE.

STATUS: ALIVE

JEN – SOME GUY, AGE 20

PRONOUNS: HE/HIM

ABILITIES: UNKNOWN

JEN IS THE HEIR TO THE PHAGOCYTE'S TITLE, THOUGH HE HAS NO IDEA WHAT THAT MEANS, AS HIS FATHER LEFT HIM WITH SOME RANDOM FAMILY AND HE NEVER LEARNED WHO HE TRULY IS. HE'S NOT A FAN OF DINOSAUR OATMEAL, SOMEHOW.

STATUS: ALIVE

MONA'S PARENT – HUMAN, AGE 37

PRONOUNS: THEY/THEM

ABILITIES: GOOD HAIR, ATTRACT NICE VAMPIRES

MONA'S PARENT IS A NONBINARY PARENT TRYING TO RAISE A WEIRD KID ALL ON THEIR OWN, WHILE MISSING THEIR SPOUSE TERRIBLY. THEY'RE VERY SAD BUT FEELING BETTER AFTER HAVING MET A CUTE AND SYMPATHETIC VAMPIRE. BUT ALSO FEELING WORSE BECAUSE THE WORLD JUST ENDED.

STATUS: ALIVE

RINGLEY'S DAD – SINGLE VAMP DAD, AGE VERY OLD

PRONOUNS: HE/HIM

ABILITIES: FLOAT, MESMERIZE, SHAPESHIFT

LIKE MONA'S PARENT, IS DOING HIS BEST TO RAISE HIS WEIRD AND HORRIBLE CHILD ALL ON HIS OWN. FOR HUNDREDS OF YEARS. BUT MAYBE THINGS WILL BE EASIER NOW THAT HE HAS MET SUCH A NICE HUMAN PERSON WHO DOESN'T MIND HOW HE IS A BAT SOMETIMES.

STATUS: VAMPIRE IN LOVE

MARTA – WITCH MOM, AGE 47

PRONOUNS: SHE/HER

ABILITIES: NECROMANCY, INTIMIDATE

MARTA IS A SINGLE MOM WHO HAS BEEN ON THE RUN WITH HER SON DUNCAN FOR AS LONG AS HE'S BEEN ALIVE, THOUGH THAT HASN'T BEEN DIFFICULT FOR A POWERFUL SORCERESS SUCH AS WAS ONCE PART OF A "BOOK CLUB" RUN BY FUGUE, WHERE SHE LEARNED SOME OF HER BASIC SKILLS IN DARK MAGICS. SHE IS THE LAST SURVIVING MEMBER OF SAID BOOK CLUB.

STATUS: ALIVE

DUNCAN – HUMAN TEEN, AGE 14

PRONOUNS: HE/HIM

ABILITIES: RUN, HIDE, TEXT

DUNCAN IS JUST YOUR AVERAGE TEEN KID WHO MIGHT BE THE HEIR TO THE ROLE OF PHAGOCYTE AND WHO'S BEEN HUNTED BY MONSTERS ALL HIS LIFE. HALF-BROTHER TO JEN, THE REAL HEIR, AND REFERRED TO BY MOST AS "THE DECOY" BECAUSE THAT'S ALL HE REALLY EVER WAS. ENJOYS THE INTERNET AND THE FRIENDS HE MEETS THERE, SINCE HE DOESN'T GO TO SCHOOL AND HIS SOCIAL LIFE IS NEARLY NOTHING.

STATUS: VERY DEAD

READER QUESTIONS

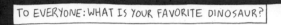
TO EVERYONE: WHAT IS YOUR FAVORITE DINOSAUR?

MONA, YOU FIRST

UH I DON'T THINK THIS IS A VERY GOOD TIME FOR QUESTIONS..?

CAN WE GET BACK TO LIKE... SAVING THE WORLD OR WHATEVER..?

NO MONA YOU HAVE TO ANSWER IT OR WE WON'T LET YOU GO AND THE WHOLE WORLD WILL DIE

OH GEEZ

UHH PTERODACTYL MAYBE??

MONA THAT'S NOT A DINOSAUR

PICK AGAIN

AAHH

OKAY ONE OF THOSE OCEAN ONES WITH THE LONG NECKS

THOSE ARE MARINE REPTILES NOT DINOSAURS

YOU ARE TERRIBLE AT THIS

AAAHH

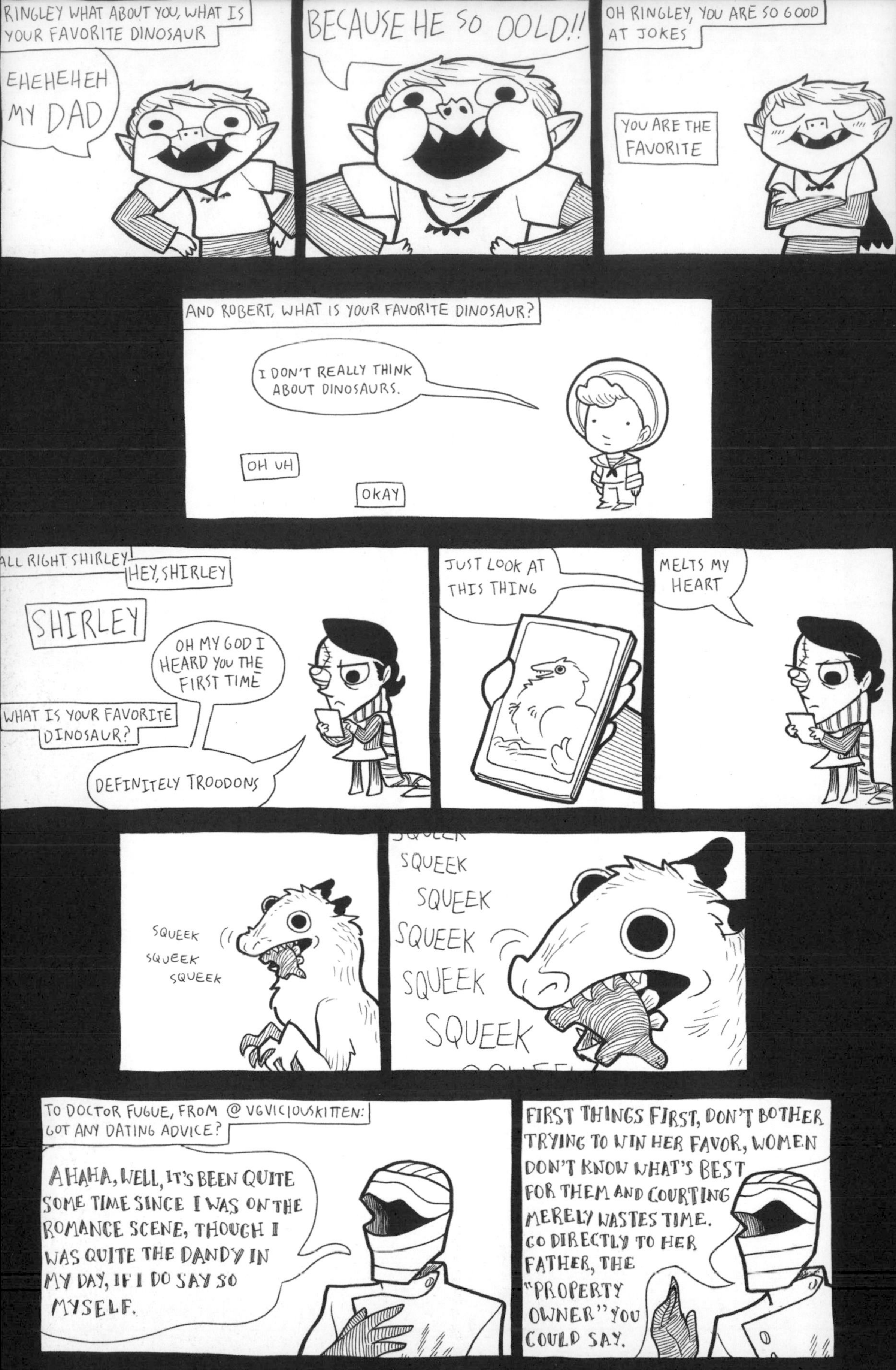
RINGLEY WHAT ABOUT YOU, WHAT IS YOUR FAVORITE DINOSAUR
EHEHEHEH MY DAD
BECAUSE HE SO OOLD!!
OH RINGLEY, YOU ARE SO GOOD AT JOKES
YOU ARE THE FAVORITE
AND ROBERT, WHAT IS YOUR FAVORITE DINOSAUR?
I DON'T REALLY THINK ABOUT DINOSAURS.
OH UH
OKAY
ALL RIGHT SHIRLEY
HEY, SHIRLEY
SHIRLEY
OH MY GOD I HEARD YOU THE FIRST TIME
WHAT IS YOUR FAVORITE DINOSAUR?
DEFINITELY TROODONS
JUST LOOK AT THIS THING
MELTS MY HEART
SQUEEK
SQUEEK
SQUEEK
SQUEEK
SQUEEK
SQUEEK
SQUEEK
SQUEEK
TO DOCTOR FUGUE, FROM @VGVICIOUSKITTEN: GOT ANY DATING ADVICE?
AHAHA, WELL, IT'S BEEN QUITE SOME TIME SINCE I WAS ON THE ROMANCE SCENE, THOUGH I WAS QUITE THE DANDY IN MY DAY, IF I DO SAY SO MYSELF.
FIRST THINGS FIRST, DON'T BOTHER TRYING TO WIN HER FAVOR, WOMEN DON'T KNOW WHAT'S BEST FOR THEM AND COURTING MERELY WASTES TIME. GO DIRECTLY TO HER FATHER, THE "PROPERTY OWNER" YOU COULD SAY.

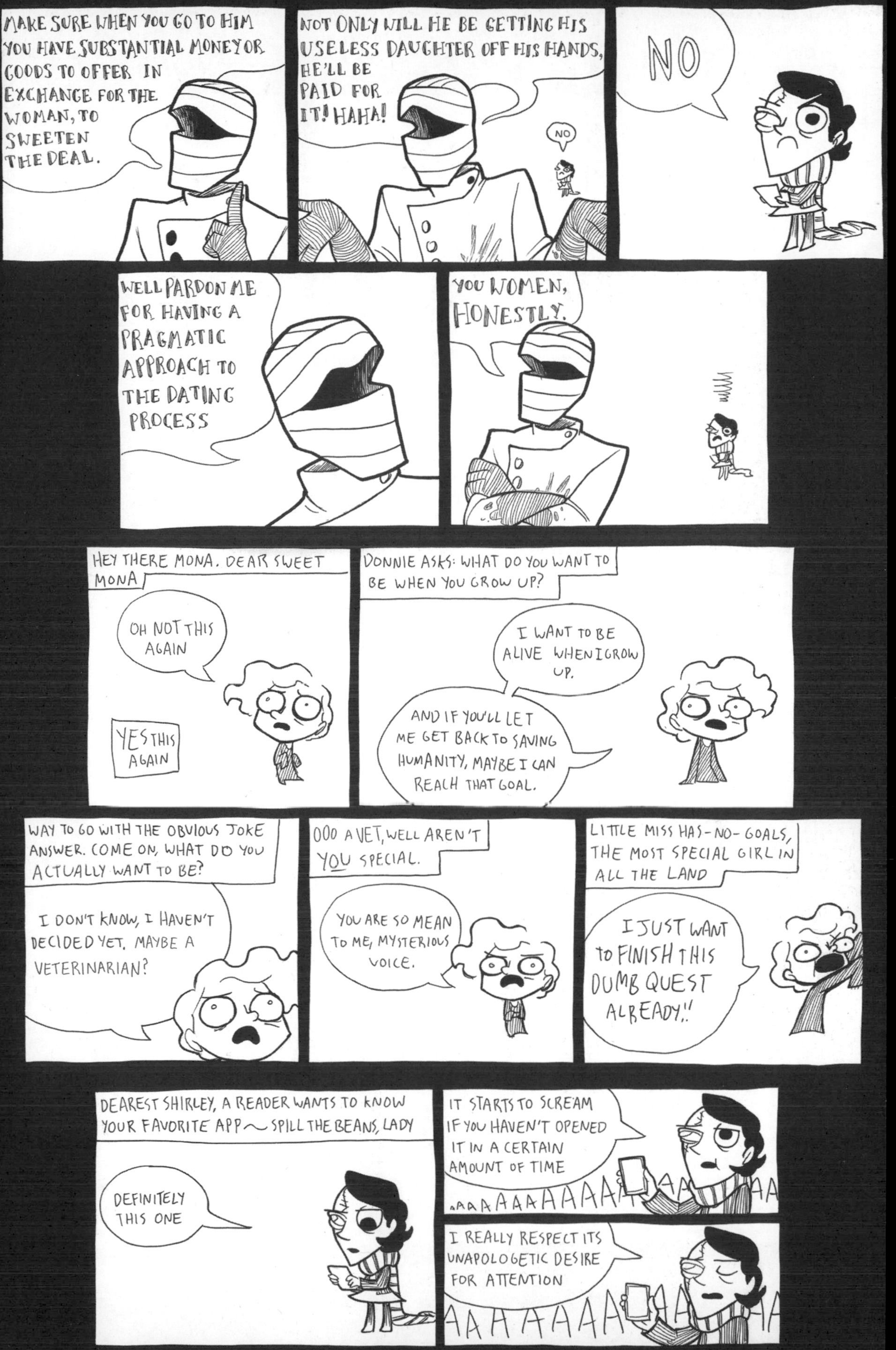
MAKE SURE WHEN YOU GO TO HIM YOU HAVE SUBSTANTIAL MONEY OR GOODS TO OFFER IN EXCHANGE FOR THE WOMAN, TO SWEETEN THE DEAL.
NOT ONLY WILL HE BE GETTING HIS USELESS DAUGHTER OFF HIS HANDS, HE'LL BE PAID FOR IT! HAHA!
NO
NO
WELL PARDON ME FOR HAVING A PRAGMATIC APPROACH TO THE DATING PROCESS
YOU WOMEN, HONESTLY.
HEY THERE MONA. DEAR SWEET MONA
OH NOT THIS AGAIN
YES THIS AGAIN
DONNIE ASKS: WHAT DO YOU WANT TO BE WHEN YOU GROW UP?
I WANT TO BE ALIVE WHEN I GROW UP.
AND IF YOU'LL LET ME GET BACK TO SAVING HUMANITY, MAYBE I CAN REACH THAT GOAL.
WAY TO GO WITH THE OBVIOUS JOKE ANSWER. COME ON, WHAT DO YOU ACTUALLY WANT TO BE?
I DON'T KNOW, I HAVEN'T DECIDED YET. MAYBE A VETERINARIAN?
OOO A VET, WELL AREN'T YOU SPECIAL.
YOU ARE SO MEAN TO ME, MYSTERIOUS VOICE.
LITTLE MISS HAS-NO-GOALS, THE MOST SPECIAL GIRL IN ALL THE LAND
I JUST WANT TO FINISH THIS DUMB QUEST ALREADY!!
DEAREST SHIRLEY, A READER WANTS TO KNOW YOUR FAVORITE APP ~ SPILL THE BEANS, LADY
DEFINITELY THIS ONE
IT STARTS TO SCREAM IF YOU HAVEN'T OPENED IT IN A CERTAIN AMOUNT OF TIME
AAAAAAAAAAAAAAA
I REALLY RESPECT ITS UNAPOLOGETIC DESIRE FOR ATTENTION
AAAAAAAAAAA

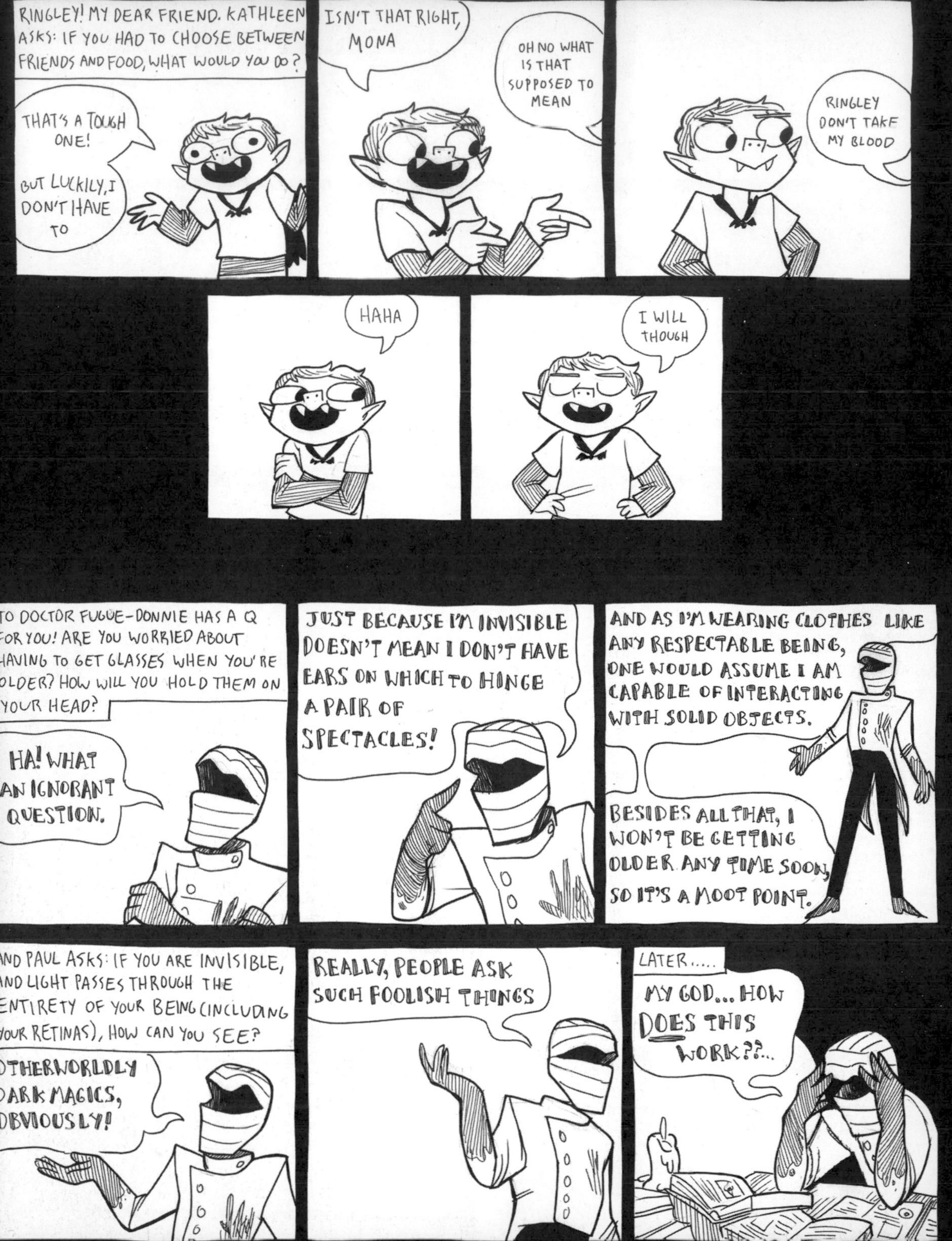
RINGLEY! MY DEAR FRIEND. KATHLEEN ASKS: IF YOU HAD TO CHOOSE BETWEEN FRIENDS AND FOOD, WHAT WOULD YOU DO?
THAT'S A TOUGH ONE!
BUT LUCKILY, I DON'T HAVE TO
ISN'T THAT RIGHT, MONA
OH NO WHAT IS THAT SUPPOSED TO MEAN
RINGLEY DON'T TAKE MY BLOOD
HAHA
I WILL THOUGH
TO DOCTOR FUGUE-DONNIE HAS A Q FOR YOU! ARE YOU WORRIED ABOUT HAVING TO GET GLASSES WHEN YOU'RE OLDER? HOW WILL YOU HOLD THEM ON YOUR HEAD?
HA! WHAT AN IGNORANT QUESTION.
JUST BECAUSE I'M INVISIBLE DOESN'T MEAN I DON'T HAVE EARS ON WHICH TO HINGE A PAIR OF SPECTACLES!
AND AS I'M WEARING CLOTHES LIKE ANY RESPECTABLE BEING, ONE WOULD ASSUME I AM CAPABLE OF INTERACTING WITH SOLID OBJECTS.
BESIDES ALL THAT, I WON'T BE GETTING OLDER ANY TIME SOON, SO IT'S A MOOT POINT.
AND PAUL ASKS: IF YOU ARE INVISIBLE, AND LIGHT PASSES THROUGH THE ENTIRETY OF YOUR BEING (INCLUDING YOUR RETINAS), HOW CAN YOU SEE?
OTHERWORLDLY DARK MAGICS, OBVIOUSLY!
REALLY, PEOPLE ASK SUCH FOOLISH THINGS
LATER.....
MY GOD... HOW DOES THIS WORK??...

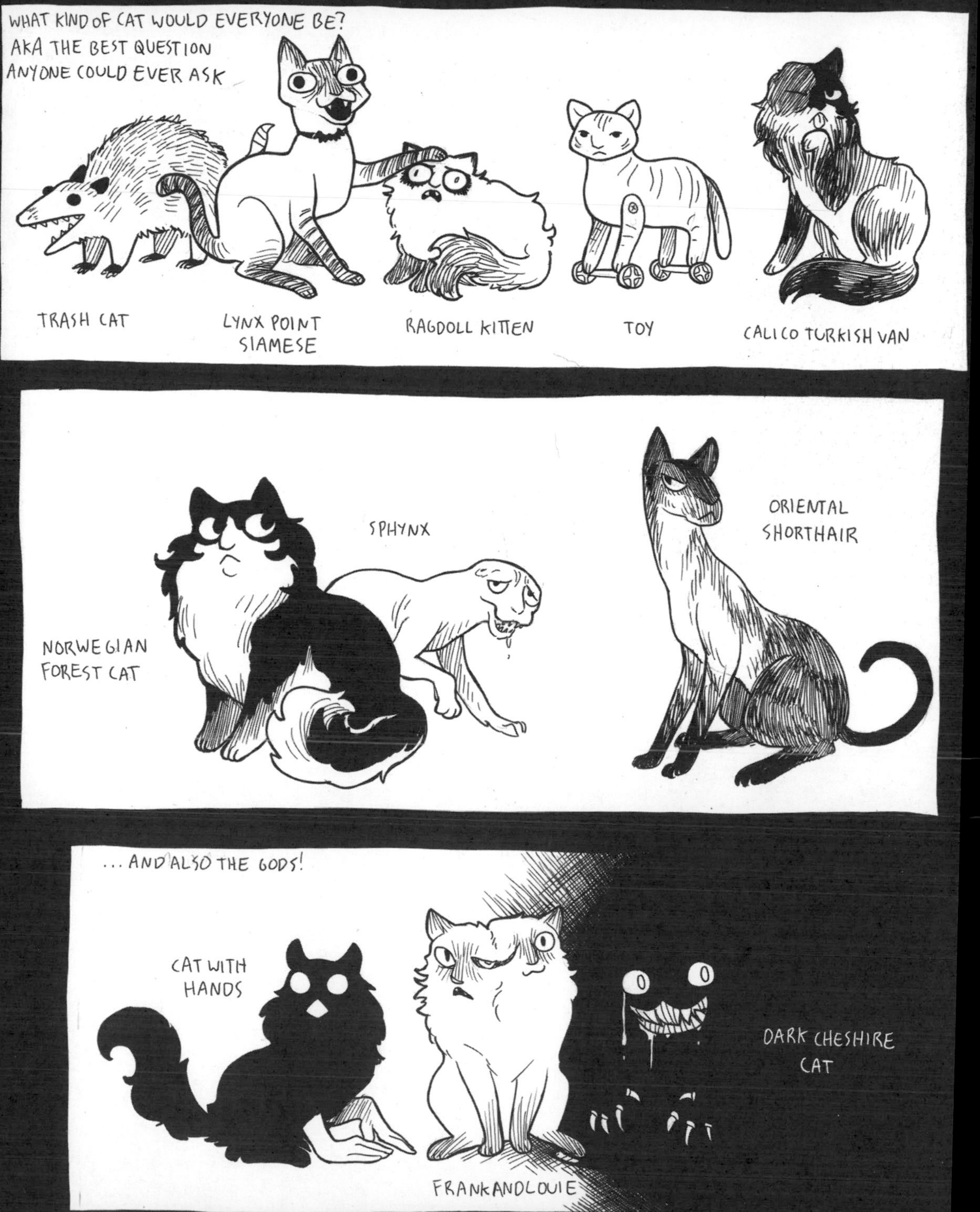
WHAT KIND OF CAT WOULD EVERYONE BE?
AKA THE BEST QUESTION ANYONE COULD EVER ASK
TRASH CAT
LYNX POINT SIAMESE
RAGDOLL KITTEN
TOY
CALICO TURKISH VAN
NORWEGIAN FOREST CAT
SPHYNX
ORIENTAL SHORTHAIR
...AND ALSO THE GODS!
CAT WITH HANDS
FRANKANDLOUIE
DARK CHESHIRE CAT

Making a Comic
Process Drawings

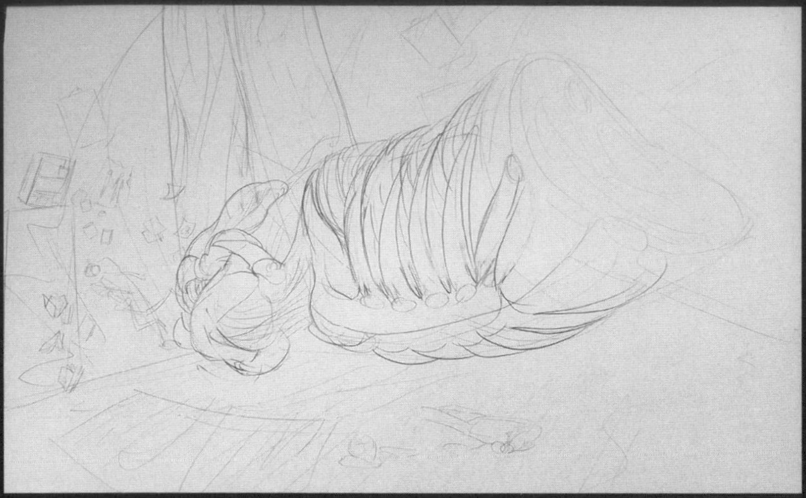

ONE: The roughs. I sketch out the background and where everything will be, along with any important details I shouldn't forget. This includes word balloons, to make sure they fit in the panel!

TWO: The pencils. I use only mechanical pencils for some reason (maybe for nice thin lines?) and draw out everything.

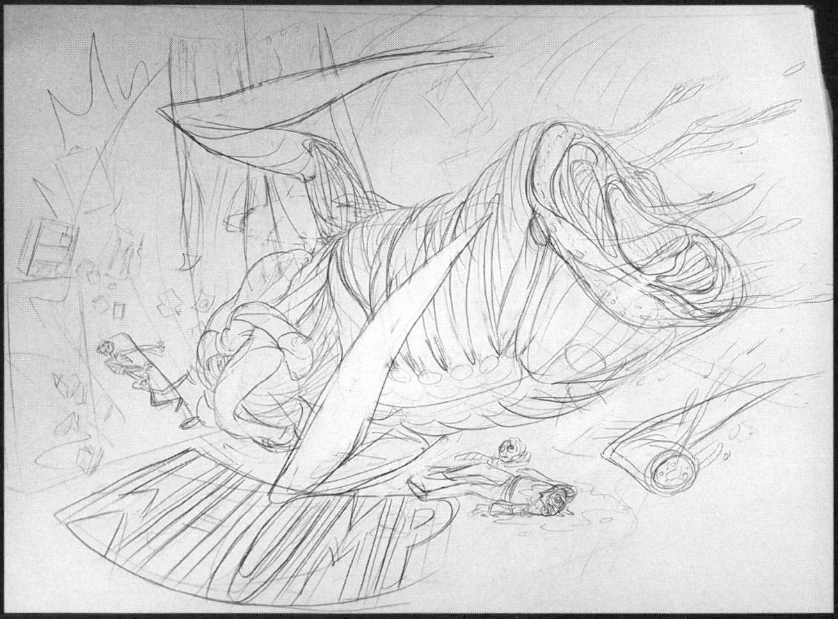
WHUMP

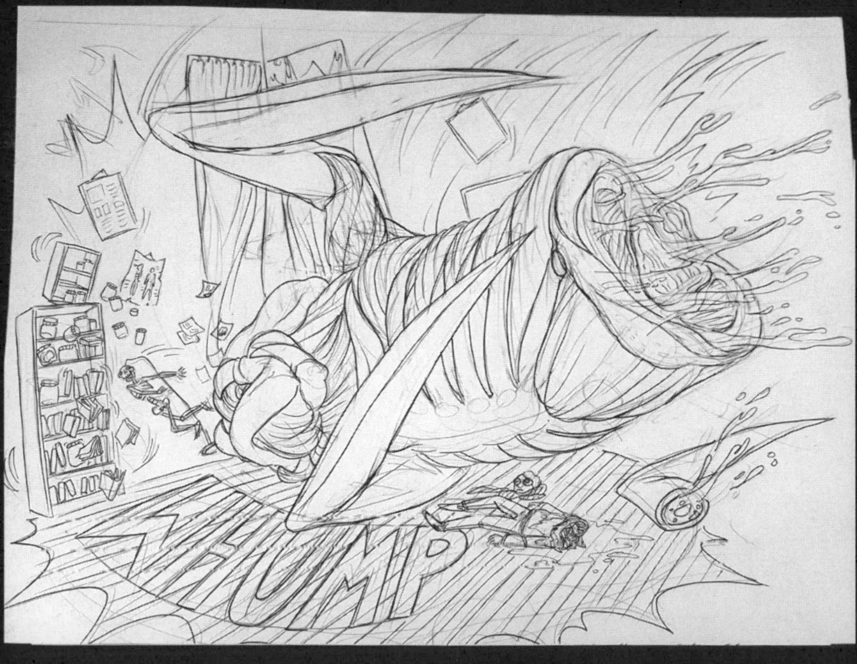
WHUMP

THREE: Primary inking. I go over all my pencil lines with pen (and add in things that were a little too fiddly for the pencils, like the books in the bookcase).

FOUR: Erasing the pencil lines. It is a surprisingly good arm workout. If I used blue pencil, I wouldn't have to deal with this, but alas, this is my method! Micron pens have shown to be one of the better pens for erasing over, they have great staying power and don't often smudge (and are great pens all around).

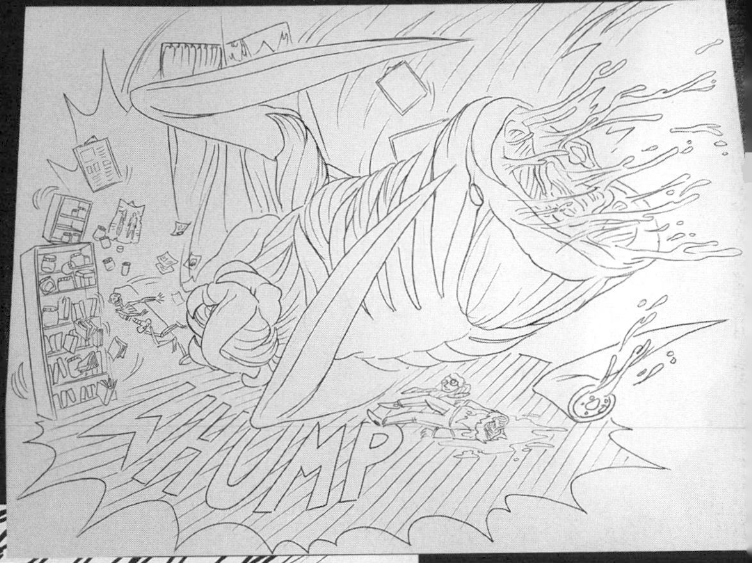
WHUMP

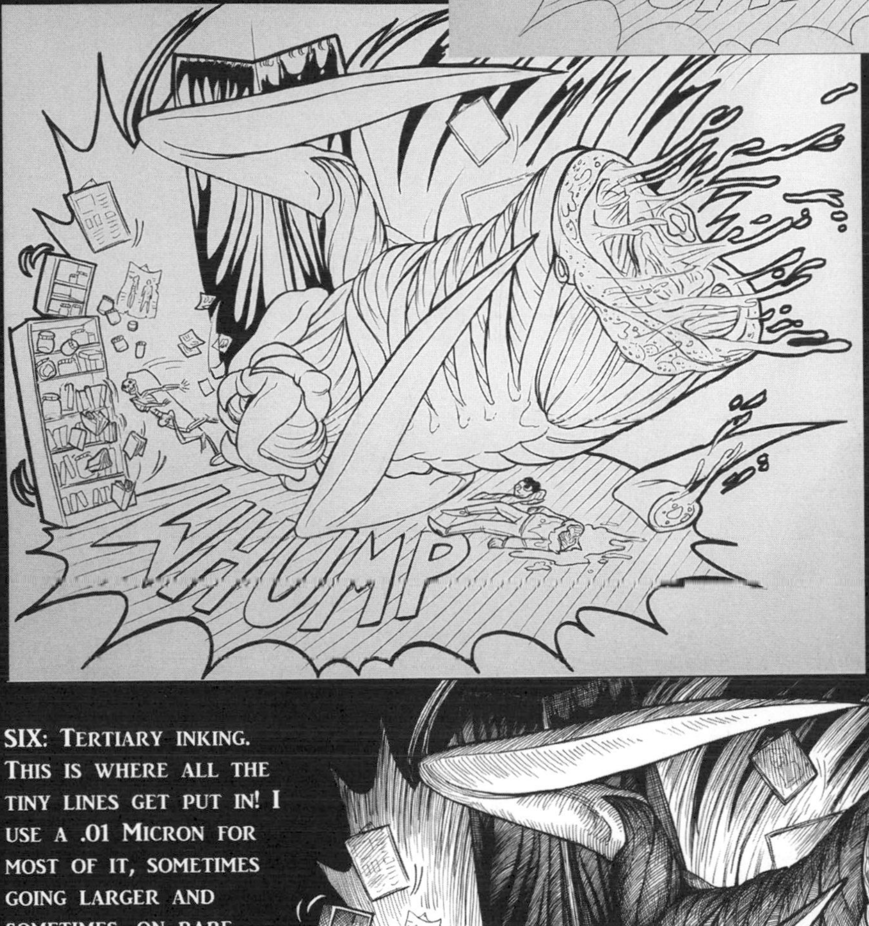
WHUMP

FIVE: Secondary inking. I use my larger pens (mostly the .08) and sharpies to thicken up certain lines to bring more life to the image, as well as filling in some of the smaller black areas.

SIX: Tertiary inking. This is where all the tiny lines get put in! I use a .01 Micron for most of it, sometimes going larger and sometimes, on rare occasions, going down to the .005 (the smallest one, great for skin tones). Then I scan it and fill in the larger black areas digitally, to save on ink.

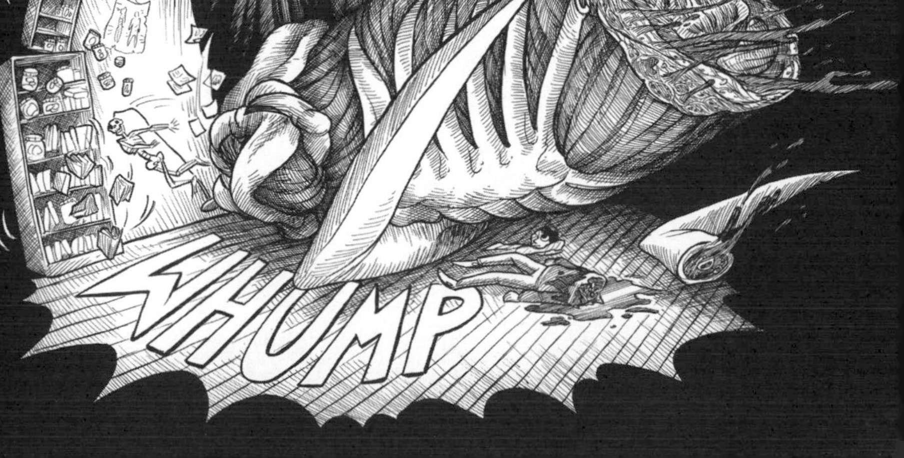
WHUMP

And thus, a panel is born.

The Last Halloween before The Last Halloween was a thing

Okay so... The Last Halloween started as several different stories I wrote in high school, and I still have a lot of the original pages I drew back then. The story that eventually became Book 1 started out as The Graveyard Ghoul Gang, a short series of tales starring Robert, Ringley, Shirley and some kid who isn't Mona.

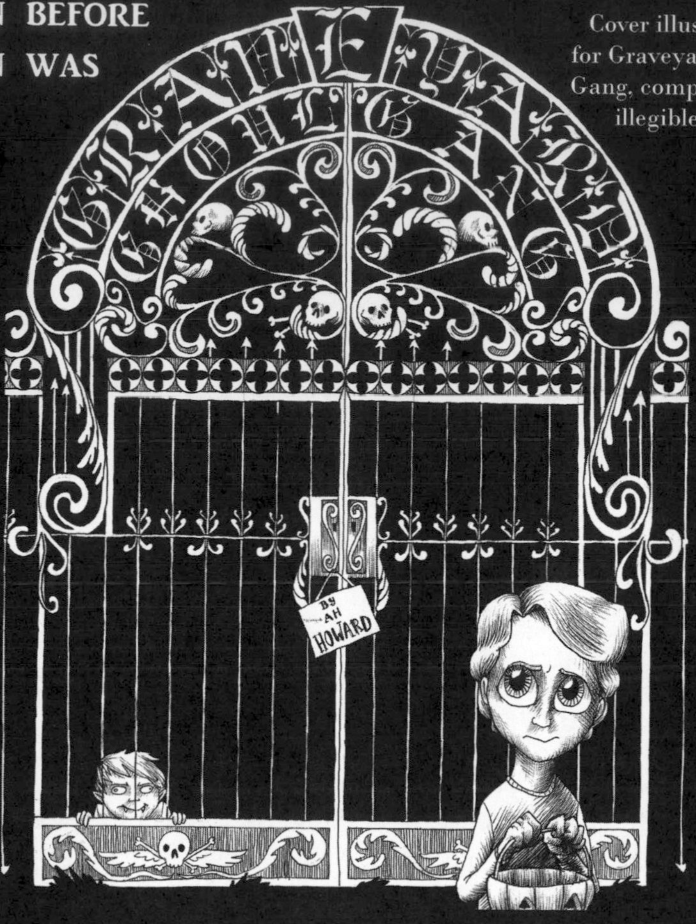
GRAVEYARD
GHOUL GANG
By AH HOWARD

Cover illustration for Graveyard Ghoul Gang, complete with illegible font

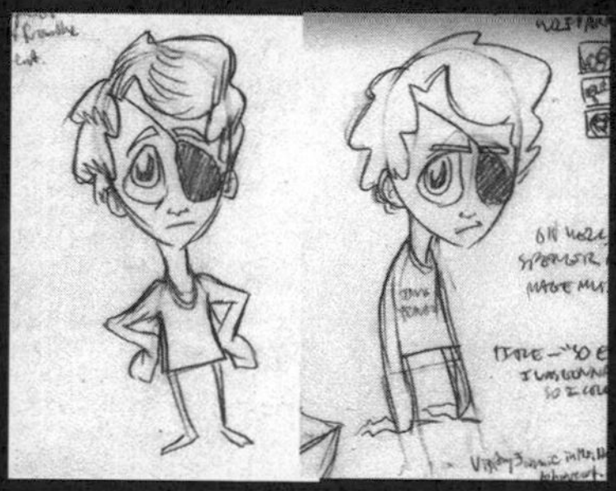

Some kid who isn't Mona

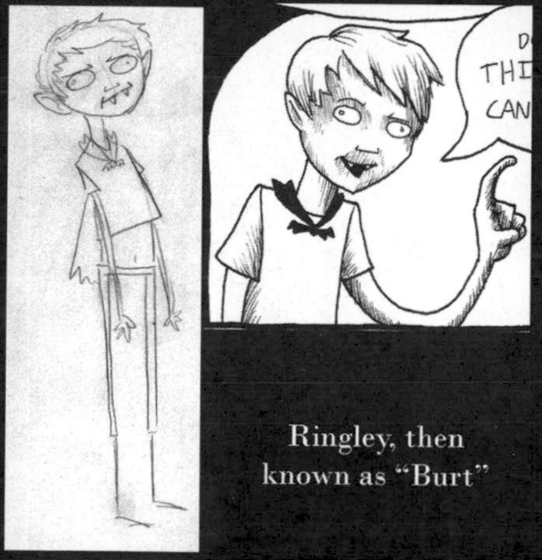

Ringley, then known as "Burt"

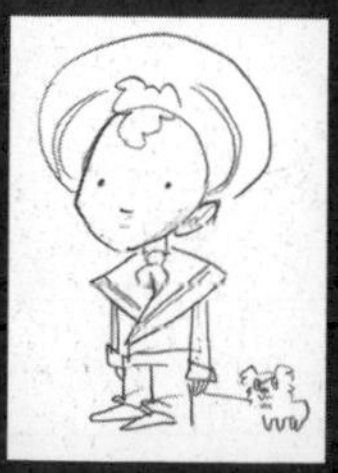

There are not many drawings of Robert pre-new stuff because I thought I was hot tamales and could just figure it out on the page. Spoilers: he looked bad.

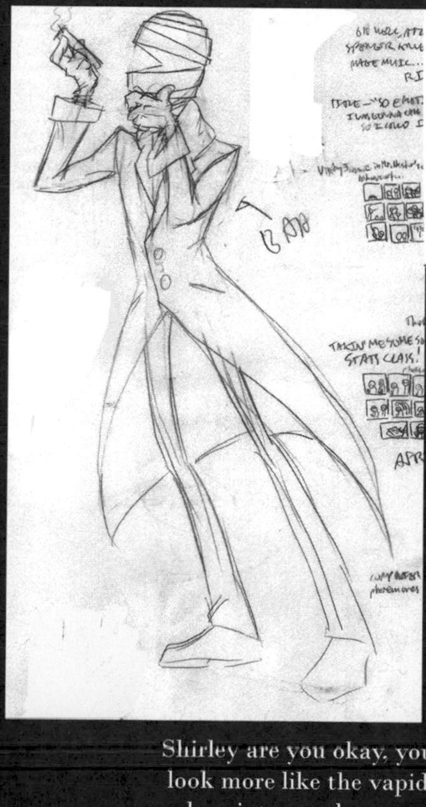

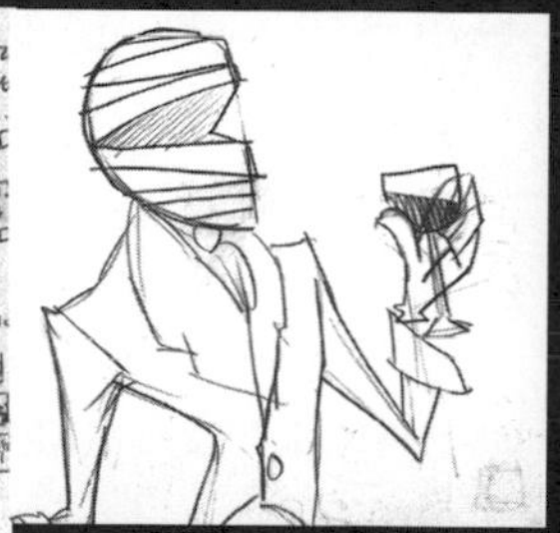

Ah, Doctor Fugue, long before he was anything more than "the invisible man". In this story he was actually competent and cool.

Shirley are you okay, you look more like the vapid love interest than an actual character.

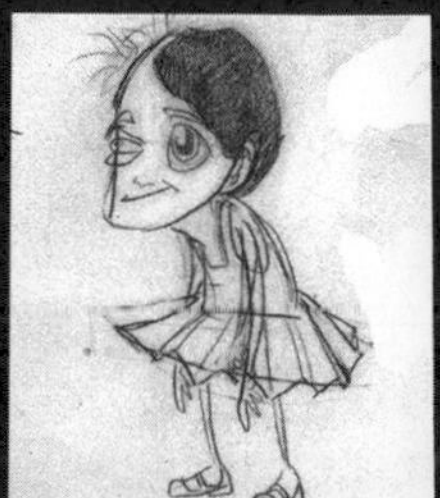

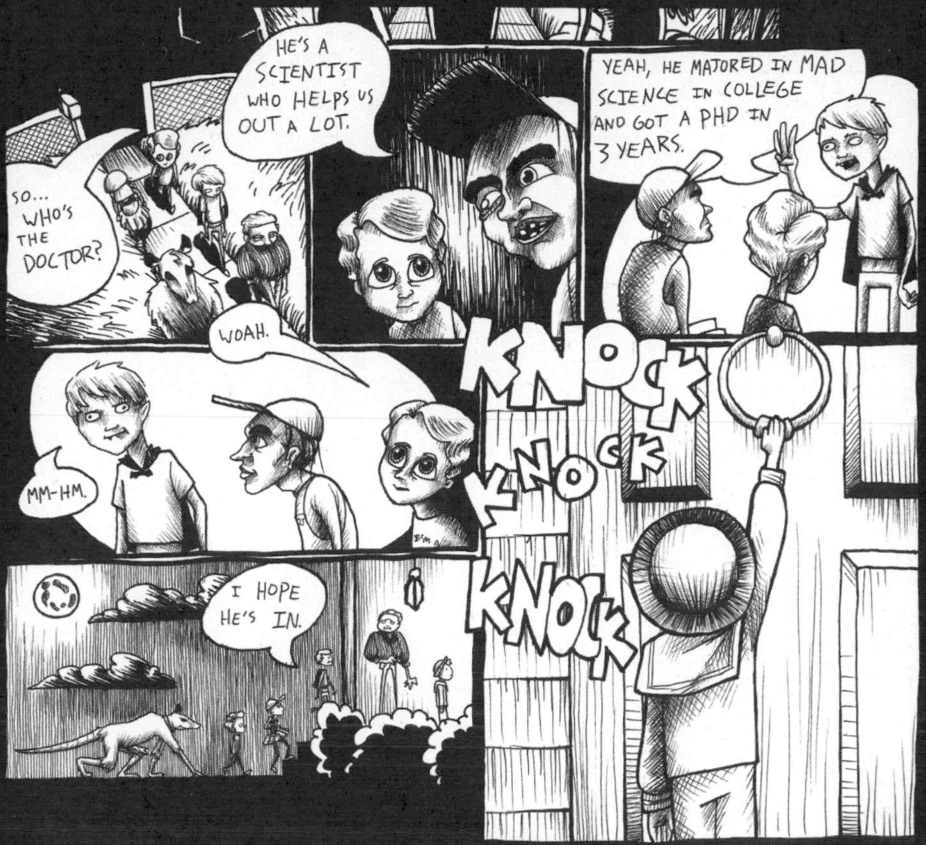
SO... WHO'S THE DOCTOR?
HE'S A SCIENTIST WHO HELPS US OUT A LOT.
YEAH, HE MATORED IN MAD SCIENCE IN COLLEGE AND GOT A PHD IN 3 YEARS.
WOAH.
MM-HM.
KNOCK
KNOCK
I HOPE HE'S IN.
KNOCK

Shirley used to have a hat? Fugue used to be competent?? I didn't know how to spell whoa??? What a time this was.

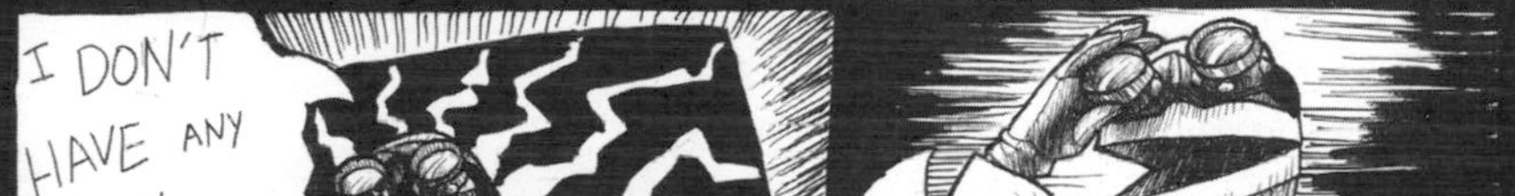
I DON'T HAVE ANY CANDY, DAMMIT!
OH, IT'S MY FAVORITE GAGGLE OF GRAVEROBBERS!
SORRY ABOUT THAT— I'VE HAD A LOT OF TRICK OR TREATERS TONIGHT.
SO, WHAT BRINGS YOU TO MY HUMBLE ABODE?

Who let these cusses in here.

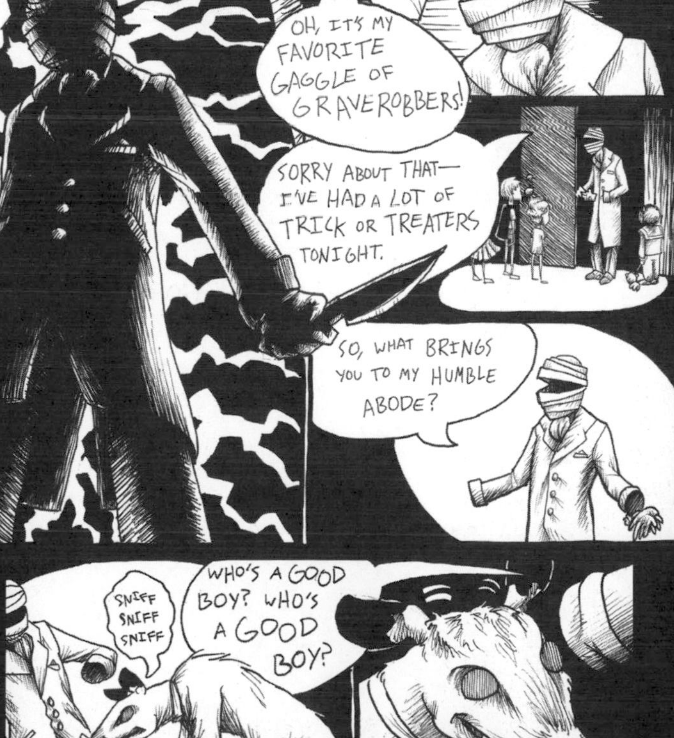
SNIFF SNIFF SNIFF
WHO'S A GOOD BOY? WHO'S A GOOD BOY?

Here's that good boy.

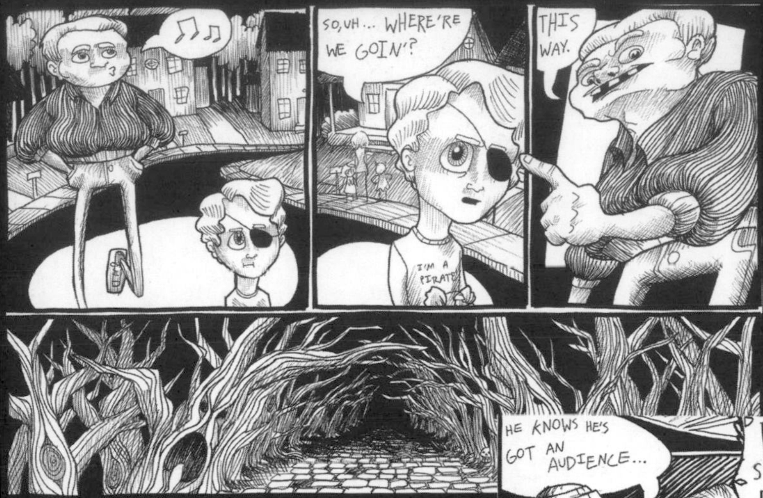
SO, UH... WHERE'RE WE GOIN'?
THIS WAY.

The kid also had an odious and cruel brother named Bryan who abandoned the kid in a graveyard for the night which is how the kid met his new friends.

The character designs are difficult to gaze upon but hey those woods look pretty nice, way to go, Past Abby.

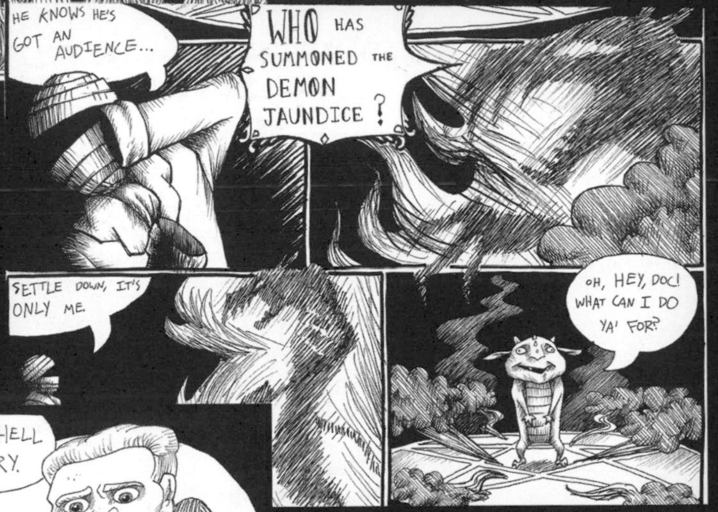
HE KNOWS HE'S GOT AN AUDIENCE...
WHO HAS SUMMONED THE DEMON JAUNDICE?
SETTLE DOWN, IT'S ONLY ME.
OH, HEY, DOC! WHAT CAN I DO YA' FOR?

Switch out the little demon for Charon and make him unhappy to see Fugue and this is basically the same interaction as in the actual comic.

Jaundice was later made into Fugue's assistant, then promptly replaced with Jangles.

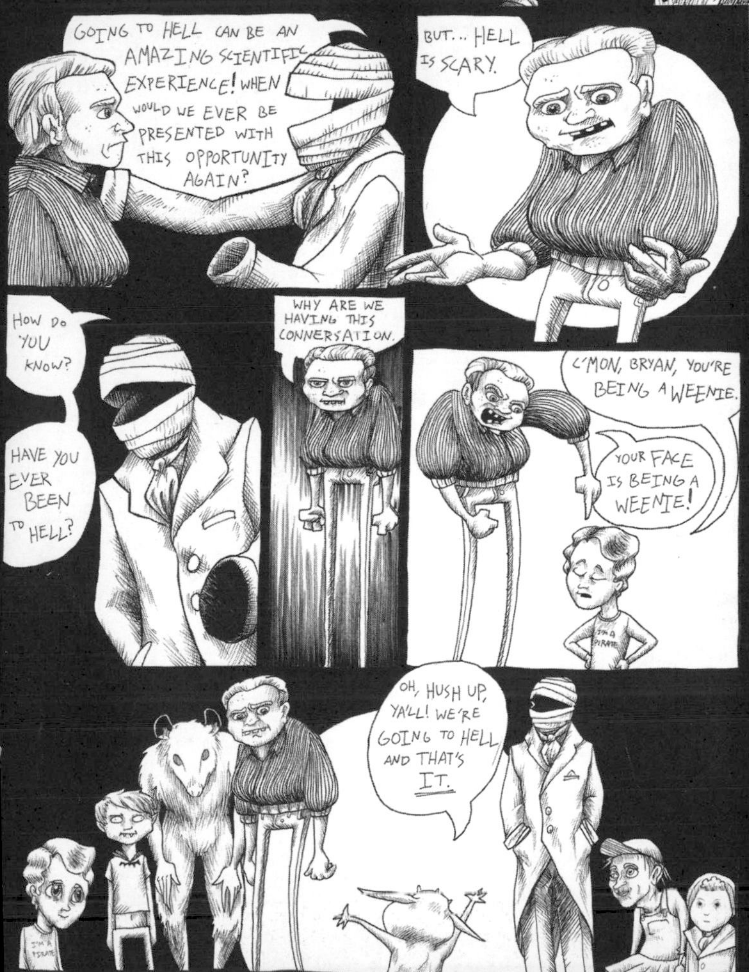
GOING TO HELL CAN BE AN AMAZING SCIENTIFIC EXPERIENCE! WHEN WOULD WE EVER BE PRESENTED WITH THIS OPPORTUNITY AGAIN?
BUT... HELL IS SCARY.
HOW DO YOU KNOW?
HAVE YOU EVER BEEN TO HELL?
WHY ARE WE HAVING THIS CONVERSATION.
C'MON, BRYAN, YOU'RE BEING A WEENIE.
YOUR FACE IS BEING A WEENIE!
OH, HUSH UP, YA'LL! WE'RE GOING TO HELL AND THAT'S IT.

And thus we have the premise of one of the original tales. They gotta go through hell to get Bryan's hideous soul back, and they were sure to have many jokes along to way.

There weren't even any monsters!!

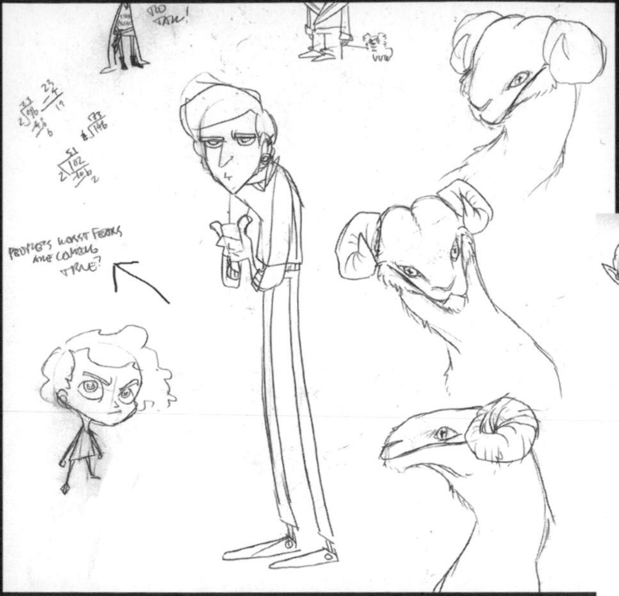
NO TAIL!
PEOPLE'S WORST FEARS ARE COMING TRUE?

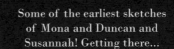

Some of the earliest sketches of Mona and Duncan and Susannah! Getting there...

The Vasquez influence seen very clearly in young Ringley.

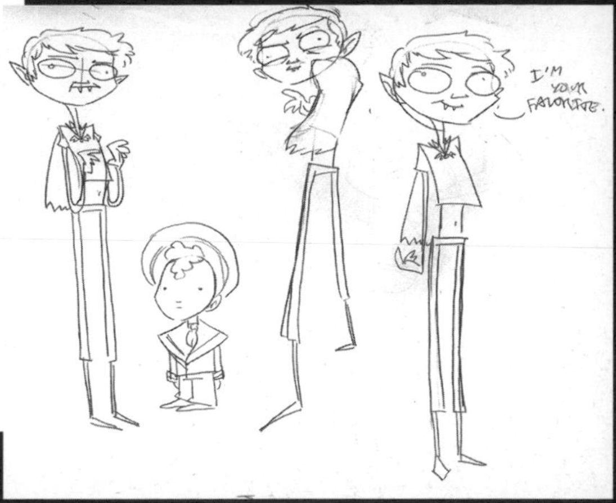
I'M YOUR FAVORITE.

Finally getting all that pesky flesh off Susannah's skull. And adding much more fear to Mona's appearance (though she was still a little boy at this point).

^(Once upon a time he was my favorite but now I do not choose between my children.)

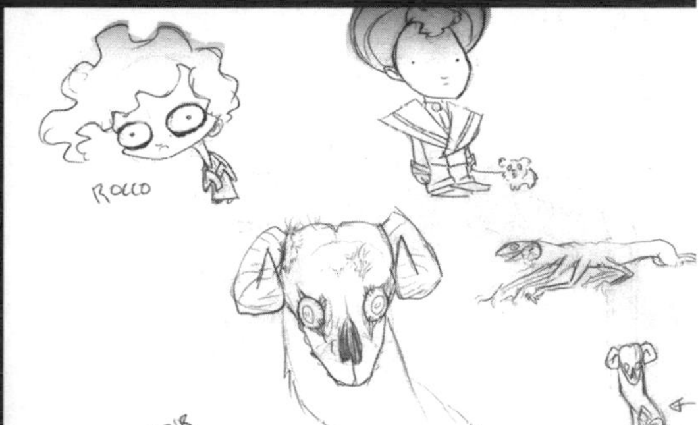
ROCCO
R's MONSTER

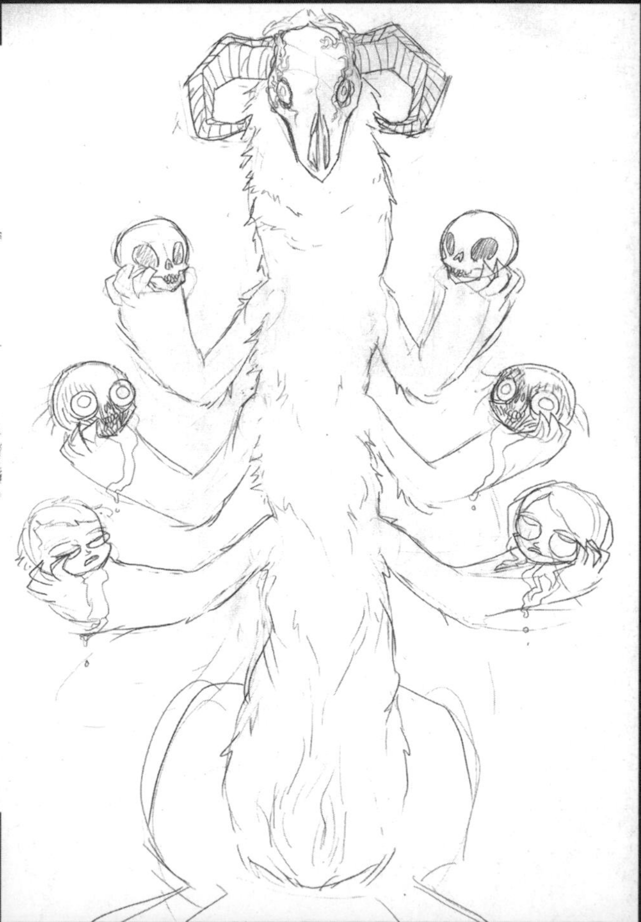

Drawn during the filming of Strip Search, mere months before the comic's launch! >

SKETCHES FROM
THE LAST HALLOWEEN: BOOK 1

The following pages contain excerpts from my sketchbook—bits and pieces of design work for some of the prominent characters and monsters as well as a storyboard here and there. Such as the image below, which contains the storyboard for Susannah's first appearance.

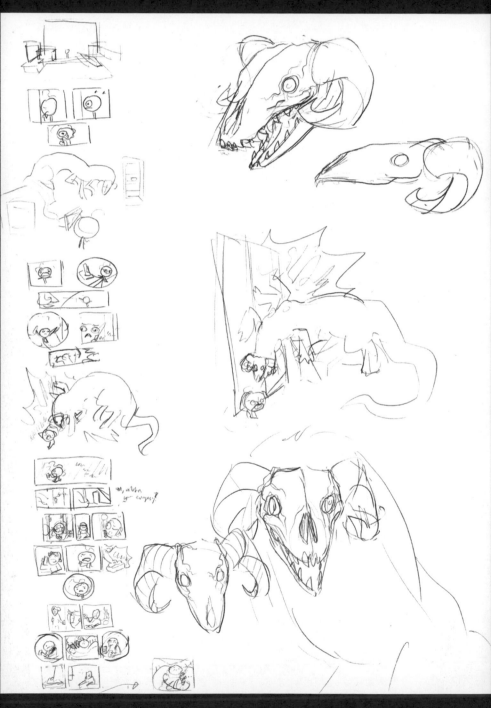

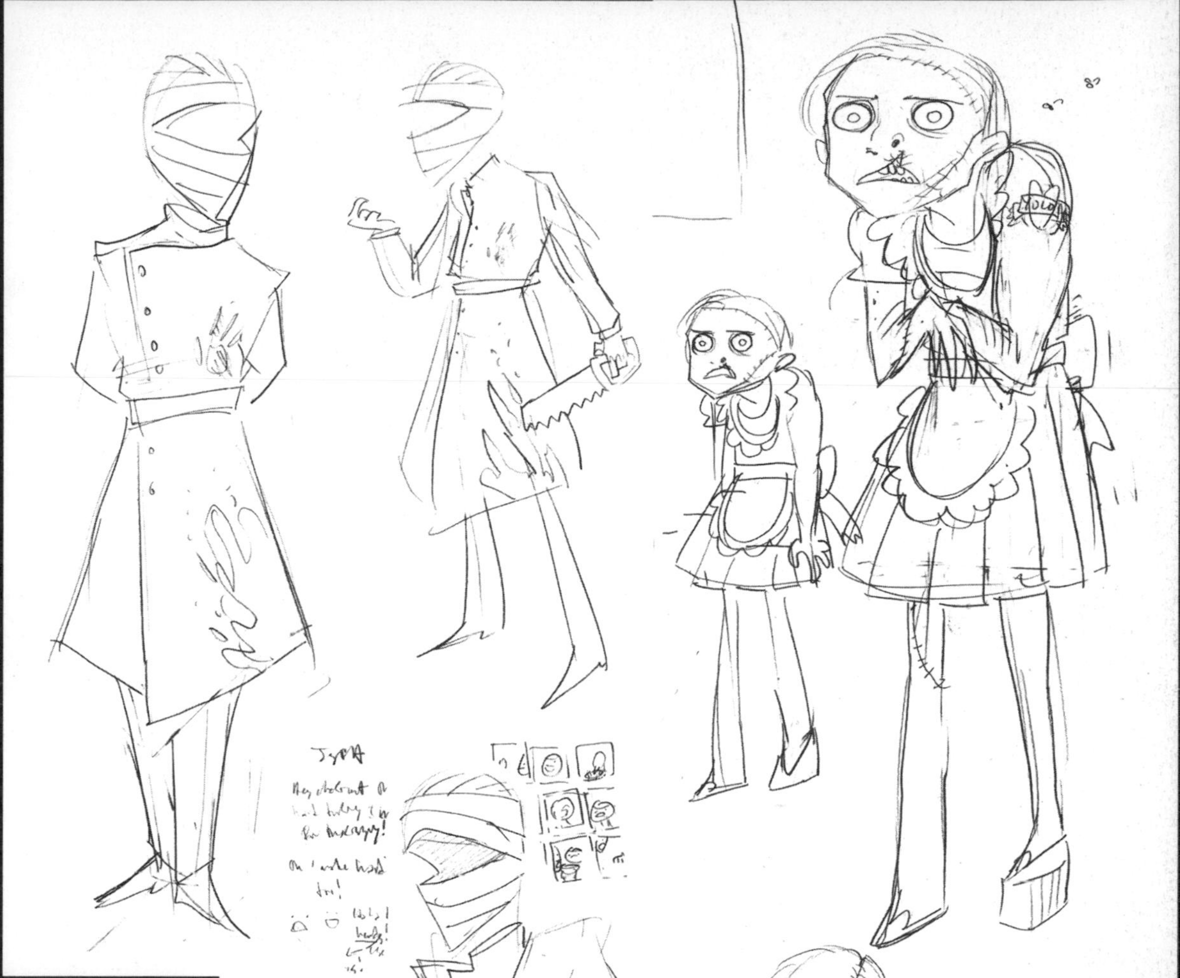

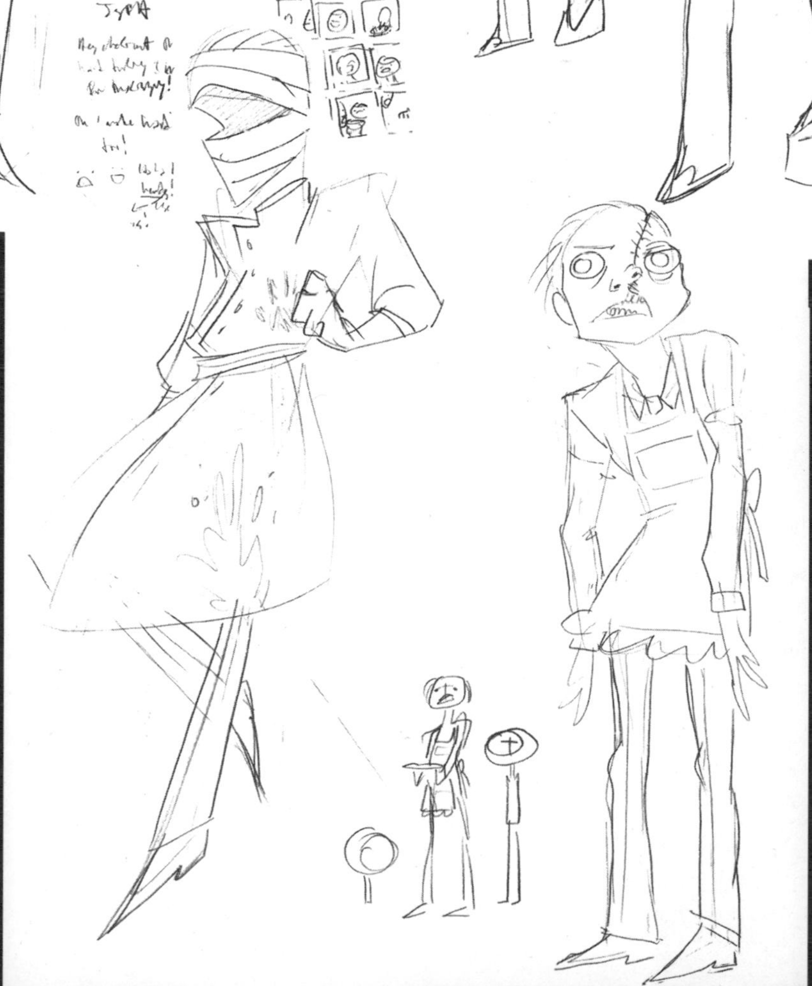

And here we have some early concepts for Fugue and Jangles. I ditched the demon Jaundice in favor of this much better Frankenstein servant during filming of the finale of Strip Search.

I kinda like Fugue's old lab coat design though...

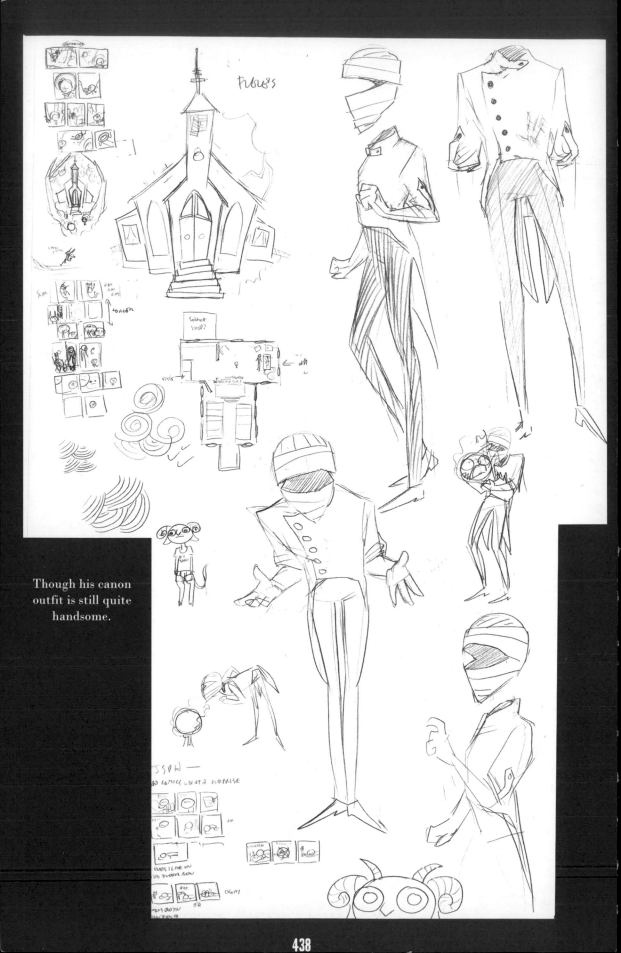

Though his canon outfit is still quite handsome.

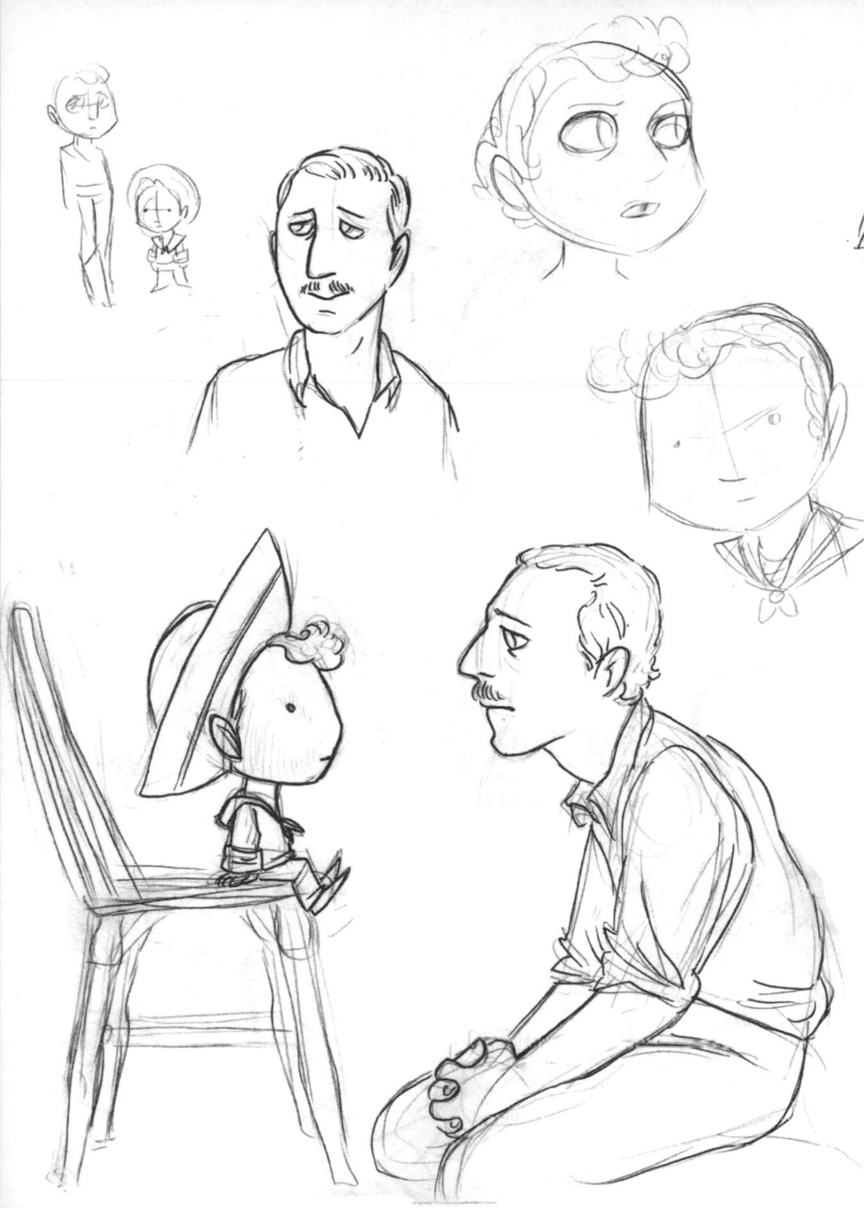

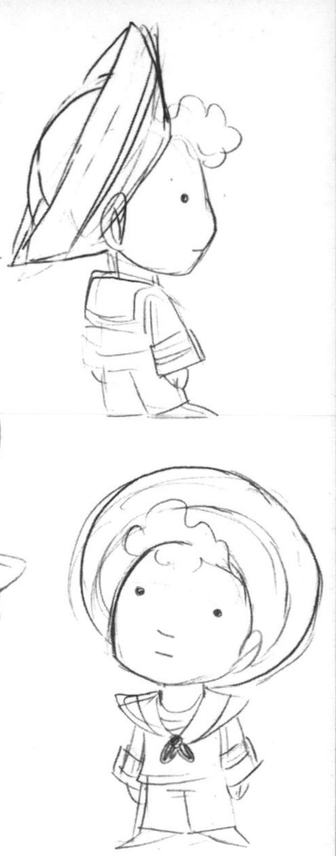

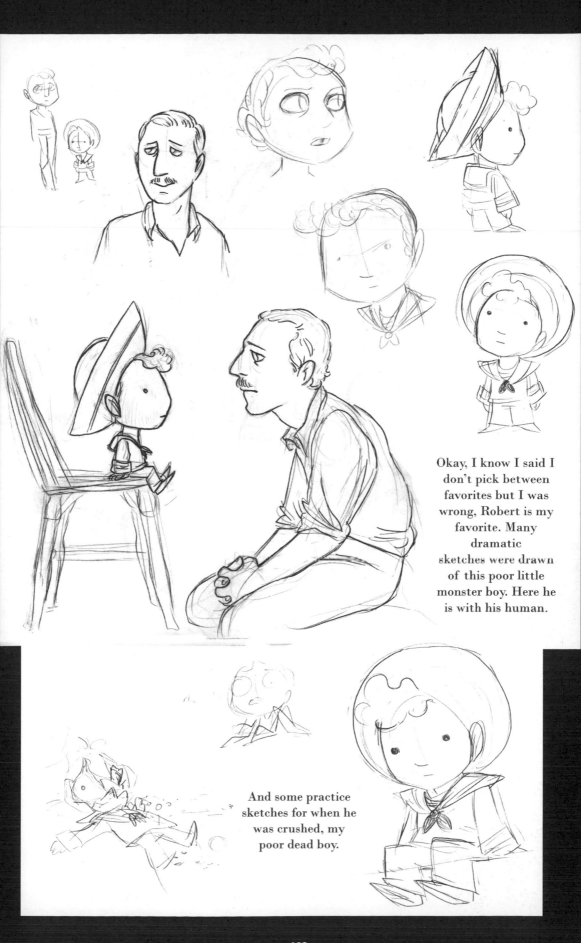

Okay, I know I said I don't pick between favorites but I was wrong, Robert is my favorite. Many dramatic sketches were drawn of this poor little monster boy. Here he is with his human.

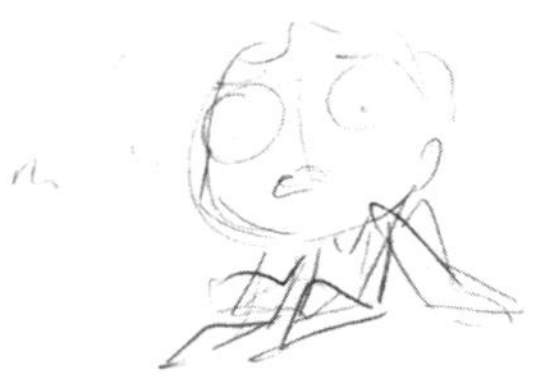

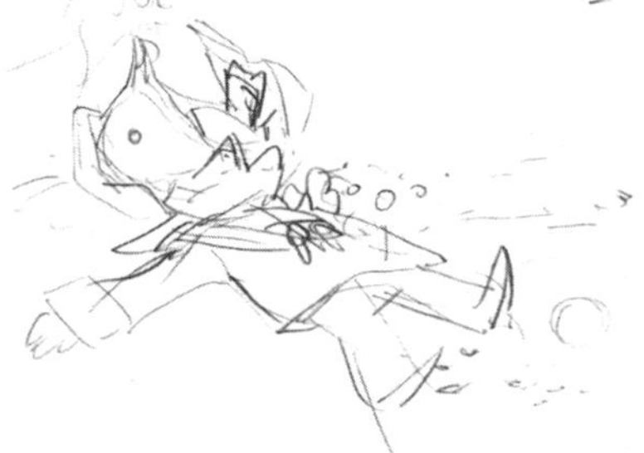

And some practice sketches for when he was crushed, my poor dead boy.

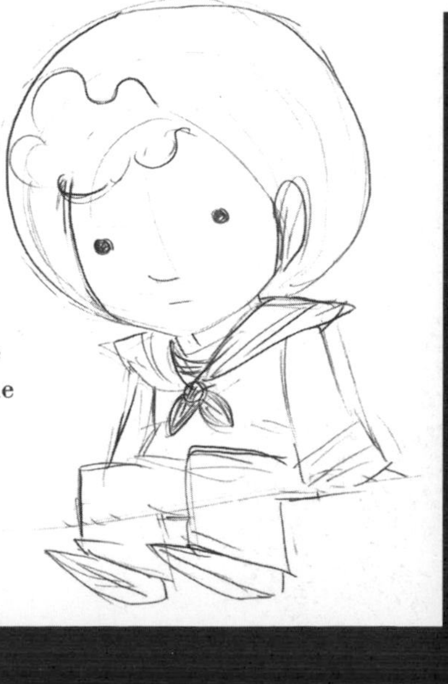

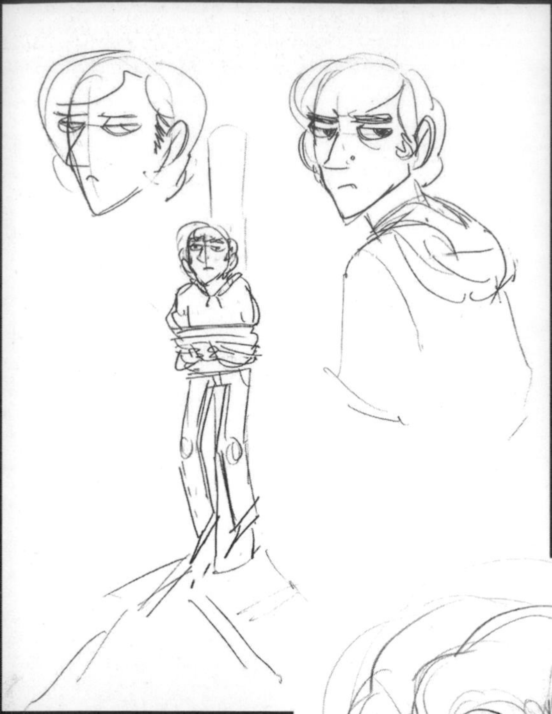

Early Duncan and early Shirduncan. I seem to have a problem with designing too many surly shoulder-length black-haired characters with narrow faces.

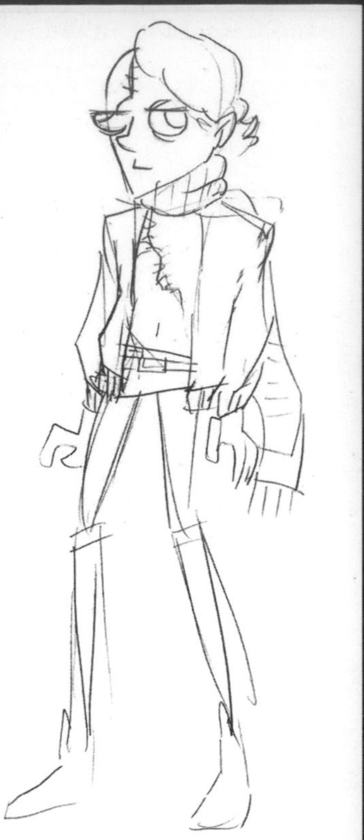

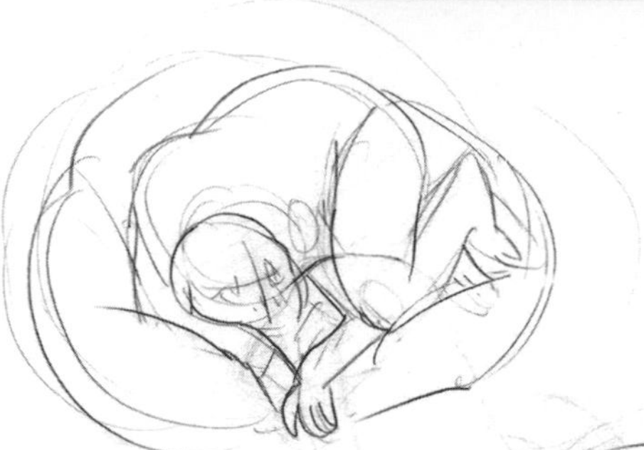

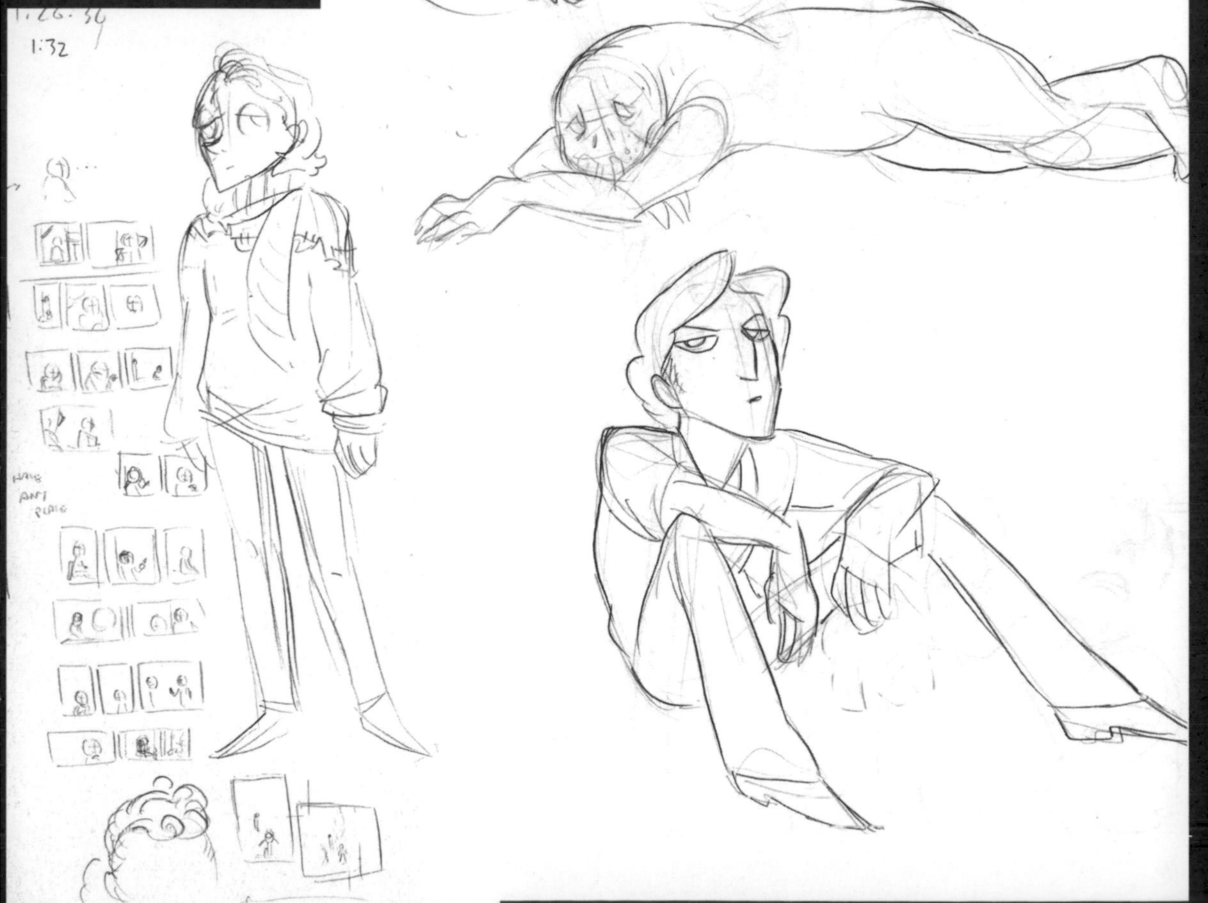

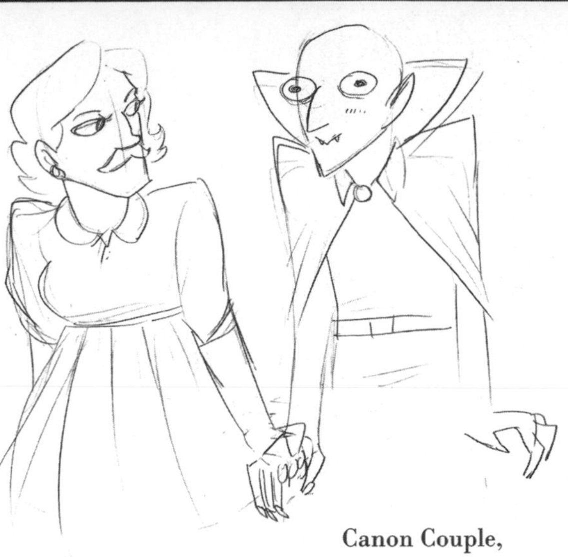

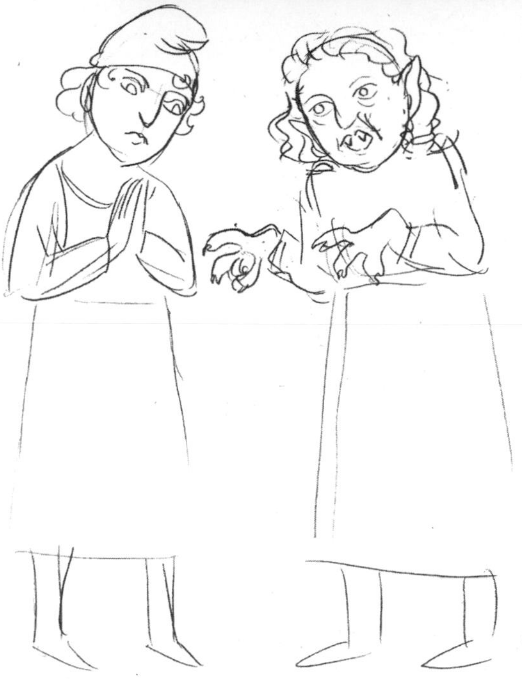

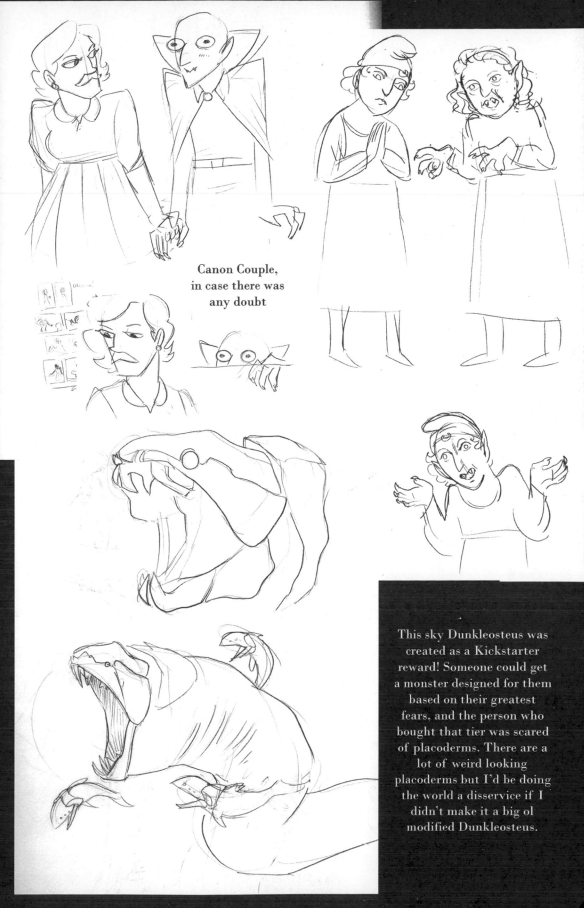

**Canon Couple,
in case there was
any doubt**

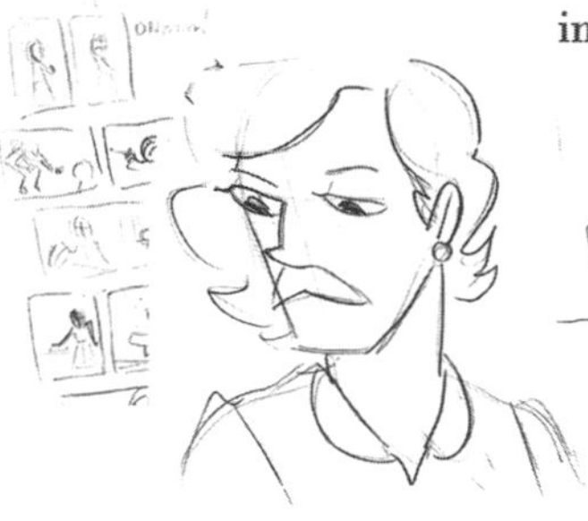

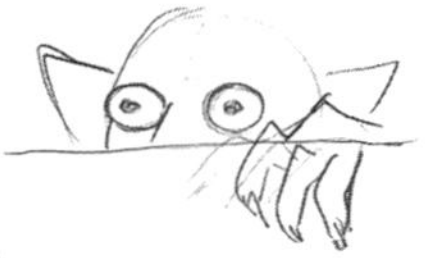

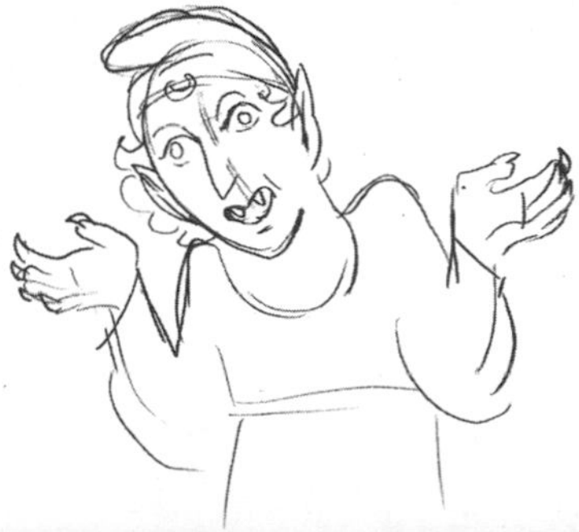

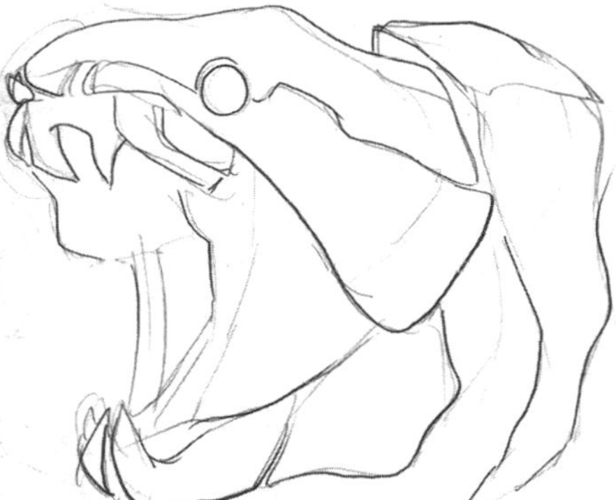

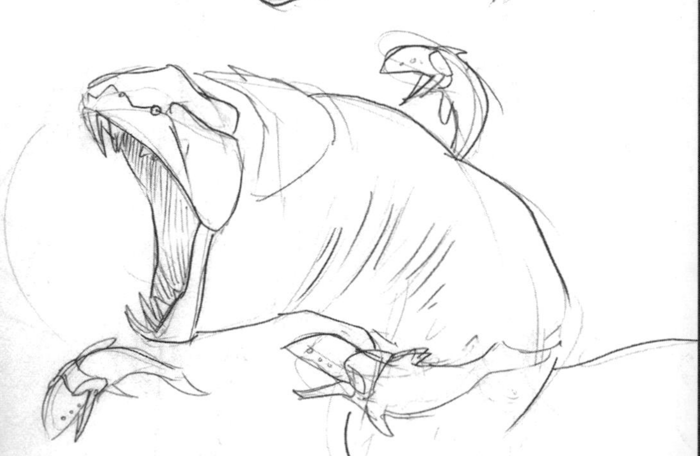

This sky Dunkleosteus was created as a Kickstarter reward! Someone could get a monster designed for them based on their greatest fears, and the person who bought that tier was scared of placoderms. There are a lot of weird looking placoderms but I'd be doing the world a disservice if I didn't make it a big ol modified Dunkleosteus.

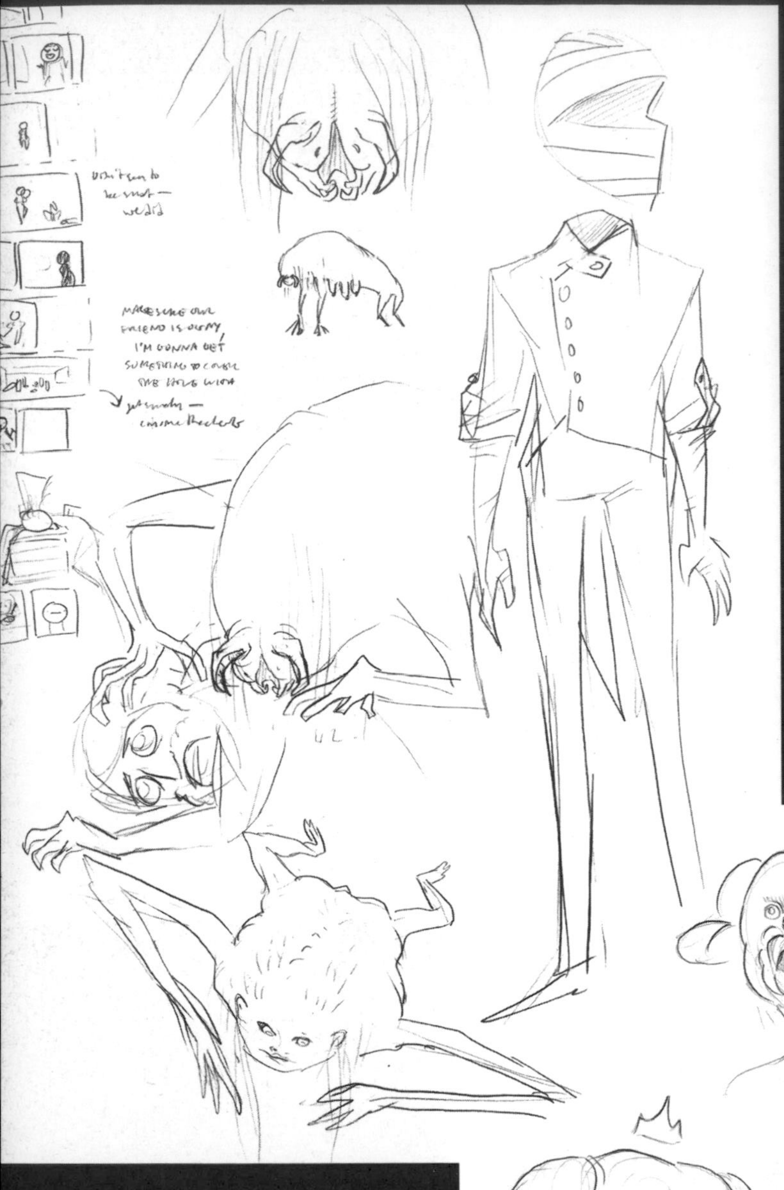

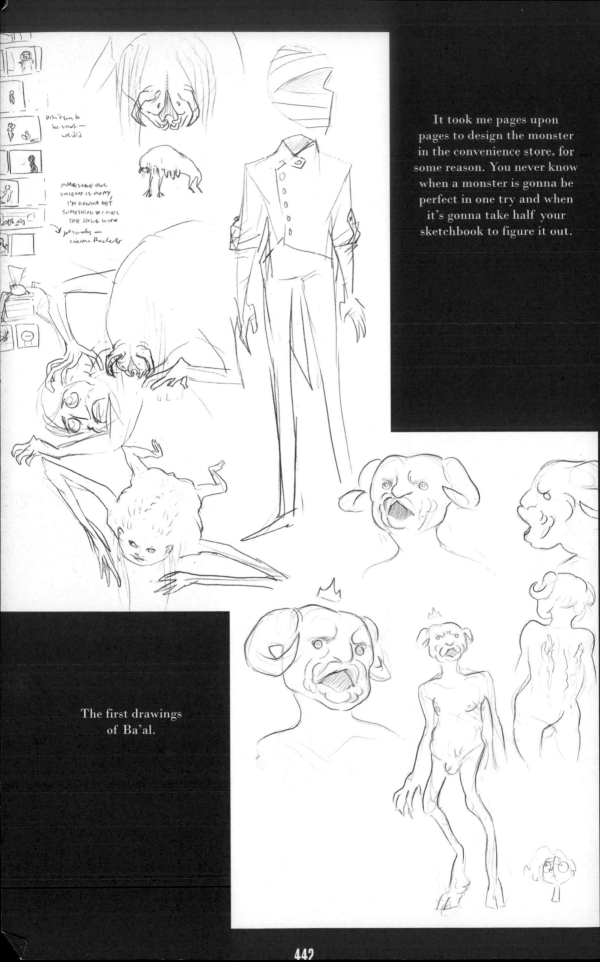

It took me pages upon pages to design the monster in the convenience store, for some reason. You never know when a monster is gonna be perfect in one try and when it's gonna take half your sketchbook to figure it out.

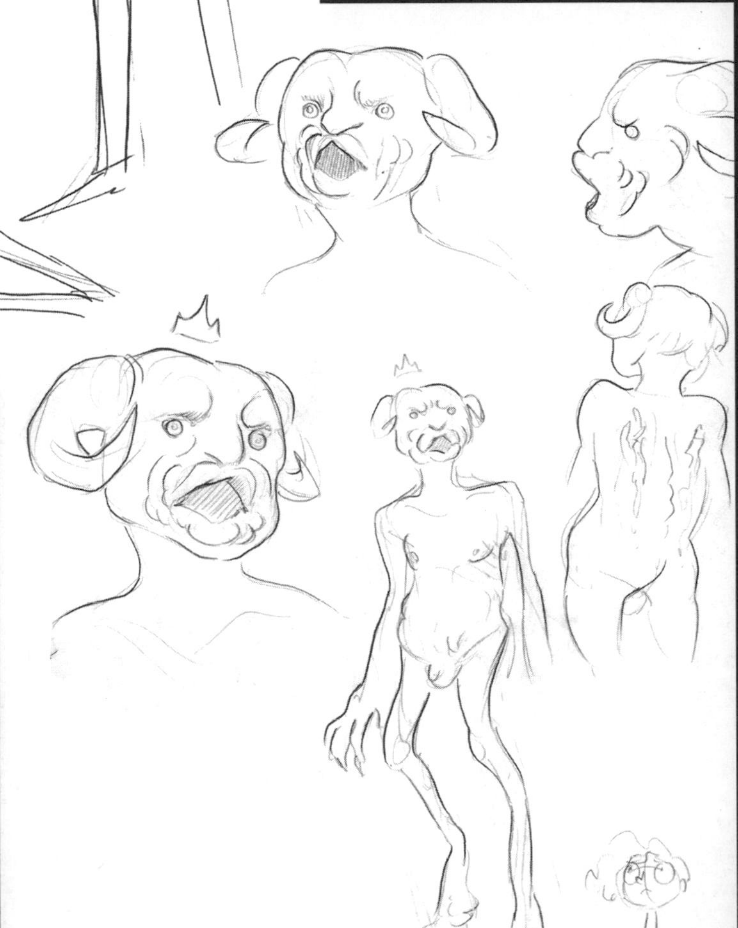

The first drawings of Ba'al.

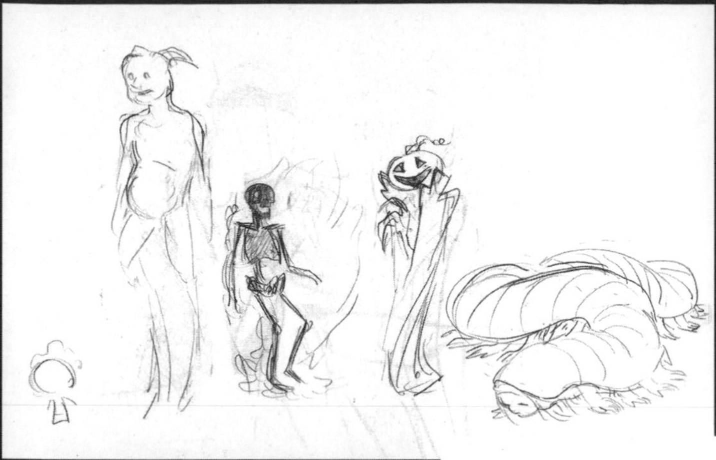

Immortals
crew!

I love them!

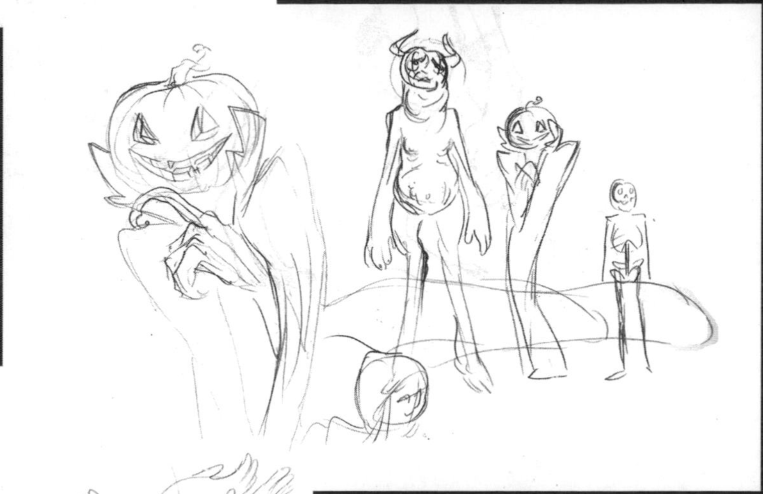

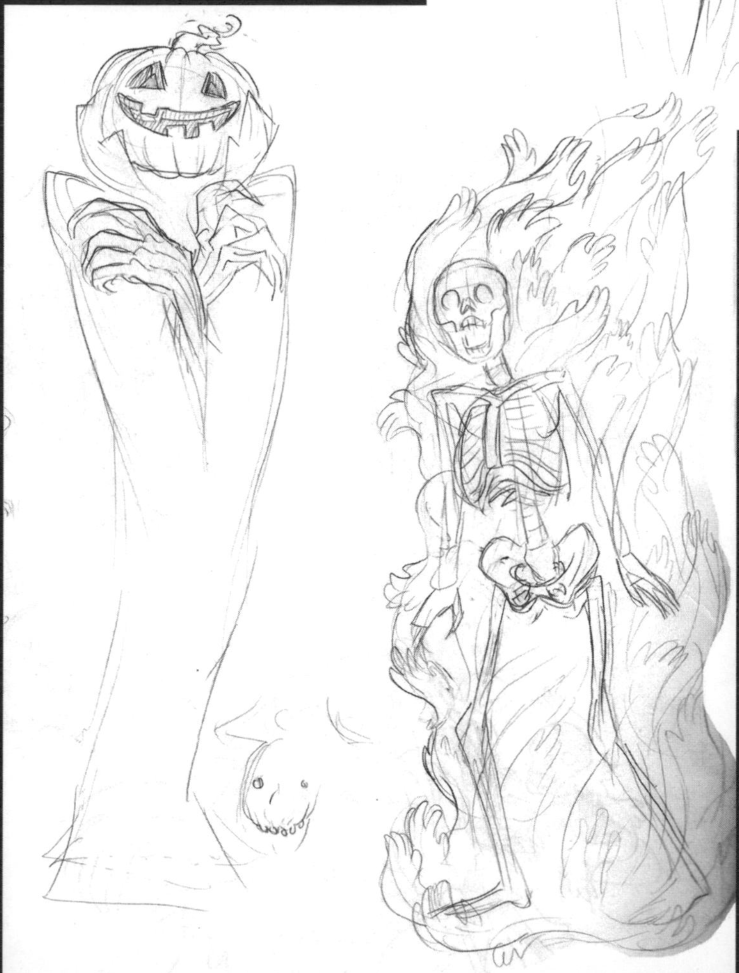

I wish they
weren't dead!!

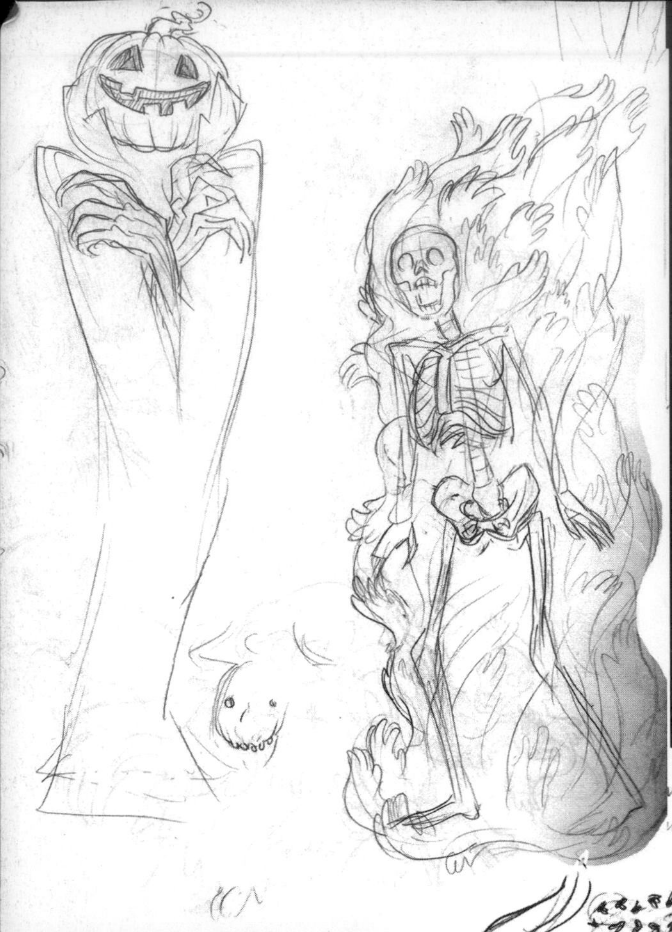

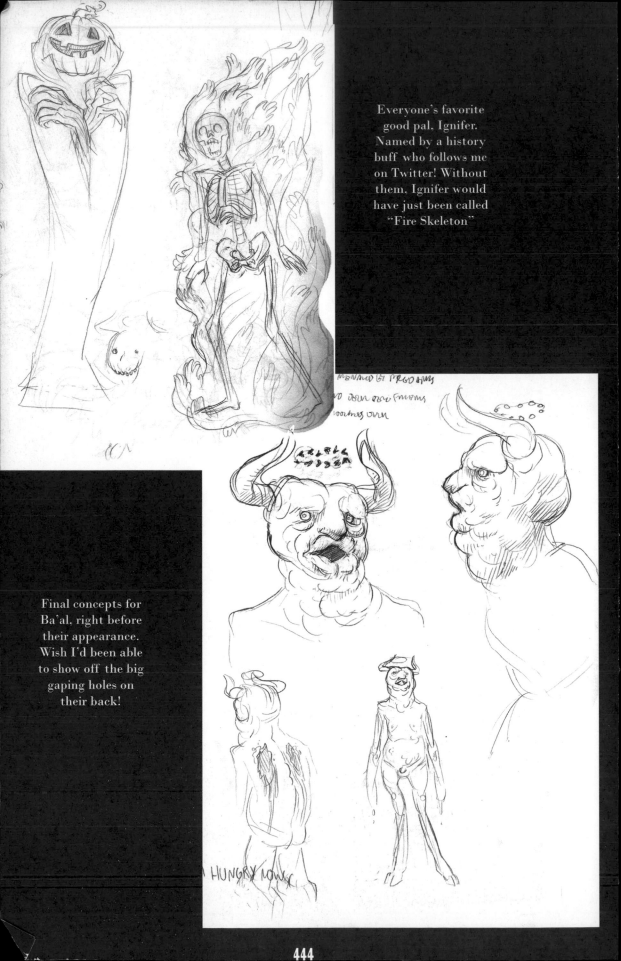

Everyone's favorite good pal, Ignifer. Named by a history buff who follows me on Twitter! Without them, Ignifer would have just been called "Fire Skeleton"

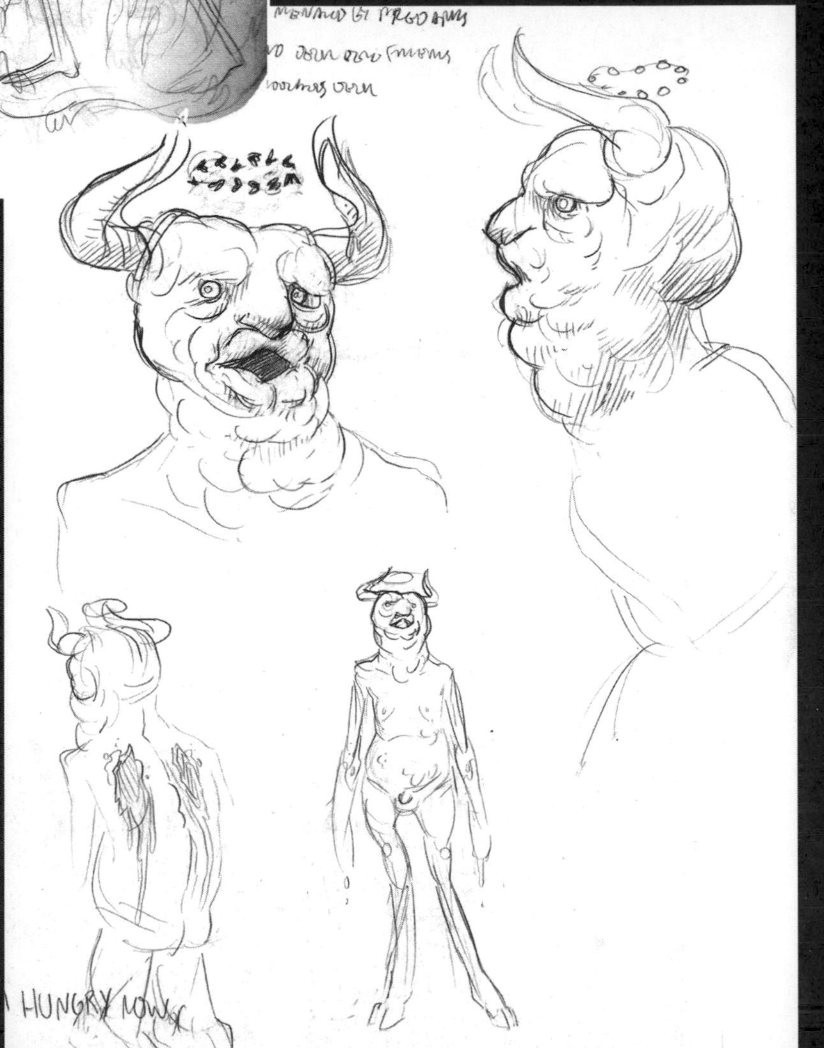
HUNGRY NOW

Final concepts for Ba'al, right before their appearance. Wish I'd been able to show off the big gaping holes on their back!

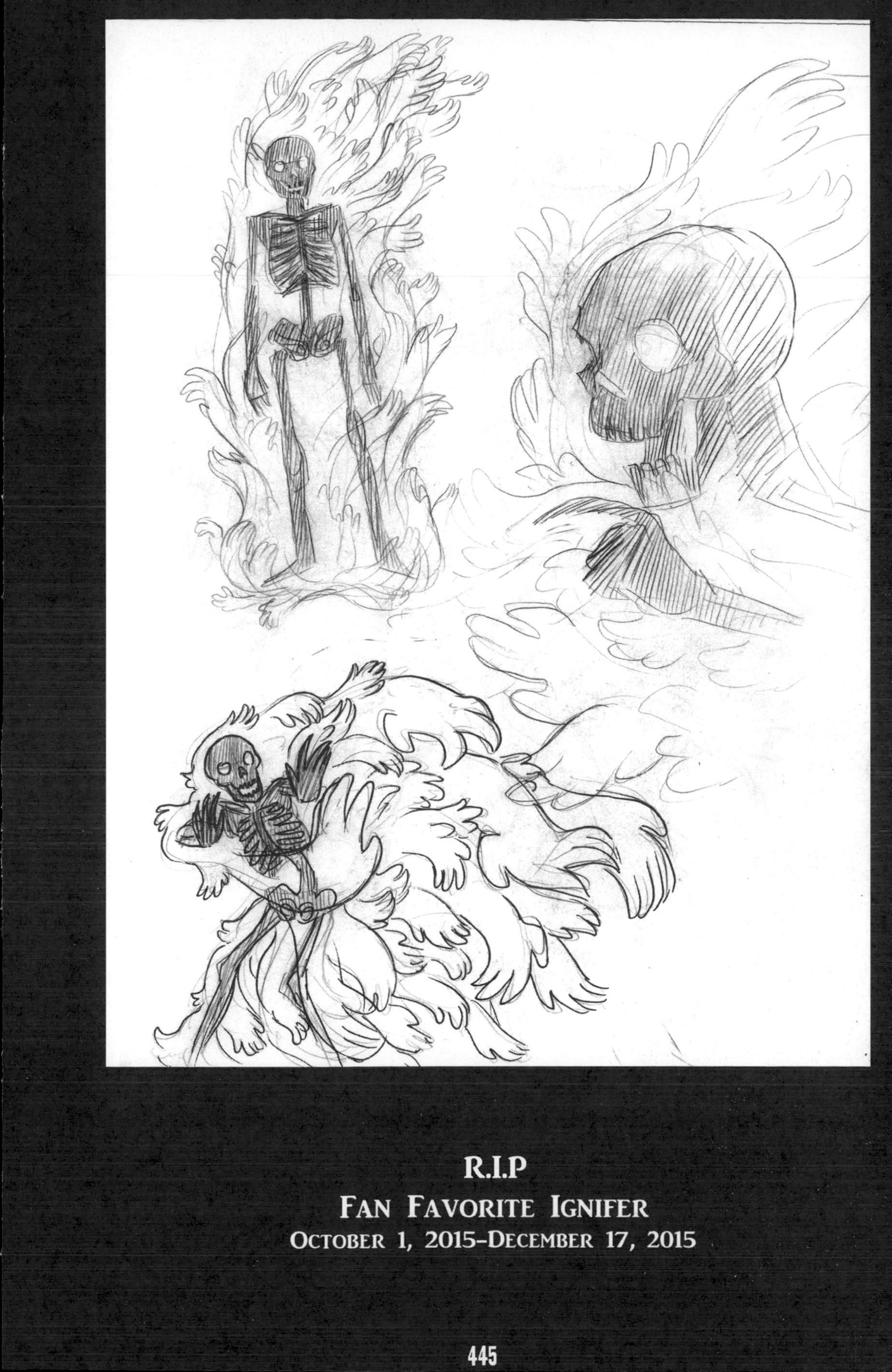

R.I.P

Fan Favorite Ignifer

October 1, 2015–December 17, 2015

About the Author

Abby Howard created the webcomics *Junior Scientist Power Hour* and *The Last Halloween*, as well as the educational series *Earth Before Us*, and the horror comic anthology *The Crossroads at Midnight* (also available from Iron Circus). She has always been drawn to the macabre, and is delighted to be bringing more horrors into the world.